Mary Ann Geadon

PENGUIN ⓟ CLASSICS

THE UNFORTUNATE TRAVELLER
AND OTHER WORKS

Thomas Nashe was born in Lowestoft in 1567, the son of a minister, and in 1573 the family moved to West Harling, near Thetford. There is no record of Nashe's schooling but in 1581 or 1582 he entered St John's College, Cambridge, where he became a Lady Margaret scholar, receiving his B.A. in 1586. He left the University in 1588 and began publishing in 1589 with *The Anatomy of Absurdity*. Nashe was strongly anti-Puritan and this together with his natural combativeness drew him into the Marlprelate controversy: *An Almond for a Parrot* (1590) is now widely accepted as his along with a number of pseudonymous pamphlets. In his defence of Robert Greene, the first and most prolific of Elizabethan professional writers, Nashe was drawn into a prolonged and bitter literary quarrel with Gabriel Harvey. The latter proved an effective target for Nashe's brilliant, satiric wit, as is shown in *Strange News* (or *The Four Letters Confuted*) and the unsparing pseudo-biography of Harvey contained in *Have with You to Saffron Walden*. The vivid social satire, *Pierce Penniless*, was the most successful of Nashe's pamphlets and went through three editions in 1592. *The Unfortunate Traveller* (1594) relating the knavish adventures of Jack Wilton is an important example of picaresque fiction and had a considerable influence on the development of the English novel. Nashe was also part-author (along with Ben Jonson among others) of *The Isle of Dogs*, which was judged by the authorities to be seditious and thus Nashe was forced to flee from London. In his writings he reveals the conflict in cultural standards which arose between the humanist values of civility and eloquence and the racy vigour of popular folk-tradition. His play *Summer's Last Will and Testament* pleads for the patronage of letters and also defends the seasonal pastimes of the countryside against the Puritan arguments for thrift. Nashe lived for most of his life in London. The date of his death is uncertain, it is known he was alive early in 1599 and dead in 1601, but it is not known how, when or where he died.

J. B. Steane was a scholar of Jesus College, Cambridge, where he read English. He is the author of *Marlowe: A Critical Study* (1964) and *Tennyson* (1966). He has also edited several Elizabethan texts, including plays by Dekker and Jonson. His edition of *Christopher Marlowe: The Complete Plays* is also published by Penguin. For some time now he has been engaged in music criticism and broadcasting, writing reviews for many music magazines and periodicals including *The Gramophone*, *The Voice* and *New Grove*. He has also written a volume on opera, *The Grand Tradition* (1974).

THOMAS NASHE

The Unfortunate Traveller

AND OTHER WORKS

Edited with an introduction by

J. B. STEANE

PENGUIN BOOKS

Penguin Books Ltd, Harmondsworth, Middlesex, England
Viking Penguin Inc., 40 West 23rd Street, New York, New York 10010, U.S.A.
Penguin Books Australia Ltd, Ringwood, Victoria, Australia
Penguin Books Canada Ltd, 2801 John Street, Markham, Ontario, Canada L3R 1B4
Penguin Books (N.Z.) Ltd, 182–190 Wairau Road, Auckland 10, New Zealand

—

Published in the Penguin English Library 1972
Reprinted 1978, 1984
Reprinted in Penguin Classics 1985

—

Introduction copyright © J. B. Steane, 1971
All rights reserved

—

Printed and bound in Great Britain by
Cox & Wyman Ltd, Reading
Set in Linotype Georgian

To Dick and Tag

CONTENTS

7

PART I

ACKNOWLEDGEMENTS
AND REFERENCES

My principal debt is to the great edition of *The Works of Thomas Nashe* by R. B. McKerrow. This is in five volumes, reprinted from the original edition (completed in 1910) with corrections and additional notes by F. P. Wilson (Oxford, 1958). The debt is pervasive; one can hardly touch Nashe without reference to McKerrow. References to his edition, in my introduction and foot-notes, are given by the initial 'M' followed by the number of the volume and the page. I have also to thank my colleague, Mr A. Woolley, for invaluable help, generously given, with Latin texts and classical allusions.

References by initial are as follows:

H. = G. R. Hibbard (ed.), *Three Elizabethan Pamphlets*, London, 1951.

M. = R. B. McKerrow (ed.), *The Works of Thomas Nashe*, V vols., Oxford, 1958.

W. = Stanley Wells (ed.), *Thomas Nashe*, The Stratford-upon-Avon Library, London, 1964.

F.P.W. = F. P. Wilson (ed.), McKerrow's *Works of Thomas Nashe*, supplementary notes, vol. V.

A.W. = A. Woolley.

In this edition, spelling and punctuation have been modernized by the present editor. Proper names have generally been left in their original form, and an explanatory note added if thought necessary.

INTRODUCTION

'THE most lively of Elizabethan journalists': an encyclopedia without much space to spend on the minor classics might well use some such phrase to qualify the inclusion in its pages of Nashe, Thomas (1567–?1601). 'Author of *The Unfortunate Traveller, Pierce Penniless his Supplication to the Devil* and *Summer's Last Will and Testament*,' (the entry might continue), 'he was reputed a formidable controversialist in his time, being involved in the Marprelate debate and in bitter conflict with Gabriel Harvey.'

Dim and dusty associations flicker and stir momentarily: the titles are not unfamiliar, the proper names not unremembered. But no, these controversies long-dead, these terms of reference ('journalist', 'in his day'), they surely suggest an essentially antiquarian interest, chilly and possibly silly, the babble of the curiosity shop; certainly a limited achievement.

It is true that Nashe is 'minor' (where 'major', among Elizabethans, means Shakespeare, Spenser, Marlowe and Jonson). His achievements, however, exceed his contemporary reputation as a mighty polemicist. And if they were merely or essentially those of the journalist, writing of the day for the day, he might be a quarry for social historians, but would not be a classic of our literature, even of the 'minor' variety.

His status and character are those of The Entertainer. He is many other things as well; or rather, many things contribute to the entertainment he offers. He is moralist, poet, story-teller, social critic (taking on All England as readily as he will the tribe of Harveys), scholar, satirist, preacher, jester: all these are part of the act. Like all great entertainers, he is a professional: he may tell us that what he is doing is 'extemporal', that he has got lost down lanes

13

and by-ways in which he is surprised to find himself, but we are ingenuous if we take him at his word, for he is in control all the time, knows where he is going and what he wants to do on the way. Like most great entertainers, he is much aware of himself and his art. He tells his tales to people whose attentive expressions he can never see; he jests to an audience whose laughter he can never hear. But he is as acutely aware of the audience and of the frail magic of his hold over them as any actor or comedian. He wills the world to dance to his tune, and knows that it can do so only if the words will dance to his pen. He is a very conscious artist, and a very good one; and that is why he is a 'classic', but 'minor'.

Much about his life and character has to be qualified in the same way. His spirit was rebellious, but his doctrine conservative; his thinking was agile, but not often deep. He was a university man, proud of his learning, but his touch was essentially popular. He was cosmopolitan in references, metropolitan in way of life, yet the work which was probably his last and in which he is his most fully and distinctively developed self is basically an encomium of the East Anglia of his birth. He was also very much alive (the energy of his writing taking an individual form, however characteristic of its period); yet in his finest poem and in much of his prose we see him in the midst of death. The 1590s were darkened by the plague, which was particularly bad in London in 1592 and 1593. In 1598 Nashe wrote casually of the time 'when I am dead and underground'; and within three or possibly two years, he was. His age, at death, cannot have been more than thirty-four.

What we know for certain about this brief life can be briefly told. The second son of a minister, Nashe was born in November 1567, at Lowestoft, from where, in 1573, the family moved to West Harling, near Thetford. There is no record concerning his schooling, but in 1581 or 1582 he went up to St John's College, Cambridge, where he became a Lady Margaret scholar, and where he gained his Bachelor's degree in 1586 He did not take his M.A., but left the University in 1588 and started publishing promptly, with *The Anatomy of Absurdity* entered in the Stationer's Register that same September. From this time on, he seems to have lived in London as far as plagues, patrons and enemies permitted. In 1592 'the fear of infection detained me with my lord in the country' (*Pierce Penniless*, p. 49); and at Christmas of that year, he tells us, 'I was in the Isle of Wight then and a great while after' (*Have with You*, M., III, 96). The 'lord' referred to in the first quotation was most probably Archbishop Whitgift, and the 'country' his palace at Croydon: *Summer's Last Will and Testament* was almost certainly written and performed there. The Isle of Wight, where he stayed at Carisbrook Castle, drew Nashe in the train of Sir George Carey, its Captain-general, and the Lady Elizabeth, Nashe's patron. He visited Lincolnshire in 1595, and on the return journey called in at Cambridge, where he 'had not been in six year before', and where he met again his old enemy Gabriel Harvey. Then in 1597 he retreated to East Anglia, where 'at Great Yarmouth [he] arrived in the latter end of August', having made London too hot to hold him; and during Lent 1598 he was still in the country writing *Lenten Stuff*. The scandal which drove him from London was aroused by a play, no longer extant, called *The Isle of Dogs*, written partly by him, and judged seditious. The Privy Council ordered a search of his lodgings, and actually imprisoned Ben Jonson (who also wrote part of it) and two members of the cast, while Nashe judiciously made himself scarce. But perhaps he had already begun to feel that he was *persona non grata* in the City, for the battle of books between himself and Harvey had become so unseemly in the eyes of authority that eventually Archbishop Whitgift and Bishop Bancroft ordered 'That all Nashe's books and Doctor Harvey's books be taken wheresoever they be found, and that none of their books be ever printed hereafter.' How the man was to live seems to have troubled nobody very much. He himself was used to poverty and had also seen the inside of a debtor's prison, though he

15

writes cheerfully enough about it ('Though I have been pinched with want – as who is not at one time or another Pierce Penniless – yet my muse never wept for want of maintenance as thine did....' Here he is again at sparring practice with Gabriel Harvey – *Strange News*, M., I, 303). Indeed, the only time we see Nashe seriously dispirited is in what he tells us of the critical period he passed through after the trouble over *The Isle of Dogs*: in the opening of *Lenten Stuff* he refers to 'such a heavy cross laid upon me, as had well near confounded me' (p. 377). Even then he rallies pretty quickly, and we gather he is on his feet again ('I have a pamphlet hot a-brooding'). But Fortune's buffets and rewards were soon to mean nothing to him. He was alive early in 1599 and dead by 1601, we know not how, when or where, but a Latin epitaph published in that year tells how black death, which would certainly have been struck dead itself if Nashe had had his pen or tongue at command, took away these his twin thunderbolts ('fulmina bina') and extinguished his vital flame, on the impartial edict of Jove himself.

He was an active professional writer for ten years, his surviving works bearing the following dates on the title-page of the first edition:

The Anatomy of Absurdity	1589 (Stationer's Register 19 September 1588)
Preface to Greene's *Menaphon*	1590 (S.R. 23 August 1598)
An Almond for a Parrot[1]	1590 (S.R. none)
Pierce Penniless	1592 (S.R. 8 August 1592)
Summer's Last Will	performed 1592
	published 1600 (S.R. 28 October 1600)
Strange News	1592 (S.R. 12 January 1592)
Christ's Tears over Jerusalem	1593 (S.R. 8 September 1593)

1. This is the only one of the Marprelate pamphlets now widely accepted as being by Nashe. McKerrow printed three others but later came to think they were not his work.

There is also the poem *The Choice of Valentines* (date unknown), and whatever share Nashe may have had in the lost play *The Isle of Dogs* (performed in 1587 before the closing of the theatres on 28 July), and in Marlowe's *Dido, Queen of Carthage*, first published in 1594. Nashe's name appears on the title-page of this play, but no internal evidence suggests shared authorship. Nashe's association with it may have been in preparing the text for the printer, or in writing some verses on Marlowe's death to be published with the first edition, and now, most unfortunately, lost. He very probably wrote, or had a hand in, other things as well, and boasts in *Strange News*: 'I have written in all sorts of humours privately, I am persuaded, more than any young man of my age in England' (M., I, 320).

He was evidently one of those men who cannot be happy for long without a pen in their hand. Yet there never was a writer whose work is less cloistered, and when the term 'journalist' is used about him it is precisely because he is a man out and around in his day: we could follow him in the morning from his room, where 'by a settee out of sight' you would find Harvey's books 'amongst old shoes and boots' (*Have with You*, M., III, 19), out into the city, by boat downstream where 'a waterman plies for his fares' (*Have with You*, M., III, 13) to the book-sellers in St Paul's churchyard, to the ordinary for a meal if there was money, to dine 'with Duke Humphrey' (*Pierce Penniless*, p. 58) if not, to the theatre in the afternoon ('the idlest time of the day', when gentlemen of the Court, captains and soldiers 'do wholly bestow themselves upon pleasure, and that pleasure they divide ... either into gaming, following of harlots, or seeing a play', *Pierce Penniless*, p. 112), and so on till lanthorn and candlelight. So much of the material for his writing comes from observant day-to-day living: the look of the people, the individual tones of their voices, the proverbs which were common wisdom to them all. As G. R. Hibbard points out, in what is to date the only full-length critical study of Nashe,[2] the habit of observing and noting must have started early, for, talking about 'aged mumping beldams', their old-wives' tales and superstitions, he says 'When I was a little child, I was a great auditor of theirs, and had all their witchcrafts at my fingers' ends, as perfect as good-morrow and good-even' (*Terrors of the Night*, p. 232).

Nor do the sketches of him by his contemporaries, or the testimony of his own writing, suggest a mere observer. Dekker, in an addition to his *News from Hell* (the 1607 version, called *A Knight's Conjuring*), describes Nashe among a company of writers in the underworld:

still haunted with the sharp and satirical spirit that followed him here upon earth. For Nashe inveighed bitterly (as he had wont to do) against dry-fisted patrons, accusing them of his untimely death, because if they had given his muse that cherishment which she most worthily deserved, he had fed to his dying day on fat capons, burnt sack and sugar, and not so desperately have ventured his life and shortened his days by keeping company with pickled herrings.

The last phrase refers to Nashe's last published work (*Lenten Stuff*, with its sub-title *In Praise of the Red Herring*[3]), but the passage reads like a portrait from life, the man depicted being recognizably that of his own writings, both critical and convivial.

A similar picture emerges from *The Three Parnassus Plays*, in the character Ingenioso. These plays (their author is anonymous), amusing and valuable for the humorous,

2. G. R. Hibbard, *Thomas Nashe, A Critical Introduction*, London, 1962.

3. Also probably a reference to Nashe's presence at the 'fatal banquet' of Rhenish wine and pickled herring that caused the death of Robert Greene, the playwright (see *Have with You*, M., I, 287–8).

sympathetic insight which they afford into the universities and the prospects and problems of their graduates, are quite clear in the personal reference to Nashe as this satirist who 'carried the deadly stockado in his pen'.[4] For one thing, he is identified by his projecting tooth: the phrase 'whose muse was armed with a gagtooth' recalls, as the editor, J. B. Leishman, points out, Harvey's sentence on Nashe: 'Take heed of the man whom Nature hath marked with a gagtooth, Art furnished with a gagtongue, and Exercise armed with a gagpen, as cruel and murderous weapons as ever drew blood.' But Ingenioso's complaints are also characteristic of Nashe. When first met, he is 'following a gouty patron by the smell, hoping to wring some water from a flint', and in the second play he is seen again cursing the way of the world:

I see wit is but a phantom and idea a quarrelling shadow, that will seldom dwell in the same room with a full purse, but commonly is the idle follower of a forlorn creature. Nay, it is a devil that will never leave a man till it hath brought him to a beggary, a malicious spirit that delights in a close libel or an open satire. Besides, it is an unfortunate thing: I have observed that that head where it dwelleth hath seldom a good hat, or the back it belongs unto, a good suit of apparel.

No doubt there is some amusement here at Nashe's expense (the pot says too much to the kettle about libels and satires, and the descent from spiritual melancholy to canny material interest is comically observed). But essentially the portrait of Ingenioso is a friendly one. He is a good fellow, who writes his pamphlets over 'a pint of wine and a pipe of tobacco'. And the serving man likes him: 'Faith, he seems a mad greek, and I have loved such lads of mettle as that seems to be from my infancy.' Although Ingenioso has the last speech in the play, Thomas Nashe in Ingenioso's person is given an epitaph earlier on by Iudicio; and it is one which with its balance and generosity speaks surely with affection:

4. *The Three Parnassus Plays*, ed. J. B. Leishman, London, 1949.

Let all his faults sleep with his mournful chest,
And there for ever let his ashes rest.
His style was witty, though it had some gall;
Some things he might have mended, so may all.
Yet this I say, that for a mother wit,
Few men have ever seen the like of it.[5]

It is a happy event that these lines should come from his own university. For, however much his popular 'image' was that of the 'mad greek', the 'lad of mettle', nevertheless he was a man of considerable learning, and his respect for scholarship was great. Almost every page of McKerrow's notes on the texts contains its allusions to Ovid, Virgil, Horace and other standard classical writers. Theologians from Augustine and Athanasius to Tyndale and Erasmus; European writers such as La Primaudaye and Castiglione; Spenser, Marlowe, Greene, Lyly, Sidney, Thomas Watson, William Warner and Sir John Davies among his near contemporaries: these were no doubt the standard authors of the educated Elizabethan, but Nashe had them in his system, not just in his notebooks, for the allusions come (in his own phrase) 'thick and three-fold' and are clearly a part of the mind. He had also read closely some more recondite works: Cornelius Agrippa's *De Incertitudine et Vanitate Scientiarum* is a frequent source of reference, a discourse on devils by Georgius Pictorius (*De Illorum Daemonum*, called the *Isagoge*) is another. Chronicles, ballads, grammars, translations, tales and plays: all sorts of reading become a part of his own writing. McKerrow lists over one hundred books by modern authors quoted in his work; and, though his classical learning is no doubt exceeded by that of his great editor, it is in some ways all the more impressive for its inaccuracies, for they suggest reliance on a memory which may be defective in detail but is plentifully stored.

Cambridge was clearly a prime influence in Nashe's life. St John's was a college with a great tradition, and Nashe several times points proudly to its former scholars and masters. It had been a notable supplier of men to Church

5. *ibid.*, p. 245.

and State: William Cecil, Lord Burghley, was the greatest
of several eminent statesmen who were also Johnsmen, and
the college produced at least twenty-six bishops during
Tudor times. 'The most flourishing society in the University at this time', L. V. Ryan calls it, writing on the 1520s
and 30s which were Ascham's time there.[6] By the 1580s,
when Nashe was up, the College had come under Calvinist
influence, and the University itself had, from mid-century
onwards, become too much a Church recruiting-centre for
broader studies to prosper. Nashe was strongly opposed to
the puritans in national as well as university life, and he
writes severely about the decline of standards at Cambridge. Cheke, Ascham and others, he says, had 'set before
our eyes a more perfect method of study':

But how ill their precepts have prospered with our idle age,
that leave the fountains of sciences to follow the rivers of Knowledge, their over-fraught studies and trifling compendiaries may
testify. For I know not how it cometh to pass, by the doting
practices of our divinity dunces, that strain to make their pupils
pulpit-men before they are reconciled to Priscian. But those
years which should be employed in Aristotle are expired in
epitomies; and well too, they may have so much catechism-
vacation to rake up a little refuse-philosophy.[7]

The complaint against 'epitomies', the second-hand
acquaintance with philosophers through other men's sum-
maries, comes from a scholar with standards; just as the
irony of the last clause comes from a critic with a pen he
knows how to use. And his criticisms have all the more
power for being voiced by a man who has just spoken, with
obvious sincerity, of his pride in the University and affection for his College. St John's, he says (echoing Ascham's
words in *The Schoolmaster*):

was as an university within itself, shining so far above all other
houses, halls and hospitals whatsoever, that no college in the
town was able to compare with the tithe of her students; having

6. L. V. Ryan, *Roger Ascham*, Stanford, 1963, pp. 16–22.
7. Preface to Greene's *Menaphon*, M., III, 317–18.

(as I have heard grave men of credit report) more candles light
in it every winter morning before four of the clock than the four-
of-the-clock bell gave strokes.[8]

This comes from the Preface to Greene's *Menaphon*, addressed 'To the Gentlemen Students' of both Universities', and written when Cambridge was a memory not above
a year old. He was to revert to it nearly ten years later in
Lenten Stuff: 'St John's ... in Cambridge, in which house
once I took up my inn for seven year together lacking a
quarter, and yet love it still, for it is and ever was the
sweetest nurse of knowledge in all that University.' [9]

The London pamphleteer still had the Cambridge scholar
within him, and it would no doubt be a source of posthumous pride to him to know that his extant writings
should eventually have become the subject of a monumental
work of scholarship in McKerrow's edition. And another
side of him might well have been quite pleased to see himself, four hundred years later, slipping into a somewhat
outside pocket at the expense of a few new pence.

He might also have been interested to note that this selection of his work contains relatively little of what won him
the reputation which stuck to him in his own time. The
'young Juvenal, that biting satirist', as Greene described him.
the Martin-queller and Harvey-baiter, has receded in vividness along with the issues involved.

The Marprelate controversy was a minor episode in one
of the great debates of English history. From Wycliff's time
to Wesley's, the reformation of the Church was a cause
that drew to it good men who wished that true religion
should prosper and abuses be checked. Such aims touched
the life of everybody in the country, and touched them at
one of the points where the basic quality of a culture is in
question. There were great things said and great things
done. Somewhere in the middle of it all, a slanging-match
blew up among some by-standers; the bishops look on, the

8. p. 476.   9. *Lenten Stuff*, p. 408.

22

people cheer and counter-cheer; it has been a bit of light relief, and it is soon over. One of the main contestants is lost again in the crowd; the other is Nashe, who is remembered for other reasons.

In 1587 Dr John Bridges wrote a tract called *Defence of the Government Established*. The contents were as little appetizing as the title, and in fact it appears to have been a bad piece of work and an embarrassment to the authorities whose defence it undertook. But some defence seemed necessary, for although the reformers were concerned about the Church, the whole power-structure was affected by an attack on one part of it. A better Church was a fine general aim, but in particular it meant better bishops – or none. The implications of this in terms of power were to become abundantly clear to the Stuarts; but even in Elizabeth's time the puritan movement was strong enough to make the government, temporal as well as spiritual, uncomfortably aware that it could not stand idly by. But then, governments are always saying that, and up to this time the situation had been niggling rather than tense. The temperature was raised, however, when, late in 1588 and throughout 1589, a series of pamphlets, eluding the Church's grip on the printing presses, appeared under the signature of Martin Marprelate, Gentleman. These disposed of the *Defence of the Government Established* without great difficulty and with much relish: *Oh, read over D. John Bridges* the fourth pamphlet was called, its popular style matching the lively title just as Bridges matched his stuffy one with a dull text. The pamphlets made a strong impression: for about the only time in its history, the puritan cause became fun.

The alarm of the Government Established was great enough for some of the Church authorities to look round for a David to take aim at this laughing Goliath. Precisely how they happened upon Nashe we do not know; his first publications, the Preface to Greene's *Menaphon* and *The Anatomy of Absurdity*, had established him as a writer best on attack, and as one with no love for the influence

23

of puritans in the universities; perhaps that was enough. In fact, several writers became involved, but in the whole pamphleteering war the only counterblow to match 'Marprelate's' own was the one now attributed with fair certainty to Nashe, *An Almond for a Parrot*.

It strikes the right note. Beginning 'Welcome, Master Martin from the dead,'[10] and much joy may you have of your stage-like resurrection,' and ending 'And so bon nute to your noddiship,' it made it clear that there were laughs to be had. And so there are. On his first page he comes up with a good story of a mean puritan of Northampton who

fetched a more thriftier precedent of funerals piping hot from the primitive church, which, including but a few words and those passing well expounded, kept his wainscot from waste and his linen from wearing; sufficeth, he tumbled his wife naked into the earth at high noon, without sheet or shroud to cover her shame, breathing over her in an audible voice: 'Naked came I out of my mother's womb, and naked shall I return again.'

He is well primed in debate-technique (gain a laugh, gain a point); the points follow, and he strikes them home unsparingly. 'Malicious hypocrite,' he is soon saying, 'didst thou so much malign the successful thrivings of the gospel, that thou shouldst filch thyself, as a new disease, into our government?' Impugn the motives of your opponent, then turn his own words against him. 'The filth of the stews, distilled into ribaldry terms, cannot confectionate a more intemperate style than his pamphlets.' He quotes a few of Martin's 'milder terms', piling them up with Dickensian relish:

wicked priests, presumptuous priests, proud prelates, arrogant bishops, horseleeches, butchers, persecutors of the truth, Lambethical whelps, Spanish inquisitors

10. In *A Countercuff to Martin Junior*, another of the pamphlets once thought to be by Nashe, the writer says 'If the monster be dead': the *Theses Martinianae*, published in July 1589, looked like a posthumous collection. But *The Protestation of Martin* came out of the Martinist press in October and showed the exequies to have been premature.

and then asks:

> Think you this miry-mouthed mate a partaker of heavenly inspiration, that thus abounds in his uncharitable railings.[11]

As for his 'ancient burlibond adjuncts' and 'unwieldy phrases', 'no true syllogism can have elbow room where they are'. There is more of this kind, and a good deal of by-play, including some that is amusingly at the expense of Philip Stubbs and his *Anatomy of Abuses* ('tickle me my Phil a little more in the flank'). Occasionally argument succeeds abuse. But generally all is subsidiary to the great denunciation, for Nashe has identified (correctly, it seems) Martin as John Penry, another Cambridge man, eight years Nashe's senior, and he proceeds to denounce, at first like Micawber on Heep:

> Pen., J. Pen., welch Pen., Pen. the protestationer, demonstrationer, supplicationer, appellationer, Pen., the father, Pen., the son, Pen. Martin Junior, Martin Martinus, Pen. the scholar of Oxford to his friend in Cambridge, Pen. *totum in toto* ...[12]

then in the language of Apemantus or Thersites:

> Predestination, that foresaw how crooked he should prove in his ways, enjoined incest to spawn him splay-footed. Eternity, that knew how awkward he should look to all honesty, consulted with conception to make him squint-eyed, and the devil, that discovered by the heaven's disposition on his birthday how great a limb of his kingdom was coming into the world, provided a rusty superficies from his mother's womb; in every part whereof these words of blessing were most artificially engraven: *Crine ruber, niger ore, brevis pede, lumine lustus.*[13]

Quoting this passage, G. R. Hibbard remarks:

11. *An Almond for a Parrot*, M., III, 347.
12. ibid., p. 365. Pamphlets were issued under the names Martin Senior and Martin Junior. The references to Oxford and Cambridge allude to the subtitle of another of the Martinist pamphlets (see M., V, 471).
13. *An Almond for a Parrot*, M., III, 366. The Latin quotation is from Martial, *Epigrams*, xii, 54 (Red hair, black face, short feet, damaged in one eye').

The whole thing is in the worst of taste, but the sheer nastiness of it all is palliated in some measure by the fantastic ingenuity of invention. The malicious invective is shot through with a kind of perverted poetry. ... Brutality of image and attitude were nothing new at the time, but the ability to combine them with the play of fancy is something peculiar to Nashe.[14]

The authorities cleared the ring when they found and dismantled the Martinist press, and when Nashe reappeared in it some two years later it was with other partners. There is a direct link between them, however. Nashe's writings had irritated one Richard Harvey, a Fellow of Pembroke College, Cambridge, and a man several years older than the upstart critic (Nashe later said he remembered him 'wondrous well' and had 'purged rheum many a time' during his philosophy lectures [15]). Harvey had written a treatise in praise of Ramus, which put him on the wrong side as far as Nashe was concerned, partly because of Ramus's Calvinism and partly because his Logic was being pushed as against Aristotle's in Cambridge by all the people whom Nashe regarded as the corrupters of the University (Ramistic logic is one of the 'newfound toys' referred to in *The Anatomy of Abuses*). Moreover, Penry, Martin Marprelate himself, was an admirer of Ramus, and Nashe had taken him to task for it in *An Almond for a Parrot*. This, together with his irreverent references to his elders in the Preface to Greene's *Menaphon*, was sufficient to provoke Harvey to public rebuke. He wrote two pamphlets in 1590, the second one being called *The Lamb of God*, insignificant enough in themselves, bearing a relationship rather like the assassination at Sarajevo to what followed. Richard Harvey drew a counter-attack from Greene, which brought in Gabriel Harvey, at which Henry Chettle reminded Nashe of his obligations to Greene: the great war was on.

It was Gabriel, Richard's brother, who became the principal on the other side. Nature had not made him a fighting man, but he was acutely conscious of himself, his deserts

14. op. cit., p. 43.
15. *Strange News*, M., I, 313 and 315.

and his disappointments, and this made him ready to lash out at an affront, and to conduct a tenacious defence. It also made him an easy and rather tempting target, for it was clear that the hurts would smart. Interestingly, the terms of his first attack on Nashe apply to himself: 'tormented with other men's felicity, and overwhelmed with his own misery' (Harvey's *Four Letters*, M., V, 84). Nashe never impresses one in this way in his writing, and the picture of him in *The Three Parnassus Plays* does not accord either. But Harvey himself certainly was a disappointed man. His university career meant everything to him, and it did not prosper. Professor in Rhetoric from 1574, he failed to become Public Orator when the appointment was made in 1581; he was passed over when he might well have become Master of Trinity Hall in 1585; and in 1592 he lost his Fellowship there. Few men would take such misfortunes in as philosophical humour as they might hope, but with Harvey his vanity must have been sadly hurt: the vanity, for instance, which made him so happy when the Queen met him and remarked that 'he looked something like an Italian' that he had to write a poem about it, and another about his kissing her hand (Nashe says he thereupon 'quite renounced his natural English accents and gestures and wrested himself wholly to the Italian punctilios, speaking our homely island tongue strangely as if he were but a raw practitioner in it', *Have with You*, p. 490). And indeed, a defensive-aggressive self-esteem speaks out throughout the controversy, and undercuts his own performance. In many ways he was more worthy than Nashe: he had some good arguments on his side, he was a genuine scholar and often very clear-headed. And not for nothing was he the friend of Spenser, who wrote of him as one:

> That, sitting like a looker-on
> Of this world's stage, dost note, with critique pen,
> The sharp dislike of each condition

Yet his character is always revealing itself as mean, vain and, in some fatal way, ridiculous. John Buxton says of him: 'he had an arrogant egotism that at times comes near to megalomania, as he reveals in the privacy of the notes so carefully written in the margins of his books.'[16] 'Tormented with other men's felicity, and overwhelmed with his own misery': he was in a glass house, with David outside fresh from his encounter with Goliath, aiming straight at the holes his own stone-throwing had made.

And Nashe hits repeatedly: to good effect in *Strange News* (or *The Four Letters Confuted*), devastatingly in *Have with You to Saffron Walden*. At the heart of that pamphlet is the famous 'Life' of Harvey: both a genuine biography in its factual reference, and, as Hibbard says, a 'mock-life'. The strength lies in the underplaying; or (if that seems a curious thing to say about so exuberant and unsparing a piece of work) in the feeling of laughter welling up from inside at the very thought of this man, somehow inherently absurd. His performance before the Queen at Audley End and his subsequent antics, his petulant, bewildered dismay when he found himself in Newgate, these are some of the 'best ones' in a life which is seen throughout as a richly comical jest-book. Sometimes it is as though Nashe had his camera with him, and, click, the expression is caught: Harvey coy and simpering, for example, 'like a proud schoolmaster when one of his boys hath made an oration before a county mayor that hath pleased' (*Have with You*, M., III, 70). His snobbery is caught, and with it, again, the foolish complacency: 'Only he tells a foolish twittle-twattle boasting tale ... of the funeral of his kinsman, Sir Thomas Smith (which word "kinsman" I wondered he caused not to be set in great capital letters)' (ibid., p. 58). The abuse is sometimes a straightforward concussion-blow on the bald pate (and Harvey had 'of late very pitifully grown bald'). More often Nashe can afford to play cat and mouse, even to adopt a 'be-kind-to-Gabriel' pose, as when, early in the pamphlet, he prints a little drawing of him. Harvey was a thin man, so Nashe considerately draws him in round hose

16. J. Buxton, *Sir Philip Sidney and the English Renaissance*, London, 1954, p. 119.

instead of his customary Venetian: 'because I would make him look more dapper and plump and round upon it, whereas otherwise he looks like a case of tooth-pikes, or a lutepin in a suit of apparel' (*Have with You*, M., III, 38).

The match resolves itself into a public entertainment (there were those who suspected it was deliberately prolonged by the participants), the interests being the wit and skill in language, and the spectacle of such contrasted characters surveying each other with such distaste. Harvey is best when dealing analytically with Nashe's prose style, at his worst when entering ham-fistedly into the thuggery ('I will batter thy carrion to dirt, whence thou camst; and squeeze thy brain to a snivel, whereof it was curdled' [17]). The contrasts of character do just a little to raise the confrontation to a level slightly higher than the merely personal and incidental. There is the bohemian against the academic; the creative against the analytic; the rashly-expensive against the cautious-mean. Behind the figures also loom two philosophies and historical trends. But, ultimately, the Harvey–Nashe quarrel takes its minor place in literature: the energy goes into devising ways and means of doing battle, not into genuine argument, and the result is that we look at these two clever and sophisticated adults and are entertained by them as we sometimes are by the ingenuities of little children.

Despite his reputation as 'the English Juvenal', however, Nashe was not one of those men who can write only if they have something to attack. Though there is a critical element in most of his work, he is not for ever, in Drayton's phrase, 'scorching and blasting' with words. His stories are told for pleasure in the telling, his jokes are cracked for the fun of them, and his whole style speaks of relish for living, not distaste.

He is also a writer with more variety than is commonly accredited him. Before turning finally to those publications which one thinks of as most essentially himself (discourses

17. *The Works of Gabriel Harvey*, ed. Grosart, II, 238.

ranging freely over morals, customs, histories, writings, and allowing a free play of wit and wisdom), we shall look at a religious homily, a 'dirty' poem, a play (and yet ''tis no play neither, but a show' [18]), and what McKerrow and Hibbard warn us must on no account be called a picaresque novel.

Yet in so far as the term 'picaresque novel' calls to mind an episodic narrative centring on the adventures of a principal character who is up to all sorts of tricks and gets himself and others into various sorts of difficulty, it is not such a misleading piece of introductory shorthand to represent *The Unfortunate Traveller* – which in fact resists categorization of any sort. It also resists attempts to find a kind of depth and organization which critics would like it to have: 'It embodies nothing that can be called a view of life' (Hibbard [19]), 'It has no organizing principle; it is not a unified work of art' (Wells [20]). And yet it does have a distinctive character of its own amongst Nashe's books, and something that goes beyond the mere facts that it comes nearest to telling a tale, as continuous, if episodic, narrative, and that its setting is European.

It is by far the most brutal of his works; cruelty is like a refrain in it, rarely out of mind for long, sometimes so gratuitous in detail as to be a far from amiable indulgence. It is true that the Elizabethans were not squeamish, that there was plenty of cruelty in their drama, and that Nashe has some bloodthirsty (and tasteless) passages elsewhere. But the sickening story of Miriam and her children (which would be an example) is incidental to *Christ's Tears over Jerusalem*; [21] and the barbaric prophetic gloating over the public disembowelling of Penry is not recognizable as thematic in *An Almond for a Parrot*: [22] whereas, in *The Un-*

18. *Summer's Last Will and Testament*, p. 148.
19. op. cit., p. 179.
20. *Thomas Nashe: Selected Works*, ed. S. Wells, London, 1964, p. 18.
21. M., II, 71.
22. M., III, 348–9.

fortunate Traveller, the execution of Cutwolfe only registers as the last and worst in a procession of cruelties. I think, too, that cruelty is present from the beginning, and that it increases in seriousness and barbarity fairly steadily. The opening pages tell of young Jack Wilton's witty tricks, how with 'a cunning shift of the seventeens' he would cadge and lie, trick, ridicule and hurt. Whether as a soft-hearted twentieth-century liberal, or as suspecting that in real life one would probably be one of his victims, I have never found Jack Wilton's practical jokes quite as mirthful as he himself (and presumably the author) thinks them to be. Of course, 'his good ass-headed Honour, mine host', 'Captain Cogswounds', the 'Switzer captain that was far gone for want of the wench' should have seen through the young whippersnapper; as he says (and it might have been Ben Jonson's proverb as well as Jack Wilton's), 'Adam never fell till God made fools.' Still, one is not altogether sorry when the tables are turned, and jolly J.W. is 'pitifully whipped for his holiday lie'.

The practical joking and pitiful whipping are, of course, in historical context, something less than cruelty and barbarism, but in a playful way they suggest a tune that is to ring out harshly and inescapably enough later in the composition. It is not long before we visit the battlefield and see 'more arms and legs scattered in the field ... than will be gathered up till Doomsday' (p. 277). If that phrase recalls some words spoken in the night before Agincourt, it will recall tones of pity, terms of thoughtfulness and responsibility. There is none of that in Nashe, however, who shows principally the interest in ingenious horrors which one associates with Lucan, and who, as he sees 'a bundle of bodies fettered together in their own bowels', reminds us of an edifying passage of Roman history in which tyrant emperors 'used to tie condemned living caitiffs face to face with dead corpses'; so, he adds (in case we should have missed the point) 'were the half-living here mixed with squeezed carcases long putrefied' (p. 276).

If one does not find a relationship between the 'tune' of

this and the frisky practical joking of the early pages, it should become clearer a few pages later when the travellers visit Germany and consider the fall of the Anabaptists. As with Jack Wilton's victims, credulity was their undoing. They saw a rainbow in the sky after they had asked for a sign, and since the rainbow was their own ensign they took it as a favourable omen, and were duly massacred. 'That which wretches would have, they easily believe': the tag matches the earlier proverb ('Adam never fell ...'), the difference being simply one of intensity, for the practical joker here is not Jack Wilton, but God or Fate, or whatever it is that is on the side of the big armies. We are not spared details: 'So ordinary at every footstep was the imbrument of iron in blood, that one could hardly discern heads from bullets, or clottred hair from mangled flesh hung with gore' (p. 286).

What is interesting is that this account *is* accompanied by some feeling of revulsion, characteristically expressed in terms of common experience in London. He has no time for the Anabaptists, he says, but to think of their slaughter is to be reminded of bear-baiting: you think a bear 'is the most cruellest of all beasts', but when he is 'too too bloodily overmatched and deformedly rent in pieces by an unconscionable number of curs, it would move compassion against kind'. As *The Unfortunate Traveller* proceeds, so do the horrors succeed one another fairly regularly, in amongst the 'reasonable conveyance of history and variety of mirth' which Nashe has promised his readers. I think that Nashe is partly indulging his own bad taste, and that of his readers, but that ultimately *The Unfortunate Traveller* is an intuitive (rather than intellectual) exploration of national character.

After the execution of Cutwolfe, Jack Wilton comes quickly home. Nashe had written a long enough book: no doubt that was the first reason. But also he has seen enough. That episode is climactic; he shakes off the dust of Italy, and although he does not rule out the possibility of a sequel, he ends: 'otherwise I will swear upon an English chronicle never to be outlandish chronicler more while I live'. There is a return, with relief, to things English; not only as being 'home', but also as being more humane. The long dissertation of 'the banished earl' ('Get thee home, my young lad: lay thy bones peaceably in the sepulchre of thy fathers; wax old in overlooking thy grounds; be at hand to close the eyes of thy kindred') is, I think, central.[23] Jack Wilton comments on it flippantly, which is in character (it is not really quite true that, in Hibbard's words, 'Jack has neither conscience nor character. As a realized human being he does not exist at all,'[24]). But the words have carried weight: they are effectively placed in the book to summarize experience and direct reaction, though Nashe is obviously conscious of his unwonted gravity (Jack's reactions to the lecture are rather like Will Summer's to the serious speeches in *Summer's Last Will*) and it is also true that the speech has the mark of set-piece oratory. Even so, it summarizes, defines and directs. The question is sometimes asked why the traveller is 'unfortunate', when he is in fact lucky as a cat with nine lives. Perhaps it is that travelling itself is 'unfortunate', the title suggesting something like Kingsley Amis's *I Like it Here*. The implicit feeling of the book is that England may have its old fools and young rogues: the one gets exploited and the other whipped, and, out of that, folk 'make themselves merry ... many a winter's evening after'. And England may also have its bear-baiting, which you may come to for amusement and be surprised to find the spectacle 'moves compassion'. But with the French battlefields, the Münster massacre, Zadoch and Zachary, and the fiendish Esdras of Granada, we, mercifully, cannot compete.

I suppose that if *The Unfortunate Traveller* failed to secure Nashe's inclusion in any reasonably comprehensive Anthology of Bad Taste, he might still gain a place through *Christ's Tears over Jerusalem* or *The Choice of Valentines*. Not that I see anything distasteful in the sheer execution,

23. *The Unfortunate Traveller*, pp. 340—47.
24. op. cit,, p. 177.

33

as opposed to the subject, of that poem. Indeed, living in the permissive sixties and (presumably) seventies, one has the opportunity (if not necessarily the intention) to compare the pornography of Nashe's age and ours. 'Adult reading', the modern book-covers would say. But inside, I do not think we would find the literary influences to be those of Ovid and Chaucer, nor would we be aware that this was a world in which

> young men in their jolly roguery
> Rose early in the morn 'fore break of day
> To seek them valentines so trim and gay.

Nor 'from out the house of venery' would there step 'a foggy three-chinned dame'; nor would we realize as we read that the author's own gratification was to be found in his success not as an aphrodisiac but as a wit. The piece survives only in manuscripts, one of them incomplete and partly in cipher; but it achieved a certain fame in its time (there is a reference in Sir John Davies's *Scourge of Folly*, 1611), and it seems worth reprinting both as a curiosity, and for what, at this date, one can see as a certain charm and freshness. In its (not unimportant) way, it even does Nashe's century some credit.

At all events, Nashe made his own apology in *Christ's Tears over Jerusalem*: 'those that have been perverted by my works, let them read this, and it shall thrice more benefit them' (M., II, 13). He does in fact cut an unwittingly comic figure in the prefatory address 'To the Reader', from which that quotation comes. He says farewell 'to fantastical satirism', desires 'to be at peace with all men', and begs pardon of all his enemies, 'even of Master Doctor Harvey'. Edward IV's death-bed reconciliations in *Richard III* and Richard's own protestations (" 'Tis death to me to be at enmity.... I thank God for my humility' [25]) come to mind all too readily: but perhaps unfairly. For there is little reason to

25. *Richard III*, II, 1.

doubt Nashe's sincerity, and the genuineness of his intentions in this homiletic work can hardly be in question when
there is so much evidence of care over structure and expression, and when the piece is so resolutely sustained (it
is easily the longest of Nashe's works. It is severely criticized in Hibbard's study: '*Christ's Tears* is a monument of
bad taste, tactlessness and unremitting over-elaboration for
which it is not easy to find a parallel; a kind of gigantic
oxymoron in which style and content, tone and intention
are consistently at odds.'[26] Actually, these strictures are
made to apply principally to the first half, the second containing some lively observation and social criticism in a
manner more naturally Nashe's own. But, although many
points are acutely noted in Hibbard's chapter, and although
Nashe's faulty taste is sometimes glaringly obvious, I still
think there is merit ignored. For example, Hibbard says
that Nashe 'seems to have had no understanding of how
much the Gospel owes to the nakedness and directness of its
prose'; yet, following on the very passage whose quotation
has led up to that remark, there are a couple of pages in
which the parable of the owner of the vineyard is told with
admirable simplicity and directness, and, what is more, with
a feeling for prose rhythms which is closely akin to that of
the Authorized Version, and which is beautiful. When
Nashe says he wishes to be God's 'pure simple orator', he
means that he desires purity and singleness of purpose,
simple in that it shall be unmixed with baser matter, including any desire for personal glory. And to a degree that is
quite remarkable with him, he does keep himself out of
the spotlight and focus it upon the objects in question
without personal intrusion. 'I hate in thy name to speak
coldly to a quick-witted generation', he says in his introductory paragraph. 'Now help, now direct', he prays at the
end of it: 'for now I transform myself from myself, to be
thy unworthy speaker to the world'. Mr Hibbard says he
didn't mean it, and that the Holy Ghost didn't listen to
him. It is, of course, a far cry from this to Milton's

26. op. cit., p. 123.

35

What in me is dark
Illumine, what is low raise and support.

Yet, if we are to suppose ourselves so well-informed about
the Holy Ghost, we might conclude that it did the same
for both men: hear and obey sometimes, turn a deaf ear
at others.

In any case, the powers above probably had little time
just then for the spiritual ambitions of reformed satirists,
for these were times of plague, and the cries of the dying
were raised to heaven day and night. This is what had
changed Nashe's tune:

How the Lord hath begun to leave our house desolate unto
us, let us enter into the consideration thereof with ourselves. At
this instant is a general plague dispersed throughout our land.
No voice is heard in our streets but that of Jeremy: 'Call for the
mourning women, that they may come and take up a lamentation for us, for death is come into our windows and entered into
our palaces.' [27]

He was writing this probably in the early autumn of 1593,
after nearly twelve months in which the plague had run
and God supposedly executed judgement. Twelve months
earlier, as the summer of 1592 was making its last will and
testament, the plague had loomed darkly, if less terribly,
as part of the backdrop to the 'show' which Nashe wrote
for the Archbishop's household at Croydon, and in which
the poet in him called out, as it never did elsewhere:

Go not yet hence, bright soul of the sad year

and:

I am sick, I must die,
Lord, have mercy upon us.

Summer's Last Will and Testament has a great deal of
charm and happiness in it, and critical discussion is always
in danger of misrepresenting it because it finds the sombre
backdrop the most interesting thing to discuss. But the

27. *Christ's Tears over Jerusalem*, M., II, 157.

whole play, not just the most famous of its lyrics ('Adieu, farewell, earth's bliss'), is deeply in the tradition of the medieval *ubi sunt* poem. The basic dramatic structure in which each of the seasons appears in turn, as in a pageant, keeps transience before us as readily as any grimmer *memento mori*. 'Forsooth, because the plague reigns in most places in this latter end of summer, Summer must come in sick,' 'All good things vanish, less than in a day,' 'This world is transitory; it was made of nothing, and it must to nothing,' 'Death waiteth at the door for thee and me,' 'Sickness, be thou my soul's physician,' 'The plague full swift goes by,' 'The worms will curse thy flesh another day,' 'withered flowers and herbs unto dead corpses, for to deck them with',

> London doth mourn, Lambeth is quite forlorn.
> Trades cry Woe worth that ever they were born ...
> From winter, plague and pestilence, good Lord deliver us.

The quotations are taken evenly from all parts of the play; and there might be many more of them. As against this, there is 'Spring, the sweet spring' (when 'Old wives a-sunning sit'); there is the joy of singing and dancing, the providence of Harvest, the mirth of Will Summers. There are also some dull patches. But when Michael Ayrton calls it 'on the whole a dull and clumsy piece' ('all Nashe's finest verse is embedded in it like diamonds in paste'),[28] one has again to exclaim against injustice, and to refer the reader to an excellent chapter by a more appreciative writer. C. L. Barber sees it as 'a kind of serio-comic *Everyman*', and presents his judgements as the outcome of a genuine reading:

> This poised two-sidedness is apparent even in the complaints about perishing: for a small example, Summer's line 'Harvest and Age have whitened my green head', links Age's sad white hair with the paling out of grain as it ripens, so that Death is connected to the consummation of harvest. The playfulness of the wit with which grain is made hair implicitly recognises that men are more durable than one season's wheaten crown – though they have their season too. In this two-sidedness, Nashe's piece

28. *The Unfortunate Traveller*, ed. M. Ayrton, London, p. 7.

anticipates Shakespeare's way of simultaneously exhibiting revel and framing it with other sorts of experience.[29]

It is not wise to risk a collocation of any writer with Shakespeare, except on the firmest ground, and in many ways Nashe is demonstrably un-Shakespearean. Yet it is a comparison which has been made also by another critic, normally fairly cautious in his praise. Walter Raleigh wrote of him in *The English Novel*:

The strongest and best of his writing . . . merits the highest praise – it is the likest of all others to Shakespeare's prose writing. The same irrepressible, inexhaustible wit, the same over-powering and often careless wealth of vocabulary, the same delight in humorous aberrations of logic distinguish both writers. And Shakespeare alone of his sixteenth century contemporaries can surpass Nashe in the double command of the springs of terror and of humour.[30]

I think the last sentence claims too much, for I do not see the springs of terror as truly being under Nashe's command at all: the quiet elegiac tone of *Summer's Last Will* comes nearer than the tortures and depravities of *The Unfortunate Traveller* in realizing the tragic qualm, but even there the intense fright and urgency of 'terror' are hardly in question.[31] But Raleigh's second sentence surely *is* just, and its truth is demonstrated on most pages of the prose works which remain for a brief consideration.

Rather than Shakespeare, however, I would suggest Dickens, if some other writer is to be invoked in order to help define Nashe's quality. It is Dickens who comes most constantly to mind as one recognizes the vividness and wit of Nashe's thumbnail character-sketches. In *Pierce Penniless*,

29. C. L. Barber, *Shakespeare's Festive Comedy*, Princeton, 1959, p. 61.

30. W. Raleigh, *The English Novel*, London, 1894.

31. Raleigh's view is also that of R. G. Howarth, who writes: 'By the intensity of his vision and his power to chill the soul with horror which is not just sensation, [Nashe] rises above mere tragedy of blood almost to the tragic plane of Webster.' (*Two Elizabethan Writers of Fiction*, Cape Town, 1956, p. 31.)

for instance, the 'old straddling usurer' with 'a huge, worm-eaten nose, like a cluster of grapes hanging downwards' (p. 58); or the affected pseudo-traveller behaving 'like a decayed earl ... all *Italianato* is his talk' when in reality he is merely some 'dapper Jack that hath been but over at Dieppe' and who will now 'wring his face round about, as a man would stir up a mustard pot, and talk English through the teeth like Jacques Scabbed-hams or Monsieur Mingo de Mousetrap' (p. 65); or the Dutchman whose education is begun so late in life 'that you shall see a great boy with a beard learn his ABC and sit weeping under the rod when he is thirty years old' (p. 39). The Dickensian touch is there in the specificity: the dapper Jack has been 'but over at Dieppe' (another writer would have said 'but over to France'); he contorts his face 'as a man would stir up a mustard pot' (the non-Dickensian writer says 'in an absurd grimace'); the weeping Dutch school-man is 'a great boy with a beard', (he could so easily have been just 'an over-grown schoolboy').

The sheer energy of the writing is also Dickensian. There is often the resourcefulness of a musician devising variations on a theme. In the opening of *Have with You to Saffron Walden*, for example, his theme is the fact that Doctor Harvey has published some more pamphlets, and the aspect that he takes up for comical exploitation is the great bulk or weight of them. Variation I is the problem of transport: 'More letters yet from the Doctor? Nay, then we shall be sure to have a whole Gravesend barge full of news ... Out upon't, here's a packet of epistling as big as a pack of woollen cloth or a stack of salt-fish. Carrier, did'st thou bring it by wain or on horseback?' 'By wain, sir, and it has cracked me three axletrees. ...' The cart, we gather, 'cried creak under them forty times every furlong.' Variation II: how to accommodate it. 'You may believe me if you will, I was fain to lift my chamber door off the hinges, only to let it in, it was so fulsome a bonarobe and terrible rounceval', (he says he weighed it first on an ironmonger's scales and found it 'counterpoiseth a cade of herrings and three Holland cheeses'). Variation III: its possible interest to athletes, and its future in sporting events. 'Credibly it was rumoured about the court that the guard meant to try masteries with it before the Queen, and instead of throwing the sledge or the hammer, to hurl it forth at the arms' length for a wager.' The zest is infectious because it appears to be so spontaneous, and one laughs with him because he scores off his opponent through what might be the observations of any impartial observer with a sense of humour. Thus a happy misprint in one of Harvey's publications is joyfully acclaimed: 'But it would seem he is ashamed of the incomprehensible corpulency thereof himself, for at the end of the 199 pages he begins with one 100 again, to make it seem little.' [32] And the laughter is Dickensian because of the penmanship: he has that rare way with the pen, whereby it can communicate zest, laughter, personality, quick shifts of mood, as though it were the actual speaking-voice of a man who (as a different kind of artist) knows that he can set the table on a roar or hold an audience, from the stalls to the gods, in the palm of his hand.

One is never so aware of this skill, of Nashe's essential character, and hence of his limitations, as in his last published writing, called *Nashe's Lenten Stuff*; and in this the comparison is not with Shakespeare or Dickens as much as with James Joyce. People who knew Joyce well sometimes say that in his last years the only passion he had was for words themselves. Granted, one does not quite feel this to be so with *Lenten Stuff* (the birch-branch-swinging prose-style takes him heavenwards, but he comes back, feet firmly on the ground, to say, for instance, that 'that which especially nourished the most prime pleasure' in him was the sight next morning in Yarmouth harbour of ships driven in by storm overnight, their sails now spread out against the sky). Nor does one feel that he could quite have said, as Joyce did with rueful realism, that all he asked of his readers was that they should spend their lifetime in the study of his works. But words *qua* words are certainly a main delight

32. *Have with You*, M., III, 33–5.

in the author's mind here: he indulges his own kind of scribbledehobble as the nonce words come thick and fast ('those greybeard huddle-duddles and crusty cum-twangs were strook with such stinging remorse of their euclionism and snudgery', p. 379), and the full vigour of the English language matches up with the zestful humour (so 'Cerdicus bellicosus Saxo' in Camden's *Britannia* becomes 'one Cerdicus, a plashing Saxon, that had revelled here and there with his battle-axe', p. 385). And Nashe is also quite ready to leave the reader standing and breathless:

> The posterior Italian and German cornugraphers stick not to applaud and canonize unnatural sodomitry, the strumpet errant, the gout, the ague, the dropsy, the sciatica, folly, drunkenness, and slovenry. The Galli Gallinacei, or cocking French, swarm every pissing while in their primer editions, *Imprimeda iour duy*, of the unspeakable healthful conducibleness of the Gomorrian great Poco a Poco, their true countryman every inch of him, the prescript laws of tennis or balonne (which is most of their gentlemen's chief livelihoods). the commodity of hoarseness, blear-eyes, scabbed hams, threadbare cloaks, potched eggs, and panados.[33]

And if one should say 'These words are not mine', Nashe would quite probably reply 'No, nor not mine now', and pass on, reflecting that a knavish speech sleeps in a foolish ear. For there is a certain cavalier indifference to the world and its opinions in this book: the dedication is to no nobleman or patron but to 'Lusty Humfrey' King, author of *An Half-Pennyworth of Wit in a Pennyworth of Paper*, and the Introduction addresses Nashe's readers, 'he care not what they be'. As to 'my huge words which I use in this book', well, he despises measured, demure, soft moderation, he says. He is following his own 'true vein' for once, and as for the rest of the world, 'you are your own men to do as you list'.

Suppose 'doing as we list' includes analysing, wresting for meaning, and, ultimately, assessing value. If we were to

33. *Lenten Stuff*, p. 403.

'analyse' the dazzling piece of apparent jabberwocky quoted above, we would find it had a meaning, and a place in the argument. Nashe's subject is 'the praise of the red herring'; and 'Why not?' he asks, seeing that there are learned treatises on every trivial and/or obscene subject under the sun, from tennis to sodomy, from fashionable ball-games to the effects of the pox. Rather like Lucky's speech in *Waiting for Godot*, the crazy jumble of words yields more on inspection; unlike that, however, it does not have a part in the expression of a view of life that finally has to be taken seriously. Nashe's writing is a performance, done for the delight of the thing itself. It is a virtuoso piece, *allegro con brio*, by a man who can make his pen move in a variety of measures: this one is, he says, 'a light friskin of my wit', whereas *Terrors of the Night*, for example, is simple and direct in style and moves at an easy walking-pace. The use of the medium fits the mood of the piece; and, of course, there is an essential artistic sensitivity and implicit success in that. 'But beyond it?' one still asks. What, ultimately, has Nashe to offer beyond the pleasures of watching a painter work with his colours, hearing a pianist go through his studies, or laughing with the others at the table as Yorick jibes and gambols?

We might, for instance, look to a critic and satirist for an underlying passion for justice, or at any rate for a radical analysis of the sources of injustice. Nashe is not entirely without either; but for understanding I would sooner go to Jonson, and for feeling to Dekker. In *Christ's Tears* he says that we should 'keep and cherish the casual poor among us' and give 'pensions to maimed soldiers and poor scholars as other nations do' (M., II, 161), but there is nothing as sympathetic as in Dekker's very comparable piece *The Seven Deadly Sins of London* or his *Work for Armourers*, and nothing so trenchant as the motto of that book: 'God help the poor, the Rich can shift'. Nashe was, in fact, curiously conservative in many ways. For levellers, who would 'take away the title of mine and thine from amongst us', he has nothing but contempt; for the pretensions of common folk, and the absurdities of seeing 'Cli. the cobbler and New. the souter jerking out their elbows in every pulpit' (*Almond for a Parrot*, M., III, 351–2), he has nothing but ridicule. Nor do we find that more general standards, such as those of kindness, common-sense, beauty or order, are invoked with much more consistency or depth of conviction.

And yet Nashe does represent something more than a collection of laughs and images, vivid lines and well-rounded sentences. What he enunciates is little to what he knows; what is explicit doctrine is little to what is expressed and communicated. *Summer's Last Will* is a branch which has grown, out of roots that have clutched: an age-old condition of life is presented, where the seasons are no mere backdrop, and where the medieval *ubi sunt* theme is given a modern realization through the imminence and urgency of the plague. Yet this is not the essential Nashe, though it is an essential part of him. The nearest he comes to a declaration of doctrine is in the introduction to *Lenten Stuff* (p. 377): 'I had as lieve have no sun as have it shine faintly', and 'not caring for ... water and wine mixed together: but give me the pure wine of itself, and that begets good blood and heats the brain throughly'. The intention voiced in this statement (for one is implied) is what *Lenten Stuff* itself achieves, without any explicit doctrine or moralizing. In its Falstaffian way ('Banish plump Jack and banish all the world') it gives us the world. We are creatures who want food and love food (the actual physical stuff that goes into our stomachs and keeps us alive): so praise the red herring. We spend our strength and our skill getting it: so praise the fishermen of East Anglia. There is splendour in our life too: 'history' (and Yarmouth has had its share), power (even the Pope likes his sea-food), love (tragically and absurdly caught up in the wrig-wrag enmity of two ancient towns which were just like Yarmouth and Lowestoft). There is also the energy which is eternal delight, and which finds expression in the writer's love for words. And this writer *knows* he may be censured for 'playing with a shuttlecock, or tossing empty bladders in the air' (but at least not every fool, he says, 'can wring juice out of a flint', and he has brought it off with 'the right trick of a workman'). But (although he himself would never say anything so pretentious) his shuttlecock, like that of all good jesters, is nothing less than this absurd globe; and his bladder nothing less than the bubble of a man's life.

Nashe is an entertainer, an artist conscious of his craft, proud of success, apprehensive of failure. But 'no man ever wrote so well', Chesterton said of Stevenson, '... who cared only about writing'. Nashe wrote of the human scene without reverence but with savour. We can at least do the same for him.

SELECT BIBLIOGRAPHY

EDITIONS OF NASHE

The Works of Thomas Nashe, ed. R. B. McKerrow, in five volumes, with corrections and supplementary notes edited by F. P. Wilson, Oxford, 1958.

Thomas Nashe (selected works), ed. Stanley Wells, The Stratford-upon-Avon Library, London, 1964.

Three Elizabethan Pamphlets (includes *The Unfortunate Traveller*), ed. G. R. Hibbard, London, 1951.

The Unfortunate Traveller (with illustrations), ed. Michael Ayrton, London, 1948.

CRITICAL WORKS

Thomas Nashe, A Critical Introduction, G. R. Hibbard, London, 1962.

Shakespeare's Festive Comedy, C. L. Barber, Princeton, 1959.

Two Elizabethan Writers of Fiction, R. G. Howarth, Cape Town, 1956.

See also

The Three Parnassus Plays, ed. J. B. Leishman, London, 1949.

The Works of Gabriel Harvey, ed. A. Grosart, The Huth Library, 1884.

PART II

I

Pierce Penniless his Supplication to the Devil

Barbaria grandis habere nihil [1]

A private Epistle of the Author to the Printer,
wherein his full meaning and purpose in publishing
this book is set forth.

FAITH, I am very sorry, sir, I am thus unawares betrayed to infamy. You write to me my book is hasting to the second impression: he that hath once broke the ice of impudence need not care how deep he wade in discredit. I confess it to be a mere toy, not deserving any judicial man's view. If it have found any friends, so it is; you know very well that it was abroad a fortnight ere I knew of it, and uncorrected and unfinished it hath offered itself to the open scorn of the world. Had you not been so forward in the republishing of it, you should have had certain epistles to orators and poets to insert to the latter end; as, namely, to the ghost of Machevill, of Tully, of Ovid, of Roscius,[2] of Pace,[3] the Duke of Norfolk's jester; and lastly, to the ghost of Robert Greene,[4] telling him what a coil [5] there is with pamphleting on him after his death. These were prepared for *Pierce Penniless* first setting forth, had not the fear of infection detained me with my lord [6] in the country.

1. 'To have nothing is the great mark of the uncultured' (Ovid). (M. suggests the tag may have been the printer's idea.)

2. Famous comic actor, defended in an oration by Cicero.

3. John Pace (*c.* 1523–90), jester to Henry VIII and later to the Duke of Norfolk.

4. Robert Greene died September 1592 (see p. 18).

5. Disturbance, 'row'.

6. M. dismisses the idea that this was Archbishop Whitgift, suggesting it was a patron, perhaps the Earl of Derby.

Now this is that I would have you to do in this second edition: first, cut off that long-tailed title,[7] and let me not in the forefront of my book make a tedious mountebank's oration to the reader, when in the whole there is nothing praiseworthy.

I hear say there be obscure imitators that go about to frame a second part to it and offer it to sell in Paul's Churchyard and elsewhere, as from me. Let me request you, as ever you will expect any favour at my hands, to get somebody to write an epistle before it, ere you set it to sale again, importing thus much: that if any such lewd device intrude itself to their hands, it is a cozenage and plain knavery of him that sells it to get money, and that I have no manner of interest or acquaintance with it. Indeed if my leisure were such as I could wish, I might haps, half a year hence, write *The Return of the Knight of the Post*[8] *from Hell*, with the devil's answer to the supplication; but as for a second part of *Pierce Penniless*, it is a most ridiculous roguery.

Other news I am advertised of, that a scald[9] trivial lying pamphlet, called *Greene's Groatsworth of Wit*,[10] is given out to be of my doing. God never have care of my soul, but utterly renounce me, if the least word or syllable in it proceeded from my pen, or if I were any way privy to the writing or printing of it. I am grown at length to see into the vanity of the world more than ever I did, and now I condemn myself for nothing so much as playing the dolt in print. Out upon it, it is odious, specially in this moralizing age, wherein everyone seeks to shew himself a politician by misinterpreting.

In one place of my book, Pierce Penniless saith but to the Knight of the Post, 'I pray how might I call you,' and they

7. The first edition was called *Piers Penniless his supplication to the Devil. Describing the over-spreading of vice, and suppression of virtue. Pleasantly interlaced with variable delights, and pathetically intermixed with conceited reproofs.*

8. *Knight of the Post*: A professional false-witness.

9. Scurvy, contemptible.

10. Entered Stationer's Register 20 September 1592.

say I meant one Howe, a knave of that trade, that I never heard of before.

The antiquaries are offended[11] without cause, thinking I go about to detract from that excellent profession, when (God is my witness) I reverence it as much as any of them all, and had no manner of allusion to them that stumble at it. I hope they will give me leave to think there be fools of that art as well as of all other. But to say I utterly condemn it as an unfruitful study, or seem to despise the excellent qualified parts of it, is a most false and injurious surmise. There is nothing that if a man list he may not wrest or pervert. I cannot forbid any to think villainously, *Sed caveat emptor*,[12] let the interpreter beware; for none ever heard me make allegories of an idle text. Write who will against me, but let him look his life be without scandal; for if he touch me never so little, I'll be as good as *The Black Book*[13] to him and his kindred.

Beggarly lies no beggarly wit but can invent. Who spurneth not at a dead dog? But I am of another metal; they shall know that I live as their evil angel, to haunt them world without end, if they disquiet me without cause.

Farewell, and let me hear from you as soon as it is come forth. I am the plague's prisoner in the country as yet: if the sickness cease before the third impression, I will come and alter whatsoever may be offensive to any man, and bring you the latter end.[14]

Your friend,

THO. NASH

Pierce Penniless His Supplication to the Devil

HAVING spent many years in studying how to live, and lived a long time without money, having tired my youth with

11. Perhaps by pp. 79–80 (M.).

12. Literally 'Let the buyer beware' (proverb).

13. Greene says he had a work of this name in preparation, which was to attack scoundrels by name and unrip their villainies (M.).

14. The Epistles mentioned on p. 49.

folly and surfeited my mind with vanity, I began at length to look back to repentance, and address my endeavours to prosperity. But all in vain I sat up late and rose early, contended with the cold, and conversed with scarcity; for all my labours turned to loss, my vulgar Muse was despised and neglected, my pains not regarded, or slightly rewarded, and I myself, in prime of my best wit, laid open to poverty.* Whereupon, in a malcontent humour, I accused my fortune, railed on my patrons, bit my pen, rent my papers, and raged in all points like a madman. In which agony tormenting myself a long time, I grew by degrees to a milder discontent; and pausing a while over my standish,[16] I resolved in verse to paint forth my passion.† Which best agreeing with the vein of my unrest, I began to complain in this sort:

> Why is't damnation to despair and die,
> When life is my true happiness' disease?
> My soul, my soul, thy safety makes me fly
> The faulty means, that might my pain appease.
> > Divines and dying men may talk of hell,
> > But in my heart her several torments dwell.

> Ah, worthless wit, to train me to this woe,
> Deceitful arts, that nourish discontent:
> Ill thrive the folly that bewitched me so;
> Vain thoughts, adieu, for now I will repent.
> > And yet my wants persuade me to proceed,
> > Since none takes pity of a scholar's need.

* *Discite qui sapitis, non haec quae scimus inertes; Sed trepidas acies, et fera bella sequi.*[15]
† *Est aliquid fatale malum per verba levare.*[17]

15. 'Learn, if you are wise, not the things which we inactive people know, but about bristling battle-lines' (Ovid).
16. Inkstand.
17. 'It is something to lighten a deadly ill by words' (Ovid).

Forgive me, God, although I curse my birth,
And ban [18] the air, wherein I breathe a wretch;
Since misery hath daunted all my mirth,
And I am quite undone through promise-breach.
  Oh friends, no friends, that then ungently frown,
  When changing Fortune casts us headlong down.*

Without redress complains my careless verse,
And Midas-ears relent not at my moan;
In some far land will I my griefs rehearse,
'Mongst them that will be mov'd when I shall groan.
  England, adieu, the soil that brought me forth;
  Adieu, unkind, where skill is nothing worth.

These rhymes thus abruptly set down, I tossed my imaginations a thousand ways to see if I could find any means to
relieve my estate; but all my thoughts consorted to this conclusion, that the world was uncharitable, and I ordained to
be miserable. Thereby I grew to consider how many base
men, that wanted those parts which I had, enjoyed content
at will and had wealth at command. I called to mind a
cobbler, that was worth five hundred pound; an hostler,
that had built a goodly inn, and might dispend forty pound
yearly by his land; a car-man in a leather pilch,[20] that had
whipped out a thousand pound out of his horse tail. 'And
have I more wit than all these?' thought I to myself, 'Am
I better born? Am I better brought up? Yea, and better
favoured? [21] And yet am I a beggar? What is the cause?
How am I crossed? Or whence is this curse?'

Even from hence, that men that should employ such as
I am, are enamoured of their own wits, and think whatever
they do is excellent, though it be never so scurvy; that learning (of the ignorant) is rated after the value of the ink and
paper, and a scrivener better paid for an obligation, than a

* *Pol me occidistis, amici.*[19]

18. Curse.
19. 'You are killing me, my friends' (Horace).
20. 'An outer garment' (NED).
21. Better looking.

scholar for the best poem he can make; that every gross-brained idiot is suffered to come into print, who if he set forth a pamphlet of the praise of pudding-pricks,[22] or write a treatise of Tom Thumb or the exploits of Untruss,[23] it is bought up thick and threefold, when better things lie dead.* How then can we choose but be needy, when there are so many drones amongst us, or ever prove rich, that toil a whole year for fair looks?

Gentle Sir Philip Sidney, thou knewest what belonged to a scholar, thou knewest what pains, what toil, what travail, conduct to perfection; well couldst thou give every virtue his encouragement, every art his due, every writer his desert; cause none more virtuous, witty, or learned than thyself.

But thou art dead in thy grave, and hast left too few successors of thy glory, too few to cherish the sons of the Muses or water those budding hopes with their plenty, which thy bounty erst planted.†

Believe me, gentlemen (for some cross mishaps have taught me experience), there is not that strict observation of honour, which hath been heretofore. Men of great calling take it of merit to have their names eternized by poets; and whatsoever pamphlet or dedication encounters them, they put it up in their sleeves, and scarce give him thanks that presents it. Much better is it for those golden pens to raise such ungrateful peasants from the dunghill of obscurity, and make them equal in fame to the worthies of old, when their doting self-love shall challenge it of duty, and not only give them nothing themselves, but impoverish liberality in others.

This is the lamentable condition of our times, that men of

* *Scribimus indocti doctique poemata passim.*[24]

†*Heu rapiunt mala fata bonos.*[25]

22. Skewers.

23. *the exploits of Untruss*: A ballad attributed to Anthony Munday (1553–1633).

24. 'Learned and ignorant, we are writing poems everywhere' (Horace).

25. 'Alas, the wicked fates snatch away good men' (Ovid).

art must seek alms of cormorants, and those that deserve best be kept under by dunces, who count it a policy to keep them bare, because they should follow their books the better; thinking belike, that, as preferment hath made themselves idle, that were erst painful in meaner places, so it would likewise slacken the endeavours of those students that as yet strive to excel in hope of advancement. A good policy to suppress superfluous liberality! But had it been practised when they were promoted, the yeomanry of the realm had been better to pass than it is, and one drone should not have driven so many bees from their honey-combs.

'Ay, ay, we'll give losers leave to talk. It is no matter what *Sic probo* [26] and his penniless companions prate, whilst we have the gold in our coffers. This is it that will make a knave an honest man, and my neighbour Crampton's strip-ling a better gentleman than his grandsire.' Oh, it is a trim thing when Pride, the son, goes before, and Shame, the father, follows after. Such precedents there are in our com-monwealth a great many; not so much of them whom learn-ing and industry hath exalted (whom I prefer before *genus et proavos*),[27] as of carterly upstarts, that out-face town and country in their velvets, when Sir Rowland Russet-coat,[28] their dad, goes sagging every day in his round gaskins of white cotton, and hath much ado, poor penny-father, to keep his unthrift elbows in reparations.

Marry, happy are they (say I) that have such fathers to work for them whilst they play; for where other men turn over many leaves to get bread and cheese in their old age, and study twenty years to distill gold out of ink, our young masters do nothing but devise how to spend, and ask coun-sel of the wine and capons how they may quickliest con-sume their patrimonies. As for me, I live secure from all

26. 'Thus I prove' (conclusion of a disputation). Here meaning 'a scholar'.

27. 'My family and ancestors' (Ovid).

28. As worn by countrymen, (hence, a name for a simple country squire).

such perturbations; for, thanks be to God, I am *vacuus viator*,[29] and care not, though I meet the Commissioners of Newmarket Heath[30] at high midnight, for any crosses,[31] images, or pictures that I carry about me, more than needs.

'Than needs,' quoth I. Nay, I would be ashamed of it if *Opus* and *Usus*[32] were not knocking at my door twenty times a week when I am not within; the more is the pity, that such a frank gentleman as I should want; but, since the dice do run so untowardly on my side, I am partly provided of a remedy. For whereas those that stand most on their honour have shut up their purses and shift us off with court-holy-bread;[33] and on the other side, a number of hypocritical hotspurs, that have God always in their mouths, will give nothing for God's sake; I have clapped up a handsome supplication to the devil and sent it by a good fellow, that I know will deliver it.

And because you may believe me the better, I care not if I acquaint you with the circumstance.

I was informed of late days, that a certain blind retailer, called the devil, used to lend money upon pawns or anything, and would let one for a need have a thousand pounds upon a statute merchant[34] of his soul; or, if a man plied him thoroughly, would trust him upon a bill of his hand, without any more circumstance. Besides, he was noted for a privy benefactor to traitors and parasites, and to advance fools and asses far sooner than any; to be a greedy pursuer of news, and so famous a politician in purchasing, that hell, which at the beginning was but an obscure village, is now become a huge city, whereunto all countries are tributary.

These manifest conjectures of plenty, assembled in one

29. 'Someone who is travelling light' (allusion to a line in Juvenal).
30. Robbers, highwaymen.
31. Coins.
32. Opus and Usus: Work and habit, combining to produce hunger.
33. Fair words.
34. Bond giving a creditor power to take his debtor's lands if debt unpaid by certain time.

commonplace of ability,[35] I determined to claw Avarice by the elbow, till his full belly gave me a full hand, and let him blood with my pen (if it might be) in the vein of liberality; and so, in short time, was this paper-monster, *Pierce Penniless*, begotten.

But, written and all, here lies the question: where shall I find this old ass, that I may deliver it? Mass, that's true; they say the lawyers have the devil and all; and it is like enough he is playing Ambodexter [36] amongst them. Fie, fie, the devil a driver in Westminster Hall? It can never be.

Now, I pray, what do you imagine him to be? Perhaps you think it is not possible he should be so grave. Oh, then you are in an error, for he is as formal as the best scrivener of them all. Marry, he doth not use to wear a nightcap, for his horns will not let him; and yet I know a hundred as well-headed as he, that will make a jolly shift with a court-cup [37] on their crowns if the weather be cold.

To proceed with my tale. To Westminster Hall I went, and made a search of enquiry, from the black gown to the buckram bag,[38] if there were any such sergeant, bencher, counsellor, attorney, or pettifogger,[39] as *Signor Cornuto Diabolo* [40] with the good face. But they all, *una voce*,[41] affirmed that he was not there; marry, whether he were at the Exchange or no, amongst the rich merchants, that they could not tell; but it was likelier of the two that I should meet with him, or hear of him at the least, in those quarters. 'I'faith, and say you so?' quoth I, 'and I'll bestow a little labour more, but I'll hunt him out.'

Without more circumstance, thither came I; and, thrusting myself, as the manner is, amongst the confusion of

35. *These manifest conjectures ... ability*: 'Having considered these means of getting money, and finding them in my power' (M.).

36. Vice in the play *Cambyses*, 1569.

37. An ash-wood dish.

38. Worn by lawyers' clerks.

39. An unqualified lawyer.

40. Facetious title with reference to the devil's horns and a suggestion of cuckoldry.

41. Unanimously.

languages, I asked, as before, whether he were there extant or no. But from one to another, 'Non novi dæmonem'[42] was all the answer I could get. At length, as fortune served, I lighted upon an old, straddling usurer, clad in a damask cassock, edged with fox fur, a pair of trunk slops,[43] sagging down like a shoemaker's wallet, and a short threadbare gown on his back, faced with moth-eaten budge;[44] upon his head he wore a filthy, coarse biggin,[45] and next it a garnish of night-caps, which a sage button-cap, of the form of a cowshard, overspread very orderly. A fat chuff it was, I remember, with a grey beard cut short to the stumps, as though it were grimed, and a huge worm-eaten nose, like a cluster of grapes hanging downwards. Of him I demanded if he could tell me any tidings of the party I sought for.

'By my troth,' quoth he, 'stripling,' and then he coughed, 'I saw him not lately, nor know I certainly where he keeps: but thus much I heard by a broker, a friend of mine, that hath had some dealings with him in his time, that he is at home sick of the gout, and will not be spoken withal under more than thou art able to give, some two or three hundred angels, at least, if thou hast any suit to him; and then, perhaps, he'll strain courtesy, with his legs in child-bed, and come forth and talk with thee; but, otherwise, *non est domi*,[46] he is busy with Mammon, and the prince of the North, how to build up his kingdom, or sending his spirits abroad to undermine the maligners of his government.'

I, hearing of this cold comfort, took my leave of him very faintly, and, like a careless malcontent that knew not which way to turn, retired me to Paul's to seek my dinner with Duke Humphrey;[47] but when I came there, the old soldier was not up. He is long a-rising, thought I, but that's all one, for he that hath no money in his purse must go dine with

42. 'I know not the devil.' 43. Loose trousers.
44. Fur. 45. Night-cap.
46. 'He is not at home.'
47. The tomb of Duke Humphrey, Duke of Gloucester, in St Paul's Cathedral was a meeting-place for gallants and petty criminals. If one failed to cadge a meal and had no money, one was said to 'dine with Duke Humphrey' (M.).

Sir John Bestbetrust [48] at the sign of the Chalk and the Post. [49]

Two hungry turns had I scarce fetched in this waste gallery, when I was encountered by a neat, pedantical fellow, in form of a citizen, who, thrusting himself abruptly into my company, like an intelligencer, [50] began very earnestly to question with me about the cause of my discontent, or what made me so sad, that seemed too young to be acquainted with sorrow. I, nothing nice [51] to unfold my estate to any whatsoever, discoursed to him the whole circumstance of my care, and what toil and pains I had took in searching for him that would not be heard of.

'Why, sir,' quoth he, 'had I been privy to your purpose before, I could have eased you of this travail; for if it be the devil you seek for, know I am his man.'

'I pray, sir, how might I call you?'

'A Knight of the Post,' quoth he, 'for so I am termed; a fellow that will swear you anything for twelve pence.* But, indeed, I am a spirit in nature and essence, that take upon me this human shape only to set men together by the ears and send souls by millions to hell.'

'Now, trust me, a substantial trade; but when do you think you could send next to your master?'

'Why, every day; for there is not a cormorant that dies, or cut-purse that is hanged, but I despatch letters by his soul to him and to all my friends in the Low Countries; [53] wherefore, if you have anything that you would have transported, give it me, and I will see it delivered.'

'Yes, marry have I,' quoth I, 'a certain supplication here unto your master, which you may peruse if it please you.' With that he opened it, and read as followeth.

Non bene conducti vendunt periuria testes. [52]

48. 'A broken-down old fellow' (M.).
49. *sign . . . Post*: On credit.
50. Spy, informer.   51. Not too particular or scrupulous.
52. 'Witnesses who have not been carefully hired sell false testimony' (Ovid).
53. Hell.

To the high and mighty Prince of Darkness, donzel [54] dell Lucifer, King of Acheron, Styx, and Phlegethon, Duke of Tartary, Marquis of Cocytus, and Lord High Regent of Limbo; his distressed orator, Pierce Penniless, wisheth increase of damnation and malediction eternal, *Per Jesum Christum Dominum nostrum.* [55]

Most humbly sueth unto your sinfulness, your single-soled [56] orator, Pierce Penniless; that whereas your impious excellence hath had the poor tenement of his purse any time this half year for your dancing school, [57] and he, notwithstanding, hath received no penny nor cross [58] for farm, according to the usual manner,* it may please your graceless majesty to consider of him, and give order to your servant Avarice he may be despatched; insomuch as no man here in London can have a dancing school without rent, and his wit and knavery cannot be maintained with nothing. Or, if this be not so plausible to your honourable infernalship, it might seem good to your hellhood to make extent upon the souls of a number of uncharitable cormorants, who, having incurred the danger of a *præmunire* [59] with meddling with matters that properly concern your own person, deserve no longer to live as men amongst men, but to be incorporated in the society of devils. By which means the mighty controller of fortune and imperious subverter of destiny, delicious gold, the poor man's god, and idol of princes, that looks pale and wan through long imprisonment, might at length be restored to his powerful monarchy, and eftsoon be set at liberty, to help his friends that have need of him.

I know a great sort of good fellows that would venture far for his freedom,† and a number of needy lawyers, who

---

* No; I'll be sworn upon a book have I not.

† *Id est*, for the freedom of gold.

54. Squire, page.
55. 'Through Jesus Christ our Lord'.   56. Poverty-stricken.
57 Proverb that the devil dances in an empty pocket.
58. Coin.
59. A writ issued for denying supremacy of the Crown.

now mourn in threadbare gowns for his thraldom, that
would go near to poison his keepers with false Latin, if that
might procure his enlargement; but inexorable iron detains
him in the dungeon of the night, so that now, poor creature, he can neither traffic with the mercers and tailors,
as he was wont, nor domineer in taverns as he ought.

The Description of Greediness

Famine, Lent, and Desolation sit in onion-skinned jackets
before the door of his indurance,[60] as a Chorus in *The
Tragedy of Hospitality*, to tell Hunger and Poverty there's
no relief for them there. And in the inner part of this ugly
habitation stands Greediness, prepared to devour all that
enter, attired in a capouch [61] of written parchment, buttoned down before with labels of wax, and lined with
sheep's fells [62] for warmness; his cap furred with cats' skins,
after the Muscovy fashion, and all to-be-tasselled with
angle-hooks,[63] instead of aglets,[64] ready to catch hold of all
those to whom he shows any humbleness. For his breeches,
they were made of the lists of broadcloths,[65] which he had
by letters patents assured him and his heirs, to the utter
overthrow of bowcases [66] and cushion makers; and bombasted [67] they were, like beer barrels, with statute merchants [68] and forfeitures.[69] But of all, his shoes were the
strangest, which, being nothing else but a couple of crab
shells, were toothed at the toes with two sharp sixpenny
nails that digged up every dunghill they came by for gold,

60. Imprisonment.   61. Capuche, hood, cowl.
62. Wool, fleece.   63. Fish-hooks.
64. Metal tag at the end of a ribbon to help threading, often
ornamental.
65. *lists of broadcloths*: Waste borders of the fine cloths used for
men's garments.
66. List would be used as stuffing for bowcases and cushions. (M.
suggests should read 'bowcasers'.)
67. Stuffed.   68. See p. 56, n. 34.
69. Loss of estates, etc., consequent upon crime or breach of agree-
ment.

and snarled at the stones as he went in the street, because they were so common for men, women, and children to tread upon, and he could not devise how to wrest an odd fine out of any of them.

Thus walks he up and down all his lifetime, with an iron crow in his hand instead of a staff, and a sergeant's mace [70] in his mouth, which night and day he still gnaws upon, and either busies himself in setting silver lime twigs to entangle young gentlemen, and casting forth silken shraps [71] to catch woodcocks,[72] or in sieving of muckhills and shop dust, whereof he will bolt a whole cartload to gain a bowed pin.

The Description of Dame Niggardize

On the other side, Dame Niggardize, his wife, in a sedge rug [73] kirtle, that had been a mat time out of mind, a coarse hempen rail about her shoulders, borrowed of the one end of a hop-bag, an apron made of almanacs out of date, such as stand upon screens, or on the backside of a door in a chandler's shop, and an old wives' pudding pan on her head, thrummed [74] with the parings of her nails, sat barrelling up the droppings of her nose, instead of oil, to saim [75] wool withal, and would not adventure to spit without half-a-dozen porringers at her elbow.

The house (or rather the hell) where these two earthworms encaptived this beautiful substance, was vast, large, strong built, and well furnished, all save the kitchen; for that was no bigger than the cook's room in a ship, with a little court chimney,[76] about the compass of a parenthesis in proclamation print; then judge you what diminutive dishes came out of this dove's-nest. So likewise of the buttery; for whereas in houses of such stately foundation, that

70. Pun on 'mace' (also a spice).
71. Baits, nets.   72. Fools.
73. 'Coarse material woven of sedge and resembling matting' (NED).
74. Ornamented.   75. To grease.
76. A small stove as found in inhospitable homes.

are built to outward show so magnificent, every office is answerable to the hall, which is principal, there the buttery was no more but a blind [77] coalhouse under a pair of stairs, wherein, uprising and downlying, was but one single, single kilderkin [78] of small beer, that would make a man, with a carouse of a spoonful, run through an alphabet of faces. Nor used they any glasses or cups, as other men, but only little farthing ounce boxes, whereof one of them filled up with froth, in manner and form of an ale-house, was a meal's allowance for the whole household.

It were lamentable to tell what misery the rats and mice endured in this hard world; how, when all supply of victuals failed them, they went a boot-haling [79] one night to Signor Greediness' bedchamber, where, finding nothing but emptiness and vastity, they encountered (after long inquisition) with a cod-piece, well dunged and manured with grease, which my pinch-fart penny-father had retained from his bachelorship, until the eating of these presents. Upon that they set, and with a courageous assault, rent it clean away from the breeches, and then carried it in triumph, like a coffin, on their shoulders betwixt them. The very spiders and dust-weavers, that wont to set up their looms in every window, decayed and undone through the extreme dearth of the place, that afforded them no matter to work on, were constrained to break,[80] against their wills, and go dwell in the country, out of the reach of the broom and the wing;[81] and generally, not a flea nor a cricket that carried any brave mind, that would stay there after he had once tasted the order of their fare. Only unfortunate gold, a predestinate slave to drudges and fools, lives in endless bondage there amongst them, and may no way be released, except you send the rot half a year amongst his keepers, and so make them away with a murrion,[82] one after another.

77. Dark and out of sight.
78. Sixteen to eighteen gallons.
79. Looting   80. Go bankrupt.   81. Feather brush.
82. Foot-and-mouth disease.

The Complaint of Pride

Oh, but a far greater enormity reigneth in the heart of the Court. Pride, the perverter of all virtue, sitteth apparelled in the merchant's spoils, and ruin of young citizens; and scorneth learning, that gave their upstart fathers titles of gentry.

The Nature of an Upstart

All malcontent sits the greasy son of a clothier,[83] and complains, like a decayed earl, of the ruin of ancient houses; whereas the weaver's loom first framed the web of his honour, and the locks of wool, that bushes and brambles have took for toll of insolent sheep, that would needs strive for the wall of a fir bush, have made him of the tenths of their tar, a squire of low degree; and of the collections of their scatterings, a Justice, *Tam Marti quam Mercurio*,[84] of Peace and of Coram.[85] He will be humorous,[86] forsooth, and have a brood of fashions by himself. Sometimes, because Love commonly wears the livery of Wit, he will be an *Inamorato Poeta*, and sonnet a whole quire of paper in praise of Lady Swine-snout, his yellow-faced mistress, and wear a feather of her rainbeaten fan for a favour, like a fore-horse. All *Italianato* is his talk, and his spade peak [87] is as sharp as if he had been a pioneer before the walls of Rouen.[88] He will despise the barbarism of his own country and tell a whole *Legend of Lies* of his travels unto Constantinople. If he be challenged to fight, for his dilatory excuse he objects that it is not the custom of the Spaniard or the German to look back to every dog that barks. You shall see a dapper jack, that hath been but over at Dieppe,

83. *son of a clothier*: Sometimes seen as an attack on Anthony Munday.

84. 'As much to Mars as to Mercury' (i.e. as much to brute force as to craft).

85. Quorum, a distinguished J.P.

86. Whimsical, eccentric.　　　　87. Cut of beard.

88. Besieged by Henry IV 1591–2.

wring his face round about, as a man would stir up a mustard pot, and talk English through the teeth, like Jacques Scabbed-hams or Monsieur Mingo de Mousetrap; when, poor slave, he hath but dipped his bread in wild boar's grease, and come home again; or been bitten by the shins by a wolf; and saith he hath adventured upon the barricades of Gurney or Guingan [89] and fought with the young Guise [90] hand to hand.

The Counterfeit Politician

Some think to be counted rare politicians and statesmen by being solitary; as who should say, 'I am a wise man, a brave man, *Secreta mea mihi; Frustra sapit, qui sibi non sapit,*[91] and there is no man worthy of my company or friendship;' when, although he goes ungartered like a malcontent cut-purse, and wears his hat over his eyes like one of the cursed crew, yet cannot his stabbing dagger, or his nitty love-lock,[92] keep him out of *The Legend of Fantastical Coxcombs.*

I pray ye, good Monsieur Devil, take some order, that the streets be not pestered with them so as they are. Is it not a pitiful thing that a fellow that eats not a good meal's meat in a week, but beggareth his belly quite and clean to make his back a certain kind of brokerly gentleman, and now and then, once or twice in a term, comes to the eighteen pence ordinary,[93] because he would be seen amongst cavaliers and brave [94] courtiers, living otherwise all the year long with salt butter and Holland cheese in his chamber, should take up a scornful melancholy in his gait and countenance, and talk as though our commonwealth were but a mockery of government, and our magistrates fools,

89. Gournay-en-Bray and Guingamp, besieged 1589 and 1591.

90. Duc de Mayenne, Henri de Guise's younger brother, captured Gournay, 1589.

91. 'My secrets are my own; he is wise in vain who does not know his own business.'

92. Long hair infested with nits.

93. Expensive eating-place.   94. Dashing.

who wronged him in not looking into his deserts, not employing him in state matters, and that, if more regard were not had of him very shortly, the whole realm should have a miss of him, and he would go (ay, marry, would he) where he should be more accounted of?

Is it not wonderful ill-provided, I say, that this disdainful companion is not made one of the fraternity of fools, to talk before great states, with some old moth-eaten politician, of mending highways and leading armies into France?

The Prodigal Young Master

A young heir or cockney,[95] that is his mother's darling, if he have played the waste-good at the Inns of the Court or about London, and that neither his student's pension nor his unthrift's credit will serve to maintain his college of whores any longer, falls in a quarrelling humour with his fortune, because she made him not King of the Indies, and swears and stares, after ten in the hundred,[96] that ne'er a such peasant as his father or brother shall keep him under: he will to the sea, and tear the gold out of the Spaniards' throats, but he will have it, by'rlady. And when he comes there, poor soul, he lies in brine, in ballast, and is lamentable sick of the scurvies; his dainty fare is turned to a hungry feast of dogs and cats, or haberdine[97] and poor John[98] at the most, and, which is lamentablest of all, that without mustard.

As a mad ruffian, on a time, being in danger of shipwreck by a tempest, and seeing all other at their vows and prayers, that if it would please God, of his infinite goodness, to deliver them out of that imminent danger, one would abjure this sin whereunto he was addicted, another make satisfaction for that violence he had committed. He, in a

95. Milksop.
96. *after ten in the hundred*: 'Swears and swaggers for all he is worth' (H.).
97. Dried cod.   98. Salt hake.

desperate jest, began thus to reconcile his soul to heaven:

'O Lord, if it may seem good to thee to deliver me from this fear of untimely death, I vow before thy throne and all thy starry host, never to eat haberdine more whilst I live.'

Well, so it fell out, that the sky cleared and the tempest ceased, and this careless wretch, that made such a mockery of prayer, ready to set foot a-land, cried out, 'Not without mustard, good Lord, not without mustard'; as though it had been the greatest torment in the world to have eaten haberdine without mustard.

But this by the way, what penance can be greater for Pride than to let it swing in his own halter? *Dulce bellum inexpertis:*[99] there's no man loves the smoke of his own country, that hath not been singed in the flame of another soil. It is a pleasant thing over a full pot to read the fable of thirsty Tantalus; but a harder matter to digest salt meats at sea, with stinking water.

The Pride of the Learned

Another misery of pride it is, when men that have good parts and bear the name of deep scholars cannot be content to participate one faith with all Christendom, but, because they will get a name to their vainglory, they will set their self-love to study to invent new sects of singularity, thinking to live when they are dead, by having their sects called after their names, as Donatists of Donatus,[100] Arians of Arius,[101] and a number more new faith-founders, that have made England the exchange of innovations, and almost as much confusion of religion in every quarter, as there was of tongues at the building of the Tower of Babel.

99. 'War is attractive to those who have never experienced it' (Pindar?).

100. Bishop of Casa Nigra, Numidia, led the first important schism of the Christian Church in 311.

101. Theologian of the fourth century, holding that Jesus was not 'of one substance' with God.

Whence, a number that fetch the articles of their belief out of Aristotle, and think of heaven and hell as the heathen philosophers, take occasion to deride our ecclesiastical state and all ceremonies of divine worship as bugbears and scarecrows,[102] because, like Herod's soldiers, we divide Christ's garment amongst us in so many pieces, and of the vesture of salvation make some of us babies' and apes' coats, others straight trusses and devil's breeches; some galligaskins[103] or a shipman's hose, like the Anabaptists[104] and adulterous Familists;[105] others, with the Martinists,[106] a hood with two faces, to hide their hypocrisy; and, to conclude, some, like the Barrowists[107] and Greenwoodians,[108] a garment full of the plague, which is not to be worn before it be new washed.

Hence atheists triumph and rejoice, and talk as profanely of the Bible, as of *Bevis of Hampton*.[109] I hear say there be mathematicians abroad that will prove men before Adam;[110] and they are harboured in high places, who will maintain it to the death that there are no devils.

It is a shame, Signor Beelzebub, that you should suffer yourself thus to be termed a bastard, or not approve to your predestinate children, not only that they have a father, but that you are he that must own them.* These are but the suburbs of the sin we have in hand: I must describe

---

* The devil hath children, as other men, but few of them know their own father.

102. *bugbears and scarecrows*: Childish superstitions.
103. Wide breeches reaching to the knees.
104. Early Baptists, first appearing in England *c.* 1534.
105. The Family of Love, a mystical section of the Anabaptists.
106. Followers of Martin Senior, who protested against abuses of the Church.
107. Followers of Henry Barrow, arrested for heresy 1586, hanged 1593.
108. Followers of John Greenwood, associated and hanged with Barrow.
109. Popular verse romance, early fourteenth century.
110. *prove men before Adam*: Show that men existed before the Biblical account (cf. p. 479).

to you a large city, wholly inhabited with this damnable enormity.

The Pride of the Artificers

In one place let me shew you a base artificer, that hath no revenues to boast on but a needle in his bosom, as brave as any pensioner or nobleman.

The Pride of Merchants' Wives

In another corner, Mistress Minx, a merchant's wife, that will eat no cherries, forsooth, but when they are at twenty shillings a pound, that looks as simperingly as if she were besmeared,[111] and jets it as gingerly as if she were dancing the Canaries.[112] She is so finical [113] in her speech, as though she spake nothing but what she had first sewed over before in her samplers,[114] and the puling accent of her voice is like a feigned treble, or one's voice that interprets to the puppets.[115] What should I tell how squeamish she is in her diet, what toil she puts her poor servants unto, to make her looking glasses in the pavement? How she will not go into the fields, to cower on the green grass, but she must have a coach for her convoy; and spends half a day in pranking herself if she be invited to any strange place? Is not this the excess of pride, Signor Satan? Go to, you are unwise if you make her not a chief saint in your calendar.

The Pride of Peasants sprung up of Nothing

The next object that encounters my eyes is some such obscure upstart gallants as without desert or service are raised from the plough to be checkmates [116] with princes. And these I can no better compare than to creatures that

---

111. Befouled. 112. A lively Spanish dance.
113. Over-refined. 114. Embroidery with a moral text.
115. *voice ... puppets*: Voice used in a puppet show.
116. Equals.

are bred *sine coitu*,[117] as crickets in chimneys; to which I
resemble poor scullions, that, from turning spit in the
chimney corner, are on the sudden hoised up from the
kitchen into the waiting chamber, or made barons of the
beeves,[118] and marquesses of the marybones;[119] some by
corrupt water, as gnats, to which we may liken brewers, that,
by retailing filthy Thames water, come in a few years to
be worth forty or fifty thousand pound; others by dead
wine, as little flying worms,[120] and so the vintners in like
case; others by slime, as frogs, which may be alluded to
Mother Bunch's[121] slimy ale, that hath made her and some
other of her fill-pot faculty so wealthy; others by dirt, as
worms, and so I know many gold-finders[122] and hostlers
come up; some by herbs, as cankers, and after the same
sort our apothecaries; others by ashes, as scarabs,[123] and
how else get our colliers the pence? Others from the putrefied flesh of dead beasts, as bees of bulls, and butchers by
fly-blown beef; wasps of horses, and hackney-men by selling their lame jades to huntsmen for carrion.

Yet am I not against it, that these men by their mechanical[124] trades should come to be sparage * gentlemen and
chuff-headed burgomasters; but that better places should be
possessed by coistrels,[125] and the cobbler's crow,[126] for crying but *Ave Caesar*, be more esteemed than rarer birds,
that have warbled sweeter notes unrewarded. But it is no
marvel, for as hemlock fatteth quails and henbane swine,
which to all other is poison, so some men's vices have power

---

* Sparagus: a flower that never groweth but through a
man's dung.

117. Without sexual intercourse. 118. Butcher's meat.
119. Marrow-bones. 120. Insects.
121. Famous ale-wife, perhaps mythical.
122. Manure-men, lavatory-cleaners. 123. Dung-beetles.
124. Manual, artisan. 125. Rascals.
126. There is a story of a bird trained to say this flattering phrase
to Augustus, and eventually brought to the Emperor because he also
said (in imitation of his trainer) *'opera et impensa periit'* ('All this
work and expense for nothing').

to advance them, which would subvert any else that should seek to climb by them; and it is enough in them, that they can pare their nails well to get them a living, whenas the seven liberal sciences [127] and a good leg will scarce get a scholar a pair of shoes and a canvas doublet.

These whelps of the first litter of gentility, these exhalations, drawn up to the heaven of honour from the dunghill of abject fortune, have long been on horseback to come riding to your Devilship; but, I know not how, like Saint George,[128] they are always mounted but never move. Here they outface town and country, and do nothing but bandy factions with their betters. Their big limbs yield the commonwealth no other service but idle sweat, and their heads, like rough-hewn globes, are fit for nothing but to be the blockhouses of sleep. Raynold the fox [129] may well bear up his tail in the lion's den, but when he comes abroad he is afraid of every dog that barks. What cur will not bawl and be ready to fly in a man's face when he is set on by his master, who, if he be not by to encourage him, he casts his tail betwixt his legs and steals away like a sheepbiter? Ulysses was a tall man [130] under Ajax' shield; but by himself he would never adventure but in the night. Pride is never built upon some pillars; and let his supporters fail him never so little, you shall find him very humble in the dust. Wit oftentimes stands instead of a chief arch to underprop it; in soldiers, strength; in women, beauty.

The Base Insinuating of Drudges and their Practice to Aspire

Drudges, that have no extraordinary gifts of body nor of mind, filch themselves into some nobleman's service, either by bribes or by flattery, and, when they are there, they so

127. The university courses of the trivium (grammar, rhetoric, logic) and the quadrivium (arithmetic, geometry, astronomy, music).
128. Pictures of St George common in pageants and as inn-signs.
129. See Spenser's *Mother Hubbard's Tale*.
130. Valiant.

labour it with cap and knee, and ply it with privy whisperings, that they wring themselves into his good opinion ere he be aware. Then do they vaunt themselves over the common multitude, and are ready to outbrave any man that stands by himself. Their lord's authority is as a rebater [131] to bear up the peacock's tail of their boasting, and anything that is said or done to the unhandsoming of their ambition is straight wrested to the name of treason. Thus do weeds grow up whiles no man regards them, and the Ship of Fools [132] is arrived in the Haven of Felicity, whilst the scouts of Envy contemn the attempts of any such small barks.

But beware you that be great men's favourites; let not a servile, insinuating slave creep betwixt your legs into credit with your lords; for peasants that come out of the cold of poverty, once cherished in the bosom of prosperity, will straight forget that ever there was a winter of want, or who gave them room to warm them. The son of a churl cannot choose but prove ingrateful, like his father. Trust not a villain that hath been miserable, and is suddenly grown happy. Virtue ascendeth by degrees of desert unto dignity. Gold and lust may lead a man a nearer way to promotion; but he that hath neither comeliness nor coin to commend him undoubtedly strides over time by stratagems,* if of a molehill he grows to a mountain in a moment. This is that which I urge; there is no friendship to be had with him that is resolute to do or suffer anything rather than to endure the destiny whereto he was born; for he will not spare his own father or brother, to make himself a gentleman.

The Pride of the Spaniard

France, Italy and Spain, are all full of these false-hearted Machivillions; but, properly, pride is the disease of the

* As by carrying tales, or playing the doughty pander.

131. Rebato, or framework of a ruff.

132. English title of a satirical Latin poem by Sebastian Brandt (1494).

Spaniard, who is born a braggart in his mother's womb.
For, if he be but seventeen years old and hath come to the
place where a field was fought (though half a year before),
he then talks like one of the giants that made war against
Heaven, and stands upon his honour, as much as if he were
one of Augustus' soldiers,[133] of whom he first instituted
the order of heralds. And let a man soothe him in this vein
of killcow [134] vanity, you may command his heart out of
his belly to make you a rasher on the coals, if you will, next
your heart.[135]

The Pride of the Italian

The Italian is a more cunning proud fellow, that hides his
humour far cleanlier, and indeed seems to take a pride in
humility, and will proffer a stranger more courtesy than he
means to perform. He hateth him deadly that takes him
at his word; as, for example, if upon occasion of meeting, he
request you to dinner or supper at his house, and that at
the first or second entreaty you promise to be his guest, he
will be the mortalest enemy you have. But if you deny him,
he will think you have manners and good bringing up, and
will love you as his brother. Marry, at the third or fourth
time you must not refuse him. Of all things he counteth it
a mighty disgrace to have a man pass jostling by him in
haste on a narrow causey [136] and ask him no leave, which
he never revengeth with less than a stab.

The Pride of the Frenchman

The Frenchman (not altered from his own nature) is wholly
compact of deceivable courtship, and for the most part

133. Augustus gave privileges to old soldiers, including the right
to wear certain badges, but this 'had little to do with heraldry in
the modern sense' (M.).

134. Boastful.

135. *next your heart*: On an empty stomach.

136. Causeway, paved part of the street.

loves none but himself and his pleasure; yet though he be the most *Grand Signeur* of them all, he will say, *A vostre service et commendemente Mounseur*, to the meanest vassal he meets. He thinks he doth a great favour to that gentleman or follower of his to whom he talks sitting on his close stool; and with that favour, I have heard, the queen mother wonted to grace the noblemen of France. And a great man of their nation coming in time past over into England, and being here very honourably received, he, in requital of his admirable entertainment, on an evening going to the privy, (as it were to honour extraordinarily our English lords appointed to attend him), gave one the candle, another his girdle, and another the paper; but they, not acquainted with this new kind of gracing, accompanying him to the privy door, set down the trash and so left him; which he, considering what inestimable kindness he extended to them therein more than usual, took very heinously.

The Pride of the Dane

The most gross and senseless proud dolts (in a different kind from all these) are the Danes, who stand so much upon their unwieldy burly-boned soldiery that they account of no man that hath not a battle-axe at his girdle to hough [137] dogs with, or wears not a cock's feather in a red thrummed [138] hat like a cavalier. Briefly, he is the best fool braggart under heaven. For besides nature hath lent him a flabberkin [139] face, like one of the four winds, and cheeks that sag like a woman's dugs over his chin-bone, his apparel is so puffed up with bladders of taffety, and his back like beef stuffed with parsley, so drawn out with ribbons and devices, and blistered with light sarsenet [140] bastings, that you would think him nothing but a swarm of butterflies if

137. To hamstring.
138. Decorated with tassels.
139. Swollen.
140. A fine silk material.

you saw him afar off.* Thus walks he up and down in his majesty, taking a yard of ground at every step, and stamps the earth so terrible, as if he meant to knock up a spirit, when, foul drunken bezzle,[141] if an Englishman set his little finger to him, he falls like a hog's-trough that is set on one end. Therefore I am the more vehement against them, because they are an arrogant, ass-headed people, that naturally hate learning and all them that love it. Yea, and for they would utterly root it out from among them, they have withdrawn all rewards from the professors thereof. Not Barbary itself is half so barbarous as they are.

The Danes Enemies to all Learning: No Rewards Amongst them for Desert

First, whereas the hope of honour maketh a soldier in England; bishoprics, deaneries, prebendaries, and other private dignities animate our divines to such excellence; the civil lawyers have their degrees and consistories of honour by themselves, equal in place with knights and esquires; the common lawyers (suppose in the beginning they are but husbandmen's sons) come in time to be chief fathers of the land, and many of them not the meanest of the Privy Council: there, the soldier may fight himself out of his skin and do more exploits than he hath doits [142] in his purse, before from a common mercenary he come to be corporal of the mould-cheese, or the lieutenant get a captainship. None but the son of a corporal must be a corporal, nor any be captain but the lawful begotten of a captain's body. Bishoprics, deaneries, prebendaries, why, they know no such functions; a sort of ragged ministers they have, of whom they count as basely as water-bearers. If

* If you know him not by any of these marks, look on his fingers and you shall be sure to find half a dozen silver rings, worth threepence apiece.

141. Tippler.

142. Small Dutch coins of little value.

any of their noblemen refrain three hours in his lifetime from drinking, to study the laws, he may perhaps have a little more government put into his hands than another; but otherwise, burgomasters and gentlemen bear all the sway of both swords, spiritual and temporal. It is death there for any but a husbandman to marry a husbandman's daughter, or a gentleman's child to join with any but the son of a gentleman. Marry, this, the King may well banish, but he cannot put a gentleman unto death in any cause whatsoever, which makes them stand upon it so proudly as they do. For fashion sake some will put their children to school, but they set them not to it till they are fourteen year old; so that you shall see a great boy with a beard learn his ABC and sit weeping under the rod when he is thirty years old.

What it is to Make Men Labour Without Hope

I will not stand to infer what a prejudice it is to the thrift of a flourishing state, to poison the growth of glory by giving it nought but the puddle water of penury to drink; to clip the wings of a high-towering falcon, who, whereas she wont in her feathered youthfulness, to look with an amiable eye upon her gray breast, and her speckled side sails, all sinewed with silver quills, and to drive whole armies of fearful fowl before her to her master's table; now she sits sadly on the ground, picking of worms, mourning the cruelty of those ungentlemanlike idle hands, that dismembered the beauty of her train.

You all know that man, insomuch as he is the image of God, delighteth in honour and worship, and all Holy Writ warrants that delight, so it be not derogatory to any part of God's own worship; now take away that delight, a discontented idleness overtakes him. For his hire, any handy-craftman, be he carpenter, joiner, or painter, will ploddingly do his day labour. But to add credit and fame to his workmanship, or to win a mastery to himself above all other, he will make a further assay in his trade than ever hitherto he did. He will have a thousand flourishes, which before he never thought upon, and in one day rid more out of hand than erst he did in ten. So in arms, so in arts; if titles of fame and glory be proposed to forward minds, or that sovereignty, whose sweetness they have not yet felt, be set in likely view for them to soar to, they will make a ladder of cord of the links of their brains, but they will fasten their hands, as well as their eyes, on the imaginative bliss which they already enjoy by admiration. Experience reproves me for a fool for dilating on so manifest a case.

The Danes are bursten-bellied sots, that are to be confuted with nothing but tankards or quart pots, and Ovid might as well have read his verses to the Getes [143] that understood him not, as a man talk reason to them that have no ears but their mouths, nor sense but of that which they swallow down their throats.* God so love me as I love the quick-witted Italians, and therefore love them the more, because they mortally detest this surly, swinish generation.

I need not fetch colours from other countries to paint the ugly visage of Pride, since her picture is set forth in so many painted faces here at home. What drugs, what sorceries, what oils, what waters, what ointments, do our curious dames use to enlarge their withered † beauties! Their lips are as lavishly red, as if they used to kiss an ochreman [144] every morning, and their cheeks sugar-candied and cherry-blushed so sweetly, after the colour of a new Lord Mayor's posts, as if the pageant of their wedlock holiday were hard at the door; so that if a painter were to draw any of their counterfeits on a table he needs no more but wet his pencil, and dab it on their cheeks, and he shall have vermilion and white enough to furnish out his work, though he leave his tar-box at home behind him. Wise was that sin-washing poet that made *The Ballad of Blue Starch*

* And that sense oftentimes makes them senseless.
† Withered flowers need much watering.

143. Ovid lived in exile among the Thracian tribe of the Getae.
144. One who deals in ochre, a colourman.

and Poking Sticks,[145] for indeed the lawn of licentiousness hath consumed all the wheat of hospitality.[146] It is said, Laurence Lucifer,[147] that you went up and down London crying then like a lantern-and-candle man.[148] I marvel no laundress would give you the washing and starching of your face for your labour, for God knows it is as black as the Black Prince.

It is suspected that you have been a great tobacco-taker in your youth, which causeth it to come so to pass; but Dame Nature, your nurse, was partly in fault, else she might have remedied it. She should have nointed your face overnight with *lac virginis*,[149] which baking upon it in bed till the morning, she might have peeled off the scale like the skin of a custard, and making a posset of verjuice[150] mixed with the oil of Tartary and camphor, bathed it in it a quarter of an hour, and you had been as fair as the flour of the frying pan. I warrant we have old hacksters in this great grandmother of corporations, Madame Troynovant,[151] that have not backbited any of their neighbours with the tooth of envy this twenty year, in the wrinkles of whose face ye may hide false dice, and play at cherry-pit in the dint of their cheeks: yet these aged mothers of iniquity will have their deformities new plastered over, and wear nosegays of yellow hair on their furies' foreheads, when age hath written, 'Ho, God be here,' on their bald, burnt-parchment pates. Pish, pish, what talk you of old age or bald pates? Men and women that have gone under the South Pole must lay off their furred night-caps[152] in spite of their teeth, and become yeomen of the vinegar bottle. A close periwig hides all the sins of an old whore-master; but the *Cucullus*

145. Entered Stationer's Register 1590. Poking sticks are instruments used in setting the plaits of a ruff.

146. *lawn ... hospitality*: All the wheat is used to make starch for dressing lawn ruffs.

147. M. suggests the name is given to Lucifer because St Laurence's Day is 10 August, in the hottest part of the year.

148. Watchman.   149. A cosmetic.

150. Crab-apple juice.   151. London, the new Troy.

152. *lay off ... night-caps*: Go bald through venereal disease.

non facit monachum,[153] 'tis not their new bonnets will keep them from the old boneache. Ware when a man's sins are written on his eyebrows, and that there is not a hairbreadth betwixt them and the falling sickness. The times are dangerous, and this is an iron age; or rather no iron age (for swords and bucklers [154] go to pawn apace in Long Lane),[155] but a tin age, for tin and pewter are more esteemed than Latin.[156] You that be wise, despise it, abhor it, neglect it, for what should a man care for gold that cannot get it?

The Commendation of Antiquaries
Laudamus veteres, sed nostris utimur annis [157]

An antiquary is an honest man, for he had rather scrape a piece of copper out of the dirt, than a crown out of Plowden's [158] standish. I know many wise gentlemen of this musty vocation, who, out of love with the times wherein they live, fall a-retailing of Alexander's stirrups, because, in verity, there is not such a strong piece of stretching leather made nowadays, nor iron so well tempered for any money. They will blow their nose in a box, and say it is the spittle that Diogenes spat in one's face; who, being invited to dinner to his house, that was neat and brave in all points as might be devised, and the grunting dog, somewhat troubled with the rheum (by means of his long fasting and staying for dinner more than wont) spat full in his host's face. And being asked the reason of it, said it was the foulest place he could spy out in all his house.

Let their mistress, or some other woman, give them a feather of her fan for her favour, and if one ask them what

153. 'The cowl does not make the monk.'
154. Being replaced by rapiers in the 1570s.
155. Noted for second-hand dealers.
156. Pun on 'latten', like brass.
157. 'We praise the days of yore, but make the most of our own' (Ovid).
158. Edmund Plowden (1518–85), a famous lawyer and writer on law.

it is they make answer, 'A plume of the Phoenix', whereof there is but one in all the whole world. A thousand gew-gaws [159] and toys have they in their chambers, which they heap up together, with infinite expense, and are made believe of them that sell them that they are rare and precious things, when they have gathered them upon some dunghill, or raked them out of the kennel by chance. I know one sold an old rope with four knots on it for four pound, in that he gave it out it was the length and breadth of Christ's tomb. Let a tinker take a piece of brass worth a halfpenny, and set strange stamps on it, and I warrant he may make it worth to him of some fantastical fool, than all the kettles that ever he mended in his life. This is the disease of our newfangled humourists, that know not what to do with their wealth. It argueth a very rusty wit, so to dote on worm-eaten eld.[160]

The Complaint of Envy

Out upon it, how long is Pride a-dressing herself? Envy, awake, for thou must appear before Nicolao Malevolo,[161] great muster-master of hell. Mark you this sly mate, how smoothly he looks? The poets were ill advised, that feigned him to be a lean, gag-toothed beldam, with hollow eyes, pale cheeks, and snaky hair; for he is not only a man, but a jolly, lusty, old gentleman, that will wink, and laugh, and jest drily, as if he were the honestest of a thousand; and I warrant you shall not hear a foul word come from him in a year. I will not contradict it, but the dog may worry a sheep in the dark and thrust his neck into the collar of clemency and pity when he hath done; as who should say, 'God forgive him, he was asleep in the shambles, when the innocent was done to death.' But openly, Envy sets a civil, fatherly countenance upon it, and hath not so much as a drop of blood in his face to attaint him of murder.

159. Ornaments, playthings.   160. Antiquity.
161. Nicolas, common name for the Devil, and allusion to Nicolai Macchiavelli.

I thought it expedient in this my supplication, to place it next to Pride; for it is his adopted son. And hence comes it, that proud men repine at others' prosperity, and grieve that any should be great but themselves. *Mens cuiusque, is est quisque;*[162] it is a proverb that is as hoary as Dutch butter. If a man will go to the devil, he may go to the devil; there are a thousand juggling tricks to be used at 'Hey pass, come aloft;'[163] and the world hath cords enough to truss up a calf that stands in one's way. Envy is a crocodile that weeps when he kills, and fights with none but he feeds on. This is the nature of this quick-sighted monster: he will endure any pains to endamage another, waste his body with undertaking exploits that would require ten men's strengths, rather than any should get a penny but himself, blear his eyes to stand in his neighbour's light, and, to conclude, like Atlas underprop heaven alone, rather than any should be in heaven that he liked not of, or come unto heaven by any other means but by him.

Philip of Spain as Great an Enemy to Mankind as the Devil

You, goodman wanderer about the world, how do ye spend your time, that you do not rid us of these pestilent members? You are unworthy to have an office if you can execute it no better. Behold another enemy of mankind, besides thyself, exalted in the South, Philip of Spain; who, not content to be the god of gold and chiefest commander of content that Europe affords, but now he doth nothing but thirst after human blood, when his foot is on the threshold of the grave. And as a wolf, being about to devour a horse, doth ballast his belly with earth that he may hang the heavier upon him, and then forcibly flies in his face, never leaving his hold till he hath eaten him up; so this wolvish, unnatural usurper, being about to devour all Christendom by invasion, doth cram his treasures with Indian earth to make his malice more forcible, and then flies in the

162. 'Individuality lies in the mind' (Cicero).
163. Familiar conjuring terms.

bosom of France and Belgia, never withdrawing his forces, as the wolf his fastening, till he hath devoured their welfare, and made the war-wasted carcases of both kingdoms a prey for his tyranny. Only poor England gives him bread for his cake,[164] and holds him out at the arm's end. His Armadoes, that like a high wood overshadowed the shrubs of our low ships, fled from the breath of our cannons, as vapours before the sun, or as the elephant flies from the ram, or the sea-whale from the noise of parched bones. The winds, envying that the air should be dimmed with such a chaos of wooden clouds, raised up high bulwarks of bellowing waves, whence death shot at their disordered navy; and the rocks with their overhanging jaws eat up all the fragments of oak that they left. So perished our foes; so the heavens did fight for us. *Præterit Hippomenes, resonant spectacula plausu.*[165]

I do not doubt, Doctor Devil, but you were present in this action, or passion rather, and helped to bore holes in ships to make them sink faster, and rinse out galley-foists with salt water, that stunk like fusty barrels with their masters' fear. It will be a good while ere you do as much for the king, as you did for his subjects. I would have ye persuade an army of gouty usurers to go to sea upon a boon voyage. Try if you can tempt Envy to embark himself in the maladventure and leave troubling the stream, that poets and good fellows may drink, and soldiers may sing *Placebo,*[166] that have murmured so long at the waters of strife.

But that will never be; for so long as Pride, Riot, and Whoredom are the companions of young courtiers, they will always be hungry and ready to bite at every dog that hath a bone given him beside themselves. Jesu, what secret grudge and rancour reigns amongst them, one being ready to despair of himself if he see the Prince but give his fellow

164. Tit for tat.
165. 'Hippomenes [a charioteer] goes past; the amphitheatre echoes with applause' (Ovid).
166. Sing 'I shall be pleased', i.e. be sycophants.

a fair look, or to die for grief if he be put down in bravery [167] never so little. Yet this custom have our false hearts fetched from other countries, that they will swear and protest love, where they hate deadly, and smile on him most kindly, whose subversion in soul they have vowed. *Fraus siblimi regnat in aula*: [168] 'tis rare to find a true friend in kings' palaces. Either thou must be so miserable that thou fall into the hands of scornful pity, or thou canst not escape the sting of envy. In one thought assemble the famous men of all ages, and tell me which of them all sat in the sunshine of his sovereign's grace, or waxed great of low beginnings, but he was spite-blasted, heaved at, and ill spoken of; and that of those that bare them most countenance.

Murder the Companion of Envy

But were Envy nought but words, it might seem to be only women's sin; but it hath a lewd mate hanging on his sleeve, called Murder, a stern fellow, that, like a Spaniard in fight, aimeth all at the heart. He hath more shapes than Proteus, and will shift himself upon any occasion of revengement into a man's dish, his drink, his apparel, his rings, his stirrups, his nosegay.

O Italy,* the academy of manslaughter, the sporting place of murder, the apothecary-shop of poison for all nations; how many kind of weapons hast thou invented for malice? Suppose I love a man's wife, whose husband yet lives, and cannot enjoy her for his jealous overlooking: physic, or rather the art of murder, as it may be used, will lend one a medicine, which shall make him away, in the nature of that disease he is most subject to, whether in the space of a year, a month, half a year, or what tract of time you will, more or less.

* Italy the storehouse of all murderous inventions.

167. Outdone in fine attire.
168. Seneca (*Hippolytus*, I, 981).

The Pasquil that was made upon this Last Pope

In Rome the papal chair is washed, every five year at the furthest, with this oil of aconitum. I pray God, the King of Spain feasted not our holy father Sextus,[169] that was last, with such conserve of henbane; for it was credibly reported he loved him not, and this that is now, is a god made with his own hands; as it may appear by the pasquil[170] that was set up of him, in manner of a note, presently after his election, *Sol, Re, Me, Fa*, that is to say, *Solus Rex me facit*; 'only the King of Spain made me Pope.' I am no chronicler of our own country, but if probable suspicion might be heard upon his oath I think some men's souls would not be canonized for martyrs, that on the earth did sway it as monarchs.*

Is it your will and pleasure, noble Lantsgrave of Limbo, to let us have less carousing to your health in poison, fewer underhand conspirings, or open quarrels executed only in words, as they are in the world nowadays: and if men will needs carouse, conspire, and quarrel, that they may make Ruffians' Hall[171] of hell, and there bandy balls of brimstone at one another's head, and not trouble our peacable paradise with their private hurly-burlies about strumpets; where no weapon, as in Adam's Paradise, should be named, but only the angel of Providence stand with a fiery sword at the gate, to keep out our enemies.

The Complaint of Wrath, a Branch of Envy

A perturbation of mind, like unto Envy, is Wrath, which looketh far lower than the former. For, whereas Envy cannot be said to be but in respect of our superiors, Wrath

---

* As Cardinal Wolsey, for example.

169. Sixtus V, Pope 1585–90. This is an unauthenticated account of his death.

170. Satire, lampoon.

171. Smithfield, 'where trials of skill were played by ordinary ruffianly people with sword and buckler' (Blount, 1674).

respecteth no degrees nor persons, but is equally armed against all that offend him. A hare-brained little dwarf* it is, with a swarth visage, that hath his heart at his tongue's end, if he be contraried, and will be sure to do no right nor take no wrong. If he be a judge or a justice (as sometimes the lion comes to give sentence against the lamb) then he swears by nothing but Saint Tyburn, and makes Newgate a noun substantive, whereto all his other works are but adjectives.† Lightly [172] he is an old man, for those years are most wayward and teatish,[173] yet be he never so old or so forward, since Avarice likewise is a fellow vice of those frail years, we must set one extreme to strive with another and allay the anger of oppression by the sweet incense of a new purse of angels, or the doting planet may have such predominance in these wicked elders of Israel, that, if you send your wife or some other female to plead for you, she may get your pardon upon promise of better acquaintance. But whist, these are the works of darkness and may not be talked of in the day-time. Fury is a heat or fire, and must be quenched with maid's water.

A Tale of a Wise Justice

Amongst other choleric wise justices, he was one, that having a play presented before him and his township by Tarlton and the rest of his fellows, Her Majesty's Servants, and they were now entering into their first merriment, as they call it, the people began exceedingly to laugh when Tarlton [174] first peeped out his head. Whereat the Justice, not a little moved, and seeing with his becks and nods he could not make them cease, he went with his staff and beat them round about unmercifully on the bare pates, in that they, being but farmers and poor country hinds, would

* Little men for the most part are most angry.

† Newgate, a common name for all prisons, as Homo is a common name for a man or a woman.

172. Probably.   173. Peevish.
174. Famous comic actor d. 1588.

presume to laugh at the Queen's Men, and make no more account of her cloth in his presence.

The Nature of the Irishman

The causes conducting unto wrath are as diverse as the actions of a man's life. Some will take on like a madman if they see a pig come to the table. Sotericus,[175] the surgeon, was choleric at the sight of sturgeon. The Irishman will draw his dagger, and be ready to kill and slay, if one break wind in his company; and so some of our Englishmen that are soldiers, if one give them the lie. But these are light matters, whereof Pierce complaineth not.

Be advertised, Master *Os fœtidum*,[176] beadle of the blacksmiths, that lawyers cannot devise which way in the world to beg, they are so troubled with brabblements and suits every term of yeomen and gentlemen that fall out for nothing. If John a Nokes [177] his hen do but leap into Elizabeth de Gappe's close, she will never leave to haunt her husband till he bring it to a *Nisi prius*.[178] One while, the parson sueth the parishioner for bringing home his tithes; another while, the parishioner sueth the parson for not taking away his tithes in time.

A Merry Tale of a Butcher and his Calves

I heard a tale of a butcher, who driving two calves over a common, that were coupled together by the necks with an oaken withe, in the way where they should pass, there lay a poor, lean mare, with a galled back; to whom they coming, as chance fell out, one of one side, and the other of the other, smelling on her, as their manner is, the midst of the withe, that was betwixt their necks, rubbed her and

175. From Sextus Empiricus (quotation in M. IV, 115).
176. Stinking mouth (the devil, breathing brimstone).
177. Used commonly as name for party in a law suit.
178. First words in writ summoning juryman to assizes; here the judgement of a court of law.

86

grated her on the sore back, that she started and rose up, and hung them both on her back as a beam; which being but a rough plaster to her raw ulcer, she ran away with them, as she were frantic, into the fens, where the butcher could not follow them, and drowned both herself and them in a quagmire. Now the owner of the mare is in law with the butcher for the loss of his mare, and the butcher interchangeably indites him for his calves. I pray ye, Timothy Tempter, be an arbitrator betwixt them, and couple them both by the necks, as the calves were, and carry them to hell on your back, and then, I hope, they will be quiet.

The chief spur unto wrath is Drunkenness, which, as the touch of an ashen bough causeth a giddiness in the viper's head, and the bat, lightly struck with the leaf of a tree, loseth his remembrance, so they, being but lightly sprinkled with the juice of the hop, become senseless, and have their reason strucken blind, as soon as ever the cup scaleth the fortress of their nose. Then run their words at random, like a dog that hath lost his master, and are up with this man and that man and generally inveigh against all men, but those that keep a wet corner for a friend, and will not think scorn to drink with a good fellow and a soldier. And so long do they practise this vein on their alebench, that when they are sober they cannot leave it. There be those that get their living all the year long by nothing but railing.

A Tale of one Friar Charles, a Foul-mouthed Knave

Not far from Chester, I knew an odd, foul-mouthed knave, called Charles the Friar, that had a face so parboiled with men's spitting on it, and a back so often knighted in Bridewell, that it was impossible for any shame or punishment to terrify him from ill-speaking. Noblemen he would liken to more ugly things than himself; some to 'After my hearty commendations',[179] with a dash over the head; others to

179. Commonplace phrase at beginning of letters, which had somehow become a joke.

gilded chines of beef, or a shoemaker sweating when he pulls on a shoe; another to an old verse in Cato, *Ad consilium ne accesseris, antequam voceris;*[180] another to a Spanish codpiece; another, that his face was not yet finished, with suchlike innumerable absurd allusions. Yea, what was he in the court but he had a comparison instead of a capcase [181] to put him in?

Upon a time, being challenged at his own weapon in a private chamber by a great personage (railing, I mean) he so far outstripped him in villainous words, and over-bandied him in bitter terms, that the name of sport could not persuade him patience, nor contain his fury in any degrees of jest, but needs he must wreak himself upon him. Neither would a common revenge suffice him, his displeasure was so infinite (and, it may be, common revenges he took before, as far as the whipcord would stretch, upon like provokements) wherefore he caused his men to take him, and bricked him up in a narrow chimney, that was *Neque maior neque minor corpore locato;*[182] where he fed him for fifteen days with bread and water through a hole, letting him sleep standing if he would, for lie or sit he could not, and then he let him out to see if he could learn to rule his tongue any better.

It is a disparagement to those that have any true spark of gentility, to be noted of the whole world so to delight in detracting, that they should keep a venomous-toothed cur and feed him with the crumbs that fall from their table, to do nothing but bite everyone by the shins that pass by. If they will needs be merry, let them have a fool and not a knave to disport them, and seek some other to bestow their alms on than such an impudent beggar.

As there be those that rail at all men, so there be those that rail at all arts, as Cornelius Agrippa *De Vanitate Scientiarum*, and a treatise that I have seen in dispraise of learn-

180. 'Don't go to the Council before you are called.'
181. Bag, valise.
182. 'Neither greater nor smaller than the body that was placed there.'

ing, where he saith it is the corrupter of the simple, the
schoolmaster of sin, the storehouse of treachery, the re-
viver of vices, and mother of cowardice; alleging many
examples, how there was never man egregiously evil but he
was a scholar; that when the use of letters was first invented
the Golden World ceased, *Facinusque invasit mortales*;[183]
how study doth effeminate a man, dim his sight, weaken
his brain, and engender a thousand diseases. Small learning would serve to confute so manifest a scandal, and I
imagine all men, like myself, so unmovably resolved of the
excellency thereof, that I will not, by the underpropping of
confutation, seem to give the idle-witted adversary so much
encouragement, as he should surmise his superficial arguments had shaken the foundation of it; against which he
could never have lifted his pen if herself had not helped
him to hurt herself.

An Invective Against Enemies of Poetry

With the enemies of Poetry, I care not if I have a bout; and
those are they that term our best writers but babbling
ballad-makers, holding them fantastical fools that have wit,
but cannot tell how to use it. I myself have been so censured
among some dull-headed divines; who deem it no more
cunning to write an exquisite poem, than to preach pure
Calvin, or distill the juice of a commentary in a quarter
sermon.* [184] Prove it when you will, you slow-spirited
saturnists,[186] that have nothing but the pilferies of your pen
to polish an exhortation withal; no eloquence but tautolo-

* *Absit arrogantia*,[185] that this speech should concern all
divines, but such dunces as abridge men of their lawful
liberty, and care not how unprepared they speak to their
auditory.

183. 'Wickedness took possession of mortals.'
184. Preaching only once a quarter.
185. 'Let arrogance be absent', (i.e. let me not be thought arrogant).
186. Morose people, as born under the melancholy influence of
Saturn.

gies, to tie the ears of your auditory unto you; no invention but here is to be noted, 'I stole this note out of Beza [187] or Marlorat';[188] no wit to move, no passion to urge, but only an ordinary form of preaching, blown up by use of often hearing and speaking; and you shall find there goes more exquisite pains and purity of wit to the writing of one such rare poem as *Rosamond* [189] than to a hundred of your dunstical [190] sermons.*

Should we (as you) borrow all out of others, and gather nothing of ourselves, our names should be baffled on every bookseller's stall, and not a chandler's mustard-pot but would wipe his mouth with our waste paper.[191] 'New herrings, new', we must cry, every time we make ourselves public, or else we shall be christened with a hundred new titles of idiotism. Nor is poetry an art whereof there is no use in a man's whole life, but to describe discontented thoughts and youthful desires; for there is no study, but it doth illustrate and beautify. How admirably shine those divines above the common mediocrity, that have tasted the sweet springs of Parnassus?

Encomium H. Smithi[192]

Silver-tongued Smith, whose well-tuned style hath made thy death the general tears of the Muses, quaintly couldst thou devise heavenly ditties to Apollo's lute, and teach stately verse to trip it as smoothly as if Ovid and thou had

---

*Such sermons I mean as our sectaries preach in ditches, and other conventicles, when they leap from the cobbler's stall to their pulpits.

187. Theodore de Bèze (1519–1605), noted Calvinist.
188. Augustin Marlorat (1506–63), also prominent among the Genevan reformers.
189. *Complaint of Rosamund* (Samuel Daniel, 1592).
190. Stupid.
191. Waste paper and books were commonly used to cover mustard pots.
192. Henry Smith (1550?–91) of St Clement Danes, London.

but one soul. Hence alone did it proceed, that thou wert such a plausible pulpit man, that before thou enteredst into the rough ways of theology, thou refinedst, preparedst, and purifidest thy mind with sweet poetry. If a simple man's censure may be admitted to speak in such an open theatre of opinions, I never saw abundant reading better mixed with delight, or sentences, which no man can challenge of profane affectation, sounding more melodious to the ear or piercing more deep to the heart.

The Fruits of Poetry

To them that demand what fruits the poets of our time bring forth or wherein they are able to prove themselves necessary to the state, thus I answer. First and foremost, they have cleansed our language from barbarism and made the vulgar sort here in London, which is the fountain whose rivers flow round about England, to aspire to a richer purity of speech than is communicated with the commonalty of any nation under heaven. The virtuous by their praises they encourage to be more virtuous, to vicious men they are as infernal hags, to haunt their ghosts with eternal infamy after death. The soldier, in hope to have his high deeds celebrated by their pens, despiseth a whole army of perils, and acteth wonders exceeding all human conjecture. Those that care neither for God nor the devil by their quills are kept in awe. *Multi famam*, saith one, *pauci conscientiam verentur.** [193] Let God see what he will, they would be loath to have the shame of the world. What age will not praise immortal Sir Philip Sidney, whom noble Salustius,[194] that thrice singular French poet, hath famoused together with Sir Nicholas Bacon, Lord Keeper, and merry Sir Thomas More, for the chief pillars of our English speech.

* Plin., lib. 3.

193. 'Many respect what other people say; few respect what their conscience tells them.'

194. Du Bartas (1544–90), author of *La Seconde Semaine*; translated into *Du Bartas His Divine Weeks* (1633).

Not so much but Chaucer's Host, Bailey in Southwark, and his Wife of Bath he keeps such a stir with in his *Canterbury Tales*, shall be talked of whilst the bath is used or there be ever a bad house in Southwark.

The Dispraise of Lay Chronigraphers

Gentles, it is not your lay chronigraphers,[195] that write of nothing but mayors and sheriffs, and the dear year, and the great frost, that can endow your names with never-dated glory, for they want the wings of choice words to fly to heaven, which we have. They cannot sweeten a discourse, or wrest admiration from men reading, as we can, reporting the meanest accident. Poetry is the honey of all flowers, the quintessence of all sciences, the marrow of wit, and the very phrase of angels. How much better is it, then, to have an elegant lawyer to plead one's cause, than a stutting [196] townsman, that loseth himself in his tale, and doth nothing but make legs; so much it is better for a nobleman, or gentleman, to have his honour's story related, and his deeds emblazoned, by a poet than a citizen.

Alas, poor Latinless authors, they are so simple they know not what they do. They no sooner spy a new ballad, and his name to it that compiled it, but they put him in for one of the learned men of our time. I marvel how the masterless [197] men that set up their bills in Paul's for services, and such as paste up their papers on every post for arithmetic and writing schools, scape eternity amongst them. I believe both they and the Knight Marshal's men,[198] that nail up mandates at the Court gate for annoying the palace with filth or making water, if they set their names to the writing, will shortly make up the number of the learned men of our time, and be as famous as the rest. For my part, I do chal-

195. Chroniclers.   196. Stuttering.
197. Unemployed, advertising for work on the doors of St Paul's.
198. Officers concerned with offences committed within twelve miles of the King's palace.

lenge no praise of learning to myself, yet have I worn a gown in the university, and so hath *caret tempus non habet moribus*;[199] but this I dare presume, that, if any Maecenas bind me to him by his bounty, or extend some round liberality to me worth the speaking of, I will do him as much honour as any poet of my beardless years shall in England. Not that I am so confident what I can do, but that I attribute so much to my thankful mind above others, which, I am persuaded, would enable me to work miracles.

On the contrary side, if I be evil entreated, or sent away with a flea in mine ear, let him look that I will rail on him soundly; not for an hour or a day, whiles the injury is fresh in my memory, but in some elaborate polished poem, which I will leave to the world when I am dead, to be a living image to all ages of his beggarly parsimony and ignoble illiberality. And let him not, whatsoever he be, measure the weight of my words by this book, where I write *Quicquid in buccam venerit*,[200] as fast as my hand can trot; but I have terms, if I be vexed, laid in steep in *aquafortis*[201] and gunpowder, that shall rattle through the skies and make an earthquake in a peasant's ears.

Put case, since I am not yet out of the theme of Wrath, that some tired jade belonging to the press, whom I never wronged in my life, hath named me expressly in print * (as I will not do him), and accused me of want of learning, upbraiding me for reviving, in an epistle of mine,[202] the reverent memory of Sir Thomas More, Sir John Cheke,[203]

* I would tell you in what book it is, but I am afraid it would make his book sell in his latter days, which hitherto hath lain dead, and been a great loss to the printer.

199. A.W. suggests that this virtually meaningless Latin is recollected but misquoted from Cicero (*In Catilinam* I, 1, 2) and that we might possibly glean 'he lacks the character and has not the time', referring to the career of a university man with no Maecenas, or great patron, behind him.

200. 'Whatever comes to my tongue' (Martial).

201. Nitric acid.

202. A reference to Nashe's Preface to *Menaphon* (see p. 476).

203. Professor of Greek, Cambridge, 1540–51.

Doctor Watson,[204] Doctor Haddon,[205] Doctor Carr,[206] Master
Ascham,[207] as if they were no meat but for his mastership's
mouth, or none but some such as the son of a ropemaker [208]
were worthy to mention them. To shew how I can rail, thus
would I begin to rail on him.

'Thou that hadst thy hood turned over thy ears,[209] when
thou wert a bachelor, for abusing of Aristotle, and setting
him up on the school gates painted with ass's ears on his
head: is it any discredit for me, thou great baboon, thou
pigmy braggart, thou pamphleteer of nothing but pæans,*
to be censured by thee, that hast scorned the Prince of
Philosophers? Thou, that in thy Dialogues soldst honey for
a halfpenny, and the choicest writers extant for cues [210]
apiece, that camest to the Logic Schools when thou wert a
freshman and writst phrases; off with thy gown and untruss, for I mean to lash thee mightily. Thou hast a brother,
hast thou not, student in almanacs? [211] Go to, I'll stand to
it, he fathered one of thy bastards (a book I mean) which,
being of thy begetting, was set forth under his name.

'Gentlemen, I am sure you have heard of a ridiculous ass
that many years since sold lies by the great, and wrote an
absurd *Astrological Discourse* [212] of the terrible conjunction
of Saturn and Jupiter; wherein, as if he had lately cast the
heavens' water or been at the anatomizing of the sky's

* Look at the chandler's shop or at the flaxwife's stall,
if you see no tow nor soap wrapped up in the title page of
such a pamphlet as 'Incerti Authoris Io Paean' ['Of uncertain
authorship . . .'].

204. Thomas Watson, 1513–84, Bishop of Lincoln.
205. Walter Haddon, 1516–72, Professor of Civil Law, Cambridge.
206. Nicholas Carr, 1524–68, Cambridge, Professor of Greek.
207. Roger Ascham, 1515–68, author of *The Scholemaster*, tutor
to Elizabeth.
208. A reference to the Harveys (Gabriel, John and Richard) who
attacked Nashe in *Lamb of God*, 1590.
209 *Thou . . . ears*: M. suggests it means he had been deprived of
his degree.   210. Half-farthings.
211. John Harvey's Almanacks for 1583 and 1589.
212. The predictions of 1583 proved false.

entrails in Surgeon's Hall, he prophesieth of such strange wonders to ensue from stars' distemperature and the unusual adultery of planets, as none but he that is bawd to those celestial bodies could ever descry. What expectation there was of it both in town and country, the amazement of those times may testify; and the rather because he pawned his credit * upon it, in these express terms: "If these things fall not out in every point as I have wrote, let me for ever hereafter lose the credit of my astronomy."

'Well, so it happened, that he happened not to be a man of his word. His astronomy broke his day with his creditors, and Saturn and Jupiter proved honester men than all the world took them for; whereupon the poor prognosticator was ready to run himself through with his Jacob's staff,[213] and cast himself headlong from the top of a globe (as a mountain) and break his neck. The whole university hissed at him; Tarlton at the theatre made jests of him; and Elderton [214] consumed his ale-crammed nose to nothing in bearbaiting him with whole bundles of ballads. Would you, in likely reason, guess it were possible for any shame-swollen toad to have the spit-proof face to live out this disgrace? It is, dear brethren, *Vivit, imo vivit;*[215] and, which is more, he is a vicar.[216]

'Poor slave, I pity thee that thou hadst no more grace but to come in my way. Why, could not you have sat quiet at home and writ catechisms, but you must be comparing me to *Martin,*[217] and exclaim against me for reckoning up the high scholars of worthy memory? *Jupiter ingeniis præbet sua numina vatum,* saith Ovid, *seque celebrari quo-*

---

*Which at home, iwis, was worth a dozen of halters at least, for if I be not deceived, his father was a ropemaker.

213. Instrument used in taking the altitude of the sun.
214. A popular, hard-drinking ballad-writer.
215. 'He lives, indeed he lives' ('imo' = 'immo'). (M. suggests it is a reminiscence of Cicero, *In Catilinam,* I, 1, 2.)
216. i.e. as rector of Chislehurst.
217. Martin Marprelate, pseudonym of author of pamphlets attacking Church of England (see Intro. pp. 22–6).

libet ore sinit.[218] Which if it be so, I hope I am *Aliquis*,[219] and those men, *quos honoris causa nominavi*,[220] are not greater than gods. Methinks I see thee stand quivering and quaking, and even now lift up thy hands to heaven, as thanking God my choler is somewhat assuaged; but thou art deceived, for however I let fall my style a little, to talk in reason with thee that hast none, I do not mean to let thee scape so.

'Thou hast wronged one for my sake, whom for the name I must love, T.N.,[221] the master-butler of Pembroke Hall, a far better scholar than thyself (in my judgment) and one that sheweth more discretion and government in setting up a size of bread, than thou in all thy whole book. Why man, think no scorn of him, for he hath held thee up a hundred times, whiles the Dean hath given thee correction, and thou hast capped and kneed him, when thou wert hungry, for a chipping.[222] But that's nothing, for hadst thou never been beholding to him nor holden up by him, he hath a beard that is a better gentleman than all thy whole body, and a grave countenance, like Cato, able to make thee run out of thy wits for fear, if he look sternly upon thee.

'I have read over thy sheepish discourse of the Lamb of God and his enemies, and entreated my patience to be good to thee whilst I read. But for all that I could do with myself (as I am sure I may do as much as another man) I could not refrain, but bequeath it to the privy, leaf by leaf as I read it, it was so ugly, dorbellical,[223] and lumpish. Mon-

218. 'Jupiter affords his divine inspiration to the minds of poets, and permits himself to be celebrated by any mouth' (Ovid).

219. 'Somebody', (i.e. 'any mouth' of the Ovid quotation).

220. 'Whom for the sake of honour I named'.

221. Thomas Nash of Eltisley, Cambridgeshire. Richard Harvey had written in the Preface to *Lamb of God*, 1590: 'Thomas Nash, one whom I never heard of before (for I cannot imagine him to be Thomas Nash our butler of Pembroke Hall, albeit peradventure not much better learned).'

222. A burnt crust.

223. A term of ridicule derived from the scholar Dorbellus, Nicholas de Orbelli (d. 1455).

strous, monstrous, and palpable, not to be spoken of in a Christian congregation; thou has scummed over the schoolmen, and of the froth of their folly made a dish of divinity brewess,[224] which the dogs will not eat. If the printer have any great dealings with thee, he were best to get a privilege betimes, *Ad imprimendum solum,*[225] forbidding all other to sell waste paper but himself, or else he will be in a woeful taking. The Lamb of God * make thee a wiser bell-wether than thou art, for else I doubt thou wilt be driven to leave all, and fall to thy father's occupation, which is, to go and make a rope to hang thyself. *Neque enim lex æquior ulla est, quam necis artifices arte perire sua.*[226] And so I leave thee till a better opportunity, to be tormented world without end of our poets and writers about London, whom thou has called piperly make-plays and make-bates; not doubting but he also, whom thou termest "the vain Paphatchet",[227] will have a flurt[228] at thee one day; all jointly driving thee to this issue, that thou shalt be constrained to go to the chief beam of thy benefice, and there beginning a lamentable speech with *cur scripsi, cur perii,*[229] end with *pravum prava decent, iuvat inconcessa voluptas,*[230] and so with a trice, truss up thy life in the string of thy sance-bell.[231] "So be it," pray Pen, Ink, and Paper, on their knees, that they may not be troubled with thee any more.'

Redeo ad vos, mei auditores,[232] have I not an indifferent pretty vein in spur-galling an ass? If you knew how ex-

* His own words.

224. Broth.
225. 'Only for printing', copyright.
226. 'For no law is fairer than that those who devise a method of killing people should die by their own methods' (Ovid).
227. The author of *Pap with a Hatchet*, probably John Lyly.
228. Gibe.
229. 'Why have I written? Why have I died?'
230. 'Immorality suits an immoral person; forbidden sensuality is pleasing' (play on *parva parvum decent*: 'little things please little minds').
231. Sanctus bell rung after the main peals.
232. 'I return to you, my listeners.'

temporal it were at this instant, and with what haste it is writ, you would say so. But I would not have you think that all this that is set down here is in good earnest, for then you go by St Giles, the wrong way to Westminster;[233] but only to shew how for a need I could rail, if I were thoroughly fired. So ho, Honiger Hammon,[234] where are you all this while, I cannot be acquainted with you? Tell me, what do you think of the case? Am I subject to the sin of Wrath I write against, or no, in whetting my pen on this block? I know you would fain have it so, but it shall not choose but be otherwise for this once. Come on, let us turn over a new leaf, and hear what Gluttony can say for herself, for Wrath hath spit his poison, and full platters do well after extreme purging.

The Complaint of Gluttony

The Roman emperors that succeeded Augustus were exceedingly given to this horrible vice, whereof some of them would feed on nothing but the tongues of pheasants and nightingales; others would spend as much at one banquet as a king's revenues came to in a year; whose excess I would decipher at large, but that a new laureate [235] hath saved me the labour, who, for a man that stands upon pains and not wit, hath performed as much as any story-dresser may do, that sets a new English nap on an old Latin apothegm. It is enough for me to lick dishes here at home, though I feed not mine eyes at any of the Roman feasts. Much good do it you, Master Dives, here in London; for you are he my pen means to dine withal. *Miserere mei*,[236] what a fat churl it is! Why, he hath a belly as big as the round church in Cambridge, a face as huge as the whole body of a base viol, and legs that, if they were hollow, a man might keep a mill

233. The hospital of St Giles in the Field was on the way to Tyburn, the place of execution.
234. Fancy name for Harvey (M. sees no special sense; J. Crow suggests 'a ludicrous perversion of Jupiter Hammon').
235. Probably satirical reference to Anthony Munday (F.P.W.).
236. 'Have mercy upon me.'

in either of them. *Experto crede,*[237] *Roberto*, there is no mast [238] like a merchant's table. *Bona fide*, it is a great misture,[239] that we have not men swine as well as beasts, for then we should have pork that hath no more bones than a pudding and a side of bacon that you might lay under your head instead of a bolster.

Nature in England is but Plain Dame, but in Spain and Italy, because they have more use of her than we, she is dubbed a Lady

It is not for nothing that other countries, whom we upbraid with drunkenness, call us bursten-bellied gluttons; for we make our greedy paunches powdering-tubs [240] of beef, and eat more meat at one meal than the Spaniard or Italian in a month. Good thrifty men, they draw out a dinner with sallets,[241] like a *Swart-rutter's* [242] suit, and make *Madonna* Nature their best caterer. We must have our tables furnished like poulters' stalls, or as though we were to victual Noah's ark again wherein there was all sorts of living creatures that ever were, or else the good-wife will not open her mouth to bid one welcome. A stranger that should come to one of our *magnificoes'* houses, when dinner were set on the board, and he not yet set, would think the goodman of the house were a haberdasher of wildfowl, or a merchant venturer of dainty meat, that sells commodity of good cheer by the great,[243] and hath factors in Arabia, Turkey, Egypt, and Barbary, to provide him of strange birds, China mustard, and odd patterns to make custards by.[244]

237. 'Believe an expert.'   238. Food for fattening swine.
239. Loss.
240. Tubs for salting or pickling meat.
241. Salads, (also a headpiece).
242. Irregular soldiers in Netherlands with black armour and blackened faces.
243. Wholesale.
244. *patterns ... by*: Patterned pastry surrounding a custard.

Lord, what a coil[245] we have, with this course and that course, removing this dish higher, setting another lower, and taking away the third. A general might in less space remove his camp, than they stand disposing of their gluttony. And whereto tends all this gourmandise, but to give sleep gross humours to feed on, to corrupt the brain, and make it unapt and unwieldy for anything?

The Roman censors, if they lighted upon a fat corpulent man, they straight away took away his horse, and constrained him to go afoot; positively concluding his carcase was so puffed up with gluttony or idleness. If we had such horse-takers amongst us, and that surfeit-swollen churls, who now ride on their foot-cloths, might be constrained to carry their flesh-budgets from place to place on foot, the price of velvet and cloth would fall with their bellies, and the gentle craft[246] (alias, the red herring's kinsmen) get more and drink less. *Plenus venter nil agit libenter, et plures gula occidit quam gladius.*[247] It is as desperate a piece of service to sleep upon a full stomach as it is to serve in face of the bullet; a man is but his breath, and that may as well be stopped by putting too much in his mouth at once, as running on the mouth of the cannon. That is verified of us, which Horace writes of an outrageous eater in his time, *Quicquid quæsierat ventri donabat avaro*; 'whatsoever he could rap or rend, he confiscated to his covetous gut.' Nay, we are such flesh-eating Saracans[248] that chaste fish may not content us, but we delight in the murder of innocent mutton, in the unpluming of pullery,[249] and quartering of calves and oxen. It is horrible and detestable; no godly fishmonger that can digest it.

245. Disturbance, trouble.
246. Shoemaking.
247. 'A full stomach does nothing willingly, and the gut has killed more than the sword' (proverb).
248. Who feasted on Christian fast-days.　　　　249. Poultry.

A Rare Witty Jest of Doctor Watson

Report, which our moderners clep²⁵⁰ floundering Fame, puts me in memory of a notable jest I heard long ago of Doctor Watson,²⁵¹ very conducible to the reproof of these fleshly-minded Belials.* He being at supper on a fasting or fish night at least, with a great number of his friends and acquaintance, there chanced to be in the company an outlandish ²⁵² doctor, who, when all other fell to such victuals (agreeing to the time) as were before them, he over-slipped them, and there being one joint of flesh on the table for such as had weak stomachs, fell freshly to it. After that hunger, half conquered, had restored him to the use of his speech, for his excuse he said to his friend that brought him thither, *'Profecto, Domine, ego sum malissimus pisca-tor,'* ²⁵³ meaning by *piscator*, a fishman (which is a liberty, as also *malissimus*, that outlandish men in their familiar talk do challenge, at least above us). *'At tu es bonissimus carnifex,'* ²⁵⁴ quoth Doctor Watson, retorting very merrily his own licentious figures upon him. So of us may it be said, we are *malissimi piscatores*, but *bonissimi carnifices*. I would English the jest for the edification of the tem-porality,²⁵⁵ but that it is not so good in English as in Latin; and though it were as good, it would not convert clubs and clouted shoon from the flesh pots of Egypt to the provant of the Low Countries; for they had rather (with the servingman) put up a supplication to the Parliament

---

* Or rather Belly-alls, because all their mind is on their belly.

250. Call.
251. Thomas Watson (1513–84), Bishop of Lincoln.
252. Foreign.
253. 'Of course, master, I am the worst fisherman' ('fisherman' sug-gesting 'fishmonger', or brothel-keeper).
254. 'But you are the best butcher' (or executioner) (part of the joke is the bad Latin, *malissimus* and *bonissimus* being unlearned solecisms).
255. Laity.

House that they might have a yard of pudding for a penny, than desire (with the baker) there might be three ounces of bread sold for a halfpenny.

The Moderation of Friar Alphonso, King Philip's Confessor

Alphonsus, King Philip's confessor, that came over with him to England, was such a moderate man in his diet, that he would feed but once a day, and at that time he would feed so slenderly and sparingly, as scarce served to keep life and soul together. One night, importunately invited to a solemn banquet, for fashion sake he sat down among the rest, but by no entreaty could be drawn to eat anything. At length, fruit being set on the board, he reached an apple out of the dish and put it in his pocket, which one marking, that sat right over against him, asked him, '*Domine, cur es solicitus in crastinum?* – Sir, why are you careful for the morrow?' Whereto he answered most soberly, '*Immo hoc facio, mi amice, ut ne sim solicitus in crastinum*. No, I do it, my friend, that I may not be careful for the morrow.' As though his appetite were a whole day contented with so little as an apple, and that it were enough to pay the morrow's tribute to nature.

The Strange Alteration of the County Molines, the Prince of Parma's Companion

Rare, and worthy to be registered to all posterities, is the County Moline's [256] (sometime the Prince of Parma's companion) altered course of life, who, being a man that lived in as great pomp and delicacy as was possible for a man to do, and one that wanted nothing but a kingdom that his

256. M. thinks Nashe may be confusing him with Henri, Duc de Joyeuse, whose entry into the Capuchin Order in 1587 attracted much attention at the time. (Other 1592 texts say that he remained in the Order 'four year', not 'twelvemonth' as in this text.)

heart could desire, upon a day entering into a deep melancholy by himself, he fell into a discursive consideration what this world was, how vain and transitory the pleasures thereof, and how many times he had offended God by surfeiting, gluttony, drunkenness, pride, whoredom, and such like, and how hard it was for him, that lived in that prosperity that he did, not to be entangled with those pleasures. Whereupon he presently resolved, twixt God and his own conscience, to forsake it and all his allurements, and betake him to the severest form of life used in their state. And with that called his soldiers and acquaintance together, and, making known his intent unto them, he distributed his living and possessions, which were infinite, amongst the poorest of them; and having not left himself the worth of one farthing under heaven, betook him to the most beggarly new erected [257] Order of the Friar Capuchines. Their institution is, that they shall possess nothing whatsoever of their own more than the clothes on their backs, continually to go barefoot, wear hair shirts, and lie upon the hard boards, winter and summer time. They must have no meat, nor ask any but what is given them voluntarily, nor must they lay up any from meal to meal, but give it to the poor, or else it is a great penalty. In this severe humility lives this devout County, and hath done this twelvemonth, submitting himself to all the base drudgery of the house, as fetching water, making clean the rest of their chambers, insomuch as he is the junior of the order. Oh, what a notable rebuke were his honourable lowliness to succeeding pride, if this prostrate spirit of his were not the servant of superstition, or he mispent not his good works on a wrong faith.

Let but our English belly-gods punish their pursy [258] bodies with this strict penance, and profess Capuchinism but one month, and I'll be their pledge they shall not grow so like dry-fats as they do. Oh, it will make them jolly long-

257. Actually founded 1525, introduced into France 1572 and spread rapidly.

258. Fat, corpulent.

winded, to trot up and down the dorter [259] stairs, and the water-tankard will keep under the insurrection of their shoulders, the hair shirt will chase whoredom out of their bones, and the hard lodging on the boards take their flesh down a button-hole lower.

But if they might be induced to distribute all their goods amongst the poor, it were to be hoped Saint Peter would let them dwell in the suburbs of heaven, whereas otherwise they must keep aloof at Pancredge, [260] and not come near the liberties by five leagues and above. It is your doing, Diotrephes [261] Devil, that these stall-fed cormorants to damnation must bung up all the wealth of the land in their snap-hance [262] bags, and poor scholars and soldiers wander in back lanes and the out-shifts of the city, with never a rag to their backs. But our trust is, that by some intemperance or other, you will turn up their heels one of these years together, and provide them of such unthrifts to their heirs, as shall spend in one week amongst good fellows what they got by extortion and oppression from gentlemen all their life-time.

The Complaint of Drunkenness

From gluttony in meats, let me descend to superfluity in drink: a sin that, ever since we have mixed ourselves with the Low Countries, is counted honourable, but, before we knew their lingering wars, was held in the highest degree of hatred that might be. Then, if we had seen a man go wallowing in the streets, or lain sleeping under the board, we would have spit at him as a toad, and called him foul drunken swine, and warned all our friends out of his com-

259. Dormitory.
260. St Pancras.
261. Third Epistle of John (v.9) refers to Diotrephes 'who loveth to have the pre-eminence among them'.
262. With snap-locks.

pany. Now, he is nobody that cannot drink *super nagulum*,*
carouse the hunter's hoop,[263] quaff *upsey freze cross*,[264]
with healths, gloves, mumps, frolics,[265] and a thousand such
domineering inventions. He is reputed a peasant and a boor
that will not take his liquor profoundly. And you shall hear
a cavalier of the first feather, a princox [266] that was but a
page the other day in the Court, and now is all-to-be-
frenchified in his soldier's suit, stand upon terms [267] with
'God's wounds, you dishonour me, sir, you do me the disgrace if you do not pledge me as much as I drunk to you;'
and, in the midst of his cups, stand vaunting his manhood,
beginning every sentence with, 'When I first bore arms',
when he never bare anything but his lord's rapier after him
in his life. If he have been over and visited a town of garrison, as a traveller or passenger, he hath as great experience as the greatest commander and chief leader in
England. A mighty deformer of men's manners and features is this unnecessary vice of all other. Let him be
indued with never so many virtues, and have as much
goodly proportion and favour as nature can bestow upon
a man, yet if he be thirsty after his own destruction, and
hath no joy nor comfort but when he is drowning his soul
in a gallon pot, that one beastly imperfection will utterly
obscure all that is commendable in him, and all his good
qualities sink like lead down to the bottom of his carousing
cups, where they will lie like lees and dregs, dead and un-
regarded of any man.

* Drinking *super nagulum*, a device of drinking new come
out of France; which is, after a man hath turned up the
bottom of the cup, to drop it on his nail, and make a pearl
with that is left; which, if it shed, and he cannot make stand
on by reason there's too much, he must drink again for his
penance.

263. A drinking term.
264. Drinking heavily, like the Frisians.
265. *gloves, mumps, frolics:* Games and pastimes associated with
drinking.
266. Young coxcomb.
267. *stand upon terms*: argue, dispute.

Clim of the Clough,[268] thou that usest to drink nothing but scalding lead and sulphur in hell, thou art not so greedy of thy night gear. Oh, but thou hast a foul swallow if it come once to carousing of human blood; but that's but seldom, once in seven year, when there's a great execution, otherwise thou art tied at rack and manger, and drinkest nothing but the *aqua vitæ* of vengeance all thy life-time. The proverb gives it forth thou art a knave, and therefore I have more hope thou art some manner of good fellow.[269] Let me entreat thee, since thou hast other iniquities enough to circumvent us withal, to wipe this sin out of the catalogue of thy subtleties; help to blast the vines, that they may bear no more grapes, and sour the wines in the cellars of merchants' store-houses, that our countrymen may not piss out all their wit and thrift against the walls.

King Edgar's Ordinance Against Drinking

King Edgar, because his subjects should not offend in swilling and bibbing, as they did, caused certain iron cups to be chained to every fountain and well's side, and at every vintner's door, with iron pins in them, to stint every man how much he should drink; and he that went beyond one of those pins forfeited a penny for every draught. And, if stories were well searched, I believe hoops in quart pots were invented to that end, that every man should take his hoop, and no more.

The Wonderful Abstinence of the Marquis of Pisana, Yet Living

I have heard it justified for a truth by great personages, that the old Marquis of Pisana,[270] who yet lives, drinks not once in seven year; and I have read of one Andron of Argos,

268. The devil, a name used in ballads (M. queries whether it could be the name of some contemporary clown or fire-eater).
269. A rowdy drunkard.
270. Unidentified.

that was so seldom thirsty, that he travelled over the hot, burning sands of Lybia, and never drank. Then why should our cold clime bring forth such fiery throats? Are we more thirsty than Spain and Italy, where the sun's force is doubled? The Germans and Low Dutch, methinks, should be continually kept moist with the foggy air and stinking mists that arise out of their fenny soil; but as their country is over-flown with water, so are their heads always over-flown with wine, and in their bellies they have standing quagmires and bogs of English beer.

The Private Laws Amongst Drunkards

One of their breed it was that writ the book *De Arte Bibendi*,[271] a worshipful treatise fit for none but Silenus and his ass [272] to set forth. Besides that volume, we have general rules and injunctions, as good as printed precepts, or statutes set down by Act of Parliament, that go from drunkard to drunkard; as still to keep your first man, not to leave any flocks in the bottom of the cup, to knock the glass on your thumb when you have done, to have some shoeing horn to pull on your wine, as a rasher off the coals or a red herring, to stir it about with a candle's end to make it taste better, and not to hold your peace while the pot is stirring.

The Eight Kinds of Drunkenness

Nor have we one or two kinds of drunkards only, but eight kinds. The first is ape drunk, and he leaps, and sings, and holloes, and danceth for the heavens. The second is lion drunk, and he flings the pots about the house, calls his hostess whore, breaks the glass windows with his dagger, and is apt to quarrel with any man that speaks to him. The third is swine drunk, heavy, lumpish, and sleepy, and cries

271. A poem by Vincentius Obsopaeus (d. 1539).
272. The tutor of Dionysus, commonly depicted as drunk and riding on an ass.

for a little more drink and a few more clothes. The fourth is sheep drunk, wise in his own conceit when he cannot bring forth a right word. The fifth is maudlin drunk when a fellow will weep for kindness in the midst of his ale, and kiss you, saying, 'By God, captain, I love thee; go thy ways, thou dost not think so often of me as I do of thee; I would (if it pleased God) I could not love thee so well as I do.' And then he puts his finger in his eye and cries. The sixth is martin [273] drunk, when a man is drunk and drinks himself sober ere he stir. The seventh is goat drunk, when, in his drunkenness, he hath no mind but on lechery. The eighth is fox drunk, when he is crafty drunk, as many of the Dutchmen be, that will never bargain but when they are drunk. All these species, and more, I have seen practised in one company at one sitting, when I have been permitted to remain sober amongst them, only to note their several humours. He that plies any one of them hard, it will make him to write admirable verses, and to have a deep casting [274] head, though he were never so very a dunce before.

The Discommodities of Drunkenness

Gentlemen, all you that will not have your brains twice sodden, your flesh rotten with the dropsy, that love not to go in greasy doublets, stockings out at the heels, and wear alehouse daggers at your backs: forswear this slavering bravery, that will make you have stinking breaths, and your bodies smell like brewers' aprons; rather keep a snuff [275] in the bottom of the glass to light you to bed withal, than leave never an eye in your head to lead you over the threshold. It will bring you in your old age to be companions with none but porters and car-men, to talk out of a cage, [276] railing as drunken men are wont, a hundred boys wondering about them; and to die suddenly, as Fol

273. A kind of monkey.
274. Calculating.
275. Drink left at the bottom of a cup.
276. A punishment for vagabonds.

Long the fencer did, drinking *aqua vitæ*. From which (as all the rest) good Lord deliver Pierce Penniless.

The Complaint of Sloth

The nurse of this enormity (as of all evils) is Idleness, or Sloth, which, having no painful providence to set himself a-work, runs headlong, with the reins in his own hand, into all lasciviousness and sensuality that may be. Men, when they are idle, and know not what to do, saith one, 'Let us go to the Stilliard [277] and drink Rhenish wine.' 'Nay, if a man knew where a good whorehouse were,' said another, 'it were somewhat like.' 'Nay,' saith the third, 'let us go to a dicing-house or a bowling-alley, and there we shall have some sport for our money.' To one of these three ('at hand', quoth pick-purse) your evil angelship, master many-headed beast, conducts them. *Ubi quid agitur*,[278] betwixt you and their souls be it, for I am no drawer, box-keeper, or pander, to be privy to their sports.

If I were to paint Sloth (as I am not seen in the sweetening) [279] by Saint John the Evangelist I swear I would draw it like a stationer that I know, with his thumb under his girdle, who, if a man come to his stall and ask him for a book, never stirs his head or looks upon him, but stands stone still and speaks not a word; only with his little finger points backwards to his boy, who must be his interpreter, and so all the day, gaping like a dumb image, he sits without motion, except at such times as he goes to dinner or supper; for then he is as quick as other three, eating six times every day.* If I would range abroad, and look in at sluggards' key-holes, I should find a number lying abed to save charges of

* *Videlicet*, before he come out of his bed, then a set breakfast, then dinner, then afternoon's nunchings, a supper, and a rere-supper.

277. A tavern near London Bridge.
278. 'Where something is being done'.
279. *seen in the sweetening*: Given to flattery.

ordinaries, and in winter, when they want firing, losing half
a week's commons together, to keep them warm in the linen.
And hold you content, this summer an under-meal[280] of
an afternoon long doth not amiss to exercise the eyes withal.
Fat men and farmers' sons, that sweat much with eating
hard cheese and drinking old wine, must have some more
ease than young boys that take their pleasure all day running up and down.

Which is Better of the Idle Glutton, or Vagrant Unthrift

Setting jesting aside, I hold it a great, disputable question,
which is a more evil man, of him that is an idle glutton at
home, or a reckless unthrift abroad? The glutton at home
doth nothing but engender diseases, pamper his flesh unto
lust, and is good for none but his own gut. The unthrift
abroad exerciseth his body at dancing school, fence school,
tennis, and all such recreations; the vintners, the victuallers,
the dicing-houses, and who not, get by him. Suppose he lose
a little now and then at play, it teacheth him wit: and how
should a man know to eschew vices, if his own experience
did not acquaint him with their inconveniences? *Omne
ignotum pro magnifico est*:[281] that villainy we have made
no assays in, we admire. Besides my vagrant reveller haunts
plays and sharpens his wits with frequenting the company
of poets; he emboldens his blushing face by courting fair
women on the sudden, and looks into all estates by conversing with them in public places. Now tell me whether of
these two, the heavy-headed, gluttonous house-dove, or this
lively, wanton, young gallant, is like to prove the wiser man,
and better member in the commonwealth? If my youth
might not be thought partial, the fine qualified gentleman,
although unstaid, should carry it clean away from the lazy
clownish drone.

280. Afternoon sleep.
281. 'Everything unfamiliar is thought wonderful' (Tacitus).

The Effects of Sloth

Sloth in nobility, courtiers, scholars, or any men, is the chiefest cause that brings them in contempt. For, as industry and unfatigable toil raiseth mean persons from obscure houses to high thrones of authority, so sloth and sluggish security causeth proud lords to tumble from the towers of their starry descents, and be trod underfoot of every inferior besonian.[282] Is it the lofty treading of a galliard, or fine grace in telling of a love tale amongst ladies, can make a man reverenced of the multitude? No, they care not for the false glistering of gay garments, or insinuating courtesy of a carpet peer;[283] but they delight to see him shine in armour, and oppose himself to honourable danger, to participate a voluntary penury with his soldiers, and relieve part of their wants out of his own purse. That is the course he that will be popular must take, which, if he neglect, and sit dallying at home, nor will be awaked by any indignities out of his love-dream, but suffer every upstart groom to defy him, set him at nought, and shake him by the beard unrevenged, let him straight take orders and be a churchman, and then his patience may pass for a virtue; but otherwise, he shall be suspected of cowardice, and not cared for of any.

The Means to Avoid Sloth

The only enemy to Sloth is contention and emulation; as to propose one man to myself, that is the only mirror of our age, and strive to out-go him in virtue. But this strife must be so tempered, that we fall not from the eagerness of praise, to the envying of their persons; for then we leave running to the goal of glory, to spurn at a stone that lies in our way; and so did Atalanta,[284] in the midst of her course, stoop to take up the golden apple that her enemy scattered in her way, and was out-run by Hippomenes. The contrary to this contention and emulation is security, peace, quiet, tran-

282. Beggar, rogue.   283. A mere courtier, no soldier.
284. A story told in Ovid, *Metamorphoses*, x.

quillity; when we have no adversary to pry into our actions, no malicious eye whose pursuing our private behaviour might make us more vigilant over our imperfections than otherwise we would be.

That state or kingdom that is in league with all the world and hath no foreign sword to vex it, is not half so strong or confirmed to endure as that which lives every hour in fear of invasion. There is a certain waste of the people for whom there is no use, but war; and these men must have some employment still to cut them off. *Nam si foras hostem non habent, domi invenient*:[285] if they have no service abroad, they will make mutinies at home. Or if the affairs of the state be such as cannot exhale all these corrupt excrements, it is very expedient they have some light toys to busy their heads withal cast before them as bones to gnaw upon, which may keep them from having leisure to intermeddle with higher matters.

The Defence of Plays

To this effect the policy of plays is very necesary, howsoever some shallow-brained censurers (not the deepest searchers into the secrets of government) mightily oppugn them. For whereas the afternoon being the idlest time of the day, wherein men that are their own masters (as gentlemen of the Court, the Inns of the Court, and the number of captains and soldiers about London) do wholly bestow themselves upon pleasure; and that pleasure they divide (how virtuously it skills[286] not) either into gaming, following of harlots, drinking, or seeing a play: is it not then better, since of four extremes all the world cannot keep them but they will choose one, that they should betake them to the least, which is plays? Nay, what if I prove plays to be no extreme, but a rare exercise of virtue? First, for the subject of them: for the most part it is borrowed out of our English

285. 'If they haven't an enemy abroad, they'll find one at home' (Livy).

286. Matters.

Chronicles, wherein our forefathers' valiant acts, that have lain long buried in rusty brass and worm-eaten books, are revived, and they themselves raised from the grave of oblivion, and brought to plead their aged honours in open presence: than which, what can be a sharper reproof to these degenerate effeminate days of ours?

How would it have joyed brave Talbot,[287] the terror of the French, to think that after he had lain two hundred years in his tomb, he should triumph again on the stage and have his bones new embalmed with the tears of ten thousand spectators at least (at several times), who, in the tragedian that represents his person, imagine they behold him fresh bleeding!

I will defend it against any cullion,[288] or club-fisted usurer of them all, there is no immortality can be given a man on earth like unto plays. What talk I to them of immortality, that are the only underminers of honour, and do envy any man that is not sprung up by base brokery like themselves? They care not if all the ancient houses were rooted out, so that, like the burgomasters of the Low Countries, they might share the government amongst them as states, and be quarter-masters of our monarchy. All arts to them are vanity; and if you tell them what a glorious thing it is to have Henry the Fifth represented on the stage, leading the French king prisoner, and forcing both him and the Dolphin[289] to swear fealty, 'Aye, but,' will they say, 'what do we get by it?', respecting neither the right of fame that is due to true nobility deceased, nor what hopes of eternity are to be proposed to adventurous minds, to encourage them forward, but only their execrable lucre, and filthy, unquenchable avarice.

They know when they are dead they shall not be brought upon the stage for any goodness, but in a merriment of the Usurer and the Devil, or buying arms of the herald, who gives them the lion, without tongue, tail, or tallents[290], because his master, whom he must serve, is a townsman, and

287. Sir John Talbot, second Earl of Shrewsbury.
288. Rascal, base fellow.   289. Dauphin.   290. Talons.

a man of peace, and must not keep any quarrelling beasts to annoy his honest neighbours.

The Use of Plays

In plays, all cozenages,[291] all cunning drifts over-gilded with outward holiness, all stratagems of war, all the cankerworms that breed on the rust of peace, are most lively anatomized. They shew the ill success of treason, the fall of hasty climbers, the wretched end of usurpers, the misery of civil dissension, and how just God is evermore in punishing of murder. And to prove every one of these allegations, could I propound the circumstances of this play and that play, if I meant to handle this theme otherwise than *obiter*.[292] What should I say more? They are sour pills of reprehension, wrapped up in sweet words.

The Confutation of Citizens' Objections Against Players

Whereas some petitioners of the Council against them object they corrupt the youth of the city, and withdraw prentices from their work, they[293] heartily wish they might be troubled with none of their youth nor their prentices; for some of them (I mean the ruder handicrafts' servants) never come abroad, but they are in danger of undoing. And as for corrupting them when they come, that's false; for no play they have encourageth any man to tumults or rebellion, but lays before such the halter and the gallows; or praiseth or approveth pride, lust, whoredom, prodigality, or drunkenness, but beats them down utterly. As for the hindrance of trades and traders of the city by them, that is an article foistered in by the vintners, alewives, and victuallers, who surmise, if there were no plays, they should have all the company that resort to them lie boozing and beer-bathing in their houses every afternoon. Nor so, nor so, good Brother Bottle-ale, for there are other places besides, where money can bestow itself. The sign of the smock will wipe your mouth clean; and yet I have heard ye have made her a

291. Tricks, frauds.   292. In passing.   293. i.e. the players.

tenant to your tap-houses. But what shall he do that hath spent himself? Where shall he haunt? Faith, when dice, lust, and drunkenness and all have dealt upon him, if there be never a play for him to go to for his penny, he sits melancholy in his chamber, devising upon felony or treason, and how he may best exalt himself by mischief.

A Player's Witty Answer to Augustus

In Augustus' time, who was the patron of all witty sports, there happened a great fray in Rome about a player, insomuch as all the city was in an uproar. Whereupon, the Emperor, after the broil was somewhat overblown, called the player before him, and asked what was the reason that a man of his quality durst presume to make such a brawl about nothing. He smilingly replied: 'It is good for thee, O Caesar, that the people's heads are troubled with brawls and quarrels about us and our light matters; for otherwise they would look into thee and thy matters.' Read Lipsius [294] or any profane or Christian politician, and you shall find him of this opinion.

A Comparison Twixt our Players and the Players Beyond the Sea

Our players are not as the players beyond sea, a sort of squirting bawdy comedians, that have whores and common courtesans to play women's parts, and forbear no immodest speech or unchaste action that may procure laughter; but our scene is more stately furnished than ever it was in the time of Roscius, our representations honourable, and full of gallant resolution, not consisting, like theirs, of a pantaloon, a whore, and a zany, but of emperors, kings and princes, whose true tragedies, *Sophocleo cothurno*,[295] they do vaunt.

294. Justus Lipsius (1547–1606), Belgian scholar. M. suspects Nashe is using his name at random.

295. 'In the Sophoclean buskin', i.e. the stately, dignified form of tragedy (Ovid).

The Due Commendation of Ned Allen

Not Roscius nor Æsop,[296] those admired tragedians that
have lived ever since before Christ was born, could ever perform more in action than famous Ned Allen.[297] I must
accuse our poets of sloth and partiality, that they will not
boast in large impressions what worthy men, above all
nations, England affords. Other countries cannot have a
fiddler break a string but they will put it in print, and the
old Romans, in the writings they published, thought scorn
to use any but domestical examples of their own home-bred
actors, scholars, and champions, and them they would
extol to the third and fourth generation: cobblers, tinkers,
fencers, none escaped them, but they mingled them all in
one gallimaufry [298] of glory.

Here I have used a like method, not of tying myself to
mine own country, but by insisting in the experience of our
time. And, if I ever write anything in Latin, as I hope one
day I shall, not a man of any desert here amongst us, but I
will have up. Tarlton,[299] Ned Allen, Knell,[300] Bently,[301] shall
be made known to France, Spain, and Italy; and not a part
that they surmounted in, more than other, but I will there
note and set down, with the manner of their habits and
attire.

The Seventh and Last Complaint of Lechery

The child of Sloth is Lechery, which I have placed last in
my order of handling: a sin that is able to make a man
wicked that should describe it; for it hath more starting
holes than a sieve hath holes, more clients than Westminster

296. Both actors flourished about 70 B.C.
297. Edward Alleyn (1566–1626), most famous tragic actor of his
time.
298. Mixture.
299. Richard Tarlton (d. 1588), chief comedian of the Queen's
players.
300. Thomas Knell (*fl.* 1586), another comic actor.
301. Mentioned by Thomas Heywood as a well-known actor.

Hall, more diseases than Newgate. Call a leet [302] at Bishops-gate, and examine how every second house in Shoreditch is maintained; make a privy search in Southwark and tell me how many she-inmates you find; nay, go where you will in the suburbs and bring me two virgins that have vowed chastity, and I'll build a nunnery.

Westminster, Westminster, much maidenhead hast thou to answer for at the day of judgment; thou hadst a sanctu-ary in thee once, but hast few saints left in thee now. Sur-geons and apothecaries, you know what I speak is true, for you live, like summoners, upon the sins of the people; tell me, is there any place so lewd, as this Lady London? Not a wench sooner creeps out of the shell, but she is of the reli-gion. Some wives will sow mandrake [303] in their gardens, and cross-neighbourhood with them is counted good fellow-ship.

The Court I dare not touch, but surely there, as in the heavens, be many falling stars and but one true Diana.[304] *Consuetudo peccandi tollit sensum peccati.*[305] Custom is a law, and lust holds it for a law to live without law. Lais, that had so many poets to her lovers, could not always pre-serve her beauty with their praises. Marble will wear away with much rain; gold will rust with moist keeping; and the richest garments are subject to time's moth-frets. Clytem-nestra,[306] that slew her husband to enjoy the adulterer Ægisthus, and bathed herself in milk every day to make her young again, had a time when she was ashamed to view herself in a looking glass, and her body withered, her mind being green. The people pointed at her for a murderer, young children hooted at her as a strumpet; shame, misery, sickness, beggary, is the best end of uncleanness.

302. Here, an official inquiry into the affairs of a ward or district.

303. A reference to Leah in *Genesis* (30, 14–16) 'hiring' Jacob to lie with her with Reuben's mandrakes (fertility symbol).

304. Goddess of chastity.

305. 'The habit of sinning takes away the sense of sin' (St Augus-tine).

306. *Lais. . . . Clytemnestra*: M. points out a confusion on N.'s part, what is said of Clytemnestra's bathing being properly applied to Lais.

Lais, Cleopatra, Helen, if our clime hath any such, noble Lord Warden of the witches and jugglers, I commend them with the rest of our unclean sisters in Shoreditch, the Spital,[307] Southwark, Westminster, and Turnbull Street,[308] to the protection of your Portership: hoping you will speedily carry them to hell, there to keep open house for all young devils that come, and not let our air be contaminated with their sixpenny damnation any longer.

Yours Devilship's
bounden execrator
PIERCE PENNILESS

'A supplication callst thou this?' quoth the Knight of the Post. 'It is the maddest supplication that ever I saw; methinks thou hast handled all the seven deadly sins in it, and spared none that exceeds his limits in any of them. It is well done to practise thy wit, but, I believe, our lord will cun[309] thee little thanks for it.'

'The worse for me,' quoth I, 'if my destiny be such to lose my labour everywhere, but I mean to take my chance, be it good or bad.' 'Well, hast thou any more that thou wouldest have me to do?' quoth he. 'Only one suit,' quoth I, 'which is this: that, sith opportunity so conveniently serves, you would acquaint me with the state of your infernal regiment; and what that hell is, where your lord holds his throne; whether a world like this, which spirits like outlaws do inhabit, who, being banished from heaven, as they are from their country, envy that any shall be more happy than they, and therefore seek all means possible, that wit or art may invent, to make other men as wretched as themselves; or whether it be a place of horror, stench, and darkness, where men see meat but can get none, or are ever thirsty and ready to swelt[310] for drink, yet have not the power to taste the cool streams that run hard at their feet; where,

307. Hospital (with allusion to venereal disease).
308. In Clerkenwell, frequented by prostitutes.
309. Give (variant of 'can').
310. Die.

permutata vicissitudine,[311] one ghost torments another by turns, and he that all his lifetime was a great fornicator, hath all the diseases of lust continually hanging upon him, and is constrained, the more to augment his misery, to have congress every hour with hags and old witches; and he that was a great drunkard here on earth, hath his penance assigned him, to carouse himself drunk with dish-wash and vinegar, and surfeit four times a day with sour ale and small beer; as so of the rest, as the usurer to swallow molten gold, the glutton to eat nothing but toads, and the murderer to be still stabbed with daggers, but never die; or whether, as some fantastical refiners of philosophy will needs persuade us, hell is nothing but error, and that none but fools and idiots and mechanical men, that have no learning, shall be damned. Of these doubts if you will resolve me, I shall think myself to have profited greatly by your company.'

He, hearing me so inquisitive in matters above human capacity, entertained my greedy humour with this answer. 'Poets and philosophers, that take a pride in inventing new opinions, have sought to renown their wits by hunting after strange conceits [312] of heaven and hell; all generally agreeing that such places there are, but how inhabited, by whom governed, or what betides them that are transported to the one or other, not two of them jump in one tale. We, that to our terror and grief do know their dotage by our sufferings, rejoice to think how these silly flies play with the fire that must burn them.

But leaving them to the labyrinth of their fond [313] curiosity, shall I tell thee in a word what hell is? It is a place where the souls of untemperate men and ill-livers of all sorts are detained and imprisoned till the general resurrection, kept and possessed chiefly by spirits, who lie like soldiers in garrison, ready to be sent about any service into the world, whensoever Lucifer, their Lieutenant General, pleaseth. For the situation of it in respect of heaven, I can no better compare it than to Calais and Dover. For, as a man stand-

311. 'Turn and turn about'.   312. Conceptions, notions.
313. Foolish.

ing upon Calais sands may see men walking on Dover cliffs, so easily may you discern heaven from the farthest part of hell, and behold the melody and motions of the angels and spirits there resident, in such perfect manner as if you were amongst them; which, how it worketh in the minds and souls of them that have no power to apprehend such felicity, it is not for me to intimate, because it is prejudicial to our monarchy.'

'I would be sorry,' quoth I, 'to importune you in any matter of secrecy; yet this I desire, if it might be done without offence, that you would satisfy me in full sort, and according to truth, what the devil is whom you serve? As also how he began, and how far his power and authority extends?'

'Percy, believe me, thou shrivest me very near [314] in this latter demand, which concerneth us more deeply than the former and may work us more damage than thou art aware of; yet in hope thou wilt conceal what I tell thee, I will lay open our whole estate plainly and simply unto thee as it is. But first I will begin with the opinions of former times, and so hasten forward to that *manifeste verum* [315] that thou seekest.

Some men there be that, building too much upon reason, persuade themselves that there are no devils at all, but that this word *dæmon* is such another moral of mischief, as the poets' Dame Fortune is of mishap. For as under the fiction of this blind goddess we aim at the folly of princes and great men in disposing of honours, that oftentimes prefer fools and disgrace wise men, and alter their favours in turning of an eye, as Fortune turns her wheel; so under the person of this old *gnathonical* [316] companion, called the devil, we shroud all subtlety masking under the name of simplicity, all painted holiness devouring widows' houses, all grayheaded foxes clad in sheep's garments; so that the devil (as they make it) is only a pestilent humour in a man, of pleasure, profit, or policy, that violently carries him away to

314. *shrivest . . . near*: Question closely.
315. 'Obvious truth'.   316. Parasitical.

vanity, villainy, or monstrous hypocrisy. Under vanity I comprehend not only all vain arts and studies whatsoever, but also dishonourable prodigality, untemperate venery, and that hateful sin of self-love, which is so common amongst us. Under villainy I comprehend murder, treason, theft, cozenage, cut-throat covetise, and such like. Lastly, under hypocrisy, all machiavellism, puritanism, and outward glozing with a man's enemy, and protesting friendship to him that I hate and mean to harm, all underhand cloaking of bad actions with commonwealth pretences and, finally, all Italianate conveyances, as to kill a man and then mourn for him, *quasi vero* [317] it was not by my consent; to be a slave to him that hath injured me, and kiss his feet for opportunity of revenge; to be severe in punishing offenders, that none might have the benefit of such means but myself; to use men for my purpose and then cast them off; to seek his destruction that knows my secrets; and such as I have employed in any murder or stratagem, to set them privily together by the ears, to stab each other mutually, for fear of bewraying me; or, if that fail, to hire them to humour one another in such courses as may bring them both to the gallows.

These, and a thousand more such sleights, hath hypocrisy learned by travelling strange countries. I will not say she puts them in practice here in England, although there be as many false brethren and crafty knaves here amongst us, as in any place. Witness the poor miller of Cambridge, that, having no room for his hen-loft but the tester [318] of his bed (and it was not possible for any hungry poulterers to come there, but they must stand upon the one side of it and so not steal them but with great hazard) had in one night, notwithstanding, when he and his wife were a-snorting, all the whole progeny of their pullery taken away, and neither of them heard any stirring. It is an odd trick, but what of that? We must not stand upon it, for we have graver matters in hand than the stealing of hens. Hypocrisy, I remember, was our text, which was one of the chief moral

317. 'As if in truth'.
318. Canopy and supporting framework.

devils our late doctors affirm to be most busy in these days.'

'And busy it is, in truth, more than any bee that I know.'

'Now you talk of a bee, I'll tell you a tale of a battledore.[319] The bear [320] on a time, being chief burgomaster of all the beasts under the lion, gan think with himself how he might surfeit in pleasure, or best husband his authority to enlarge his delight and contentment. With that he began to pry and to smell through every corner of the forest for prey, to have a thousand imaginations with himself what dainty morsel he was master of, and yet had not tasted. Whole herds of sheep had he devoured, and was not satisfied; fat oxen, heifers, swine, calves, and young kids, were his ordinary viands. He longed for horse-flesh, and went presently to a meadow, where a fat cammell [321] was grazing, whom, fearing to en-counter with force, because he was a huge beast and well shod, he thought to betray under the colour of demanding homage, hoping that, as he should stoop to do him trew-age,[322] he might seize upon his throat and stifle him before he should be able to recover himself from his false em-brace. But therein he was deceived; for, coming unto this stately beast with this imperious message, instead of doing homage unto him, he lifted up one of his hindmost heels and struck him such a blow on the forehead that he over-threw him. Thereat not a little moved and enraged that he should be so dishonoured by his inferior, as he thought, he consulted with the ape how he might be revenged.

The ape abhorring him by nature, because he overlooked him so lordly and was by so many degrees greater than he was, advised him [323] to dig a pit with his paws right in the way where this big-boned gentleman should pass, that so

319. *bee ... battledore*: 'To tell a B from a battledore' (proverbial reference to illiteracy).

320. M. thinks the bear may represent the Earl of Leicester (d. 1588); the fox being Cartwright or Martin (i.e. the puritans); the chameleon, Martin Marprelate or Penry; the bees the Anglican clergy. See Introduction, pp. 22–6.

321. Some kind of horse.   322. Homage.

323. i.e. the bear.

stumbling and falling in, he might lightly skip on his back, and bridle him, and then he come and seize on him at his pleasure. No sooner was this persuaded than performed; for envy, that is never idle, could not sleep in his wrath or over-slip the least opportunity till he had seen the confusion of his enemy. Alas, goodly creature, that thou mightest no longer live! What availeth thy gentleness, thy prowess, or the plentiful pasture wherein thou wert fed, since malice triumphs over all thou commandest? Well may the mule rise up in arms, and the ass bray at the authors of thy death: yet shall their fury be fatal to themselves, before it take hold on these traitors. What needeth more words? The devourer feeds on his captive and is gorged with blood.

But as avarice and cruelty are evermore thirsty, so fared it with this hungry usurper; for having fleshed his ambition with this treacherous conquest, he passed along through a grove, where a herd of deer were a-ranging; whom, when he had steadfastly surveyed from the fattest to the leanest, he singled out one of the fairest of the company, with whom he meant to close up his stomach instead of cheese. But because the woodmen were ever stirring thereabout, and it was not possible for one of his coat to commit such outrage undescried, and that if he were espied, his life were in peril (though not with the lion, whose eyes he could blind as he list, yet with the lesser sort of the brutish commonalty, whom no flattery might pacify), therefore he determined slily and privily to poison the stream where this jolly forester wonted to drink. And as he determined, so he did. Whereby it fell out that when the sun was ascended to his height and all the nimble citizens of the wood betook them to their lair, this youthful lord of the lawns, all faint and malcontent (as prophesying his near approaching mishap by his languishing) with a lazy wallowing pace, strayed aside from the rest of his fellowship and betook him all carelessly to the corrupted fountain that was prepared for his funeral.

Ah, woe is me, this poison is pitiless! What need I say more, since you know it is death with whom it encounters?

And yet cannot all this expense of life set a period [324] to insatiable murder; but still it hath some anvil to work upon, and overcasts all opposite prosperity, that may any way shadow his glory.

Too long it were to rehearse all the practices of this savage blood-hunter: how he assailed the unicorn as he slept in his den, and tore the heart out of his breast ere he could awake; how he made the lesser beasts lie in wait one for the other, and the crocodile to cope with the basilisk, that when they had interchangeably weakened each other he might come and insult over them both as he list. But these were lesser matters, which daily use had worn out of men's mouths, and he himself had so customably practised that often [325] exercise had quite abrogated the opinion of sin, and impudency thoroughly confirmed an undaunted defiance of virtue in his face. Yet new-fangled lust, that in time is weary of welfare and will be as soon cloyed with too much ease and delicacy, as poverty with labour and scarcity, at length brought him out of love with this greedy bestial humour, and now he affected a milder variety in his diet. He had bethought him what a pleasant thing it was to eat nothing but honey another while, and what great store of it there was in that country.

Now did he cast in his head, that if he might bring the husbandmen of the soil in opinion that they might buy honey cheaper than being at such charges in keeping of bees, or that those bees which they kept were most of them drones, and what should such idle drones do with such stately hives or lie sucking at such precious honeycombs; that if they were took away from them, and distributed equally abroad, they would relieve a great many of painful labourers that had need of them, and would continually live serviceable at their command, if they might enjoy such a benefit. Nay more, let them give wasps but only the wax and dispose of the honey as they think good, and they shall hum and buzz a thousand times louder than they, and have the hive fuller

324. A close, full-stop.
325. Frequent.

at the year's end (with young ones, I mean) than the bees are wont in ten year.

To broach this device, the fox was addressed like a shepherd's dog, and promised to have his patent sealed to be the King's poulterer for ever, if he could bring it to pass. "Faith," quoth he, "and I'll put it in a venture, let it hap how it will." With that he grew in league with an old chameleon, that could put on all shapes, and imitate any colour as occasion served, and him he addressed, sometime like an ape to make sport, and then like a crocodile to weep, sometime like a serpent to sting, and by and by like a spaniel to fawn, that with these sundry forms, applied to men's variable humours, he might persuade the world he meant as he spake, and only intended their good, when he thought nothing less. In this disguise, these two deceivers went up and down and did much harm under the habit of simplicity, making the poor silly swains believe they were cunning physicians and well seen in all cures, that they could heal any malady, though never so dangerous, and restore a man to life that had been dead two days, only by breathing upon him. Above all things they persuaded them that the honey that their bees brought forth was poisonous and corrupt, by reason that those flowers and herbs out of which it was gathered and exhaled were subject to the infection of every spider and venomous canker, and not a loathsome toad, how detestable soever, but reposed himself under their shadow and lay sucking at their roots continually; whereas in other countries, no noisome or poisonous creature might live, by reason of the imputed goodness of the soil, or careful diligence of the gardeners above ours, as for example, Scotland, Denmark, and some more pure parts of the seventeen provinces.

These persuasions made the good honest husbandmen to pause, and mistrust their own wits very much, in nourishing such dangerous animals. But yet, I know not how, antiquity and custom so over-ruled their fear, that none would resolve to abandon them on the sudden till they saw a further inconvenience. Whereby my two cunning philosophers were driven to study Galen anew, and seek out splenative simples,[326] to purge their popular patients of the opinion of their old traditions and customs; which, how they wrought with the most part that had least wit, it were a world to tell. For now nothing was canonical but what they spake, no man would converse with his wife but first asked their advice, nor pare his nails, nor cut his beard, without their prescription. So senseless, so wavering is the light unconstant multitude, that will dance after every man's pipe, and sooner prefer a blind harper that can squeak out a new hornpipe, than Alcinous'[327] or Apollo's variety, that imitates the right strains of the Dorian melody. I speak this to amplify the novel folly of the headlong vulgar, that making their eyes and ears vassals to the *legerdemain* of these juggling mountebanks, are presently drawn to contemn art and experience in comparison of the ignorance of a number of audacious idiots.

The fox can tell a fair tale, and covers all his knavery under conscience, and the chameleon can address himself like an angel whensoever he is disposed to work mischief by miracles: but yet in the end, their secret drifts are laid open, and Linceus' eyes, that see through stone walls, have made a passage into the close coverture of their hypocrisy.

For one day, as these two devisers were plotting by themselves how to drive all the bees from their honeycombs by putting wormwood in all their hives, and strewing henbane and rue in every place where they resort, a fly that passed by and heard all their talk, stomaching the fox of old, for that he had murdered so many of his kindred with his flail-driving tail, went presently and buzzed in Linceus' ears the whole purport of their malice; who, awaking his hundred eyes at these unexpected tidings, gan pursue them wheresoever they went, and trace their intents as they proceeded into action; so that ere half their baits were cast forth, they were apprehended and imprisoned, and all their whole counsel detected. But long ere this, the bear, impatient of

326. Medicinal herbs acting on the spleen.
327. A harper sang at the banquet given by Alcinous to Ulysses.

delays and consumed with an inward grief in himself that he might not have his will of a fat hind that outran him, he went into the woods all melancholy and there died for pure anger, leaving the fox and the chameleon to the destiny of their desert, and mercy of their judges. How they scaped I know not, but some say they were hanged, and so we'll leave them.

How likest thou of my tale, friend Percy? Have I not described a right earthly devil unto thee in the discourse of this bloody-minded bear? Or canst thou not attract [328] the true image of hypocrisy under the description of the fox and the chameleon?'

'Yes, very well,' quoth I, 'but I would gladly have you return to your first subject, since you have moved doubts in my mind, which you have not yet discussed.'

'Of the sundry opinions of the devil, thou meanest, and them that imagine him to have no existence, of which sort are they that first invented the proverb, *homo homini dæmon*: [329] meaning thereby, that that power which we call the devil, and the ministering spirits belonging to him and to his kingdom, are tales and fables, and mere bugbears to scare boys; and that there is no such essence at all, but only it is a term of large content, describing the rancour, grudge, and bad dealing of one man toward another: as, namely, when one friend talks with another subtly, and seeks to dive into his commodity, that he may deprive him of it craftily; when the son seeks the death of the father, that he may be enfeoffed in his wealth; and the step-dame goes about to make away her son-in-law, that her children may inherit; when brothers fall at jars for portions, and shall, by open murder or privy conspiracy, attempt the confusion of each other, only to join house to house, and unite two livelihoods in one; when the servant shall rob his master, and men put in trust start away from their oaths and vows, they care not how.

328. Gather, take in.
329. 'Man a devil to man'. (In this section on demons N. is following a tract called the *Isagoge* by Georgius Pictorius, 1563.)

In such cases and many more, may one man be said to be a devil to another, and this is the second opinion. The third is that of Plato, who not only affirmeth that there are devils, but divided them into three sorts, every one a degree of dignity above the other. The first are those whose bodies are compact of the purest airy element, combined with such transparent threads, that neither they do partake so much fire as should make them visible to sight, or have any such affinity with the earth, as they are able to be pressed or touched; and these he setteth in the highest incomprehensible degree of heaven. The second he maketh these whom Apuleius[330] doth call reasonable creatures, passive in mind and eternal in time, being those *apostata*[331] spirits that rebelled with Beelzebub; whose bodies, before their fall, were bright and pure all like to the former; but, after their transgression, they were obscured with a thick, airy matter, and ever after assigned to darkness. The third he attributes to those men that, by some divine knowledge or understanding, seeming to aspire above mortality, are called *dæmona*, (that is) gods: for this word *dæmon* containeth either, and Homer in every place doth use it both for that omnipotent power that was before all things, and the evil spirit that leadeth men to error: so doth Syrianus[332] testify, that Plato was called *dæmon*, because he disputed of deep commonwealth matters, greatly available to the benefit of his country; and also Aristotle because he wrote at large of all things subject to moving and sense.'

'Then belike,' quoth I, 'you make this word *dæmon* a capable[333] name of gods, of men, and of devils, which is far distant from the scope of my demand; for I do only enquire of the devil, as this common appellation of the devil signifieth a malignant spirit, enemy to mankind, and a hater of God and all goodness.'

'Those are the second kind,' said he, 'usually termed detractors or accusers, that are in knowledge infinite, inso-

---

330. In *De Deo Socratis*. 331. Rebellious, treacherous.
332. (?) Syrianus of Alexandria (*fl.* 435).
333. Comprehensive.

much as, by the quickness of their wits and agreeable mixtures of the elements, they so comprehend those seminary virtues to men unknown, that those things which, in course of time or by growing degrees, nature of itself can effect, they, by their art and skill in hastening the works of nature, can contrive and compass in a moment: as the magicians of Pharaoh, who, whereas nature, not without some interposition of time and ordinary causes of conception, brings forth frogs, serpents, or any living thing else, they, without all such distance of space, or circumscription of season, even in a thought, as soon as their king commanded, covered the land of Egypt with this monstrous increase.

Of the original of us spirits the scripture most amply maketh mention; namely, that Lucifer, before his fall an archangel, was a clear body, compact of the purest and brightest of the air, but after his fall he was veiled with a grosser substance, and took a new form of dark and thick air, which he still retaineth. Neither did he only fall, when he strove with Michael, but drew a number of angels to his faction; who, joint partakers of his proud revolt, were likewise partakers of his punishment, and all thrust out of heaven together by one judgment: who ever since do nothing but wander about the earth, and tempt and enforce frail men to enterprise all wickedness that may be, and commit most horrible and abominable things against God.

Marvel not that I discover so much of our estate unto thee; for the scripture hath more than I mention, as St Peter, where he saith that "God spared not his angels that sinned," and in another place, where he saith that "they are bound with the chains of darkness, and thrown headlong into hell": which is not meant of any local place in the earth, or under the waters, for, as Austin [334] affirmeth, we do inhabit the region under the moon, and have the thick air assigned us as a prison, from whence we may with small labour cast our nets where we list. Yet are we not so at our disposition, but that we are still commanded by Lucifer, although we are in number infinite, who, retaining that

334. St Augustine.

pride wherewith he arrogantly affected the majesty of God, hath still his ministering angels about him, whom he employs in several charges, to seduce and deceive as him seemeth best; as those spirits which the Latins call *Iovios* and *Antemeridianos*, to speak out of oracles, and make the people worship them as gods, when they are nothing but deluding devils that covet to have a false deity ascribed unto them, and draw men unto their love by wonders and prodigies, that else would hate them deadly, if they knew their malevolence and envy. Such a monarchizing spirit it was that said to Christ, "If thou wilt fall down and worship me, I will give thee all the kingdoms of the earth." And such a spirit it was that possessed the Lybian Sapho, and the Emperor Diocletian, who thought it the blessedest thing that might be, to be called God. For the one, being weary of human honour and inspired with a supernatural folly, taught little birds, that were capable of speech, to pronounce distinctly, *Magnus deus Sapho*;[335] that is to say, 'A great god is Sapho,' which words, when they had learnt readily to carol and were perfect in their note, he let them fly at random, that so dispersing themselves everywhere, they might induce the people to count of him as a god. The other was so arrogant that he made his subjects fall prostrate on their faces, and lifting up their hands to him as to heaven, adore him as omnipotent.

The second kind of devils which he most employeth, are those northern *Marcii*, called the spirits of revenge, and the authors of massacres, and seedsmen of mischief; for they have commission to incense men to rapines, sacrilege, theft, murder, wrath, fury, and all manner of cruelties, and they command certain of the southern spirits, as slaves, to wait upon them, as also great Arioch, that is termed the spirit of revenge.

These know how to dissociate the love of brethren, and to break wedlock bands with such violence that they may not be united, and are predominant in many other domestical mutinies; of whom if thou list to hear more, read the

335. Misreading for Psaphon (M.).

thirty ninth chapter of *Ecclesiasticus*. The prophet Esay [336] maketh mention of another spirit, sent by God to the Egyptians, to make them stray and wander out of the way, that is to say, the spirit of lying, which they call Bolychym. The spirits that entice men to gluttony and lust are certain watery spirits of the West, and certain southern spirits as Nefrach and Kelen, which for the most part prosecute unlawful loves and cherish all unnatural desires. They wander through lakes, fish-ponds, and fens, and overwhelm ships, cast boats upon anchors, and drown men that are swimming. Therefore are they counted the most pestilent, troublesome, and guileful spirits that are; for by the help of Alrynach, a spirit of the West, they will raise storms, cause earthquakes, whirlwinds, rain, hail, or snow in the clearest day that is; and if ever they appear to any man, they come in women's apparel. The spirits of the air will mix themselves with thunder and lightning, and so infect the clime where they raise any tempest, that suddenly great mortality shall ensue to the inhabitants from the infectious vapours which arise from their motions. Of such St John maketh mention in the ninth chapter of the *Apocalypse*. Their patron is Mereris, who beareth chief rule about the middle time of the day.

The spirits of the fire have their mansions under their regions of the moon, that whatsoever is committed to their charge they may there execute, as in their proper consistory,[337] from whence they cannot start. The spirits of the earth keep, for the most part, in forests and woods, and do hunters much noyance, and sometime in the broad fields, where they lead travellers out of the right way, or fright men with deformed apparitions, or make them run mad through excessive melancholy, like Ajax Telemonius,[338] and so prove hurtful to themselves, and dangerous to others. Of

336. Isaiah.
337. *proper consistory*: Own council.
338. Said to have gone mad when adjudged less worthy than Ulysses in the Trojan War, and to have committed suicide in desperation.

this number the chief are Samaab and Achymael, spirits of the East, that have no power to do any great harm, by reason of the unconstancy of their affections. The under-earth spirits are such as lurk in dens and little caverns of the earth, and hollow crevices of mountains, that they may dive into the bowels of the earth at their pleasure. These dig metals and watch treasures, which they continually transport from place to place, that none should have use of them. They raise winds that vomit flames and shake the foundation of buildings; they dance in rounds in pleasant lawns and green meadows, with noises of music and minstrelsy, and vanish away when any comes near them. They will take upon them any similitude but of a woman, and terrify men in the likeness of dead men's ghosts in the night-time; and of this quality and condition the necromancers hold Gaziel, Fegor, and Anarazel, southern spirits, to be.

Besides, there are yet remaining certain lying spirits, who, although all be given to lie by nature, yet are they more prone to that vice than the rest, being named Pythonists, of whom Apollo comes to be called Pytheus. They have a prince as well as other spirits, of whom mention is made in the *Third Book of Kings*, when he saith he will be a lying spirit in the mouth of all Ahab's prophets; from which those spirits of iniquity do little differ, which are called the vessels of wrath, that assist Belial (whom they interpret a spirit without yoke or controller) in all damnable devices and inventions. Plato reports them to be such as first devised cards and dice, and I am in the mind that the monk was of the same order, that found out the use of gunpowder and the engines of war thereto belonging. Those that write of these matters call this Belial Chodar of the East, that hath all witches' and conjurers' spirits under his jurisdiction, and gives them leave to help jugglers in their tricks, and Simon Magus [339] to do miracles; always provided they bring a soul home to their master for his hire.

Yet are not these all, for there are spirits called spies and tale-carriers, obedient to Ascaroth, whom the Greeks call

339. Leader of a religious sect in the first century A.D. (see Acts 8, 5).

daimona, and St John, *the accuser of the brethren*: also tempters, who, for their interrupting us in all our good actions are called our evil angels. Above all things they hate the light and rejoice in darkness, disquieting men maliciously in the night and sometimes hurt them by pinching them or blasting them as they sleep. But they are not so much to be dreaded as other spirits, because if a man speak to them they flee away and will not abide. Such a spirit Plinius Secundus telleth of, that used to haunt a goodly house in Athens that Athenodorus hired. And such another Suetonius describeth to have long hovered in Lamianus' garden, where Caligula lay buried, who, for because he was only covered with a few clods and unreverently thrown amongst the weeds, he marvellously disturbed the owners of the garden, and would not let them rest in their beds, till by his sisters, returned from banishment, he was taken up and entombed solemnly.

Pausanias avoucheth, amongst other experiments, that a certain spirit called Zazilus doth feed upon dead men's corses, that are not deeply interred in the earth as they ought. Which to confirm, there is a wonderful accident set down in the Danish history of Asuitus and Asmundus, who, being two famous friends well known in those parts, vowed one to another, that which of them two outlived the other should be buried alive with his friend that first died. In short space Asuitus fell sick and yielded to nature; Asmundus, compelled by the oath of his friendship, took none but his horse and his dog with him, and transported the dead body into a vast cave under the earth, and there determined, having victualled himself for a long time, to finish his days in darkness and never depart from him that he loved so dearly.

Thus shut up and enclosed in the bowels of the earth, it happened Ericus, King of Sweveland, to pass that way with his army, not full two months after; who, coming to the tomb of Asuitus, and suspecting it a place where treasure was hidden, caused his pioneers with their spades and mattocks to dig it up. Whereupon was discovered the loathsome body of Asmundus, all to-besmeared with dead men's filth, and his visage most ugly and fearful; which, imbrued [340] with congealed blood and eaten and torn like a raw ulcer, made him so ghastly to behold that all the beholders were affrighted. He, seeing himself restored to light, and so many amazed men stand about him, resolved their uncertain perplexity in these terms.

"Why stand you astonished at my unusual deformities, when no living man converseth with the dead but is thus disfigured? But other causes have effected this change in me; for I know not what audacious spirit, sent by Gorgon from the deep, hath not only most ravenously devoured my horse and my dog, but also hath laid his hungry paws upon me, and tearing down my cheeks, as you see, hath likewise rent away one of mine ears. Hence is it that my mangled shape seems so monstrous, and my human image obscured with gore in this wise. Yet scaped not this fell harpy from me unrevenged; for as he assailed me, I raught his head from his shoulders, and sheathed my sword in his body."'

'Have spirits their visible bodies,' said I, 'that may be touched, wounded, or pierced? Believe me, I never heard that in my life before this.'

'Why,' quoth he, 'although in their proper essence they are creatures incorporal, yet can they take on them the induments [341] of any living body whatsoever, and transform themselves into all kind of shapes, whereby they may more easily deceive our shallow wits and senses. So testifies Basilius, that they can put on a material form when they list. Socrates affirmeth that his *dæmon* did oftentimes talk with him, and that he saw him and felt him many times. But Marcus Cherronesius, a wonderful discoverer of devils, writeth that those bodies which they assume are distinguished by no difference of sex, because they are simple, and the discernance of sex belongs to bodies compound. Yet are they flexible, motive [342] and apt for any configura-

340. Defiled, stained.
341. Material attributes.
342. Capable of movement.

tion; but not all of them alike, for the spirits of the fire and air have this power above the rest. The spirits of the water have slow bodies resembling birds and women, of which kind the Naiads and Nereids [343] are much celebrated amongst poets. Nevertheless, however they are restrained to their several similitudes, it is certain that all of them desire no form or figure so much as the likeness of a man, and do think themselves in heaven when they are enfeoffed in that hue; wherefore I know no other reason but this, that man is the nearest representation to God, insomuch as the scripture saith, "He made man after his own likeness and image;" and they, affecting by reason of their pride to be as like God as they may, contend most seriously to shroud themselves under that habit.'

'But, I pray, tell me this, whether are there (as Porphyrius holdeth) good spirits as well as evil?'

'Nay, certainly,' quoth he, 'we are all evil, let Porphyrius, Proclus, Apuleius, or the Platonists dispute to the contrary as long as they will; which I will confirm to thy capacity by the names that are everywhere given us in the scripture. For the devil, which is the *summum genus* [344] to us all, is called *diabolus, quasi deorsum ruens*,[345] that is to say, falling downward, as he that, aspiring too high, was thrown from the top of felicity to the lowest pit of despair; and Satan, that is to say, an adversary, who, for the corruption of his malice, opposeth himself ever against God, who is the chiefest good; in *Job*, Behemoth and Leviathan; and in the ninth chapter of the *Apocalypse*, Apolyon, that is to say, a subverter, because the foundation of those virtues, which our high maker hath planted in our souls, he undermineth and subverteth; a serpent for his poisoning, a lion for his devouring, a furnace, for that by his malice the elect are tried, who are vessels of wrath and salvation; in *Esay*, a siren, a lamia, a screech-owl, an ostrich; in the *Psalms*, an adder, a basilisk, a dragon; and lastly in the gospel, Mammon, Prince

343. *Naiads and Nereids*: Nymphs of rivers and seas.
344. 'The highest form'.
345. 'Devil, as falling from above'.

of this World, and the Governor of Darkness. So that, by the whole course of condemning names that are given us, and no one instance of any favourable title bestowed upon us, I positively set down that all spirits are evil. Now, where-as the divines attribute unto us these good and evil spirits, the good to guide us from evil, and the evil to draw us from goodness, they are not called spirits, but angels; of which sort was Raphael, the good angel of Tobias, who exiled the evil spirit Asmodeus into the desert of Egypt, that he might be the more secure from his temptation.'

'Since we have entered thus far into the devil's common-wealth, I beseech you certify me thus much, whether have they power to hurt granted them from God, or from them-selves; can they hurt as much as they will?'

'Not so,' quoth he, 'for although that devils be most mighty spirits, yet can they not hurt but permissively, or by some special dispensation. As, when a man is fallen into the state of an outlaw, the law dispenseth with them that kill him, and the Prince excludes him from the protection of a subject, so, when a man is a relapse from God and his laws, God withdraws his providence from watching over him, and authoriseth the devil, as his instrument, to assault him and torment him, so that whatsoever he doth is *limitata potestate*,[346] as one saith; insomuch as a hair cannot fall from our heads, without the will of our heavenly father.

The devil could not deceive Ahab's prophets, till he was licensed by God, nor exercise his tyranny over Job till he had given him commission, nor enter into the herd of swine till Christ bade them go. Therefore need you not fear the devil any whit, as long as you are in the favour of God, who reineth him so strait, that except he let him loose he can do nothing. This manlike proportion, which I now retain, is but a thing of sufferance, granted unto me to plague such men as hunt after strife, and are delighted with variance.'

'It may be so very well, but whether have you that skill to foretell things to come, that is ascribed unto you?'

'We have,' quoth he, 'sometimes. Not that we are privy

346. 'With limited power'.

136

to the eternal counsel of God, but for that by the sense of
our airy bodies, we have a more refined faculty of foreseeing
than men possibly can have that are chained to such heavy
earthly moulder; or else for that by the incomparable per-
nicity [347] of those airy bodies, we not only outstrip the swift-
ness of men, beasts, and birds, whereby we may be able to
attain to the knowledge of things sooner than those that
by the dullness of their earthly sense come a great way behind us. Hereunto may we adjoin our long experience in
the course of things from the beginning of the world, which
men want, and therefore cannot have that deep conjecture
that we have. Nor is our knowledge any more than conjecture; for prescience only belongeth to God, and that
guess that we have, proceedeth from the compared disposition of heavenly and earthly bodies, by whose long observed
temperature we do divine many times as it happens; and
therefore do we take upon us to prophesy, that we may purchase estimation to our names, and bring men in admiration
with that we do, and so be counted for gods. The miracles
we work are partly contrived by illusion, and partly assisted
by that supernatural skill we have in the experience of
nature above all other creatures.'

'But against these illusions of your subtlety, and vain
terrors you inflict, what is our chief refuge?'

'I shall be accounted a foolish devil anon if I bewray the
secrets of our kingdom, as I have begun; yet I speak no more
than learned clerks have written, and as much as they have
set down will I shew thee.

Origen, in his treatise against Celsus, saith there is nothing better for him that is vexed with spirits, than the naming
of Jesu, the true God, for he avoucheth he hath seen divers
driven out of men's bodies by that means. Athanasius, in
his book *De variis questionibus*, saith, "The presentest
remedy against the invasion of evil spirits, is the beginning
of the sixty seventh Psalm, *Exsurgat Deus, et dissipentur
inimici eius.*" [348] Cyprian counsels men to adjure spirits only

347. Quickness.
348. 'Let God arise, and his enemies shall be scattered.'

by the name of the true God. Some hold that fire is a preservative for this purpose, because when any spirit appeareth, the lights by little and little go out, as it were of their own accord, and the tapers are by degrees extinguished; others by invocating upon God by the name of *Vehiculum ignis superioris*,[349] and often rehearsing the articles of our faith. A third sort are persuaded that the brandishing of swords is good for this purpose, because Homer feigneth that Ulysses, sacrificing to his mother, wafted his sword in the air to chase the spirits from the blood of the sacrifice; and Sibylla, conducting Æneas to hell, begins her charm in this sort:

> *Procul, o procul, este, prophani*:
> *Tuque invade viam, vaginaque erripe ferrum.*[350]

Philostratus reporteth, that he and his companions meeting that devil which artists entitle Apollonius,[351] as they came one night from banqueting, with such terms as he is cursed in holy writ, they made him run away howling. Many in this case extol perfume of *calamentum, pæonia, menta, palma Christi* and *appius*.[352] A number prefer the carrying of red coral about them, or of *artemisia, hypericon, ruta, verbena*: and to this effect many do use the jingling of keys, the sound of the harp, and the clashing of armour. Some of old time put great superstition in characters, curiously engraved in their *pentagonon*, but they are all vain, and will do no good, if they be otherwise used than as signs of covenant between the devil and them. Nor do I affirm all the rest to be infallible prescriptions, though sometime they have their use; but that the only assured way to resist their attempts is prayer and faith, gainst which all the devils in hell cannot prevail.'

349. 'A vehicle of fire from above.
350. 'Away, now stand away, you uninitiated ones ... But you [Aeneas], draw your sword from the scabbard and fare forth' (*Aeneid*, VI, 258, 260, translated by C. Day Lewis).
351. M. points out that N. has mistranslated from the *Isagoge*, and is probably thinking of Apollyon (Revelation 9, 11).
352. Names of plants.

'Enough, gentle spirit, I will importune thee no further, but commit this supplication to thy care; which, if thou deliver accordingly, thou shalt at thy return have more of my custom; for by that time I will have finished certain letters to divers orators and poets, dispersed in your dominions.'

'That as occasion shall serve; but now I must take leave of you, for it is term time, and I have some business. A gentleman, a friend of mine that I never saw before, stays for me, and is like to be undone if I come not in to bear witness on his side: wherefore *Bazilez manus*,[353] till our next meeting.'

Gentle reader, *tandem aliquando* [354] I am at leisure to talk to thee. I dare say thou hast called me a hundred times dolt for this senseless discourse: it is no matter, thou dost but as I have done by a number in my days. For who can abide a scurvy peddling poet to pluck a man by the sleeve at every third step in Paul's Churchyard,[355] and when he comes in to survey his wares, there's nothing but purgations and vomits wrapped up in waste paper. It were very good the dog-whipper [356] in Paul's would have a care of this in his unsavoury visitation every Saturday; for it is dangerous for such of the Queen's liege people, as shall take a view of them fasting.

Look to it, you booksellers and stationers, and let not your shops be infected with any such goose giblets or stinking garbage, as the jigs of newsmongers. And especially such of you as frequent Westminster Hall, let them be circumspect what dunghill papers they bring thither: for one bad pamphlet is enough to raise a damp that may poison a whole term, or at the least a number of poor clients, that have no money to prevent ill air by breaking their fasts ere they come thither. Not a base ink-dropper, or scurvy plodder at

353. 'I kiss your hand' (Spanish: '*beso las manos*').
354. 'Sometime eventually'.
355. Where books were sold.
356. A man employed to drive dogs away.

Noverint,[357] but nails his asses' ears on every post, and comes off with a long *circumquaque* [358] to the gentlemen readers; yea, the most excrementory dish-lickers of learning are grown so valiant in impudency, that now they set up their faces (like Turks) of gray paper, to be spit at for silver games [359] in Finsbury Fields.[360]

Whilst I am talking, methinks I hear one say, 'What a fop is this, he entitles his book *A Supplication to the Devil*, and doth nothing but rail on idiots, and tells a story of the nature of spirits!' Have patience, good sir, and we'll come to you by and by. Is it my title you find fault with? Why, have you not seen a town surnamed by the principal house in the town, or a nobleman derive his barony from a little village where he hath least land? So fareth it by me in christening of my book. But some will object, 'Whereto tends this discourse of devils, or how is it induced?' Forsooth, if thou wilt needs know my reason, this it is. I bring Pierce Penniless to question with the devil, as a young novice would talk with a great traveller, who, carrying an Englishman's appetite to enquire of news, will be sure to make what use of him he may, and not leave anything unasked, that he can resolve him of. If then the devil be tedious in discoursing, impute it to Pierce Penniless that was importunate in demanding; or, if I have not made him so secret and subtle in his art as devils are wont, let that of Lactantius be mine excuse, *lib*. 2. *cap*. 16. *de Origenis errore*,[361] where he saith, the devils have no power to lie to a just man, and if they adjure them by the majesty of the high God, they will not only confess themselves to be devils, but also tell their names as they are.

---

357. *plodder at* Noverint: Scrivener or petty lawyer (writs began with the words '*noverint universi*': 'let all men know').

358. Circumlocution.

359. 'Would appear to be some kind of pitch and toss, in which a Turk's head cut out of grey paper was the mark' (H.).

360. Popular recreation and sporting grounds.

361. *De Origine Erroris* (N. appears to have supposed the book was a treatise against Origen).

Deus bone, what a vein am I fallen into? 'What, an Epistle
to the Readers in the end of thy book? Out upon thee for
an arrant block, where learnedst thou that wit?' O sir, hold
your peace: a felon never comes to his answer before the
offence be committed. Wherefore, if I, in the beginning of
my book, should have come off with a long apology to excuse myself, it were all one as if a thief, going to steal a
horse, should devise by the way as he went, what to speak
when he came at the gallows. Here is a crossway, and I
think it good here to part. Farewell, farewell, good Parenthesis, and commend me to Lady Vanity, thy mistress.

'Now, Pierce Penniless, if for a parting blow thou hast
ere a trick in thy budget more than ordinary, be not dainty
of it for a good patron will pay for all.' Ay, where is he?
Promissis quilibet dives esse potest.[362] But cap and thanks
is all our courtiers' payment; wherefore I would counsel
my friends to be more considerate in their dedications, and
not cast away so many months' labour on a clown that knows
not how to use a scholar: for what reason have I to bestow
any of my wit upon him that will bestow none of his wealth
upon me? Alas, it is easy for a goodly tall fellow that shineth
in his silks, to come and outface a poor simple pedant in a
threadbare cloak, and tell him his book is pretty, but at this
time he is not provided for him: marry, about two or three
days hence if he come that way, his page shall say he is not
within, or else he is so busy with my Lord How-call-ye-him,
and my Lord What-call-ye-him, that he may not be spoken
withal. These are the common courses of the world, which
every man privately murmurs at, but none dares openly
upbraid, because all artists for the most part are base-minded
and like the Indians that have store of gold and precious
stones at command yet are ignorant of their value, and
therefore let the Spaniards, the Englishmen and everyone
load their ships with them without molestation; so they,
enjoying and possessing the purity of knowledge, a treasure

362. 'You promise riches to anyone who wants them' (adapted from
Ovid, *Ars Amatoris*, I, 443–4).

far richer than the Indian mines, let every proud Thraso [363] be partaker of their perfections, repaying them no profit, and gild himself with the titles they give him, when he will scarce return them a good word for their labour. Give an ape but a nut, and he will look your head for it; or a dog a bone, and he'll wag his tail; but give me one of my young masters a book, and he will put off his hat and blush, and so go his way.

Yes, now I remember me, I lie; for I know him that had thanks for three years' work, and a gentleman that bestowed much cost in refining of music, and had scarce fiddler's wages for his labour. We want an Aretine [364] here among us, that might strip these golden asses out of their gay trappings, and after he had ridden them to death with railing, leave them on the dunghill for carrion. But I will write to his ghost by my carrier, and I hope he'll repair his whip and use it against our English peacocks, that painting themselves with church spoils, like mighty men's sepulchres, have nothing but atheism, schism, hypocrisy, and vainglory, like rotten bones lie lurking within them. Oh, how my soul abhors these buckram giants,[365] that having an outward face of honour set upon them by flatterers and parasites, have their inward thoughts stuffed with straw and feathers, if they were narrowly sifted.

Far be it, bright stars of nobility and glistering attendants on the true Diana,[366] that this my speech should be any way injurious to your glorious magnificence: for in you live those sparks of Augustus' liberality, that never sent any away empty; and science's seven-fold throne, well-nigh ruined by riot and avarice, is mightily supported by your plentiful largesse, which makes poets to sing such goodly hymns of your praise, as no envious posterity may forget.

But from general fame let me digress to my private ex-

363. Braggart, (character in Terence's *Eunuch*).
364. Pietro Aretino (1492–1554), commonly regarded as champion of the writer, as well as being famous for his *Sonetti Lusuriosi*.
365. Effigies as used in pageants (H.).
366. Goddess of chastity; here Queen Elizabeth.

perience, and, with a tongue unworthy to name a name of such worthiness, affectionately emblazon to the eyes that wonder, the matchless image of honour, and magnificent rewarder of virtue, Jove's eagle-borne Ganymede, thrice noble Amyntas.[367] In whose high spirit, such a deity of wisdom appeareth, that if Homer were to write his Odyssey new (where, under the person of Ulysses, he describeth a singular man of perfection, in whom all ornaments both of peace and war are assembled in the height of their excellence), he need no other instance to augment his conceit, than the rare carriage of his honourable mind. Many writers and good wits are given to commend their patrons and benefactors, some for prowess, some for policy, others for the glory of their ancestry and exceeding bounty and liberality; but if my unable pen should ever enterprise such a continuate task of praise, I would embowel a number of those wind-puffed bladders and disfurnish their bald pates of the periwigs poets have lent them, that so I might restore glory to his right inheritance, and these stolen titles to their true owners. Which, if it would so fall out (as time may work all things), the aspiring nettles, with their shady tops, shall no longer overdrip the best herbs, or keep them from the smiling aspect of the sun, that live and thrive by his comfortable beams; none but desert should sit in fame's grace, none but Hector be remembered in the chronicles of prowess, none but thou, most courteous Amyntas, be the second mystical argument of the knight of the Red Cross.

Oh decus atque ævi gloria summa tui.[368]

And here, heavenly Spenser, I am most highly to accuse thee of forgetfulness, that in that honourable catalogue of our English heroes, which insueth the conclusion of thy famous *Faerie Queene*, thou wouldst let so special a pillar of nobility pass unsaluted. The very thought of his far-

367. Probably the Earl of Derby, alluded to by that name in Spenser's *Colin Clout*, 1595.
368. 'O ornament and great glory of your age' (Ovid).

derived descent and extraordinary parts, wherewith he astonieth the world and draws all hearts to his love, would have inspired thy forwearied Muse with new fury to proceed to the next triumphs of thy stately goddess. But as I, in favour of so rare a scholar, suppose, with this counsel he refrained his mention in this first part, that he might with full sail proceed to his due commendation in the second. Of this occasion, long since I happened to frame a sonnet, which, being wholly intended to the reverence of this renowned Lord, to whom I owe all the utmost powers of my love and duty, I meant here for variety of style to insert.

> Perusing yesternight, with idle eyes,
>   The fairy singer's stately tuned verse,
> And viewing after chapmen's wonted guise,[369]
>   What strange contents the title did rehearse:
> I straight leapt over to the latter end,
>   Where like the quaint comedians of our time,
> That when their play is done do fall to rhyme,
>   I found short lines to sundry nobles penn'd;
> Whom he as special mirrors singled forth,
>   To be the patrons of his poetry:
> I read them all, and reverenc'd their worth,
>   Yet wonder'd he left out thy memory.
>   But therefore guess'd I he suppress'd thy name,
>   Because few words might not comprise thy fame.

Bear with me, gentle poet, though I conceive not aright of thy purpose, or be too inquisitive into the intent of thy oblivion: for, however my conjecture may miss the cushion,[370] yet shall my speech savour of friendship, though it be not allied to judgment.

Tantum hoc molior,[371] in this short digression, to acquaint our countrymen that live out of the echo of the Court, with a common knowledge of his invaluable virtues, and show myself thankful (in some part) for benefits received; which,

369. *And viewing ... guise*: Presumably, looking over the advertised goods, as merchant and traders do.
370. *miss the cushion*: Go wide of the mark.
371. 'Thus much do I labour'.

since words may not countervail, that are the usual lip labour of every idle discourser, I conclude with that of Ovid:

> *Accipe per longos tibi qui deserviat annos,*
> *Accipe, qui pura novit amare fide.*[372]

And if my zeal and duty, though all too mean to please, may by any industry be reformed to your gracious liking, I submit the simplicity of my endeavours to your service, which is all my performance may proffer, or my ability perform.

> *Præbeat Alcinoi poma benignus ager,*
> *Officium pauper numeret studiumque fidemque.*[373]

And so I break off this endless argument of speech abruptly.

FINIS

372. 'Accept [someone] who will serve you for long years; accept [someone] who knows how to love with pure faith' (Ovid).

373. 'The kindly earth affords Alcinous fruits; the poor man reckons only his duties and obligations' (Ovid). (Alcinous: King of Phoeacia, proverbially well provided by the gods.)

2

A PLEASANT COMEDY CALLED

Summer's Last Will and Testament

[*Enter Will Summers in his fool's coat but half on, coming out*]

WILL SUMMERS:[1] *Noctem peccatis, et fraudibus obiice nubem.*[2] There is no such fine time to play the knave in as the night. I am a goose, or a ghost at least; for what with turmoil of getting my fool's apparel, and care of being perfect,[3] I am sure I have not yet supped tonight. Will Summers' ghost I should be, come to present you with *Summer's Last Will and Testament*. Be it so, if my cousin Ned[4] will lend me his chain and his fiddle. Other, stately-paced Prologues use to attire themselves within.[5] I, that have a toy[6] in my head more than ordinary, and use to go without money, without garters, without girdle, without a hat-band,[7] without points[8] to my hose, without a knife to my dinner, and make so much use of this word 'without'[9] in everything, will here dress me without. Dick Huntley[10] cries 'Begin, begin,' and all the whole house 'For shame, come away', when I had my things but now brought me out of the laundry. God forgive me, I did not see my lord before! I'll set a good face on it, as though what I had talked idly all this while

1. Became Court Fool 1525; d. 1560.
2. 'I cast a cloud over the sins and deceptions of the night' (Horace).
3. Knowing my part by heart.
4. May have been the name of the Fool of this household.
5. i.e. in the actors' dressing-room.
6. Idea, fancy (note also ending of The Epilogue, p. 206).
7. 'To wear a hat without a band was a mark of eccentricity' (M.).
8. Lacing (i.e. to keep them up).
9. i.e. on the stage (as opposed to 'within').
10. (?) The prompter.

were my part. So it is, *boni viri*,[11] that one fool presents another. And I, fool by nature and by art, do speak to you in the person of the idiot our playmaker. He, like a fop and an ass, must be making himself a public laughing-stock, and have no thank for his labour, where other *Magisterii*, whose invention is far more exquisite, are content to sit still and do nothing. I'll show you what a scurvy Prologue he had made me, in an old vein of similitudes. If you be good fellows, give it the hearing, that you may judge of him thereafter.

THE PROLOGUE

'At a solemn feast of the *Triumviri* in Rome, it was seen and observed that the birds ceased to sing, and sat solitary on the house-tops, by reason of the sight of a painted serpent set openly to view. So fares it with us novices that here betray our imperfections. We, afraid to look on the imaginary serpent of Envy, painted in men's affections, have ceased to tune any music of mirth to your ears this twelvemonth, thinking that, as it is the nature of the serpent to hiss, so childhood and ignorance would play the goslings, contemning[12] what they understood not. Their censures we weigh not, whose senses are not yet unswaddled. The little minutes will be continually striking, though no man regard them. Whelps will bark before they can see, and strive to bite before they have teeth. Politianus speaketh of a beast who, while he is cut on the table, drinketh and represents the motions and voices of a living creature. Suchlike foolish beasts are we, who, whilst we are cut, mocked, and flouted at, in every man's common talk, will notwithstanding proceed to shame ourselves to make sport. No man pleaseth all: we seek to please one. Didymus[13] wrote four thou-

11. 'Good men'.
12. Despising.
13. References in Cornelius Agrippa (the source of other allusions in this speech) and Seneca.

sand books, or, as some say, six thousand, of the art of grammar. Our author hopes it may be as lawful for him to write a thousand lines of as light a subject. Socrates, whom the Oracle pronounced the wisest man of Greece, sometimes danced. Scipio and Lelius by the seaside played at pebble-stone.[14] *Semel insanivimus omnes.*[15] Every man cannot, with Archimedes, make a heaven of brass,[16] or dig gold out of the iron-mines of the law. Such odd trifles as mathematicians' experiments be (artificial flies to hang in the air by themselves, dancing balls, an egg-shell that shall climb up to the top of a spear,[17] fiery-breathing gourds), *poeta noster*[18] professeth not to make. *Placeat sibi quisque licebit.*[19] What's a fool but his bable? Deep-reaching wits, here is no deep stream for you to angle in. Moralisers,[20] you that wrest a never-meant meaning out of everything, applying all things to the present time, keep your attention for the common stage, for here are no quips in characters[21] for you to read. Vain glozers,[22] gather what you will. Spite, spell backwards what thou canst. As the Parthians fight, flying away, so will we prate and talk, but stand to nothing that we say.'

How say you, my masters, do you not laugh at him for a coxcomb? Why, he hath made a Prologue longer than his play! Nay, 'tis no play neither, but a show.[23] I'll be sworn, the Jig of Rowland's God-son[24] is a giant in com-

14. A game like chuckstone (M.).

15. 'All of us have been mad at some time' (Mantuanus).

16. A kind of planetarium, mentioned by Cicero.

17. *an egg-shell ... spear*: A trick described in Thomas Lupton's *Thousand Notable Things*, 1579.

18. 'Our poet'.

19. 'Everyone may please himself' (adapted from Ovid).

20. Term for allegory-hunters.

21. *quips in characters*: Personal allusions (M.).

22. Interpreters.   23. Entertainment.

24. *the jig ... God-son*: Possibly a reference to a lost work by John Wolf called *Rowlands' Godson Moralized*, 1592; perhaps to a ballad called *Rowland's Godson*. Jig: 'rhymed dialogue presenting a comic plot danced and sung by two or more characters' (M.).

parison of it. What can be made of Summer's last will
and testament? Such another thing as Gillian of Brains-
ford's will,[25] where she bequeathed a score of farts
amongst her friends. Forsooth, because the plague [26]
reigns in most places in this latter end of summer, Summer must come in sick. He must call his officers to
account, yield his throne to Autumn, make Winter his
executor, with tittle-tattle Tom boy: God give you
goodnight in Watling Street.[27] I care not what I say now,
for I play no more than you hear, and some of that you
heard too (by your leave) was extempore. He were as
good have let me had the best part, for I'll be revenged
on him to the uttermost, in this person of Will Summers,
which I have put on to play the Prologue, and mean not
to put off till the play be done. I'll sit as a Chorus and
flout the actors and him at the end of every scene. I know
they will not interrupt me, for fear of marring of all. But
look to your cues, my masters, for I intend to play the
knave in cue,[28] and put you besides all your parts, if you
take not the better heed. Actors, you rogues, come away,
clear your throats, blow your noses, and wipe your
mouths ere you enter, that you may take no occasion to
spit or to cough, when you are *non plus*.[29] And this I bar,
over and besides: that none of you stroke your beards
to make action, play with your cod-piece points, or stand
fumbling on your buttons, when you know not how to
bestow your fingers. Serve God and act cleanly. A fit of
mirth and an old song first, if you will.

[*Enter Summer, leaning on Autumn's and Winter's shoulders, and attended on with a train of satyrs and wood-
nymphs singing. Vertumnus also following him.*]

25. *Jill of Brentford's Testament*, by Robert Copland. Reprinted
1871.

26. See Introduction, pp. 36–7.

27. *God give ... Watling Street*: M. interprets as meaning 'worse
luck' or 'a bad thing for us'. Significance of Watling Street unknown.

28. In humour or temper (Grosart).

29. Nonplussed, not knowing what to do.

Fair Summer droops, droop men and beasts therefore:
So fair a summer look for never more.
All good things vanish, less than in a day,
Peace, plenty, pleasure, suddenly decay.
  Go not yet away, bright soul of the sad year;
  The earth is hell when thou leav'st to appear.

What, shall those flowers that deck'd thy garland erst,
Upon thy grave be wastefully dispers'd?
O trees, consume your sap in sorrow's source;
Streams, turn to tears your tributary course.
  Go not yet hence, bright soul of the sad year;
  The earth is hell, when thou leav'st to appear.

[*The satyrs and wood-nymphs go out singing, and leave
Summer and Winter and Autumn with Vertumnus on the
stage.*]

WILL SUMMERS: A couple of pretty boys, if they would
wash their faces and were well breeched an hour or two.
The rest of the green men have reasonable voices, good
to sing catches, or the great Jowben [30] by the fire's side,
in a winter's evening. But let us hear what Summer can
say for himself, why he should not be hissed at.

SUMMER: What pleasure alway lasts? No joy endures:
Summer I was, I am not as I was;
Harvest and age have whit'ned my green head:
On Autumn now and Winter must I lean.
Needs must he fall whom none but foes uphold.
Thus must the happiest man have his black day:
Omnibus una manet nox, et calcanda semel via lethi. [31]
This month have I lain languishing a-bed,
Looking each hour to yield my life and throne;
And died I had in deed unto the earth,
But that Eliza, England's beauteous Queen,
On whom all seasons prosperously attend,
Forbad the execution of my fate,

30. Unknown (perhaps 'Jew Ben', M.).
31. 'One night awaits all, and all must tread death's path once'
(Horace).

Until her joyful progress [32] was expired.
For her doth Summer live, and linger here,
And wisheth long to live to her content:
But wishes are not had when they wish well.
I must depart, my death-day is set down:
To these two must I leave my wheaten crown.
So unto unthrifts rich men leave their lands,
Who in an hour consume long labour's gains.
True is it that divinest Sidney sung,
'Oh, he is marred, that is for others made.' [33]
Come near, my friends, for I am near my end.
In presence of this honourable train,
Who love me (for I patronize their sports),
Mean I to make my final testament:
But first I'll call my officers to count,
And of the wealth I gave them to dispose,
Know what is left, I may know what to give.
Vertumnus then, that turn'st the year about,
Summon them one by one to answer me;
First Ver, the Spring, unto whose custody
I have committed more than to the rest:
The choice of all my fragrant meads and flowers,
And what delights so'er nature affords.

VERTUMNUS: I will, my Lord. Ver, lusty Ver, by the name
of lusty Ver, come into the court! Or lose a mark in
issues.[34]

_Enter Ver with his train, overlaid with suits of green moss,
representing short grass, singing._]

THE SONG

Spring, the sweet spring, is the year's pleasant king,
Then blooms each thing, then maids dance in a ring;
Cold doth not sting, the pretty birds do sing,
Cuckoo, jug jug, pu we, to witta woo.

32. The Queen visited Newbury, Circencester, Woodstock and
Oxford during August and September 1592.
33. _Arcadia_, 1590 edition.
34. Be fined a mark for non-attendance.

The palm and may make country houses gay,
Lambs frisk and play, the shepherds pipe all day,
And we hear aye birds tune this merry lay,
Cuckoo, jug, jug, pu we, to witta woo.

The fields breathe sweet, the daisies kiss our feet,
Young lovers meet, old wives a-sunning sit;
In every street these tunes our ears do greet,
Cuckoo, jug, jug, pu we, to witta woo.
    Spring, the sweet spring.

WILL SUMMERS: By my troth, they have voices as clear as crystal. This is a pretty thing, if it be for nothing but to go a-begging with.

SUMMER: Believe me, Ver, but thou art pleasant bent. This humour should import a harmless mind: Know'st thou the reason why I sent for thee?

VER: No, faith, nor care not whether I do or no. If you will dance a galliard, so it is: if not

    Falangtado,[35] Falangtado, to wear the black and yellow:[36]

    Falangtado, Falangtado, my mates are gone; I'll follow.

SUMMER: Nay, stay awhile, we must confer and talk.

Ver, call to mind I am thy sovereign Lord,
And what thou hast, of me thou hast and hold'st.
Unto no other end I sent for thee,
But to demand a reckoning at thy hands,
How well or ill thou hast employed my wealth.

VER: If that be all, we will not disagree:
A clean trencher and a napkin you shall have presently.

WILL SUMMERS: The truth is, this fellow hath been a tapster in his days.

[*Ver goes in and fetcheth out the hobby-horse and the morris-dance, who dance about.*]

SUMMER: How now? Is this the reckoning we shall have?

WINTER: My lord, he doth abuse you: brook it not.

---

35. This and variants were common as refrains in popular songs.
36. *black and yellow*: Representing constancy and (here) sadness.

AUTUMN: *Summa totalis*,[37] I fear, will prove him but a fool.

VER: About, about, lively! Put your horse to it, rein him harder, jerk him with your wand! Sit fast, sit fast, man! Fool, hold up your bable [38] there!

WILL SUMMERS: Oh, brave Hall! [39] Oh, well said, Butcher! Now for the credit of Worcestershire.[40] The finest set of morris-dancers that is between this and Streatham. Marry, methinks there is one of them danceth like a cloyther's [41] horse, with a wool-pack on his back. You, friend, with the hobby-horse, go not too fast, for fear of wearing out my lord's tile-stones with your hob-nails.

VER: So, so, so; trot the ring twice over, and away. May it please my lord, this is the grand capital sum; but there are certain parcels [42] behind, as you shall see.

SUMMER: Nay, nay, no more; for this is all too much.

VER: Content yourself, we'll have variety.

[*Here enter three clowns and three maids, singing this song, dancing.*]

> Trip and go, heave and ho,
> Up and down, to and fro,
> From the town to the grove,
> Two and two let us rove
> A-maying, a-playing:
> Love hath no gainsaying:
> So merrily trip and go.

WILL SUMMERS: Beshrew my heart, of a number of ill legs I never saw worse dancers! How blest are you, that the wenches of the parish do not see you!

37. 'The sum of all'.

38. Commonly emended from 'ladle' (but ladles were sometimes carried by fool or hobby-horse to collect money – M.).

39. Possibly a reference to a taborer of that name.

40. M. conjectures the morris dancers were Worcestershire men, perhaps some of Whitgift's servants brought with him from Worcester, where he was Bishop till 1583.

41. Clothier's.   42. Items.

SUMMER: Presumptuous Ver, uncivil-nurtured boy,
Think'st I will be derided thus of thee?
Is this th'account and reckoning that thou mak'st?

VER: Troth, my lord, to tell you plain, I can give you no
other account: *nam quae habui, perdidi*[43] – what I had,
I have spent on good fellows; in these sports you have
seen, which are proper to the spring, and others of like
sort (as giving wenches green gowns,[44] making garlands
for fencers, and tricking up children gay) have I bestowed
all my flowery treasure and flower of my youth.

WILL SUMMERS: A small matter. I know one spent, in less
than a year, eight and fifty pounds in mustard, and another that ran in debt in the space of four or five year
above fourteen thousand pound in lute strings[45] and
grey paper.

SUMMER: Oh monstrous unthrift, who e'er heard the like?
The sea's vast throat, in so short tract of time,
Devoureth nor consumeth half so much.
How well mightst thou have liv'd within thy bounds!

VER: What talk you to me of living within my bounds? I
tell you, none but asses live within their bounds: the
silly beasts, if they be put in a pasture that is eaten bare
to the very earth and where there is nothing to be had
but thistles, will rather fall soberly to those thistles and
be hunger-starved, than they will offer to break their
bounds; whereas the lusty courser, if he be in a barren
plot and spy better grass in some pasture near adjoining,
breaks over hedge and ditch, and to go, ere he will be
pent in, and not have his belly full. Peradventure the
horses lately sworn to be stolen[46] carried that youthful
mind, who, if they had been asses, would have been yet
extant.

43. Adapted from Terence.
44. Throwing them down on the grass (M.).
45. Credulous borrowers would be 'paid' in such goods by owners
in lieu of money (they would be represented as having a certain value
though they were in fact virtually unsaleable).
46. *horses . . . stolen*: Perhaps horses stolen by Germans, followers
of Count Mompelgard, between Reading and Windsor.

WILL SUMMERS: Thus we may see, the longer we live, the more we shall learn. I ne'er thought honesty an ass till this day.

VER: This world is transitory; it was made of nothing, and it must to nothing. Wherefore, if we will do the will of our high Creator, whose will it is that it pass to nothing, we must help to consume it to nothing. Gold is more vile than men. Men die in thousands, and ten thousands, yea, many times in hundred thousands, in one battle. If then the best husband be so liberal of his best handiwork, to what end should we make much of a glittering excrement, or doubt to spend at a banquet as many pounds as He spends men at a battle? Methinks I honour Geta, the Roman Emperor, for a brave-minded fellow, for he commanded a banquet to be made him of all meats under the sun, which were served in after the order of the alphabet, and the clerk of the kitchen following the last dish, which was two mile off from the foremost, brought him an index of their several names; neither did he pingle [47] when it was set on the board, but for the space of three days and three nights never rose from the table.

WILL SUMMERS: Oh intolerable lying villain, that was never begotten without the consent of a whetstone!

SUMMER: Ungracious man, how fondly [48] he argueth!

VER: Tell me, I pray, wherefore was gold laid under our feet in the veins of the earth, but that we should contemn it and tread upon it, and so consequently tread thrift under our feet? It was not known till the Iron Age, *donec facinus invasit mortales*,[49] as the poet says, and the Scythians always detested it. I will prove it, that an unthrift of any comes nearest a happy man insomuch as he comes nearest to beggary. Cicero saith *summum bonum* consists in *omnium rerum vacatione*, that it is the chiefest felicity that may be to rest from all labours. Now, who

47. Eat without appetite or squeamishly.
48. Foolishly.
49. 'Till crime corrupted men'.

155

doeth so much *vacare a rebus*? Who rests so much? Who hath so little to do, as the beggar?

> Who can sing so merry a note,
> As he that cannot change a groat?

Cui nil est, nil deest: [50] 'he that hath nothing, wants nothing.' On the other side, it is said of the carl [51] *Omnia habeo, nec quicquam habeo*: 'I have all things, yet want everything.' *Multi mihi vitio vertunt, quia egeo*, saith Marcus Cato in Aulus Gellius, *at ego illis, quia nequeunt egere*: 'Many upbraid me,' saith he, 'because I am poor; but I upbraid them because they cannot live if they were poor.' It is a common proverb *divesque miserque* ('a rich man, and a miserable'): *nam natura paucis contenta* ('none so contented as the poor man'). Admit that the chiefest happiness were not rest or ease, but knowledge, as Herillus, Alcidamas and many of Socrates' followers affirm. Why, *paupertas omnes perdocet artes*: 'poverty instructs a man in all arts', it makes a man hardy and venturous, and therefore it is called of the poets *Paupertas audax*,[52] 'valiant poverty'. It is not so much subject to inordinate desires as wealth or prosperity. *Non habet unde suum paupertas pascat amorem*: [53] 'poverty hath not wherewithal to feed lust.' All the poets were beggars. All alchemists and all philosophers are beggars: *Omnia mea mecum porto*,[54] quoth Bias, when he had nothing but bread and cheese in a leathern bag, and two or three books in his bosom. Saint Francis: a holy saint, and never had any money. It is madness to dote upon muck. That young man of Athens (Aelianus makes mention of) may be an example to us, who doted so extremely on the image of fortune, that, when he might not enjoy it, he died for sorrow. The earth yields all her fruits together,

50. Terence, *Eunuch*, II, 2, 12.
51. Churl, niggard.
52. Horace, *Epistolae*, II, 2, 31.
53. Ovid, *Remedia Amoris*, 749.
54. 'All my possessions I carry with me' (Cicero).

and why should not we spend them together? I thank
heavens on my knees, that have made me an unthrift.

SUMMER: Oh vanity itself! Oh wit ill-spent!
So study thousands not to mend their lives,
But to maintain the sin they most affect,
To be hell's advocates gainst their own souls.
Ver, since thou giv'st such praise to beggary,
And hast defended it so valiantly,
This be thy penance: thou shalt ne'er appear,
Or come abroad, but Lent shall wait on thee;
His scarcity may countervail thy waste.
Riot may flourish, but finds want at last.
Take him away, that knoweth no good way,
And lead him the next way to woe and want. [*Exit Ver*.]
Thus in the paths of knowledge many stray,
And from the means of life fetch their decay.

WILL SUMMERS: Heigh ho! Here is a coil [55] indeed to
bring beggars to stocks. I promise you truly, I was almost
asleep; I thought I had been at a sermon. Well, for this
one night's exhortation, I vow (by God's grace) never to
be good husband while I live. But what is this to the
purpose? 'Hur come to Powl,' as the Welshman says,
'and hur pay an halfpenny for hur seat, and hur hear the
preacher talge, and a talge very well, by gis; but yet a
cannot make hur laugh. Go ae theatre and hear a Queen's
Fice, and he make hur laugh, and laugh hur belly-full.'
So we came hither to laugh and be merry, and we hear
a filthy beggarly oration in the praise of beggary. It is a
beggarly poet that writ it; and that makes him so much
commend it, because he knows not how to mend himself.
Well, rather than he shall have no employment but lick
dishes, I will set him a-work myself, to write in praise
of the art of stooping, and how there was never any
famous thresher, porter, brewer, pioneer, or carpenter,
that had straight back. Repair to my chamber, poor fellow, when the play is done, and thou shalt see what I will
say to thee.

55. Trouble, disturbance.

SUMMER: Vertumnus, call Solstitium.

VERTUMNUS: Solstitium, come into the court.

[*without* [56]]: Peace there below, make room for master Solstitium!

[*Enter Solstitium like an aged hermit, carrying a pair of balances with an hour-glass in either of them; one hourglass white, the other black. He is brought in by a number of shepherds playing upon recorders.*]

SOLSTITIUM: All hail to Summer, my dread sovereign lord.

SUMMER: Welcome, Solstitium. Thou art one of them
To whose good husbandry we have referred
Part of those small revenues that we have.
What hast thou gain'd us? What hast thou brought in?

SOLSTITIUM: Alas, my lord, what gave you me to keep,
But a few days' eyes in my prime of youth?
And those I have converted to white hairs.
I never lov'd ambitiously to climb,
Or thrust my hand too far into the fire.
To be in heaven, sure, is a blessed thing;
But, Atlas-like, to prop heaven on one's back
Cannot but be more labour than delight.
Such is the state of men in honour plac'd:
They are gold vessels made for servile uses,
High trees that keep the weather from low houses,
But cannot shield the tempest from themselves.
I love to dwell betwixt the hills and dales;
Neither to be so great to be envied,
Nor yet so poor the world should pity me.
Inter utrumque tene, medio tutissimus ibis. [57]

SUMMER: What dost thou with those balances thou
bear'st?

SOLSTITIUM: In them I weigh the day and night alike.
This white glass is the hour-glass of the day,
This black one the just measure of the night.
One more than other holdeth not a grain:
Both serve time's just proportion to maintain.

56. M.'s emendation. Q. has '*court without*: "Peace"'.
57. 'Stay between the two; you are safest in the middle' (Ovid).

SUMMER: I like thy moderation wondrous well;
   And this thou balance, weighing the white glass
   And black with equal poise and steadfast hand,
   A pattern is to princes and great men,
   How to weigh all estates indifferently,
   The Spiritualty and Temporalty alike:
   Neither to be too prodigal of smiles,
   Nor too severe in frowning without cause.
   If you be wise, you monarchs of the earth,
   Have two such glasses still before your eyes;
   Think, as you have a white glass running on,
   Good days, friends' favour, and all things at beck,
   So, this white glass run out (as out it will),
   The black comes next; your downfall is at hand.
   Take this of me, for somewhat I have tried:
   A mighty ebb follows a mighty tide.
   But say, Solstitium, hadst thou nought besides?
   Nought but days' eyes and fair looks gave I thee?
SOLSTITIUM: Nothing, my lord, nor aught more did I
   ask.
SUMMER: But hadst thou always kept thee in my sight,
   Thy good deserts, though silent, would have asked.
SOLSTITIUM: Deserts, my lord, of ancient servitors
   Are like old sores, which may not be ripp'd up.
   Such use these times have got, that none must beg,
   But those that have young limbs to lavish fast.
SUMMER: I grieve no more regard we had of thee.
   A little sooner hadst thou spoke to me,
   Thou hadst been heard, but now the time is past:
   Death waiteth at the door for thee and me.
   Let us go measure out our beds in clay:
   Nought but good deeds hence shall we bear away.
   Be, as thou wert, best steward of my hours,
   And so return unto thy country bowers.
[*Here Solstitium goes out with his music, as he comes in.*]
WILL SUMMERS: Fie, fie, of honesty, fie! Solstitium is an
   ass, perdy! This play is a gallimaufry.[58] Fetch me some

58. Mixture, formless concoction.

drink, somebody. What cheer, what cheer, my hearts? Are you not thirsty with listening to this dry sport? What have we to do with scales [59] and hour-glasses, except we were bakers or clock-keepers? I cannot tell how other men are addicted, but it is against my profession to use any scales but such as we play at with a bowl, or keep any hours but dinner or supper. It is a pedantical thing to respect times and seasons. If a man be drinking with good fellows late, he must come home, for fear the gates be shut. When I am in my warm bed, I must rise to prayers, because the bell rings. I like no such foolish customs. Actors, bring now a black jack, and a rundlet [60] of Rhenish wine, disputing of the antiquity of red noses. Let the prodigal child come out in his doublet and hose all greasy, his shirt hanging forth, and ne'er a penny in his purse, and talk what a fine thing it is to walk summerly, or sit whistling under a hedge and keep hogs. Go forward in grace and virtue to proceed; but let us have no more of these grave matters.

SUMMER: Vertumnus, will Sol come before us?

VERTUMNIUS: Sol, sol, ut, re, me, fa, sol,
Come to church while the bell toll.

[*Enter Sol, very richly attired, with a noise of musicians before him.*]

SUMMER: Ay, marry, here comes majesty in pomp,
Resplendent Sol, chief planet of the heavens.
He is our servant, looks he ne'er so big.

SOL: My liege, what crav'st thou at thy vassal's hands?

SUMMER: Hypocrisy, how it can change his shape!
How base is pride from his own dunghill put!
How I have rais'd thee, Sol, I list [61] not tell,
Out of the ocean of adversity,
To sit in height of honour's glorious heaven,
To be the eye-sore of aspiring eyes;
To give the day her life from thy bright looks,
And let nought thrive upon the face of earth,

59. Ninepins (kayles).   60. Small barrel.
61. Desire, choose.

From which thou shalt withdraw thy powerful smiles.
What hast thou done deserving such high grace?
What industry, or meritorious toil,
Canst thou produce to prove my gift well-plac'd?
Some service or some profit I expect:
None is promoted but for some respect.

SOL: My lord, what needs these terms betwixt us two?
Upbraiding ill beseems your bounteous mind:
I do you honour for advancing me.
Why, 'tis credit for your excellence,
To have so great a subject as I am.
This is your glory and magnificence,
That, without stooping of your mightiness,
Or taking any whit from your high state,
You can make one as mighty as yourself.

AUTUMN: Oh arrogance exceeding all belief!
Summer my lord, this saucy upstart Jack,
That now doth rule the chariot of the sun,
And makes all stars derive their light from him,
Is a most base insinuating slave,
The son of parsimony and disdain,
One that will shine on friends and foes alike,
That under brightest smiles hideth black showers,
Whose envious breath doth dry up springs and lakes,
And burns the grass, that beasts can get no food.

WINTER: No dunghill hath so vild an excrement,
But with his beams he will forthwith exhale.
The fens and quagmires tithe to him their filth;
Forth purest mines he sucks a gainful dross;
Green ivy-bushes [62] at the vintner's doors
He withers, and devoureth all their sap.

AUTUMN: Lascivious and intemperate he is.
The wrong of Daphne [63] is a well-known tale·
Each evening he descends to Thetis' lap,[64]

62. The vintner's sign.
63. *wrong of Daphne*: She was seduced by Apollo (the sun god),
and changed to a bay-tree.
64. The ocean.

The while men think he bathes him in the sea.
Oh, but when he returneth whence he came
Down to the west, then dawns his deity
Then doubled is the swelling of his looks.
He overloads his car with orient gems,
And reigns his fiery horses with rich pearl;
He terms himself the god of poetry,
And setteth wanton songs unto the lute.

WINTER: Let him not talk, for he hath words at will,
And wit to make the baddest matter good.

SUMMER: Bad words, bad wit; oh, where dwells faith or
truth?
Ill usury my favours reap from thee,
Usurping Sol, the hate of heaven and earth.

SOL: If Envy unconfuted may accuse,
Then Innocence must uncondemned die.
The name of martyrdom offence hath gained,
When Fury stopp'd a froward judge's ears.
Much I'll not say (much speech much folly shows),
What I have done, you gave me leave to do.
The excrements you bred, whereon I feed;
To rid the earth of their contagious fumes,
With such gross carriage did I load my beams;
I burnt no grass, I dried no springs and lakes,
I suck'd no mines, I wither'd no green boughs,
But when, to ripen harvest, I was forc'd
To make my rays more fervent than I wont.
For Daphne's wrongs, and scapes in Thetis' lap,
All gods are subject to the like mishap.
Stars daily fall ('tis use is all in all)
And men account the fall but nature's course.
Vaunting my jewels, hasting to the west,
Or rising early from the grey-ey'd morn,
What do I vaunt but your large bountihood,
And show how liberal a lord I serve?
Music and poetry, my two last crimes,
Are those two exercises of delight,
Wherewith long labours I do weary out.

The dying swan is not forbid to sing.
The waves of Heber play'd on Orpheus' [65] strings,
When he, sweet music's trophy, was destroy'd.
And as for poetry, words' eloquence,
(Dead Phaeton's three sisters' [66] funeral tears,
That by the gods were to electrum [67] turn'd),
Not flint, or rocks of icy cinders framed,
Deny the source of silver-falling streams.
Envy envieth not outcry's unrest:
In vain I plead; well is to me a fault,
And these my words seem the slight web of art,
And not to have the taste of sounder truth.
Let none but fools be car'd for of the wise;
Knowledge's own children knowledge most despise.

SUMMER: Thou know'st too much to know to keep the
   mean
He that sees all things oft sees not himself.
The Thames is witness of thy tyranny,
Whose waves thou hast exhaust for winter showers.
The naked channel plains her of thy spite,
That laid'st her entrails unto open sight.
Unprofitably born to man and beast,
Which like to Nilus yet doth hide his head,
Some few years since thou let'st o'erflow these walks,
And in the horse-race headlong ran at race,
While in a cloud thou hid'st thy burning face.
Where was thy care to rid contagious filth,
When some men wetshod, with his waters, droop'd?
Others that ate the eels his heat cast up
Sicken'd and died, by them empoisoned.
Sleep'st thou, or keep'st thou then Admetus' sheep, [68]
Thou driv'st not back these flowings to the deep?

65. *Heber . . . Orpheus*: Orpheus' severed head, still singing, floated on the River Hebrus.

66. The Heliades, who wept unceasingly for Phaeton (killed by Zeus) and were changed into poplars.

67. Amber (their tears oozing from the trees were hardened into amber by Helios).

68. Kept for a while by Apollo in Thessaly.

SOL: The winds, not I, have floods and tides in chase.
   Diana, whom our fables call the moon,
   Only commandeth o'er the raging main.
   She leads his wallowing offspring up and down;
   She waning, all streams ebb; as in the year
   She was eclips'd, when that the Thames was bare.
SUMMER: A bare conjecture, builded on perhaps!
   In laying thus the blame upon the moon,
   Thou imitat'st subtle Pythagoras,
   Who, what he would the people should believe,
   The same he wrote with blood upon a glass,
   And turn'd it opposite gainst the new moon;
   Whose beams, reflecting on it with full force,
   Show'd all those lines, to them that stood behind,
   Most plainly writ in circle of the moon.
   And then he said: 'Not I, but the new moon,
   Fair Cynthia, persuades you this and that.'
   With like collusion shalt thou not blind me;
   But for abusing both the moon and me,
   Long shalt thou be eclipsed by the moon,
   And long in darkness live, and see no light.
   Away with him, his doom hath no reverse.
SOL: What is eclips'd will one day shine again.
   Though Winter frowns, the Spring will ease my pain.
   Time from the brow doth wipe out every stain.   [*Exit Sol.*]
WILL SUMMERS: I think the sun is not so long in passing
   through the twelve signs, as the son of a fool hath been
   disputing here about 'had I wist'. Out of doubt, the poet
   is bribed of some that have a mess of cream to eat before my lord go to bed yet, to hold him half the night
   with riff-raff of the rumming of Eleanor.[69] If I can tell
   what it means, pray God I may never get breakfast more
   when I am hungry. Troth, I am of opinion he is one of
   those hieroglyphical writers that by the figures of beasts,
   planets, and of stones, express the mind as we do in
   A.B.C.; or one that writes under hair, as I have heard

69. *riff-raff . . . Eleanor*: Nonsensical, crude verse with reference to
Skelton's *Tunning of Elinor Rumming*.

of a certain notary Histiaeus, who, following Darius in
the Persian wars and desirous to disclose some secrets of
import to his friend Aristagoras, that dwelt afar off, found
out this means. He had a servant that had been long
sick of a pain in his eyes, whom, under pretence of curing
his malady, he shaved from one side of his head to the
other, and with a soft pencil wrote upon his scalp, as on
parchment, the discourse of his business, the fellow all
the while imagining his master had done nothing but
noint his head with a feather. After this, he kept him
secretly in his tent, till his hair was somewhat grown,
and then willed him to go to Aristagoras into the country and bid him shave him, as he had done, and he should
have perfect remedy. He did so. Aristagoras shaved him
with his own hands, read his friend's letter, and when
he had done, washed it out, that no man should perceive
it else, and sent him home to buy him a night-cap. If I
wist there were any such knavery, or Peter Bales' *Brachy-
graphy*,[70] under Sol's bushy hair, I would have a barber,
my host of 'The Murrion's Head',[71] to be his interpreter,
who would whet his razor on his Richmond cap,[72] and
give him the terrible cut,[73] like himself, but he would
come as near as a quart pot to the construction of it. To
be sententious, not superfluous, Sol should have been beholding to the barber, and not the beard-master. Is it
pride that is shadowed under this two-legged sun, that
never came nearer heaven than Dubber's Hill?[74] That
pride is not my sin, Sloven's Hall where I was born be
my record. As for covetousness, intemperance and exac-
tion, I meet with nothing in a whole year but a cup of
wine, for such vices to be conversant in. *Pergite porro*,[75]
my good children, and multiply the sins of your

70. Stenography, as invented probably by Bales (1547?–1610), or
plagiarized by him from Timothy Bright (1531?–1615).
71. Like 'The Saracen's Head' ('murrion' = blackamoor).
72. Meaning unknown.
73. Haircut to make a man look terrible to his enemies.
74. Duppa's Hill, near Croydon.   75. 'Contrive'.

absurdities, till you come to the full measure of the
grand hiss, and you shall hear how we will purge rheum
with censuring your imperfections.

SUMMER: Vertumnus, call Orion.

VERTUMNUS: Orion, Urion, Arion!

My lord thou must look upon.

Orion, gentleman dog-keeper, huntsman, come into the
court! Look you bring all hounds, and no bandogs.[76]
Peace there, that we may hear their horns blow!

[*Enter Orion like a hunter, with a horn about his neck, all
his men after the same sort hallooing and blowing their
horns.*]

ORION: Sirrah, was't thou that call'd us from our game?

How durst thou (being but a petty god)

Disturb me in the entrance of my sports?

SUMMER: 'Twas I, Orion, caus'd thee to be call'd.

ORION: 'Tis I, dread Lord, that humbly will obey.

SUMMER: How haps't thou leftst the heavens, to hunt
below?

As I remember, thou wert Hireus' [77] son,

Whom of a huntsman Jove chose for a star,

And thou art call'd the dog-star, art thou not?

AUTUMN: Pleaseth your honour, heaven's circumference

Is not enough for him to hunt and range,

But with those venom-breathed curs he leads,

He comes to chase health from our earthly bounds.

Each one of those foul-mouthed mangy dogs

Governs a day (no dog but hath his day),

And all the days by them so governed,

The dog-days hight.[78] Infectious fosterers

Of meteors [79] from carrion that arise,

And putrefied bodies of dead men,

Are they engender'd to that ugly shape,

76. Fierce dogs, e.g. mastiffs.
77. Hyrieus, the son of Neptune and Alcyone.
78. Are called.
79. Loosely used, here referring to the *ignis fatuus* (phosphorescent
light from decaying matter).

Being nought else but preserv'd corruption.
'Tis these that, in the entrance of their reign,
The plague and dangerous agues have brought in.
They arre [80] and bark at night against the moon,
For fetching in fresh tides to cleanse the streets.
They vomit flames, and blast the ripen'd fruits:
They are Death's messengers unto all those
That sicken while their malice beareth sway.
ORION: A tedious discourse, built on no ground;
A silly fancy, Autumn, hast thou told,
Which no philosophy doth warrantize,
No old received poetry confirms.
I will not grace thee by confuting thee;
Yet in a jest (since thou railest so gainst dogs)
I'll speak a word or two in their defence.[81]
That creature's best that comes most near to men:
That dogs of all come nearest, thus I prove.
First, they excel us in all outward sense,
Which no one of experience will deny;
They hear, they smell, they see better than we.
To come to speech, they have it questionless,
Although we understand them not so well.
They bark as good old Saxon as may be,
And that in more variety than we;
For they have one voice when they are in chase,
Another, when they wrangle for their meat,
Another, when we beat them out of doors.
That they have reason, this I will allege:
They choose those things that are most fit for them,
And shun the contrary all that they may;
They know what is for their own diet best,
And seek about for't very carefully;
At sight of any whip they run away,
As runs a thief from noise of hue and cry;

80. Onomatopoeic word for the snarling of dogs.
81. M. points out that the whole passage is derived from Sextus
Empericus' *Pyrrhoniae Hyptotyposes*, probably in a lost English
translation.

Nor live they on the sweat of others' brows,
But have their trades to get their living with,
Hunting and coney-catching, two fine arts.
Yea, there be of them, as there be of men,
Of every occupation more or less:
Some carriers, and they fetch; some watermen,
And they will dive and swim when you bid them;
Some butchers, and they do worry sheep by night;
Some cooks, and they do nothing but turn spits.
Chrysippus holds dogs are logicians,
In that, by study and by canvassing,
They can distinguish twixt three several things:
As when he cometh where three broad ways meet,
And of those three hath stay'd at two of them,
By which he guesseth that the game went not,
Without more pause he runneth on the third;
Which, as Chrysippus saith, insinuates
As if he reason'd thus within himself:
'Either he went this, that, or yonder way,
But neither that, nor yonder, therefore this.'
But whether they logicians be or no,
Cynics they are, for they will snarl and bite;
Right courtiers to flatter and to fawn;
Valiant to set upon the enemies,
Most faithful and constant to their friends;
Nay, they are wise, as Homer witnesseth,
Who, talking of Ulysses coming home,
Saith all his household but Argus, his dog,
Had quite forgot him. Ay, and his deep insight
Nor Pallas' art [82] in altering of his shape,
Nor his base weeds, nor absence twenty years,
Could go beyond, or any way delude.
That dogs physicians are, thus I infer:
They are ne'er sick, but they know their disease,
And find out means to ease them of their grief;
Special good surgeons to cure dangerous wounds,

82. Pallas disguised Ulysses as a poor beggar to avoid recognition
by Penelope's suitors.

For, strucken with a stake into the flesh,
This policy they use to get it out:
They trail one of their feet upon the ground,
And gnaw the flesh about, where the wound is,
Till it be clean drawn out; and then, because
Ulcers and sores kept foul are hardly cur'd,
They lick and purify it with their tongue,
And well observe Hippocrates' old rule;
'The only medicine for the foot is rest,'
For if they have the least hurt in their feet,
They bear them up and look they be not stirr'd
When humours rise, they eat a sovereign [83] herb,
Whereby what cloys their stomachs they cast up,
And, as some writers of experience tell,
They were the first invented vomiting.
Sham'st thou not, Autumn, unadvisedly
To slander such rare creatures as they be?
SUMMER: We call'd thee not, Orion, to this end,
To tell a story of dogs' qualities.
With all thy hunting how are we enrich'd?
What tribute payest thou us for thy high place?
ORION: What tribute should I pay you out of nought?
Hunters do hunt for pleasure, not for gain.
While dog-days last, the harvest safely thrives;
The sun burns hot, to finish up fruits' growth;
There is no blood-letting to make men weak.
Physicians with their *Cataposia,*
Recipe Elinctoria,
Masticatorum and *Cataplasmata;*[84]
Their gargarisms,[85] clysters,[86] and pitched cloths,[87]
Their perfumes, syrups, and their triacles,[88]
Refrain to poison the sick patients,
And dare not minister till I be out.

---

83. Remedial.
84. Cataposia . . . Cataplasmata: Pills, poultices, medicines to purge phlegm.
85. Gargles.   86. Enemas (sometimes suppositories).
87. Medicated plugs.   88. Salves.

Then none will bathe, and so are fewer drown'd;
All lust is perilsome, therefore less us'd.
In brief, the year without me cannot stand:
Summer, I am thy staff and thy right hand.

SUMMER: A broken staff, a lame right hand I had,
If thou wert all the stay that held me up.
Nihil violentum perpetuum:[89]
'No violence that liveth to old age.'
Ill-governed star, that never bod'st good luck,
I banish thee a twelve-month and a day,
Forth of my presence. Come not in my sight,
Nor show thy head, so much as in the night.

ORION: I am content, though hunting be not out;
We will go hunt in hell for better hap.
One parting blow, my hearts, unto our friends,
To bid the fields and huntsmen all farewell.
Toss up your bugle horns unto the stars:
Toil findeth ease: peace follows after wars.   [*Exit*]
[*Here they go out, blowing their horns and hallooing, as
they came in.*]

WILL SUMMERS: Faith, this scene of Orion is right
prandium caninum, 'a dog's dinner', which as it is without wine, so here's a coil about dogs without wit. If I had
thought the Ship of Fools [90] would have stayed to take in
fresh water at the Isle of Dogs, I would have furnished
it with a whole kennel of collections to the purpose. I
have had a dog myself, that would dream and talk in his
sleep, turn round like Ned Fool,[91] and sleep all night in
a porridge-pot. Mark but the skirmish between Sixpence [92] and the fox, and it is miraculous how they overcome one another in honourable courtesy. The fox,
though he wears a chain, runs as though he were free,
mocking us (as it is a crafty beast) because we, having a

89. Proverbial.
90. A reference to Brandt's *Stultifera Navis*, 1494; translated in 1509.
91. Perhaps the name of the fool in Whitgift's household, perhaps
general like Tom-fool (M.). (cf. p. 146, n. 4.)
92. Probably popular term for a dog.

lord and master to attend on, run about at our pleasures, like masterless men. Young Sixpence, the best page his master hath, plays a little and retires. I warrant he will not be far out of the way when his master goes to dinner. Learn of him, you diminutive urchins, how to behave yourselves in your vocation. Take not up your standings in a nut-tree, when you should be waiting on my lord's trencher. Shoot but a bit at butts; play but a span at points.[93] Whatever you do, *memento mori*: remember to rise betimes in the morning.

SUMMER: Vertumnus, call Harvest.

VERTUMNUS: Harvest, by west, and by north, by south and southeast,

Show thyself like a beast.

Goodman Harvest, yeoman, come in and say what you can.

Room for the scythe and the sickles there!

[*Enter Harvest with a scythe on his neck, and all his reapers with sickles, and a great black bowl with a posset in it borne before him. They come in singing.*]

THE SONG

Merry, merry, merry, cherry, cherry, cherry,
    Trowl the black bowl to me.
        Hey derry, derry, with a poop and a lerry,
        I'll trowl it again to thee.
Hooky, hooky, we have shorn,
    And we have bound,
And we have brought Harvest
    Home to town.

SUMMER: Harvest, the bailie of my husbandry,
    What plenty hast thou heap'd into our barns?
    I hope thou hast sped well, thou art so blithe.

HARVEST: Sped well or ill, sir, I drink to you on the same.
    Is your throat clear to help us to sing 'Hooky, hooky'?
[*Here they all sing after him.*]

93. (?) Backgammon.

Hooky, hooky, we have shorn,
And we have bound,
And we have brought Harvest
Home to town.

AUTUMN: Thou Corydon, why answer'st not direct?

HARVEST: Answer? Why, friend, I am no tapster, to say 'Anon, anon, sir'. But leave you to molest me, goodman tawny leaves, for fear (as the proverb says, 'leave is light') so I mow off all your leaves with my scythe.

WINTER: Mock not and mow not too long, you were best, For fear we whet not your scythe upon your pate.

SUMMER: Since thou art so perverse in answering,
Harvest, hear what complaints are brought to me.
Thou art accused by the public voice,
For an engrosser [94] of the common store:
A carl,[95] thou hast no conscience, nor remorse,
But dost impoverish the fruitful earth,
To make thy garners rise up to the heavens.
To whom givest thou? Who feedeth at thy board?
No almës, but unreasonable gain,
Digests what thy huge iron teeth devour:
'Small beer, coarse bread', the hinds and beggars cry,
Whilst thou withholdest both the malt and flour,
And giv'st us bran and water, fit for dogs.

HARVEST: Hooky, hooky! If you were not my lord, I would say you lie. First and foremost, you say I am a grocer. A grocer is a citizen. I am no citizen, therefore no grocer. A hoarder-up of grain: that's false, for not so much but my elbows eat wheat every time I lean on them. A carl: that is as much to say as a coney-catcher of good fellowship. For that one word you shall pledge me a carouse; eat a spoonful of the curd to allay your choler. My mates and fellows, sing no more 'Merry, merry', but weep out a lamentable 'Hooky, Hooky', and let your sickles cry:

94. Hoarder.
95. Miser.

  Sick, sick, and very sick,
   And sick, and for the time;
  For Harvest your master is
   Abus'd without reason or rhyme.

I have no conscience, I? I'll come nearer to you, and yet
I am no scab, nor a louse. Can you make proof wherever
I sold away my conscience, or pawned it? I think I have
given you the pose:[96] blow your nose, Master Constable.
But to say that I impoverish the earth, that I rob the
man in the moon, that I take a purse on the top of Paul's
steeple: by this straw and thread, I swear you are no
gentleman, no proper man, no honest man, to make me
sing 'Oh man in desperation'.[97]

SUMMER: I must give credit unto what I hear,
For other than I hear, attract I nought.

HARVEST: Ay, ay: nought seek, nought have.
An ill husband is the first step to a knave.
You object I feed none at my board. I am sure if you were
a hog you would never say so, for, surreverence of their
worships, they feed at my stable table every day. I keep
good hospitality for hens and geese. Gleaners are oppressed with heavy burdens of my bounty:

  They rake me and eat me to the very bones,
  Till there be nothing left but gravel and stones.

And yet I give no alms, but devour all? They say, when a
man cannot hear well, 'You hear with your harvest ears.'[98]
But if you heard with your harvest ears, that is, with the
ears of corn which my alms-cart scatters, they would tell
you that I am the very poor man's box of pity, that there
are more holes of liberality open in Harvest's heart than
in a sieve or a dust-box. Suppose you were a craftsman, or

96. A pun on a cold in the head and a puzzle.
97. A popular tune of a melancholy character often referred to.
98. Proverbial ('You had on your harvest ears, thick of hearing,'
Heywood's Proverbs).

an artificer, and should come to buy corn of me, you should have bushels of me: not like the baker's loaf that should weigh but six ounces, but usury for your money, thousands for one. [99] What would you have more? Eat me out of my apparel if you will, if you suspect me for a miser.

SUMMER: I credit thee, and think thou wert belied. But tell me, hadst thou a good crop this year?

HARVEST: Hay, God's plenty, which was so sweet and so good, that when I jerted [100] my whip and said to my horses but 'Hay', they would go as they were mad.

SUMMER: But 'hay' alone thou say'st not, but 'Hay-ree'.

HARVEST: I sing 'hay-ree', that is 'hay and rye', meaning that they shall have hay and rye their belly-fulls, if they will draw hard. So we say 'Wa hay', when they go out of the way, meaning that they shall want hay if they will not do as they should do.

SUMMER: How thrive thy oats, thy barley and thy wheat?

HARVEST: My oats grow like a cup of beer that makes the brewer grow rich; my rye, like a cavalier that wears a huge feather in his cap but hath no courage in his heart, had a long stalk, a goodly husk, but nothing so great a kernel as it was wont. My barley, even as many a novice is crossbitten as soon as ever he peeps out of the shell, so was it frost-bitten in the blade, yet picked up his crumbs again afterward, and bade 'Fill pot, hostess', in spite of a dear year. As for my pease and my fetches, [101] they are famous and not to be spoken of.

AUTUMN: Ay, ay, such country buttoned-caps as you do want no fetches to undo great towns.

HARVEST: Will you make good your words, that we want no fetches?

WINTER: Ay, that he shall.

HARVEST: Then fetch us a cloak-bag, to carry away yourself in.

99. *baker's loaf . . . thousands for one*: Meaning unknown.
100. Jerked, cracked.
101. Vetches.

SUMMER: Plough-swains are blunt, and will taunt bitterly.
Harvest, when all is done, thou art the man,
Thou doest me the best service of them all.
Rest from thy labours till the year renews,
And let the husbandmen sing of thy praise.

HARVEST: Rest from my labours, and let the husbandmen
sing of my praise? Nay, we do not mean to rest so. By
your leave, we'll have a largesse amongst you ere we part.

ALL: A largesse, a largesse, a largesse!

WILL SUMMERS: Is there no man that will give them a hiss
for a largesse?[102]

HARVEST: No, that there is not, goodman Lundgis.[103] I see
charity waxeth cold, and I think this house be her habitation, for it is not very hot. We are as good even put up our
pipes and sing 'Merry, merry', for we shall get no money.

[*Here they go out all singing.*]

Merry, merry, merry, cherry, cherry, cherry,
Trowl the black bowl to me.
Hey derry, derry, with a poop and a lerry,
I'll trowl it again to thee.
Hooky, hooky, we have shorn and we have bound,
And we have brought Harvest Home to town.

WILL SUMMERS: Well, go thy ways, thou bundle of straw.
I'll give thee this gift: thou shalt be a clown while thou
liv'st. As lusty as they are, they run on the score with
George's wife for their posset, and God knows who shall
pay Goodman Yeomans for his wheatsheaf. They may
sing well enough 'Trowl the black bowl to me, trowl the
black bowl to me', for a hundred to one but they will be
all drunk ere they go to bed. Yet of a slavering fool that
hath no conceit in anything but in carrying a wand in his
hand with commendation when he runneth by the highway side, this stripling Harvest hath done reasonable well.

102. A pun on large 'S'.
103. 'A long slim awkward fellow . . . a lout, a laggard, a lingerer'
(NED).

Oh that somebody had had the wit to set his thatched suit
on fire, and so lighted him out. If I had had but a jet ring
on my finger, I might have done with him what I list. I had
spoiled him, I had took his apparel prisoner; for, it being
made of straw, and the nature of jet to draw straw unto
it, I would have nailed him to the pommel of my chair
till the play were done and then have carried him to my
chamber door, and laid him at the threshold as a wisp, or
a piece of mat, to wipe my shoes on every time I come up
dirty.

SUMMER: Vertumnus, call Bacchus!

VERTUMNUS: Bacchus, Baccha, Bacchum, god Bacchus,
god fatback!

Baron of double beer and bottle ale,
Come in and show thy nose that is nothing pale.

Back, back there, god barrel-belly may enter!
[*Enter Bacchus riding upon an ass trapped in ivy, himself
dressed in vine-leaves, and a garland of grapes on his head,
his companions having all jacks in their hands and ivy garlands on their heads. They come in singing.*]

THE SONG
Monsieur Mingo[104] for quaffing doth surpass,
In cup, in can, or glass.
God Bacchus, do me right,
And dub me Knight Domingo.

BACCHUS: Wherefore didst thou call me, Vertumnus? Hast
any drink to give me? One of you hold my ass while I
light. Walk him up and down the hall, till I talk a word or
two.

SUMMER: What, Bacchus? Still *animus in patinis*,[105] no
mind but on the pot?

BACCHUS: Why, Summer, Summer, how wouldst do but
for rain? What is a fair house without water coming to it?

104. Domingo, popular term for drunkard.
105. 'His mind is on his dinner' (Terence).

Let me see how a smith can work if he have not his trough standing by him. What sets an edge on a knife? The grindstone alone? No, the moist element poured upon it, which grinds out all gaps, sets a point upon it, and scours it as bright as the firmament. So, I tell thee, give a soldier wine before he goes to battle, it grinds out all gaps, it makes him forget all scars and wounds, and fight in the thickest of his enemies as though he were but at foils amongst his fellows. Give a scholar wine, going to his book, or being about to invent, it sets a new point on his wit, it glazeth it, it scours it, it gives him acumen. Plato saith *vinum esse fomitem quemdam, et incitabilem ingenii virtutisque*.[106] Aristotle saith: *Nulla est magna scientia absque mixtura dementiae*: 'There is no excellent knowledge without mixture of madness.' And what makes a man more mad in the head than wine? *Qui bene vult poyein, debet ante pinyen*: 'he that will do well must drink well.' *Prome, prome, potum prome*: 'Ho, butler, a fresh pot!' *Nunc est bibendum, nunc pede libero terra pulsanda*.[107] A pox on him that leaves his drink behind him! Hey, *Rendezvous*![108]

SUMMER: It is wine's custom to be full of words: I prithee, Bacchus, give us *vicissitudinem loquendi*.[109]

BACCHUS: A fiddlestick! Ne'er tell me I am full of words. *Faecundi calices, quem non fecere disertum?*[110] *Aut epi, aut abi*: 'either take your drink, or you are an infidel.'

SUMMER: I would about thy vintage question thee. How thrive thy vines? Hadst thou good store of grapes?

BACCHUS: *Vinum quasi venenum*. Wine is poison to a sick body; a sick body is no sound body; *ergo*, wine is a pure thing and is poison to all corruption. Trilill, the hunters'

---

106. 'Wine is a sort of kindling and tinder to the brain and the faculties' (Aulus Gellius).

107. 'Now is the time for drinking and for beating the ground with unrestrained feet' (Horace).

108. Probably a drinking term.

109. 'A conversational interchange'.

110. 'Eloquent cups, whom have they not made a good speaker!'

hoop[111] to you. I'll stand to it, Alexander was a brave man and yet an arrant drunkard.

WINTER: Fie, drunken sot, forget'st thou where thou art? My Lord asks thee what vintage thou hast made.

BACCHUS: Our vintage was a vintage, for it did not work upon the advantage.[112] It came in the vanguard of summer,

> And winds and storms met it by the way,
> And made it cry 'Alas and welladay'.

SUMMER: That was not well, but all miscarried not?

BACCHUS: Faith, shall I tell you no lie? Because you are my countryman and so forth, and a good fellow is a good fellow, though he have never a penny in his purse. We had but even pot-luck, a little to moisten our lips, and no more. That same Sol is a pagan and a proselyte.[113] He shined so bright all summer that he burned more grapes than his beams were worth, were every beam as big as a weaver's beam. *A fabis abstinendum*:[114] faith, he should have abstained. For what is flesh and blood without his liquor?

AUTUMN: Thou want'st no liquor, nor no flesh and blood. I pray thee, may I ask without offence? How many tuns of wine hast in thy paunch? Methinks that belly, built like a round church, Should yet have some of Julius Caesar's wine. I warrant, 'twas not broach'd this hundred year.

BACCHUS: Hearest thou, dough-belly? Because thou talk'st, and talk'st, and dar'st not drink to me a black jack, wilt thou give me leave to broach this little kilderkin[115] of my corpse against thy back? I know thou art but a micher,[116]

---

111. *the hunters' hoop*: Apparently a drink measure.

112. *Our vintage ... advantage*: M. believes there is something wrong with the text.

113. A convert to Judaism.

114. Literally 'Abstaining from beans'; one of Pythagoras' enigmatical precepts.

115. A half-barrel (sixteen to eighteen gallons).

116. Petty thief, general term of contempt.

and dar'st not stand me. *A vous, Monsieur Winter,* a frolic upsey-freeze. Cross, ho! *Super nagulum!* [117]
[*Knocks the jack upon his thumb.*]

WINTER: Grammercy, Bacchus, as much as though I did. For this time thou must pardon me perforce.

BACCHUS: What, give me the disgrace? Go to, I am no pope to pardon any man. *Ran, ran, tarra:* cold beer makes good blood. Saint George for England: somewhat is better than nothing! Let me see: hast thou done me justice? Why so, thou art a king, though there were no more kings in the cards but the knave. Summer, wilt thou have a demi-culverin,[118] that shall cry 'Hufty Tufty' and make thy cup fly fine meal in the element? [119]

SUMMER: No, keep thy drink, I pray thee, to thyself.

BACCHUS: This Pupillonian in the fool's coat shall have a cast of martins and a whiff.[120] To the health of Captain Rinocerotry![121] Look to it, let him have weight and measure.

WILL SUMMERS: What an ass is this! I cannot drink so much, though I should burst.

BACCHUS: Fool, do not refuse your moist sustenance. Come, come, dog's head in the pot,[122] do what you are born to!

WILL SUMMERS: If you will needs make me a drunkard against my will, so it is. I'll try what burthen my belly is of.

BACCHUS: Crouch, crouch on your knees, fool, when you pledge god Bacchus.

[*Here Will Summers drinks, and they sing about him. Bacchus begins*]

ALL: Monsieur Mingo for quaffing did surpass,
    In cup, in can, or glass.

---

117. *upsey-freeze.* ... Super nagulum: Drinking terms (for *super nagulum* see *Pierce Penniless,* N.'s note, p. 105).
118. A small gun or cannon.
119. *make thy cup ... element:* Meaning unknown.
120. *This Pupillonian ... whif:* Meaning unknown.
121. Meaning unknown.
122. *dog's ... pot:* Glutton, term of abuse.

BACCHUS: Ho, well shot! A toucher,[123] a toucher! For quaffing Toy doth pass, in cup, in can, or glass.

ALL: God Bacchus do him right,
And dub him knight.

[*Here he dubs Will Summers with the black jack.*]

BACCHUS: Rise up, Sir Robert Tosspot.

SUMMER: No more of this, I hate it to the death.
No such deformer of the soul and sense
As is this swinish damn'd-born drunkenness.
Bacchus, for thou abusest so earth's fruits,
Imprisoned live in cellars and in vaults.
Let none commit their counsels unto thee;
Thy wrath be fatal to thy dearest friends;
Unarmed run upon thy foeman's swords;
Never fear any plague before it fall;
Dropsies and watery tympanies[124] haunt thee,
Thy lungs with surfeiting be putrefied,
To cause thee have an odious stinking breath.
Slaver and drivel like a child at mouth;
Be poor and beggarly in thy old age;
Let thy own kinsmen laugh when thou complain'st,
And many tears gain nothing but blind scoffs.
This is the guerdon[125] due to drunkenness;
Shame, sickness, misery, follow excess.

BACCHUS: Now on my honour, Sim Summer, thou art a bad member, a dunce, a mongrel, to discredit so worshipful an art after this order. Thou hast cursed me, and I will bless thee. Never cup of nippitaty[126] in London come near thy niggardly habitation. I beseech the gods of good fellowship, thou may'st fall into a consumption with drinking small beer. Every day may'st thou eat fish, and let it stick in the midst of thy maw for want of a cup of wine to swim away in. Venison be venenum[127] to thee, and may that vintner have the plague in his house that sells thee a drop

123. 'A bowl which touches the jack' (NED); here a pun on 'jack' meaning a drinking vessel.
124. Swellings.   125. Reward.
126. Strong ale.   127. Poison.

of claret to kill the poison of it. As many wounds may'st thou have as Caesar had in the Senate House, and get no white wine to wash them with. And to conclude, pine away in melancholy and sorrow, before thou hast the fourth part of a dram of my juice to cheer up thy spirits.

SUMMER: Hale him away! He barketh like a wolf. It is his drink, not he, that rails on us.

BACCHUS: Nay, soft, brother Summer. Back with that foot. Here is a snuff[128] in the bottom of the jack, enough to light a man to bed withal. We'll leave no flocks behind us, whatsoever we do.

SUMMER: Go drag him hence, I say, when I command.

BACCHUS: Since we must needs go, let's go merrily. Farewell, Sir Robert Tosspot. Sing amain 'Monsieur Mingo' whilst I mount up my ass.

[*Here they go out singing 'Monsieur Mingo' as they came in.*]

WILL SUMMERS: Of all gods, this Bacchus is the ill-favourd'st, misshapen god that ever I saw. A pox on him, he hath christened me with a new nickname of Sir Robert Tosspot, that will not part from me this twelvemonth. Ned Fool's clothes are so perfumed with the beer he poured on me that there shall not be a Dutchman[129] within twenty mile, but he'll smell out and claim kindred of him. What a beastly thing is it, to bottle up ale in a man's belly, when a man must set his guts on a gallon pot last, only to purchase the alehouse title of a boon companion? 'Carouse, pledge me and you dare!' 'Swounds, I'll drink with thee for all thou art worth!' It is even as two men should strive who should run furthest into the sea for a wager. Methinks these are good household terms: 'Will it please you to be here, sir? I commend me to you. Shall I be so bold as trouble you? Saving your tale, I drink to you.' And if these were put in practice but a year or two in taverns, wine would soon fall from six and twenty pound a tun, and be beggar's money, a penny a quart, and

128. Dregs (and candle end).
129. A reference to the Dutch as proverbial drunkards.

take up his inn with waste beer in the alms tub. I am a
sinner as others: I must not say much of this argument.
Everyone, when he is whole, can give advice to them that
are sick. My masters, you that be good fellows, get you
into corners and sup off your provender closely. Report
hath a blister on her tongue; open taverns are tell-tales.
Non peccat quicunque potest peccasse negare.[130]

SUMMER: I'll call my servants to account, said I?
A bad account: worse servants no man hath.
Quos credis fidos effuge, tutus eris:[131]
The proverb I have prov'd to be too true.
Totidem domi hostes habemus, quot servos.[132]
And that wise caution of Democritus:
Servus necessaria possessio, non autem dulcis:[133]
Now here fidelity and labour dwells.
Hope-young [134] heads count to build on had-I-wist.
Conscience but few respect; all hunt for gain.
Except the camel have his provender
Hung at his mouth, he will not travel on.
Tyresias to Narcissus promised
Much prosperous hap and many golden days,
If of his beauty he no knowledge took.
Knowledge breeds pride, pride breedeth discontent.
Black discontent, thou urgest to revenge.
Revenge opes not her ears to poor men's prayers.
That dolt destruction is she without doubt,
That hales her forth and feedeth her with nought.
Simplicity and plainness, you I love:
Hence, double diligence, thou mean'st deceit.
Those that now serpent-like creep on the ground,
And seem to eat the dust, they crouch so low,
If they be disappointed of their prey,

130. 'The man that denies that he has sinned does not sin' (Ovid).
131. 'Flee from the people you believe are faithful, and you will
be safe' (Ovid).
132. 'As many enemies have we at home as we have servants'
(Seneca).
133. 'A slave is a necessary possession, but not a pleasant one.'
134. 'Young hopefuls always reckon to prosper out of ignorance.'

Most traitorously will trace [135] their tails and sting.
Yea, such as, like the lapwing, build their nests
In a man's dung, come up by drudgery,
Will be the first that, like that foolish bird,
Will follow him with yelling and false cries.
Well sung a shepherd, that now sleeps in skies,
'Dumb swans do love, and not vain chattering pies.' [136]
In mountains, poets [137] say, Echo is hid,
For her deformity and monstrous shape.
Those mountains are the houses of great lords,
Where Stentor [138] with his hundred voices sounds
A hundred trumps at once with rumour filled.
A woman they imagine her to be,
Because that sex keeps nothing close they hear;
And that's the reason magic writers [139] frame
There are more witches women than of men,
For women generally, for the most part,
Of secrets more desirous are than men,
Which having got, they have no power to hold.
In these times had Echo's first fathers lived,
No woman, but a man, she had been feign'd
(Though women yet will want [140] no news to prate).
For men, mean men, the scum and dross of all,
Will talk and babble of they know not what,
Upbraid, deprave, and taunt they care not whom.
Surmises pass for sound approved truths;
Familiarity and conference,
That were the sinews of societies,
Are now for underminings only us'd,
And novel wits, that love none but themselves,

135. Raise.
136. *Dumb swans ... pies*: Adapted from Sidney's *Astrophel and Stella*, sonnet fifty-four.
137. e.g. Ovid (*Metamorphoses*, II, 395–401).
138. A Greek in the Trojan War who could shout as loud as fifty men.
139. e.g. Cornelius Agrippa (*De Incertitudine et Vanitate Scientiarum*).
140. Lack.

Think wisdom's height as falsehood slyly couch'd,
Seeking each other to o'erthrow his mate.
Oh friendship, thy old temple is defac'd.
Embracing every guileful courtesy [141]
Hath overgrown fraud-wanting honesty.
Examples live but in the idle schools:
Sinon [142] bears all the sway in princes' courts.
Sickness, be thou my soul's physician:
Bring the apothecary Death with thee.
In earth is hell, true hell felicity,
Compared with this world, the den of wolves.

AUTUMN: My lord, you are too passionate without cause.
WINTER: Grieve not for that which cannot be recall'd.
Is it your servants' carelessness you plain? [143]
Tully, by one of his own slaves was slain.
The husbandman close in his bosom nurs'd
A subtle snake, that after wraught his bane.[144]

AUTUMN: *Servos fideles liberalitas facit;*[145]
Where on the contrary, *servitutem*: [146]
Those that attend upon illiberal lords,
Whose covetise yields nought else but fair looks,
Even of those fair looks make their gainful use.
For, as in Ireland[147] and in Denmark both,
Witches for gold will sell a man a wind,
Which, in the corner of a napkin wrapp'd,
Shall blow him safe unto what coast he will,
So make ill servants sale of their lord's wind,[148]
Which, wrapp'd up in a piece of parchment,

141. *Embracing ... courtesy*: Hazlitt emends to read 'Embracing envy, guileless courtesy . . .'
142. Persuaded the Trojans to take in the wooden horse; used here as typical traitor.
143. Complain of.
144. *wraught his bane*: Made the poison that killed him.
145. 'Generosity makes servants faithful' (Plautus).
146. Slavery (i.e. harshness in the master makes mere servitude).
147. M. suggests Iceland, with which there is some authority to associate this legend.
148. Also means 'favours'.

Blows many a knave forth danger of the law.
SUMMER: Enough of this: let me go make my will.
  Ah, it is made; although I hold my peace,
  These two will share betwixt them what I have.
  The surest way to get my will perform'd,
  Is to make my executor my heir;
  And he, if all be given him, and none else,
  Unfallibly will see it well perform'd.
  Lions will feed, though none bid them go to.
  Ill grows the tree affordeth ne'er a graft.
  Had I some issue to sit in my throne,
  My grief would die, death should not hear me groan.
  But when perforce these must enjoy my wealth,
  Which thank me not, but enter't as a prey,
  Bequeath'd it is not, but clean cast away.
  Autumn, be thou successor of my seat:
  Hold, take my crown – look how he grasps for it!
  Thou shalt not have it yet – but hold it too.
  Why should I keep that needs I must forgo?
WINTER: Then (duty laid aside) you do me wrong.
  I am more worthy of it far than he.
  He hath no skill nor courage for to rule;
  A weather-beaten bankrout [149] ass it is,
  That scatters and consumeth all he hath;
  Each one do pluck from him without control.
  He is nor hot nor cold, a silly soul,
  That fain would please each party, if so he might.
  He and the Spring are scholars' favourites.
  What scholars are, what thriftless kind of men,
  Yourself be judge, and judge of him by them.
  When Cerberus was headlong drawn from hell,
  He voided a back poison from his mouth,
  Called aconitum, whereof ink was made;
  That ink, with reeds first laid on dried barks,
  Serv'd men a while to make rude works withal,
  Till Hermes, secretary to the gods,
  Or Hermes Trismegistus, as some will,

149. Bankrupt.

Weary with graving in blind characters,
And figures of familiar beasts and plants,
Invented letters to write withal.
In them he penn'd the fables of the gods,
The giants' war, and thousand tales besides.
After each nation got these toys in use,
There grew up certain drunken parasites,
Term'd poets, which, for a meal's meat or two,
Would promise monarchs immortality.
They vomited in verse all that they knew,
Found causes and beginnings of the world,
Fetch'd pedigrees of mountains and of floods
From men and women whom the gods transform'd.
If any town or city they pass'd by
Had in compassion (thinking them mad men)
Forborne to whip them, or imprison them,
That city was not built by human hands,
'Twas raised by music, like Megara walls.[150]
Apollo, poets' patron, founded it,
Because they found one fitting favour there;
Musaeus, Linus, Homer, Orpheus,
Were of this trade, and thereby won their fame.

WILL SUMMERS: *Fama malum, quo non velocius ullum.*[151]

WINTER: Next them, a company of ragged knaves,
Sun-bathing beggars, lazy hedge-creepers,
Sleeping face-upwards in the fields all night,
Dream'd strange devices of the sun and moon;
And they, like gypsies, wandering up and down,
Told fortunes, juggled, nicknamed all the stars,
And were of idiots term'd philosophers.
Such was Pythagoras the silencer,[152]
Prometheus, Thales Milesius,

150. Built by Alcathous, with the assistance of Apollo, who rested his lyre on the 'singing stone'.
151. 'Ill-rumour, than which nothing is swifter' (Virgil).
152. Five years' silence is said to have been required of pupils in the school of Pythagoras.

Who would all things of water should be made,[153]
Anaximander, Anaximenes,
That positively said the air was god,
Zenocrates, that said there were eight gods,
And Cratoniates Alcmeon too,
Who thought the sun and moon and stars were gods;
The poorer sort of them, that could get nought,
Profess'd, like beggarly Franciscan friars,
And the strict order of the Capuchins,
A voluntary wretched poverty,
Contempt of gold, thin fare, and lying hard;
Yet he that was most vehement in these,
Diogenes the cynic and the dog,
  Was taken coining money in his cell.

WILL SUMMERS: What an old ass was that! Methinks, he
should have coined carrot roots rather; for, as for money,
he had no use for't, except it were to melt, and solder up
holes in his tub withal.

WINTER: It were a whole Olympiad's work to tell
How many devilish (*ergo* armed) arts,
Sprung all, as vices, of this idleness;
For even as soldiers not employed in wars,
But living loosely in a quiet state,
Not having wherewithal to maintain pride,
Nay, scarce to find their bellies any food,
Nought but walk melancholy, and devise
How they may cozen merchants, fleece young heirs,
Creep into favour by betraying men,
Rob churches, beg waste toys, court city dames,
(Who shall undo their husbands for their sakes),
The baser rabble how to cheat and steal,
And yet be free from penalty of death,
So those word-warriors, lazy star-gazers,
Us'd to no labour but to louse [154] themselves,
Had their heads fill'd with cozening fantasies,

153. *Thales Milesius ... made*: again from Cornelius Agrippa
(*De Incertitudine*).
154. Ruin, destroy (archaic verb 'lose').

They plotted how to make their poverty
Better esteem'd of than high sovereignty.
They thought how they might plant a heaven on earth,
Whereof they would be principal low gods,
That heaven they called Contemplation,
As much to say as a most pleasant sloth;
Which better I cannot compare than this,
That if a fellow licensed to beg
Should all his lifetime go from fair to fair,
And buy gape-seed,[155] having no business else.
That contemplation, like an aged weed,
Engender'd thousand sects, and all those sects
Were but as these times, cunning shrouded rogues:
Grammarians some; and wherein differ they
From beggars, that profess the pedlars' French?
The poets next, slovenly tatter'd slaves,
That wander, and sell ballets in the streets.
Historiographers others there be,
And they, like lazars by the highway-side,
That for a penny, or a half-penny,
Will call each knave a good-fac'd gentleman,
Give honour unto tinkers for good ale,
Prefer a cobbler fore the Black Prince far,
If he bestow but blacking of their shoes;
And, as it is the spital-houses' guise
Over the gate to write their founders' names,
Or on the outside of their walls at least,
In hope by their examples others mov'd
Will be more bountiful and liberal;
So in the forefront of their chronicles,
Or *peroratione operis*,[156]
They learning's benefactors reckon up:
Who built this college, who gave that free-school,
What king or queen advanced scholars most,
And in their times what writers flourished;
Rich men and magistrates, whilst yet they live,

155. Go sight-seeing.
156. 'In the work's peroration'.

They flatter palpably, in hope of gain.
Smooth-tongued orators, the fourth in place,
Lawyers our commonwealth entitles them,
Mere swashbucklers and ruffianly mates,
That will for twelve pence make a doughty fray,
Set men for straws together by the ears.
Sky-measuring mathematicians,
Gold-breathing alchemists also we have,
Both which are subtle witty humorists,
That get their meals by telling miracles,
Which they have seen in travelling the skies;
Vain boasters, liars, make-shifts, they are all,
Men that, removed from their inkhorn terms,
Bring forth no action worthy of their bread.
What should I speak of pale physicians?
Who as Fismenus *non Nasutus* [157] was
(Upon a wager that his friends had laid)
Hir'd to live in a privy a whole year;
So are they hir'd for lucre and for gain,
All their whole life to smell on excrements.

WILL SUMMERS: Very true, for I have heard it for a
proverb many a time and oft: *Hunc os foetidum*,[158] fah,
he stinks like a physician!

WINTER: Innumerable monstrous practices
Hath loitering contemplation brought forth more,
Which 'twere too long particular to recite.
Suffice, they all conduce unto this end:
To banish labour, nourish slothfulness,
Pamper up lust, devise newfangled sins.
Nay, I will justify there is no vice,
Which learning and vild knowledge brought not in,
Or in whose praise some learned have not wrote.
The art of murther Machiavel hath penn'd;
Whoredom hath Ovid to uphold her throne,

157. *Fismenus* non Nasutus: A character without a nose, and having
no sense of smell.

158. (Perhaps this should read 'Huic'.) 'This stinking mouth'; a
phrase used in association with the Devil.

And Aretine of late in Italy,
Whose *Cortigiana*[159] toucheth bawds their trade.
Gluttony Epicurus doth defend,
And books of th'art of cookery confirm,
Of which Platina[160] hath not writ the least.
Drunkenness of his good behaviour
Hath testimonial from where he was born:
That pleasant work *De Arte Bibendi*[161]
A drunken Dutchman spew'd out few years since.
Nor wanteth Sloth, although sloth's plague be want,
His paper pillars for to lean upon:
The Praise of Nothing pleads his worthiness:
Folly Erasmus sets a flourish on.
For baldness, a bald ass I have forgot
Patch'd up a pamphletary periwig.
Slovenry Grobianus magnifieth;
Sodomitry a cardinal commends,
And Aristotle necessary deems.
In brief, all books, divinity except,
Are nought but tables of the devil's laws,
Poison wrapt up in sugared words,
Man's pride, damnation's props, the world's abuse.
Then censure, good my lord, what bookmen are,
If they be pestilent members in a state.
He is unfit to sit at stern of state
That favours such as will o'erthrow his state.
Blest is that government where no art thrives.
Vox populi, vox Dei:
'The vulgar's voice, it is the voice of God.'
Yet Tully saith: *Non est consilium in vulgo, non ratio,
Non discrimen, non differentia*:[162]
'The vulgar have no learning, wit, nor sense.'
Themistocles, having spent all his time
In study of philosophy and arts,
And noting well the vanity of them,

159. 'The Courtesan'. 160. Bartholomaeus Sacchi, *fl.* 1475.
161. 'On the Art of Drinking' (V. Obsopaeus, 1536).
162. Cicero, *Pro Plancio* (defence of Gnaius Plancius), IV, 9.

Wish'd, with repentance for his folly past,
Some would teach him th'art of oblivion,
How to forget the arts that he had learn'd.
And Cicero, whom we alleg'd before,
As saith Valerius, stepping into old age,
Despised learning, loathed eloquence.
Naso,[163] that could speak nothing but pure verse,
And had more wit than words to utter it,
And words as choice as ever poet had,
Cried and exclaim'd in bitter agony,
When knowledge had corrupted his chaste mind:
Discite, qui sapitis, non haec quae scimus inertes,
Sed trepidas acies, et fera bella sequi.[164]
'You that be wise, and ever mean to thrive,
Oh, study not these toys we sluggards use,
But follow arms, and wait on barbarous wars.'
Young men, young boys, beware of schoolmasters,
They will infect you, mar you, blear your eyes;
They seek to lay the curse of God on you,
Namely, confusion of languages,
Wherewith those that the Tower of Babel built
Accursed were in the world's infancy.
Latin, it was the speech of infidels.
Logic hath nought to say in a true cause.
Philosophy is curiosity;
And Socrates was therefore put to death,
Only for he was a philosopher.
Abhor, contemn, despise these damned snares.

WILL SUMMERS: Out upon it, who would be a scholar?
Not I, I promise you. My mind always gave me this learn-
ing was such a filthy thing, which made me hate it so as
I did. When I should have been at school, construing
Batte, mi fili, mi fili, mi batte, I was close under a hedge,
or under a barn wall, playing at span counter[165] or jack

163. Ovid (Ovidius Naso, 43 B.C.–A.D. 17).
164. *Amores*, III, 8, 25–6.
165. One player throws his counter; another has to throw within a
a span of it.

in a box. My master beat me, my father beat me, my mother gave me bread and butter, yet all this would not make me a squitter-book.[166] It was my destiny: I thank her as a most gorgeous goddess, that she hath not cast me away upon gibridge.[167] Oh, in what a mighty vein am I now against horn-books![168] Here, before all this company, I profess myself an open enemy to ink and paper. I'll make it good upon the accidence body, that in speech is the devil's *Pater noster*. Nouns and pronouns, I pronounce you as traitors to boys' buttocks. Syntaxis and prosodia, you are tormenters of wit, and good for nothing but to get a schoolmaster twopence a week. Hang copies; fly out, phrase books; let pens be turned to pick-tooths! Bowls, cards and dice, you are the true liberal sciences! I'll ne'er be a goosequill, gentlemen, while I live.

SUMMER: Winter, with patience unto my grief
I have attended thy invective tale.
So much untruth wit never shadowed.
Gainst her own bowels thou art's weapons turn'st.
Let none believe thee that will ever thrive;
Words have their course, the wind blows where it lists;
He errs alone, in error that persists.
For thou gainst Autumn such exceptions tak'st,
I grant his over-seer thou shalt be,
His treasurer, protector, and his staff.
He shall do nothing without thy consent;
Provide thou for his weal and his content.

WINTER: Thanks, gracious lord; so I'll dispose of him,
As it shall not repent you of your gift.

AUTUMN: On such conditions no crown will I take.
I challenge Winter for my enemy,
A most insatiate miserable carl,
That, to fill up his garners to the brim,
Cares not how he endangereth the earth;
What poverty he makes it to endure!
He over-bars the crystal streams with ice,

166. Bookworm.   167. Gibberish, nonsense.
168. Schoolboys' textbooks.

That none but he and his may drink of them.
All for a foul back-winter [169] he lays up;
Hard craggy ways and uncouth slippery paths
He frames, that passengers may slide and fall.
Who quaketh not that heareth but his name?
Oh, but two sons he hath, worse than himself:
Christmas the one, a pinch-back,[170] cut-throat churl,
That keeps no open house, as he should do,
Delighteth in no game or fellowship,
Loves no good deeds, and hateth talk,
But sitteth in a corner turning crabs,
Or coughing o'er a warmed pot of ale;
Back-winter th'other, that's his n'own sweet boy,
Who like his father taketh in all points.[171]
An elf [172] it is, compact of envious pride,
A miscreant, born for a plague to men,
A monster, that devoureth all he meets.
Were but his father dead, so he would reign;
Yea, he would go good near [173] to deal by him
As Nabuchodonozor's ungracious son
Evilmerodach by his father dealt,
Who, when his sire was turned to an oxe,
Full greedily snatch'd up his sovereignty,
And thought himself a king without control.
So it fell out, seven years expir'd and gone,
Nabuchodonozor came to his shape again,
And dispossess'd him of his regiment;
Which my young prince no little grieving at,
When that his father shortly after died,
Fearing lest he should come from death again,
As he came from an oxe to be a man,
Will'd that his body, spoil'd of coverture,[174]

169. The return of wintry conditions late in the season.
170. Pinchbeck, miser.
171. *Who like . . . points*: Who takes after his father in everything.
172. Mischievous creature.
173. Very near.
174. Taken out of its grave.

Should be cast forth into the open fields,
For birds and ravens to devour at will,
Thinking, if they bare every one of them
A bill full of his flesh into their nests,
He would not rise to trouble him in haste.

WILL SUMMERS: A virtuous son, and I'll lay my life on't,
he was a cavalier and a good fellow.[175]

WINTER: Pleaseth your honour, all he says is false.
For my own part, I love good husbandry,
But hate dishonourable covetise.
Youth ne'er aspires to virtue's perfect growth,
Till his wild oats be sown; and so the earth,
Until his weeds be rotted with my frosts,
Is not for any seed or tillage fit.
He must be purged that hath surfeited:
The fields have surfeited with summer fruits;
They must be purg'd, made poor, oppress'd with snow,
Ere they recover their decayed pride.
For overbarring of the streams with ice,
Who locks not poison from his children's taste?
When Winter reigns, the water is so cold,
That it is poison, present death to those
That wash, or bathe their limbs in his cold streams.
The slipp'rier that ways are under us,
The better it makes us to heed our steps,
And look ere we presume too rashly on.
If that my sons have misbehav'd themselves,
A God's name let them answer't fore my lord.

AUTUMN: Now I beseech your Honour it may be so.

SUMMER: With all my heart. Vertumnus, go for them.

[Exit Vertumnus.]

WILL SUMMERS: This same Harry Baker [176] is such a
necessary fellow to go on errands, as you shall not find
in a country. It is pity but he should have another silver
arrow, if it be but for crossing the stage with his cap
on.

175. A dashing gallant and a good chap (often used ironically).
176. Perhaps the actor's name.

194

SUMMER: To weary out the time until they come,
Sing me some doleful ditty to the lute,
That may complain my near-approaching death.

THE SONG

Adieu, farewell earth's bliss,
This world uncertain is,
Fond are life's lustful joys,
Death proves them all but toys,
None from his darts can fly;
I am sick, I must die:
  Lord, have mercy on us.

Rich men, trust not in wealth,
Gold cannot buy you health;
Physick himself must fade.
All things to end are made,
The plague full swift goes by;
I am sick, I must die:
  Lord, have mercy on us.

Beauty is but a flower,
Which wrinkles will devour,
Brightness falls from the air,[177]
Queens have died young and fair,
Dust hath closed Helen's eye.
I am sick, I must die:
  Lord, have mercy on us.

Strength stoops unto the grave,
Worms feed on Hector brave,
Swords may not fight with fate,
Earth still holds ope her gate.
Come, come, the bells do cry.
I am sick, I must die:
  Lord, have mercy on us.

177. M. mentions the possibility that this is a misprint for 'hair'.

Wit with his wantonness,
Tasteth death's bitterness:
Hell's executioner
Hath no ears for to hear
What vain art can reply.
I am sick, I must die:
    Lord, have mercy on us.

Haste therefore each degree,
To welcome destiny:
Heaven is our heritage,
Earth but a player's stage,
Mount we unto the sky.
I am sick, I must die:
    Lord, have mercy on us.

SUMMER: Beshrew me, but thy song hath moved me.

WILL SUMMERS: Lord, have mercy on us. How lamentable
'tis!

[*Enter Vertumnus with Christmas and Backwinter.*]

VERTUMNUS: I have dispatched, my Lord. I have brought
you them you sent me for.

WILL SUMMERS: What say'st thou? Hast thou made a
good batch? [178] I pray thee, give me a new loaf.

SUMMER: Christmas, how chance thou com'st not as the
rest,
Accompanied with some music, or some song?
A merry carol would have grac'd thee well;
Thy ancestors have us'd it heretofore.

CHRISTMAS: Ay, antiquity was the mother of ignorance.
This latter world, that sees but with her spectacles, hath
spied a pad [179] in those sports more than they could.

SUMMER: What, is't against thy conscience for to sing?

CHRISTMAS: No, nor to say, by my troth, if I may get a
good bargain.

178. Taking up the sound of the word 'dispatched', leading to pun
on 'baker', name of the actor who played Vertumnus.
179. Toad (cf., popular expression 'a toad in the straw').

SUMMER: Why, thou should'st spend; thou should'st not care to get. Christmas is god of hospitality.

CHRISTMAS: So will he never be of good husbandry. I may say to you, there is many an old god that is now grown out of fashion. So is the god of hospitality.

SUMMER: What reason canst thou give he should be left?

CHRISTMAS: No other reason but that Gluttony is a sin, and too many dunghills are infectious. A man's belly was not made for a powdering-beef tub.[180] To feed the poor twelve days and let them starve all the year after would but stretch out the guts wider than they should be, and so make famine a bigger den in their bellies than he had before. I should kill an oxe and have some such fellow as Milo[181] to come and eat it up at a mouthful; or, like the Sybarites,[182] do nothing all one year but bid guests against the next year. The scraping of trenchers you think would put a man to no charges. It is not a hundred pound a year would serve the scullions in dishclouts. My house stands upon vaults; it will fall if it be overladen with a multitude. Besides, have you never read of a city that was undermined and destroyed by moles?[183] So, say I keep hospitality and bid me a whole fair of beggars[184] to dinner every day, what with making legs[185] when they thank me at their going away, and settling their wallets handsomely on their backs, they would shake as many lice on the ground as were able to undermine my house and undo me utterly. It is their prayers would built it again, if it were overthrown by this vermin, would it? I pray: who began feasting and gourmandize first, but Sardanapalus, Nero, Heliogabalus,

180. Tub for salting and pickling beef.

181. Trained himself to carry a bull; the story of his eating a whole ox is in Athenaeus, *Deipnosophistae*, X.

182. N. refers again in margin note to *Lenten Stuff* ('The Sybarites never would make any banquet under a twelve month's warning').

183. *city ... moles*: Thessalia, according to Lyly (M.).

184. *bid me ... beggars*: Emended from 'a whole fair of beggars bid me'.

185. Bowing.

Commodus, tyrants, whoremasters, unthrifts? Some call them Emperors, but I respect no crowns but crowns in the purse. Any man may wear a silver crown that hath made a fray in Smithfield, and lost but a piece of his brain-pan. And to tell you plainly, your golden crowns are little better in substance and many times got after the same sort.

SUMMER: Gross-headed sot, how light he makes of state!

AUTUMN: Who treadeth not on stars, when they are fallen?
Who talketh not of states, when they are dead?
A fool conceits [186] no further than he sees;
He hath no sense of aught but what he feels.

CHRISTMAS: Ay, ay, such wise men as you come to beg at such fool's doors as we be.

AUTUMN: Thou shut'st thy door. How should we beg of thee?
No alms but thy sink carries from thy home.

WILL SUMMERS: And I can tell you, that's as plentiful alms for the plague as the sheriff's tub [187] to them of Newgate.

AUTUMN: For feasts thou keepest none; cankers thou feed'st.
The worms will curse thy flesh another day,
Because it yieldeth them no fatter prey.

CHRISTMAS: What worms do another day I care not, but I'll be sworn a whole kilderkin of single-beer I will not have a worm-eaten nose like a pursuivant [188] while I live. Feasts are but puffing up of the flesh, the purveyors for diseases: travail, cost, time, ill-spent. Oh, it were a trim thing to send as the Romans did, round about the world for provision for one banquet. I must rig ships to Samos for peacocks, to Paphos for pigeons, to Austria for oysters, to Phasis for pheasants, to Arabia for phoenixes, to Meander for swans, to the Orcades for geese, to Phrygia for woodcocks, to Malta for cranes, to the Isle of Man for puffins, to Ambracia for goats, to Tartole for lamp-

186. Imagines.
187. A basket for scraps to be distributed among the poor.
188. Messenger, attendant.

reys, to Egypt for dates, to Spain for chestnuts: and all
for one feast!

WILL SUMMERS: Oh sir, you need not. You may buy them
at London better cheap.

CHRISTMAS: *Liberalitas liberalitate perit*:[189] Love me a
little and love me long. Our feet must have wherewithal
to fend the stones; our backs, walls of wool to keep out
the cold that besiegeth our warm blood; our doors must
have bars, our doublets must have buttons. Item: for
an old sword to scrape the stones before the door with,
three half-pence; for stitching a wooden tankard that was
burst – these water-bearers will empty the conduit and
a man's coffers at once. Not a porter that brings a man
a letter but will have his penny. I am afraid to keep past
one or two servants, lest, hungry knaves, they should rob
me. And those I keep, I warrant I do not pamper up too
lusty: I keep them under with red herring and poor-
john [190] all the year long. I have dammed up all my chimneys for fear (though I burn nothing but small coal) my
house should be set on fire with the smoke. I will not
deny, but once in a dozen year, when there is a great rot
of sheep, and I know not what to do with them, I keep
open-house for all the beggars, in some of my out-yards.
Marry, they must bring bread with them: I am no baker.

WILL SUMMERS: As good men as you, and have thought
no scorn to serve their prenticeships on the pillory.

SUMMER: Winter, is this thy son? Hear'st how he talks?

WINTER: I am his father, therefore may not speak. But
otherwise I could excuse his fault.

SUMMER: Christmas, I tell thee plain, thou art a snudge,[191]
And wert not that we love thy father well,
Thou should'st have felt what 'longs to avarice.
It is the honour of nobility
To keep high days and solemn festivals,
Then, to set their magnificence to view,
To frolic open with their favourites,

189. 'Generosity dies through generosity.'
190. Cheap hake.   191. Miser.

And use their neighbours with all courtesy.
When thou in hugger-mugger [192] spend'st thy wealth.
Amend thy manners, breathe thy rusty gold:
Bounty will win thee love when thou art old.

WILL SUMMERS: Ay, that bounty would I fain meet to
borrow money of. He is fairly blest nowadays that scapes
blows when he begs. *Verba dandi et reddendi* [193] go together in the grammar rule. There is no giving but with
condition of restoring:

> Ah, *Benedicite*,[194]
> Well is he hath no necessity
> Of gold ne of sustenance;
> Slow good hap comes by chance;
> Flattery best fares;
> Arts are but idle wares;
> Fair words want giving hands;
> The lento [195] begs that hath no lands.
> Fie on thee, thou scurvy knave,
> That hast nought and yet goest brave; [196]
> A prison be thy deathbed,
> Or be hang'd all save the head.

SUMMER: Backwinter, stand forth!

VERTUMNUS: Stand forth, stand forth! Hold up your
head, speak out!

BACKWINTER: What, should I stand? Or whither should
I go?

SUMMER: Autumn accuseth thee of sundry crimes,
Which here thou art to clear or to confess.

BACKWINTER: With thee or Autumn have I nought to do:
I would you were both hanged face to face.

SUMMER: Is this the reverence that thou ow'st to us?

192. Secrecy.
193. The two verbs would be found on the same page on the standard
Latin grammar of the time.
194. Mild exclamation, common in medieval plays.
195. Lazy idler.
196. Finely dressed.

BACKWINTER: Why not? What art thou? Shalt thou always
    live?

AUTUMN: It is the veriest dog in Christendom.

WINTER: That's for he barks at such a knave as thou.

BACKWINTER: Would I could bark the sun out of the
    sky,
  Turn moon and stars to frozen meteors,
  And make the ocean a dry land of ice;
  With tempests of my breath turn up high trees,
  On mountains heap up second mounts of snow,
  Which, melted into water, might fall down,
  As fell the deluge on the former world.
  I hate the air, the fire, the Spring, the year,
  And whatsoe'er brings mankind any good.
  Oh that my looks were lightning to blast fruits!
  Would I with thunder presently might die,
  So I might speak in thunder to slay men.
  Earth, if I cannot injure thee enough,
  I'll bite thee with my teeth, I'll scratch thee thus;
  I'll beat down the partition with my heels,
  Which, as a mud-vault, severs hell and thee.
  Spirits, come up! 'Tis I that knock for you,
  One that envies the world far more than you.
  Come up in millions; millions are too few
  To execute the malice I intend.

SUMMER: *O scelus inauditum, O vox damnatorum!* [197]
  Not raging Hecuba, whose hollow eyes
  Gave suck to fifty sorrows [198] at one time,
  That midwife to so many murders was,
  Us'd half the execrations that thou dost.

BACKWINTER: More will I use, if more I may prevail.
  Backwinter comes but seldom forth abroad,
  But when he comes, he pincheth to the proof.
  Winter is mild; his son is rough and stern.
  Ovíd could well write of my tyranny,
  When he was banish'd to the frozen zone.

197. 'Oh unheard-of reprobate, oh voice of the damned!'
198. A reference to the fifty sons and fifty daughters of Priam.

SUMMER: And banish'd be thou from my fertile bounds.
Winter, imprison him in thy dark cell,
Or, with the winds, in bellowing caves of brass,
Let stern Hippotades [199] lock him up safe,
Ne'er to peep forth, but when thou, faint and weak,
Want'st him to aid thee in thy regiment.
BACKWINTER: I will peep forth, thy kingdom to supplant.
My father I will quickly freeze to death,
And then sole monarch will I sit, and think
How I may banish thee, as thou dost me.
WINTER: I see my downfall written in his brows.
Convey him hence to his assigned hell.
Fathers are given to love their sons too well.

[*Exit Backwinter.*]

WILL SUMMERS: No, by my troth, nor mothers neither. I am sure I could never find it. This Backwinter plays a railing part to no purpose; my small learning finds no reason for it, except as a backwinter or an after-winter is more raging-tempestuous and violent than the beginning of winter, so he brings him in stamping and raging as if he were mad, when his father is a jolly, mild, quiet old man, and stands still and does nothing. The court accepts of your meaning. You might have writ in the margent of your play-book: 'Let there be a few rushes laid in the place where Backwinter shall tumble,[200] for fear of raying his clothes.' Or set down: 'Enter Backwinter with his boy bringing a brush after him to take off the dust if need require.' But you will ne'er have any wardrobe-wit while you live. I pray you hold the book well;[201] we will not *nonplus* in the latter end of the play.
SUMMER: This is the last stroke my tongue's clock must strike,
My last will, which I will that you perform;
My crown I have dispos'd already of.

199. Aeolus, keeper of the winds.
200. *a few rushes ... tumble*: It is suggested that Backwinter struggles to resist arrest.
201. Prompt efficiently.

Item; I give my wither'd flowers and herbs
Unto dead corses, for to deck them with.
My shady walks to great men's servitors,
Who in their masters' shadows walk secure.
My pleasant open air and fragrant smells
To Croydon and the grounds abutting round.
My heat and warmth to toiling labourers,
My long days to bondmen and prisoners,
My short nights to young married souls,
My drought and thirst to drunkards' quenchless throats.
My fruits to Autumn, my adopted heir,
My murmuring springs, musicians of sweet sleep,
To murmuring malcontents, with their well-tuned cares,
Channel'd in a sweet-falling quaterzaine,[202]
Do lull their ears asleep, listening themselves.
And finally (oh words, now cleanse your course),
Unto Eliza, that most sacred dame,
Whom none but saints and angels ought to name,
All my fair days remaining I bequeath,
To wait upon her till she be return'd.
Autumn, I charge thee, when that I am dead,
Be press'd and serviceable at her beck,
Present her with thy goodliest ripen'd fruits,
Unclothe no arbours where she ever sat,
Touch not a tree thou thinkst she may pass by.
And Winter, with thy writhen frosty face,
Smoothe up thy visage when thou look'st on her;
Thou never look'st on such bright majesty.
A charmed circle draw about her court,
Wherein warm days may dance and no cold come;
On seas let winds make war, not vex her rest,
Quiet enclose her bed, thought fly her breast.
Ah, gracious Queen, though Summer pine away,
Yet let thy flourishing stand at a stay;
First droop this universal's aged frame,
Ere any malady thy strength should tame.

202. A poem of fourteen lines, more loosely constructed than a
sonnet.

Heaven raise up pillars to uphold thy hand,
Peace may have still his temple in thy land.
Lo, I have said; this is the total sum.
Autumn and Winter, on your faithfulness
For the performance I do firmly build.
Farewell, my friends; Summer bids you farewell,
Archers and bowlers, all my followers,
Adieu, and dwell with desolation;
Silence must be your master's mansion.
Slow marching thus, descend I to the fiends.
Weep, heavens; mourn, earth; here Summer ends.
[*Here the satyrs and wood-nymphs carry him out, singing as he came in.*]

THE SONG

Autumn hath all the Summer's fruitful treasure;
Gone is our sport, fled is poor Croydon's pleasure.
Short days, sharp days, long nights come on apace;
Ah, but who shall hide us from the Winter's face?
Cold doth increase, the sickness will not cease,
And here we lie, God knows, with little ease:
    From winter, plague and pestilence, good Lord,
      deliver us.
London doth mourn, Lambeth is quite forlorn,
Trades cry 'Woe worth' that ever they were born,
The want of term is town and city's harm;
Close chambers we do want, to keep us warm;
Long banished must we live from our friends;
This low-built house [203] will bring us to our ends.
    From winter, plague and pestilence, good Lord,
      deliver us.

WILL SUMMERS: How is't, how is't? You that be of the graver sort, do you think these youths worthy of a *Plaudite* for praying for the Queen and singing of the

---

203. M. quotes Henry VIII on Otford House which 'standeth low and is rheumatic, like unto Croyden, where I could never be without sickness'.

Litany? They are poor fellows, I must needs say, and have bestowed great labour in sewing leaves, and grass, and straw, and moss upon cast suits.[204] You may do well to warm your hands with clapping, before you go to bed, and send them to the tavern with merry hearts. Here is a pretty boy comes with an Epilogue, to get him audacity.[205]

[*Enter a little boy with an Epilogue.*]

I pray you sit still a little and hear him say his lesson without book. It is a good boy; be not afraid; turn thy face to my lord. Thou and I will play at pouch[206] tomorrow morning for a breakfast. Come and sit on my knee, and I'll dance thee, if thou canst not endure to stand.

THE EPILOGUE

Ulysses, a dwarf, and the prolocutor for the Graecians, gave me leave, that am a pigmy, to do an embassage to you from the cranes.[207] Gentlemen, for kings are no better, certain humble animals called our actors commend them unto you; who, what offence they have committed I know not (except it be in purloining some hours out of time's treasury that might have been better employed), but by me, the agent for their imperfections, they humbly crave pardon, if haply some of their terms have trodden awry, or their tongues stumbled unwittingly on any man's content. In much corn is some cockle; in a heap of coin here and there a piece of copper. Wit hath his dregs as well as wine; words their waste, ink his blots, every speech his parenthesis; poetical fury, as well crabs as sweetings for his summer fruits. *Nemo sapit omnibus horis.*[208] Their

---

204. Worn-out clothes.
205. Give him practice and confidence.
206. A children's game, also called slatter-pouch.
207. *pigmy . . . cranes*: Herodotus describes the pigmies and cranes as being in a perpetual state of war, therefore embassies would sometimes be necessary.
208. 'Nobody knows all hours' (Pliny).

folly is deceased; their fear is yet living. Nothing can kill an ass but cold; cold entertainment, discouraging scoffs, authorized disgraces, may kill a whole litter of young asses of them here at once, that have travelled thus far in impudence, only in hope to sit a-sunning in your smiles. The Romans dedicated a temple to the fever quartane, thinking it some great god, because it shook them so; and another to ill-fortune *in Exquilliis*, a mountain in Rome, that it should not plague them at cards and dice. Your Graces' frowns are to them shaking fevers, your least disfavours the greatest ill-fortune that may betide them. They can build no temples; but themselves and their best endeavours, with all prostrate reverence, they here dedicate and offer up wholly to your service. *Sic bonus, O, Faelixque tuis.*[209] To make the gods merry, the celestial clown Vulcan tuned his polt-foot [210] to the measures of Apollo's lute, and danced a limping galliard in Jove's starry hall. To make you merry, that are the gods of art and guides unto heaven, a number of rude Vulcans, unwieldy speakers, hammer-headed clowns (for so it pleaseth them in modesty to name themselves) have set their deformities to view, as it were in a dance here before you. Bear with their wants, lull melancholy asleep with their absurdities, and expect hereafter better fruits of their industry. Little creatures often terrify great beasts; the elephant flieth from a ram, the lion from a cock and from fire, the crocodile from all sea-fish, the whale from the noise of parched bones; light toys chase great cares. The great fool Toy hath marred the play: goodnight, gentlemen; I go.

[*Let him be carried away.*]

WILL SUMMERS: Is't true, jackanapes, do you serve me so? As sure as this coat is too short for me, all the points of your hose for this are condemned to my pocket, if you and I ere play at span-counter [211] more. *Valete, spec-*

209. 'Be good to your friends, and bring them good fortune (Virgil).
210. Club-foot.
211. See pp. 165, 191.

tatores;[212] pay for this sport with a *plaudite*, and the next time the wind blows from this corner, we will make you ten times as merry.

Barbarus hic ego sum, quia non intelligor ulli.[213]

FINIS

212. 'Farewell, spectators'.
213. 'I am a barbarian here, for nobody understands me' (Ovid).

3

The Terrors of the Night

OR

A DISCOURSE OF APPARITIONS

A LITTLE to beguile time idly discontented, and satisfy some of my solitary friends here in the country, I have hastily undertook to write of the weary fancies of the night, wherein if I weary none with my weak fancies, I will hereafter lean harder on my pen and fetch the pedigree of my praise from the utmost of pains.

As touching the terrors of the night, they are as many as our sins. The night is the devil's Black Book, wherein he recordeth all our transgressions. Even as, when a condemned man is put into a dark dungeon, secluded from all comfort of light or company, he doth nothing but despairfully call to mind his graceless former life, and the brutish outrages and misdemeanours that have thrown him into that desolate horror; so when night in her rusty dungeon hath imprisoned our eye-sight, and that we are shut separately in our chambers from resort, the devil keepeth his audit in our sin-guilty consciences, no sense but surrenders to our memory a true bill of parcels [1] of his detestable impieties. The table [2] of our heart is turned to an index of iniquities, and all our thoughts are nothing but texts to condemn us.

The rest we take in our beds is such another kind of rest as the weary traveller taketh in the cool soft grass in summer, who thinking there to lie at ease and refresh his tired limbs, layeth his fainting head unawares on a loathsome nest of snakes.

---

1. *bill of parcels*: List, catalogue.
2. Tablet for writing memoranda or inscriptions.

Well have the poets termed night the nurse of cares, the mother of despair, the daughter of hell.

Some divines have had this conceit, that God would have made all day and no night, if it had not been to put us in mind there is a hell as well as a heaven.

Such is the peace of the subjects as is the peace of the Prince under whom they are governed. As God is entitled the Father of Light, so is the devil surnamed the Prince of Darkness, which is the night. The only peace of mind that the devil hath is despair, wherefore we that live in his nightly kingdom of darkness must needs taste some disquiet.

The raven and the dove that were sent out of Noah's Ark to discover the world after the general deluge may well be an allegory of the day and the night. The day is our good angel, the dove, that returneth to our eyes with an olive branch of peace in his mouth, presenting quiet and security to our distracted souls and consciences; the night is that ill angel the raven, which never cometh back to bring any good tidings of tranquillity: a continual messenger he is of dole and misfortune. The greatest curse[3] almost that in the scripture is threatened is that the ravens shall pick out their eyes in the valley of death. This cursed raven, the night, pecks out men's eyes in the valley of death. It hindreth them from looking to heaven for succour, where their Redeemer dwelleth; wherefore no doubt it is a time most fatal and unhallowed. This being proved, that the devil is a special predominant planet of the night, and that our creator for our punishment hath allotted it him as his peculiar signory and kingdom, from his inveterate envy I will amplify the ugly terrors of the night. The names importing his malice, which the scripture is plentiful of, I will here omit, lest some men should think I went about to conjure. Sufficeth us to have this heedful knowledge of him, that he is an ancient malcontent, and seeketh to make any one desperate like himself. Like a cunning fowler, to this end he

3. 'The eye that mocketh at his father, and despiseth to obey his mother, the ravens of the valley shall pick it out, and the young eagles shall eat it' (*Proverbs*, 30, 17).

spreadeth his nets of temptation in the dark, that men might not see to avoid them. As the poet saith:

> *Quae nimis apparent retia vitat avis.*[4]
> (Too open nets even simple birds do shun)

Therefore in another place (which it cannot be but the devil hath read) he counseleth thus:

> *Noctem peccatis et fraudibus obiice nubem.*[5]
> (By night-time sin, and cloak thy fraud with clouds)

When hath the devil commonly first appeared unto any man but in the night?

In the time of infidelity, when spirits were so familiar with men that they called them *Dii Penates*, their household Gods or their Lares, they never sacrificed unto them till sunsetting. The Robin Goodfellows, elves, fairies, hobgoblins of our latter age, which idolatrous former days and the fantastical world of Greece y-clepped[6] fawns, satyrs, dryads, and hamadryads, did most of their merry pranks in the night. Then ground they malt, and had hempen shirts for their labours, danced in rounds in green meadows, pinched maids in their sleep that swept not their houses clean, and led poor travellers out of their way notoriously.

It is not to be gainsaid but the devil can transform himself into an angel of light, appear in the day as well as in the night, but not in this subtle world of Christianity so usual as before. If he do, it is when men's minds are extraordinarily thrown down with discontent, or inly terrified with some horrible concealed murder or other heinous crime close smothered in secret. In the day he may smoothly in some mild shape insinuate, but in the night he takes upon himself like a tyrant. There is no thief that is half so hardy in the day as in the night; no more is the devil. A general principle it is, he that doth ill hateth the light.

This Machiavellian trick hath he in him worth the not-

---

4. Ovid, *Remedia Amoris*, 516.
5. Horace, *Epistolae*, i, 16, 62.   6. Called, named.

ing, that those whom he dare not united or together encounter, disjoined and divided he will one by one assail in their sleep. And even as ruptures and cramps do then most torment a man when the body with any other disease is distempered, so the devil, when with any other sickness or malady the faculties of our reason are enfeebled and distempered, will be most busy to disturb us and torment us.

In the quiet silence of the night he will be sure to surprise us, when he unfallibly knows we shall be unarmed to resist, and that there will be full auditory granted him to undermine or persuade what he lists.[7] All that ever he can scare us with are but Seleucus' airy castles,[8] terrible bugbear brags, and nought else, which with the least thought of faith are quite evanished and put to flight. Neither in his own nature dare he come near us, but in the name of sin and as God's executioner. Those that catch birds imitate their voices; so will he imitate the voices of God's vengeance, to bring us like birds into the net of eternal damnation.

Children, fools, sick-men or madmen, he is most familiar with, for he still delights to work upon the advantage, and to them he boldly revealeth the whole astonishing treasury of his wonders.

It will be demanded why in the likeness of one's father or mother, or kinsfolks, he oftentimes presents himself unto us.

No other reason can be given of it but this, that in those shapes which he supposeth most familiar unto us, and that we are inclined to with a natural kind of love, we will sooner harken to him than otherwise.

Should he not disguise himself in such subtle forms of affection, we would fly from him as a serpent, and eschew him with that hatred he ought to be eschewed. If any ask why he is more conversant and busy in churchyards and places where men are buried than in any other places, it is to make us believe that the bodies and souls of the departed

7. Desires, chooses.
8. An untraced allusion (Seleucus was one of Alexander's generals).

rest entirely in his possession and the peculiar power of death is resigned to his disposition.[9] A rich man delights in nothing so much as to be uncessantly raking in his treasury, to be turning over his rusty gold every hour. The bones of the dead, the devil counts his chief treasury, and therefore is he continually raking amongst them; and the rather he doth it, that the living which hear it should be more unwilling to die, insomuch as after death their bones should take no rest.

It was said of Catiline, *Vultum gestavit in manibus*: with the turning of a hand he could turn and alter his countenance. Far more nimble and sudden is the devil in shifting his habit; his form he can change and cog[10] as quick as thought.

What do we talk of one devil? There is not a room in any man's house but is pestered and close-packed with a camp-royal of devils. Chrisostom saith the air and earth are three parts inhabited with spirits. Hereunto the philosopher alluded when he said nature made no voidness in the whole universal; for no place (be it no bigger than a pockhole in a man's face) but is close thronged with them. Infinite millions of them will hang swarming about a worm-eaten nose.

Don Lucifer himself, their grand Capitano, asketh no better throne than a blear eye to set up his state in. Upon a hair they will sit like a nit,[11] and overdredge a bald pate like a white scurf. The wrinkles in old witches' visages they eat out to entrench themselves in.

If in one man a whole legion of devils have been billetted, how many hundred thousand legions retain to a term in London? If I said but to a tavern, it were an infinite thing. In Westminster Hall a man can scarce breathe for them; for in every corner they hover as thick as motes in the sun.

The Druids that dwelt in the Isle of Man, which are famous for great conjurers, are reported to have been lousy with familiars.[12] Had they but put their finger and their

9. At his disposal.   10. Cheat (as at cards or dice).
11. Small insect, possibly here gnat.
12. Familiar spirits, devils.

thumb into their neck, they could have plucked out a whole nest of them.

There be them that think every spark in a flame is a spirit, and that the worms which at sea eat through a ship are so also; which may very well be, for have not you seen one spark of fire burn a whole town and a man with a spark of lightning made blind or killed outright? It is impossible the guns should go off as they do, if there were not a spirit either in the fire or in the powder.

Now for worms: what makes a dog run mad but a worm in his tongue? [13] And what should that worm be but a spirit? Is there any reason such small vermin as they are should devour such a vast thing as a ship, or have the teeth to gnaw through iron and wood? No, no, they are spirits, or else it were incredible.

Tullius Hostilius,[14] who took upon him to conjure up Jove by Numa Pompilius' books, had no sense to quake and tremble at the wagging and shaking of every leaf but that he thought all leaves are full of worms, and those worms are wicked spirits.

If the bubbles in streams were well searched, I am persuaded they would be found to be little better. Hence it comes that mares, as Columella reporteth, looking their forms in the water run mad. A flea is but a little beast, yet if she were not possessed with a spirit, she could never leap and skip so as she doth. Froisard saith the Earl of Foix had a familiar that presented itself unto him in the likeness of two rushes fighting one with another. Not so much as Tewkesbury mustard [15] but hath a spirit in it or else it would never bite so. Have we not read of a number of men that have ordinarily carried a familiar or a spirit in a ring instead of a spark of a diamond? Why, I tell ye we cannot

13. 'A vermiform cartilage under the tongue, believed to be a parasite' (M.).

14. King of Rome (673–42 B.C.) (There is no reference in Livy or Pliny to his trembling.)

15. cf. Falstaff on Poins: 'His wit as thick as Tewksbury mustard' *2 Henry IV*, II, iv, 240.

break a crumb of bread so little as one of them will be if they list.

From this general discourse of spirits, let us digress and talk another while of their separate natures and properties.

The spirits of the fire which are the purest and perfectest are merry, pleasant, and well-inclined to wit, but nevertheless giddy and unconstant.

Those whom they possess they cause to excel in whatever they undertake. Or poets or boon companions they are, out of question.

Socrates' genius was one of this stamp, and the dove [16] wherewith the Turks hold Mohamet their prophet to be inspired. What their names are and under whom they are governed *The Discovery of Witchcraft* hath amplified at large, wherefore I am exempted from that labour. But of the divinest quintessence of metals and of wines are many of these spirits extracted. It is almost impossible for any to be encumbered with ill spirits who is continually conversant in the excellent restorative distillations of wit and of alchemy. Those that ravenously englut themselves with gross meats and respect not the quality but the quantity of what they eat, have no affinity with these spirits of the fire.

A man that will entertain them must not pollute his body with any gross carnal copulation or inordinate beastly desires, but love pure beauty, pure virtue, and not have his affections linsey-wolsey,[17] intermingled with lust and things worthy of liking.

As for example, if he love good poets he must not countenance ballad-makers; if he have learned physicians he must not favour horse-leeches and mountebanks. For a bad spirit and a good can never endure to dwell together.

Those spirits of the fire, however I term them comparatively good in respect of a number of bad, yet are they not simply well-inclined, for they be by nature ambitious, haughty, and proud; nor do they love virtue for itself any

16. Mahomet was said to feed a dove by the ear and to receive from the dove God's secrets in return.

17. Mixed, like this material woven of coarse wool and flax.

whit, but because they would overquell and outstrip others with the vain-glorious ostentation of it. A humour of monarchizing and nothing else it is, which makes them affect rare qualified studies.[18] Many atheists are with these spirits inhabited.

To come to the spirits of the water, the earth and the air: they are dull phlegmatic drones, things that have much malice without any great might. Drunkards, misers and women they usually retain to. Water, you all know, breedeth a medley kind of liquor called beer; with these watery spirits they were possessed that first invented the art of brewing. A quagmire consisting of mud and sand sendeth forth the like puddly mixture.

All rheums, poses,[19] sciaticas, dropsies and gouts are diseases of their phlegmatic engendering. Sea-faring men of what sort soever are chief entertainers of those spirits. Greedy vintners likewise give hospitality to a number of them; who, having read no more scripture than that miracle of Christ's turning water into wine in Canaan, think to do a far stranger miracle than ever he did, by turning wine into water.

Alehouses and cooks' shady pavilions, by watery spirits are principally upholden.

The spirits of the earth are they which cry 'All bread and no drink', that love gold and a buttoned cap above heaven. The worth in nought they respect, but the weight; good wits they naturally hate, insomuch as the element of fire, their progenitor, is a waste-good and a consumer. If with their earth-ploughing snouts they can turn up a pearl out of a dunghill, it is all they desire. Witches have many of these spirits and kill kine with them. The giants and chieftains of those spirits are powerful sometimes to bring men to their ends, but not a jot of good can they do for their lives.

Soldiers with these terrestial spirits participate part of their essence; for nothing but iron and gold, which are earth's excrements, they delight in. Besides, in another

18. *rare . . . studies*: Studies of a recondite character.
19. Head cold, catarrh.

kind they may be said to participate with them, insomuch as they confirm them in their fury and congeal their minds with a bloody resolution. Spirits of the earth they were that entered into the herd of swine in the gospel. There is no city merchant or country purchaser, but is haunted with a whole host of these spirits of the earth. The Indies is their metropolitan realm of abode.

As for the spirits of the air, which have no other visible bodies or form, but such as by the unconstant glimmering of our eyes is begotten, they are in truth all show and no substance, deluders of our imagination and naught else. Carpet knights, politic statesmen, women and children they most converse with. Carpet knights they inspire with a humour of setting big looks on it, being the basest cowards under heaven, covering an ape's heart with a lion's case, and making false alarums when they mean nothing but a may-game. Politic statesmen they privily incite to blear the world's eyes with clouds of commonwealth pretences, to broach any enmity or ambitious humour of their own under a title of their country's preservation; to make it fair or foul when they list, to procure popularity, or induce a preamble to some mighty piece of prowling, to stir up tempests round about, and replenish heaven with prodigies and wonders, the more to ratify their avaricious religion. Women they underhand instruct to pounce and bolster out their brawn-fallen deformities, to new parboil with painting their rake-lean withered visages, to set up flax shops on their foreheads when all their own hair is dead and rotten, to stick their gums round with comfits when they have not a tooth left in their heads to help them to chide withal.

Children they seduce with garish objects, and toyish babies, abusing them many years with slight vanities. So that you see all their whole influence is but thin overcast vapours, flying clouds dispersed with the least wind of wit or understanding.

None of these spirits of the air or the fire have so much predominance in the night as the spirits of the earth and the water; for they feeding on foggy-brained melancholy engender thereof many uncouth terrible monsters. Thus much observe by the way, that the grossest part of our blood is the melancholy humour, which in the spleen congealed whose office is to disperse it, with his thick steaming fenny vapours casteth a mist over the spirit and clean bemasketh the fantasy.

And even as slime and dirt in a standing puddle engender toads and frogs and many other unsightly creatures, so this slimy melancholy humour, still still thickening as it stands still, engendreth many misshapen objects in our imaginations. Sundry times we behold whole armies of men skirmishing in the air: dragons, wild beasts, bloody streamers, blazing comets, fiery streaks, with other apparitions innumberable. Whence have all these their conglomerate matter but from fuming meteors that arise from the earth? So from the fuming melancholy of our spleen mounteth that hot matter into the higher region of the brain, whereof many fearful visions are framed. Our reason even like drunken fumes it displaceth and intoxicates, and yields up our intellective apprehension to be mocked and trodden under foot by every false object or counterfeit noise that comes near it. Herein specially consisteth our senses' defect and abuse, that those organical parts, which to the mind are ordained ambassadors, do not their message as they ought, but, by some misdiet or misgovernment being distempered, fail in their report and deliver up nothing but lies and fables.

Such is our brain oppressed with melancholy, as is a clock tied down with too heavy weights or plummets; which as it cannot choose but monstrously go a-square or not go at all, so must our brains of necessity be either monstrously distracted or utterly destroyed thereby.

Lightly this extremity of melancholy never cometh, but before some notable sickness; it faring with our brains as with bees, who, as they exceedingly toil and turmoil before a storm or change of weather, so do they beat and toil and are infinitely confused before sickness.

Of the effects of melancholy I need not dilate, or discourse how many encumbered with it have thought themselves birds and beasts, with feathers and horns and hides; others, that they have been turned into glass; others, that if they should make water they should drown all the world; others, that they can never bleed enough.

Physicians in their circuit every day meet with far more ridiculous experience. Only it shall suffice a little by the way to handle one special effect of it, which is dreams.

A dream is nothing else but a bubbling scum or froth of the fancy, which the day hath left undigested; or an after-feast made of the fragments of idle imaginations.

How many sorts there be of them no man can rightly set down, since it scarce hath been heard there were ever two men that dreamed alike. Divers have written diversely of their causes, but the best reason among them all that I could ever pick out was this: that as an arrow which is shot out of a bow is sent forth many times with such force that it flieth far beyond the mark whereat it was aimed, so our thoughts, intensively fixed all the daytime upon a mark we are to hit, are now and then overdrawn with such force that they fly beyond the mark of the day into the confines of the night. There is no man put to any torment, but quaketh and trembleth a great while after the executioner hath withdrawn his hand from him. In the daytime we torment our thoughts and imaginations with sundry cares and devices; all the night-time they quake and tremble after the terror of their late suffering, and still continue thinking of the perplexities they have endured. To nothing more aptly can I compare the working of our brains after we have unyoked and gone to bed than to the glimmering and dazzling of a man's eyes when he comes newly out of the bright sun into the dark shadow.

Even as one's eyes glimmer and dazzle when they are withdrawn out of the light into darkness, so are our thoughts troubled and vexed when they are retired from labour to ease, and from skirmishing to surgery.

You must give a wounded man leave to groan while he is in dressing. Dreaming is no other than groaning, while sleep our surgeon hath us in cure.

He that dreams merrily is like a boy new breeched, who leaps and danceth for joy his pain is passed. But long that joy stays not with him, for presently after, his master, the day, seeing him so jocund and pleasant, comes and does as much for him again, whereby his hell is renewed.

No such figure [20] as the first chaos whereout the world was extraught,[21] as our dreams in the night. In them all states, all sexes, all places, are confounded[22] and meet together.

Our cogitations run on heaps like men to part a fray where every one strikes his next fellow. From one place to another without consultation they leap, like rebels bent on a head.[23] Soldiers just up and down [24] they imitate at the sack of a city, which spare neither age nor beauty: the young, the old, trees, steeples and mountains, they confound in one gallimaufry.[25]

Of those things which are most known to us, some of us that have moist brains make to ourselves images of memory. On those images of memory whereon we build in the day, comes some superfluous humour of ours, like a jackanapes, in the night, and erects a puppet stage or some such ridiculous idle childish invention.

A dream is nothing else but the echo of our conceits [26] in the day.

But otherwhile it falls out that one echo borrows of another; so our dreams, the echoes of the day, borrow of any noise we hear in the night.

As for example: if in the dead of the night there be any rumbling, knocking or disturbance near us, we straight dream of wars or of thunder. If a dog howl, we suppose we are transported into hell, where we hear the complaint of damned ghosts. If our heads lie double or uneasy, we imagine we uphold all heaven with our shoulders, like Atlas.

20. Nothing is so like.   21. Made, derived.
22. Thrown into disorder, confusion.
23. Rushing ahead, headlong.   24. Completely, exactly.
25. A jumble, a mixture; literally a hash or stew made of odds and ends.
26. Ideas, thoughts.

If we be troubled with too many clothes, then we suppose the night mare rides us.

I knew one that was cramped, and he dreamed that he was torn in pieces with wild horses; and another, that having a black sant [27] brought to his bedside at midnight, dreamt he was bidden to dinner at Ironmongers' Hall.

Any meat that in the daytime we eat against our stomachs, begetteth a dismal dream. Discontent also in dreams hath no little predominance; for even as from water that is troubled, the mud dispersingly ascendeth from the bottom to the top, so when our blood is chased, disquieted and troubled all the light imperfect humours of our body ascend like mud up aloft into the head.

The clearest spring a little touched is creased with a thousand circles; as those momentary circles for all the world, such are our dreams.

When all is said, melancholy is the mother of dreams, and of all terrors of the night whatsoever. Let it but affirm it hath seen a spirit, though it be but the moonshine on the wall, the best reason we have cannot infringe it.

Of this melancholy there be two sorts: one that, digested by our liver, swimmeth like oil above water and that is rightly termed women's melancholy, which lasteth but for an hour and is, as it were, but a copy of their countenance; the other sinketh down to the bottom like the lees of the wine, and that corrupteth all the blood and is the causer of lunacy. Well-moderated recreations are the medicine to both: surfeit or excessive study the causers of either.

There were gates in Rome out of which nothing was carried but dust and dung, and men to execution; so, many of the gates of our senses serve for nothing but to convey our excremental vapours and affrighting deadly dreams, that are worse than executioners unto us.

Ah, woe be to the solitary man that hath his sins continually about him, that hath no withdrawing place from the devil and his temptations.

Much I wonder how treason and murder dispense with

27. Black sanctus; noisy discordant singing.

the darkness of the night, how they can shrive themselves to it, and not rave and die. Methinks they should imagine that hell embraceth them round, when she overspreads them with her black pitchy mantle.

Dreams to none are so fearful, as to those whose accusing private guilt expects mischief every hour for their merit. Wonderful superstitious are such persons in observing every accident that befalls them; and that their superstition is as good as an hundred furies to torment them. Never in this world shall he enjoy one quiet day, that once hath given himself over to be her slave. His ears cannot glow, his nose itch, or his eyes smart, but his destiny stands upon her trial, and till she be acquitted or condemned he is miserable.

A cricket or a raven keep him forty times in more awe than God or the devil.

If he chance to kill a spider, he hath suppressed an enemy; if a spinner creep upon him, he shall have gold rain down from heaven. If his nose bleed, some of his kinsfolks is dead; if the salt fall right against him, all the stars cannot save him from some immediate misfortune.

The first witch was Proserpine,[28] and she dwelt half in heaven and half in hell; half-witches are they that pretending any religion, meddle half with God and half with the devil. Meddling with the devil I call it, when ceremonies are observed which have no ground from divinity.

In another kind, witches may be said to meddle half with GOD and half with the Devil, because in their exorcisms, they use half scripture and half blasphemy.

The greatest and notablest heathen sorcerers that ever were, in all their hellish adjurations used the name of the one true and everliving God; but such a number of damned potestates[29] they joined with him, that it might seem the stars had darkened the sun, or the moon was eclipsed by candlelight.

Of all countries under the sky, Persia was most addicted unto dreams. Darius, King of the Medes and Persians, before

28. 'Accepting, I suppose, her identification with Hecate' (M.).
29. Spiritual powers.

his fatal discomfiture, dreamt he saw an estrich[30] with a winged crown overrunning the earth and devouring his jewel-coffer as if it had been an ordinary piece of iron. The jewel-coffer was by Alexander surprised,[31] and afterward Homer's works in it carried before him, even as the mace or purse is customably carried before our Lord Chancellor.

Hannibal dreamed a little before his death that he was drowned in the poisonous Lake Asphaltites,[32] when it was presently his hap within some days' distance, to seek his fate by the same means in a vault under the earth.

In India, the women very often conceive by devils in their sleep.

In Iceland, as I have read and heard, spirits in the likeness of one's father or mother after they are deceased do converse with them as naturally as if they were living.

Other spirits like rogues they have among them, destitute of all dwelling and habitation, and they chillingly complain if a constable ask them *Chevala*[33] in the night, that they are going unto Mount Hecla[34] to warm them.

That Mount Hecla a number conclude to be hell mouth; for near unto it are heard such yellings and groans as Ixion,[35] Titius,[36] Sisyphus[37] and Tantalus[38] blowing all in one trumpet of distress could never conjoined bellow forth.

Bondmen in Turkey or in Spain are not so ordinarily sold as witches sell familiars there. Far cheaper may you buy a wind amongst them than you can buy wind[39] or fair words in the Court. Three knots in a thread, or an odd[40] grandam's

30. Ostrich. 31. Captured.
32. The Dead Sea, Asphaltites. 33. *Qui va là?*
34. Thought to be an abode of lost souls, because of the 'lamenting' noise made by the ice in the sea near-by.
35. Pinned to a wheel for the attempted rape of Hera.
36. Tityus, son of Earth, condemned, also for attempted rape, to have his liver pecked perpetually by vultures.
37. A proverbial trickster, condemned to roll a boulder up a hill.
38. Served the gods with the flesh of his son at a banquet, and was condemned to perpetual hunger and thirst.
39. Favour. 40. M. suggests 'old'.

blessing in the corner of a napkin will carry you all the world over.

We when we frown knit our brows, but let a wizard there knit a noose or a riding snarl[41] on his beard, and it is hail, storm and tempest a month after.

More might be spoken of the prodigies this country sends forth, if it were not too much erring from my scope. Whole islands they have of ice, on which they build and traffic as on the mainland.

Admirable, above the rest, are the incomprehensible wonders of the bottomless Lake Vether,[42] over which no fowl flies but is frozen to death, nor any man passeth but he is senselessly benumbed like a statue of marble.

All the inhabitants round about it are deafened with the hideous roaring of his waters when the winter breaketh up, and the ice in his dissolving gives a terrible crack like to thunder, whenas out of the midst of it, as out of Mont-Gibell,[43] a sulphureous stinking smoke issues, that wellnigh poisons the whole country.

A poison light on it, how come I to digress to such a dull, lenten, northern clime, where there is nothing but stock-fish, whetstones and cods' heads? Yet now I remember me: I have not lost my way so much as I thought, for my theme is the terrors of the night, and Iceland is one of the chief kingdoms of the night, they having scarce so much day there as will serve a child to ask his father blessing. Marry, with one commodity they are blest: they have ale that they carry in their pockets like glue, and ever when they would drink, they set it on fire and melt it.

It is reported that the Pope long since gave them a dispensation to receive the sacrament in ale, insomuch as, for their uncessant frosts there, no wine but was turned to red emayle[44] as soon as ever it came amongst them.

Farewell, frost: as much to say as 'Farewell, Iceland', for I have no more to say to thee.

41. *a riding snarl*: A slip-knot.
42. Lake Vetter or Wetter in Sweden.
43. Aetna.　　　　　44. Enamel.

I care not much if I dream yet a little more, and to say the troth, all this whole tractate is but a dream, for my wits are not half awaked in it; and yet no golden dream, but a leaden dream is it, for in a leaden standish [45] I stand fishing all day, but have none of Saint Peter's luck to bring a fish to the hook that carries any silver in the mouth. And yet there be of them that carry silver in the mouth too, but none in the hand; that is to say, are very bountiful and honourable in their words, but (except it be to swear indeed) no other good deeds come from them.

Filthy Italianate compliment-mongers they are who would fain be counted the Court's *Gloriosos*, and the refined judges of wit; when if their wardrobes and the withered bladders of their brains were well searched, they have nothing but a few moth-eaten cod-piece suits, made against the coming of Mounsier,[46] in the one, and a few scraps of outlandish proverbs in the other, and these alone do buckler them from the name of beggars and idiots. Otherwhile perhaps they may keep a coil [47] with the spirit of Tasso, and then they fold their arms like braggarts, writhe their necks *alla Neapolitano*, and turn up their eye-balls like men entranced.

Come, come, I am entranced from my text, I wote well, and talk idly in my sleep longer than I should. Those that will harken any more after dreams, I refer them to Artimidorus, Synesius, and Cardan, with many others which only I have heard by their names, but I thank God had never the plodding patience to read, for if they be no better than some of them I have perused, every weatherwise old wife might write better.

What sense is there that the yoke of an egg should signify gold, or dreaming of bears, or fire, or water, debate and anger, that everything must be interpreted backward as witches say their *Pater Noster*, good being the character of bad, and bad of good?

45. Inkstand.
46. *against ... Mounsier*: In readiness for the arrival in England of the Duke of Anjou, a suitor of the Queen, in 1581.
47. Make noisy conversation.

As well we may calculate from every accident in the day, and not go about any business in the morning till we have seen on which hand the crow sits.

'Oh Lord,' I have heard many a wise gentlewoman say, 'I am so merry and have laughed so heartily, that I am sure ere long to be crossed with some sad tidings or other' – all one as if men coming from a play should conclude, 'Well, we have seen a comedy today, and therefore there cannot choose but be a tragedy tomorrow.'

I do not deny but after extremity of mirth follow many sad accidents, but yet those sad accidents, in my opinion, we merely pluck on with the fear of coming mischief, and those means we in policy most use to prevent it soonest enwrap us in it; and that was Satan's trick in the old world of gentilism [48] to bring to pass all his blind prophecies.

Could any men set down certain rules of expounding of dreams, and that their rules were general, holding in all as well as in some, I would begin a little to list to them; but commonly that which is portentive in a king is but a frivolous fancy in a beggar, and let him dream of angels, eagles, lions, griffons, dragons never so, all the augury under heaven will not allot him so much as a good alms.

Some will object unto me for the certainty of dreams, the dreams of Cyrus, Cambyses, Pompey, Caesar, Darius and Alexander. For those I answer that they were rather visions than dreams, extraordinarily sent from heaven to foreshow the translation [49] of monarchies.

The Greek and Roman histories are full of them, and such a stir they keep with their augurers and soothsayers, how they foretold long before by dreams and beasts' and birds' entrails the loss of such a battle, the death of such a captain or emperor, when, false knaves, they were all as prophet Calchas,[50] pernicious traitors to their country and them that put them in trust, and were many times hired by

48. Paganism.
49. Change, transference.
50. The high-priest of Troy who, believing that the city was doomed, defected to the Greeks.

the adverse part to dishearten and discourage their masters by such conycatching [51] riddles as might in truth be turned any way.

An easy matter was it for them to prognosticate treasons and conspiracies, in which they were underhand inlinked themselves; and however the world went, it was a good policy for them to save their heads by the shift, for if the treasons chanced afterwards to come to light, it would not be suspected they were practisers in them, insomuch as they revealed them; or if they should by their confederates be appealed [52] as practisers, yet might they plead and pretend it was done but of spite and malice to supplant them for so bewraying and laying open their intents.

This trick they had with them besides, that never till the very instant that any treason was to be put in execution, and it was so near at hand that the Prince had no time to prevent it, would they speak one word of it, or offer to disclose it. Yea, and even then such unfit seasons for their colourable [53] discovery would they pick forth, as they would be sure he should have no leisure to attend it.

But you will ask why at all as then, they should step forth to detect it. Marry, to clear themselves to his successors, that there might be no revenge prosecuted on their lives.

So did Spurina, the great astrologer; even as Caesar in the midst of all his business was going hastily to the Senate House, he popped a bill in his hand of Brutus' and Cassius' conspiracy, and all the names of those that were colleagued with them.

Well he might have thought that in such haste by the highway side, he would not stay to peruse any schedules, and well he knew and was ascertained that as soon as ever he came into the Capitol the bloody deed was to be accomplished.

Shall I impart unto you a rare secrecy how these great famous conjurors and cunning men ascend by degrees to foretell secrets as they do? First and foremost they are men

51. Tricking, deceptive.   52. Accused.
53. Deceitful.

which have had some little sprinkling of grammar learning in their youth, or at least I will allow them to have been surgeons' or apothecaries' prentices; these, I say, having run through their thrift at the elbows, and riotously amongst harlots and make-shifts spent the annuity of halfpenny ale that was left them, fall a-beating their brains how to botch up an easy gainful trade, and set a new nap [54] on an old occupation.

Hereupon presently they rake some dunghill for a few dirty boxes and plasters, and of toasted cheese and candles' ends temper up a few ointments and syrups; which having done, far north or into some such rude simple country they get them and set up.

Scarce one month have they stayed there, but what with their vaunting and prating, and speaking fustian [55] instead of Greek, all the shires round about do ring with their fame; and then they begin to get them a library of three or four old rusty manuscript books, which they themselves nor any else can read, and furnish their shops with a thousand *quid pro quos*, that would choke any horse, besides some waste trinkets in their chambers hung up, which may make the world half in jealousy they can conjure.

They will evermore talk doubtfully, as if there were more in them than they meant to make public, or was appliable to every common man's capacity; when, God be their rightful judge, they utter all that they know and a great deal more.

To knit up their knaveries in short (which in sooth is the hangman's office and none's else), having picked up their crumbs thus prettily well in the country, they draw after a time a little nearer and nearer to London; and at length into London they filch themselves privily – but how? Not in the heart of the City will they presume at first dash to hang out their rat-banners, but in the skirts and outshifts [56] steal out a sign over a cobbler's stall, like aqua vitae sellers, and stocking menders.

54. Surface, pile, of material. 55. Gibberish.
56. *skirts and outshifts*: Suburbs, outskirts.

Many poor people they win to believe in them, who have not a barrelled herring or a piece of poor-john that looks ill on it, but they will bring the water that he was steeped in unto them in an urinal, and crave their judgement whether he be rotten, or merchant and chapmanable,[57] or no. The bruit[58] of their cunning thus travelling from ale-house to ale-house at length is transported in the great hilts of one or other country serving-man's sword to some good tavern or ordinary;[59] where it is no sooner alive, but it is greedily snatched up by some dappert Monsieur Diego, who lives by telling of news, and false dice, and it may be hath a pretty insight into the cards also, together with a little skill in his Jacob's staff[60] and his compasses, being able at all times to discover a new passage to Virginia.

This needy gallant, with the qualities aforesaid, straight trudgeth to some nobleman's to dinner, and there enlargeth the rumour of this new physician, comments upon every glass and vial that he hath, raleth on our Galenists, and calls them dull gardeners and hay-makers in a man's belly, compares them to dogs, who when they are sick eat grass, and says they are no better than pack or malt-horses, who, if a man should knock out their brains, will not go out of the beaten highway; whereas his horse-leach will leap over the hedge and ditch of a thousand Dioscorides[61] and Hippocrates,[62] and give a man twenty poisons in one, but he would restore him to perfect health. With this strange tale the nobleman inflamed desires to be acquainted with him; what does me he, but goes immediately and breaks with[63] this mountebank, telling him if he will divide his gains with him, he will bring him in custom with such and such states, and he shall be countenanced in the Court as he would desire. The hungry druggier, ambitious after prefer-

57. *merchant and chapmanable*: Saleable, marketable.
58. News, reputation.　　　　　　59. Eating house.
60. The 'astronomer's staff' for taking the altitude of the sun.
61. Author of *Materia Medica* (first or second century A.D.).
62. Famous Greek physician (c. 460–377 B.C.).
63. Confides in.

ment, agrees to anything, and to Court he goes; where, being come to interview, he speaks nothing but broken English like a French doctor, pretending to have forgotten his natural tongue by travel, when he hath never been farther than either the Low Countries or Ireland, enforced thither to fly either for getting a maid with child, or marrying two wives. Sufficeth he set a good face on it, and will swear he can extract a better balsamum out of a chip than the balm of Judea; yea, all receipts and authors you can name he syllogizeth of, and makes a pish at,[64] in comparison of them he hath seen and. read; whose names if you ask, he claps you in the mouth with half-a-dozen spruce titles, never till he invented them heard of by any Christian. But this is most certain: if he be of any sect, he is a metal-brewing Paracelsian,[65] having not passed one or two probatums [66] for all diseases. Put case he be called to practise, he excuseth it by great cures he hath in hand; and will not encounter an infirmity but in the declining, that his credit may be more authentical, or else when by some secret intelligence he is throughly instructed of the whole process of his unrecoverable extremity, he comes gravely marching like a judge, and gives peremptory sentence of death; whereby he is accounted a prophet of deep prescience.

But how he comes to be the devil's secretary, all this long tale unrips not.

In secret be it spoken, he is not so great with the devil as you take it. It may be they are near akin, but yet you have many kindred that will do nothing for one another; no more will the devil for him, except it be to damn him.

This is the *Tittle est amen* [67] of it: that when he waxeth stale, and all his pisspots are cracked and will no longer hold water, he sets up a conjuring school and undertakes to play the bawd to Lady Fortune.

64. Speaks contemptuously of.

65. Paracelsus (*c.* 1490–1541) extended the study of minerals in medical use.   66. Proven remedies.

67. Tittle est amen. Words given at the end of the alphabet in horn-books, or reading manuals, i.e. the conclusion.

Not a thief or a cut-purse, but a man that he keeps doth associate with, and is of their fraternity; only that his master when anything is stolen may tell who it is that hath it. In petty trifles having gotten some credit, great peers entertain him for one of their privy council, and if they have any dangerous enterprise in hand, they consult with him about success.

All malcontents intending any invasive violence against their Prince and country run headlong to his oracle. Contrary factions enbosom unto him their inwardest complots, whilst he like a crafty jack-a-both-sides, as if he had a spirit still at his elbow, reciprocally embowelleth to the one what the other goes about, receiving no intelligence from any familiar, but their own mouths. I assure you most of our chief noted augurers and soothsayers in England at this day, by no other art but this gain their reputation.

They may very well pick men's purses, like the unskilfuller cozening kind of alchemists, with their artificial and ceremonial magic, but no effect shall they achieve thereby, though they would hang themselves. The reason is, the devil of late is grown a puritan and cannot away with [68] any ceremonies; he sees all princes have left off their states, and he leaves off his state too and will not be invocated with such solemnity as he was wont.

Private and disguised, he passeth to and fro, and is in a thousand places in an hour.

Fair words cannot any longer beguile him, for not a cue [69] of courtesy will he do any man, except it be upon a flat bill of sale, and so he chaffers with wizards and witches every hour.

Now the world is almost at an end, he hath left form and is all for matter; and like an embroiderer or a tailor, he maketh haste of work against a good time, which is the Day of Judgment. Therefore, you goodmen exorcisers, his old

68. Cannot tolerate.
69. A jot, the smallest amount.

acquaintance, must pardon him, though (as heretofore) he stay not to dwell upon compliments.

In diebus illis[70] when Corineus[71] and Gogmagog[72] were little boys, I will not gainsay but he was wont to jest and sport with country people, and play the Goodfellow amongst kitchen-wenches, sitting in an evening by the fireside making of possets, and come a-wooing to them in the likeness of a cooper, or a curmudgeonly purchaser; and sometimes he would dress himself like a barber, and wash and shave all those that lay in such a chamber. Otherwhile, like a stale cutter of Queen-hive,[73] he would justle men in their own houses, pluck them out of bed by the heels, and dance in chains from one chamber to another. Now there is no goodness in him but miserableness and covetousness.

Sooner he will pare his nails cleanly than cause a man to dream of a pot of gold, or a money-bag that is hid in the eaves of a thatched house.

(Here is to be noted, that it is a blessed thing but to dream of gold, though a man never have it.)

Such a dream is not altogether ridiculous or impertinent, for it keeps flesh and blood from despair. All other are but as dust we raise by our steps, which awhile mounteth aloft and annoyeth our eye-sight, but presently disperseth and vanisheth.

Señor Satan, when he was a young stripling and had not yet gotten perfect audacity to set upon us in the daytime, was a sly politician in dreams; but those days are gone with him, and now that he is thoroughly steeled in his scutchery,[74] he plays above-board boldly, and sweeps more stakes than ever he did before.

I have rid a false gallop these three or four pages. Now I care not if I breathe me and walk soberly and demurely half-a-dozen turns, like a grave citizen going about to take the air.

70. Once upon a time.   71. A Trojan captain.
72. A giant, killed by Corineus.
73. A rowdy from Queenhithe, (a rough neighbourhood).
74. Knavery.

To make a shaft or a bolt [75] of this drumbling [76] subject of dreams, from whence I have been tossed off and on I know not how, this is my definitive verdict: that one may as well by the smoke that comes out of a kitchen guess what meat is there a-broach, as by paraphrasing on smoky dreams pre-ominate of future events. Thus far notwithstanding I'll go with them: physicians by dreams may better discern the distemperature of their pale clients, than either by urine or ordure.

He that is inclining to a burning fever shall dream of frays, lightning and thunder, of skirmishing with the devil and a hundred such-like. He that is spiced with the gout or the dropsy frequently dreameth of fetters and manacles and being put on the bilbows, that his legs are turned to marble or adamant, and his feet, like the giants that scaled heaven, kept under with Mount Ossa and Pelion and erst-while that they are fast locked in quagmires. I have heard aged mumping [77] beldams as they sat warming their knees over a coal scratch over the argument very curiously, and they would bid young folks beware on what day they pared their nails, tell what luck everyone should have by the day of the week he was born on; show how many years a man should live by the number of wrinkles on his forehead, and stand descanting not a little of the difference in fortune when they are turned upward and when they are bent down-ward; 'him that had a wart on his chin', they would confi-dently ascertain he should 'have no need of any of his kin'; marry, they would likewise distinguish between the standing of the wart on the right side and on the left. When I was a little child, I was a great auditor of theirs, and had all their witchcrafts at my fingers' ends, as perfect as good-morrow and good-even.

Of the signification of dreams, whole catalogues could I re-cite of theirs, which here there is no room for; but for a glance to this purpose this I remember they would very soberly affirm, that if one at supper eat birds, he should

75. *To make ... bolt*: To make something definite.
76. Mumbling, droning.   77. Toothless mumbling.

dream of flying; if fish, of swimming; if venison, of hunting, and so for the rest; as though those birds, fish, and venison being dead and digested did fly, swim and hold their chase in their brains; or the solution of our dreams should be nought else but to express what meats we ate overnight.

From the unequal and repugnant mixture of contrarious meats, I jump with them, many of our mystic cogitations procede; and even as fire maketh iron like itself, so the fiery inflammations of our liver or stomach transform our imaginations to their analogy and likeness.

No humour in general in our bodies overflowing or abounding, but the tips of our thoughts are dipped in his tincture. And as when a man is ready to drown, he takes hold of anything that is next him, so our fluttering thoughts, when we are drowned in deadly sleep, take hold and co-essence themselves with any overboiling humour which sourceth highest in our stomachs.

What heed then is there to be had of dreams that are no more but the confused giddy action of our brains, made drunk with the inundation of humours?

Just such-like impostures as is this art of exposition of dreams are the arts of physiognomy and palmistry, wherein who beareth most palm and praise is the palpablest fool and crepundio.[78] Lives there any such slow, ice-brained, beef-witted gull, who by the rivelled bark or outward rind of a tree will take upon him to forespeak how long it shall stand, what mischances of worms, caterpillars, boughs breaking, frost bitings, cattle rubbing against, it shall have? As absurd is it, by the external branched seams or furrowed wrinkles in a man's face or hand, in particular or general to conjecture and foredoom of his fate.

According to every one's labour or exercise, the palm of his hand is writhen and plaited,[79] and every day alters as he alters his employments or pastimes; wherefore well may we collect[80] that he which hath a hand so brawned and

78. A rattler or empty talker.   79. Wrinkled and entwined.
80. Conclude, gather.

interlined useth such-and-such toils or recreations; but for the mind or disposition, we can no more look into through it than we can into a looking glass through the wooden case thereof.

So also our faces, which sundry times with surfeits, grief, study or intemperance are most deformedly whelked and crumpled; there is no more to be gathered by their sharp embossed joiner's antique work or ragged overhangings or pitfalls but that they have been laid up in sloven's press, and with miscarriage and misgovernment are so fretted and galled.

My own experience is but small, yet thus much I can say by his warrantize that those fatal brands of physiognomy which condemn men for fools and for idiots, and on the other side for treacherous circumventers and false brothers, have in a hundred men I know been verified in the contrary.

So Socrates, the wisest man of Greece, was censured by a wrinkle-wizard [81] for the lumpishest blockhead that ever went on two legs; whom though the philosopher in pity vouchsafed with a nice distinction of art and nature to raise and recover, when he was utterly confounded with a hiss and a laughter, yet sure his insolent simplicity might lawfully have sued out his patent of exemption, for he was a forlorn creature, both in discretion and wit-craft.

Will you have the sum of all: some subtle humourist, to feed fantastic heads with innovations and novelties, first invented this trifling childish glose upon dreams and physiognomy; wherein he strove only to boast himself of a pregnant probable conceit beyond philosophy or truth.

Let but any man who is most conversant in the superstition of dreams reckon me one that hath happened just, and I'll set down a hundred out of histories that have perished to foolery.

To come to late days. Lewis the xj. dreamt that he swam in blood on the top of the Alps, which one Father Robert, a holy hermit of his time, interpreted to be present death

81. Zopyrus, a quack physiognomist.

in his next wars against Italy, though he lived and prospered in all his enterprises a long while after.

So Charles the Fifth, sailing to the siege of Tunis, dreamt that the City met him on the sea like an Argosy, and overwhelmed his whole navy; when by Cornelius Agrippa, the great conjurer, who went along with him, it was expounded to be the overthrow of that famous expedition. And thereupon Agrippa offered the Emperor, if it pleased him to blow up the City by art magic in the air before his eyes without any farther jeopardy of war or beseiging. The Emperor utterly refused it and said since it was God's wars against an infidel, he would never borrow aid of the devil.

Some have memorized that Agrippa seeing his counsel in that case rejected, and that the Emperor, notwithstanding his unfortunate presage, was prosperous and successful, within few days after died frantic and desperate.

Alphonso, King of Naples, in like case, before the rumour of the French King's coming into Italy, had a vision in the night presented unto him of Aeneas' ghost having Turnus in chase, and Juno Pronuba coming betwixt them, and parting them; whereby he guessed that by marriage their jarring kingdoms should be united. But far otherwise it fell out, for the French King came indeed and he was driven thereby into such a melancholy ecstasy that he thought the very fowls of the air would snatch his crown from him, and no bough or arbour that overshadowed him but enclosed him and took him prisoner, and that not so much but the stones of the street sought to justle him out of his throne.

These examples I allege, to prove there is no certainty in dreams, and that they are but according to our devisings and meditations in the daytime.

I confess the saints and martyrs of the Primitive Church had unfallible dreams fore-running their ends, as Policarpus and other; but those especially proceeded from heaven and not from any vaporous dreggy parts of our blood or our brains.

For this cause the Turks banish learning from amongst

them, because it is every day setting men together by the ears, moving strange contentions and alterations, and making his professors faint-hearted and effeminate. Much more requisite were it that out of our civil Christian commonwealths we severely banish and exterminate those fabulous commentaries on toyish fantasies which fear-benumb and effeminate the hearts of the stoutest, cause a man without any ground to be jealous of his own friends and his kinsfolks, and withdraw him from the search and insight into more excellent things, to stand all his whole life sifting and winnowing dry rubbish chaff, whose best bottom quintescence proves in the end but sandy gravel and cockle.

Molestations and cares enough the ordinary course of our life tithes of his own accord unto us, though we seek not a knot in a bulrush,[82] or stuff not our night-pillows with thistles to increase our disturbance.

In our sleep we are aghasted and terrified with the disordered skirmishing and conflicting of our sensitive faculties. Yet with this terror and aghastment cannot we rest ourselves satisfied, but we must pursue and hunt after a further fear in the recordation and too busy examining our pains over-passed.

Dreams in my mind if they have any premonstrances in them, the preparative fear of that they so premonstrate and denounce is far worse than the mischief itself by them denounced and premonstrated.

So there is no long sickness but is worse than death, for death is but a blow and away, whereas sickness is like a Chancery suit, which hangs two or three year ere it can come to a judgment.

Oh, a consumption is worse than a *Capias ad Ligatum*;[83] to nothing can I compare it better than to a reprieve after a man is condemned, or to a boy with his hose about his heels, ready to be whipped, to whom his master stands preaching a long time all law and no gospel ere he proceed

82. *seek not ... bulrush*: Don't go looking for trouble.
83. Possibly a mistake for 'Capias Utligatum', 'a writ directing the arrest of an outlaw' (M.).

to execution. Or rather it is as a man should be roasted to death and melt away by little and little, whiles physicians like cooks stand stuffing him out with herbs and basting him with this oil and that syrup.

I am of the opinion that to be famished to death is far better, for his pain in seven or eight days is at an end, whereas he that is in a consumption continues languishing many years ere death have mercy on him.

The next plague and the nearest that I know in affinity to a consumption is long depending hope frivolously defeated, than which there is no greater misery on earth, and so *per consequens* no men in earth more miserable than courtiers. It is a cowardly fear that is not resolute enough to despair. It is like a poor hunger-starved wretch at sea, who still in expectation of a good voyage endures more miseries than Job. He that writes this can tell, for he hath never had good voyage in his life but one, and that was to a fortunate blessed island near those pinacle rocks called the Needles. Oh, it is a purified continent, and a fertile plot fit to seat another paradise, where, or in no place, the image of the ancient hospitality is to be found.

While I live I will praise it and extol it for the true magnificence and continued honourable bounty that I saw there.

Far unworthy am I to spend the least breath of commendation in the extolling so delightful and pleasant a Tempe,[84] or once to consecrate my ink with the excellent mention of the thrice-noble and illustrious chieftain under whom it is flourishingly governed.

That rare ornament of our country, learned Master Camden,[85] whose desertful name is universally admired throughout Christendom, in the last re-polished edition of his *Britannia* hath most elaborate and exactly described the sovereign plenteous situation of that isle, as also the inestimable happiness it inherits, it being patronized and care-

84. Beautiful valley in Thessaly.
85. William Camden (1551–1623), antiquary and historian. His *Britannia* was first published in 1586.

fully protected by so heroical and courageous a comman-der.[86]

Men that have never tasted that full spring of his liber-ality, wherewith, in my most forsaken extremities, right graciously he hath deigned to revive and refresh me, may rashly, at first sight, implead[87] me of flattery and not esteem these my fervent terms as the necessary repayment of due debt, but words idly begotten with good looks, and in an over-joyed humour of vain hope slipped from me by chance; but therein they shall show themselves too uncivil injurious, both to my devoted observant duty and the con-dign[88] dear purchased merit of his glory.

Too base a ground is this, whereon to embroider the rich story of his eternal renown; some longer-lived tractate I reserve for the full blaze of his virtues, which here only in the sparks I decipher. Many embers of encumbrances have I at this time, which forbid the bright flame of my zeal to mount aloft as it would. Perforce I must break from it, since other turbulent cares sit as now at the stern of my invention. Thus I conclude with this chance-medley parenthesis, that whatsoever minutes' intermission I have of calmed content, or least respite to call my wits together, principal and im-mediate proceedeth from him.

Through him my tender wainscot study door is delivered from much assault and battery. Through him I look into and am looked on in the world, from whence otherwise I were a wretched banished exile. Through him all my good, as by a conduit head, is conveyed unto me; and to him all my endeavours, like rivers, shall pay tribute as to the ocean.

Did Ovid entitle Carus, a nobleman of Rome, the only constant friend he had, in his ungrateful extrusion among the Getes, and writ to him thus:

Qui quod es id vere Care vocaris? [89]

86. Sir George Carey   87. Accuse, prosecute.
88. Worthy, deserving.
89. 'Are you called Carey [*Carus* = dear] because that is what you are?'

238

and in another elegy:

> *O mihi post nullos Care memorande sodales?* [90]

Much more may I acknowledge all redundant prostrate vassalage to the royal descended family of the Careys, but for whom my spirit long ere this had expired, and my pen served as a poniard to gall my own heart.

Why do I use so much circumstance, and in a stream on which none but gnats and flies do swim sound Fame's trumpet like Triton to call a number of foolish skiffs and light cock-boats [91] to parley?

Fear, if I be not deceived, was the last pertinent matter I had under my displing,[92] from which I fear I have strayed beyond my limits; and yet fear hath no limits, for to hell and beyond hell it sinks down and penetrates.

But this was my position, that the fear of any expected evil is worse than the evil itself, which by divers comparisons I confirmed.

Now to visions and apparitions again, as fast as I can trudge.

The glasses of our sight, in the night, are like the prospective glasses one Hostius made in Rome, which represented the images of things far greater than they were. Each mote in the dark they make a monster, and every slight glimmering a giant.

A solitary man in his bed is like a poor bed-red lazar lying by the highway-side unto whose displayed wounds and sores a number of stinging flies do swarm for pastance [93] and beverage. His naked wounds are his inward heart-griping woes, the wasps and flies his idle wandering thoughts; who to that secret smarting pain he hath already do add a further sting of impatience and new-lance his sleeping griefs and vexations.

Questionless, this is an unrefutable consequence, that the

---

90. 'After all my companions are gone, I will remember you, oh Carus.'
91. Small ship's-boats.   92. Discipline, in my charge.
93. Food, or possibly recreation, pastime.

man who is mocked of his fortune, he that hath consumed his brains to compass prosperity and meets with no counter-vailment [94] in her likeness, but hedge wine and lean mutton and peradventure some half-eyed good looks that can hardly be discerned from winking; this poor piteous perplexed miscreant either finally despairs, or like a lank frost-bitten plant loseth his vigour or spirit by little and little; any terror, the least illusion in the earth, is a Cacodaemon unto him. His soul hath left his body; for why, it is flying after these airy incorporate courtly promises, and glittering painted allurements, which when they vanish to nothing, it likewise vanisheth with them.

Excessive joy no less hath his defective and joyless operations, the spleen [95] into water it melteth; so that except it be some momentary bubbles of mirth, nothing it yields but a cloying surfeit of repentance.

Divers instances have we of men whom too much sudden content and over-ravished delight hath brought untimely to their graves.

Four or five I have read of, whom the very extremity of laughter hath bereft of their lives; whereby I gather that even such another pernicious sweet, superfluous mirth is to the sense as a surfeit of honey to a man's stomach, than the which there is nothing more dangerous.

Be it as dangerous as it will, it cannot but be an easy kind of death. It is like one that is stung with an aspis, who in the midst of his pain falls delighted asleep, and in that suavity of slumber surrenders the ghost; whereas he whom grief undertakes to bring to his end, hath his heart gnawen in sunder by little and little with vultures, like Prometheus.

But this is nothing, you will object, to our journey's end of apparitions. Yes, altogether; for of the overswelling superabundance of joy and grief we frame to ourselves most of our melancholy dreams and visions.

There is an old philosophical common proverb, *Unus-quisque fingit fortunam sibi*: everyone shapes his own for-

94. Compensation.
95. The seat of laughter.

tune as he lists. More aptly may it be said: everyone shapes his own fears and fancies as he list.

In all points our brains are like the firmament, and exhale in every respect the like gross mistempered vapours and meteors: of the more foeculent [96] combustible airy matter whereof, affrighting forms and monstrous images innumerable are created, but of the slimy unwieldier drossy part, dull melancholy or drowsiness.

And as the firmament is still moving and working, so uncessant is the wheeling and rolling on of our brains, which every hour are tempering some new piece of prodigy or other, and turmoiling, mixing and changing the course of our thoughts.

I write not this for that I think there are no true apparitions or prodigies, but to show how easily we may be flouted if we take not great heed with our own antique suppositions. I will tell you a strange tale tending to this nature; whether of true melancholy or true apparition, I will not take upon me to determine.

It was my chance in February last to be in the country some threescore mile off from London, where a gentleman of good worship and credit falling sick, the very second day of his lying down he pretended to have miraculous waking visions, which before I enter to describe, thus much I will inform ye by the way, that at the reporting of them he was in perfect memory, nor had sickness yet so tyrannized over him to make his tongue grow idle. A wise, grave, sensible man he was ever reputed, and so approved himself in all his actions in his life-time. This which I deliver, with many preparative protestations, to a great man of this land he confidently avouched. Believe it or condemn it as you shall see cause, for I leave it to be censured indifferently.

The first day of his distemperature, he visibly saw, as he affirmed, all his chamber hung with silken nets and silver hooks, the devil, as it should seem, coming thither a-fishing. Whereupon, every *Pater-Noster*-while,[97] he looked whether

96. Normally means impure, dreggy.
97. *every . . . while*: In the time it takes to say the Lord's Prayer.

in the nets he should be entangled, or with the hooks ensnared. With the nets he feared to be strangled or smothered, and with the hooks to have his throat scratched out and his flesh rent and mangled. At length, he knew not how, they suddenly vanished and the whole chamber was cleared. Next a company of lusty sailors, every one a shirker [98] or a swaggerer at the least, having made a brave voyage, came carousing and quaffing in large silver cans to his health. Fellows they were that had good big pop mouths [99] to cry 'port, ahelm, Saint George', and knew as well as the best what belongs to haling of bolings [100] yare [101] and falling on the starboard buttock.

But to the issue of my tale. Their drunken proffers he utterly put by, and said he highly scorned and detested both them and their hellish disguisings; which notwithstanding, they tossed their cups to the skies, and reeled and staggered up and down the room like a ship shaking in the wind.

After all they danced lusty gallant [102] and a drunken Danish lavalto [103] or two, and so departed. For the third course, rushed in a number of stately devils, bringing in boisterous [104] chests of massy treasure betwixt them. As brave they were as Turkish janissaries,[105] having their apparel all powdered with gold and pearl, and their arms as it were bemailed with rich chains and bracelets, but faces far blacker than any ball of tobacco, great glaring eyes that had whole shelves of Kentish oysters in them, and terrible wide mouths, whereof not one of them but would well have made a case for Molenax'[106] great globe of the world.

98. A rogue, swindler.
99. 'A mouth able to utter an exclamation with a sharp outburst' (NED).
100. Bowlines, ropes passed from the sail to the bow.
101. Tight and neat.
102. *lusty gallant*: A dance.
103. La volta, a boisterous Italian dance.
104. Strong.   105. The Sultan's guard.
106. Emeric Molyneux of Lambeth constructed a globe in 1592.

These lovely youths and full of favour, having stalked up and down the just measures of a sinkapace,[107] opened one of the principal chests they brought, and out of it plucked a princely royal tent, whose empearled shining canopy they quickly advanced on high, and with all artificial magnificence adorned like a state; which performed, pompous Lucifer entered, imitating in goodly stature the huge picture[108] of Laocoon at Rome, who sent unto him a gallant ambassador, signifying thus much, that if he would serve him, he should have all the rich treasure that he saw there, or any further wealth he would desire.

The gentleman returned this mild answer, that he knew not what he was, whether an angel or a wicked fiend, and if an angel, he was but his fellow servant, and no otherwise to be served or regarded; if a fiend, or a devil, he had nothing to do with him, for God had exalted and redeemed him above his desperate outcast condition, and a strong faith he had to defy and withstand all his juggling temptations. Having uttered these words, all the whole train of them invisibly avoided, and he never set eye on them after.

Then did there, for the third pageant, present themselves unto him an inveigling troop of naked virgins, thrice more amiable and beautiful than the bright vestals that brought in Augustus' Testament to the Senate after his decease; but no vestal-like ornament had they about them, for from top to toe bare despoiled they were, except some one or two of them that ware masks before their faces, and had transparent azured lawn veils before the chief jewel-houses of their honours.

Such goodly lustful bonarobaes[109] they were, by his report, as if any sharp-eyed painter had been there to peruse them, he might have learned to exceed divine Michael Angelo in the true bosk[110] of a naked, or curious Tuns[111] in quick life,

107. *Cinquepace*, a lively French dance.
108. i.e. in statuary.
109. Courtesans.
110. Sketch.
111. This may refer to the Dutch painter Willem Tons (M.).

whom the great masters of that art do term the sprightly
old man.

Their hair they ware loose unrolled about their shoulders,
whose dangling amber trammels reaching down beneath
their knees seemed to drop balm on their delicious bodies,
and ever as they moved to and fro, with their light windy
wavings, wantonly to correct their exquisite mistresses.

Their dainty feet in their tender birdlike trippings
enamelled, as it were, the dusty ground; and their odoriferous breath more perfumed the air than ordnance would
that is charged with amomum, musk, civet and amber-
greece.[112]

But to leave amplifications and proceed. Those sweet be-
witching naked maids, having majestically paced about the
chamber, to the end their natural unshelled shining mother
pearl proportions might be more imprintingly apprehended,
close to his bedside modestly blushing they approached,
and made impudent proffer unto him of their lascivious
embraces. He, obstinately bent to withstand these their
sinful allurements, no less than the former, bad them go
seek entertainment of hotter bloods, for he had not to
satisfy them. A cold comfort was this to poor wenches no
better clothed, yet they hearing what to trust to, very sorrowfully retired and shrunk away.

Lo, in the fourth act there sallied out a grave assembly of
sober-attired matrons, much like the virgins of Mary Mag-
dalen's order in Rome, which vow never to see man, or the
chaste daughters of Saint Philip.[113]

With no incontinent courtesy did they greet him, but
told him if he thought good they would pray for him.

Thereupon, from the beginning to the ending he unfolded
unto them how he had been mightily haunted with wicked
illusions of late, but nevertheless, if he could be persuaded
that they were angels or saints, their invocations could not

112. Ambergris, perfume from waxlike substance found in tropical
seas.
113. 'And the same man had four daughters, virgins, which did
prophesy' (*Acts*, XXI, 9).

hurt him; yea, he would add his desire to their requests to make their prayers more penetrably enforcing.

Without further parley, upon their knees they fell most devoutly and for half-an-hour never ceased extensively to intercessionate G O D for his speedy recovery.

Rising up again on the right hand of his bed, there appeared a clear light, and with that he might perceive a naked slender foot offering to steal betwixt the sheets in to him.

At which instant, entered a messenger from a knight of great honour thereabouts, who sent him a most precious extract quintessence to drink; which no sooner he tasted, but he thought he saw all the fore-named interluders at once hand-over-head leap, plunge and drown themselves in puddles and ditches hard by, and he felt perfect ease.

But long it lasted not with him, for within four hours after, having not fully settled his estate in order, he grew to trifling dotage, and raving died within two days following.

God is my witness, in all this relation I borrow no essential part from stretched-out invention, nor have I one jot abused my informations; only for the recreation of my readers, whom loath to tire with a coarse home-spun tale that should dull them worse than Holland cheese, here and there I welt and gard [114] it with allusive exornations [115] and comparisons; and yet methinks it comes off too gouty and lumbering.

Be it as it will, it is like to have no more allowance of English for me. If the world will give it any allowance of truth, so it is. For then I hope my excuse is already lawfully customed and authorized, since Truth is ever drawn and painted naked, and I have lent her but a leathern patched cloak at most to keep her from the cold; that is, that she come not off too lamely and coldly.

Upon the accidental occasion of this dream or apparition (call or miscall it what you will, for it is yours as freely as any waste paper that ever you had in your lives) was this

114. *welt and gard*: Adorn, trim.
115. Decorations, embellishments.

pamphlet (no bigger than an old preface) speedily botched up and compiled.

Are there any doubts which remain in your mind undigested, as touching this incredible narration I have unfolded? Well, doubt you not, but I am mild and tractable and will resolve you in what I may.

First, the house where this gentleman dwelt stood in a low marish ground, almost as rotten a climate as the Low Countries, where their misty air is as thick as mould butter, and the dew lies like frothy barm on the ground. It was noted over and besides to have been an unlucky house to all his predecessors, situate in a quarter not altogether exempted from witches. The abrupt falling into his sickness was suspicious, proceeding from no apparent surfeit or misdiet. The outrageous tyranny of it in so short a time bred thrice more admiration and wonder, and his sudden death incontinent [116] ensuing upon that his disclosed dream or vision, might seem some probable reason to confirm it, since none have such palpable dreams or visions but die presently after.

The like to this was Master Alington's vision [117] in the beginning of Her Majesty's reign; than the which there is nothing more ordinarily bruited.[118] Through Greek and Roman commonplaces to this purport I could run, if I were disposed to vaunt myself like a ridiculous pedant of deep reading in Fulgosius,[119] Licosthenes [120] and Valerius.[121]

Go no further than the Court, and they will tell you of a mighty worthy man of this land, who riding in his coach from London to his house was all the way haunted with a

116. Immediately.

117. Richard Allington, a merchant, on his death-bed had a vision in which those who had paid him usury money demanded repayment. 'This he did and died with a good conscience' (M.).

118. Talked about.

119. Gianbatista Fregoso, Doge of Genoa, whose book published in 1509 has a section on dreams.

120. Conrad Wolffhart (1518–61).

121. Possibly Valerius Maximus, but there were many others.

couple of hogs, who followed him close, and do what his men could, they might not drive them from him. Wherefore at night he caused them to be shut up in a barn and commanded milk to be given them; the barn door was locked, and the key safely kept, yet were they gone by morning, and no man knew how.

A number of men there be yet living who have been haunted by their wives after their death about forswearing themselves and undoing their children of whom they promised to be careful fathers; whereof I can gather no reason but this, that women are born to torment a man both alive and dead.

I have heard of others likewise, that besides these night-terrors, have been, for whole months together, whithersoever they went or rid, pursued by weasels and rats, and oftentimes with squirrels and hares, that in the travelling of three hundred mile have still waited on their horse heels.

But those are only the exploits and stratagems of witches, which may well astonish a little at first sight, but if a man have the least heart or spirit to withstand one fierce blast of their bravadoes, he shall see them shrink faster than northern cloth,[122] and outstrip time in dastardly flight.

Fie, fie, was ever poor fellow so far benighted in an old wive's tale of devils and urchins![123] Out upon it, I am weary of it, for it hath caused such a thick fulsome serena [124] to descend on my brain that now my pen makes blots as broad as a furred stomacher, and my muse inspires me to put out my candle and go to bed; and yet I will not neither, till, after all these nights' revels I have solemnly bid you goodnight, as much to say as tell you how you shall have a good night, and sleep quietly without affrightment and annoyance.

First and foremost, drink moderately, and dice and drab

122. Proverbial, cf. 'Charing-Cross was old, and old things must shrink as well as new Northern cloth' (*Westward Ho!* 2. 1) (M.).

123. Goblins, elves (which might take the form of an 'urchin' or hedgehog).

124. Evening rain. A 'serena' was considered harmful.

not away your money prodigally and then foreswear yourselves to borrow more.

You that be poor men's children, know your own fathers;
and though you can shift and cheat yourselves into good
clothes here about town, yet bow your knees to their
leathern bags and russet coats, that they may bless you from
the ambition of Tyburn.

You that bear the name of soldiers and live basely swaggering in every ale-house, having no other exhibition but
from harlots and strumpets, seek some new trade, and leave
whoring and quarrelling, lest besides the nightly guilt of
your own bankrout consciences, Bridewell or Newgate prove
the end of your cavaliering.

You, whosoever or wheresoever you be, that live by spoil-
ing and overreaching young gentlemen, and make but a
sport to deride their simplicities to their undoing, to you
the night at one time or other will prove terrible, except
you forthwith think on restitution; or if you have not your
night in this world, you will have it in hell.

You that are married and have wives of your own, and
yet hold too near friendship with your neighbours', set up
your rests [125] that the night will be an ill neighbour to your
rest and that you shall have as little peace of mind as the
rest. Therefore was Troy burnt by night, because Paris by
night prostituted Helena, and wrought such treason to
Prince Menelaus.

You that are Machiavellian vain fools, and think it no wit
or policy but to vow and protest what you never mean, that
travel for nothing else but to learn the vices of other countries and disfigure the ill English faces that God hath given
you with Tuscan glicks [126] and apish tricks: the night is for
you a black saunt [127] or a matachine, [128] except you presently
turn and convert to the simplicity you were born to.

You that can cast a man into an Italian ague when you

125. *set . . . rests*: Be assured, make up your mind to it.
126. Jests (variant of 'gleek').
127. Black sanctus, noisy discordant singing.
128. A sword dance performed in fantastic costume.

list, and imitate with your diet-drinks any disease or infirmity, the night likewise hath an infernal to act before ye.

Traitors that by night meet and consult how to walk in the day undiscovered, and think those words of Christ revealed and laid open: to you no less the night shall be as a night owl to vex and torment you.

And finally, on you judges and magistrates, if there be any amongst you that do wrest all the law into their own hands, by drawing and receiving every man's money into their hands, and making new golden laws of their own, which no prince nor parliament ever dreamed of; that look as just as Jehovah by day, enthronizing grave zeal and religion on the elevated whites of their eyes, when by night corrupt gifts and rewards rush in at their gates in whole armies, like northern carriers coming to their inn; that instead of their books turn over their bribes, for the deciding of causes, adjudging him the best right that brings the richest present unto them. If any such there be, I say, as in our Commonwealth I know none, but have read of in other states, let them look to have a number of unwelcome clients of their own accusing thoughts and imaginations that will betray them in the night to every idle fear and illusion.

Therefore are the terrors of the night more than of the day, because the sins of the night surmount the sins of the day.

By night-time came the Deluge over the face of the whole earth; by night-time Judas betrayed Christ, Tarquin ravished Lucretia.

When any poet would describe a horrible tragical accident, to add the more probability and credence unto it, he dismally beginneth to tell how it was dark night when it was done and cheerful daylight had quite abandoned the firmament.

Hence it is, that sin generally throughout the scripture is called the works of darkness; for never is the devil so busy as then, and then he thinks he may as well undiscovered walk abroad, as homicides and outlaws.

Had we no more religion than we might derive from

heathen fables, methinks those doleful quiristers of the night, the scritch-owl, the nightingale, and croaking frogs, might overawe us from any insolent transgression at that time. The first for her lavish blabbing of forbidden secrets, being for ever ordained to be a blab of ill-news and misfortune, still is crying out in our ears that we are mortal and must die. The second puts us in mind of the end and punishment of lust and ravishment.[129] And the third and last, that we are but slime and mud, such as those watery creatures are bred of; and therefore why should we delight to add more to our slime and corruption, by extraordinary surfeits and drunkenness?

But these are nothing neither in comparison. For he whom in the day heaven cannot exhale, the night will never help; she only pleading for her old grandmother hell. as well as the day for heaven.

Thus I shut up my treatise abruptly: that he who in the day doth not good works enough to answer the objections of the night, will hardly answer at the Day of Judgment.

FINIS

129. *The second ... ravishment*: i.e. Philomela, changed by the gods into a nightingale, having been ravished by Tereus.

4

The Unfortunate Traveller

OR

THE LIFE OF JACK WILTON

Qui audiunt audita dicunt

To the Right Honourable Lord Henry Wriothesley,
Earl of Southampton, and Baron of Tichfield.

INGENUOUS[1] honourable lord, I know not what blind custom methodical antiquity hath thrust upon us, to dedicate
such books as we publish to one great man or other. In
which respect, lest any man should challenge these my
papers as goods uncustomed, and so extend upon them as
forfeit to contempt, to the seal of your excellent censure, lo
here I present them to be seen and allowed. Prize them
as high or as low as you list: if you set any price on them, I
hold my labour well satisfied. Long have I desired to
approve my wit unto you. My reverent dutiful thoughts
(even from their infancy) have been retainers to your glory.
Now at last I have enforced an opportunity to plead my
devoted mind.

All that in this fantastical treatise I can promise, is some
reasonable conveyance of history, and variety of mirth. By
divers of my good friends have I been dealt with to employ
my dull pen in this kind, it being a clean different vein from
other my former courses of writing. How well or ill I have
done in it, I am ignorant (the eye that sees round about
itself sees not into itself): only your Honour's applauding
encouragement hath power to make me arrogant. Incomprehensible is the heighth of your spirit, both in heroical
resolution and matters of conceit.[2] Unreprievably perisheth
that book whatsoever to waste paper, which on the diamond

1. Ingenious.   2. Imagination, creativeness.

rock of your judgment disasterly chanceth to be ship-wrecked. A dear lover and cherisher you are, as well of the lovers of poets themselves. Amongst their sacred number I dare not ascribe myself, though now and then I speak English; that small brain I have, to no further use I convert, save to be kind to my friends and fatal to my enemies. A new brain, a new wit, a new style, a new soul will I get me, to canonize your name to posterity, if in this my first attempt I be not taxed of presumption.

Of your gracious favour I despair not, for I am not alto-gether Fame's outcast. This handful of leaves I offer to your view, to the leaves on trees I compare, which, as they cannot grow of themselves except they have some branches or boughs to cleave to, and with whose juice and sap they be evermore recreated and nourished, so, except these un-polished leaves of mine have some branch of nobility where-on to depend and cleave, and with the vigorous nutriment of whose authorized commendation they may be continu-ally fostered and refreshed, never will they grow to the world's good liking, but forthwith fade and die on the first hour of their birth. Your Lordship is the large-spreading branch of renown, from whence these my idle leaves seek to derive their whole nourishing: it resteth you either scorn-fully shake them off, as worm-eaten and worthless, or in pity preserve them and cherish them for some little summer fruit you hope to find amongst them.

Your Honour's in all humble service:

THO: NASHE.

THE INTRODUCTION TO THE DAPPER
MONSIEUR PAGES OF THE COURT

Gallant squires, have amongst you! At mumchance[3] I mean not, for so I might chance come to short commons, but at *novus, nova, novum*,[4] which is in English, 'news of the maker'. A proper fellow page of yours, called Jack Wilton,

3. A card game.
4. Pun on 'novum' (new) and 'novem' (a dice game).

by me commends him unto you, and hath bequeathed for waste paper here amongst you certain pages of his misfortunes. In any case keep them preciously as a privy token of his good will towards you. If there be some better than other, he craves you would honour them in their death so much as to dry and kindle tobacco with them. For a need he permits you to wrap velvet pantofles in them also, so they be not woe-begone at the heels, or weather-beaten, like a black head with grey hairs, or mangy at the toes, like an ape about the mouth. But as you love good fellowship and ames-ace,[5] rather turn them to stop mustard pots than the grocers should have one patch of them to wrap mace [6] in: a strong, hot, costly spice it is, which above all things he hates. To any use about meat or drink put them to and spare not, for they cannot do their country better service. Printers are mad whoresons; allow them some of them for napkins.

Just a little nearer to the matter and the purpose. Memorandum: every one of you after the perusing of this pamphlet is to provide him a case of poniards, that if you come in company with any man which shall dispraise it or speak against it, you may straight cry 'Sic respondeo', and give him the stockado. It stands not with your honours, I assure ye, to have a gentleman and a page abused in his absence. Secondly, whereas you were wont to swear men on a pantofle [7] to be true to your puissant order, you shall swear them on nothing but this chronicle of the King of Pages henceforward. Thirdly, it shall be lawful for any whatsoever to play with false dice in a corner on the cover of this foresaid Acts and Monuments. None of the fraternity of the minorites shall refuse it for a pawn in the times of famine and necessity. Every stationer's stall they pass by, whether by day or by night, they shall put off their hats to and make a low leg in regard their grand printed Capitano is there entombed. It shall be flat treason for any of this fore-

5. Throw of two aces, the lowest possible; or perhaps a dice game.
6. Pun on the sergeant or bailiff's mace.
7. As an initiation ceremony for undergraduates.

mentioned catalogue of the point-trussers once to name him within forty foot of an alehouse; marry, the tavern is honourable. Many special grave articles more had I to give you in charge, which your Wisdoms waiting together at the bottom of the Great Chamber stairs, or sitting in a porch (your parliament house), may better consider of than I can deliver. Only let this suffice for a taste to the text and a bit to pull on a good wit with, as a rasher on the coals is to pull on a cup of wine.

Hey-pass, come aloft! Every man of you take your places, and hear Jack Wilton tell his own tale.

THE UNFORTUNATE TRAVELLER

About that time that the terror of the world and fever quartane of the French, Henry the Eight (the only true subject of chronicles), advanced his standard against the two hundred and fifty towers of Turney and Turwin,[8] and had the Emperor and all the nobility of Flanders, Holland and Brabant as mercenary attendants on his full-sailed fortune, I, Jack Wilton, a gentleman at least, was a certain kind of an appendix or page, belonging or appertaining in or unto the confines of the English Court; where what my credit was, a number of my creditors that I cozened can testify. *Coelum petimus stultitia*[9]: which of us all is not a sinner? Be it known to as many as will pay money enough to peruse my story, that I followed the Court or the camp, or the camp and the Court, when Turwin lost her maidenhead and opened her gates to more than Jane Trosse[10] did. There did I (soft, let me drink before I go any further) reign sole King of the Cans and Black-jacks, Prince of the Pigmies, County Palatine of Clean Straw and Provant, and, to conclude, Lord High Regent of Rashers of the Coals and Red-herring Cobs.[11] *Paulô maiora canamus.*[12] Well, to

8. Tournai and Térouanne (1513).
9. 'We seek the heavens in our stupidity' (Horace).
10. Reference unknown.   11. Heads.
12. 'Let us sing of matters a little more important' (Virgil).

the purpose. What stratagemical acts and monuments do you think an ingenious infant of my years might enact? You will say, it were sufficient if he slur a die,[13] pawn his master to the utmost penny, and minister the oath of the pantofle artificially. These are signs of good education, I must confess, and arguments of 'In grace and virtue' to proceed. Oh, but *Aliquid latet quod non patet*;[14] there's a further path I must trace.

Examples confirm: list, lordings, to my proceedings.

Whosoever is acquainted with the state of a camp understands that in it be many quarters, and yet not so many as on London Bridge. In those quarters are many companies: 'much company, much knavery', as true as that old adage, 'much courtesy, much subtlety'. Those companies, like a great deal of corn, do yield some chaff: the corn are cormorants, the chaff are good fellows which are quickly blown to nothing with bearing a light heart in a light purse. Amongst this chaff was I winnowing my wits to live merrily, and by my troth so I did. The Prince could but command men spend their blood in his service; I could make them spend all the money they had for my pleasure. But poverty in the end parts friends. Though I was prince of their purses, and exacted of my unthrift subjects as much liquid allegiance as any keisar in the world could do, yet where it is not to be had, the king must lose his right. Want cannot be withstood; men can do no more than they can do. What remained then but the fox's case must help when the lion's skin is out at the elbows.

There was a lord in the camp. Let him be a Lord of Misrule if you will, for he kept a plain alehouse without welt or guard of any ivy-bush,[15] and sold cider and cheese by pint and by pound to all that came (at the very name of cider I can but sigh, there is so much of it in Rhenish wine

13. 'A method of cheating at dice by throwing so that the die slides without turning' (M.).
14. 'Something is hidden which is not obvious.'
15. Sacred to Bacchus.

nowadays). Well, *Tendit ad sydera virtus*: [16] there's great virtue belongs, I can tell you, to a cup of cider, and very good men have sold it, and at sea it is *Aqua coelestis*.[17] But that's neither here nor there: if it had no other patron but this peer of quart pots to authorize it, it were sufficient. This great lord, this worthy lord, this noble lord, thought no scorn (Lord have mercy upon us) to have his great velvet breeches larded with the droppings of this dainty liquor; and yet he was an old servitor, a cavalier of an ancient house, as might appear by the arms of his ancestors, drawn very amiably in chalk on the inside of his tent door.

He and no other was the man I chose out to damn with a lewd moneyless device. For, coming to him on a day as he was counting his barrels and setting the price in chalk on the head of them, I did my duty very devoutly, and told his aley Honour I had matters of some secrecy to impart unto him, if it pleased him to grant me private audience. 'With me, young Wilton,' quod he; 'marry, and shalt! Bring us a pint of cider of a fresh tap into The Three Cups here – wash the pot.' So into a back room he led me, where, after he had spit on his finger and picked off two or three motes [18] off his old moth-eaten velvet cap, and sponged and wrung all the rheumatic drivel from his ill-favoured goat's-beard, he bad me declare my mind, and thereupon he drank to me on the same. I up with a long circumstance, alias a cunning shift of the seventeens, and discoursed unto him what entire affection I had borne him time out mind, partly for the high descent and lineage from whence he sprung, and partly for the tender care and provident respect he had of poor soldiers; that, whereas the vastity of that place (which afforded them no indifferent supply of drink or of victuals) might humble them to some extremity and so weaken their hands, he vouchsafed in his own person to be a victualler to the camp (a rare example of magnificence and honourable courtesy), and diligently provided that with-

16. Allusion to '*tendit in ardua virtus*' (Ovid).
17. 'Water of the heavens', name of a restorative drug.
18. Specks of dust.

out far travel every man might for his money have cider and cheese his bellyful. Nor did he sell his cheese by the way [19] only, or his cider by the great, but abased himself with his own hands to take a shoemaker's knife (a homely instrument for such a high personage to touch) and cut it out equally, like a true justiciary, in little pennyworths, that it would do a man good for to look upon. So likewise of his cider, the poor man might have his moderate draught of it (as there is a moderation in all things) as well for his doit [20] or his dandiprat [21] as the rich man for his half-souse or his denier. 'Not so much,' quoth I, 'but this tapster's linen apron which you wear to protect your apparel from the imperfections of the spigot, most amply bewrays your lowly mind. I speak it with tears: too few noblemen have we that will drink in linen aprons. Why, you are every child's fellow. Any man that comes under the name of a soldier and a good fellow, you will sit and bear company to the last pot; yea, and you take in as good part of the homely phrase of "Mine host, here's to you" as if one saluted you by all the titles of your barony. These considerations, I say, which the world suffers to slip by in the channel of forgetfulness, have moved me, in ardent zeal of your welfare, to forewarn you of some dangers that have beset you and your barrels.'

At the name of dangers he start up, and bounced with his fist on the board so hard that his tapster overhearing him cried 'Anon, anon, sir, by and by', and came and made a low leg and asked him what he lacked. He was ready to have stricken his tapster for interrupting him in attention of this his so much desired relation, but for fear of displeasing me he moderated his fury, and, only sending for the other fresh pint, willed him look to the bar and come when he is called, with a devil's name. Well, at his earnest importunity, after I had moistened my lips to make my lie run glib to his journey's end, forward I went as followeth.

19. By the two to three hundredweight.
20. A coin worth about a farthing.
21. A coin which varied in value. A little later than this it was worth only one tenth of a penny.

'It chanced me the other night, amongst other pages, to attend where the King with his lords and many chief leaders sat in council. There, amongst sundry serious matters that were debated, and intelligences from the enemy given up, it was privily imformed (no villains to these privy informers!) that you, even you that I now speak to, had. . . . Oh, would I had no tongue to tell the rest! By this drink, it grieves me so I am not able to repeat it . . .'

Now was my drunken lord ready to hang himself for the end of the full point; and over my neck he throws himself very lubberly, and entreated me, as I was a proper young gentleman and ever looked for pleasure at his hands, soon to rid him out of this hell of suspense, and resolve him of the rest. Then fell he on his knees, wrung his hands, and I think on my conscience wept out all the cider that he had drunk in a week before. To move me to have pity on him, he rose and put his rusty ring on my finger, gave me his greasy purse with that single money that was in it, promised to make me his heir, and a thousand more favours, if I would expire the misery of his unspeakable tormenting uncertainty. I, being by nature inclined to Mercy (for indeed I knew two or three good wenches of that name), bad him harden his ears and not make his eyes abortive before their time, and he should have the inside of my breast turned outward, hear such a tale as would tempt the utmost strength of life to attend it, and not die in the midst of it.

'Why,' quoth I, 'myself that am but a poor childish wellwiller of yours, with the very thought that a man of your desert and state by a number of peasants and varlets should be so injuriously abused in hugger-mugger,[22] have wept all my urine upward. The wheel under our city bridge carries not so much water over the city as my brain hath welled forth gushing streams of sorrow. I have wept so immoderately and lavishly that I thought verily my palate had been turned to Pissing Conduit[23] in London. My eyes have been drunk, outrageously drunk, with giving but ordinary inter-

22. Secrecy.
23. Near junction of Threadneedle St and Cornhill.

course through their sea-circled islands to my distilling dreariment. What shall I say? That which malice hath said is the mere overthrow and murther of your days. Change not your colour: none can slander a clear conscience to itself. Receive all your fraught of misfortune in at once.

'It is buzzed in the King's head that you are a secret friend to the enemy, and, under pretence of getting a licence to furnish the camp with cider and suchlike provant, you have furnished the enemy, and in empty barrels sent letters of discovery and corn innumerable.'

I might well have left here, for by this time his white liver had mixed itself with the white of his eye, and both were turned upwards as if they had offered themselves a fair white for death to shoot at. The truth was, I was very loth mine host and I should part with dry lips. Wherefore the best means that I could imagine to wake him out of his trance was to cry loud in his ear: 'Ho, host, what's to pay? Will no man look to the reckoning here?' And in plain verity it took expected effect for, with the noise, he started and bustled, like a man that had been scared with fire out of his sleep, and ran hastily to his tapster and all-to-belaboured him about the ears for letting gentlemen call so long and not look in to them. Presently he remembered himself, and had like to fall into his memento[24] again but that I met him half-ways and asked his Lordship what he meant to slip his neck out of the collar so suddenly and, being revived, strike his tapster so hastily.

'Oh,' quoth he, 'I am bought and sold for doing my country such good service as I have done! They are afraid of me because my good deeds have brought me into such estimation with the commonalty. I see, I see, it is not for the lamb to live with the wolf.'

The world is well amended, thought I, with your Cidership: such another forty years' nap together as Epeminedes[25] had would make you a perfect wise man.

'Answer me,' quoth he, 'my wise young Wilton. Is it true

24. Brown study (M.), reverie, daze.
25. His sleep lasted forty years, or, according to Pliny, fifty-seven.

that I am thus underhand dead and buried by these bad tongues?'

'Nay,' quoth I, 'you shall pardon me, for I have spoken too much already. No definitive sentence of death shall march out of my well-meaning lips. They have but lately sucked milk, and shall they so suddenly change their food and seek after blood?'

'Oh, but,' quoth he, 'a man's friend is his friend. Fill the other pint, tapster. What said the King? Did he believe it when he heard it? I pray thee say. I swear by my nobility, none in the world shall ever be made privy that I received any light of this matter by thee.'

'That firm affiance,' quoth I, 'had I in you before, or else I would never have gone so far over shoes to pluck you out of the mire. Not to make many words, since you will needs know, the King says flatly you are a miser and a snudge,[26] and he never hoped better of you.'

'Nay then,' quoth he, 'questionless some planet that loves not cider hath conspired against me.'

'Moreover, which is worse, the King hath vowed to give Turwin one hot breakfast only with the bungs that he will pluck out of your barrels. I cannot stay at this time to report each circumstance that passed, but the only counsel that my long-cherished, kind inclination can possibly contrive, is now in your old days to be liberal. Such victuals or provision as you have, presently distribute it frankly amongst poor soldiers. I would let them burst their bellies with cider and bathe in it, before I would run into my Prince's ill opinion for a whole sea of it. The hunter pursuing the beaver for his stones, he bites them off and leaves them behind for him to gather up, whereby he lives quiet. If greedy hunters and hungry tale-tellers pursue you, it is for a little pelf that you have. Cast it behind you, neglect it, let them have it, lest it breed a farther inconvenience. Credit my advice; you shall find it prophetical. And thus have I discharged the part of a poor friend.'

With some few like phrases of ceremony ('Your Honour's

26. Skinflint.

poor suppliant' and so forth, and 'Farewell, my good youth, I thank thee and will remember thee') we parted.

But the next day I think we had a deal of cider, cider in bowls, in scuppets,[27] in helmets. And, to conclude, if a man would have filled his boots full, there he might have had it. Provant thrust itself into poor soldiers' pockets whether they would or no. We made five peals of shot into the town together of nothing but spigots and faucets [28] of discarded empty barrels. Every under-foot soldier had a distenanted tun, as Diogenes had his tub to sleep in. I myself got as many confiscated tapsters' aprons as made me a tent as big as any ordinary commander's in the field. But, in conclusion, my well-beloved Baron of double-beer got him humbly on his mary-bones [29] to the King, and complained he was old and stricken in years, and had never an heir to cast at a dog, wherefore if it might please His Majesty to take his lands into his hands, and allow him some reasonable pension to live on, he should be marvellously well pleased. As for wars, he was weary of them; yet, as long as his Highness ventured his own person, he would not flinch a foot, but make his withered body a buckler to bear off any blow advanced against him.

The King, marvelling at this alteration of his cider-merchant (for so he often pleasantly termed him), with a little further talk bolted out the whole complotment. Then was I pitifully whipped for my holiday lie, though they made themselves merry with it many a winter's evening after.

For all this, his good ass-headed Honour, mine host, persevered in his former request to the King to accept his lands and allow him a beadsmanry [30] or out-brothership of brachet;[31] which through his vehement instancy took effect, and the King jestingly said, since he would needs have it so,

27. A kind of shovel (M.).
28. *spigots and faucets*: Tops of beer and wine barrels.
29. Marrow bones, knees.
30. Tenancy of an almshouse.
31. *out-brothership of brachet*: 'What "mine host" is wanting is perhaps the care of a kennel of bitch hounds in the country near one of the royal palaces' (F.P.W.).

he would distrain on part of his land for impost of cider, which he was behind with.

This was one of my famous achievements, insomuch as I never light upon the like famous fool. But I have done a thousand better jests, if they had been booked in order as they were begotten. It is pity posterity should be deprived of such precious records; and yet there is no remedy; and yet there is too, for when all fails, well fare a good memory. Gentle readers (look you be gentle now, since I have called you so), as freely as my knavery was mine own, it shall be yours to use in the way of honesty.

Even in this expedition of Turwin (for the King stood not long a-thrumming of buttons there) it happened me fall in (I would it had fallen out otherwise for his sake) with an ugly mechanical[32] Captain. You must think in an army, where truncheons are in their state-house, it is a flat stab once to name a Captain without cap in hand. Well, suppose he was a Captain, and had never a good cap of his own, but I was fain to lend him one of my lord's cast velvet caps and a weather-beaten feather wherewith he threatened his soldiers afar off, as Jupiter is said with the shaking of his hair to make heaven and earth to quake. Suppose out of the parings[33] of a pair of false dice I apparelled both him and myself many a time and oft. And surely, not to slander the devil, if any man ever deserved the golden dice[34] the King of the Parthians sent to Demetrius, it was I: I had the right vein of sucking up a die twixt the dints of my fingers; not a crevice in my hand but could swallow a quater trey[35] for a need; in the line of life many a dead lift did there lurk, but it was nothing towards the maintenance of a

32. Vulgar.

33. Earnings, profits, ('the gains from false dice are compared to those from clipping coin', Maxwell).

34. 'And it [dice play] was accounted so great a reproach among the noblest men, that the King of the Parthians sent golden dice to King Demetrius, for a reproach of his lightness' (Cornelius Agrippa quoted by M.).

35. *quater trey*: Dice loaded so that four or three would come up (M.).

family. This Monsieur Capitano ate up the cream of my earnings, and *Crede mihi, res est ingeniosa dare*:[36] 'Any man is a fine fellow as long as he hath any money in his purse.' That money is like the marigold, which opens and shuts with the sun: if fortune smileth or one be in favour, it floweth; if the evening of age comes on, or he falls into disgrace, it fadeth and is not to be found. I was my craft's master though I were but young, and could as soon decline *Nominativo hic asinus*[37] as a greater clerk. Wherefore I thought it not convenient my soldado should have my purse any longer for his drum to play upon, but I would give him Jack Drum's entertainment[38] and send him packing.

This was my plot. I knew a piece of service of intelligence which was presently to be done, that required a man with all his five senses to effect it, and would overthrow any fool that should undertake it. To this service did I animate and egg my foresaid costs and charges, alias Senior Velvet-cap, whose head was not encumbered with too much forecast. And coming to him in his cabin about dinner-time, where I found him very devoutly paring of his nails for want of other repast, I entertained him with this solemn oration.

'Captain, you perceive how near both of us are driven. The dice of late are grown as melancholy as a dog; high men and low men both prosper alike; langrets,[39] fulhams[40] and all the whole fellowship of them will not afford a man his dinner. Some other means must be invented to prevent imminent extremity. My state, you are not ignorant, depends on trencher service. Your advancement must be derived from the valour of your arm. In the delays of siege, desert hardly gets a day of hearing: 'tis gowns must direct and guns enact all the wars that is to be made against walls. Resteth no way for you to climb suddenly, but by doing

36. 'Believe me, to give is a mark of genius' (Ovid).
37. In tables used for learning Latin declensions the form would run *Nominativo hic magister*' (or *dominus*), not *asinus*.
38. Expulsion with violence.
39. False dice, longer on the three and four than other sides.
40. Dice loaded at the corner.

some rare stratagem, the like not before heard of; and fitly at this time occasion is offered.

There is a feat the King is desirous to have wrought on some great man of the enemy's side. Marry, it requireth not so much resolution as discretion to bring it to pass; and yet resolution enough should be shown in it too, being so full of hazardous jeopardy as it is. Hark in your ear. Thus it is: without more drumbling [41] or pausing, if you will undertake it and work it through-stitch [42] (as you may, ere the King hath determined which way to go about it), I warrant you are made while you live; you need not care which way your staff falls. If it prove not so, then cut off my head.'

Oh my auditors, had you seen him how he stretched out his limbs, scratched his scabbed elbows at this speech, how he set his cap over his eyebrows like a politician, and then folded his arms one in another and nodded with the head, as who would say 'Let the French beware, for they shall find me a devil. . . .' If, I say, you had seen but half the action that he used, of shrucking up his shoulders, smiling scornfully, playing with his fingers on his buttons and biting the lip, you would have laughed your face and your knees together. The iron being hot, I thought to lay on load, for in any case I would not have his humour cool. As before I laid open unto him the brief sum of the service, so now I began to urge the honourableness of it and what a rare thing it was to be a right politician, how much esteemed of kings and princes, and how divers of mean parentage have come to be monarchs by it. Then I discoursed of the qualities and properties of him in every respect; how, like the wolf, he must draw the breath from a man long before he be seen; how, like a hare, he must sleep with his eyes open; how, as the eagle in his flying casts dust in the eyes of crows and other fowls for to blind them, so he must cast dust in the eyes of his enemies, delude their sight by one means or other, that they dive not into his subtleties; how he must be familiar with all and trust none; drink,

41. Idling, time-wasting.   42. Thoroughly.

carouse and lecher with him out of whom he hopes to wring any matter; swear and forswear rather than be suspected; and, in a word, have the art of dissembling at his fingers' ends as perfect as any courtier.

'Perhaps,' quoth I, 'you may have some few greasy cavaliers that will seek to dissuade you from it, and they will not stick to stand on their three-halfpenny honour, swearing and staring that a man were better be a hangman than an intelligencer, and call him a sneaking eavesdropper, a scraping hedge-creeper, and a piperly pickthank.[43] But you must not be discouraged by their talk, for the most part of these beggarly contemners of wit are huge burly-boned butchers like Ajax, good for nothing but to strike right-down blows on a wedge with a cleaving-beetle, or stand hammering all day upon bars of iron. The whelps of a bear never grow but sleeping, and these bear-wards, having big limbs, shall be preferred though they do nothing. You have read stories' (I'll be sworn he never looked in book in his life) 'how many of the Roman worthies were there that have gone as spials into their enemy's camp? Ulysses, Nestor, Diomede went as spies together in the night into the tents of Rhesus, and intercepted Dolon, the spy of the Trojans. Never any discredited the trade of intelligencers but Judas, and he hanged himself. Danger will put wit into any man. Architas made a wooden dove to fly; by which proportion I see no reason that the veriest block in the world should despair of anything. Though nature be contrary inclined, it may be altered; yet usually those whom she denies her ordinary gifts in one thing, she doubles them in another. That which the ass wants in wit, he hath in honesty: who ever saw him kick or winch,[44] or use any jade's tricks? Though he live an hundred years you shall never hear that he breaks pasture. Amongst men, he that hath not a good wit lightly [45] hath a good iron memory, and he that hath neither of both hath some bones to carry

43. Sycophant.
44. Kick restlessly or impatiently (NED).
45. Often, probably.

burthens. Blind men have better noses than other men; the bull's horns serve him as well as hands to fight withal; the lion's paws are as good to him as a pole-axe to knock down any that resist him; the boar's tushes serve him in better stead than a sword and buckler; what need the snail care for eyes when he feels the way with his two horns as well as if he were as quick-sighted as a decipherer? There is a fish that having no wings supports herself in the air with her fins. Admit that you had neither wit nor capacity (as sure, in my judgment, there is none equal unto you in idiotism), yet if you have simplicity and secrecy, serpents themselves will think you a serpent; for what serpent is there but hides his sting? And yet, whatsoever be wanting, a good plausible tongue in such a man of employment can hardly be spared, which, as the fore-named serpent with his winding tail fetcheth in those that come near him, so with a ravishing tale it gathers all men's hearts unto him; which if he have not, let him never look to engender by the mouth, as ravens and doves do; that is, mount or be great by undermining. Sir, I am ascertained that all these imperfections I speak of in you have their natural resiance.[46] I see in your face that you were born, with the swallow, to feed flying, to get much treasure and honour by travel. None so fit as you for so important an enterprise: our vulgar politicians are but flies swimming on the stream of subtlety superficially in comparison of your singularity. Their blind narrow eyes cannot pierce into the profundity of hypocrisy. You alone, with Palamede,[47] can pry into Ulysses' mad counterfeiting. You can discern Achilles from a chamber-maid,[48] though he be decked with his spindle and distaff. As Jove dining with Lycaon could not be beguiled with human flesh dressed like meat,[49] so no human brain may go beyond you, none beguile you. You gull all; all fear you, love you, stoop to you.

46. Residence.

47. Palamedes detected Ulysses' feigned madness.

48. Disguised himself as a woman to avoid conscription for the Trojan War.

49. Lycaon and his fifty godless sons were killed by Jove for attempting to deceive him in this way.

Therefore, good sir, be ruled by me: stoop your fortune so low as to bequeath yourself wholly to this business.'

This silver-sounding tale made such sugared harmony in his ears that with the sweet meditation what a more than miraculous politician he should be and what kingly promotion should come tumbling on him thereby, he could have found in his heart to have packed up his pipes and to have gone to heaven without a bait.[50] Yea, he was more inflamed and ravished with it than a young man called Taurimontanus was with the Phrygian melody: who was so incensed and fired therewith that he would needs run presently upon it and set a courtesan's house on fire that had angered him.

No remedy there was but I must help to furnish him with money. I did so, as who will not make his enemy a bridge of gold to fly by? Very earnestly he conjured me to make no man living privy to his departure, in regard of his place and charge, and on his honour assured me his return should be very short and successful. 'Ay, ay, shorter by the neck,' thought I. In the meantime, let this be thy posy:[51] 'I live in hope to scape the rope.'

Gone he is. God send him good shipping to Wapping, and by this time, if you will, let him be a pitiful poor fellow and undone for ever. For mine own part, if he had been mine own brother I could have done no more for him than I did; for, straight after his back was turned, I went in all love and kindness to the Marshal General of the field, and certified him that such a man was lately fled to the enemy, and got his place begged for another immediately. What became of him after you shall hear. To the enemy he went and offered his service, railing egregiously against the King of England. He swore, as he was a gentleman and a soldier, he would be revenged on him; and let but the King of France follow his counsel, he would drive him from Turwin walls yet ere three days to an end. All these were good humours, but the tragedy followeth. The French King hearing of such a prating fellow that was come, desired to see

50. Without a stop for food.   51. Rhymed motto.

him, but yet he feared treason, willing one of his minions to take upon him his person, and he would stand by as a private person while he was examined. Why should I use any idle delays? In was Captain Gogswounds brought, after he was throughly searched. Not a louse in his doublet was let pass but was asked *Quevela*? [52] and charged to stand in the King's name. The moulds of his buttons they turned out to see if they were not bullets covered over with thread. The cod-piece in his devil's breeches [53] (for they were then in fashion) they said plainly was a case for a pistol. If he had had ever a hobnail in his shoes, it had hanged him, and he should never have known who had harmed him. But as luck was, he had no mite of any metal about him. He took part with none of the Four Ages, neither the Golden Age, the Silver Age, the Brazen, nor the Iron Age; only his purse was aged in emptiness, and I think verily a puritan, for it kept itself from any pollution of crosses. [54] Standing before the supposed King, he was asked what he was and wherefore he came. To which, in a glorious bragging humour, he answered that he was a gentleman, a captain commander, a chief leader, that came from the King of England upon discontentment. Questioned of the particular cause, he had not a word to bless himself with, yet fain he would have patched out a polt-foot [55] tale, but, God knows, it had not one true leg to stand on.

Then began he to smell on the villain so rammishly [56] that none there but was ready to rent him in pieces, yet the minion-king kept in his choler, and propounded unto him further what of the King of England's secrets (so advantage-able) he was privy to, as might remove him from the siege of Turwin in three days. He said divers, divers matters which asked longer conference, but in good honesty they were lies which he had not yet stamped. [57] Hereat the true King stepped forth and commanded to lay hands on the

52. 'Who goes there?'
53. Loosely fitting trousers.
54. On the back of many coins.
55. Club-foot.
56. With a bad smell.
57. Coined.

lozel,[58] and that he should be tortured to confess the truth, for he was a spy and nothing else.

He no sooner saw the wheel and the torments set before him, but he cried out like a rascal and said he was a poor Captain in the English camp, suborned by one Jack Wilton, a nobleman's page, and no other, to come and kill the French King in a bravery [59] and return, and that he had no other intention in the world.

This confession could not choose but move them all to laughter, in that he made it as light a matter to kill their King and come back, as to go to Islington and eat a mess of cream and come home again; nay, and besides he protested that he had no other intention, as if that were not enough to hang him.

Adam never fell till God made fools. All this could not keep his joints from ransacking on the wheel, for they vowed either to make him a confessor or a martyr with a trice. When still he sung all one song, they told the King he was a fool, and that some shrewd head had knavishly wrought on him. Wherefore it should stand with his honour to whip him out of the camp and send him home. That persuasion took place, and soundly was he lashed out of their liberties and sent home by a herald with this message: that so the King his Master hoped to whip home all the English fools very shortly. Answer was returned that that shortly was a long lie, and they were shrewd fools that should drive the Frenchman out of his kingdom, and make him glad, with Corinthian Dionysius,[60] to play the schoolmaster.

The herald being dismissed, our afflicted intelligencer was called *coram nobis*.[61] How he sped, judge you; but something he was adjudged too. The sparrow for his lechery liveth but a year; he for his treachery was turned on the toe,[62] *Plura dolor prohibet*.[63]

58. Scoundrel.   59. Out of bravado, as a 'dare'.
60. Tyrant of Syracuse, who fled and took up a teaching post.
61. 'Into our presence'.   62. Flogged (M.).
63. 'Grief prevents [my saying] more' (Ovid)).

Here let me triumph awhile and ruminate a line or two on the excellence of my wit; but I will not breathe neither till I have disfraughted all my knavery.

Another Switzer Captain that was far gone for want of the wench, I led astray most notoriously, for he being a monstrous unthrift of battle-axes (as one that cared not in his anger to bid fly out scuttles to five score of them) and a notable emboweller of quart pots, I came disguised unto him in the form of a half-crown wench, my gown and attire according to the custom then in request. Iwis I had my courtsies in cue, or in quart pot rather, for they dived into the very entrails of the dust, and I simpered with my countenance like a porridge pot on the fire when it first begins to seethe. The sobriety of the circumstance is that after he had courted me and all, and given me in the earnest-penny of impiety some six crowns at the least for an antipast [64] to iniquity, I feigned an impregnable excuse to be gone, and never came at him after.

Yet left I not here, but committed a little more scutchery.[65] A company of coistral [66] clerks (who were in band with Satan, and not of any soldier's collar nor hat-band) pinched a number of good minds to God-ward of their provant.[67] They would not let a dram of dead-pay [68] over-slip them; they would not lend a groat of the week to come to him that had spent his money before this week was done. They outfaced the greatest and most magnanimous servitors in their sincere and finigraphical [69] clean shirts and cuffs. A louse, that was any gentleman's companion, they thought scorn of. Their near-bitten beards must in a devil's name be dewed every day with rose-water. Hogs could have ne'er a hair on their backs for making them rubbing brushes to rouse their crab-lice. They would in no wise per-

64. Foretaste.
65. Knavery (NED); (to scutch = to beat, lash).
66. Base.
67. *pinched . . . provant*: Stole from some godly, righteous folk.
68. Officers would draw the pay of dead soldiers.
69. Fastidious, finicking.

mit that the motes in the sunbeams should be full-mouthed beholders of their clean finified [70] apparel. Their shoes shined as bright as a slike-stone;[71] their hands troubled and foiled [72] more water with washing than the camel doth, that never drinks till the whole stream be troubled. Summarily, never any were so fantastical the one half as they.

My masters, you may conceive of me what you list, but I think confidently I was ordained God's scourge from above for their dainty finicality. The hour of their punishment could no longer be prorogued,[73] but vengeance must have at them at all aventures.[74] So it was, that the most of these above-named goose-quill braggadoches [75] were mere cowards and cravens, and durst not so much as throw a penful of ink into the enemy's face, if proof were made. Wherefore on the experience of their pusillanimity, I thought to raise the foundation of my roguery.

What did I now, but one day made a false alarum in the quarter where they lay, to try how they would stand to their tackling, and with a pitiful outcry warned them to fly, for there was treason afoot, they were environed and beset. Upon the first watchword of treason that was given, I think they betook them to their heels very stoutly, left their pen and inkhorns and paper behind them for spoil, resigned their desks, with the money that was in them, to the mercy of the vanquisher, and in fine left me and my fellows (their fool-catchers) lords of the field. How we dealt with them, their disburdened desks can best tell; but this I am assured, we fared the better for it a fortnight of fasting-days after.

I must not place a volume in the precincts of a pamphlet. Sleep an hour or two, and dream that Turney and Turwin is won, that the King is shipped again into England,[76] and

70. Carefully looked after, adorned.
71. Stone used for smoothing or polishing.
72. Fouled.
73. Deferred.
74. *at all aventures*: Whatever happened.
75. Braggarts.
76. *King . . . England*: Towards the end of September 1513.

that I am close at hard meat [77] at Windsor or at Hampton
Court. What, will you in your indifferent opinions allow me
for my travel no more signory over the pages than I had
before? Yes, whether you will part with so much probable
friendly suppose or no, I'll have it in spite of your hearts.
For your instruction and godly consolation, be informed that
at that time I was no common squire, no undertrodden torch-
bearer. I had my feather in my cap as big as a flag in the
fore-top; my French doublet gelt [78] in the belly as though
(like a pig ready to be spitted) all my guts had been plucked
out; a pair of side-paned hose [79] that hung down like two
scales filled with Holland cheeses; my long stock that sat
close to my dock [80] and smothered not a scab or a lecherous
hairy sinew on the calf of the leg; my rapier pendant like a
round stick fastened in the tacklings, for skippers the better
to climb by; my cape cloak of black cloth overspreading
my back like a thornback or an elephant's ear, that hangs
on his shoulders like a country huswife's banskin [81] which
she thirls her spindle on; and in consummation of my
curiosity, my hands without gloves, all a more [82] French,
and a black budge edging of a beard on the upper lip, and
the like sable auglet [83] of excrements in the rising of the
angle [84] of my chin. I was the first that brought in the order
of passing into the Court which I derived from the common word *Qui passa?* and the herald's phrase of arms
passant, thinking in sincerity he was not a gentleman, nor
his arms current, who was not first passed by the pages. If
any prentice or other came into the Court that was not a
gentleman, I thought it was an indignity to the pre-
eminence of the Court to include such a one, and could not

77. *at hard meat*: Put out to fodder, i.e. in confinement or retire-
ment.

78. Let out, cut.

79. 'Hose decorated with stripes of coloured cloth at the sides –
or does "side" here mean "wide"?' (M.).

80. Buttocks.   81. Leather apron.

82. *all a more*: M. suggests '*à la mode*'.

83. Tassel.

84. Quartos (1594) have 'anckle'.

be salved except we gave him Arms Passant to make him a gentleman.

Besides, in Spain none pass any far way but he must be examined what he is and give threepence for his pass.

In which regard, it was considered of by the common table of the cupbearers, what a perilsome thing it was to let any stranger or outdweller approach so near the precincts of the Prince as the Great Chamber, without examining what he was and giving him his pass. Whereupon we established the like order, but took no money of them as they did; only, for a sign that he had not passed our hands unexamined, we set a red mark on their ears, and so let them walk as authentical.

I must not discover what ungodly dealing we had with the black jacks,[85] or how oft I was crowned King of the Drunkards with a court cup. Let me quietly descend to the waning of my youthful days, and tell a little of the sweating sickness [86] that made me in a cold sweat take my heels and run out of England.

This sweating sickness was a disease that a man then might catch and never go to a hot-house. Many masters desire to have such servants as would work till they sweat again, but in those days he that sweat never wrought again. That scripture then was not thought so necessary which says 'Earn thy living with the sweat of thy brows,' for then they earned their dying with the sweat of their brows. It was enough if a fat man did but truss his points to turn him over the perch.[87] Mother Cornelius' tub,[88] why, it was like hell; he that came into it never came out of it.

Cooks that stand continually basting their faces before the fire, were now all cashiered with this sweat into kitchen stuff. Their hall fell into the King's hands for want of one of the trade to uphold it.

Felt-makers and furriers, what the one with the hot steam

85. Large leather beer jugs.
86. M. lists five epidemics between 1485 and 1551.
87. to turn ... perch: 'To do for him' (M.).
88. Tubs used for curing venereal disease by sweating.

of their wool new taken out of the pan, and the other with the contagious heat of their slaughter budge [89] and coney [90] skins, died more thick than of the pestilence. I have seen an old woman at that season, having three chins, wipe them all away one after another, as they melted to water, and left herself nothing of a mouth but an upper chap. Look how in May or the heat of summer we lay butter in water for fear it should melt away, so then were men fain to wet their clothes in water as dyers do, and hid themselves in wells from the heat of the sun.

Then happy was he that was an ass, for nothing will kill an ass but cold, and none died but with extreme heat. The fishes called sea-stars, that burn one another by excessive heat, were not so contagious as one man that had the sweat was to another. Masons paid nothing for hair to mix their lime, nor glovers to stuff their balls with, for then they had it for nothing; it dropped off men's heads and beards faster than any barber could shave it. Oh, if hair breeches had then been in fashion, what a fine world had it been for tailors; and so it was a fine world for tailors nevertheless, for he that could make a garment slightest and thinnest carried it away. Cutters, I can tell you, then stood upon it to have their trade one of the twelve companies, for who was it then that would not have his doublet cut to the skin and his shirt cut into it too, to make it more cold. It was as much as a man's life was worth once to name a frieze jerkin; it was high treason for a fat gross man to come within five miles of the Court. I heard where they died up all in one family, and not a mother's child escaped, insomuch as they had but an Irish rug locked up in a press, and not laid upon any bed neither. If those that were sick of this malady slept of it, they never waked more. Physicians with their simples [91] in this case waxed simple fellows, and knew not which way to bestir them.

89. Budge is a cheap fur from lambskin; 'slaughter budge' perhaps fur from the slaughter-house (M.).
90. Rabbit.
91. Medicines made out of one constituent.

Galen[92] might go shoe the gander[93] for any good he could do; his secretaries had so long called him divine that now he had lost all his virtue upon earth. Hippocrates[94] might well help almanack-makers, but here he had not a word to say: a man might sooner catch the sweat with plodding over him to no end, than cure the sweat with any of his impotent principles. Paracelsus,[95] with his spirit of the buttery[96] and his spirits of minerals, could not so much as say 'God amend him' to the matter. *Plus erat in artifice quam arte*:[97] 'there was more infection in the physician himself than his art could cure.' This mortality first began amongst old men, for they, taking a pride to have their breasts loose basted with tedious beards, kept their houses so hot with their hairy excrements, that not so much but their very walls sweat out saltpeter with the smothering perplexity. Nay, a number of them had marvellous hot breaths, which sticking in the briars of their bushy beards could not choose but, as close air long imprisoned, engender corruption.

Wiser was our Brother Bankes[98] of these latter days, who made his juggling horse a cut, for fear if at any time he should foist,[99] the stink sticking in his thick bushy tail might be noisome to his auditors. Should I tell you how many pursuivants with red noses, and sergeants with precious faces,[100] shrunk away in this sweat, you would not believe me. Even as the salamander with his very sight blasteth apples on the trees, so a pursuivant or a sergeant at this

92. *c.* A.D. 130–200, Greek physician, most famous of ancient authorities.

93. 'Undertake a useless or absurd task' (M.).

94. *fl. c.* 400 B.C., 'the Father of Medicine'.

95. *c.* 1490–1541, great German physician, also much involved in alchemy and superstitious doctrine.

96. Familiar spirits supposed to be carried in the pommel of his sword.

97. 'There was more in the artificer than the artefact.'

98. Marocco was the name of the wonderful performing horse trained by the Scottish showman Bankes (*fl.* 1588–1637).

99. 'Silently break wind' (NED).

100. Red faced, as with drink.

present, with the very reflex of his fiery faces,[101] was able to spoil a man afar off. In some places of the world there is no shadow of the sun: *Diebus illis*[102] if it had been so in England, the generation of Brute[103] had died all and some. To knit up this description in a pursenet,[104] so fervent and scorching was the burning air which enclosed them, that the most blessed man then alive would have thought that God had done fairly by him if He had turned him to a goat, for goats take breath, not at the mouth or nose only, but at the ears also.

Take breath how they would, I vowed to tarry no longer among them. As at Turwin I was a demi-soldier in jest, so now I became a martialist in earnest. Over sea with my implements I got me, where hearing the King of France and the Switzers were together by the ears, I made towards them as fast as I could, thinking to thrust myself into that faction that was strongest. It was my good luck or my ill, I know not which, to come just to the fighting of the battle, where I saw a wonderful spectacle of bloodshed on both sides. Here unwieldly Switzers wallowing in their gore like an oxe in his dung; there the sprightly French sprawling and turning on the stained grass like a roach new taken out of the stream. All the ground was strewed as thick with battle-axes as the carpenter's yard with chips: the plain appeared like a quagmire, overspread as it was with trampled dead bodies. In one place might you behold a heap of dead murthered men overwhelmed with a falling steed instead of a tombstone; in another place a bundle of bodies fettered together in their own bowels. And as the tyrant Roman Emperor used to tie condemned living caitiffs face to face to dead corpses, so were the half-living here mixed with squeezed carcases long putrefied. Any man might give

101. Pun on the term *'fieri facias'*, a writ served on a debtor.
102. 'In those days'.
103. Descendants of Brute, legendary founder of London (the New Troy).
104. Bag-shaped net, the mouth of which can be drawn together with cords.

arms that was an actor in that battle, for there were more arms and legs scattered in the field that day than will be gathered up till Doomsday. The French King himself in this conflict was much distressed; the brains of his own men sprinkled in his face; thrice was his courser slain under him, and thrice was he struck on the breast with a spear. But in the end, by the help of the Venetians, the Helvetians or Switzers were subdued, and he crowned a victor, a peace concluded, and the city of Millaine [105] surrendered unto him as a pledge of reconciliation.

That war thus blown over, and the several bands dissolved, like a crow that still follows aloof where there is carrion, I flew me over to Münster [106] in Germany, which an Anabaptistical brother named John Leiden kept at that instant against the Emperor and the Duke of Saxony. Here I was in good hope to set up my staff for some reasonable time, deeming that no city would drive it to a siege, except they were able to hold out. And prettily well had these Münsterians held out, for they kept the Emperor and the Duke of Saxony play for the space of a year, and longer would have done but that Dame Famine came amongst them, whereupon they were forced by messengers to agree upon a day of fight, when, according to their Anabaptistical error, they might all be new christened in their own blood.

That day come, flourishing entered John Leiden the botcher into the field, with a scarf made of lists like a bow-case, a cross on his breast like a thread-bottom, a round-twilted tailor's cushion buckled like a tankard-bearer's device to his shoulders for a target, the pyke whereof was a pack-needle, a tough prentice's club for his spear, a great brewer's cow [107] on his back for a corslet,[108] and on his head for a helmet a huge high shoe with the bottom turned upwards, embossed as full of hobnails as ever it might stick. His men were all

105. Milan.
106. The Anabaptist uprising took place here in 1534.
107. Probably the cowl, or wooden covering over the chimney of a malt-house.
108. Body-armour.

base handicrafts, as cobblers and curriers [109] and tinkers, whereof some had bars of iron, some hatchets, some cool-staves, [110] some dung-forks, some spades, some mattocks, some wood-knives, some addises [111] for their weapons. He that was best provided had but a piece of rusty brown bill bravely fringed with cobwebs to fight for him. Perchance here and there you might see a fellow that had a canker-eaten skull [112] on his head, which served him and his ancestors for a chamber-pot two hundred years, and another that had bent a couple of iron dripping-pans armour-wise to fence his back and his belly; another that had thrust a pair of dry old boots as a breastplate before his belly of his doublet, because he would not be dangerously hurt; another that had twilted [113] all his truss full of counters, thinking, if the enemy should take him, he would mistake them for gold and so save his life for his money. Very devout asses they were, for all they were so dunstically [114] set forth, and such as thought they knew as much of God's mind as richer men. Why, inspiration was their ordinary familiar, [115] and buzzed in their ears like a bee in a box every hour what news from heaven, hell and the land of whipper-ginnie. [116] Displease them who durst, he should have his mittimus [117] to damnation *ex tempore*. [118] They would vaunt there was not a pea's difference betwixt them and the apostles: they were as poor as they, of as base trades as they, and no more inspired than they, and with God there is no respect of persons. Only herein may seem some little diversity to lurk: that Peter wore a sword, and they count it flat hell-fire for

109. Leather workers, colouring and dressing the leather after tanning.

110. Cowl-staves, sticks used for carrying burdens.

111. Adzes.

112. Armour in the form of a skull-cap.

113. Quilted.

114. Duncically, in the manner of a fool.

115. Familiar spirit.

116. Purgatory (OED); also meant a loose woman.

117. Commital, deliverance over.

118. On the spot, without more ado.

any man to wear a dagger; nay, so grounded and gravelled[119] were they in this opinion, that now, when they should come to battle, there's never a one of them would bring a blade, no, not an onion blade, about him, to die for it. It was not lawful, said they, for any man to draw the sword but the magistrate; and in fidelity (which I had wellnigh forgot), Jack Leiden, their magistrate, had the image or likeness of a piece of a rusty sword, like a lusty lad, by his side. Now I remember me, it was but a foil neither, and he wore it to show that he should have the foil of his enemies, which might have been an oracle for his two-hand interpretation. *Quid Plura*?[120] His battle is pitched. By pitched I do not mean set in order, for that was far from their order; only as sailors do pitch their apparel to make it storm-proof, so had most of them pitched their patched clothes to make them impierceable: a nearer way than to be at the charges of armour by half. And in another sort he might be said to have pitched the field, for he had pitched or rather set up his rest whether to fly if they were discomfited.

Peace, peace there in the belfry: service begins. Upon their knees before they join falls John Leiden and his fraternity very devoutly. They pray, they howl, they expostulate with God to grant them victory, and use such unspeakable vehemence a man would think them the only well-bent men under heaven. Wherein let me dilate a little more gravely than the nature of this history requires or will be expected of so young a practitioner in divinity: that not those that intermissively[121] cry 'Lord, open unto us, Lord, open unto us' enter first into the Kingdom; that not the greatest professors have the greatest portion in grace; that all is not gold that glisters. When Christ said 'The Kingdom of Heaven must suffer violence' he meant not the violence of long babbling prayers, nor the violence of tedious invective sermons without wit, but the violence of faith, the violence of good works, the violence of patient suf-

119. 'Stuck in the mud'.   120. 'What more [can I say]?'
121. Intermittently.

fering. The ignorant snatch the Kingdom of Heaven to themselves with greediness, when we with all our learning sink into hell.

Where did Peter and John, in the third of the Acts, find the lame cripple but in the gate of the temple called Beautiful? In the beautifullest gates of our temple, in the fore-front of professors, are many lame cripples, lame in life, lame in good works, lame in everything. Yet will they always sit at the gates of the temple. None be more forward than they to enter into matters of reformation, yet none more behindhand to enter into the true temple of the Lord by the gates of good life.

You may object that those which I speak against are more diligent in reading the Scriptures, more careful to resort unto sermons, more sober in their looks, more modest in their attire than any else. But I pray you let me answer you: doth not Christ say that before the Latter Day the sun shall be turned into darkness and the moon into blood? Whereof what may the meaning be but that glorious sun of the Gospel shall be eclipsed with the dim cloud of dissimulation; that that which is the brightest planet of salvation shall be a means of error and darkness? And the moon shall be turned into blood: those that shine fairest, make the simplest show, seem most to favour religion, shall rent out the bowels of the Church, be turned into blood, and all this shall come to pass before the notable day of the Lord, whereof this age is the eve?

Let me use a more familiar example, since the heat of a great number hath outraged so excessively. Did not the devil lead Christ to the pinnacle or highest place of the temple to tempt him? If he led Christ, he will lead a whole army of hypocrites to the top or highest part of the temple, the highest step of religion and holiness, to seduce them and subvert them. I say unto you that which this our tempted Saviour with many other words besought his disciples: 'Save yourselves from this froward generation. Verily, verily, the servant is not greater than his master.' Verily, verily, sinful men are not holier than holy Jesus, their maker. That holy Jesus again repeats this holy sentence: 'Remember the words I said unto you: the servant is not holier nor greater than his master'; as if he should say: 'Remember them, imprint in your memory, your pride and singularity will make you forget them, the effects of them many years hence will come to pass.' 'Whosoever will seek to save his soul shall lose it': whosoever seeks by headlong means to enter into heaven and disannul God's ordinance shall, with the giants [122] that thought to scale heaven in contempt of Jupiter, be overwhelmed with Mount Ossa and Pelion, and dwell with the devil in eternal desolation.

Though the High Priest's office was expired when Paul said unto one of them 'God rebuke thee, thou painted sepulchre', yet when a stander-by reproved him saying 'Revilest thou the High Priest?' he repented and asked for-giveness.

That which I suppose, I do not grant. The lawfulness of the authority they oppose themselves against is sufficiently proved. Far be it my under-age arguments should intrude themselves as a green weak prop to support so high a build-ing. Let it suffice, if you know Christ you know his Father also; if you know Christianity you know the fathers of the Church also. But a great number of you, with Philip, have been long with Christ and have not known him, have long professed yourselves Christians and have not known his true ministers. You follow the French and Scottish fashion and faction, and in all points are like the Switzers, *Qui quaerunt cum qua gente cadunt*,[123] 'that seek with what nation they may first miscarry'.

In the days of Nero there was an odd fellow that had found out an exquisite way to make glass as hammerproof as gold. Shall I say that the like experiment he made upon glass, we have practised on the Gospel? Ay, confidently will I. We have found out a sleight to hammer it to any heresy whatsoever. But those furnaces of falsehood and hammer-heads of heresy must be dissolved and broken as his was,

122. The Gigantes, eventually defeated by Hercules.
123. Adapted from Lucan (*Pharsalia*, XVIII, 504–5).

or else I fear me the false glittering glass of innovation will be better esteemed of than the ancient gold of the Gospel.

The fault of faults is this: that your dead-born faith is begotten by too-too infant fathers. Cato,[124] one of the wisest men in Roman histories canonized, was not born till his father was fourscore years old. None can be a perfect father of faith and beget men aright unto God, but those that are aged in experience, have many years imprinted in their mild conversation, and have, with Zachaeus, sold all their possessions of vanities to enjoy the sweet fellowship, not of the human, but spiritual Messias.

Ministers and pastors, sell away your sects and schisms to the decrepit Churches in contention beyond sea. They have been so long inured to war, both about matters of religion and regiment, that now they have no peace of mind but in troubling all other men's peace. Because the poverty of their provinces will allow them no proportionable maintenance for higher callings of ecclesiastical magistrates, they would reduce us to the precedent of their rebellious persecuted beggary: much like the sects of philosophers called Cynics, who when they saw they were born to no lands or possessions, nor had any possible means to support their estates, but they must live despised and in misery, do what they could, they plotted and consulted with themselves how to make their poverty better esteemed of than rich dominion and sovereignty. The upshot of their plotting and consultation was this: that they would live to themselves, scorning the very breath or company of all men. They professed, according to the rate of their lands, voluntary poverty, thin fare and lying hard, contemning and inveighing against all those as brute beasts whatsoever whom the world had given any reputation for riches or prosperity. Diogenes was one of the first and foremost of the ringleaders of this rusty morosity, and he, for all his nice dogged disposition and blunt deriding of worldly dross and the gross felicity of fools, was taken notwithstanding a little after very fairly a-coining money in his cell. So fares it up and down

124. A confusion on Nashe's part, pointed out by M. (IV, 269).

with our cynical reformed foreign Churches. They will digest no grapes of great bishoprics forsooth, because they cannot tell how to come by them. They must shape their coats, good men, according to their cloth, and do as they may, not as they would; yet they must give us leave here in England that are their honest neighbours, if we have more cloth than they, to make our garment somewhat larger.

What was the foundation or groundwork of this dismal declining of Münster, but the banishing of their Bishop, their confiscating and casting lots for Church livings, as the soldiers cast lots for Christ's garments, and, in short terms, their making the house of God a den of thieves? The house of God a number of hungry Church-robbers in these days have made a den of thieves. Thieves spend loosely what they have gotten lightly; sacrilege is no such inheritance; Dionysius was ne'er the richer for robbing of Jupiter of his golden coat – he was driven in the end to play the schoolmaster at Corinth. The name of religion, be it good or bad that is ruinated, God never suffers unrevenged. I'll say of it as Ovid said of eunuchs:

> *Qui primus pueris genitalia membra recidit,*
> *Vulnera quae fecit debuit ipse pati.*

> Who first deprived young boys of their best part,
> With self-same wounds he gave he ought to smart.[125]

So would he that first gelt [126] religion or church-livings had been first gelt himself or never lived. Cardinal Wolsey is the man I aim at: *Qui in suas poenas ingeniosus erat,*[127] 'first gave others a light to his own overthrow'. How it prospered with him and his instruments that after wrought for themselves, chronicles largely publish, though not apply; and some parcel of their punishment yet unpaid I do not doubt but will be required of their posterity.

To go forward with my story of the overthrow of that

125. Marlowe's translation of Ovid's *Amores* (*Elegies*), II, 3, 3–4.
126. Gelded.
127. 'Who was resourceful in devising his own punishment' (adapted from Ovid, *Tristia*, II, 342).

usurper John Leiden. He and all his army, as I said before, falling prostrate on their faces and fervently given over to prayer, determined never to cease or leave soliciting of God till He had showed them from heaven some manifest miracle of success.

Not that it was a general received tradition both with John Leiden and all the crew of Cnipperdollings and Müncers,[128] if God at any time at their vehement outcries and clamours did not condescend to their requests, to rail on Him and curse Him to His face, to dispute with Him and argue Him of injustice for not being so good as His word with them, and to urge His many promises in the scripture against Him: so that they did not serve God simply, but that He should serve their turns. And after that tenure are many content to serve as bondmen to save the danger of hanging. But he that serves God aright, whose upright conscience hath for his mot *Amor est mihi causa sequendi*[129] ('I serve because I love'), he says *Ego te potius, Domine, quam tua dona sequar*[130] ('I'll rather follow thee, Oh Lord, for thine own sake than for any covetous respect of that thou canst do for me').

Christ would have no followers but such as forsake all and follow him, such as forsake all their own desires, such as abandon all expectations of reward in this world, such as neglected and contemned their lives, their wives and children in comparison of him, and were content to take up their cross and follow him.

These Anabaptists had not yet forsook all and followed Christ. They had not forsook their own desires of revenge and innovation. They had not abandoned their expectation of the spoil of their enemies. They regarded their lives. They looked after their wives and children. They took not up their crosses of humility and followed him, but would cross him, upbraid him and set him at nought if he assured not by some sign their prayers and supplications. *Deteriora*

128. Knipperdolink and Müncer, anabaptist leaders at Münster.
129. 'Love is my reason for following' (Ovid).
130. Ovid, *Heroides*, XVII, 70.

sequuntur: [131] they followed God as daring Him. God heard their prayers, *Quod petitur poena est*: [132] 'it was their speedy punishment that they prayed for'. Lo, according to the sum of their impudent supplications, a sign in the heavens appeared, the glorious sign of the rainbow, which agreed just with the sign of their ensign that was a rainbow likewise.

Whereupon, assuring themselves of victory (*Miseri quod volunt, facile credunt*: [133] 'That which wretches would have they easily believe'), with shouts and clamours they presently ran headlong on their well-deserved confusion.

Pitiful and lamentable was their unpitied and well-performed slaughter. To see even a bear, which is the most cruellest of all beasts, too too bloodily overmatched and deformedly rent in pieces by an unconscionable number of curs, it would move compassion against kind, and make those that, beholding him at the stake yet uncoped with, wished him a suitable death to his ugly shape, now to re-call their hard-hearted wishes and moan him suffering as a mild beast, in comparison of the foul-mouthed mastiffs, his butchers. Even such comparsion did those overmatched ungracious Münsterians obtain of many indifferent eyes, who now thought them, suffering, to be sheep brought innocent to the shambles, whenas before they deemed them as a number of wolves up in arms against the shepherds.

The Emperials themselves that were their executioners, like a father that weeps when he beats his child, yet still weeps and still beats, not without much ruth and sorrow prosecuted that lamentable massacre. Yet drums and trumpets sounding nothing but stern revenge in their ears made them so eager that their hands had no leisure to ask counsel of their effeminate eyes. Their swords, their pikes, their bills, their bows, their calivers slew, empierced, knocked down,

131. 'They follow the worse path', adapted from Ovid (*Metamorphoses*, VII, 20–21: *video meliora, probaque; Deteriora sequor*: 'I see and applaud what is better; I practise the worse').

132. 'What is sought is punishment' (Ovid).

133. Adapted from Seneca, *Hercules Furens*, 313.

shot through and overthrew as many men every minute of the battle as there falls ears of corn before the scythe at one blow. Yet all their weapons so slaying, empiercing, knocking down, shooting through, overthrowing, dis-soul-joined not half so many as the hailing thunder of the great ordinance. So ordinary at every footstep was the imbrument of iron in blood, that one could hardly discern heads from bullets, or clottred hair from mangled flesh hung with gore.

This tale must at one time or other give up the ghost, and as good now as stay longer. I would gladly rid my hands of it cleanly if I could tell how, for what with talking of cobblers, tinkers, rope-makers, botchers and dirt-daubers, the mark is clean out of my muse's mouth, and I am as it were more than duncified twixt divinity and poetry. What is there more as touching this tragedy that you would be resolved of? Say quickly, for now is my pen on foot again. How John Leiden died, is that it? He died like a dog: he was hanged and the halter paid for. For his companions, do they trouble you? I can tell you, they troubled some men before, for they were all killed and none escaped; no, not so much as one to tell the tale of the rainbow. Hear what it is to be Anabaptists, to be Puritans, to be villains. You may be counted illuminate botchers [134] for a while, but your end will be 'Good people, pray for us.'

With the tragical catastrophe of this Münsterian conflict did I cashier the new vocation of my cavaliership. There was no more honourable wars in Christendom then towards. Wherefore, after I had learned to be half-an-hour in bidding a man *bonjour* in German sunonimas,[135] I travelled along the country towards England as fast as I could.

What with wagons and bare ten-toes having attained to Middleborough (good Lord, see the changing chances of us knights-arrant infants [136]), I met with the Right Honourable Lord Henry Howard, Earl of Surrey,[137] my late master. Jesu,

134. Enlightened reformers.
135. Synonyms.
136. Young knights errant.
137. 1517?–47 (executed). Never in Italy (M.).

I was persuaded I should not be more glad to see heaven than I was to see him. Oh, it was a right noble lord, liberality itself, if in this iron age there were any such creature as liberality left on the earth, a prince in content because a poet without peer.

Destiny never defames herself but when she lets an excellent poet die. If there be any spark of Adam's paradised perfection yet embered up in the breasts of mortal men, certainly God hath bestowed that His perfectest image on poets. None come so near to God in wit, none more contemn the world. *Vatis avarus non temere est animus*, saith Horace, *versus amat, hoc studet unum*: 'Seldom have you seen any poet possessed with avarice, only verses he loves, nothing else he delights in.' And as they contemn the world, so contrarily of the mechanical world are none more contemned. Despised they are of the world, because they are not of the world: their thoughts are exalted above the world of ignorance and all earthly conceits.

As sweet angelical quiristers they are continually conversant in the heaven of arts. Heaven itself is but the highest height of knowledge. He that knows himself and all things else knows the means to be happy; happy, thrice happy, are they whom God hath doubled His spirit upon and given a double soul unto to be poets.

My heroical master exceeded in this supernatural kind of wit. He entertained no gross earthly spirit of avarice, nor weak womanly spirit of pusillanimity and fear that are feigned to be of the water, but admirable, airy and fiery spirits, full of freedom, maganimity and bountihood. Let me not speak any more of his accomplishments for fear I spend all my spirits in praising him, and leave myself no vigour of wit or effects of a soul to go forward with my history.

Having thus met him I so much adored, no interpleading was there of opposite occasions, but back I must return and bear half-stakes with him in the lottery of travel. I was not altogether unwilling to walk along with such a good purse-bearer, yet musing what changeable humour had so suddenly seduced him from his native soil to seek out needless perils in those parts beyond sea, one night very boldly I demanded of him the reason that moved him thereto.

'Ah,' quoth he, 'my little page, full little canst thou perceive how far metamorphosed I am from myself since I last saw thee. There is a little god called love, that will not be worshipped of any leaden brains, one that proclaims himself sole king and emperor of piercing eyes, and chief sovereign of soft hearts. He it is that, exercising his empire in my eyes, hath exorcised and clean conjured me from my content.

'Thou knowest stately Geraldine,[138] too stately, I fear, for me to do homage to her statue or shrine. She it is that has come out of Italy to bewitch all the wise men of England. Upon Queen Catherine Dowager[139] she waits, that hath a dowry of beauty sufficient to make her wooed of the greatest kings in Christendom. Her high exalted sunbeams have set the phoenix nest of my breast on fire, and I myself have brought Arabian spiceries of sweet passions and praises to furnish out the funeral flame of my folly. Those who were condemned to be smothered to death by sinking down into the soft bottom of an high-built bed of roses, never died so sweet a death as I should die if her rose-coloured disdain were my death's-man.[140]

'Oh, thrice imperial Hampton Court, Cupid's enchanted castle, the place where I first saw the perfect omnipotence of the Almighty expressed in mortality, tis thou alone that, tithing all other men solace in thy pleasant situation, affordest me nothing but an excellent-begotten sorrow out of the chief treasury of all thy recreations.

'Dear Wilton, understand that there it was where I first

---

138. M. quotes Surrey's 'Geraldine' sonnet, starting 'From Tuscane came my lady's worthy race: Fair Florence was sometime her ancient seat.'

139. Catherine of Aragon or Catherine Parr, though Elizabeth Fitzgerald was in the household of neither but in that of Catherine Howard (M.).

140. Executioner.

set eye on my more than celestial Geraldine. Seeing her, I admired her; all the whole receptacle of my sight was unhabited with her rare worth. Long suit and uncessant protestations got me the grace to be entertained. Did never unloving servant so prenticelike obey his never-pleased mistress as I did her. My life, my wealth, my friends, had all their destiny depending on her command.

'Upon a time I was determined to travel. The fame of Italy and an especial affection I had unto poetry, my second mistress, for which Italy was so famous, had wholly ravished me unto it. There was no dehortment [141] from it, but needs thither I would. Wherefore, coming to my mistress as she was then walking with other ladies of estate in paradise at Hampton Court, I most humbly besought her of favour that she would give me so much gracious leave to absent myself from her service, as to travel a year or two into Italy. She very discreetly answered me that if my love were so hot as I had often avouched, I did very well to apply the plaster of absence unto it, for absence, as they say, causeth forgetfulness. "Yet nevertheless, since it is Italy, my native country, you are so desirous to see, I am the more willing to make my will yours. *I, pete Italiam*: 'Go and seek Italy', with Aeneas. But be more true than Aeneas: I hope that kind wit-cherishing climate will work no change in so witty a breast. No country of mine shall it be more, if it conspire with thee in any new love against me. One charge I will give thee, and let it be rather a request than a charge: when thou comest to Florence, the fair city from whence I fetched the pride of my birth, by an open challenge defend my beauty against all comers.

'"Thou hast that honourable carriage in arms that it shall be no discredit for me to bequeath all the glory of my beauty to thy well-governed arm. Fain would I be known where I was born; fain would I have thee known where fame sits in her chiefest theatre. Farewell, forget me not. Continued deserts will eternize me unto thee; thy wishes shall be expired when thy travel shall be once ended."

141. Discussion.

Here did my tears step out before words, and intercepted the course of my kind-conceived speech, even as wind is allayed with rain. With heart-scalding sighs I confirmed her parting request, and avowed myself hers while living heat allowed me to be mine own. *Hinc illae lachrimae*: [142] here hence proceedeth the whole cause of my peregrination.'

Not a little was I delighted with this unexpected love story, especially from a mouth out of which was nought wont to march but stern precepts of gravity and modesty. I swear unto you I thought his company the better by a thousand crowns because he had discarded those nice terms of chastity and continency. Now I beseech God love me so well as I do a plain-dealing man. Earth is earth, flesh is flesh, earth will to earth, and flesh unto flesh. Frail earth, frail flesh, who can keep you from the work of your creation?

Dismissing this fruitless annotation *pro et contra*: towards Venice we progressed, and took Rotterdam in our way, that was clean out of our way. There we met with aged learning's chief ornament that abundant and superingenious clerk Erasmus, as also with merry Sir Thomas More,[143] our countryman, who was come purposely over a little before us to visit the said grave father Erasmus. What talk, what conference we had then it were here superfluous to rehearse; but this I can assure you – Erasmus in all his speeches seemed so much to mislike the indiscretion of princes in preferring of parasites and fools, that he decreed with himself to swim with the stream and write a book forthwith in commendation of folly.[144] Quick-witted Sir Thomas More travelled in a clean contrary province, for he seeing most commonwealths corrupted by ill custom, and that principalities were nothing but great piracies which, gotten by violence and murther, were maintained by private undermining and bloodshed, that in the chiefest flourishing

142. 'Hence those tears' (Terence).
143. Erasmus and More met in England (1497 and 1508), and at Calais (1520) but are not known to have met in Rotterdam (M.).
144. *a book . . . folly: Encomium Moriae*, 1509.

kingdoms there was no equal or well-divided weal one with
another, but a manifest conspiracy of rich men against poor
men, procuring their own unlawful commodities under the
name and interest of the commonwealth, he concluded with
himself to lay down a perfect plot of a commonwealth or
government which he would entitle his *Utopia*.[145]

So left we them to prosecute their discontented studies,
and made our next journey to Wittenberg.

At the very point of our entrance into Wittenberg, we
were spectators of a very solemn scholastical entertainment
of the Duke of Saxony thither. Whom, because he was the
chief patron of their university, and had took Luther's part
in banishing the Mass and all like papal jurisdiction out of
their town, they crouched unto extremely. The chief ceremonies of their entertainment were these: first, the heads
of their university (they were greats heads, of certainty) met
him in their hooded hypocrisy and doctorly accoutrements,
secundum formum statuti,[146] where by the orator of the
university, whose pickerdevant[147] was very plentifully be-
sprinkled with rose water, a very learned, or rather, ruthful,
oration was delivered (for it rained all the while) signifying
thus much – that it was all by patch and by piecemeal stolen
out of Tully, and he must pardon them though in emptying
their phrase-books the world emptied his entrails; for they
did it not in any ostentation of wit (which God knows, they
had not) but to show the extraordinary good will they bare
the Duke (to have him stand in the rain till he was through
wet). A thousand *quemadmodums* and *quapropters*[148] he
came over him with. Every sentence he concluded with *Esse
posse videatur*.[149] Through all the Nine Worthies[150] he ran

145. First published in Latin, 1516. Translated into English, 1551.
146. 'According to the form of the decree'.
147. Picke-davant, short pointed beard.
148. quemadmodums *and* quapropters: 'In-so-far-ases' and 'where-
fores'.
149. Imitators of Cicero sought to achieve this particular rhythm
at the end of their periods.
150. Joshua, David, Judas Maccabeus, Hector, Alexander, Julius
Caesar, Arthur, Charlemagne and Godfrey of Bouillon.

with praising and comparing him. Nestor's years he assured him of under the broad seal of their supplications and with that crow-trodden [151] verse in Virgil, *Dum iuga montis aper*,[152] he packed up his pipes and cried *Dixi*.[153]

That pageant overpast, there rushed upon him a miserable rabblement of junior graduates that all cried upon him mightily in their gibrige, like a company of beggars, 'God save your Grace, God save your Grace, Jesus preserve your Highness, though it be but for an hour!'

Some three half-pennyworth of Latin here also had he thrown at his face, but it was choice stuff, I can tell you, as there is a choice even amongst rags gathered up from the dung-hill. At the town's end met him the burghers and dunstical incorporationers [154] of Wittenberg in their distinguished liveries, their distinguished livery faces, I mean, for they were most of them hot-livered drunkards and had all the coat colours of sanguine, purple, crimson, copper, carnation, that were to be had, in their countenances. Filthy knaves, no cost had they bestowed on the town for his welcome, saving new-painted their houghs [155] and boozing-houses, which commonly are fairer than their churches, and over their gates set the town arms carousing a whole health to the Duke's arms, which sounded gulping after this sort: *Vanhotten, slotten, irk bloshen glotten gelderslike.* Whatever the words were, the sense was this: 'Good drink is a medicine for all diseases.'

A bursten-belly inkhorn orator called Vanderhulke [156] they picked out to present him with an oration; one that had a sulphurous big swollen large face like a Saracen, eyes like two Kentish oysters, a mouth that opened as wide every time he spake as one of those old knit trap doors, a beard as

151. Term of abuse.

152. 'As long as the wild boar loves the mountain ridges' (i.e. for ever) (Virgil).

153. 'I have spoken.'

154. Members of the Corporation.

155. Taverns, places of resort.

156. Used as a name for Gabriel Harvey in *Have with You to Saffron Walden*, III, 31, 10.

though it had been made of a bird's nest plucked in pieces, which consisteth of straw, hair and dirt mixed together. He was apparelled in black leather new-liquored and a short gown without any gathering in the back, faced before and behind with a boisterous bear-skin, and a red night-cap on his head. To this purport and effect was this brocking [157] double-beer oration.

'Right noble Duke (*ideo nobilis quasi no bilis*, for you have no bile or choler in you), know that our present incorporation of Wittenberg, by me the tongue-man of their thankfulness, a townsman by birth, a free German by nature, an orator by art, and a scrivener by education, in all obedience and chastity, most bountifully bid you welcome to Wittenberg. Welcome, said I? Oh orificial rhetoric, wipe thy everlasting mouth and afford me a more Indian metaphor than that, for the brave princely blood of a Saxon! Oratory, uncask the barred hutch of thy compliments, and with the triumphantest trope in thy treasury do trewage unto him! What impotent speech with his eight parts may not specify, this unestimable gift, holding his peace, shall as it were (with tears I speak it) do whereby as it may seem or appear to manifest or declare, and yet it is, and yet it is not, and yet it may be a diminutive oblation meritorious to your high pusillanimity and indignity. Why should I go gadding and fizgigging [158] after firking flantado amphibologies? [159] Wit is wit, and good will is good will. With all the wit I have, I here, according to the premisses, offer up unto you the city's general good will, which is a gilded can, in manner and form following, for you and the heirs of your body lawfully begotten to drink healths in. The scholastical squitterbooks [160] clout you up canopies and foot-cloths of verses. We that are good fellows and live as merry as cup and can, will not verse upon you as they do, but must do as we can, and entertain you if it be but with a plain empty can. He

157. M. suggests variant of 'broking', a vague term of abuse.
158. Gadding about.
159. Frisking, flaunting equivocations.
160. Contemptuous term for academics.

hath learning enough that hath learned to drink to his first man.

'Gentle Duke, without paradox be it spoken, thy horses at our own proper costs and charges shall knead up to the knees all the while thou art here in spruce-beer and Lubeck liquor. Not a dog thou bringest with thee but shall be banqueted with Rhenish wine and sturgeon. On our shoulders we wear no lamb-skin or miniver like these academics, yet we can drink to the confusion of thy enemies. Good lamb's wool have we for their lamb-skins, and for their miniver, large minerals in our coffers. Mechanical men they call us, and not amiss, for most of us being *Maechi*,[161] that is, cuckolds and whoremasters, fetch our antiquity from the temple of Maecha, where Mahomet was hung up. Three parts of the world, America, Affrike, and Asia, are of this our mechanic religion. Nero, when he cried *O quantus artifex pereo*,[162] professed himself of our freedom, insomuch as *artifex* is a citizen or craftsman, as well as *carnifex* a scholar or hangman. Pass on by leave into the precincts of our abomination. Bonny Duke, frolic in our bower, and persuade thyself that even as garlic hath three properties – to make a man wink, drink and stink – so we will wink on thy imperfections, drink to thy favourites, and all thy foes shall stink before us. So be it. Farewell.'

The Duke laughed not a little at this ridiculous oration, but that very night as great an ironical occasion was ministered, for he was bidden to one of the chief schools to a comedy handled by scholars. *Acolastus, the Prodigal Child*[163] was the name of it, which was so filthily acted, so leathernly set forth, as would have moved laughter in Heraclitus. One, as if he had been planing a clay floor, stampingly trod the stage so hard with his feet that I thought verily he

161. *Moechi* (Greek): adulterers (with a punning reference later to men of Mecca, where Mahomet's body in its iron coffin was said to have been drawn up to the temple roof by great loadstones).

162. 'What an artist perishes in me' (Suetonius).

163. A play by Gulielmus Gnapheus, or Fullonius, a Dutch scholar written in Latin, translated into English for schools, 1540. ('*Acolastus*' means 'The unpunished'.)

had resolved to do the carpenter that set it up some utter shame. Another flung his arms like cudgels at a pear tree, insomuch as it was mightily dreaded that he would strike the candles that hung above their heads out of their sockets and leave them all dark. Another did nothing but wink and make faces. There was a parasite, and he with clapping his hands and thripping [164] his fingers seemed to dance an antic to and fro. The only thing they did well was the prodigal child's hunger, most of their scholars being hungerly kept. And surely you would have said they had been brought up in Hog's Academy to learn to eat acorns, if you had seen how sedulously they fell to them. Not a jest had they to keep their auditors from sleeping but of swill and draff. Yes, now and then the servant put his hand into the dish before his master and almost choked himself, eating slovenly and ravenously to cause sport.

The next day they had solemn disputations, where Luther and Carolostadius scolded level coil. [165] A mass of words I wot well they heaped up against the Mass and the Pope, but farther particulars of their disputations I remember not. I thought verily they would have worried one another with words, they were so earnest and vehement. Luther had the louder voice; Carolostadius went beyond him in beating and bouncing with his fists. *Quae supra nos, nihil ad nos*: [166] they uttered nothing to make a man laugh, therefore I will leave them. Marry, their outward gestures would now and then afford a man a morsel of mirth: of those two I mean not so much, as of all the other train of opponents and respondents. One pecked like a crane with his forefinger at every half-syllable he brought forth, and nodded with his nose like an old singing-man teaching a young quirister to keep time. Another would be sure to wipe his mouth with his handkerchief at the end of every full

164. Snapping.

165. *scolded level coil*: argued, 'shouted the odds' ('level coil' from French *lever le cul*, a party game). Luther and Carolostadius are said to have met in a disputation at Lipsia, 1519.

166. 'Things which are above us do not concern us' (proverb).

point, and ever when he thought he had cast a figure so curiously [167] as he dived over head and ears into his auditors' admiration, he would take occasion to stroke up his hair, and twine up his mustachios twice or thrice over, while they might have leisure to applaud him. A third wavered and waggled his head, like a proud horse playing with his bridle, or, as I have seen some fantastical swimmer, at every stroke, train his chin side-long over his left shoulder. A fourth sweat and foamed at the mouth for very anger his adversary had denied that part of the syllogism which he was not prepared to answer. A fifth spread his arms like an usher that goes before to make room, and thripped with his finger and his thumb when he thought he had tickled it with a conclusion. A sixth hung down his countenance like a sheep, and stuttered and slavered very pitifully when his invention was stepped aside out of the way. A seventh gasped and gaped for wind and groaned in his pronunciation as if he were hard bound with some bad argument. Gross plodders they were all, that had some learning and reading, but no wit to make use of it. They imagined the Duke took the greatest pleasure and contentment under heaven to hear them speak Latin, and as long as they talked nothing but Tully he was bound to attend them. A most vain thing it is in many universities at this day, that they count him excellent eloquent who stealeth, not whole phrases, but whole pages out of Tully. If of a number of shreds of his sentences he can shape an oration, from all the world he carries it away,[168] although in truth it be no more than a fool's coat of many colours. No invention or matter have they of their own, but tack up a style of his stale gallimaufries. The leaden-headed Germans first began this, and we Englishmen have surfeited of their absurd imitation. I pity Nizolius [169] that had nothing to do but pick threads' ends out of an old overworn garment.

167. Expressed himself so ingeniously.
168. He is reckoned the world champion.
169. Marius Nizolius (?1498–1576), author of *Thesaurus Ciceronianus*, 1535.

This is but by the way: we must look back to our disputants. One amongst the rest, thinking to be more conceited [170] than his fellows, seeing the Duke have a dog he loved well, which sat by him on the tarras, [171] converted all his oration to him, and not a hair of his tail but he combed out with comparisons: so to have courted him, if he were a bitch, had been very suspicious. Another commented and descanted on the Duke's staff, new-tipping it with many quaint epithets. Some cast his nativity and promised him he should not die until the Day of Judgment. Omitting further superfluities of this stamp, in this general assembly we found intermixed that abundant scholar Cornelius Agrippa. [172] At that time he bare the fame to be the greatest conjurer in Christendom. Scoto, [173] that did the juggling tricks before the Queen, never came near him one quarter in magic reputation. The doctors of Wittenberg, doting on the rumour that went of him, desired him before the Duke and them to do something extraordinary memorable.

One requested to see pleasant Plautus, and that he would show them in what habit he went, and with what countenance he looked when he ground corn in the mill. Another had half a month's mind [174] to Ovid and his hook nose. Erasmus, who was not wanting in that honourable meeting, requested to see Tully in that same grace and majesty he pleaded his oration *pro Roscio Amerino*, [175] affirming that till in person he beheld his importunity of pleading, he would in no wise be persuaded that any man could carry away a manifest case with rhetoric so strangely. To Erasmus' petition he easily condescended, and willing the doctors at such an hour to hold their convocation and everyone to keep him in his place without moving, at the time prefixed, in

170. Imaginative, quick-witted.
171. Terrace.
172. 1486–1535 b. Cologne, his lectures on the Cabala gaining him reputation as a magician.
173. An Italian juggler and conjurer who visited England between 1576 and 1583.
174. *half a month's mind*: An inclination, or fancy, to.
175. Famous oration of the youthful Cicero.

entered Tully, ascended his pleading-place, and declaimed verbatim the forenamed oration, but with such astonishing amazement, with such fervent exaltation of spirit, with such soul-stirring gestures, that all his auditors were ready to instal his guilty client for a god.

Great was the concourse of glory Agrippa drew to him with this one feat. And indeed he was so cloyed with men that came to behold him that he was fain, sooner than he would, to return to the Emperor's Court from whence he came, and leave Wittenberg before he would. With him we travelled along, having purchased his acquaintance a little before. By the way as we went, my master and I agreed to change names. It was concluded betwixt us that I should be the Earl of Surrey and he my man, only because in his own person, which he would not have reproached, he meant to take more liberty of behaviour; as for my carriage, he knew he was to tune it at a key either high or low, as he list.

To the Emperor's Court we came, where our entertainment was every way plentiful. Carouses we had in whole gallons instead of quart pots. Not a health was given us but contained well-near a hogshead.[176] The customs of the country we were eager to be instructed in, but nothing we could learn but this: that ever at the Emperor's coronation there is an ox roasted with a stag in the belly, and that stag in his belly hath a kid, and that kid is stuffed full of birds. Some courtiers, to weary out time, would tell us further tales of Cornelius Agrippa, and how when Sir Thomas More, our countryman, was there, he showed him the whole destruction of Troy in a dream. How, the Lord Cromwell being the King's Ambassador there, in like case, in a perspective glass he set before his eyes King Henry the Eighth with all his lords on hunting in his forest at Windsor, and (when he came into his study and was very urgent to be partaker of some rare experiment, that he might report when he came into England) he willed him amongst two thousand great books down which he list, and begin to read one line in any place, and without book he would rehearse twenty leaves

176. About fifty gallons.

following. Cromwell did so, and in many books tried him, when in everything he exceeded his promise and conquered his expectation. To Charles the Fifth, then Emperor, they reported how he showed the Nine Worthies (David, Solomon, Gideon and the rest) in that similitude and likeness that they lived upon earth. My master and I, having by the highway-side gotten some reasonable familiarity with him, upon this access of miracles imputed to him, resolved to request him something in our own behalfs. I, because I was his suborned lord and master, desired him to see the lively image of Geraldine, his love, in the glass, and what at that instant she did and with whom she was talking. He showed her us without any more ado, sick weeping on her bed, and resolved all into devout religion for the absence of her lord. At the sight thereof he could in no wise refrain, though he had took upon him the condition of a servant, but he must forthwith frame this extemporal ditty: [177]

All soul, no earthly flesh, why dost thou fade?
All gold, no worthless dross, why look'st thou pale?
Sickness, how dar'st thou one so fair invade,
Too base infirmity to work her bale?
    Heaven be distemper'd since she grieved pines,
    Never be dry, these my sad plaintive lines.

Perch thou, my spirit, on her silver breasts,
And with their pain-redoubled music-beatings,
Let them toss thee to world where all toil rests,
Where bliss is subject to no fear's defeatings:
    Her praise I tune whose tongue doth tune the spheres,
    And gets new muses in her hearer's ears.

Stars fall to fetch fresh light from her rich eyes,
Her bright brow drives the sun to clouds beneath.
Her hairs' reflex with red streaks paints the skies,
Sweet morn and evening dew flows from her breath:
    Phoebe rules tides, she my tears' tides forth draws,
    In her sick-bed love sits and maketh laws.

177. This was printed in *England's Parnassus*, 1600, signed T. Nash (reading 'paint' for 'paints' v.3. 'falls' for 'flows' v.3).

Her dainty limbs tinsel her silk soft sheets,
Her rose-crown'd cheeks eclipse my dazzled sight;
Oh glass, with too much joy my thoughts thou greets,
And yet thou showest me day but by twilight:
   I'll kiss thee for the kindness I have felt,
   Her lips one kiss would unto nectar melt.

Though the Emperor's Court and the extraordinary edifying company of Cornelius Agrippa might have been arguments of weight to have arrested us a little longer there, yet Italy still stuck as a great mote in my master's eye; he thought he had travelled no further than Wales till he had took survey of that country which was such a curious moulder of wits.

To cut off blind ambages [178] by the highway-side, we made a long stride and got to Venice in short time; where having scarce looked about us, a precious supernatural pander, apparelled in all points like a gentleman, and having half-a-dozen several languages in his purse, entertained us in our own tongue very peraphrastically and eloquently, and maugre [179] all other pretended acquaintance would have us in a violent kind of courtesy to be the guests of his appointment. His name was Petro de Campo Frego, a notable practitioner in the policy of bawdry. The place whither he brought us was a pernicious courtesan's house named Tabitha the Temptress's, a wench that could set as civil a face on it as chastity's first martyr, Lucretia. What will you conceit to be in any saint's house that was there to seek? Books, pictures, beads, crucifixes, why, there was a haberdasher's shop of them in every chamber. I warrant you should not see one set of her neckercher perverted or turned awry, not a piece of a hair displaced. On her beds there was not a wrinkle of any wallowing to be found; her pillows bare out as smooth as a groaning wife's belly, and yet she was a Turk and an infidel, and had more doings than all her neighbours besides. Us for our money they used like emperors. I was

178. 'Circuitous ways leading nowhither' (M.).
179. In spite of.

master, as you heard before, and my master, the Earl, was but as my chief man whom I made my companion. So it happened (as iniquity will out at one time or other) that she, perceiving my expenses had no more vents than it should have, fell in with my supposed servant, my man, and gave him half a promise of marriage if he would help to make me away, that she and he might enjoy the jewels and wealth that I had.

The indifficulty of the condition thus she explained unto him. Her house stood upon vaults, which in two hundred years together were never searched; who came into her house none took notice of. His fellow servants that knew of his master's abode there should be all dispatched by him, as from his master, into sundry parts of the city about business, and, when they returned, answer should be made that he lay not there any more but had removed to Padua since their departure and thither they must follow him. 'Now', quoth she, 'if you be disposed to make him away in their absence, you shall have my house at command. Stab, poison, or shoot him through with a pistol, all is one; into the vault he shall be thrown when the deed is done.' On my bare honesty, it was a crafty quean, for she had enacted with herself, if he had been my legitimate servant, as he was one that served and supplied my necessities, when he had murthered me, to have accused him of the murther, and made all that I had hers, as I carried all my master's wealth, money, jewels, rings, or bills of exchange continually about me. He very subtly consented to her stratagem at the first motion: kill me he would, that heavens could not withstand, and a pistol was the predestinate engine which must deliver the parting blow. God wot, I was a raw young squire, and my master dealt judasly with me, for he told me but everything that she and he agreed of. Wherefore, I could not possibly prevent it, but as a man would say avoid it. The execution day aspired to his utmost devolution, into my chamber came my honourable attendant, with his pistol charged by his side, very suspiciously and sullenly. Lady Tabitha and Petro de Campo Frego, her pander, followed him at the hard heels.

At their entrance I saluted them all very familiarly and merrily, and began to impart unto them what disquiet dreams had disturbed me the last night. 'I dreamt', quoth I, 'that my man Brunquell [180] here (for no better name got he of me) came into my chamber with a pistol charged under his arm to kill me, and that he was suborned by you, Mistress Tabitha, and my very good friend here, Petro de Campo Frego. God send it turn to good, for it hath affrighted me above measure.' As they were ready to enter into a colourable [181] commonplace of the deceitful frivolousness of dreams, my trusty servant Brunquell stood quivering and quaking every joint of him, and, as it was before compacted between us, let his pistol drop from him on the sudden, wherewith I started out of my bed and drew my rapier and cried 'Murther, murther!' which made goodwife Tabitha ready to bepiss her.

My servant (or my master, which you will), I took roughly by the collar, and threatened to run him through incontinent if he confessed not the truth. He, as it were stricken with remorse of conscience (God be with him, for he could counterfeit most daintly), down on his knees asked me forgiveness, and impeached Tabitha and Petro de Campo Frego as guilty of subornation. I very mildly and gravely gave him audience; rail on them I did not after his tale was ended, but said I would try what the law could do. Conspiracy by the custom of their country was a capital offence, and what custom or justice might afford they should be all sure to feel. 'I could,' quoth I, 'acquit myself otherwise, but it is not for a stranger to be his own carver in revenge.' Not a word more with Tabitha, but die she would before God or the devil would have her. She sounded [182] and revived, and then sounded again, and after she revived again, sighed heavily, spoke faintly and pitifully, yea, and so pitifully as, if a man had not known the pranks of harlots before, he would have melted into commiseration. Tears,

180. Perhaps a reference to a character called Bruquell, a dwarf servant in *Palmendos*, a play popular in England from 1589 (M.).
181. Plausible.   182. Swooned.

sighs, and doleful-tuned words could not make any forcible claim to my stony ears. It was the glittering crowns that I hungered and thirsted after, and with them for all her mock holyday gestures she was fain to come off, before I condescended to any bargain of silence. So it fortuned (fie upon that unfortunate word of Fortune) that this whore, this quean, this courtesan, this common of ten thousand, so bribing me not to bewray her, had given me a great deal of counterfeit gold, which she had received of a coiner to make away a little before, amongst the gross sum of my bribery. I, silly milksop, mistrusting no deceit, under an angel of light took what she gave me, n'er turned it over, for which (Oh falsehood in fair show) my master and I had like to have been turned over.[183] He that is a knight errant, exercised in the affairs of ladies and gentlewomen, hath more places to send money to than the devil hath to send his spirits to.

There was a delicate wench named Flavia Aemilia lodging in Saint Mark's Street at a goldsmith's, which I would fain have had to the grand test to try whether she were cunning in alchemy or no. Ay me, she was but a counterfeit slip,[184] for she not only gave me the slip, but had wellnigh made me a slip-string.[185] To her I sent my gold to beg an hour of grace: ah, graceless fornicatress, my hostess and she were confederate, who having gotten but one piece of my ill gold in their hands, devised the means to make me immortal. I could drink for anger till my head ached to think how I was abused. Shall I shame the devil and speak the truth? To prison was I sent as principal, and my master as accessory; nor was it to a prison neither, but to the Master of the Mint's house, who, though partly our judge, and a most severe upright justice in his own nature, extremely seemed to condole our ignorant estate, and without all[186] peradventure a present redress he had ministered, if certain of our countrymen, hearing an English Earl was appre-

183. Murdered.   184. Counterfeit coin.
185. Noose for hanging, (also meant truant).
186. In spite of everything.

hended for coining, had not come to visit us. An ill planet brought them thither, for at the first glance they knew the servant of my secrecies to be the Earl of Surrey, and I (not worthy to be named I) an outcast of his cup or pantofles. Thence, thence sprung the full period of our infelicity. The Master of the Mint, our whilom refresher and consolation, now took part against us: he thought we had a mint in our heads of mischievous conspiracies against their state. Heavens bear witness with us it was not so (heavens will not always come to witness when they are called).

To a straiter ward were we committed: that which we have imputatively transgressed must be answered. Oh, the heathen hey-pass [187] and the intrinsical legerdemain [188] of our special approved good pander, Petro de Campo Frego! He, although he dipped in the same dish with us every day, seeming to labour our cause very importunately, and had interpreted for us to the state from the beginning, yet was one of those treacherous Brother Trulies,[189] and abused us most clerkly. He interpreted to us with a pestilence, for whereas we stood obstinately upon it, we were wrongfully detained and that it was naught but a malicious practice of sinful Tabitha, our late hostess, he, by a fine coney-catching corrupt translation, made us plainly to confess and cry *Miserere*, ere we had need of our neck-verse.[190]

Detestable, detestable, that the flesh and the devil should deal by their factors. I'll stand to it, there is not a pander but hath vowed paganism. The devil himself is not such a devil as he, so be he perform his function aright. He must have the back of an ass, the snout of an elephant, the wit of a fox, and the teeth of a wolf; he must fawn like a spaniel, crouch like a Jew, leer like a sheepbiter. If he be half a puritan and have scripture continually in his mouth, he speeds the better. I can tell you it is a trade of great promotion, and

187. Rigmarole.

188. *intrinsical legerdemain*: Secretive trickery.

189. (?) A name for Puritans (M.).

190. The opening verse of Psalm 51, often repeated before an execution.

let none ever think to mount by service in foreign courts or creep near to some magnifique lords, if they be not seen in this science. Oh, it is the art of arts, and ten thousand times goes beyond the intelligencer.[191] None but a staid, grave, civil man is capable of it. He must have exquisite courtship in him or else he is not old who;[192] he wants the best point in his tables.

God be merciful to our pander (and that were for God to work a miracle): he was seen in all the seven liberal deadly sciences, not a sin but he was as absolute in as Satan himself. Satan could never have supplanted us so as he did. I may say to you he planted in us the first Italianate wit that we had. During the time we lay close and took physic in this castle of contemplation, there was a magnifico's wife of good calling sent to bear us company. Her husband's name was Castaldo; she hight [193] Diamante. The cause of her committing was an ungrounded jealous superstition which her doting husband had conceived of her chastity. One Isaac Medicus, a Bergomast,[194] was the man he chose to make him a monster,[195] who being a courtier, and repairing to his house very often, neither for love of him nor his wife, but only with a drift to borrow money of a pawn of wax and parchment,[196] when he saw his expectation deluded, and that Castaldo was too chary for him to close with, he privily, with purpose of revenge, gave out amongst his copesmates [197] that he resorted to Castaldo's house for no other end but to cuckold him, and doubtfully he talked that he had and he had not obtained his suit. Rings which he borrowed of a light courtesan that he used to, he would fain to be taken from her fingers, and, in sum, so handled the matter that Castaldo exclaimed: 'Out, whore! strumpet! six-penny hackster! [198] Away with her to prison!'

191. Informer, spy. 192. 'Old so-and-so' (M.).
193. Was called.
194. Bergomask, native of Bergamo (M.).
195. Cuckold him.
196. *Pawn of wax and parchment*: Written security.
197. Confederates. 198. Cheap prostitute.

As glad were we almost as if they had given us liberty, that fortune lent us such a sweet pew-fellow. A pretty round-faced wench was it, with black eyebrows, a high fore-head, a little mouth, and a sharp nose; as fat and plum, every part of her, as a plover, a skin as sleek and soft as the back of a swan; it doth me good when I remember her. Like a bird she tripped on the ground, and bare out her belly as majestical as an estrich. With a lickerous rolling eye fixed piercing in the earth, and sometimes scornfully darted on the t'one side,[199] she figured forth a high discontented dis-dain; much like a prince puffing and storming at the treason of some mighty subject fled lately out of his power. Her very countenance repiningly wrathful, and yet clear and unwrinkled, would have confirmed the clearness of her con-science to the austerest judge in the world. If in anything she were culpable, it was in being too melancholy chaste, and showing herself as covetous of her beauty as her hus-band was of his bags. Many are honest because they know not how to be dishonest; she thought there was no pleasure in stolen bread because there was no pleasure in an old man's bed. It is almost impossible that any woman should be excellently witty and not make the utmost penny of her beauty. This age and this country of ours admits of some miraculous exceptions, but former times are my constant informers. Those that have quick motions of wit have quick motions in everything: iron only needs many strokes, only iron wits are not won without a long siege of entreaty. Gold easily bends; the most ingenious minds are easiest moved; *Ingenium nobis molle Thalai dedit* [200] saith Psapho to Phao. Who hath no merciful mild mistress, I will maintain, hath no witty but a clownish, dull, phlegmatic puppy to his mistress.

This magnifico's wife was a good loving soul that had mettle enough in her to make a good wit of, but being never removed from under her mother's and her husband's wing,

199. To one side.
200. 'Thalia [one of the Muses] gave me a mind easily moved' (Ovid).

it was not moulded and fashioned as it ought. Causeless distrust is able to drive deceit into a simple woman's head. I durst pawn the credit of a page, which is worth ames ace [201] at all times, that she was immaculate honest till she met with us in prison. Marry, what temptations she had then, when fire and flax were put together, conceit with yourselves, but hold my master excusable.

Alack, he was too virtuous to make her vicious; he stood upon religion and conscience, what a heinous thing it was to subvert God's holy ordinance. This was all the injury he would offer her: sometimes he would imagine her in a melancholy humour to be his Geraldine, and court her in terms correspondent. Nay, he would swear she was his Geraldine, and take her white hand and wipe his eyes with it, as though the very touch of her might staunch his anguish. Now would he kneel and kiss the ground as holy ground which she vouchsafed to bless from barrenness by her steps. Who would have learned to write an excellent passion might have been a perfect tragic poet had he but attended half the extremity of his lament. Passion upon passion would throng one on another's neck. He would praise her beyond the moon and stars, and that so sweetly and ravishingly as I persuade myself he was more in love with his own curious-forming fancy than her face; and truth it is, many become passionate lovers only to win praise to their wits.

He praised, he prayed, he desired and besought her to pity him that perished for her. From this his entranced mistaking ecstasy could no man remove him. Who loveth resolutely will include everything under the name of his love. From prose he would leap into verse, and with these or such-like rhymes assault her:

> If I must die, Oh, let me choose my death:
> Suck out my soul with kisses, cruel maid;
> In thy breasts crystal balls embalm my breath:
> Dole it all out in sighs when I am laid.

201. The lowest throw in a dice game.

Thy lips on mine like cupping-glasses clasp,
Let our tongues meet and strive as they would sting;
Crush out my wind with one straight girting [202] grasp;
Stabs on my heart keep time whilst thou dost sing.
Thy eyes like searing irons burn out mine,
In thy fair tresses stifle me outright,
Like Circes change me to a loathsome swine,
So I may live for ever in thy sight.
    Into heaven's joys none can profoundly see,
    Except that first they meditate on thee.

Sadly and verily, if my master said true, I should, if I were a wench, make many men quickly immortal. What is't, what is't for a maid fair and fresh to spend a little lipsalve on a hungry lover? My master beat the bush and kept a coil and a prattling, but I caught the bird: [203] simplicity and plainness shall carry it away in another world. God wot he was Petro Desperato, when I, stepping to her with a Dunstable [204] tale, made up my market. A holy requiem to their souls that think to woo a woman with riddles. I had some cunning plot, you must suppose, to bring this about. Her husband had abused her, and it was very necessary she should be revenged. Seldom do they prove patient martyrs who are punished unjustly: one way or other they will cry quittance whatsoever it cost them. No other apt means had this poor she-captivated Cicely, to work her hoddy-peak [205] husband a proportionable plague for his jealousy, but to give his head his full loading of infamy. She thought she would make him complain for something, that now was so hard bound with an heretical opinion. How I dealt with her, guess, gentle reader, *subaudi* [206] that I was in prison and she my silly jailor.

Means there was made after a month's or two durance

---

202. Encircling.
203. *beat the bush ... caught the bird*: M. quotes Heywood's Proverbs: 'And while I at length debate and beat the bush, there shall step in other men and catch the bird.'
204. Simple, plain.   205. Cuckolded.
206. 'Understand' (as used in old grammar books).

by Mr John Russell,[207] a gentleman of King Henry the
Eighth's chamber, who then lay lieger[208] at Venice for
England, that our cause should be favourably heard. At that
time was Monsieur Petro Aretino[209] searcher and chief In-
quisitor to the college of courtesans. Divers and sundry ways
was this Aretino beholding to the King of England, especially for, by this foresaid John Russell, a little before, he
had sent him a pension of four hundred crowns yearly
during his life. Very forcibly was he dealt withal, to strain
the utmost of his credit for our delivery out of prison. Nothing at his hands we sought but that the courtesan might
be more narrowly sifted and examined. Such and so extraordinary was his care and industry herein, that, within few
days after, Mistress Tabitha and her pander cried *Peccavi,
confiteor*, and we were presently discharged, they for
example sake executed. Most honourably, after our enlargement, of the state were we used, and had sufficient recompense for all our troubles and wrongs

Before I go any further, let me speak a word or two of
this Aretine. It was one of the wittiest knaves that ever God
made. If out of so base a thing as ink there may be extracted
a spirit, he writ with nought but the spirit of ink, and his
style was the spirituality of arts and nothing else; whereas
all others of his age were but the lay temporalty of inkhorn
terms.[210] For indeed they were mere temporisers and no
better. His pen was sharp-pointed like a poniard; no leaf he
wrote on but was like a burning-glass to set on fire all his
readers. With more than musket-shot did he charge his
quill, where he meant to inveigh. No hour but he sent a
whole legion of devils into some herd of swine or other. If

207. (?1486–1555) accompanied Howard (Surrey) in a naval expedition against the French in 1522.

208. Was ledger (resident) ambassador.

209. (1492–1554) dedicated Volume II of his letters to Henry VIII
in 1542. There appears no evidence for the appointment Nashe speci-
fies, and Henry's gift was of 300 scudi sent through the ambassador.
Later N. confuses Pietro with the poet Bernardo Accolti, called
l'unico Aretino.

210. Pedantic expression.

Martial[211] had ten muses, as he saith of himself, when he but tasted a cup of wine, he had ten score when he determined to tyrannize; ne'er a line of his but was able to make a man drunken with admiration. His sight pierced like lightning into the entrails of all abuses. This I must needs say, that most of his learning he got by hearing the lectures at Florence. It is sufficient that learning he had and a conceit exceeding all learning, to quintessence everything which he heard. He was no timorous servile flatterer of the commonwealth wherein he lived. His tongue and his invention were forborne; what they thought, they would confidently utter. Princes he spared not, that in the least point transgressed. His life he contemned[212] in comparison of the liberty of speech. Whereas some dull-brain maligners of his accuse him of that treatise *De Tribus Impostoribus Mundi*,[213] which was never contrived without a general council of devils, I am verily persuaded it was none of his, and of my mind are a number of the most judicial Italians. One reason is this: because it was published forty years after his death, and he never in his lifetime wrote anything in Latin. Certainly I have heard that one of Machevel's followers and disciples was the author of that book, who, to avoid discredit, filched it forth under Aretine's name a great while after he had sealed up his eloquent spirit in the grave. Too much gall did that wormwood of Ghibelline wits put in his ink, who engraved that rhubarb epitaph[214] on this excellent poet's tombstone. Quite forsaken of all good angels was he, and utterly given over to artless envy. Four universities honoured Aretine with these rich titles: *Il*

211. Perhaps a reference to the *Epigrams*, XI, 6, 12–13. (Translation: 'I can't achieve anything when too sober, but when in my cups fifteen poets will come to my aid.')

212. Despised.

213. An imperfect edition of 1598 contains attacks upon Moses, Christ and Mahomet.

214. An Italian verse translated 'Here lies Aretino, a bitter poison to the human race, whose tongue pierced both the living and dead. He said nothing ill of God, excusing himself by saying he did not know Him.'

flagello de' principi, *Il veritiero*, *Il divino*, and *L'unico Aretino*.[215]

The French King, Francis the First, he kept in such awe, that to chain his tongue he sent him a huge chain of gold, in the form of tongues fashioned. Singularly hath he commented of the humanity of Christ.[216] Besides, as Moses set forth his Genesis, so hath he set forth his Genesis also, including the contents of the whole Bible. A notable treatise hath he compiled, called *I sette Psalmi poenetentiarii*.[217] All the Thomasos have cause to love him, because he hath dilated so magnificently of the life of Saint Thomas.[218] There is a good thing that he hath set forth, *La vita della virgine Maria*,[219] though it somewhat smell of superstition, with a number more, which here, for tediousness, I suppress. If lascivious he were, he may answer with Ovid, *Vita verecunda est, musa iocosa mea est*: 'My life is chaste, though wanton be my verse.' Tell me, who is travelled in histories: what good poet is, or ever was there, who hath not had a little spice of wantonness in his days? Even Beza [220] himself, by your leave. Aretine, as long as the world lives, shalt thou live. Tully, Virgil, Ovid, Seneca were never such ornaments to Italy as thou hast been. I never thought of Italy more religiously than England till I heard of thee. Peace to thy ghost, and yet methinks so indefinite a spirit should have no peace or intermission of pains, but be penning ditties to the archangels in another world. Puritans, spew forth the venom of your dull inventions. A toad swells with thick troubled poison; you swell with poisonous perturbations. Your malice hath not a clear dram of any inspired disposition.

215. 'The Scourge of Princes', 'The Truthful', 'The Divine', 'The Unique Aretino' (properly the title of Bernardo Accolti).

216. *La Umanità di Christo*, 1535.

217. 'The seven penitential psalms': *I sette Salmi de la Penitentia di David*, 1534.

218. *La Vita di San Tomaso, Signor d'Aquino*, 1543.

219. *La Vita di Maria Vergine*, 1539.

220. Theodore de Bèze, who repented later of the Latin poems written in his dissipated youth.

My principal subject plucks me by the elbow. Diamante, Castaldo's ye magnifico's wife, after my enlargement, proved to be with child, at which instant there grew an unsatiable famine in Venice wherein, whether it were for mere niggardise or that Castaldo still ate out his heart with jealousy, Saint Anne be our record, he turned up the heels very devoutly. To Master Aretine after this once more very dutifully I appealed, requested him of favour, acknowledged former gratuities. He made no more humming or halting, but, in despite of her husband's kinsfolks, gave her her *Nunc dimittis*, and so established her free of my company.

Being out, and fully possessed of her husband's goods, she invested me in the state of a monarch. Because the time of childbirth drew nigh, and she could not remain in Venice but discredited, she decreed to travel withersoever I would conduct her. To see Italy throughout was my proposed scope, and that way if she would travel, have with her, I had wherewithal to relieve her.

From my master by her full-hand provokement, I parted without leave: the state of an earl he had thrust upon me before, and now I would not abate him an ace of it. Through all the cities passed I by no other name but the young Earl of Surrey; my pomp, my apparel, train and expense was nothing inferior to his; my looks were as lofty, my words as magnifical. Memorandum: that Florence being the principal scope of my master's course, missing me, he journeyed thither without interruption. By the way as he went, he heard of another Earl of Surrey besides himself, which caused him make more haste to fetch me in, whom he little dreamed of had such art in my budget to separate the shadow from the body. Overtake me at Florence he did, where, sitting in my pontificalibus [221] with my courtesan at supper, like Antony and Cleopatra when they quaffed standing bowls of wine spiced with pearl together, he stole in ere we sent for him, and bad much good it us, and asked us whether we wanted any guests. If he had asked me whether I would have hanged myself, his question had been more

221. Splendour.

acceptable. He that had then ungartered me might have plucked out my heart at my heels.

My soul, which was made to soar upward, now sought for passage downward; my blood, as the rushing Sabine maids, surprised on the sudden by the soldiers of Romulus, ran to the noblest of blood amongst them for succour, that were in no less (if not greater) danger, so did it run for refuge to the noblest of his blood about my heart assembled, that stood in more need itself of comfort and refuge. A trembling earthquake or shaking fever assailed either of us; and I think unfeinedly, if he, seeing our faintheart agony, had not soon cheered and refreshed us, the dogs had gone together by the ears under the table for our fear-dropped limbs.

Instead of menacing or affrighting me with his sword or his frowns for my superlative presumption, he burst out into laughter above ela,[222] to think how bravely napping he had took us, and how notably we were damped and struck dead in the nest with the unexpected view of his presence.

'Ah,' quoth he, 'my noble Lord' (after his tongue had borrowed a little leave of his laughter), 'is it my luck to visit you thus unlooked for? I am sure you will bid me welcome, if it be but for the name's sake. It is a wonder to see two English earls of one house at one time together in Italy.' I hearing him so pleasant, began to gather up my spirits, and replied as boldly as I durst: 'Sir, you are welcome. Your name which I borrowed I have not abused. Some large sums of money this my sweet mistress Diamante hath made me master of, which I knew not how better to employ for the honour of my country than by spending it munificently under your name. No Englishman would I have renowned for bounty, magnificence and courtesy but you; under your colours all my meritorious works I was desirous to shroud. Deem it no insolence to add increase to your fame. Had I basely and beggarly, wanting ability to support any part of your royalty, undertook the

222. Literally very high-pitched, above e-la, the highest note of the scale; therefore 'immoderately'.

estimation of this high calling, your allegement of injury had been the greater, and my defence less authorized. It will be thought but a policy of yours thus to send one before you who, being a follower of yours, shall keep and uphold the estate and port of an earl. I have known many earls myself that in their own persons would go very plain, but delighted to have one that belonged to them (being loaden with jewels, apparelled in cloth of gold and all the rich embroidery that might be) to stand bareheaded unto him; arguing thus much, that if the greatest men went not more sumptuous, how more great than the greatest was he that could command one going so sumptuous. A nobleman's glory appeareth in nothing so much as in the pomp of his attendants. What is the glory of the sun, but that the moon and so many millions of stars borrow their lights from him? If you can reprehend me of any one illiberal licentious action I have disparaged your name with, heap shame on me prodigally; I beg no pardon or pity.'

Non veniunt in idem pudor et amor: [223] he was loth to detract from one that he loved so. Beholding with his eyes that I clipped not the wings of his honour, but rather increased them with additions of expense, he entreated me as if I had been an ambassador. He gave me his hand and swore he had no more hearts but one, and I should have half of it, in that I so enhanced his obscured reputation. 'One thing', quoth he, 'my sweet Jack, I will entreat thee (it shall be but one), that, though I am well pleased thou shouldest be the ape of my birthright – as what nobleman hath not his ape and his fool? – yet that thou be an ape without a clog,[224] not carry thy courtesan with thee.' I told him that a king could do nothing without his treasury; this courtesan was my purse-bearer, my countenance and supporter. My earldom I would sooner resign than part with such a special benefactor. 'Resign it I will, however, since I am thus challenged of stolen goods by the true owner. Lo, into my former state I return again; poor Jack Wilton and

223. 'Shame and love do not tend in the same direction' (Ovid).
224. Piece of wood fastened to the leg.

your servant am I, as I was at the beginning, and so will I persever to my life's ending.'

That theme was quickly cut off, and other talk entered in place, of what I have forgot, but talk it was and talk let it be and talk it shall be, for I do not mean here to remember it. We supped, we got to bed, rose in the morning, on my master I waited, and the first thing he did after he was up, he went and visited the house where his Geraldine was born, at sight whereof he was so impassioned that in the open street, but for me, he would have made an oration in praise of it. Into it we were conducted, and shewed each several room thereto appertaining. Oh, but when he came to the chamber where his Geraldine's clear sunbeams first thrust themselves into this cloud of flesh and acquainted mortality with the purity of angels, then did his mouth overthrow with magnificats; his tongue thrust the stars out of heaven, and eclipsed the sun and moon with comparisons. Geraldine was the soul of heaven, sole daughter and heir to *primus motor*.[225] The alchemy of his eloquence, out of the incomprehensible drossy matter of clouds and air distilled no more quintessence than would make his Geraldine complete fair. In praise of the chamber that was so illuminatively honoured with her radiant conception, he penned this sonnet:

> Fair room, the presence of sweet beauty's pride,
> The place the sun upon the earth did hold,
> When Phaeton his chariot did misguide,
> The tower where Jove rain'd down himself in gold,
>   Prostrate, as holy ground I'll worship thee;
> Our Lady's chapel henceforth be thou nam'd;
> Here first Love's queen put on mortality,
> And with her beauty all the world inflam'd.
>   Heaven's chambers harbouring fiery cherubins,
> Are not with thee in glory to compare;
> Lightning it is, not light, which in thee shines,
> None enter thee but straight intranced are.
>   Oh, if Elizium be above the ground,
>   Then here it is, where nought but joy is found.

225. First mover: this sonnet was printed in *England's Parnassus*, 1600, signed Th.N.

Many other poems and epigrams in that chamber's patient alabaster enclosure, which her melting eyes long sithence had softened, were curiously engraved. Diamonds thought themselves *Dii mundi*[226] if they might but carve her name on the naked glass. With them on it did he anatomize these body-wanting mots: [227] *Dulce puella malum est; Quod fugit ipse sequor; Amor est mihi causa sequendi; O infelix ego; Cur vidi? cur perii? Non patienter amo. Tantum patiatur amari*. After the view of these venereal monuments, he published a proud challenge in the Duke of Florence's court against all comers, whether Christians, Turks, Jews or Saracens, in defence of his Geraldine's beauty. More mildly was it accepted in that she whom he defended was a town-born child of that city, or else the pride of the Italian would have prevented him ere he should have come to perform it. The Duke of Florence nevertheless sent for him and demanded him of his estate and the reason that drew him thereto, which when he was advertised of to the full, he granted all countries whatsoever, as well enemies and outlaws as friends and confederates, free access and regress into his dominions unmolested until that insolent trial were ended.

The right honourable and ever renowned Lord Henry Howard, Earl of Surrey, my singular good lord and master, entered the lists after this order. His armour was ill intermixed with lilies and roses, and the bases thereof bordered with nettles and weeds, signifying stings, crosses and overgrowing encumbrances in his love; his helmet round-proportioned like a gardener's water-pot, from which seemed to issue forth small threads of water, like cittern strings, that not only did moisten the lilies and roses, but did fructify as well the nettles and weeds, and made them overthrow their

226. 'Gods of the earth'.
227. Sayings from Ovid's *Amores, Heroides* and *Metamorphoses* translated: 'A girl is a sweet evil', 'I pursue what flies from me', 'Love is the reason for my following', 'O unhappy me', 'Why have I seen? Why have I perished?', 'I do not love patiently', 'Only let her be patient to be loved'.

liege lords. Whereby he did import thus much, that the tears that issued from his brains, as those artificial distillations issued from the well-counterfeit water-pot on his head, watered and gave life as well to his mistress' disdain (resembled to nettles and weeds) as increase of glory to her care-causing beauty (comprehended under the lilies and roses). The symbol thereto annexed was this: *Ex lachrimis lachrimae*.[228] The trappings of his horse were pounced and bolstered out with rough-plumed silver plush, in full proportion and shape of an estrich. On the breast of the horse were the foreparts of this greedy bird advanced, whence, as his manner is, he reached out his long neck to the reins of the bridle, thinking they had been iron, and still seemed to gape after the golden bit, and ever as the courser did raise or curvet,[229] to have swallowed it half in. His wings, which he never useth but running, being spread full sail, made his lusty steed as proud under him as he had been some other Pegasus, and so quiveringly and tenderly were these his broad wings bound to either side of him, that, as he paced up and down the tilt-yard in his majesty ere the knights were entered, they seemed wantonly to fan in his face and make a flickering sound, such as eagles do, swiftly pursuing their prey in the air. On either of his wings, as the estrich hath a sharp goad or prick wherewith he spurreth himself forward in his sail-assisted race, so this artificial estrich, on the inbent knuckle of the pinion of either wing, had embossed crystal eyes affixed, wherein wheelwise were circularly ingrafted sharp pointed diamonds, as rays from those eyes derived, that like the rowal of a spur ran deep into his horse sides, and made him more eager in his course.

Such a fine dim shine did these crystal eyes and these round-enranked diamonds make through their bollen[230] swelling bowers of feathers as if it had been a candle in a paper lantern, or a glow-worm in a bush by night, glistering through the leaves and briars. The tail of the estrich being short and thick served very fitly for a plume to trick up his

228. 'From tears, more tears'.   229. Leap in a curvet.
230. Swollen, inflated.

horse-tail with, so that every part of him was as naturally coapted [231] as might be. The word to this device was *Aculeo alatus*: [232] 'I spread my wings only spurred with her eyes'. The moral of the whole is this: that, as the estrich, the most burning-sighted bird of all others, insomuch as the female of them hatcheth not her eggs by covering them but by the effectual rays of her eyes, as he, I say, outstrippeth the nimblest trippers of his feathered condition in footmanship (only spurred on with the needle-quickening goad under his side), so he, no less burning-sighted than the estrich, spurred on to the race of honour by the sweet rays of his mistress' eyes, persuaded himself he should outstrip all other in running to the goal of glory, only animated and incited by her excellence. And as the estrich will eat iron, swallow any hard metal whatsoever, so would he refuse no iron adventure, no hard task whatsoever, to sit in the grace of so fair a commander. The order of his shield was this: it was framed like a burning-glass, beset round with flame-coloured feathers, on the outside whereof was his mistress' picture adorned as beautiful as art could portraiture; on the inside, a naked sword tied in a true loveknot; the mot, *Militat omnis amans.*[233] Signifying that in a true-loveknot his sword was tied to defend and maintain the features of his mistress.

Next him entered the Black Knight, whose beaver was pointed all torn and bloody, as though he had new come from combatting with a bear; his headpiece seemed to be a little oven fraught full with smothering flames, for nothing but sulphur and smoke voided out at the clefts of his beaver. His bases were all embroidered with snakes and adders, engendered of the abundance of innocent blood that was shed. His horse trappings were throughout bespangled with honey spots, which are no blemishes but ornaments. On his shield he bare the sun full shining on a dial at his going down; the word, *Sufficit tandem.*[234]

231. Fitted, suited.   232. 'Winged by a sting'.
233. 'Every lover is a soldier' (Ovid).
234. 'Ultimately it is sufficient'.

After him followed the Knight of the Owl, whose armour was a stubbed tree overgrown with ivy, his helmet fashioned like an owl sitting on the top of this ivy. On his bases were wrought all kind of birds, as on the ground, wondering about him; the word, *Ideo mirum quia monstrum.*[235] His horse's furniture was framed like a cart, scattering whole sheaves of corn amongst hogs; the word, *Liberalitas liberalitate perit.*[236] On his shield, a bee entangled in sheep's wool; the mot, *Frontis nulla fides.*[237] The fourth that succeeded was a well-proportioned knight in an armour imitating rust, whose headpiece was prefigured like flowers growing in a narrow pot, where they had not any space to spread their roots or disperse their flourishing. His bases embellished with open armed hands scattering gold amongst truncheons; the word, *Cura futuri est.*[238] His horse was harnessed with leaden chains, having the outside gilt, or at least saffroned instead of gilt, to decipher a holy or golden pretence of a covetous purpose; the sentence, *Cani capilli mei compedes.*[239] On his target[240] he had a number of crawling worms kept under by a block; the faburthen,[241] *Speramus lucent.*[242] The fifth was the Forsaken Knight, whose helmet was crowned with nothing but cypress and willow garlands. Over his armour he had Hymen's nuptial robe, dyed in a dusky yellow, and all-to-be-defaced and discoloured with spots and stains. The enigma, *Nos quoque floruimus*, as who should say 'We have been in fashion.' His steed was adorned with orange tawny eyes, such as those have that have the yellow jandies,[243] that make all things yellow they look upon; with this brief,[244] *Qui invident egent*, 'Those that envy are hungry.' The sixth was the Knight of

235. 'Wonderful because monstrous'.
236. 'Liberality carries the seeds of its own destruction' (St Jerome).
237. 'You can't take anything at face value' (Juvenal).
238. 'Care is a thing of the future' (Ovid).
239. 'My white hairs are my fetters.'
240. A light shield or buckler.
241. Fauxbourdon (here 'theme' or 'motto').
242. 'We hope, they shine.'
243. Jaundice.   244. Device, motto.

the Storms, whose helmet was round-moulded like the moon, and all his armour like waves, whereon the shine of the moon, sleightly silvered, perfectly represented moonshine in the water. His bases were the banks or shores that bounded in the streams. The spoke [245] was this, *Frustra pius*, as much to say as 'fruitless service'. On his shield he set forth a lion driven from his prey by a dunghill cock. The word, *Non vi sed voce*: 'not by violence but by voice'.

The seventh had, like the giants that sought to scale heaven in despite of Jupiter, a mount overwhelming his head and whole body; his bases outlaid with arms and legs which the skirts of that mountain left uncovered. Under this did he characterize a man desirous to climb to the heaven of honour, kept under with the mountain of his prince's command; and yet had he arms and legs exempted from the suppression of that mountain. The word, *Tu mihi criminis author* [246] (alluding to his prince's command): 'Thou art the occasion of my imputed cowardice.' His horse was trapped in the earthly strings of tree-roots, which, though their increase was stubbed down to the ground, yet were they not utterly deaded, but hoped for an after-resurrection. The word, *Spe alor*: [247] 'I hope for a spring.' Upon his shield he bare a ball, stricken down with a man's hand that it might mount. The word, *Ferior ut efferar*: 'I suffer myself to be contemned because I will climb.'

The eighth had all his armour throughout engrailed like a crabbed briary hawthorn bush, out of which notwithstanding sprung (as a good child of an ill father) fragrant blossoms of delightful may flowers, that made, according to the nature of may, a most odoriferous smell. In the midst of this, his snowy curled top, round wrapped together, on the ascending of his crest, sat a solitary nightingale close encaged, with a thorn at her breast, having this mot in her mouth: *Luctus monumenta manebunt*.[248] At the foot of

245. Word, 'mot'.
246. Ovid, *Metamorphoses*, XV, 40.
247. 'I am sustained by hope.'
248. 'Monuments of grief will remain.'

this bush represented on his bases lay a number of black swollen toads gasping for wind, and summer-lived grasshoppers gaping after dew, both which were choked with excessive drought for want of shade. The word, *Non sine vulnere viresco*: [249] 'I spring not without impediments', alluding to the toads and suchlike that erst lay sucking at his roots, but now were turned out and near choked with drought. His horse was suited in black sandy earth, as adjacent to this bush, which was here and there patched with short burnt grass, and as thick ink-dropped with toiling ants and emmets as ever it might crawl, who, in the full of the summer moon (ruddy garnished on his horse's forehead) hoarded up their provision of grain against winter. The word, *Victrix fortunae sapientia*: [250] 'Providence prevents misfortune.' On his shield he set forth the picture of death doing alms-deeds to a number of poor desolate children. The word, *Nemo alius explicat*: [251] 'No other man takes pity upon us.' What his meaning was herein I cannot imagine, except death had done him and his brethren some great good turn in ridding them of some untoward parent or kinsman that would have been their confusion; for else I cannot see how death should have been said to do almsdeeds, except he had deprived them suddenly of their lives, to deliver them out of some further misery; which could not in any wise be, because they were yet living.

The ninth was the Infant Knight, who on his armour had enamelled a poor young infant put into a ship without tackling, masts, furniture, or anything. This weather-beaten or ill-apparelled ship was shadowed on his bases, and the slender compass of his body set forth the right picture of an infant. The waves wherein the ship was tossed were fretted on his steed's trappings so movingly that ever as he offered to bound or stir they seemed to bounce and toss and sparkle brine out of their hoary silver billows. The mot, *Inopem me*

249. 'I flourish not without wound' (from Plautus).
250. 'Wisdom, the conqueror of fortune'.
251. Literally 'No one else unfolds'.

copia fecit: [252] as much as to say as 'The rich prey makes the thief.'

On his shield he expressed an old goat that made a young tree to wither only with biting it; the word thereto, *Primo extinguor in aevo*: [253] 'I am frost-bitten ere I come out of the blade.'

It were here too tedious to manifest all the discontented or amorous devices that were used in this tournament; the shields only of some few I will touch, to make short work. One bare for his impress the eyes of young swallows coming again after they were plucked out, with this mot, *Et addit et addimit*: 'Your beauty both bereaves and restores my sight.' Another, a siren smiling when the sea rageth and ships are overwhelmed, including a cruel woman that laughs, sings and scorns at her lover's tears and the tempests of his despair. The word, *Cuncta pereunt*: 'All my labour is ill-employed.' A third, being troubled with a curst,[254] a treacherous and wanton wife, used this similitude. On his shield he caused to be limned Pompey's ordinance for parricides, as namely, a man put into a sack with a cock, a serpent and an ape, interpreting that his wife was a cock for her crowing, a serpent for her stinging, and an ape for her unconstant wantonness, with which ill qualities he was so beset that thereby he was thrown into a sea of grief. The word, *Extremum malorum mulier*: 'The utmost of evils is a woman.' A fourth, who, being a person of suspected religion, was continually haunted with intelligencers and spies that thought to prey upon him for that he had, he could not devise which way to shake them off but by making away that he had. To obscure this, he used no other fancy but a number of blind flies, whose eyes the cold had enclosed. The word, *Aurum reddit acutissimum*: 'Gold is the only physic for the eyesight.' A fifth, whose mistress was fallen into a consumption and yet would condescend to no treaty of love, emblazoned for his complaint grapes that withered

252. 'Abundance has made me needy' (Ovid).
253. Adapted from Ovid, *Metamorphoses*, III, 470.
254. Ill-tempered, shrewish.

for want of pressing. The ditty to the mot, *Quid regna sine usu*.[255] I will rehearse no more, but I have an hundred other. Let this be the upshot of those shows: they were the admirablest that ever Florence yielded.

To particularise their manner of encounter were to describe the whole art of tilting. Some had like to have fallen over their horse necks and so break their necks in breaking their staves. Others ran at a buckle instead of a button, and peradventure whetted their spears' points, idly gliding on their enemy's sides, but did no other harm. Others ran across at their adversary's left elbow, yea, and by your leave sometimes let not the lists scape scot-free, they were so eager. Others, because they would be sure not to be unsaddled with the shock, when they came to the spear's utmost proof, they threw it over the right shoulder and so tilted backward, for forward they durst not. Another had a monstrous spite at the pommel of his rival's saddle, and thought to have thrust his spear twixt his legs without rasing any skin, and carried him clean away on it as a cool-staff.[256] Another held his spear to his nose, or his nose to his spear, as though he had been discharging his caliver, and ran at the right foot of his fellow's steed. Only the Earl of Surrey, my master, observed the true measures of honour and made all his encounters new-scour their armour in the dust; so great was his glory that day as Geraldine was thereby eternally glorified. Never such a bountiful master came amongst the heralds: not that he did enrich them with any plentiful purse-largesse, but that by his stern assaults he tithed them more rich offals [257] of bases, of helmets, of armour, than the rent of their offices came to in ten years before.

What would you have more? The trumpets proclaimed him master of the field; the trumpets proclaimed Geraldine the exceptionless fairest of women. Everyone strived to magnify him more than other. The Duke of Florence,

255. 'What use are kingdoms without the ability to enjoy them?' (Ovid).
256. Cowlstaff.
257. 'Leavings' (M.).

whose name (as my memory serveth me) was Paschal de' Medicis,[258] offered him such large proffers to stay with him as it were incredible to report. He would not; his desire was, as he had done in Florence, so to proceed throughout all the chief cities in Italy. If you ask why he began not this at Venice first, it was because he would let Florence, his mistress' native city, have the maidenhead of his chivalry. As he came back again, he thought to have enacted something there worthy the annals of posterity, but he was debarred both of that and all his other determinations, for, continuing in feasting and banqueting with the Duke of Florence and the princes of Italy there assembled, posthaste letters came to him from the King his master to return as speedily as he could possible into England. Whereby his fame was quite cut off by the shins, and there was no reprieve but *Bazelus manus*,[259] he must into England; and I with my courtesan travelled forward in Italy.

What adventures happened him after we parted, I am ignorant; but Florence we both forsook, and I, having a wonderful ardent inclination to see Rome, the Queen of the world and metropolitan mistress of all other cities, made thither with my bag and baggage as fast as I could.

Attained thither, I was lodged at the house of one Johannes de Imola, a Roman cavaliero. Who, being acquainted with my courtesan's deceased doting husband, for his sake used us with all the familiarity that might be. He showed us all the monuments that were to be seen, which are as many as there have been emperors, consuls, orators, conquerors, famous painters or players in Rome. Till this day not a Roman, if he be a right Roman indeed, will kill a rat, but he will have some registered remembrance of it.

There was a poor fellow during my remainder there, that, for a new trick that he had invented of killing cimices [260]

---

258. Either Alexander dei Medici, ruler of Florence from 1530 to 1537, or Cosimo (1537–74) (M.).

259. 'Kiss the hands' (Spanish: *'beso las manos'*).

260. Plural of cimex, a bed-bug.

and scorpions, had his mountebank banner hung up on a
high pillar, with an inscription about it longer than the
King of Spain's style. I thought these cimices, like the
Cimbrians, had been some strange nation he had brought
under, and they were no more but things like lice, which
alive have the most venomous sting that may be, and being
dead do stink out of measure; Saint Austin [261] compareth
heretics unto them. The chiefest thing that my eyes delighted in, was the Church of the Seven Sibyls, [262] which is a
most miraculous thing, all their prophecies and oracles being
there enrolled, as also the beginning and ending of their
whole catalogue of the heathen gods, with their manner of
worship. There are a number of other shrines and statues
dedicated to the emperors, and withal some statues of
idolatry reserved for detestation.

I was at Pontius Pilate's house and pissed against it. The
name of the place I remember not, but it is as one goes to
Saint Paul's Church not far from the Jews' Piazza. [263] There
is the prison yet packed up together (an old rotten thing)
where the man that was condemned to death and could
have nobody come to him and succour him but was
searched, was kept alive a long space by sucking his daughter's breasts.

These are but the shop-dust of the sights that I saw, and
in truth I did not behold with any care hereafter to report,
but contented my eye for the present, and so let them pass.
Should I memorize half the miracles which they there told
me had been done about martyrs' tombs, or the operations
of the earth of the sepulchre and other relics brought from
Jerusalem, I should be counted the most monstrous liar that
ever came in print. The ruins of Pompey's theatre, reputed
one of the nine wonders of the world, Gregory the Sixth's

261. Augustine.
262. Meaning unknown. The Sistine Chapel has five sibyls with
scrolls, painted by Michelangelo; Dover Wilson suggests Nashe may
be drawing on a traveller's story referring to these.
263. Emendation of 'the jems piazza', suggested by M., referring
to the Piazza Giudea.

tomb,[264] Priscilla's grate,[265] or the thousands of pillars arreared amongst the rased foundations of old Rome, it were frivolous to specify, since he that hath but once drunk with a traveller talks of them. Let me be a historiographer of my own misfortunes, and not meddle with the continued trophies of so old a triumphing city.

At my first coming to Rome, I, being a youth of the English cut, ware my hair long, went apparelled in light colours, and imitated four or five sundry nations in my attire at once; which no sooner was noted, but I had all the boys of the city in a swarm wondering about me.

I had not gone a little farther, but certain officers crossed the way of me, and demanded to see my rapier; which when they found (as also my dagger) with his point unblunted, they would have haled me headlong to the strappado, but that with money I appeased them, and my fault was more pardonable in that I was a stranger, altogether ignorant of their customs.

Note, by the way, that it is the use in Rome for all men whatsoever to wear their hair short; which they do not so much for conscience sake, or any religion they place in it, but because the extremity of the heat is such there that, if they should not do so, they should not have a hair left on their heads to stand upright when they were scared with sprites. And he is counted no gentleman amongst them that goes not in black; they dress their jesters and fools only in fresh colours and say variable garments do argue unsteadiness and unconstancy of affections.

The reason of their strait ordinance for carrying weapons without points is this: the bandittos, which are certain outlaws that lie betwixt Rome and Naples, and besiege the passage, that none can travel that way without robbing. Now and then, hired for some few crowns, they will steal to Rome and do a murther, and betake them to their heels

264. Probably a printer's mistake for Gregory XI (suggestion by E. S. de Beer and J. C. Maxwell).

265. De Beer suggests this may be a mistake for the burial place of S. Francesca Romana.

again. Disguised as they go, they are not known from strangers; sometimes they will shroud themselves under the habit of grave citizens. In this consideration, neither citizen or stranger, gentleman, knight, marquis, or any, may wear any weapon endamageable, upon pain of the strappado. I bought it out; let others buy experience of me better cheap.

To tell you of the rare pleasures of their gardens, their baths, their vineyards, their galleries, were to write a second part of *The Gorgeous Gallery of Gallant Devices*.[266] Why, you should not come into any man's house of account, but he had fish-ponds and little orchards on the top of his leads. If by rain or any other means those ponds were so full they need to be sluiced or let out, even of their superfluities they made melodious use, for they had great wind instruments instead of leaden spouts, that went duly on consort only with this water's rumbling descent.

I saw a summer banqueting house belonging to a merchant, that was the marvel of the world, and could not be matched except God should make another paradise. It was built round of green marble like a theatre without; within there was a heaven and earth comprehended both under one roof. The heaven was a clear overhanging vault of crystal, wherein the sun and moon and each visible star had his true similitude, shine, situation and motion, and, by what enwrapped art I cannot conceive, these spheres in their proper orbs observed their circular wheelings and turnings, making a certain kind of soft angelical murmuring music in their often windings and going about; which music the philosophers say in the true heaven, by reason of the grossness of our senses, we are not capable of. For the earth, it was counterfeited in that likeness that Adam lorded over it before his fall. A wide, vast, spacious room it was, such as we would conceit Prince Arthur's hall to be, where he feasted all his Knights of the Round Table together every Pentecost. The floor was painted with the beautifullest

266. *The Gorgeous Gallery of Gallant Inventions*, a poetical miscellany by Thomas Proctor, 1578 (M.).

flowers that ever man's eye admired; which so lively [267] were delineated that he that viewed them afar off and had not directly stood poringly over them, would have sworn they had lived indeed. The walls round about were hedged with olives and palm trees, and all other odoriferous fruit-bearing plants, which at any solemn entertainment dropped myrrh and frankincense. Other trees, that bare no fruit, were set in just order one against another, and divided the room into a number of shady lanes, leaving but one over-spreading pine tree arbour where we sat and banqueted.

On the well-clothed boughs of this conspiracy of pine trees against the resembled sunbeams were perched as many sorts of shrill-breasted birds as the summer hath allowed for singing men in her sylvan chapels. Who, though they were bodies without souls, and sweet-resembled substances without sense, yet by the mathematical experiments of long silver pipes secretly inrinded in the entrails of the boughs whereon they sat, and undiscernibly conveyed under their bellies into their small throats sloping, they whistled and freely carolled their natural field note. Neither went those silver pipes straight, but, by many-edged, unsundered writhings and crankled wanderings aside, strayed from bough to bough into an hundred throats. But into this silver pipe so writhed and wandering aside, if any demand how the wind was breathed, forsooth the tail of the silver pipe stretched itself into the mouth of a great pair of bellows, where it was close soldered and bailed about with iron, it could not stir or have any vent betwixt. These bellows, with the rising and falling of leaden plummets wound up on a wheel, did beat up and down uncessantly, and so gathered in wind, serving with one blast all the snarled pipes to and fro of one tree at once. But so closely were all those organis-ing implements obscured in the corpulent trunks of the trees that every man there present renounced conjectures of art and said it was done by enchantment.

One tree for his fruit bare nothing but enchained chirp-ing birds, whose throats being conduit-piped with squared

267. M.'s suggested emendation for 'lineally'.

narrow shells, and charged syringe-wise [268] with searching sweet water driven in by a little wheel for the nonce, that fed it afar off, made a spirting sound, such as chirping is, in bubbling upwards through the rough crannies of their closed bills.

Under tuition of the shade of every tree that I have signified to be in this round hedge, on delightful leavy cloisters lay a wild tyrannous beast asleep all prostrate; under some, two together, as the dog nuzzling his nose under the neck of the deer, the wolf glad to let the lamb lie upon him to keep him warm, the lion suffering the ass to cast his leg over him, preferring one honest unmannerly friend before a number of crouching pickthanks. [269] No poisonous beast there reposed (poison was not before our parent Adam transgressed). There were no sweet-breathing panthers that would hide their terrifying heads to betray; no men-imitating hyenas that changed their sex to seek after blood. Wolves, as now when they are hungry eat earth, so then did they feed on earth only and abstained from innocent flesh. The unicorn did not put his horn into the stream to chase away venom before he drank, [270] for then there was no such thing extant in the water or on the earth. Serpents were as harmless to mankind as they are still one to another; the rose had no cankers, the leaves no caterpillars, the sea no sirens, the earth no usurers. Goats then bare wool, as it is recorded in Sicily they do yet. The torrid zone was habitable; only jays loved to steal gold and silver to build their nests withal, and none cared for covetous clientry or running to the Indies. As the elephant understands his country speech, so every beast understood what man spoke. The ant did not hoard up against winter, for there was no winter, but a perpetual spring, as Ovid [271] saith. No frosts to make the green almond tree counted rash and improvident in budding soonest of all other; or the mulberry tree a strange politician in

268. Like a syringe.
269. Sycophants.
270. The horn was held to be an antidote for poison.
271. 'Ver erat aeternum' (Metamorphoses, I, 107).

blooming late and ripening early. The peach tree at the first planting was fruitful and wholesome, whereas now, till it be transplanted, it is poisonous and hateful. Young plants for their sap had balm; for their yellow gum, glistering amber. The evening dewed not water on flowers, but honey. Such a golden age, such a good age, such an honest age, was set forth in this banqueting house.

Oh Rome, if thou hast in thee such soul-exalting objects, what a thing is heaven in comparison of thee, of which Mercator's globe [272] is a perfecter model than thou art? Yet this I must say to the shame of us Protestants: if good works may merit heaven, they do them, we talk of them. Whether superstition or no makes them unprofitable servants, that let pulpits decide; but there you shall have the bravest ladies, in gowns of beaten gold, washing pilgrims' and poor soldiers' feet, and doing nothing, they and their waiting-maids, all the year long, but making shirts and bands for them against [273] they come by in distress. Their hospitals are more like noblemen's houses than otherwise; so richly furnished, clean kept and hot perfumed, that a soldier would think it a sufficient recompense for all his travel and his wounds, to have such a heavenly retiring place. For the Pope and his pontificalibus I will not deal with; only I will dilate unto you what happened whilst I was in Rome.

So it fell out that, it being a vehement hot summer when I was a sojourner there, there entered such a hotspurred [274] plague as hath not been heard of. Why, it was but a word and a blow, 'Lord have mercy upon us', and he was gone. Within three quarters of a year in that one city there died of it a hundred thousand: look in Lanquet's *Chronicle* [275] and you shall find it. To smell of a nosegay that was poisoned, and turn your nose to a house that had the plague, it was all

272. Gerardus Mercator designed a pair of globes, 1541–51, in common use in England in 1592.

273. In case.

274. Fiery.

275. T. Lanquet (1545). M. quotes 'a pestilence in Rome which consumed an 100 thousand' under the year 1522.

one. The clouds, like a number of cormorants that keep their corn till it stink and is musty, kept in their stinking exhalations till they had almost stifled all Rome's inhabitants. Physicians' greediness of gold made them greedy of their destiny. They would come to visit those with whose infirmity their art had no affinity; and even as a man with a fee should be hired to hang himself, so would they quietly go home and die presently after they had been with their patients. All day and all night long, car-men did nothing but go up and down the streets with their carts, and cry 'Have you any dead bodies to bury?' And had many times out of one house their whole loading. One grave was the sepulchre of seven score; one bed was the altar whereon whole families were offered.

The walls were hoared and furred with the moist scorching steam of their desolation. Even as, before a gun is shot off, a stinking smoke funnels out and prepares the way for him, so before any gave up the ghost, death arrayed in a stinking smoke stopped his nostrils and crammed itself full into his mouth that closed up his fellow's eyes, to give him warning to prepare for his funeral. Some died sitting at their meat, others as they were asking counsel of the physician for their friends. I saw at the house where I was hosted, a maid bring her master warm broth for to comfort him, and she sink down dead herself ere he had half eat it up.

During this time of visitation, there was a Spaniard, one Esdras of Granado, a notable banditto, authorised by the Pope because he had assisted him in some murthers. This villain, colleagued with one Bartol, a desperate Italian, practised to break into those rich men's houses in the night where the plague had most reigned, and if there were none but the mistress and maid left alive, to ravish them both and bring away all the wealth they could fasten on. In an hundred chief citizens' houses where the hand of God had been, they put this outrage in ure.[276] Though the women so ravished cried out, none durst come near them for fear of

276. Into practice.

331

catching their deaths by them, and some thought they cried out only with the tyranny of the malady. Amongst the rest, the house where I lay he invaded, where all being snatched up by sickness but the good wife of the house, a noble and chaste matron called Heraclide, and her zany and I and my courtesan, he, knocking at the door late in the night, ran in to the matron and left me and my love to the mercy of his companion, who finding me in bed (as the time required) ran at me full with his rapier, thinking I would resist him, but, as good luck was, I escaped him and betook me to my pistol in the window uncharged. He, fearing it had been charged, threatened to run her through if I once offered but to aim at him. Forth the chamber he dragged her, holding his rapier at her heart, whilst I cried out 'Save her, kill me! And I'll ransom her with a thousand ducats.' But lust prevailed; no prayers would be heard. Into my chamber I was locked, and watchmen charged (as he made semblance when there was none there) to knock me down with their halberds if I stirred but a foot down the stairs. Then threw I myself pensive again on my pallet,[277] and dared all the devils in hell, now I was alone, to come and fight with me one after another in defence of that detestable rape. I beat my head against the walls and called them bawds, because they would see such a wrong committed and not fall upon him.

To return to Heraclide below, whom the ugliest of all blood-suckers, Esdras of Granado, had under shrift.[278] First he assailed her with rough means, and slew her zany at her foot that stepped before her in rescue. Then when all armed resist was put to flight, he assayed [279] her with honey speech, and promised her more jewels and gifts than he was able to pilfer in an hundred years after. He discoursed unto her how he was countenanced and borne out by the Pope, and how many execrable murthers with impunity he had executed on

277. Mattress.
278. At his mercy (the period for prayer and confession before execution).
279. Tried, tempted.

them that displeased him. 'This is the eight-score house,' quoth he, 'that hath done homage unto me, and here I will prevail or I will be torn in pieces.' 'Ah,' quoth Heraclide with a heart-renting sigh, 'art thou ordained to be worse plague to me than the plague itself? Have I escaped the hands of God to fall into the hands of man? Hear me, Jehova, and be merciful in ending my misery! Dispatch me incontinent,[280] dissolute homicide, death's usurper! Here lies my husband stone cold on the dewy floor. If thou beest of more power than God to strike me speedily, strike home, strike deep, send me to heaven with my husband. Ay me, it is the spoil of my honour thou seekest in my soul's troubled departure; thou art some devil sent to tempt me. Avoid from me, Satan! My soul is my saviour's. To him I have bequeathed it; from him can no man take it. Jesu, Jesu, spare me indefiled for thy spouse! Jesu, Jesu, never fail those that put their trust in thee!'

With that, she fell in a swoon, and her eyes in their closing seemed to spawn forth in their outward sharp corners new-created seed pearl, which the world before never set eye on. Soon he rigorously revived her, and told her that he had a charter above scripture; she must yield, she should yield, see who durst remove her out of his hands. Twixt life and death thus she faintly replied:

'How thinkest thou, is there a power above thy power? If there be, He is here present in punishment and on thee will take present punishment if thou persistest in thy enterprises. In the time of security, every man sinneth, but when death substitutes one friend his special bailie to arrest another by infection, and disperseth his quiver into ten thousand hands at once, who is it but looks about him? A man that hath an unevitable huge stone hanging only by a hair over his head, which he looks, every Pater-Nosterwhile,[281] to fall and pash[282] him in pieces, will not he be submissively sorrowful for his transgressions, refrain himself from

280. Without delay.
281. As long as it takes to say the Lord's Prayer.
282. Crush.

333

the least thought of folly, and purify his spirit with contrition and penitence? God's hand like a huge stone hangs inevitably over thy head. What is the plague but death playing the Provost Marshal, to execute all those that will not be called home by any other means? This my dear knight's body is a quiver of his arrows, which already are shot into thee invisibly. Even as the age of goats is known by the knots on their horns, so think the anger of God apparently visioned or shown unto thee in the knitting of my brows. A hundred have I buried out of my house, at all whose departures I have been present. A hundred's infection is mixed with my breath. Lo, now I breathe upon thee, a hundred deaths come upon thee. Repent betimes; imagine there is a hell though not a heaven. That hell thy conscience is thoroughly acquainted with, if thou hast murdered half so many as thou unblushingly braggest. As Mecoenas in the latter end of his days was seven years without sleep, so these seven weeks have I took no slumber. My eyes have kept continual watch against the devil, my enemy. Death I deemed my friend (friends fly from us in adversity); death, the devil, and all the ministering spirits of temptation are watching about thee to entrap thy soul, by my abuse, to eternal damnation. It is thy soul thou mayest save, only by saving mine honour. Death will have thy body infallibly for breaking into my house, that he had selected for his private habitation. If thou ever camest of a woman, or hopest to be saved by the seed of a woman, pity a woman. Deers oppressed with dogs, when they cannot take soil, run to men for succour: to whom should women in their disconsolate and desperate estate run but to men, like the deer, for succour and sanctuary? If thou be a man, thou wilt succour me; but if thou be a dog and a brute beast, thou wilt spoil me, defile me and tear me. Either renounce God's image, or renounce the wicked mind thou bearest.'

These words might have moved a compound heart of iron and adamant, but in his heart they obtained no impression. For he sitting in his chair of state against the door all the while that she pleaded, leaning his overhanging gloomy eyebrows on the pommel of his unsheathed sword, he never looked up or gave her a word. But when he perceived she expected his answer of grace or utter perdition, he start up and took her currishly by the neck, asking how long he should stay for her Ladyship. 'Thou tell'st me,' quoth he, 'of the plague and the heavy hand of God, and thy hundred infected breaths in one. I tell thee I have cast the dice an hundred times for the galleys in Spain and yet still missed the ill chance. Our order of casting is this: if there be a general or captain new come home from the wars, and hath some four or five hundred crowns overplus of the King's in his hand, and his soldiers all paid, he makes proclamation that whatsoever two resolute men will go to dice for it and win the bridle or lose the saddle, to such a place let them repair, and it shall be ready for them. Thither go I, and find another such needy squire resident. The dice run, I win, he is undone. I winning have the crowns; he losing is carried to the galleys. This is our custom, which a hundred times and more hath paid me custom of crowns, when the poor fellows have gone to Gehenna,[283] had coarse bread and whipping cheer all their life after. Now thinkest thou that I, who so oft have escaped such a number of hellish dangers, only depending upon the turning of a few pricks, can be scare-bugged with the plague? What plague canst thou name worse than I have had? Whether diseases, imprisonment, poverty, banishment, I have passed through them all. My own mother gave I a box of the ear to, and brake her neck down a pair of stairs, because she would not go in to a gentleman when I bad her. My sister I sold to an old leno,[284] to make his best of her. Any kinswoman that I have, knew I she were not a whore, myself would make her one. Thou art a whore; thou shalt be a whore, in spite of religion or precise [285] ceremonies.'

Therewith he flew upon her and threatened her with his sword, but it was not that he meant to wound her with. He

283. Hell. 284. Pander.
285. Puritanical.

grasped her by the ivory throat and shook her as a mastiff
would shake a young bear, swearing and staring he would
tear out her weasand if she refused. Not content with that
savage constraint, he slipped his sacrilegious hand from her
lily lawn-skinned neck and enscarfed it in her long silver
locks which with struggling were unrolled. Backward he
dragged her, even as a man backward would pluck a tree
down by the twigs, and then, like a traitor that is drawn to
execution on a hurdle, he traileth her up and down the
chamber by those tender untwisted braids, and setting his
barbarous foot on her bare snowy breast, bad her yield or
have her wind stamped out. She cried 'Stamp, stifle me in
my hair, hang me up by it on a beam and so let me die,
rather than I should go to heaven with a beam in my eye.'
'No,' quoth he, 'nor stamped nor stifled nor hanged, nor to
heaven shalt thou go, till I have had my will of thee. Thy
busy arms in these silken fetters I'll enfold.' Dismissing
her hair from his fingers and pinioning her elbows there-
withal, she struggled, she wrested, but all was in vain. So
struggling and so resisting, her jewels did sweat, signifying
there was poison coming towards her. On the hard boards
he threw her, and used his knee as an iron ram to beat ope
the two-leaved gate of her chastity. Her husband's dead
body he made a pillow to his abomination. Conjecture the
rest, my words stick fast in the mire and are clean tired;
would I had never undertook this tragical tale. Whatsoever
is born, is born to have an end. Thus ends my tale: his
whorish lust was glutted, his beastly desire satisfied. What
in the house of any worth was carriageable, he put up, and
went his way.

Let not your sorrow die, you that have read the proem
and narration of this elegiacal history. Show you have quick
wits in sharp conceit of compassion. A woman that hath
viewed all her children sacrificed before her eyes, and after
the first was slain wiped the sword with her apron to
prepare it for the cleanly murther of the second, and so
on forward till it came to the empiercing of the seventeenth
of her loins, will you not give her great allowance of

anguish? This woman, this matron, this forsaken Heraclide, having buried fourteen children in five days, whose
eyes she howlingly closed and caught many wrinkles with
funeral kisses, besides having her husband within a day
after laid forth as a comfortless corse, a carrionly block,
that could neither eat with her, speak with her nor weep
with her: is she not to be borne withal though her body
swell with a timpany [286] of tears, though her speech be as
impatient as unhappy Hecuba's, though her head rave and
her brain dote? Devise with yourselves that you see a corse
rising from his hearse after he is carried to church, and
such another suppose Heraclide to be, rising from the couch
of enforced adultery.

Her eyes were dim, her cheeks bloodless, her breath smelt
earthy, her countenance was ghastly. Up she rose after she
was deflowered, but loth she rose, as a reprobate soul rising
to the Day of Judgment. Looking on the t'one side as she
rose, she spied her husband's body lying under her head.
Ah, then she bewailed as Cephalus when he had killed
Procris unwittingly, or Oedipus when ignorantly he had
slain his father and known his mother incestuously. This was
her subdued reason's discourse:

'Have I lived to make my husband's body the bier to
carry me to hell? Had filthy pleasure no other pillow to
lean upon but his spreaded limbs? On thy flesh my fault
shall be imprinted at the day of resurrection. Oh beauty,
the bait ordained to ensnare the irreligious! Rich men are
robbed for their wealth; women are dishonested for being
too fair. No blessing is beauty, but a curse. Cursed be the
time that ever I was begotten. Cursed be the time that my
mother brought me forth to tempt. The serpent in Paradise
did no more. The serpent in Paradise is damned sem-
piternally: why should not I hold myself damned (if pre-
destination's opinions be true) that am predestinate to this
horrible abuse? The hog dieth presently if he loseth an
eye; with the hog have I wallowed in the mire, I have lost
my eye of honesty, it is clean plucked out with a strong

286. Literally a swelling of the abdomen.

hand of unchastity. What remaineth but I die? Die I will, though life be unwilling. No recompense is there for me to redeem my compelled offence, but with a rigorous compelled death. Husband, I'll be thy wife in heaven. Let not thy pure deceased spirit despise me when we meet, because I am tyrannously polluted. The devil, the belier of our frailty and common accuser of mankind, cannot accuse me, though he would, of unconstrained submitting. If any guilt be mine, this is my fault, that I did not deform my face, ere it should so impiously allure.'

Having passioned thus awhile, she hastily ran and looked herself in her glass, to see if her sin were not written on her forehead. With looking she blushed, though none looked upon her but her own reflected image.

Then began she again: 'Heu quam difficile est crimen non prodere vultu.[287] "How hard is it not to bewray a man's fault by his forehead." Myself do but behold myself, and yet I blush. Then, God beholding me, shall not I be ten times more ashamed? The angels shall hiss at me, the saints and martyrs fly from me. Yea, God Himself shall add to the devil's damnation, because he suffered such a wicked creature to come before Him. Agamemnon, thou wert an infidel, yet when thou went'st to the Trojan War, thou left'st a musician at home with thy wife, who by playing the foot Spondaeus [288] till thy return might keep her in chastity. My husband going to war with the devil and his enticements, when he surrendered left no musician with me, but mourning and melancholy. Had he left any, as Aegisthus killed Agamemnon's musician ere he could be successful, so surely would he have been killed ere this Aegisthus surceased. My distressed heart, as the hart whenas he loseth his horns is astonied and sorrowfully runneth to hide him-

287. Ovid, Metamorphoses, II, 447.
288. M. quotes Cornelius Agrippa: 'King Agamemnon, also going to the Trojan war, left at home a musician that played the Dorian tune, who with the foot spondeus preserved his wife Clitemnestra in chastity and honesty, wherefore she could not be deflowered by Aegisthus before he had wickedly slain the musician.'

self, so be thou afflicted and distressed. Hide thyself under the Almighty's wings of mercy. Sue, plead, entreat: grace is never denied to them that ask. It may be denied; I may be a vessel ordained to dishonour.

'The only repeal we have from God's undefinite chastisement is to chastise ourselves in this world. And I will; nought but death be my penance, gracious and acceptable may it be. My hand and my knife shall manumit[289] me out of the horror of mind I endure. Farewell, life that hast lent me nothing but sorrow. Farewell, sin-sowed flesh, that hast more. weeds than flowers, more woes than joys. Point, pierce, edge, enwiden, I patiently afford thee a sheath. Spur forth my soul to mount post to heaven. Jesu, forgive me; Jesu, receive me!'

So, throughly stabbed, fell she down and knocked her head against her husband's body, wherewith he, not having been aired his full four-and-twenty hours, start as out of a dream; whiles I, thorough a cranny of my upper chamber unsealed, had beheld all this sad spectacle. Awaking, he rubbed his head to and fro, and wiping his eyes with his hand, began to look about him. Feeling something lie heavy on his breast, he turned it off, and getting upon his legs, lighted a candle.

Here beginneth my purgatory. For he, good man, coming into the hall with the candle, and spying his wife with her hair about her ears, defiled and massacred, and his simple zany Capestrano run through, took a halberd in his hand, and running from chamber to chamber to search who in his house was likely to do it, at length found me lying on my bed, the door locked to me on the outside, and my rapier unsheathed in the window. Wherewith he straight conjected it was I, and calling the neighbours hard by, said I had caused myself to be locked into my chamber after that sort, sent away my courtesan whom I called my wife. and made clean my rapier, because I would not be suspected.

Upon this was I laid in prison, should have been hanged, was brought to the ladder, had made a ballad for my fare-

289. Release, free.

well in a readiness, called *Wilton's Wantonness*, and yet, for all that, scaped dancing in a hempen circle. He that hath gone through many perils and returned safe from them makes but a merriment to dilate them. I had the knot under my ear. There was fair play; the hangman had one halter, another about my neck was fastened to the gallows, the riding device [290] was almost thrust home, and his foot on my shoulder to press me down, when I made my saint-like confession as you have heard before, that such and such men at such an hour brake into the house, slew the zany, took my courtesan, locked me into my chamber, ravished Heraclide, and finally how she slew herself.

Present at the execution was there a banished English earl, who, hearing that a countryman of his was to suffer for such a notable murder, came to hear his confession and see if he knew him. He had not heard me tell half of that I have recited but he craved audience and desired the execution might be stayed.

'Not two days since it is, gentlemen and noble Romans,' said he, 'since, going to be let blood in a barber's shop against the infection, all on sudden in a great tumult and uproar was there brought in one Bartol, an Italian, grievously wounded and bloody. I, seeming to commiserate his harms, courteously questioned him with what ill debtors he had met, or how or by what casualty he came to be so arrayed. "Oh," quoth he, "long have I lived sworn brothers in sensuality with one Esdras of Granado: five hundred rapes and murders have we committed betwixt us. When our iniquities were grown to the height, and God had determined to countercheck our amity, we came to the house of Johannes de Imola" (whom this young gentleman hath named). There did he justify all those rapes in manner and form as the prisoner here hath confessed. But lo, an accident after, which neither he nor this audience is privy to. Esdras of Granado, not content to have ravished the matron Heraclide and robbed her, after he had betook him from thence to his heels, lighted on his companion Bartol with his cour-

290. The slip knot.

tesan, whose pleasing face he had scarce winkingly glanced on, but he picked a quarrel with Bartol to have her from him. On this quarrel they fought. Bartol was wounded to the death, Esdras fled, and the fair dame left to go whither she would. This, Bartol in the barber's shop freely acknowleged, as both the barber and his man and other here present can amply depose.'

Deposed they were. Their oaths went for current. I was quit by proclamation. To the banished earl I came to render thanks, when thus he examined and schooled me:

'Countryman, tell me, what is the occasion of thy straying so far out of England to visit this strange nation? If it be languages, thou may'st learn them at home; nought but lasciviousness is to be learned here. Perhaps, to be better accounted of than other of thy condition, thou ambitiously undertakest this voyage: these insolent fancies are but Icarus' feathers, whose wanton wax, melted against the sun, will betray thee into a sea of confusion.

'The first traveller was Cain, and he was called a vagabond runagate on the face of the earth. Travel (like the travail wherein smiths put wild horses when they shoe them) is good for nothing but to tame and bring men under.

'God had no greater curse to lay upon the Israelites, than by leading them out of their own country to live as slaves in a strange land. That which was their curse, we Englishmen count our chief blessedness. He is nobody, that hath not travelled: we had rather live as slaves in another land, crouch and cap and be servile to every jealous Italian's and proud Spaniard's humour, where we may neither speak, look, nor do anything but what pleaseth them, than live as freemen and lords in our country.

'He that is a traveller must have the back of an ass to bear all, a tongue like the tail of a dog to flatter all, the mouth of a hog to eat what is set before him, the ear of a merchant to hear all and say nothing. And if this be not the highest step of thraldom, there is no liberty or freedom.

'It is but a mild kind of subjection to be the servant of one master at once; but when thou hast a thousand thousand masters, as the veriest botcher, tinker, or cobbler freeborn will domineer over a foreigner and think to be his better or master in company, then shalt thou find there is no such hell as to leave thy father's house, thy natural habitation, to live in the land of bondage.

'If thou dost but lend half a look to a Roman's or Italian's wife, thy porridge shall be prepared for thee, and cost thee nothing but thy life. Chance some of them break a bitter jest on thee and thou retort'st it severely or seemest discontented, go to thy chamber and provide a great banquet, for thou shalt be sure to be visited with guests in a mask the next night, when in kindness and courtship thy throat shall be cut, and the doers return undiscovered. Nothing so long of memory as a dog; these Italians are old dogs and will carry an injury a whole age in memory. I have heard of a box on the ear that hath been revenged thirty year after. The Neapolitan carrieth the bloodiest mind, and is the most secret fleering[291] murderer; whereupon it is grown to a common proverb, "I'll give him the Neapolitan shrug," when one intends to play the villain and make no boast of it.

'The only precept that a traveller hath most use of and shall find most ease in is that of Epicharchus,[292] *Vigila, et memor sis ne quid credas*: "Believe nothing, trust no man yet seem thou as thou swallowedst all, suspectedst none, but wert easy to be gulled by everyone." *Multi fallere docuerunt* (as Seneca saith) *dum timent falli*: "Many by showing their jealous suspect of deceit have made men seek more subtle means to deceive them."

'Alas, our Englishmen are the plainest-dealing souls that ever God put life in. They are greedy of news, and love to be fed in their humours[293] and hear themselves flattered the best that may be. Even as Philemon, a comic poet, died with extreme laughter at the conceit of seeing an ass eat figs, so have the Italians no such sport as to see poor English

291. Fawning, jeering.
292. Epicharmus, Greek comedian, born *c.* 540 B.C.
293. *Fed in their humours*: Encouraged in their peculiarities.

asses, how soberly they swallow Spanish figs,[294] devour any hook bated for them. He is not fit to travel that cannot, with the Candians, live on serpents, make nourishing food even of poison. Rats and mice engender by licking one another; he must lick, he must crouch, he must cog, lie and prate, that either in the Court or a foreign country will engender and come to preferment. Be his feature what it will, if he be fair spoken he winneth friends. *Non formosus erat, sed erat facundus Ulysses*: [295] "Ulysses, the long traveller, was not amiable, but eloquent." Some allege they travel to learn wit, but I am of this opinion: that, as it is not possible for any man to learn the art of memory, whereof Tully, Quintilian, Seneca and Hermannus Buschius have written so many books, except he have a natural memory before, so it is not possible for any man to attain any great wit by travel except he have the grounds of it rooted in him before. That wit which is thereby to be perfected or made staid is nothing but *Experientia longa malorum*,[296] 'the experience of many evils', the experience that such a man lost his life by this folly, another by that; such a young gallant consumed his substance on such a courtesan; these courses of revenge a merchant of Venice took against a merchant of Ferrara; and this point of justice was showed by the duke upon the murtherer. What is here but we may read in books, and a great deal more too, without stirring our feet out of a warm study?

> *Vobis alii ventorum praelia narrent* (said Ovid)
> *Quasque Scilla infestet, quasve Charybdis aquas.*
> "Let others tell you wonders of the wind,
> How Scylla or Charybdis is inclined."
>   – *vos quod quisque loquetur*
> *Credite.* "Believe you what they say, but never try."

So let others tell you strange accidents, treasons, poisonings,

294. 'A poisoned fig used as a secret way of destroying an obnoxious person' (NED).
295. Ovid, *Ars Amatoris*, II, 123.
296. cf. '*Patientia longa memorum*' (Ovid, *Tristia*, V, 12, 31).

close packings in France, Spain and Italy; it is no harm for you to hear of them, but come not near them.

'What is there in France to be learned more than in England, but falsehood in fellowship, perfect slovenry, to love no man but for my pleasure, to swear *Ah par la mort Dieu* when a man's hams are scabbed? For the idle traveller, I mean not for the soldier, I have known some that have continued there by the space of half-a-dozen years, and when they come home they have hid a little wearish [297] lean face under a broad French hat, kept a terrible coil [298] with the dust in the street in their long cloaks of grey paper, and spoke English strangely. Nought else have they profited by their travel, save learnt to distinguish of the true Bordeaux grape, and know a cup of neat Gascoigne wine from wine of Orleance. Yea, and peradventure this also, to esteem of the pox as a pimple, to wear a velvet patch on their face, and walk melancholy with their arms folded.

'From Spain what bringeth our traveller? A skull-crowned hat of the fashion of an old deep porringer, a diminutive alderman's ruff with short strings like the droppings of a man's nose, a close-bellied doublet coming down like a peak behind as far as the crupper, and cut off before by the breast-bone like a partlet or neckercher, a wide pair of gaskins which ungathered would make a couple of women's riding kirtles, huge hangers [299] that have half a cow-hide in them, a rapier that is lineally descended from half-a-dozen dukes at the least. Let his cloak be as long or as short as you will; if long, it is faced with Turkey grogeran [300] ravelled; if short, it hath a cape like a calf's tongue and is not so deep in his whole length, nor hath so much cloth in it, I will justify, as only the standing cape of a Dutchman's cloak. I have not yet touched all, for he hath in either shoe as much taffatie for his tyings as would serve for an ancient; which serveth

297. Wizened, sickly-looking.
298. Tumult, disturbance.
299. 'Loops or straps on a sword-belt from which the sword was hung' (OED).
300. Grogram, coarse silk fabric.

him (if you will have the mystery of it) of the own accord for a shoe-rag. A soldier and a braggart he is (that's concluded). He jetteth strouting,[301] dancing on his toes with his hands under his sides. If you talk with him, he makes a dishcloth of his own country in comparison of Spain, but if you urge him more particularly wherein it exceeds, he can give no instance but 'in Spain they have better bread than any we have'; when, poor hungry slaves, they may crumble it into water well enough and make misers [302] with it, for they have not a good morsel of meat except it be salt piltchers to eat with it all the year long, and, which is more, they are poor beggars and lie in foul straw every night.

'Italy, the paradise of the earth and the epicure's heaven, how doth it form our young master? It makes him to kiss his hand like an ape, cringe his neck like a starveling, and play at heypass, repass come aloft,[303] when he salutes a man. From thence he brings the art of atheism, the art of epicurising, the art of whoring, the art of poisoning, the art of sodomitry. The only probable good thing they have to keep us from utterly condemning it is that it maketh a man an excellent courtier, a curious carpet knight; which is, by interpretation, a fine close lecher, a glorious hypocrite. It is now a privy note amongst the better sort of men, when they would set a singular mark or brand on a notorious villain, to say he hath been in Italy.

'With the Dane and the Dutchman I will not encounter, for they are simple honest men, that, with Danaus' daughters,[304] do nothing but fill bottomless tubs and will be drunk and snort in the midst of dinner. He hurts himself only that goes thither; he cannot lightly be damned, for the vintners, the brewers, the malt-men, the alewives pray for him. 'Pitch and pay,[305] they will pray all day; score and borrow, they

301. Strutting.

302. Sop made with breadcrumbs.

303. *play ... aloft*: Recite mumbo-jumbo as before conjurer's tricks.

304. The forty-nine daughters of Danaus murdered their husbands and were condemned to collect water in sieves for ever.

305. *Pitch and pay*: Pay cash.

will wish him much sorrow.' But lightly a man is ne'er the better for their prayers, for they commit all deadly sin for the most part of them in mingling their drink, the vintners in the highest degree.

'Why jest I in such a necessary persuasive discourse? I am a banished exile from my country, though near linked in consanguinity to the best: an earl born by birth, but a beggar now as thou seest. These many years in Italy have I lived an outlaw. Awhile I had a liberal pension of the Pope, but that lasted not, for he continued not; one succeeded him in his chair that cared neither for Englishmen nor his own countrymen. Then was I driven to pick up my crumbs among the cardinals, to implore the benevolence and charity of all the dukes of Italy, whereby I have since made a poor shift to live, but so live as I wish myself a thousand times dead.

> *Cum patriam amisi, tunc me periisse putato* [306]
> "When I was banished, think I caught my bane."

The sea is the native soil to fishes; take fishes from the sea, they take no joy, nor thrive, but perish straight. So likewise the birds removed from the air, the abode whereto they were born, the beasts from the earth, and I from England. Can a lamb take delight to be suckled at the breasts of a she-wolf? I am a lamb nourished with the milk of wolves, one that, with the Ethiopians inhabiting over against Meroe, feed on nothing but scorpions. Use is another nature, yet ten times more contentive were nature, restored to her kingdom from whence she is excluded. Believe me, no air, no bread, no fire, no water doth a man any good out of his own country. Cold fruits never prosper in a hot soil, nor hot in a cold. Let no man for any transitory pleasure sell away the inheritance he hath of breathing in the place where he was born. Get thee home, my young lad; lay thy bones peaceably in the sepulchre of thy fathers; wax old in overlooking thy grounds; be at hand to close the eyes of thy

306. Ovid, *Tristia*, III, 3, 53.

kindred. The devil and I am desperate, he of being restored to heaven, I of being recalled home.'

Here he held his peace and wept. I, glad of any opportunity of a full point to part from him, told him I took his counsel in worth; what lay in me to requite in love should not be lacking. Some business that concerned me highly called me away very hastily, but another time I hoped we should meet. Very hardly he let me go, but I earnestly overpleading my occasions, at length he dismissed me, told me where his lodging was, and charged me to visit him without excuse very often.

Here's a stir, thought I to myself, after I was set at liberty, that is worse than an upbraiding lesson after a breeching. Certainly if I had bethought me like a rascal as I was, he should have had an Ave Marie of me for his cynic exhortation. God plagued me for deriding such a grave fatherly advertiser. List the worst throw of ill lucks. Tracing up and down the city to seek my courtesan till the evening began to grow very well in age, it thus fortuned. The element, as if it had drunk too much in the afternoon, poured down so profoundly that I was forced to creep like one afraid of the watch close under the pentices,[307] where the cellar door of a Jew's house called Zadoch, over which in my direct way I did pass, being unbarred on the inside, over head and ears I fell into it, as a man falls in a ship from the orlop into the hold, or as in an earthquake the ground should open and a blind man come feeling pad pad over the open gulf with his staff, should tumble on a sudden into hell. Having worn out the anguish of my fall a little with wallowing up and down, I cast up mine eyes to see under what continent I was, and lo, oh destiny, I saw my courtesan kissing very lovingly with a prentice.

My back and my sides I had hurt with my fall, but now my head swelled and ached worse than both. I was even gathering wind to come upon her with a full blast of contumely, when the Jew, awaked with the noise of my fall, came hastily bustling down the stairs, and, raising his other

307. Penthouses.

347

tenants, attached[308] both the courtesan and me for breaking his house and conspiring with his prentice to rob
him.

It was then the law in Rome that if any man had a felon
fallen into his hands, either by breaking into his house or
robbing him by the highway, he might choose whether he
would make him his bondman or hang him. Zadoch, as all
Jews are covetous, casting with himself he should have no
benefit by casting me off the ladder, had another policy in
his head. He went to one Doctor Zacherie, the Pope's physician, that was a Jew and his countryman likewise, and told
him he had the finest bargain for him that might be. 'It is
not concealed from me,' saith he, 'that the time of your
accustomed yearly anatomy is at hand, which it behoves
you under forfeiture of the foundation of your college very
carefully to provide for. The infection is great and hardly
will you get a sound body to deal upon: you are my countryman, therefore I come to you first. Be it known unto you, I
have a young man at home fallen to me for my bondman,
of the age of eighteen, of stature tall, straight-limbed, of as
clear a complexion as any painter's fancy can imagine. Go
to, you are an honest man and one of the scattered children
of Abraham. You shall have him for five hundred crowns.'
'Let me see him,' quoth Doctor Zacharie, 'and I will give
you as much as another.' Home he sent for me; pinioned and
shackled, I was transported alongst the street, where, passing
under Juliana's (the Marquis of Mantua's wife's) window,
that was a lusty *bona roba*, one of the Pope's concubines, as
she had her casement half open, she looked out and spied
me. At the first sight she was enamoured with my age and
beardless face, that had in it no ill sign of physiognomy
fatal to fetters. After me she sent to know what I was,
wherein I had offended, and whither I was going. My conducts resolved them all. She having received this answer,
with a lustful collachrimation lamenting my jewish pre-
munire,[309] that body and goods I should light into the

308. Arrested.
309. A legal charge, a difficulty, a scrape.

348

hands of such a cursed generation, invented the means of my release.

But first I'll tell you what betided me after I was brought to Doctor Zacharie's. The purblind Doctor put on his spectacles and looked upon me; and when he had throughly viewed my face, he caused me to be stripped naked, to feel and grope whether each limb were sound and my skin not infected. Then he pierced my arm to see how my blood ran; which essays and searchings ended, he gave Zadoch his full price and sent him away, then locked me up in a dark chamber till the day of anatomy.

Oh, the cold sweating cares which I conceived after I knew I should be cut like a French summer doublet! Methought already the blood began to gush out at my nose. If a flea on the arm had but bit me, I deemed the instrument had pricked me. Well, well, I may scoff at a shrewd turn, but there's no such ready way to make a man a true Christian as to persuade himself he is taken up for an anatomy. I'll depose I prayed then more than I did in seven year before. Not a drop of sweat trickled down my breast and my sides, but I dreamt it was a smooth-edged razor tenderly slicing down my breast and sides. If any knocked at door, I supposed it was the beadle of Surgeons' Hall come for me. In the night I dreamed of nothing but phlebotomy,[310] bloody fluxes, incarnatives,[311] running ulcers. I durst not let out a wheal [312] for fear through it I should bleed to death. For meat in this distance I had plumporridge of purgations ministered me one after another to clarify my blood, that it should not lie cloddered in the flesh. Nor did he it so much for clarifying physic as to save charges. Miserable is that mouse that lives in a physician's house. Tantalus lives not so hunger-starved in hell as she doth there. Not the very crumbs that fall from his table, but Zacharie sweeps together and of them moulds up a manna. Of the ashy parings of his bread, he would make conserve of chippings. Out

310. Blood-letting, 'bleeding'.
311. Usually medicines to help a wound to heal.
312. Pimple.

of bones, after the meat was eaten off, he would alchemize an oil that he sold for a shilling a dram. His snot and spittle a hundred times he hath put over to his apothecary for snow-water. Any spider he would temper to perfect Mithridate.[313] His rheumatic eyes when he went in the wind, or rose early in a morning, dropped as cool alum water as you would request. He was Dame Niggardize' sole heir and executor. A number of old books had he, eaten with the moths and worms. Now all day would not he study a dodkin,[314] but pick those worms and moths out of his library and of their mixture make a preservative against the plague. The liquor out of his shoes he would wring, to make a sacred balsamum against barrenness.

Spare we him a line or two, and look back to Juliana, who, conflicted in her thoughts about me very doubtfully, adventured to send a messenger to Doctor Zacharie in her name, very boldly to beg me of him, and if she might not beg me, to buy me with what sums of money soever he would ask. Zacharie jewishly and churlishly denied both her suits, and said if there were no more Christians on the earth, he would thrust his incision knife into his throat-bole immediately. Which reply she taking at his hands most despitefully, thought to cross him over the shins with as sore an overwhart [315] blow ere a month to an end. The Pope (I know not whether at her entreaty or no) within two days after fell sick. Doctor Zacharie was sent for to minister unto him, who, seeing a little danger in his water, gave him a gentle comfortive for the stomach and desired those near about him to persuade his Holiness to take some rest and he doubted not but he would be forthwith well. Who should receive this mild physic of him but the concubine Juliana, his utter enemy! She, being not unprovided of strong poison, at that instant in the Pope's outward chamber so mingled it, that when his grand-sublimity-taster came to

313. Antidote against poisons.
314. A doit, small Dutch coin of little value (i.e. he wouldn't give any time to study).
315. Overthwart, a side-blow.

relish it, he sank down stark dead on the pavement. Herewith the Pope called Juliana, and asked her what strong-concocted broth she had brought him. She kneeled down on her knees and said it was such as Zacharie the Jew had delivered her with his own hands, and therefore if it misliked his Holiness she craved pardon. The Pope, without further sifting into the matter, would have had Zacharie and all the Jews in Rome put to death, but she hung about his knees, and with crocodile tears desired him the sentence might be lenified, and they be all but banished at the most. 'For Doctor Zacharie,' quoth she, 'your ten-times ungrateful physician, since notwithstanding his treacherous intent, he hath much art and many sovereign simples, oils, gargarisms,[316] and syrups in his closet and house that may stand your Mightiness in stead, I beg all his goods only for your Beatitude's reservation and good.' This request at the first was sealed with a kiss, and the Pope's edict without delay proclaimed throughout Rome, namely, that all foreskin clippers, whether male or female, belonging to the Old Jewry, should depart and avoid upon pain of hanging, within twenty days after the date thereof.

Juliana, two days before the proclamation came out, sent her servants to extend upon Zacharie's territories, his goods, his movables, his chattels and his servants; who performed their commission to the utmost tittle, and left him not so much as master of an old urinal-case or a candle-box. It was about six o'clock in the evening when those boot-halers entered. Into my chamber they rushed, when I sat leaning on my elbow and my left hand under my side, devising what a kind of death it might be, to be let blood till a man die. I called to mind the assertion of some philosophers, who said the soul was nothing but blood. Then, thought I, what a thing were this, if I should let my soul fall and break his neck into a basin. I had but a pimple rose with heat in that part of the vein where they use to prick, and I fearfully misdeemed it was my soul searching for passage. Fie upon it, a man's breath to be let out at a back door, what a villainy

316. Gargles.

it is! To die bleeding is all one as if a man should die piss-ing. Good drink makes good blood, so that piss is nothing but blood under age. Seneca and Lucan were lobcocks [317] to choose that death of all other: a pig or a hog or any edible brute beast a cook or a butcher deals upon dies bleeding. To die with a prick, wherewith the faintest-hearted woman under heaven would not be killed, oh God, it is infamous.

In this meditation did they seize upon me. In my cloak they muffled me that no man might know me, nor I see which way I was carried. The first ground I touched after I was out of Zacharie's house was the Countess Juliana's chamber. Little did I surmise that fortune reserved me to so fair a death. I made no other reckoning all the while they had me on their shoulders, but that I was on horseback to heaven, and carried to church on a bier, excluded for ever from drinking any more ale or beer. Juliana scornfully questioned them thus, as if I had fallen into her hands beyond expecta-tion: 'What proper apple-squire [318] is this you bring so sus-piciously into my chamber? What hath he done? Or where had you him?' They answered likewise afar off, that in one of Zacharie's chambers they found him close prisoner, and thought themselves guilty of the breach of her Ladyship's commandment if they should have left him. 'Oh,' quoth she, 'ye love to be double-diligent, or thought peradventure that I, being a lone woman, stood in need of a love. Bring you me a princocks [319] beardless boy (I know not whence he is, nor whither he would) to call my name in suspense? I tell you, you have abused me, and I can hardly brook it at your hands. You should have led him to the magistrate; no commission received you of me but for his goods and his servants.' They besought her to excuse their error, proceed-ing of duteous zeal, no negligent fault. 'But why should not I conjecture the worst?' quoth she. 'I tell you troth, I am half in a jealousy he is some fantastic youngster who hath hired you to dishonour me. It is a likely matter that such a man as Zacharie should make a prison of his house! By your

317. Bumpkins, fools.   318. Harlot's attendant (M.).
319. A forward youth, a coxcomb.

leave, sir gallant, under lock and key shall you stay with me till I have enquired farther of you. You shall be sifted throughly ere you and I part. Go, maid, show him to the farther chamber at the end of the gallery that looks into the garden. You, my trim panders, I pray guard him thither as you took pains to bring him hither. When you have so done, see the doors be made fast and come your way.' Here was a wily wench had her liripoop [320] without book. She was not to seek in her knacks and shifts: such are all women, each of them hath a cloak for the rain and can bear her husband's eyes as she list.

Not too much of this Madam Marquess at once. Let me dilate a little what Zadoch did with my courtesan after he had sold me to Zacharie. Of an ill tree I hope you are not so ill-sighted in grafting to expect good fruit. He was a Jew, and entreated her like a Jew. Under shadow of enforcing her to tell how much money she had of his prentice so to be trained to his cellar, he stripped her and scourged her from top to toe tantara. [321] Day by day he digested his meat with leading her the measures. A diamond delphinical dry lecher it was. The Ballet of the Whipper [322] of late days here in England was but a scoff in comparison of him. All the colliers of Romford, who hold their corporation by yarking the blind bear at Paris garden, [323] were but bunglers to him. He had the right agility of the lash; there were none of them could make the cord come aloft with a twang half like him. Mark the ending, mark the ending.

The tribe of Judah is adjudged from Rome to be trudging; they may no longer be lodged there. All the Album-

320. Role, part in a play.

321. Trumpet sound, but used colloquially to suggest lecherous feeling.

322. M. refers to a ballad entered in the Stationers Register, 16 February 1590/1: 'A Ballad entitled all the merry pranks of him that whips men in the highways'.

323. Proverbially dishonest and brutal. The practice of whipping a chained blind bear after bull-baiting or bear-baiting was not uncommon. F.P.W. points out that Dekker associated it with colliers in *Work for Armourers*, 1609.

azers, Rabisaks, Gideons, Tebiths, Benhadads, Benrodans, Zedekiahs, Halies of them were banquerouts [324] and turned out of house and home. Zacharie came running to Zadoch's in sackcloth and ashes presently after his goods were confiscated, and told him how he was served, and what decree was coming out against them all. Descriptions, stand by: here is to be expressed the fury of Lucifer when he was turned over heaven-bar for a wrangler.[325] There is a toad-fish, which taken out of the water swells more than one would think his skin could hold, and bursts in his face that toucheth him. So swelled Zadoch, and was ready to burst out of his skin and shoot his bowels like chain-shot full at Zacharie's face for bringing him such baleful tidings. His eyes glared and burnt blue like brimstone and aqua vitae set on fire in an eggshell. His very nose lightened glow-worms; his teeth crashed and grated together like the joints of a high building cracking and rocking like a cradle whenas a tempest takes her full butt against his broadside. He swore, he cursed, and said:

'These be they that worship that crucified God of Nazareth. Here's the fruits of their new-found gospel: sulphur and gunpowder carry them all quick to Gehenna! I would spend my soul willingly to have that triple-headed Pope with all his sin-absolved whores and oil-greased priests borne with a black sant [326] on the devils' backs in procession to the pit of perdition. Would I might sink presently into the earth, so I might blow up this Rome, this whore of Babylon, into the air with my breath. If I must be banished, if those heathen dogs will needs rob me of my goods, I will poison their springs and conduit-heads, whence they receive all their water round about the city. I'll tice all the young children into my house that I can get, and, cutting their throats, barrel them up in powdering-beef tubs, and so send them to victual the Pope's galleys. Ere the officers come to extend, I'll bestow an hundred pound on a dole of bread, which I'll cause to be kneaded with scorpion's oil that will

324. Bankrupts.   325. As a trouble-maker.
326. A noisy, burlesque hymn.

354

kill more than the plague. I'll hire them that make their wafers or sacramentary gods, to minge [327] them after the same sort, so in the zeal of their superstitious religion shall they languish and droop like carrion. If there be ever a blasphemous conjurer that can call the winds from their brazen caves and make the clouds travail before their time, I'll give him the other hundred pounds to disturb the heavens a whole week together with thunder and lightning, if it be for nothing but to sour all the wines in Rome and turn them to vinegar. As long as they either have oil or wine, this plague feeds but pinglingly [328] upon them.'

'Zadoch, Zadoch,' said Doctor Zacharie, cutting him off, 'thou threat'nest the air, whilst we perish here on earth. It is the Countess Juliana, the Marquis of Mantua's wife, and no other, that hath complotted our confusion. Ask not how, but insist in my words, and assist in revenge.'

'As how? As how?' said Zadoch, shrugging and shrubbing. [329] 'More happy than the patriarchs were I if, crushed to death with the greatest torments Rome's tyrants have tried, there might be quintessenced out of me one quart of precious poison. I have a leg with an issue; shall I cut it off, and from his fount of corruption extract a venom worse than any serpent's? If thou wilt, I'll go to a house that is infected, where, catching the plague and having got a running sore upon me, I'll come and deliver her a supplication and breathe upon her. I know my breath stinks so already that it is within half a degree of poison. I'll pay her home if I perfect it with any more putrefaction.'

'No, no, brother Zadoch,' answered Zacharie, 'that is not the way. Canst thou provide me ere a bondmaid endued with singular and divine qualified beauty, whom as a present from our synagogue thou mayest commend unto her, desiring her to be good and gracious unto us?'

'I have, I am for you,' quoth Zadoch. 'Diamante, come forth. Here's a wench,' said he, 'of as clean a skin as Susanna. She hath not a wem on her flesh from the sole of the foot

327. (?) Mix, (NED gives 'to discharge as urine').
328. With little appetite.   329. Scratching.

to the crown of the head. How think you, Master Doctor, will she not serve the turn?'

'She will,' said Zacharie, 'and therefore I'll tell you what charge I would have committed to her. But I care not if I disclose it only to her. Maid (if thou beest a maid), come hither to me. Thou must be sent to the Countess of Mantua's about a small piece of service, whereby, being now a bondwoman, thou shalt purchase freedom and gain a large dowry to thy marriage. I know thy master loves thee dearly, though he will not let thee perceive so much. He intends after he is dead to make thee his heir, for he hath no children. Please him in that I shall instruct thee, and thou art made for ever. So it is, that the Pope is far out of liking with the Countess of Mantua, his concubine, and hath put his trust in me, his physician, to have her quietly and charitably made away. Now, I cannot intend it, for I have many cures in hand which call upon me hourly. Thou, if thou beest placed with her as her waiting-maid or cup-bearer, mayest temper poison with her broth, her meat, her drink, her oils, her syrups, and never be bewrayed. I will not say whether the Pope hath heard of thee, and thou mayest come to be his leman in her place if thou behave thyself wisely. What, hast thou the heart to go thorough with it or no?'

Diamante, deliberating with herself in what hellish servitude she lived with the Jew, and that she had no likelihood to be released of it, but fall from evil to worse if she omitted this opportunity, resigned herself over wholly to be disposed and employed as seemed best unto them. Thereupon, without further consultation, her wardrop was richly rigged, her tongue smooth filed and new edged on the whetstone, her drugs delivered her, and presented she was by Zadoch, her master, to the Countess, together with some other slight newfangles, as from the whole congregation, desiring her to stand their merciful mistress and solicit the Pope for them, that through one man's ignorant offence were all generally in disgrace with him, and had incurred the cruel sentence of loss of goods and of banishment.

Juliana, liking well the pretty round face of my black-browed Diamante, gave the Jew better countenance than otherwise she would have done, and told him for her own part she was but a private woman, and could promi..e nothing confidently of his Holiness; for though he had suffered himself to be overruled by her in some humours, yet in this that touched him so nearly, she knew not how he would be inclined; but what lay in her either to pacify or persuade him, they should be sure of, and so craved his absence.

His back turned, she asked Diamante what country-woman she was, what friends she had, and how she fell into the hands of that Jew. She answered that she was a magnifico's daughter of Venice, stolen when she was young from her friends, and sold to this Jew for a bond-woman, 'who,' quoth she, 'hath used me so jewishly and tyrannously that for ever I must celebrate the memory of this day wherein I am delivered from his jurisdiction. Alas' (quoth she, deep sighing), 'why did I enter into any mention of my own mis-usage? It will be thought that that which I am now to reveal proceeds of malice, not truth. Madam, your life is sought by these Jews that sue to you. Blush not, nor be troubled in your mind, for with warning I shall arm you against all their intentions. Thus and thus' (quoth she) 'said Doctor Zacharie unto me. This poison he delivered me. Before I was called in to them, such and such consultation through the crevice of the door hard-locked did I hear betwixt them. Deny it if they can, I will justify it. Only I beseech you to be favourable lady unto me, and let me not fall again into the hands of those vipers.'

Juliana said little but thought unhappily. Only she thanked her for detecting it, and vowed, though she were her bondwoman, to be a mother unto her. The poison she took of her, and set it up charily on a shelf in her closet, thinking to keep it for some good purposes; as, for example, when I was consumed and worn to the bones through her abuse, she would give me but a dram too much, and pop me into a privy. So she had served some of her paramours ere

357

that, and, if God had not sent Diamante to be my redeemer, undoubtedly I had drunk of the same cup.

In a leaf or two before was I locked up. Here in this page the foresaid goodwife Countess comes to me. She is no longer a judge but a client. How she came, in what manner of attire, with what immodest and uncomely words she courted me, if I should take upon me to enlarge, all modest ears would abhor me. Some inconvenience she brought me to by her harlotlike behaviour, of which enough I can never repent me.

Let that be forgiven and forgotten. Fleshly delights could not make her slothful or slumbering in revenge against Zadoch. She set men about him to incense and egg him on in courses of discontentment, and other supervising espials to ply, follow and spur forward those suborning incensers Both which played their parts so that Zadoch, of his own nature violent, swore by the ark of Jehovah to set the whole city on fire ere he went out of it. Zacharie, after he had furnished the wench with the poison, and given her instructions to go to the devil, durst not stay one hour for fear of disclosing, but fled to the Duke of Burbon,[330] that after sacked Rome, and there practised with his Bastardship all the mischief against the Pope and Rome that envy could put into his mind. Zadoch was left behind for the hangman. According to his oath, he provided balls of wildfire in a readiness, and laid trains of gunpowder in a hundred several places of the city to blow it up, which he had set fire to and also bandied his balls abroad, if his attendant spies had not taken him with the manner. To the straitest prison in Rome he was dragged, where from top to toe he was clogged with fetters and manacles. Juliana informed the Pope of Zacharie's and his practice. Zacharie was sought for, but *Non est inventus*:[331] he was packing long before. Commandment was given that Zadoch, whom they had under hand and seal of lock and key, should be executed with all the fiery torments that could be found out.

330. Charles de Bourbon, killed in an assault on Rome, 1527.
331. Legal term, used by a sheriff unable to make an arrest.

I'll make short work, for I am sure I have wearied all my readers. To the execution place was he brought, where first and foremost he was stripped; then on a sharp iron stake fastened in the ground he had his fundament pitched, which stake ran up along into the body like a spit. Under his arm-holes two of like sort. A great bonfire they made round about him, wherewith his flesh roasted, not burned; and ever as with the heat his skin blistered, the fire was drawn aside and they basted him with a mixture of aqua fortis, alum water and mercury sublimatum,[332] which smarted to the very soul of him, and searched him to the marrow. Then did they scourge his back parts so blistered and blasted with burning whips of red-hot wire. His head they nointed over with pitch and tar and so inflamed it. To his privy members they tied streaming fireworks. The skin from the crest of the shoulder, as also from his elbows, his huckle bones, his knees, his ankles, they plucked and gnawed off with sparkling pincers. His breast and his belly with seal-skins they grated over, which as fast as they grated and rawed, one stood over and laved with smith's cindery water [333] and aqua vitae. His nails they half raised up, and then underpropped them with sharp pricks, like a tailor's shop window half-open on a holiday. Every one of his fingers they rent up to the wrist; his toes they brake off by the roots, and let them still hang by a little skin. In conclusion, they had a small oil fire, such as men blow light bubbles of glass with, and beginning at his feet, they let him lingeringly burn up limb by limb, till his heart was consumed, and then he died. Triumph, women; this was the end of the whipping Jew, contrived by a woman, in revenge of two women, herself and her maid.

I have told you, or should tell you, in what credit Dia-mante grew with her mistress. Juliana never dreamed but she was an authentical maid. She made her the chief of her bed-chamber; she appointed none but her to look in to me, and serve me of such necessaries as I lacked. You must suppose when we met there was no small rejoicing on either part,

332. Mercuric chloride.
333. From the forge, sometimes used medicinally.

much like the three brothers that went three several ways to seek their fortunes and at the year's end at those three crossways met again and told one another how they sped. So after we had been long asunder seeking our fortunes, we commented one to another most kindly, what cross haps had encountered us. Ne'er a six hours but the Countess cloyed me with her company. It grew to this pass, that either I must find out some miraculous means of escape or drop away in a consumption, as one pined for lack of meat. I was clean spent and done; there was no hope of me.

The year held on his course to doomsday, when Saint Peter's Day [334] dawned. That day is a day of supreme solemnity in Rome, when the Ambassador of Spain comes and presents a milk-white jennet to the Pope, that kneels down upon his own accord in token of obeisance and humility before him, and lets him stride on his back as easy as one strides over a block. With this jennet is offered a rich purse of a yard length, full of Peter pence. No music that hath the gift of utterance, but sounds all the while. Copes and costly vestments deck the hoarsest and beggarliest singing-man. Not a clerk or sexton is absent, no, nor a mule nor a footcloth belonging to any Cardinal but attends on the tail of the triumph. The Pope himself is borne in his pontificalibus thorough the Burgo (which is the chief street in Rome) to the Ambassador's house to dinner, and thither resorts all the assembly; where if a poet should spend all his lifetime in describing a banquet, he could not feast his auditors half so well with words, as he doth his guests with junkets.

To this feast Juliana addressed herself like an angel; in a litter of green needlework wrought like an arbour and open on every side was she borne by four men, hidden under cloth rough-plushed and woven like eglantine and woodbine. At the four corners it was topped with four round crystal cages of nightingales. For footmen, on either side of her went four virgins clad in lawn, with lutes in their hands, playing. Next before her, two and two in order, a hundred

334. 29 June.

pages in suits of white cypress and long horsemen's coats of cloth of silver; who, being all in white, advanced every one of them her picture, enclosed in a white round screen of feathers, such as is carried over great princesses' heads when they ride in summer to keep them from the heat of the sun. Before them went a fourscore beadwomen she maintained, in green gowns, scattering strewing-herbs and flowers. After her followed the blind, the halt, and the lame, sumptuously apparelled like lords. And thus passed she on to St Peter's.

Interea quid agitur domi: 'How is't at home all this while?' My courtesan is left my keeper, the keys are committed unto her, she is mistress *fac totum*. Against our Countess we conspire, pack up all her jewels, plate, money that was extant, and to the waterside send them. To conclude: courageously rob her and run away. *Quid non auri sacra fames*?:[335] 'What defame will not gold salve?' He mistook himself that invented the proverb, *Dimicandum est pro aris et focis*, for it should have been *pro auro et fama*: not 'for altars and fires we must contend', but for 'gold and fame'.

Oars nor wind could not stir nor blow faster than we toiled out of Tiber. A number of good fellows would give size ace and the dice,[336] that with as little toil they could leave Tyburn behind them. Out of ken we were, ere the Countess came from the feast. When she returned and found her house not so much pestered as it was wont, her chests, her closets and her cupboards broke open to take air, and that both I and my keeper was missing, oh, then she fared like a frantic bacchanal; she stamped, she stared, she beat her head against the walls, scratched her face, bit her fingers and strewed all the chamber with her hair. None of her servants durst stay in her sight, but she beat them out in heaps and bad them go seek, search they knew not where, and hang themselves and never look her in the face more if they did not hunt us out.

335. Adapted from Virgil, *Aeneid*, III, 56–7.
336. *size ace and the dice*: 'All they possess' (a reference to a game; precise meaning unknown).

After her fury had reasonably spent itself, her breast began to swell with the mother,[337] caused by her former fretting and chafing, and she grew very ill at ease. Whereupon she knocked for one of her maids, and bad her run into her closet and fetch her a little glass that stood on the upper shelf, wherein there was *spiritus vini.* The maid went, and mistaking took the glass of poison which Diamante had given her and she kept in store for me. Coming with it as fast as her legs could carry her, her mistress at her return was in a swound and lay for dead on the floor, whereat she shrieked out and fell a-rubbing and chafing her very busily. When that would not serve, she took a key and opened her mouth, and having heard that *spiritus vini* was a thing of mighty operation, able to call a man from death to life, she took the poison, and verily thinking it to be *spiritus vini* (such as she was sent for), poured a large quantity of it into her throat and jogged on her back to digest it. It revived her with a very vengeance, for it killed her outright: only she awakened and lift up her hands, but she spake ne'er a word. Then was the maid in my grandame's beans,[338] and knew not what should become of her. I heard the Pope took pity on her and because her trespass was not voluntary but chance-medley,[339] he assigned her no other punishment but this, to drink out the rest of the poison in the glass that was left, and so go scot-free. We, careless of these mischances, held on our flight, and saw no man come after us but we thought had pursued us. A thief, they say, mistakes every bush for a true man; the wind rattled not in any bush by the way as I rode, but I straight drew my rapier. To Bologna with a merry gale we posted, where we lodged ourselves in a blind street out of the way and kept secret many days. But when we perceived we sailed in the haven, that the wind was laid, and no alarum made after us, we boldly came abroad. And one day, hearing of a more desperate murtherer than Cain that was to be executed, we followed

337. Choking in the throat (cf. Lear's 'hysterica passio').
338. (?) Great to-do (M.).
339. Misused legal term, here meaning inadvertent.

the multitude and grutched [340] not to lend him our eyes at his last parting.

Who should it be but one Cutwolfe, a wearish [341] dwarfish writhen-faced cobbler, brother to Bartol the Italian that was confederate with Esdras of Granado, and at that time stole away my courtesan when he ravished Heraclide.

It is not so natural for me to epitomize his impiety, as to hear him in his own person speak upon the wheel where he was to suffer.

Prepare your ears and your tears, for never till this thrust I any tragical matter upon you. Strange and wonderful are God's judgments; here shine they in their glory. Chaste Heraclide, thy blood is laid up in heaven's treasury. Not one drop of it was lost, but lent out to usury. Water poured forth sinks down quietly into the earth, but blood spilt on the ground sprinkles up to the firmament. Murder is wide-mouthed and will not let God rest till he grant revenge. Not only the blood of the slaughtered innocent, but the soul, ascendeth to His throne, and there cries out and exclaims for justice and recompense. Guiltless souls that live every hour subject to violence, and with your despairing fears do much impair God's providence, fasten your eyes on this spectacle that will add to your faith. Refer all your oppressions, afflictions and injuries to the even-balanced eye of the Almighty; He it is that when your patience sleepeth will be most exceeding mindful of you.

This is but a gloss upon the text. Thus Cutwolfe begins his insulting oration:

'Men and people that have made holiday to behold my pained flesh toil on the wheel, expect not of me a whining penitent slave that shall do nothing but cry and say his prayers, and so be crushed in pieces. My body is little, but my mind is as great as a giant's. The soul which is in me is the very soul of Julius Caesar by reversion. My name is Cutwolfe, neither better nor worse by occupation than a poor cobbler of Verona. Cobblers are men, and kings are no more. The occasion of my coming hither at this present is to have

340. Begrudged.   341. Wizened.

a few of my bones broken (as we are all born to die) for being the death of the Emperor of homicides, Esdras of Granado. About two years since in the streets of Rome, he slew the only and eldest brother I had, named Bartol, in quarrelling about a courtesan. The news brought to me as I was sitting in my shop under a stall, knocking in of tacks, I think, I raised up my bristles, sold pritchel,[342] sponge, blacking tub and punching iron, bought me a rapier and pistol, and to go I went. Twenty months together I pursued him, from Rome to Naples, from Naples to Caiete, passing over the river, from Caiete to Sienna, from Sienna to Florence, from Florence to Parma, from Parma to Pavia, from Pavia to Sion, from Sion to Geneva, from Geneva back again towards Rome, where in the way it was my chance to meet him in the nick here in Bologna, as I will tell you how. I saw a great fray in the streets as I passed along, and many swords walking, whereupon drawing nearer and enquiring who they were, answer was returned me it was that notable banditto, Esdras of Granado. Oh, so I was tickled in the spleen with that word! My heart hopped and danced, my elbows itched, my fingers frisked. I wist not what should become of my feet, nor knew what I did for joy. The fray parted, I thought it not convenient to single him out (being a sturdy knave) in the street, but to stay till I had got him at more advantage. To his lodging I dogged him, lay at the door all night where he entered, for fear he should give me the slip any way. Betimes in the morning I rung the bell and craved to speak with him. Now to his chamber door I was brought, where knocking, he rose in his shirt and let me in, and when I was entered bad me lock the door and declare my arrant,[343] and so he slipped to bed again.

'"Marry, this", quoth I, 'is my arrant. Thy name is Esdras of Granado, is it not? Most treacherously thou slew'st my brother Bartol about two years ago in the streets of Rome. His death am I come to revenge. In quest of thee ever since, above three thousand miles have I travelled. I have begged to maintain me the better part of the way, only

342. Tool for cutting holes.   343. Errand.

because I would intermit no time from my pursuit in going back for money. Now have I got thee naked in my power. Die thou shalt, though my mother and my grandmother dying did entreat for thee. I have promised the devil thy soul within this hour, break my word I will not: in thy breast I intend to bury a bullet. Stir not, quinch [344] not, make no noise, for if thou dost it will be the worse for thee."

'Quod Esdras: "Whatever thou beest at whose mercy I lie, spare me, and I will give thee as much gold as thou wilt ask. Put me to any pains, my life reserved, and I willingly will sustain them. Cut off my arms and legs and leave me as a lazar to some loathsome spital, where I may but live a year to pray and repent me. For thy brother's death, the despair of mind that hath ever since haunted me, the guilty gnawing worm of conscience I feel may be sufficient penance. Thou canst not send me to such a hell as already there is in my heart. To dispatch me presently is no revenge; it will soon be forgotten. Let me die a lingering death; it will be remembered a great deal longer. A lingering death may avail my soul, but it is the illest of ills that can befortune my body. For my soul's health I beg my body's torment. Be not thou a devil to torment my soul and send me to eternal damnation. Thy overhanging sword hides heaven from my sight. I dare not look up, lest I embrace my death's wound unawares. I cannot pray to God and plead to thee both at once. Ay me, already I see my life buried in the wrinkles of thy brows. Say but I shall live, though thou meanest to kill me. Nothing confounds like to sudden terror; it thrusts every sense out of office. Poison wrapped up in sugared pills is but half a poison; the fear of death's looks are more terrible than his stroke. The whilst I view death, my faith is deaded; where a man's fear is, there his heart is. Fear never engenders hope: how can I hope that heaven's Father will save me from the hell everlasting, when He gives me over to the hell of thy fury?

' "Heraclide, now think I on thy tears sown in the dust, thy tears that my bloody mind made barren. In revenge of thee,

344. Move, flinch.

God hardens this man's heart against me. Yet I did not slaughter thee, though hundreds else my hand hath brought to the shambles. Gentle sir, learn of me what it is to clog your conscience with murder, to have your dreams, your sleeps, your solitary walks troubled and disquieted with murther. Your shadow by day will affright you; you will not see a weapon unsheathed, but immediately you will imagine it is predestinate for your destruction.

' "This murther is a house divided within itself. It suborns a man's own soul to inform against him. His soul, being his accuser, brings forth his two eyes as witnesses against him, and the least eye-witness is unrefutable. Pluck out my eyes if thou wilt, and deprive my traitorous soul of her two best witnesses. Dig out my blasphemous tongue with thy dagger: both tongue and eyes will I gladly forgo to have a little more time to think on my journey to heaven.

' "Defer awhile thy resolution. I am not at peace with the world, for even but yesterday I fought and in my fury threatened further vengeance. Had I a face to ask forgiveness, I should think half my sins were forgiven. A hundred devils haunt me daily for my horrible murthers. The devils when I die will be loth to go to hell with me, for they desired of Christ he would not send them to hell before their time. If they go not to hell, into thee they will go and hideously vex thee for turning them out of their habitation. Wounds I contemn, life I prize light; it is another world's tranquillity which makes me so timorous – everlasting damnation, everlasting howling and lamentation. It is not from death I request thee to deliver me, but from this terror of torment's eternity. Thy brother's body only I pierced unadvisedly; his soul meant I no harm to at all. My body and soul both shalt thou cast away quite, if thou dost at this instant what thou may'st. Spare me, spare me, I beseech thee. By thy own soul's salvation I desire thee, seek not my soul's utter perdition. In destroying me thou destroyest thyself and me."

'Eagerly I replied after this long suppliant oration: "Though I knew God would never have mercy upon me except I had mercy on thee, yet of thee no mercy would I have. Revenge in our tragedies is continually raised from hell: of hell do I esteem better than heaven, if it afford me revenge. There is no heaven but revenge. I tell thee, I would not have undertook so much toil to gain heaven, as I have done in pursuing thee for revenge. Divine revenge, of which, as of the joys above, there is no fulness or satiety. Look how my feet are blistered with following thee from place to place. I have riven my throat with overstraining it to curse thee. I have ground my teeth to powder with grating and grinding them together for anger when any hath named thee. My tongue with vain threats is bollen, and waxen too big for my mouth. My eyes have broken their strings with staring and looking ghastly as I stood devising how to frame or set my countenance when I met thee. I have near spent my strength in imaginary acting on stone walls what I determined to execute on thee. Entreat not: a miracle may not reprieve thee. Villain, thus march I with my blade into thy bowels."

' "Stay, stay!" exclaimed Esdras, "and hear me but one word further. Though neither for God nor man thou carest, but placest thy whole felicity in murther, yet of thy felicity learn how to make a greater felicity. Respite me a little from thy sword's point, and set me about some execrable enterprise that may subvert the whole state of Christendom and make all men's ears tingle that hear of it. Command me to cut all my kindred's throats, to burn men, women and children in their beds in millions, by firing their cities at midnight. Be it Pope, Emperor or Turk that displeaseth thee, he shall not breath on the earth. For thy sake will I swear and forswear, renounce my baptism and all the interest I have in any other sacrament. Only let me live how miserable soever, be it in a dungeon amongst toads, serpents and adders, or set up to the neck in dung. No pains I will refuse however prorogued to have a little respite to purify my spirit. Oh hear me, hear me, and thou canst not be hardened against me!"

'At this his importunity I paused a little, not as retiring

from my wreakful resolution, but going back to gather
more forces of vengeance. With myself I devised how to
plague him double for his base mind. My thoughts travelled
in quest of some notable new Italianism, whose murderous
platform might not only extend on his body, but his soul
also. The groundwork of it was this: that whereas he had
promised for my sake to swear and forswear and commit
Julian-like violence on the highest seals of religion, if he
would but this far satisfy me he should be dismissed from
my fury. First and foremost, he should renounce God and
His laws, and utterly disclaim the whole title or interest he
had in any covenant of salvation. Next, he should curse
Him to His face, as Job was willed by his wife, and write an
absolute firm obligation of his soul to the devil, without condition or exception. Thirdly and lastly, having done this, he
should pray to God fervently never to have mercy upon him
or pardon him.

'Scarce had I propounded these articles unto him, but he
was beginning his blasphemous abjurations. I wonder the
earth opened not and swallowed us both, hearing the bold
terms he blasted forth in contempt of Christianity. Heaven
hath thundered when half less contumelies against it have
been uttered. Able they were to raise saints and martyrs from
their graves and pluck Christ himself from the right hand
of his Father. My joints trembled and quaked with attending them; my hair stood upright and my heart was turned
wholly to fire. So affectionately and zealously did he give
himself over to infidelity, as if Satan had gotten the upper
hand of our High Maker. The vein in his left hand that is
derived from the heart with no faint blow he pierced, and
with the full blood that flowed from it writ a full obligation of his soul to the devil. Yea, he more earnestly prayed
unto God never to forgive his soul than many Christians do
to save their souls. These fearful ceremonies brought to an
end, I bad him ope his mouth and gape wide. He did so (as
what will not slaves do for fear?). Therewith made I no
more ado, but shot him full into the throat with my pistol.
No more spake he after; so did I shoot him that he might

never speak after or repent him. His body being dead looked as black as a toad; the devil presently branded it for his own. This is the fault that hath called me hither; no true Italian but will honour me for it. Revenge is the glory of arms and the highest performance of valour; revenge is whatsoever we call law or justice. The farther we wade in revenge, the nearer come we to the throne of the Almighty. To His sceptre it is properly ascribed; His sceptre He lends unto man when He lets one man scourge another. All true Italians imitate me in revenging constantly and dying valiantly. Hangman, to thy task, for I am ready for the utmost of thy rigour.'

Herewith all the people, outrageously incensed, with one conjoined outcry yelled mainly : 'Away with him, away with him ! Executioner, torture him, tear him, or we will tear thee in pieces if thou spare him !'

The executioner needed no exhortation hereunto, for of his own nature was he hackster good enough. Old excellent he was at a boneache. At the first chop with his wood-knife would he fish for a man's heart and fetch it out as easily as a plum from the bottom of a porridge pot. He would crack necks as fast as a cook cracks eggs; a fiddler cannot turn his pin so soon as he would turn a man off the ladder. Bravely did he drum on this Cutwolfe's bones, not breaking them outright but, like a saddler knocking in of tacks, jarring on them quaveringly with his hammer a great while together. No joint about him but with a hatchet he had for the nonce he disjointed half, and then with boiling lead soldered up the wounds from bleeding. His tongue he pulled out, lest he should blaspheme in his torment. Venomous stinging worms he thrust into his ears to keep his head ravingly occupied. With cankers scruzed [345] to pieces he rubbed his mouth and his gums. No limb of his but was lingeringly splintered in shivers. In this horror left they him on the wheel as in hell, where, yet living, he might behold his flesh legacied amongst the fowls of the air.

Unsearchable is the book of our destinies. One murder

345. Crushed, squeezed.

begetteth another; was never yet bloodshed barren from the beginning of the world to this day. Mortifiedly abjected and daunted was I with this truculent [346] tragedy of Cutwolfe and Esdras. To such straight life did it thenceforward incite me that ere I went out of Bologna I married my courtesan, performed many alms-deeds, and hasted so fast out of the Sodom of Italy, that within forty days I arrived at the King of England's camp [347] twixt Ardes and Guines in France, where he with great triumphs met and entertained the Emperor and the French King and feasted many days. And so, as my story began with the King at Tournay and Turwin, I think meet here to end it with the King at Ardes and Guines. All the conclusive epilogue I will make is this: that if herein I have pleased any, it shall animate me to more pains in this kind.

Otherwise I will swear upon an English Chronicle
never to be outlandish Chronicler more
while I live. Farewell as many
as wish me well.

FINIS

346. Cruel, savage.
347. Field of the Cloth of Gold, 1520, the English camp being at Guisnes, the French at Ard.

5

Nashe's Lenten Stuff [1]

CONTAINING

The Description and first
Procreation and Increase of the Town of
Great Yarmouth [2] in Norfolk

With a new play never played before,
of the praise of the
RED HERRING

Fit of all Clerks of Noblemen's
kitchens to be read; and not unnecessary
by all serving men that have short
board-wages to be remembered.

Famam peto per undas. [3]

To his worthy good patron, Lusty Humfrey, [4]
according as the townsmen do christen him;
Little Numps, as the Nobility and Courtiers do name him;
and Honest Humfrey, as all his friends and acquaintance
esteem him, King of the Tobacconists *hic & ubique,* [5] and
a singular Mecaenas [6] to the Pipe and the Tabour
(as his patient livery attendant can witness) his
bounden Orator T. N. most prostrately offers
up this tribute of ink and paper.

1. A familiar phrase for provision (for eating etc.) during Lent;
appropriate here because the work was begun in Lent 1598, though
finished towards the end of the year.
2. Where Nashe stayed after leaving London to avoid arrest after
the condemnation of the play *Isle of Dogs* in the summer of 1597 (see
Introduction p. 15).
3. 'I seek fame through the waves.'
4. Humfrey King, author of *An Halfpenny-worth of Wit in a
Pennyworth of Paper.*
5. 'Here and everywhere'.
6. The great patron of classical times (here used humorously, apparently with reference to King's liking for morris-dancing).

371

MOST courteous, unlearned lover of poetry, and yet a poet thyself, of no less price than H.S.,[7] that in honour of Maid Marian gives sweet Margaret for his Empress and puts the sow most saucily upon some great personage, whatever she be, bidding her (as it runs in the old song) 'Go from my garden, go, for there no flowers for thee doth grow': these be to notify to your Diminutive Excelsitude and Compendiate Greatness what my zeal is towards you, that in no straiter bonds would be pounded[8] and enlisted, than in an Epistle Dedicatory.

To many more lusty-blood Bravamente signors,[9] with Cales beards[10] as broad as scullers' maples[11] that they make clean their boats with, could I have turned it over, and had nothing for my labour, some fair words except of 'Good sir, will it please you to come near and drink a cup of wine?' After my return from Ireland[12] I doubt not but my fortunes will be of some growth to requite you. In the meantime my sword is at your command. And, before God, money so scatteringly runs here and there upon *utensilia*, furnitures,[13] ancients,[14] and other necessary preparations (and, which is a double charge, look how much tobacco we carry with us to expel cold, the like quantity of stavesacre[15] we must provide us of to kill lice in that rugged country of rebels), that I say unto you, in the word[16] of a martialist, we cannot do as we would. I am no incredulous Didymus, but have more

7. Identity uncertain; M. suggests a reference to the H.S. mentioned on the title-page of Sidney's *Arcadia*.

8. Enclosed.

9. M. suggests that it is in the style of such swaggering bloods that the following passage is written.

10. 'Presumably some fashion set by those who had taken part in the Cadiz expedition of 1596' (M.).

11. Mops.

12. Sometimes thought to be an autobiographical reference by Nashe, but more probably, as M. believes, part of the character of a 'bravamente signor'.

13. Equipment.

14. Ensigns.

15. A flower used to deter vermin.

16. *in the word*: On the word.

faith to believe they have no coin than they have means to
supply themselves with it; and so leave them.

To any other carpetmonger[17] or primrose knight of primero[18] bring I a dedication; and[19] the dice overnight have not
befriended him, he sleeps five days and five nights to new-
skin his beauty, and will not be known he is awaked till
his men upon their own bonds (a dismal world for trencher-
men when their master's bond shall not be so good as theirs)
have took up commodities or fresh droppings of the mint
for him. And then: what then? He pays for the ten dozen of
balls he left upon the score at the tennis court; he sends for
his barber to depure, decurtate[20] and sponge him, whom having not paid a twelvemonth before, he now rains down eight
quarter-angels into his hand, to make his liberality seem
greater, and gives him a cast[21] riding jerkin and an old
Spanish hat into the bargain, and God's peace be with him.

The chamber is not rid of the smell of his feet, but the
greasy shoemaker with his squirrels'-skin and a whole stall
of ware upon his arm enters and wrencheth his legs for an
hour together, and after shows his tally.[22] By St Loy, that
draws deep,[23] and by that time his tobacco merchant is made
even with, and he hath dined at a tavern and slept his
undermeal at a bawdy house, his purse is on the heild,[24] and
only forty shillings he hath behind to try his fortune with
at the cards in the presence; which if it prosper, the Court
cannot contain him, but to London again he will, to revel
it and have two plays in one night, invite all the poets and
musicians to his chamber the next morning; where, against
their coming,[25] a whole heap of money shall be bespread
upon the board, and all his trunks opened to show his rich

17. Carpet knight (cf. armchair politician).
18. *primrose ... primero*: A flowery creature only good for playing
cards (primero was a popular card-game).
19. If.
20. *depure, decurtate*: Purify, cut (shorten).
21. Worn, cast-off.   22. Bill, account.
23. Makes its mark (on his purse).
24. *on the heild*: In decline.
25. *against their coming*: In preparation for their arrival.

373

suits. But the devil a whit [26] he bestows on them, save bottle-ale and tobacco, and desires a general meeting.

The particular of it is that bounty is bankrupt, and Lady Sensuality licks all the fat from the seven liberal sciences,[27] that poetry, if it were not a trick to please my Lady,[28] would be excluded out of Christian burial, and, instead of wreaths of laurel to crown it with, have a bell with a cock's-comb clapped on the crown of it by old Johannes de Indagines [29] and his choir of dorbellists.[30] Wherefore the premisses [31] considered (I pray you consider of that word 'premisses', for somewhere I have borrowed it) neither to rich, noble, right worshipful or worshipful, of spiritual or temporal, will I consecrate this work, but to thee and thy capering humour alone, that, if thy stars had done thee right, they should have made thee one of the mightiest princes of Germany; not for thou canst drive a coach or kill an oxe so well as they, but that thou art never well but when thou art amongst the retinue of the muses, and there spendest more in the twinkling of an eye than in a whole year thou gettest by some grazierly gentility thou followest. A king thou art by name, and a king of good fellowship by nature, whereby I ominate [32] this encomion of the King of Fishes was predestinate to thee from thy swaddling clothes. Hug it, ingle [33] it, kiss it and cull [34] it now thou hast it, and renounce eating of green beef [35] and garlic till Martlemas, if it be not the next style to *The Strife of Love in a Dream* [36] or *The Lamentable Burning of Teverton*.[37]

26. *devil a whit*: Nothing.

27. The university courses of the Trivium and Quadrivium.

28. *if ... Lady*: If it were not regarded as a little pleasure for the ladies.

29. A fifteenth-century monk.

30. Term of ridicule derived from a fifteenth-century scholar, called Dorbellus.

31. M. suggests a mocking reference to Richard Harvey's use of the word in his *Lamb of God*.   32. Presume, infer.

33. Caress, fondle.   34. Pluck, gather.   35. Unsalted.

36. A translation from the Italian, by one R.D., written in a style comparable to Nashe's own.

37. A book or ballad about the Tiverton fire of 1598.

Give me good words I beseech thee, though thou givest
me nothing else, and thy words shall stand for thy deeds;
which I will take as well in worth, as if they were the deeds
and evidences of all the land thou hast. Here I bring you a
red herring; if you will find drink to it, there an end, no
other detriments will I put you to. Let the can of strong ale
your constable, with the toast his brown bill,[38] and sugar and
nutmegs his watchmen, stand in a readiness to entertain me
every time I come by your lodging. In Russia there are no
presents but of meat or drink: I present you with meat,
and you, in honourable courtesy to requite me, can do no
less than present me with the best morning's draught of
merry-go-round [39] in your quarters. And so I kiss the shadow
of your feet's shadow, amiable donzel,[40] expecting your
sacred poem of the *Hermit's Tale*,[41] that will restore the
golden age amongst us, and so upon my soul's knees
          I take my leave.

Yours for a whole last [42] of red
Herrings.
TH. NASHE.

To his Readers, he cares not what they be.

'*Nashe's Lenten Stuff*'. And why '*Nashe's Lenten Stuff*'?
Some scabbed scald [43] squire replies, 'Because I had money
lent me at Yarmouth, and I pay them again in praise of
their town and the red herring.' And if it were so, Goodman Pig-wiggen,[44] were not that honest dealing? Pay thou all
thy debts so if thou canst for thy life. But thou art a ninny-
hammer; that is not it. Therefore, Nickneacave,[45] I call it

38. A halberd used by the watch.
39. Strong ale.
40. Young gentleman, squire.
41. The subtitle of King's *An Halfpenny-worth of Wit in a Penny-worth of Paper*.
42. Twelve barrels.   43. 'Scurvy', contemptible.
44. Fanciful comic name, also used by Drayton.
45. Presumably a mildly abusive term (cf. 'noodle').

Nashe's Lenten Stuff as well for it was most of my study
the last Lent, as that we use so to term any fish that takes
salt, of which the red herring is one the aptest. 'Oh, but,'
saith another John Dringle,[46] 'there is a book of the *Red Herring's Tale* printed four terms since, that made this stale.'
Let it be a tale of haberdine if it will; I am nothing entailed thereunto. I scorn it, I scorn it, that my works should
turn tail to any man. Head, body, tail and all of a red herring you shall have of me, if that will please you; or if that
will not please you, stay till Easter Term and then, with the
answer to the Trim Tram,[47] I will make you laugh your hearts
out. Take me at my word, for I am the man that will do it.
This is a light friskin of my wit, like the praise of injustice,
the fever quartan, Busiris, or Phalaris,[48] wherein I follow the
trace of the famousest scholars of all ages, whom a wan-
tonizing humour once in their lifetime hath possessed to
play with straws and turn mole-hills into mountains.

Every man can say Bee to a Battledore,[49] and write in
praise of virtue and the seven liberal sciences, thresh corn
out of the full sheaves and fetch water out of the Thames;
but out of dry stubble to make an after-harvest and a plentiful crop without sowing, and wring juice out of a flint, that's
Pierce a-God's name,[50] and the right trick of a workman.

Let me speak to you about my huge words which I use in
this book, and then you are your own men to do what you
list. Know it is my true vein to be *tragicus Orator*, and of
all styles I most affect and strive to imitate Aretine's,[51] not

46. Fool (as also used in *HWY*, M. III. 13. 2).

47. *answer to the Trim Tram*: A written reply to an attack on himself, called *The Trimming of Tom Nashe*.

48. *the praise ... Phalaris*: Reference to learned treatises about
trivia.

49. *Bee to a Battledore*: Proverbial (cf. *Pierce Penniless*, n. 319),
the 'Bee' being the letter B and the phrase referring presumably to
very elementary learning.

50. *that's Pierce a-God's name*: That's an achievement truly up to
my standard, as you know it from *Pierce Penniless*.

51. cf. Nashe's admiration of Aretino expressed in *The Unfortunate
Traveller*, p. 309).

caring for this demure, soft *mediocre genus*, that is like water and wine mixed together. But give me pure wine of itself, and that begets good blood and heats the brain thoroughly. I had as lieve have no sun as have it shine faintly, no fire as a smothering fire of small coals, no clothes rather than wear linsey wolsey.[52]

Apply it for me, for I am called away to correct the faults
of the press, that escaped in my
absence from the Prin-
ting-house.

THE PRAISE OF THE RED HERRING

The strange turning of *The Isle of Dogs*[1] from a comedy to a tragedy two summers past, with the troublesome stir which happened about it, is a general rumour that hath filled all England, and such a heavy cross laid upon me as had well near confounded me. I mean, not so much in that it sequestered me from the wonted means of my maintenance, which is as great a maim to any man's happiness as can be feared from the hands of misery, or the deep pit of despair whereinto I was fallen, beyond my greatest friends' reach to recover me; but that in my exile and irksome discontented abandonment, the silliest miller's thumb or contemptible stickle-bank[2] of my enemies is as busy nibbling about my fame as if I were a dead man thrown amongst them to feed upon.

So I am, I confess, in the world's outward appearance, though perhaps I may prove a cunninger diver than they are aware; which if it so happen, as I am partly assured, and that I plunge above water once again, let them look to it, for I will put them in brine, or a piteous pickle, every one. But let that pass (though they shall find I will not let

52. *linsey wolsey*: Poor cloth of mixed wool and flax.
1. See Introduction p. 15.
2. Stickleback, i.e. the smallest, most insignificant of creatures.

it pass when time serves, I having a pamphlet hot a-brooding that shall be called *The Barber's Warming Pan*), and to the occasion afresh of my falling in alliance with this lenten argument. That infortunate imperfect embrion of my idle hours, *The Isle of Dogs* before mentioned, breeding unto me such bitter throws in the teeming [3] as it did, and the tempests that arose at his birth so astonishing outrageous and violent as if my brain had been conceived of another Hercules, I was so terrified with my own increase, like a woman long travailing to be delivered of a monster, that it was no sooner born but I was glad to run from it.[4] Too inconsiderate headlong rashness this may be censured in me, in being thus prodigal in advantaging my adversaries but my case is no smothered secret, and with light cost of rough-cast rhetoric it may be tolerably plastered over, if under the pardon and privilege of incensed higher powers it were lawfully indulgenced me freely to advocate my own astrology.

Sufficeth what they in their grave wisdoms shall proscribe I in no sort will seek to acquit, nor presumptuously attempt to dispute against the equity of their judgments, but, humble and prostrate, appeal to their mercies. Avoid or give ground I did. *Scriptum est*:[5] I will not go from it; and *post varios casus*,[6] variant knight-errant adventures and outroads and inroads, at Great Yarmouth in Norfolk I arrived in the latter end of autumn. Where having scarce looked about me, my presaging mind said to itself: '*Hic Favonius serenus est, hic Auster imbricus*;[7] this is a predestinate fit place for Pierce Penniless to set up his staff in.' Therein not much diameter to my divining hopes did the event sort itself, for six weeks first and last, under that predominant constellation of Aquarius or Jove's Nectar-filler,[8] took I up my

3. Birthpangs, pains in the breeding.
4. See Introduction p. 15.
5. 'It is written'.
6. 'After various mishaps'.
7. 'Here is the calm west wind, here the rainy south' (Plautus).
8. Ganymede, identified with Aquarius (the water-bearer) as a constellation.

repose, and there met with such kind entertainment and benign hospitality when I was *Una litera plusquam medicus*,[9] as Plautus saith, and not able to live to myself with my own juice, as some of the crumbs of it (like the crumbs in a bushy beard after a great banquet) will remain in my papers to be seen when I am dead and under ground; from the bare perusing of which, infinite posterities of hungry poets shall receive good refreshing, even as Homer by Galataeon was pictured vomiting in a basin in the temple that Ptolomy Philopater erected to him, and the rest of the succeeding poets after him greedily lapping up what he disgorged.

That good old blind bibber of Helicon, I wot well, came a-begging to one of the chief cities of Greece,[10] and promised them vast corpulent volumes of immortality if they would bestow upon him but a tender out-brother's annuity of mutton and broth, and a pallet to sleep on; and with derision they rejected him. Whereupon he went to their enemies with the like proffer, who used him honourably, and whom he used so honourably that to this day, though it be three thousand year since, their name and glory flourish green in men's memory through his industry. I trust you make no question but those dull-pated pennyfathers,[11] that in such dudgeon-scorn rejected him, drank deep of the sour cup of repentance for it, when the high flight of his lines in common bruit[12] was ooyessed.[13] Yea, in the word of one no more wealthy than he was (wealthy, said I? nay, I'll be sworn he was a grand juryman in respect of me), those greybeard huddle-duddles[14] and crusty cumtwangs[15] were struck with such stinging remorse of their

---

9. 'One letter more than a doctor'.

10. Homer went first to Cyme, where he and his offers to immortalize the town were rejected, and thence to Phocaea where he was accepted and after which he named his poem The Phocaeid.

11. Misers, skinflints.   12. Reputation.

13. Proclaimed as by cries of 'Oyez' (NED).

14. Decrepit old men (NED), probably N.'s coinage.

15. 'An obsolete term of contempt' (NED).

miserable euclionism [16] and snudgery,[17] that he was not yet cold in his grave but they challenged him to be born amongst them, and they and six cities more entered a sharp war about it, everyone of them laying claim to him as their own. And to this effect hath Buchanan [18] an epigram:

> *Urbes certarunt septem de patria Homeri,*
> *Nulla domus vivo patria nulla fuit.*

> Seven cities strove whence Homer first should come;
> When living, he no country had nor home.

I allege this tale to show how much better my luck was than Homer's, though all the King of Spain's Indies will not create me such a niggling hexameter-founder as he was, in the first proclaiming of my bankrout indigence and beggary to bend my course to such a courteous-compassionate clime as Yarmouth, and to warn others that advance their heads above all others, and have not respected, but rather flatly opposed themselves against the friar mendicants of our profession, what their amercements [19] and unreprievable penance will be, except they tear ope their oyster-mouthed pouches quickly, and make double amends for their parsimony. I am no Tiresias or Calchas to prophesy, but yet I cannot tell: there may be more resounding bell-metal in my pen than I am aware, and if there be, the first peal of it is Yarmouth's. For a pattern or tiny sample what my elaborate performance would be in this case, had I a full-sailed gale of prosperity to encourage me (whereas at the dishumoured composing hereof I may justly complain with Ovid, *Anchora iam nostram non tenet ulla ratem*,[20] my state is so tossed and weather-beaten that it hath now no anchor-hold left to cleave unto), I care not if, in a

16. Stinginess (from Euçleon, a miser, chief character in Plautus' *Autularia*).

17. Miserliness ('snudge', a miser).

18. George Buchanan (1506–82). Not an epigram but from an elegy (M.).

19. Penalties, fines.

20. 'No anchor now holds our boat' (Ovid).

dim far-off launce-skip,[21] I take the pains to describe this superiminent [22] principal metropolis of the red fish.

A town it is that in rich situation exceedeth many cities, and without the which, *caput gentis*,[23] the swelling battlements of Gurguntus,[24] a head city of Norfolk and Suffolk, would scarce retain the name of a city, but become as ruinous and desolate as Thetford [25] or Ely; out of an hill or heap of sand reared and enforced from the sea most miraculously, and by the singular policy and uncessant inestimable expense of the inhabitants, so firmly piled and rampiered against the fumish [26] waves' battery, or suing the least action of recovery, that it is more conjectural of the twain, the land with a writ of an *Eiectione firma* [27] will get the upper hand of the ocean than the ocean one crow's skip prevail against the continent. Forth of the sands thus strugglingly as it exalteth and lifts up his glittering head, so of the neighbouring sands no less semblably, whether in recordation of their worn-out affinity or no, I know not, it is so inamorately protected and patronized, that they stand as a trench or guard about it in the night, to keep off their enemies. Now, in that drowsy empire of the pale-faced Queen of Shades, malgre [28] letting drive upon their barricadoes, or impetuously contending to break through their chain or bar, but they entomb and ballast with sudden destruction.

In this transcursive reportory,[29] without some observant glance I may not dully overpass the gallant beauty of their haven, which, having but as it were a welt of land, or, as Master Camden [30] calls it, *lingulam terrae*, a little tongue of

21. Landscape.   22. Pre-eminent.
23. Capital city.
24. King Gurgunt, founder of Norwich.
25. Former seat of East-Anglian kings.
26. Foaming, seething.
27. Writ of ejectment from a holding (here, from terra firma, M. suggests).
28. In spite of.
29. Cursory account.
30. William Camden (1551–1623) in *Britannia*, 1594 edition.

the earth betwixt it and the wide main, sticks not [31] to
manage arms and hold his own undefeasibly [32] against that
universal unbounded empery of surges, and so hath done for
this hundred year. Two mile in length it stretcheth his
winding currents, and then meets with a spacious river or
backwater that feeds it. A narrow channel or isthmus in
rash view [33] you would opinionate it. When this I can
devoutly aver, I beholding it with both my eyes this last
fishing, six hundred reasonable barks and vessels of good
burden,[34] with a vantage, it hath given shelter to at once
in her harbour, and most of them riding abreast before the
quay betwixt the bridge and the south gate. Many bows'
length beyond the mark my pen roves not, I am certain. If
I do, they stand at my elbow that can correct me. The
delectable lusty sight and movingest object methought it
was, that our Isle sets forth, and nothing behind in number with the invincible Spanish Armada, though they were
not such Gargantuan boisterous gullyguts [35] as they, though
ships and galliasses [36] they would have been reckoned in
the navy of King Edgar, who is chronicled and registered
with three thousand ships of war to have scoured the narrow seas and sailed round about England every summer.
That which especiallest nourished the most prime pleasure
in me was after a storm when they were driven in swarms,
and lay close pestered [37] together as thick as they could
pack. The next day following, if it were fair, they would
cloud the whole sky with canvas, by spreading their drab-
bled sails in the full clew [38] abroad a-drying, and make a
braver show with them than so many banners and streamers
displayed against the sun on a mountain top.

But how Yarmouth, of itself so innumerable populous and

31. Does not hesitate.   32. Undefeatably.

33. At a quick glance.   34. The carrying capacity of a ship.

35. Gluttons.

36. Large ships, bigger than a galley, used chiefly in war.

37. Crowded.

38. *in the full clew*: Spread wide (a clew is the corner of the sail
by which it is spread out and attached to the lower yard).

replenished, and in so barren a plot seated, should not only supply her inhabitants with plentiful purveyance of sustenance, but provant and victual [39] moreover this monstrous army of strangers, was a matter that egregiously bepuzzled and entranced my apprehension. Hollanders, Zelanders, Scots, French, Western men, Northern men, besides all the hundreds and wapentakes [40] nine miles compass, fetch the best of her viands and mangery from her market. For ten weeks together this rabble rout of outlandishers are billeted with her; yet in all that while the rate of no kind of food is raised, nor the plenty of their markets one pint of butter rebated, and at the ten weeks' end, when the camp is broken up, no impression of any dearth left, but rather more store than before. Some of the town dwellers have so large an opinion of their settled provision that, if all Her Majesty's fleet at once should put into their bay, within twelve days' warning with so much double beer, beef, fish and biscuit, they would bulk them as they could wallow away with.

Here I could break out into a boundless race of oratory, in shrill trumpeting and concelebrating the royal magnificence of her government, that for state and strict civil ordering scant admitteth any rivals; but I fear it would be a theme displeasant to the grave modesty of the discreet present magistrates, and therefore consultively [41] I overslip [42] it. Howsoever, I purpose not in the like respect to leap over the laudable pedigree of Yarmouth, but will fetch her from her swaddling clouts or infancy, and reveal to you when and by whom she was first wrought out of the ocean's arms, and start up and aspired to such starry sublimity; as also acquaint you with the notable immunities, franchises, privileges she is endowed with beyond all her confiners, by the descentine [43] line of kings from the Conquest.

There be of you, it may be, that will account me a palterer, for hanging out the sign of the red herring in my title page, and no such feast towards for ought you can see. Soft and

39. Provide and feed.   40. Subdivisions of the counties.
41. Purposely, advisedly.
42. Leave out.   43. Descending.

fair, my masters, you must walk and talk before dinner an hour or two, the better to whet your appetites to taste of such a dainty dish as the red herring. And that you may not think the time tedious, I care not if I bear you company and lead you a sound walk round about Yarmouth and show you the length and breadth of it.

The masters' and bachelors' commencement dinners at Cambridge and Oxford are betwixt three and four in the afternoon, and the rest of the antecedence of the day worn out in disputations. Imagine this the act or commencement of the red herring, that proceedeth bachelor, master and doctor all at once, and therefore his disputations must be longer. But to the point, may it please the whole generation of my auditors to be advertised how that noble earth where the town of Great Yarmouth is now mounted, and where so much fish is sold, in the days of yore hath been the place where you might have catched fish and as plain a sea within this six hundred year as any boat could tumble in, and so was the whole level of the marshes betwixt it and Norwich. *An. Do.* 1000 or thereabouts (as I have scraped out of worm-eaten parchment) and in the reign of Canutus (he that died drunk at Lambeth[44] or Lome-hith), somewhat before or somewhat after, not a prenticeship of years varying, *Caput extulit undis,*[45] the sands set up shop for themselves; and from that moment to this sextine century (or let me be not taken with a lie, five hundred ninety-eight, that wants but a pair of years to make me a true man) they would no more live under the yoke of the sea, or have their heads washed with his bubbly spume or barber's balderdash,[46] but clearly quitted, disterminated,[47] and relegated themselves from his inflated capriciousness of playing the dictator over them.

The northern wind was the clanging trumpeter, who, with

44. In Holinshead's Chronicle it is Hardicanute, Canute's son, who died 'with a pot in his hand' at a feast in Lambeth (M.).
45. 'Raised his head out of the waves' (Virgil and Ovid).
46. Frothy liquid (NED).
47. Separated as by a boundary.

the terrible blast of his throat, in one yellow heap or plump,[48] clustered or congested them together, even as the western gales in Holland right over against them have wrought unruly havoc and threshed and swept the sands so before them that they have choked or clammed up the middle walk or door of the Rhene, and made it as stable a clodmould or turf-ground as any hedger can drive stake in. Caster, two mile distant from this new Yarmouth we entreat of, is inscribed to be that old Yarmouth whereof there are specialties to be seen in the oldest writers, and yet some visible apparent tokens remain of a haven that ran up to it, and there had his entrance into the sea (by aged fishermen commonly termed 'Grub's Haven'), though now it be gravelled up and the stream or tide-gate turned another way. But this is most warrantable: the alpha of all the Yarmouths it was, and not the omega correspondently, and from her withered root they branch the high ascent of their genealogy. *Omnium rerum vicissitudo est*:[49] one's falling is another's rising, and so fell it out with that ruined dorp[50] or hamlet which after it had relapsed into the Lord's hands for want of reparations,[51] and there were not men enough in it to defend the shore from invasion, one Cerdicus, a plashing[52] Saxon, that had revelled here and there with his battleaxe, on the bordering banks of the decrepit over-worn village now surnamed Gorlstone, threw forth his anchor, and, with the assistance of his spear instead of a pikestaff, leapt aground like a sturdy brute, and his yeomen bold cast their heels in their neck,[53] and frisked it after him, and thence sprouteth that obscene appellation of Sarding[54] Sands, with the draff of the carterly hoblobs[55] thereabouts concoct[56] or disgeast[57] for a scripture verity, when the right Christen-

48. A bunch, cluster, or clump.
49. 'There is mutability in all things' (Terence).
50. Village.
51. Maintenance, repair-work.
52. Sea-going.
53. *Cast their heels in their neck*: Leapt.
54. Swiving, or copulating.   55. Yokels.
56. Heated, matured.   57. Digested.

dom of it is Cerdick Sands, or Cerdick Shore, of Cerdicus so denominated, who was the first maylord or captain of the morris dance that on those embenched shelves [58] stamped his footing, where cods and dogfish swom (not a warp of weeks [59] forerunning), and till he had given the onset, they balked [60] them as quicksands. By and by, after his jumping upon them, the Saxons, for that Garianonum, or Yarmouth, that had given up the ghost, in those slimy plashy fields of Gorlstone trowelled up [61] a second Yarmouth, abutting on the west side of the shore of this Great Yarmouth that is. But feeling the air to be unwholesome and disagreeing with them, to the overwhart [62] brink or verge of the flood, that writ all one style of Cerdick Sands, they dislodged with bag and baggage, and there laid the foundation of a third Yarmouth *Quam nulla potest abolere vetustas*,[63] that I hope will hold up her head till doomsday.

In this Yarmouth, as Master Camden saith, there were seventy inhabitants, or householders, that paid scot and lot in the time of Edward the Confessor, but a chronographical Latin table, which they have hanging up in their Guildhall, of all their transmutations from their cradlehood, infringeth this a little, and flatters her she is a great deal younger; in a fair text hand texting unto us how, in the Scepterdom of Edward the Confessor, the sands first began to grow into sight at a low water, and more shoulder at the mouth of the river Hirus or Jerus, whereupon it was dubbed Iernmouth or Yarmouth. And then there were two channels, one on the north, another on the south, wherethrough the fishermen did wander and waver up to Norwich and divers parts of Suffolk and Norfolk, all the fenny Lerna betwixt, that with reeds is so embristled, being (as I have forspoke or spoken

58. Banked-up land round the coast.
59. A month, (a warp meaning a tale of four).
60. Avoided.
61. Built, 'flung up'.
62. Opposite.
63. 'Which no ageing can destroy' (adapted from Ovid).

tofore) *Madona Amphitrite,* fluctuous demeans or fee simple.[64]

From the City of Norwich on the east part, it is sixteen mile disjunct or dislocated. And though betwixt the sea and the salt flood it be interposed, yet in no place about it can you dig six-foot deep, but you shall have a gushing spring of fresh or sweet water for all uses, as apt and accommodate as Saint Winifred's Well,[65] or Tower Hill water at London, so much praised and sought after. My tables [66] are not yet one quarter emptied of my notes out of their table, which because it is, as it were, a sea rutter [67] diligently kept amongst them from age to age, of all their ebbs and flows, and winds that blew with or against them, I tie myself to more precisely, and thus it leadeth on.

In the time of King Harold and William the Conqueror, this sand of Yarmouth grew to a settled lump, and was as dry as the sands of Arabia, so that thronging theatres of people, as well aliens as Englishmen, hived thither about the selling of fish and herring, from Saint Michael to Saint Martin, and there built sutlers' [68] booths and tabernacles, to canopy their heads in from the rheum of the heavens, or the clouds-dissolving cataracts. King William Rufus having got the golden wreath about his head, one Herbertus, Bishop of the See of Norwich, hearing of the gangs of good fellows that hurtled and hustled thither as thick as it had been to the shrine of Saint Thomas à Becket or our Lady of Walsingham, builded a certain chapel there for the service of God and salvation of souls.

In the reign of King Henry the First, King Stephen, King Henry the Second and Richard de corde Lion, the apostasy of the sands from the yalping world was so great that they

64. *Fluctuous . . . simple*: 'Something is evidently wrong with the text. The simplest emendation would be to read "Madonna Amphitrite's fluctuous demeans", but the phrase is too clumsy to be quite satisfactory' (M.). 'Demeans' would then presumably be 'demesnes' going with 'fee simple' and meaning land in legal possession.

65. At Holywell in Flintshire.

66. Note-books.   67. Sailing chart.

68. Provision sellers to the army.

joined themselves to the mainland of Eastflege, and whole
tribes of males and females trotted, barged it thither, to
build and inhabit, which the said kings (whiles they wielded
their swords temporal) animadvertized of, assigned a ruler
or governor over them, thāt was called the King's Provost;
and that manner of provostship or government remained in
full force and virtue all their four throneships, alias a hundred year, even till the inauguration of King John, in whose
days the forwritten Bishop of Norwich, seeing the num-
brous increase of souls of both kinds that there had framed
their nests, and meant not to forsake them till the Soul
Bell [69] tolled them thence, pulled down his chapel, and
what by himself and the devout oblations and donatives of
the fishermen upon every return with their nets full, re-
edified and raised it to a church of that magnitude as, under
minsters and cathedrals, very queasy it admits any hail-
fellow-well-met.[70] And the Church of St Nicholas he hal-
lowed it, whence Yarmouth Road [71] is nicknamed the Road of
Saint Nicholas. King John, to comply and keep consort with
his ancestors in furthering of this new water-work, in the
ninth year of the engirting his annointed brows with the
refulgent ophir circle, and Anno 1209, set a fresh gloss upon
it, of the town or free borough of Yarmouth, and furnished
it with many substantial privileges and liberties, to have and
to hold the same of him and his race for fifty-five pound
yearly. In Anno 1240 it perched up to be governed by
bailies, and in a narrower limit than the forty years under-
meal [72] of the seven sleepers,[73] it had so much tow to her
distaff and was so well lined and bumbasted,[74] that in a sea
battle her ships and men conflictèd [75] the cinq ports, and

69. Passing-bell.
70. Does not recognize any church as being on a footing with
itself unless it be a cathedral or minster.
71. Harbour.
72. Afternoon sleep.
73. The seven martyred brothers of Ephesus who slept for two (or
three) hundred years before returning to life.
74. Padded with stuffing.
75. Challenged.

therein so laid about them that they burnt, took and spoiled the most of them, whereof such of them as were sure flights (saving a reverence of their manhoods) ran crying and complaining to King Henry the Second, who, with the advice of his council, set a fine of a thousand pound on the Yarmouth men's heads for that offence, which fine in the tenth of his reign he dispensed with and pardoned.

Edward the First and Edward the Second likewise let them lack for no privileges, changing it from a borough to a port town, and there setting up a custom house with the appurtenances for the loading and unloading of ships. Henry the Third in the fortieth of his empery cheered up their bloods with two charters more, and in Anno 1262 and forty-five of his court-keeping, he permitted them to wall in their town and moat it about with a broad ditch and to have a prison or jail in it. In the swing of his trident he constituted two Lords Admirals over the whole navy of England, which he disposed in two parts: the one to bear sway from the Thames' mouth northward, called the northern navy, the other to shape his course from the Thames' mouth to the westward, termed the western navy. And over this northern navy, for Admiral, commissionated one John Peerbrown, burgess of the town of Yarmouth, and over the western navy one Sir Robert Laburnus, knight.

But Peerbrown did not only hold his office all the time of that king, doing plausible service, but was again re-admiral'd by Edward the Third, and so died. In the fourteenth of whose reign he met with the French King's navy, being four-hundred sail, near to the haven of Sluse, and there so sliced and slashed them and tore their planks to mammocks [76] and their lean guts to kite's meat that their best mercy was fire and water which hath no mercy, and not a victualler or a drumbler [77] of them hanging in the wind aloof, but was rib-roasted or had some of his ribs crushed with their stone-darting engines, no ordinance then being invented. This Edward the Third, of his propensive mind

76. Shreds, pieces.
77. A small fast vessel used as a transport (NED).

towards them, united to Yarmouth Kirtley Road, from it seven mile vacant, and, sowing in the furrows that his predecessors had entered, hained [78] the price of their privileges and not brought them down one barley kernel.

Richard the Second, upon a discord twixt Leystofe and Yarmouth, after divers lawdays and arbitrary mandates to the counties of Suffolk and Norfolk directed about it, in proper person 1385 came to Yarmouth, and, in his parliament the year ensuing, confirmed unto it the liberties of Kirtley Road, the only motive of all their contention. Henry the Fifth, or the fifth of the Henries that ruled over us, abridged them not a mite of their purchased prerogatives, but permitted them to build a bridge over their haven and aided and furthered them in it. Henry the Sixth, Edward the Fourth, Henry the Seventh and King Henry the Eight, with his daughters Queen Mary and our *Chara deum soboles*,[79] Queen Elizabeth, have not withered up their hands in signing and subscribing to their requests, but our virgin rectoress most of all hath showered down her bounty upon them, granting them greater grants than ever they had, besides by-matters of the clerk of the marketship,[80] and many other benevolences towards the reparation of their port. This and every town hath his backwinters or frosts that nip it in the blade (as not the clearest sun-shine but hath his shade, and there is a time of sickness as well as of health). The backwinter, the frost-biting, the eclipse or shade, and sickness of Yarmouth was a great sickness or plague in it 1348, of which in one year seven thousand and fifty people toppled up their heels there. The new building at the west end of the church was begun there 1330, which, like the imperfect works of King's College in Cambridge, or Christchurch in Oxford, have too costly large foundations to be ever finished.

It is thought, if the town had not been so scourged and

78. Raised.
79. 'Dear offspring of the gods' (Virgil).
80. Yarmouth had been given rights in the appointment of this inspecting officer.

eaten up by that mortality, out of their own purses they would have proceeded with it, but now they have gone a nearer way to the wood, for with wooden galleries in the church that they have, and stairy degrees of seats in them, they make as much room to sit and hear as a new west-end would have done.

The length and breadth of Yarmouth I promised to show you. Have with you,[81] have with you! But first look wistly [82] upon the walls, which, if you mark, make a stretched-out quadrangle with the haven. They are in compass, from the south cheans[83] to the north cheans, two thousand, one hundred and fourscore yards. They have towers upon them sixteen; mounts underfonging [84] and enflanking them two of old, now three, which have their thundering tools to compel Diego Spaniard to duck and strike the wind cholic in his paunch if he prance too near them and will not vail [85] to the Queen of England. The compass about the wall of this new mount is five-hundred foot, and in the measure of yards eight-score and seven. The breadth of the foundation nine foot; the depth within ground eleven. The heighth to the setting thereof fifteen foot, and in the breadth, at the setting of it, five foot three inches, and the procerous [86] stature of it (so embaling [87] and girdling in this mount) twenty foot and six inches. Gates to let in her friends and shut out her enemies Yarmouth hath ten; lanes sevenscore. As for her streets, they are as long as threescore streets in London, and yet they divide them but into three. Void ground in the town from the walls to the houses, and from the houses to the haven, is not within the verge of my geometry. The liberties of it on the fresh water one way, as namely from Yarmouth to St Toolies [88] in Beckles water, are ten mile, and from Yarmouth to Hardlie Cross another way, ten mile. In all which fords or meanders none can attach,[89]

81. 'Coming directly'.   82. Closely.
83. (?) Chines.   84. Supporting from below.
85. Show respect to, (literally 'take off hat to').
86. Lofty.   87. Enclosing in a ring.
88. Corruption of St Olave's.   89. Seize, arrest.

arrest, distress, but their officers; and if any drown themselves in them, their crowners[90] sit upon them.

I had a crotchet in my head, here to have given the reins to my pen, and run astray throughout all the coast towns of England, digging up their dilapidations, and raking out of the dust-heap or charnel house of tenebrous eld the rottenest relic of their monuments, and bright-scoured the canker-eaten brass of their first bricklayers and founders, and commented and paralogized[91] on their condition in the present and in the pretertense;[92] not for any love or hatred I bear them, but that I would not be snibbed[93] or have it cast in my dish that therefore I praise Yarmouth so rantantingly,[94] because I never elsewhere baited my horse, or took my bow and arrows and went to bed. Which leasing,[95] had I been let alone, I would have put to bed with a recumbentibus,[96] by uttering the best that with a safe conscience mought be uttered of the best or worst of them all; and notwithstanding all at best that tongue could speak or heart could think of them, they should bate me an ace of[97] Yarmouth. Much braintossing and breaking of my skull it cost me, but farewell it; and farewell the bailies of the cinq ports, whose primordiat[98] *Genethliaca*[99] was also dropping out of my inkhorn with the silver ore of their baronry by William the Conqueror conveyed over to them at that nick[100] when he firmed and rubricked the Kentishmen's gavelkind[101] of the son to inherit at fifteen, and the felony of the father not to draw a foot of land from the son, and amongst the sons the portion to be equally distributed; and if there were no sons, much good do it the daughters, for they were to share it after the same tenure, and might alienate it how they would, either by legacy or bargain, without the consent of the lord.

90. Coroners.
91. (?) Criticized.
92. Past.
93. Rebuked, snubbed.
94. Extravagantly.
95. Loss.
96. Knock-out blow.
97. *Bate . . . of*: 'Not come up to' (M.).
98. Earliest.
99. Birthday, horoscope.
100. Moment.
101. Laws governing tenure and inheritance of land.

To shun spite I smothered these dribblements, and re-frained to descant how William the Conqueror, having heard the proverb of Kent and Christendom,[102] thought he had won a country as good as all Christendom when he was enfeoffed [103] of Kent, for which, to make it sure unto him after he was entailed thereunto, nought they asked they needed to ask twice, it being enacted ere the words came out of their mouth. Of that profligated labour yet my breast pants and labours. A whole month's mind of revolving meditation I ravelling out therein (as ravelling out signifies *Penelopes telam retexere*,[104] the unweaving of a web before woven and contexted). It pities me, it pities me, that in cutting of so fair a diamond as Yarmouth, I have not a casket of dusky Cornish diamonds by me, and a box of muddy foils, the better to set it forth. *Ut nemo miser nisi comparatus, sic nihil pro mirifico nisi cum aliis conferatur. Cedite soli, stellae scintillantes; soli Garrianano cedite, reliqua oppida veligera, sedium navalium speciocissimo. Sed redeo ad ver-naculum.*[105]

All commonwealths assume their prenominations [106] of their common divided weal, as where one man hath not too much riches, and another man too much poverty. Such was Plato's community, and Lycurgus' [107] and the old Romans' laws of measuring out their fields, their meads, their pastures and houses, and meeting out to every one his child's portion.

102. M. quotes Lyly's *Mother Bomby*, III, 4, 5: 'I can live in Christendom as well as in Kent,' adding that although the saying is common it is still not adequately explained.

103. In possession of the fief, the due from the land.

104. 'Penelope unwinding the warp' (Cicero). A reference to the story of Ulysses' wife, hard pressed by suitors in his absence.

105. 'As no one is wretched unless compared [sc. to someone else], so nothing appears wonderful unless it is compared with other things. Give ground before the sun, ye shining stars; give way, remaining sail-bearing towns, before the most splendid of naval bases. But I re-turn now to the vernacular' (M. says the Latin is 'apparently Nashe's own').

106. Giving a first name.

107. Famous orator and financial administrator in Athens, *c.* 330 B.C.

To this *Commune bonum* (or every horse his loaf) Yarmouth in propinquity is as the buckle to the thong, and the next finger to the thumb. Not that it is sib or cater-cousins [108] to any mongrel Democratia, in which one is all and all is one, but that in her, as they are not all one, so one or two there pockets not up all the pieces; there being two hundred in it worth three hundred pound apiece, with poundage and shillings to the lurched,[109] set aside the bailiffs, four and twenty,[110] and eight and forty. Put out mine eye, who can, with such another brag of any sea-town within two hundred mile of it. But this common good within itself is nothing to the common good it communicates to the whole state. Shall I particularize unto you *quibus viis et modis*,[111] how and wherein? There is my hand to, I will do it; and this is my *exordium*.[112] A town of defence it is to the counties of Suffolk and Norfolk against the enemies (so accounted at the first granting of their liberties), and by the natural strength of the situation so apparent, being both environed with many sands, and now of late by great charge much more fortified than in ancient times. All the realm it profiteth many ways, as by the free fare of herring chiefly, maintained by the fishermen of Yarmouth themselves, by the great plenty of salted fish there, not so little two years past as four hundred thousand, wherein were employed about fourscore sail of barks of their own.

By the furnishing forth of forty boats for mackerel at the spring of the year when all things are dearest, which is a great relief to all the country thereabouts, and soon after Bartlemew-tide,[113] a hundred and twenty sail of their own for herrings, and forty sail of other ships and barks trading

108. Blood-relations or close friends.

109. *Poundage ... lurched*: 'Some contribution to the poor-rate or possibly to a special fund appropriated to the relief of those whose ships had met with disaster' (M.'s suggestion).

110. Norwich had twenty-four aldermen and forty-eight members of the Common Council.

111. By which ways and means.

112. Beginning (of speech or exposition).

113. St Bartholomew's Day, 24 August.

Newcastle, the Low Countries and other voyages. Norwich, at Her Majesty's coming in progress thither,[114] presented her with a show of knitters on a high stage placed for the nonce. Yarmouth, if the like occasion were, could clap up as good a show of netbraiders, or those that have no clothes to wrap their hides in or bread to put in their mouths but what they earn and get by braiding of nets (not so little as two thousand pound they yearly dispersing amongst the poor women and children of the country for the spinning of twine to make them with, besides the labour of the inhabitants in working them); and, for a commodious green place near the seashore to mend and dry them, no Salisbury Plain or Newmarket Heath (though they have no vicinity or neighbourhood with the sea, or scarce with any ditch or pond of freshwater) may overpeer or outcrow her, there being above five thousand pounds worth of them at a time upon her dens [115] a-sunning. A convenient quay within her haven she hath, for the delivery of nets and herrings, where you may lie afloat at a low water (I beseech you do not so in the Thames), many serviceable mariners and seafaring men she traineth up (but of that in the herring).

The marishes and lower grounds lying upon the three rivers that vagary [116] up to her, comprehending many thousand acres, by the vigilant preservation of their haven are increased in value more than half, which else would be a *Maeotis palus*,[117] a meer or lake of eels, frogs and wildducks. The City of Norwich, as in the Preludium hereof I had a twitch at, fares ne'er the worse for her, nor would fare so well if it were not for the fish of all sorts that she cloyeth her with, and the fellowship of their haven, into which their three rivers infuse themselves, and through which their goods and merchandise from beyond seas are keeled up with small cost to their very thresholds, and to many good towns on this side and beyond. I would be loth to build a labyrinth in the gatehouse of my book, for you to lose yourselves in, and therefore I shred off many things. We will but cast over

114. This was in 1578.   115. Denes, sandy coastland.
116. Wander.   117. Sea of Asaph.

the bill of her charge, and talk a word or two of her buildings, and break up and go to breakfast with the red herring.
The haven hath cost in these twenty-eight years, six-and-
twenty thousand, two hundred and six-and-fifty pound, four
shillings and five pence. Fortification and poulder [118] since
Anno 1587, two thousand marks, and sea-service in Anno
1588, eight hundred pounds, the Portingale voyage [119] a
thousand pound, the voyage to Cales [120] as much.

It hath lost by the Dunkerkers [121] a thousand pound, by
the Frenchmen three thousand, by Wafting [122] eight hundred, by the Spaniards and other losses not rated, at the
least three thousand more. The continual charge of the
town in maintenance of their haven, five hundred pounds a
year, *Omnibus annis* for ever, the feefarm [123] of the town
fifty-five pound, and five pound a year above for Kirtley
Road. The continual charge of the bridge over the haven,
their walls and a number of other odd reckonings we deal
not with; towards all which they have not in certain
revenues above fifty or three-score pounds a year, and that
is in houses. The yearly charge towards the provision of
fish for Her Majesty one thousand pounds; as for arable
matters of tillage and husbandry, and grazing of cattle,
their barren sands will not bear them, and they get not a
beggar's noble by one or other of them, but their whole
harvest is by sea.

It were to be wished that other coasters were so industrious as the Yarmouth, in winning the treasure of fish out
of those profundities, and then we should have twenty eggs a
penny, and it would be as plentiful a world as when abbeys
stood. And now, if there be any plentiful world, it is
in Yarmouth. Her sumptuous porches and garnished buildings are such as no port town in our British circumference

118. Powder.   119. This was in 1589.
120. Cadiz, the expedition of 1596.
121. Dunkirk pirates.
122. 'The word ordinarily meant "passage" or "passage-money"'
(M.).
123. Rent.

(nay, take some port city's overplus into the bargainer) may suitably stake with, or adequate.[124]

By the proportion of the east surprised Gades or Cales divers have tried their cunning to configurate a twinlike image of it,[125] both in the correlative analogy of the span-broad rows running betwixt, as also of the skirt or lappet [126] of earth whereon it stands; herein only limiting the difference, that the houses here are not such flat custard crowns at the top as they are. But I for my part cast it aside as too obscure a canton to demonstrate and take the altitude by of so Elizian a habitation as Yarmouth. Of a bouncing side-wasted [127] parish in Lancashire we have a flying voice dispersed, where they go nine mile to church every Sunday, but parish-for-parish throughout Lancashire, Cheshire, or Wingandecoy,[128] both for numbers in gross of honest householders, youthful courageous valiant spirits, and substantial grave burghers, Yarmouth shall drop vie [129] with them to the last Edward groat they are worth. I am posting to my proposed scope, or else I could run ten quire of paper out of breath, in further traversing her rights and dignities.

But of that fraught I must not take in too liberal, in case I want stowage for my red herring, which I rely upon as my wealthiest loading. Farewell, flourishing Yarmouth, and be every day more flourishing than other until the latter day. Whiles I have my sense or existence, I will persist in loving thee, and so with this abrupt *Post script* I leave thee. I have not travelled far, though conferred with farthest travellers, from our own realm. I have turned over Venerable Bede, and plenteous beadrolls [130] of fiery annals following on the back of him. Polidore Vergil, Buchanan, Camden's *Britannia*,

124. Be equal to.

125. *By the proportion ... image of it*: 'This seems to make no sense, Cadiz was taken by the Spaniards in April 1596, and retaken for the French by the Earl of Essex on 21 June of the same year. But it does not seem there was any surprise' (M.).

126. Flap or fold.   127. Broad.

128. Virginia, the native term for which was Wingandecoa.

129. A gambling term (to 'vic' was to wager) (M.).

130. Long series.

and most records of friends or enemies I have searched, as concerning the later model of it; none of the inland parts thereof but I have traded them as frequently as the middle walk in Paul's,[131] or my way to bed every night, yet for aught I have read, heard or seen, Yarmouth, regal Yarmouth, of all maritime towns that are no more but fisher towns, solely reigneth sans peer.

Not anywhere is the Word severer practised, the preacher reverentlier observed and honoured, justice sounder ministered, and a warlike people peaceablier demeanoured, betwixt this and the Grand Cathay, and the strand of Prester John.

Adieu, adieu, ten-thousand-fold delicate paramour of Neptune; the next year my standish [132] may happen to address another voyage unto thee, if this have any acceptance. Now it is high heaking time,[133] and be the winds never so easterly adverse and the tide fled from us, we must violently tow and hale in our redoubtable Sophy [134] of the floating kingdom of Pisces, whom so much as by name I should not have acknowledged, had it not been that I mused how Yarmouth should be invested in such plenty and opulence, considering that in Mr Hakluyt's [135] *English Discoveries* I have not come in ken of one mizzen-mast of a man-of-war bound for the Indies or Mediterranean stern-bearer sent from her zenith or meridian, mercurial-breasted [136] Mr Harborne [137] always excepted, a rich spark of eternity first lighted and enkindled at Yarmouth, or there first bred and brought forth to see the light, who since, in the hottest degrees of

131. The nave of St Paul's, a popular meeting place.

132. Writing materials.

133. NED suggests time to draw in the haking, a special kind of fishing net.

134. Name for the Persian monarch.

135. Richard Hakluyt (1552–1616) first published *The Principal Navigations, Voyages and Discoveries of the English Nation* in 1589.

136. Those born under Mercury were supposed to possess an aptitude for commerce (M.).

137. William Harborne (d. 1617), first English ambassador to Turkey.

Leo, hath echoing noised the name of our island and of
Yarmouth so Tritonly that not an infant of the curtailed
skinclipping pagans but talk of London as frequently as of
their prophet's tomb at Maecha, and as much worships our
maidenpeace as it were but one sun that shined over them
all. Our first ambassador was he to the Behemoth of Constantinople, and as Moses was sent from the omnipotent
God of heaven to persuade with Sultan Pharoah to let the
children of Israel go, so from the prepotent goddess of the
earth, Eliza, was he sent to set free the English captives and
open unto us the passage into the Red Sea and Euphrates.
How impenetrable [138] he was in mollifying the adamantinest
tyranny of mankind and hourly crucifier of Jesus Christ
crucified, and rooter up of Palestine, those that be scrutinous
to pry into, let them resolve the digests of our English
discoveries cited up in the precedence, and be document-
ized most locupletely.[139] Of him and none but him, who,
in valuation is worth eighteen huge Argosies full of our
present-dated misshapen childish travellers, have I took
scent or come in the wind of, that ever Yarmouth unshelled
or engendered to weather it on, till they lost the North
Star, or sailed just Antipodes against us. Nor, walking in
her streets so many weeks together, could I meet with
any of these swaggering captains (captains that wore a
whole ancient [140] in a scarf, which made them go heave-
shouldered,[141] it was so boisterous), or huftytufty [142] youthful
ruffling comrades, wearing every one three yards of feather
in his cap for his mistress' favour, such as we stumble on at
each second step at Plymouth, Southampton and Ports-
mouth, but an universal merchantly formality in habit,
speech, gestures, though little merchandise they beat their
heads about, Queen Norwich for that going between them
and home.

At length (oh, that length of the full-point spoils me; all
gentle readers, I beseech you pardon me) I fell a-communing
hereupon with a gentleman, a familiar of mine, and he eft-

138. Here means successful.   139. Richly.   140. Ensign.
141. With raised shoulders.   142. Swaggering.

soons defined unto me that the red herring was this old
Ticklecob or *Magister fac totum*, that brought in the red
ruddocks [143] and the grummel [144] seed as thick as oatmeal,
and made Yarmouth for argent to put down the City of
Argentine. 'Do but convert', said he, 'the slenderest twinkling reflex of your eye-sight to this flinty ring that engirts it,
these towered walls, portcullised gates, and gorgeous archi-
tectures that condecorate and adorn it, and then perponder
of the red herring's priority and prevalence, who is the only
unexhaustible mine that hath raised and begot all this, and
minutely to riper maturity fosters and cherisheth it. The
red herring alone it is that countervails the burdensome
detriments of our haven, which every twelve-month devours
a Justice of Peace's living, in wears and banks to beat off the
sand and overthwart ledging [145] and fencing it in; that
defrays all impositions and outward payments to Her
Majesty (in which Yarmouth gives not the wall to [146] six,
though sixteen moth-eaten burgess towns, that have daubers
and thatchers to their mayors, challenge in parliament the
upper hand of it), and, for the vanward or suburbs of my narration, that empalls [147] our sage senators or Ephori [148] in
princely scarlet as pompous ostentive as the *Vinti quater* [149]
of Lady Troynovant. [150] Wherefore,' quoth he, 'if there be in
thee any whit of that unquenchable sacred fire of Apollo
(as all men repute) and that Minerva amongst the number
of her heirs hath adopted thee, or thou wilt commend thy
muse to sempiternity, and have images and statues erected
to her after her unstringed silent interment and obsequies,
rouse thy spirits out of this drowsy lethargy of melancholy
they are drenched in, and wrest them up to the most out-
stretched airy strain of elocution to chant and carol forth

143. Gold coins.
144. Gromwell seed, symbolizing profit.
145. *Overthwart ledging*: System of protective cross-bars.
146. *Gives ... to*: Will not admit the superiority of.
147. Cloaks.
148. Magistrates (in Sparta).
149. The London aldermen, or possibly sheriffs.
150. 'New Troy', i.e. London.

the *Alteza* and excelsitude of this monarchal floody *Induperator.'* [151]

Very tractable to this lure I was trained, and put him not to the full anviling of me with any sound hammering persuasion, in that at the first sight of the top-gallant towers of Yarmouth, and a week before he had broken any of these words betwixt his teeth, my muse was ardently inflamed to do it some right; and how to bring it about fitter I knew not than in the praise of the red herring, whose proper soil and nursery it is. But this I must give you to wit, however I have took it upon me: that never since I spouted ink was I of worse aptitude to go through with such a mighty Marchbrewage as you expect, or temper you one right cup of that ancient wine of Falernum, which would last forty year, or consecrate to your fame a perpetual temple of the pinetrees of Ida,[152] which never rot. For besides the loud bellowing prodigious flaw [153] of indignation stirred up against me in my absence and extermination from the upper region of our celestial regiment, which hath dung [154] me in a manner down to the infernal bottom of desolation, and so troubledly bemuddled with grief and care every cell or organ-pipe of my purer intellectual faculties, that no more they consort with any ingenuous playful merriments, of my note-books and all books else here in the country I am bereaved, whereby I might enamel and hatch-over this device more artificially and masterly, and attire it in his true orient varnish and tincture. Wherefore heart and good will, a workman is nothing without his tools. Had I my topics by me instead of my learned counsel to assist me, I might haps marshal my terms in better array, and bestow such costly coquery [155] on this Marine Magnifico as you

151. Imperator.
152. A mountain range in the neighbourhood of Troy, covered with woods and said, by the poets, to have been frequented by the gods during the Trojan war.
153. A squall.
154. Beaten, knocked (past tense of 'ding').
155. Cookery.

would prefer him before tart and galingale,[156] which Chaucer [157] preheminentest encomionizeth [158] above all junketries [159] or confectionaries whatsoever.

Now you must accept of it as the place serves, and, instead of comfits and sugar to strew him with, take well in worth a farthing worth of flour to white him over and wamble [160] him in, and I having no great pieces to discharge for his benvenue, or welcoming in, with this volley of Rhapsodies or small shot he must rest pacified, and so *ad rem*,[161] spur cut through thick and thin, and enter the triumphal chariot of the red herring.

HOMER of rats and frogs hath heroicked it.[162] Other oaten pipers after him in praise of the gnat, the flea, the hazel-nut, the grasshopper, the butterfly, the parrot, the popinjay, Philip-sparrow, and the cuckoo; the wantoner sort of them sing descant on their mistress' glove, her ring, her fan, her looking glass, her pantofle,[163] and on the same jury I might impanel Johannes Secundus,[164] with his book of the two hundred kind of kisses. Philosophers come sneaking in with their paradoxes of poverty, imprisonment, death, sickness, banishment and baldness, and as busy they are about the bee, the stork, the constant turtle, the horse, the dog, the ape, the ass, the fox and the ferret. Physicians deafen our ears with the *Honorificabilitudinitatibus* [165] of their heavenly panachaea,[166] their sovereign guaiacum,[167] their glisters,[168]

156. Aromatic wood used in cooking and medicine.

157. 'A cooke they hadde with hem for the nones. To boille the chiknes with the marybones And poudre marchant tart and galingale' (*Canterbury Tales*, Prologue, 381).

158. Eulogizes.

159. Banquets or perhaps delicacies.

160. Roll.

161. To the thing itself.

162. *The Battle of Frogs and Mice.*

163. Slippers (often high-heeled).

164. 1511–36, a Dutch poet.

165. Used by Dante in *De vulgari eloquentia* and by earlier writers.

166. Panacea, or supposed remedy for all ills.

167. Tree from the West Indies; its wood is used in medicine.

168. Clysters, commonly an enema.

their triacles,[169] their mithridates[170] of forty several poisons compacted, their bitter rhubarb and torturing stibium.[171]

The posterior [172] Italian and German cornugraphers [173] stick not to [174] applaud and cannonize unnatural sodomitry, the strumpet errant, the gout, the ague, the dropsy, the sciatica, folly, drunkenness, and slovenry. The Galli Gallinacei, or cocking French, swarm every pissing while [175] in their primer editions, *Imprimeda iour duy*[176] of the unspeakable healthful conducibleness [177] of the Gomorrian [178] great *Poco, a Poco*,[179] their true countryman every inch of him, the prescript laws of tennis or balonne [180] (which is most of their gentlemen's chief livelihoods), the commodity of hoarseness, blear-eyes, scabbed hams, threadbare cloaks, potched eggs, and panados.[181] Amongst our English harmonious calinos [182] one is up with the excellence of the brown bill [183] and the long bow; another plays his prizes in print, in driving it home with all weapons in right of the noble science of defence; a third writes passing enamorately of the nature of white-meats,[184] and justifies it under his hand to be bought and sold everywhere, that they exceed

169. Treacles, compounds used as remedies for many diseases.

170. Another general medicine, the name deriving from Mithridates VI of Pontus, supposedly proof against all poisons.

171. Antimony, metallic substance used in alchemy.

172. Later.

173. Writers of the horn (i.e. the arts of cuckoldry). (See note on this passage: Introduction pp. 41–2.)

174. Do not hesitate to.

175. 'In frequent use' (M. gives references to *Gammer Gurton's Needle* and *The Two Gentlemen of Verona*).

176. *Imprimé aujourd'hui.*

177. (?) Advantageousness.   178. Gonorrhoea.

179. *Poco, a poco*: Little by little (the gradual effects of venereal diseases).

180. Game played with a balloon.

181. Panada is a dish in which a basin of boiled bread is flavoured with sugar, fruit or spices.

182. (?) Beggars with faked diseases or infirmities, or perhaps a reference to the popular song 'Calino costure me' (F.P.W.).

183. A halberd.

184. Milk, butter, curds and cheese.

nectar and ambrosia; a fourth comes forth with something in praise of nothing; a fifth of an enflamed heel [185] to coppersmith's hall, all-to-berhymes [186] it of the diversity of red noses, and the hierarchy of the rose magnificat. A sixth sweeps behind the door all earthly felicities, and makes baker's malkins [187] of them, if they stand in competency with a strong dozen of points; marry, they must be points of the matter, you must consider, whereof the foremost cod-piss point is the crane's proverb in painted clothes, 'Fear God and obey the King'; and the rest, some have tags and some have none. A seventh sets a tobacco pipe instead of a trumpet to his mouth, and of that divine drug proclaimeth miracles. An eighth capers it up to the spheres in commen-dation of dancing. A ninth offers sacrifice to the goddess Cloaca,[188] and disports himself very scholarly and wittily about the reformation of close-stools [189] and houses of office,[190] and spicing and embalming their rank entrails that they stink not. A tenth sets forth remedies of toasted turves against famine.

To these I might wedge in Cornelius the Brabantine [191] who was feloniously suspected in '87 for penning a discourse of tuftmockados, and a country gentleman of my acquain-tance who is launching forth a treatise as big-garbed as the French Academy of *The Cornucopia of a Cow* and what an advantageable creature she is, beyond all the four-footed rabblement of herbagers and grass-champers (day nor night that she can rest for filing [192] and tampering about it), as also a sworn brother of his that so bebangeth poor paper in laud of a bag-pudding,[193] as a switzer [194] would not believe

185. F.P.W. suggests read 'zeal'.
186. Makes up a set of rhyming verses.
187. Mops for cleaning ovens.
188. A reference to Sir John Davies's *Orchestra, or a Poem of Danc-ing*, 1596.
189. 'A chamber utensil enclosed in a stool or box' (NED).
190. Privies.
191. Said to have published an *Enconium of Tuftmockados* in 1582.
192. M. suggests 'fussing'.   193. Pudding boiled in a bag.
194. A Swiss (thought of as especially credulous).

it. Neither of their decads are yet stamped, but ere mid-summer term they will be, if their words be sure payment, and then tell me if our English sconces [195] be not right Sheffield [196] or no.

The application of this whole catalogue of waste authors is no more but this: *Quot capita tot sententiae* [197] ('so many heads, so many whirligigs').[198] And if all these have terlery-ginked [199] it so frivolously of they recked not what, I may *cum gratia et priveligio* [200] pronounce it, that a red herring is wholesome in a frosty morning, and rake up some few scattered syllables together in the exornation [201] and polishing of it. No more excursions and circumquaques [202] but *totaliter ad appositum*.[203]

That English merchandise is most precious which no country can be without. If you ask Suffolk, Essex, Kent, Sussex, or Lemster or Cotswold what merchandise that should be, they will answer you it is the very same which Polidore Vergil calls *Vae aureum vellus*,[204] the true golden fleece of our wool and English cloth, and naught else. Other engrating [205] upland cormorants [206] will grunt out it is *grana paradisi*,[207] our grain or corn, that is most sought after. The westerners and northerners that it is lead, tin and iron. 'Butter and cheese, butter and cheese!' saith the farmer. But from every one of these I dissent and will stoutly bide by it, that, to trowl in the cash throughout all nations of christendom, there is no fellow to the red herring. The

195. Heads or helmets.   196. Good metal.

197. 'So many heads, so many opinions'.

198. Toys, like tops, for spinning (metaphorically: fancy, far-fetched ideas).

199. Meaning uncertain, but cf. *Strange News*: 'Turlery ginkes, in a light foot jig, libels in commendation of little wit very loftily' (M. Vol. I, 296). Also Harvey's description of *SN* as 'a Turlery-ginks of conceit' (M. Vol. IV, 178).

200. With grace and favour.

201. Adornment, embellishment.

202. Circumlocutions.   203. 'Keeping to the point'.

204. 'Woe to the Golden Fleece'.   205. Ingratiating.

206. Greedy folk.

207. Grains of paradise, an African spice.

French, Spanish, and Italian have wool enough of their own whereof they make cloth to serve their turn, though it be somewhat coarser than ours. For corn, none of the east parts but surpasseth us. Of lead and tin is the most scarcity in foreign dominions, and plenty with us, though they are not utterly barren of them. As for iron, about Isenborough [208] and other places of Germany they have quadruple the store that we have. As touching butter and cheese, the Hollanders cry 'By your leave, we must go before you'; and the Transalpiners with their lordly parmasin (so named of the city of Parma in Italy where it is first clout-crushed [209] and made) shoulder in for the upper hand as hotly. Whenas, of our appropriate glory of the red herring, no region twixt the poles artic and antartic may, can, or will rebate from us one scruple.

On no coast like ours is it caught in such abundance, nowhere dressed in his right cue but under our horizon; hosted,[210] roasted and toasted here alone it is, and as well powdered and salted as any Dutchman would desire. If you articulate with me of the gain or profit of it, without the which the newfanglest rarity, that nobody can boast of but ourselves, after three days gazing is reversed over to children for babies to play with. Behold, it is every man's money, from the King to the courtier. Every householder or goodman Baltrop,[211] that keeps a family in pay, casts for it as one of his standing provisions. The poorer sort make it three parts of their sustenance; with it, for his denier, [212] the patchedest leather *piltche labaratho* [213] may dine like a Spanish duke, when the niggardliest mouse [214] of beef will cost him sixpence. In the craft of catching or taking it, and smudging [215] it merchant and chapmanable [216] as it should be, it sets a-work thousands, who live all the rest of the year

208. Eisenburg in Hungary (?) (M.)
209. Crushed or pressed in the curd.
210. Dried in an oast or kiln.   211. Meaning unknown.
212. Penny.
213. Leather-coated labourer.
214. Morsel.   215. Smoking.
216. *merchant and chapmanable*: Saleable.

gaily well by what in some few weeks they scratch up then, and come to bear office of questman [217] and scavenger in the parish where they dwell; which they could never have done, but would have begged or starved with their wives and brats had not this captain of the squamy [218] cattle so stood their good lord and master. Carpenters, shipwrights, makers of lines, ropes, and cables, dressers of hemp, spinners of thread, and net-weavers it gives their handfuls to, sets up so many salt-houses to make salt, and salt upon salt; keeps in earnings the cooper, the brewer, the baker, and numbers of other people, to gill, wash and pack it, and carry it, and recarry it.

In exchange of it from other countries they return wine and woads, for which is always paid ready gold, with salt, canvas, vitre,[219] and a great deal of good trash.[220] Her Majesty's tributes and customs this *Semper Augustus*[221] of the seas' finny freeholders augmenteth and enlargeth uncountably, and to the increase of navigation for her service he is no enemy.

Voyages of purchase or reprisals, which are now grown a common traffic, swallow up and consume more sailors and mariners than they breed, and lightly not a slop of a rope-haler they send forth to the Queen's ships, but he is first broken to the sea in the herring man's skiff or cock-boat, where having learned to brook all waters, and drink as he can out of a tarry can, and eat poor-john out of swuttie [222] platters, when he may get it, without butter or mustard, there is no ho [223] with him, but, once heartened thus, he will needs be a man of war, or a tobacco-taker, and wear a silver whistle. Some of these for their haughty climbing come home with wooden legs, and some with none, but leave body and all behind. Those that escape to bring news tell of nothing but eating tallow and young blackamoors, of five and five to a rat in every mess, and the ship-boy to the

217. Inspector.   218. Scaly.
219. Glass.   220. Valuables.
221. Title used by Roman Emperors.
222. (?) Sooty, dirty.   223. *no ho*: No stopping.

tail, of stopping their noses when they drank stinking water that came out of the pump of the ship, and cutting a greasy buff jerkin in tripes and broiling it for their dinners. Divers Indian adventures have been seasoned with direr mishaps, not having for eight days' space the quantity of a candle's end among eight-score to grease their lips with; and landing in the end to seek food, by the cannibal savages they have been circumvented, and forced to yield their bodies to feed them.

Our mitred Archpatriarch, Leopold Herring, exacts no such muscovian vassalage of his liegemen, though he put them to their trumps [224] other while, and scuppets [225] not his benefice into their mouths with such freshwater facility as Master Ascham in his *Schoolmaster* would imply. His words are these in his censure upon Varro: 'He enters not,' saith he, 'into any great depth of eloquence, but as one carried in a small low vessel by himself very nigh the common shore, not much unlike the fishermen of Rie, or herring men of Yarmouth, who deserve by common men's opinion small commendation for any cunning sailing at all.' Well, he was Her Majesty's schoolmaster, and a St John's man in Cambridge, in which house once I took up my inn for seven year together lacking a quarter, and yet love it still, for it is and ever was the sweetest nurse of knowledge in all that University. Therefore I will keep fair quarter with him, and expostulate the matter more tamely. *Memorandum non ab uno*: [226] I vary not a minim from him, that, in the captious mystery of Monsieur Herring, low vessels will not give their heads for the washing,[227] holding their own pell-mell in all weathers as roughly as vaster timber-men, though not so near the shore as, through ignorance of the coast, he soundeth, nor one man by himself alone to do everything, which is the opinion of one man by himself alone, and not believed of any other. Five to one, if he were alive, I would beat against him, since one without five is as good as none,

224. Put them in difficulties.   225. Shovels.
226. M. suggests should read '*abnuo*': 'I do not disagree'.
227. *give ... washing*: Submit to insult.

408

to govern the most eggshell shallop that floateth, and spread
her nets and draw them in. As stiffly could I controvert it
with him about pricking his card so badly in Cape Norfolk
or *Sinus Yarmouthiensis* and discrediting our countrymen
for shorecreepers, like these Colchester oystermen, or
whiting-mongers and sprot-catchers.[228] Solyman Herring,
would you should persuade yourselves, is loftier minded
and keepeth more aloof than so. And those that are his
followers, if they will seek him where he is, more than common danger they must incur in close driving under the
sands which alternately or betwixt times, when he is disposed to ensconce himself, are his entrenched randevowe [229]
or castle of retiring; and otherwhile forty or threescore
leagues in the roaring territory they are glad on their wooden
horses to post after him, and scour it with their ethiope
pitchboards [230] till they be windless in his quest and pursuing. Returning from waiting on him, have with you to the
Adriatic and abroad everywhere far and near to make port-
sail [231] of their perfumed smoky commodities, and, that toil
rocked asleep, they are for Ultima Thule,[232] the north-seas,
or Iceland, and thence yerk over [233] that worthy *Pallamede
don pedro de linge*,[234] and his worshipful nephew Hugo
Haberdine,[235] and a trundle-tail [236] tyke [237] or shaugh [238]
or two, and towards Michlemas scud home to catch herring
again. This argues they should have some experience of
navigation, and are not such halcyons to build their nests
all on the shore as Master Ascham supposeth.

Rie is one of the ancient towns belonging to the cinq

228. Sprat-catchers.
229. Rendezvous.
230. *ethiope pitchboards*: 'Fanciful name for a ship' (NED).
231. Sale by auction, or public sale.
232. Here probably meaning Iceland (see Virgil, *Georgics* I, 30).
233. 'Yerk' could mean stitch, lash out, beat, jerk, push, pull. Basic
sense here probably 'to capture'.
234. The ling is a kind of codfish found in northern seas. Further
meaning untraced.
235. Large cod used for salting.   236. Curly-tailed.
237. A dog, usually a mongrel.   238. Icelandic lapdog.

ports, yet limpeth cinq ace [239] behind Yarmouth, and it will sink when Yarmouth riseth, and yet, if it were put in the balance against Yarmouth, it would rise when Yarmouth sinketh; and to stand threshing no longer about it, Rie is rye and no more but rye, and Yarmouth wheat compared with it. Wherefore had he been a right clerk of the market, he would have set a higher price on the one than the other, and set that one of highest price above the other.

Those that deserve by common men's opinion small commendation for any cunning sailing at all are not the Yarmouthers (however there is a foul fault in the print escaped, that curstly squinteth and leereth that way) but the bonny northern cobbles of his country, with their Indian canoes or boats like great beef-trays or kneading-troughs, firking [240] as flight [241] swift thorough the glassy fields of Thetis as if it were the land of ice, and sliding over the boiling desert so early, and never bruise one bubble of it, as though they contended to outstrip the light-foot tripper in the *Metamorphosis*, [242] who would run over the ripe-bending ears of corn and never shed or perish one kernel. No such iron-fisted cyclops to hew it out of the flint and run thorough anything as these frost-bitten crabtree-faced lads, spun out of the hards [243] of the tow, which are Donzel [244] Herring's lackeys at Yarmouth every fishing.

Let the careeringest [245] billow confess and absolve itself, before it prick up his bristles against them, for, if it come upon his dancing horse, and offer to tilt it with them, they will ask no trustier lances than their oars to beat out the brains of it and stop his throat from belching.

These rubs [246] removed, on with our game as fast as we may, and to the gain of the red herring again another

239. Throw of five and one at dice, i.e. 'a good throw', 'a good way'.

240. Speeding.   241. An arrow.

242. Ovid, *Metamorphoses*, X, 654–5; and Virgil, *Aeneid*, VIII, 808–11 (M.).

243. Refuse of flax, hemp, etc. (M.).

244. A young gentleman.

245. Swiftest.   246. Hindrances.

crash.[247] Item: if it were not for this Huniades[248] of the
liquid element, that word Quadragesima, or Lent, might be
clean sponged out of the calendar, with rogation weeks,
saints' eves, and the whole ragman's rule of fasting days;
and fishmongers might keep Christmas all the year for any
overlavish takings they should have of clowns and clouted
shoes,[249] and the rubbish menialty, their best customers;
and their bloody adversaries, the butchers, would never
leave cleaving it out in the whole chines,[250] till they had got
a Lord Mayor of their company as well as they. Nay, out of
their wits they would be haunted with continual takings
and stand cross-gagged with knives in their mouths from
one Shrove Tuesday to another, and wear candles'-ends in
their hats at midsummer, having no time to shave their
pricks[251] or wash their flyblown aprons, if Domingo Rufus[252]
or Sacrapant[253] Herring caused not the dice to run contrary.

The Romish rotten Pythagoreans or Carthusian friars,
that mump[254] on nothing but fish, in what a phlegmatic
predicament would they be, did not his counterpoison
of the spitting-sickness (sixtyfold more restorative than
bezer[255]) patch them out and preserve them; which, being
double-roasted and dried as it is, not only sucks up all
rheumatic inundations, but is a shoeing horn[256] for a pint of
wine over-plus.

The sweet smack that Yarmouth finds in it, and how it
hath made it *Lippitudo Atticae*[257] (as it was said of Aegina,
her near adjacent confronter), the blemish and stain of all

247. Music or a dance.

248. After John Hunyade (*c.* 1400–56), hero of wars against the
Turks.

249. *clowns . . . shoes*: Peasants, boors.

250. Joints of meat from the animals' backbones.

251. Skewers.

252. Domingo was a name for a drunkard; Rufus is the red herring.

253. A magician in Peele's *Old Wives' Tale*.

254. Munch.   255. Bezoar, antidote for poisons.

256. For drawing liquor.

257. Conjunctivitis, common in Attica. Pericles called Aegina the
eyesore of the Piraeus (Aristotle, *Rhet.* III, 10).

her salt-water sisters in England, and multiplied it from a mole-hill of sand to a cloud-crowned Mount Teneriffe, abbreviately and meetly according to my old Sarum plain-song [258] I have harped upon, and that, if there were no other certificate or instance of the inlinked consanguinity twixt him and Lady Lucar,[259] is *instar mille*,[260] worth a million of witnesses, to exemplify the riches of him. The poets were trivial that set up Helen's face for such a top-gallant summer maypole for men to gaze at, and strouted [261] it out so in their buskined braves [262] of her beauty, whereof the only Circe's Heypass and Repass [263] was that it drew a thousand ships to Troy, to fetch her back with a pestilence. Wise men in Greece in the meanwhile to swagger so about a whore!

Eloquious [264] hoary-beard father Nestor, you were one of them, and you, Master Ulysses, the prudent dwarf of Pallas, another, of whom it is iliadized that your very nose dropped sugar candy, and that your spittle was honey. Natalis Comes,[265] if he were above ground, would be sworn upon it. As loud a ringing miracle as the attractive melting eye of that strumpet can we supply therewith of our dappert Pie-mont Huldrick [266] Herring, which draweth more barques to Yarmouth Bay than her beauty did to Troy. Oh, he is attended upon most Babylonically; and Xerxes so over-cloyed not the Hellespont with his foists, galleys and brigan-dines, as he mantleth the narrow seas with his retinue, being not much behind, in the check-roll of his janissaries and contributories, with eagle-soaring Bullingbroke, that at his removing of household into banishment (as Father Froissart

258. Form of service in use before publication of the English *Prayer Book*.

259. Lucre (after a character in *Three Ladies of London* by R. Wilson).

260. 'Like a thousand'. ₁   261. Strutted.

262. *buskined braves*: Swaggering style.

263. *Circe's Heypass and Repass*: Magician's hocus pocus.

264. Eloquent.

265. Sixteenth-century Italian author of the standard work on mythology.

266. St Ulrich, on whose day fish were offered in churches.

threaps us down [267]) was accompanied with 40,000 men, women and children weeping, from London to the land's end at Dover. A colony of critical Zenos,[268] should they sinnow [269] their syllogistical cluster-fists [270] in one bundle to confute and disprove moving, were they, but during the time they might lap up a mass of buttered fish, in Yarmouth one fishing, such a violent motion of toiling myrmidons [271] they should be spectators of and a confused stirring to and fro of a Lepantalike hoste of undefatigable flood-bickerers and foam-curbers, that they would not move or stir one foot till they had declaimed and abjured their bedrid spital [272] positions. In verament and sincerity, I never crowded through this confluent herring fair, but it put me in memory of the great year of jubilee in Edward the Third's time, in which it is sealed and delivered under the hands of a public notary, three hundred thousand people roamed to Rome for purgatory pills and paternal venial benedictions, and the ways beyond sea were so bunged up with your daily orators or beadsmen and your crutched or crouchant friars or cross-creepers and barefoot penitentiaries, that a snail could not wriggle in her horns betwixt them. Small things we may express by great, and great by small, though the greatness of the red herring be not small (as small a hop-on-my-thumb he seemeth). It is with him as with great personages, which from their high estate and not their high statures propagate the elevate titles of their gogmagognes.[273] Cast [274] his state who will, and they shall find it to be very high-coloured (as high-coloured as his complexion if I said there were not a pimple to be abated). In Yarmouth he hath set up his state house, where one quarter of a year he keeps open court for Jews and Gentiles.

267. Contradicts us.
268. Zeno of Citium illustrated a point of argument by opening and closing his fist, and Zeno of Elea argued the unreality of motion.
269. Sinew, clench.
270. Close-fisted, grasping folk.
271. Warriors who took Troy.
272. Hospital.
273. Greatness.   274. Reckon up.

To fetch him in,* in Trojan equipage, some of every of the Christcross alphabet [275] of outlandish cosmopoli furrow up the rugged brine, and sweep through his tumultuous ooze, will or nill he, rather than in tendering their allegiance they should be benighted with tardity. For our English Mikrokosmos or Phoenician Dido's hide of ground,[276] no shire, county, count palatine,[277] or quarter of it, but rigs out some oaken squadron or other to waft him along Cleopatrian † Olympickly ‡ and not the diminutivest nook or cruise of them but is parturient [278] of the like super-officiousness,§ arming forth though it be but a catch or pink,[279] no capabler than a rundlet [280] or washing bowl to imp [281] the wings of his convoy. Holy Saint Taubard, in what droves the gouty-bagged Londoners hurry down and dye the watchet [282] air of an iron russet hue with the dust that they raise in hot-spurred rowelling it on [283] to perform compliments unto him. One beck more to the baillies of the cinq ports, whom I were a ruder barbarian than Smill, the Prince of the Crims and Nagayans,[284] if in this action I should forget (having had good cheer at their tables more than once or twice whiles I loitered in this paragonless [285] fish town). City,

* The fatal wooden horse at Troy fetched in with such pomp.
  † Cleopatra's glorious sailing to meet Antony.
  ‡ The solemn bringing of the champions at Olympus.
  § Tugging forth by the strength of their arms.

275. The figure of the cross was commonly placed at the beginning of the alphabet in the hornbooks.

276. The 'bull's hide' of ground purchased by Dido when she fled from Tyre to Carthage (*Aeneid*, I, 367–8).

277. County palatine, dignitaries attached to the Crown, such as the Earl of Chester and the Duke of Lancaster.

278. Pregnant, productive.

279. Small fishing boat.   280. Small barrel.

281. Strengthen (by engrafting feathers).

282. Pale blue.

283. Spurring on (rowel: the extremity of the spur).

284. Hackluyt refers to a ruthless 'Tartar prince called Murse Smille', *Principal Navigations*, 1589.

285. Unsurpassed, peerless.

town, country, Robin Hood and Little John, and who not,
are industrious and careful to squire and safe conduct him
in; but in ushering him in, next to the baillies of Yarmouth,
they trot before all, and play the provost marshals, helping
to keep good rule the first three weeks of his ingress, and
never leave roaring it out with their brazen horn as long as
they stay, of the freedoms and immunities sourcing from
him. Being thus entered or brought in, the consistorians [286]
or settled standers of Yarmouth commence intestate [287] wars
amongst themselves who should give him the largest hospitality, and gather about him as flocking to handsel [288]
him and strike him good luck as the sweetkin madams did
about valiant Sir Walter Manny, the martial tutor unto the
Black Prince (he that built Charterhouse), who being upon
the point of a hazardous journey into France, either to win
the horse or lose the saddle, as it runs in the proverb,[289]
and taking his leave at Court in a suit of mail from top to
toe, all the ladies clung about him and would not let him
stretch out a step, till they had enfettered him with their
variable favours, and embroidered over his armour like a
gaudy summer mead, with their scarves, bracelets, chains,
ouches;[290] in generous reguerdonment [291] whereof he sacra-
mentally obliged himself, that, had the French King as
many giants in his country as he hath pears or grapes, and
they stood all enranged on the shore to interdict his dis-
embarking, through the thickest thorny quickset of them he
would pierce, or be tossed up to heaven on their spears, but,
in honour of those debonair Idalian nymphs and their
spangled trappings, he would be the first man should set
foot in his kingdom, or unsheathe steel against him. As he
promised, so was his* manly blade's execution, and, in

* Manny *quasi* Manly, and from him I take it the Mannies
of Kent are descended.

286. Inhabitants.
287. Presumably an error, probably 'intestine', internal.
288. Greet with a gift as token of good will.
289. 'What they got in the bridle, they lost in the saddle.'
290. Clasps, brooches.   291. Recompense.

emulation of him, whole herds of knights and gentlemen closed up their right eyes with a piece of silk every one, and vowed never to uncover them or let them see light till, in the advancement of their mistress's beauties, they had enacted with their brandished bilbowblades [292] some chivalrous Bellerophon's [293] trick at arms, that from Salomons Islands to St Magnus' corner [294] might cry clang again. Oh it was a brave age then, and so it is ever, where there are offensive wars, and not defensive, and men fight for the spoil and not in fear to be spoiled, and are as lions seeking out their prey, and not as sheep that lie still whiles they are preyed on.

The red herring is a legate of peace, and so abhorrent from unnatural bloodshed that if, in his quarrel or bandying who should harbing him, there be any hewing or slashing or trials of life and death, there where that hangman embowelling is, his pursuivants or baillies return *non est inventus*; [295] out of one bailiwick he is fled, never to be fastened on there more. The Scottish jockies [296] or redshanks [297] (so surnamed of their immoderate raunching [298] up the red shanks or red herrings) uphold and make good the same. Their clack or gabbling to this purport: '*How*, in diebus illis,[299] *when Robert de Breaux,*[300] *their gud king, sent his dear heart to the haly land, for reason he caud not gang thider himself, (or then or thereabout or whilom before or whilom after, it matters not) they had the staple or fruits of the herring in their road or channel, till a foul ill feud arose amongst his sectaries and servitors, and there was*

292. Finely tempered swords of Bilbao.
293. Owner of Pegasus, slayer of the Chimera.
294. By London Bridge, a centre for proclamations.
295. The form in which a sheriff reported his inability to make a required arrest, the man not being within his jurisdiction or bailiwick.
296. Jocks, lads.
297. Supposedly because the highlanders' legs were reddened by exposure.
298. Cutting, tearing.
299. Once upon a time (in those days).
300. Robert the Bruce.

mickle tule,[301] *and a black world, and a deal of whin-yards* [302] *drawn about him, and many sackless* [303] *wights and praty barns run through the tender weambs, and fra thence ne sarry tale of a herring in thilk sound they caud grip.*' This language or parley have I usurped from some of the deftest lads in all Edinborough town, which it will be no impeachment for the wisest to turn loose for a truth, without any diffident wrestling with it.

The sympathy thereunto in our frothy streams we have took napping. Wherefore, without any further bolstering or backing, this Scottish history may bear palm.[304] And if any further bolstering or backing be required, it is evident by the confession of the six-hundred Scottish witches executed in Scotland at Bartelmewtide was twelve-month, that in Yarmouth Road they were altogether in a plump [305] on Christmas Eve was two year, when the great flood was, and there stirred up such tornadoes and furicanoes of tempests, in envy (as I collect) that the staple of the herring from them was translated to Yarmouth, as will be spoke of there whiles any winds or storms and tempests chafe and puff in the lower region.[306]

They and all the seafaring towns under our temperate zone of peace may well envy her prosperity, as a general envy encompassing it. Kings, noblemen, it cleaves unto, that walk upright and are anything happy; and even amongst mean artificers it thrusts in his foot, one of them envying another if he have a knack above another, or his gains be greater, and, if in his art they cannot disgrace him, they will find a starting hole in his life that shall confound him. For example: there is * a mathematical smith or artificer in Yarmouth that hath made a lock and key that weighs but three farthings, and a chest with a pair of knit gloves in

* John Thurkle.

301. Grief (*deuil*). 302. Short-swords.
303. Innocent. 304. Win applause.
305. Flock, shoal.
306. On earth, as opposed to 'the upper air' which was unaffected by storms.

417

the till of it, whose whole poise is no more but a groat. Now, I do not think but all the smiths in London, Norwich or York, if they heard of him, would envy him if they could not outwork him.

Hydra herring will have everything * Sybarite-dainty, where he lays knife aboard, or he will fly them, he will not look upon them. Stately born, stately sprung he is, the best blood of the Ptolemies no statelier, and with what state he hath been used from his swaddling clouts I have reiterated unto you, and, which is a not-above-*ela,* stately Hyperion or the lordly sun, the most rutilant [308] planet of the seven,[309] in Lent when Heralius [310] Herring enters into his chief reign and sceptredom, skippeth and danceth the goat's jump [311] on the earth for joy of his entrance. Do but mark him on your walls any morning at that season, how he sallies and lavoltoes,[312] and you will say I am no fabler. Of so eye-bewitching deaurate [313] ruddy dye is the skincoat of this lantsgrave,[314] that happy is that nobleman who for his colours in armoury can nearest imitate his chimical [315] temper. Nay, which is more, if a man should tell you that god Hymen's saffron-coloured robe were made of nothing but red herrings' skins, you would hardly believe him. Such is the obduracy and hardness of heart of a number of infidels in these days, they will tear herrings out of their skins as fast as one of these exchequer-tellers can turn over a heap of money; but his virtues, both exterior and interior, they have no more taste of than of a dish of stockfish.

Somewhere I have snatched up a jest of a king that was

* The Sybarites [307] never would make any banquet under a twelve month's warning.

307. Inhabitants of a city in S. Italy, proverbial for luxury.
308. Shining.
309. i.e. the spheres.
310. Meaning unknown.
311. A capriol, a jump which horses could be trained to perform.
312. Dances the lavolta.
313. Gilded, golden.
314. Landgrave, a German count or prince.
315. Alchemical.

desirous to try what kind of flesh-meat was most nutritive-prosperous with a man's body, and to that purpose he commanded four hungry fellows in four separate rooms by themselves to be shut up for a year and a day, whereof the first should have his gut bombasted with beef and nothing else till he cried 'Hold, belly, hold,' and so the second to have his paunch crammed with pork, the third with mutton, and the fourth with veal. At the twelvemonth's end they were brought before him, and he enquired of every one orderly what he had eat. Therewith out stepped the stallfed foreman that had been at host with the fat oxe, and was grown as fat as an oxe with tiring on the sirloins, and baft [316] in his face 'Beef, beef, beef'. Next the Norfolk hog or the swine-worrier, who had got him a sagging pair of cheeks like a sow's paps that give suck, with the plentiful mast set before him, came lazily waddling in and puffed out 'Pork, pork, pork'. Then the sly sheep-biter issued into the midst, and summer-setted [317] and flipflapt [318] it twenty times above ground, as light as a feather, and cried 'Mitton, mitton, mitton'. Last the Essex calf or lagman, [319] who had lost the calves of his legs with gnawing on the horselegs, shuddering and quaking, limped after, with a visage as pale as a piece of white leather, and a staff in his hand and a kerchief on his head, and very lamentably vociferated 'Veal, veal, veal'. A witty toy of his noble Grace it was, and different from the recipes and prescriptions of our modern physicians, that to any sick languishers, if they be able to waggle their chaps, propound veal for one of the highest nourishers.

But had his principality gone through with fish as well as flesh, and put a man to livery with the red herring but as long, he would have come in * 'Hurrey, [320] Hurrey, Hur-

----

* As much to say as Urrey, Urrey, Urrey, one of the principal places where the herring is caught.

316. Barked.   317. Somersaulted.
318. Made a series of somersaults.
319. The last man.
320. Harrow; a cry of denunciation.

rey', as if he were harrying and chasing his enemies, and Bevis of Hampton,[321] after he been out of his diet, should not have been able to have stood before him. A choleric parcel of food it is, that whoso ties himself to rack and manger to for five summers and five winters, he shall beget a child that will be a soldier and a commander before he hath cast his first teeth, and an Alexander, a Julius Caesar, a Scanderbeg,[322] a Barbarossa he will prove ere he aspire to thirty.

But to think on a red herring, such a hot stirring meat it is, is enough to make the cravenest dastard proclaim fire and sword against Spain. The most intenerate [323] virgin-wax phisnomy, that taints his throat with the least rib of it, it will embrawn and iron-crust his flesh, and harden his soft bleeding veins as stiff and robustious as branches of coral. The art of kindling of fires that is practised in the smoking or parching of him is old dog [324] against the plague. Too foul-mouthed I am to becollow [325] or becollier [326] him with such chimney sweeping attributed of smoking and parching. Will you have the secret of it? This well-meaning *Pater patriae*, and providitor and supporter of Yarmouth, which is the lock and key of Norfolk, looking pale and sea-sick at his first landing, those that be his stewards or necessariest men about him, whirl him in a thought out of the raw cold air, to some stew or hot-house, where immuring himself for three or four days, when he unhouseth him or hath cast off his shell, he is as freckled about the gills, and looks as red as a fox, clum,[327] and is more surly to be spoken with than ever he was before, and, like Lais of Corinth,[328] will smile upon no man except he may have his own asking. There are that number of herrings vented out of Yarmouth every year,

321. Popular verse-romance, early fourteenth century.

322. Kastriota, fifteenth-century Albanian patriot (derived from 'Iskander-Bey', the Turkish name for him).

323. Tender.   324. Skilled.

325. Blacken.

326. Impute the dirtiness of the collier's trade, commonly reckoned to involve much cheating.

327. (?) Silent.   328. A courtesan.

though the grammarians make no plural number of Halec, as not only they are more by two thousand last than our own land can spend, but they fill all other lands, to whom at their own prices they sell them, and happy is he that can first lay hold of them.

And how can it be otherwise? For if Cornish pilchards, otherwise called fumadoes, taken on the shore of Cornwall from July to November, be so saleable as they are in France, Spain and Italy, which are but counterfeits to the red herring, as copper to gold, or ockamie [329] to silver, much more their elbows itch for joy, when they meet with the true gold, the true red herring itself. No true flying fish but he, or if there be, that fish never flies but when his wings are wet, and the red herring flies best when his wings are dry. Throughout Belgia, High Germany, France, Spain and Italy he flies, and up into Greece and Africa, South and South-west estritch-like, walks his stations,[330] and the sepulchre palmers or pilgrims, because he is so portable, fill their scrips [331] with them; yea no dispraise to the blood of the Ottomans, the Nabuchedonesor of Constantinople and giantly Antaeus,[332] that never yawneth nor neezeth,[333] but he affrighteth the whole earth, gormandizing, muncheth him up for imperial dainties, and will not spare his idol Mahomet a bit with him, no, not though it would fetch him from heaven forty years before his time; whence, with his dove that he taught to peck barley out of his ear, and brought his disciples into a fool's paradise that it was the Holy Ghost in her similitude, he is expected every minute to descend, but I am afraid as he was troubled with the falling sickness in his lifetime, in self manner it took him in his mounting up to heaven and so *ab inferno nulla redemptio*,[334] he is fallen backward into hell and they are never more like to hear of him.

329. Alchemy.   330. Goes his rounds.
331. Wallets, satchels.
332. Libyan giant, defeated by Hercules.
333. Sneezes.
334. 'There is no redemption from the inferno.'

Whiles I am shuffling and cutting with these long-coated Turks, would any antiquary would explicate unto me this remblere [335] or quiddity,[336] whether those turbanto * grout-heads,[337] that hang all men by the throats on iron hooks, even as our towers hang all their herrings by the throats on wooden spits, first learned it of our herring men, or our herring men of them. Why the Alcheronship of that Belzabub of Saracens, Rhinoceros Zelim aforesaid, should so much delight in this shiny animal, I cannot guess, except he had a desire to imitate Midas in eating of gold, or Dionysius in stripping Jupiter out of his golden coat. And, to shoot my fool's bolt amongst you, that fable of Midas eating gold had no other shadow or inclusive pith in it, but he was of a queasy stomach and nothing he could fancy but this new-found gilded fish, which Bacchus at his request gave him (though it were not known here two thousand year after, for it was the delicates of the gods, and no mortal food till of late years). Midas, unexperienced of the nature of it, for he was a fool that had ass's ears, snapped it up at one blow, and because in the boiling or seething of it in his maw he felt it commotion a little and upbraid him, he thought he had eaten gold indeed, and thereupon directed his orisons to Bacchus afresh, to help it out of his crop again, and have mercy upon him and recover him. He, propensive inclining to Midas' devotion in everything, in lieu of the friendly hospitalities drunken Silenus, his companion, found at his hands when he strayed from him, bad him but go wash himself in the river Pactolus, that is, go wash it down soundly with flowing cups of wine, and he should be as well as ever he was. By the turning of the river Pactolus into gold, after he had rinsed and clarified himself in it (which is the close of the fiction) is signified that, in regard of that blessed operation of the juice of the grape in him, from that

---

* Turbanto, the great lawn roll Turks wear about their heads.

335. Puzzle, riddle.   336. Quibble.
337. Turbaned blockheads.

day forth in nothing but golden cups he would drink or quaff it, whereas in wooden mazers[338] and Agathocles'[339] earthen stuff they trillild it off before, and that was the first time that any golden cups were used.

Follow this tract in expounding the tale of Dionysius[340] and Jupiter, and you cannot go amiss. No such Jupiter, no such golden-coated image was there; but it was a plain golden-coated herring, without welt or gard, whom, for the strangeness of it, they (having never beheld a beast of that hue before) in their temples enshrined for a God, and insomuch as Jupiter had shown them such slippery pranks more than once or twice, in shifting himself into sundry shapes, and raining himself down in gold into a woman's lap, they thought this too might be a trick of youth in him, to alter himself into the form of this golden Scaliger[341] or red herring. And therefore, as to Jupiter, they fell down on their marybones,[342] and lift up their hay-cromes[343] unto him. Now King Dionysius being a good wise fellow, for he was afterwards a schoolmaster and had played the coachman to Plato and spit in Aristippus the philosopher's face many a time and oft, no sooner entered the temple and saw him sit under his canopy so budgely,[344] with a whole gold-smith's stall of jewels and rich offerings at his feet, but to him he stepped and plucked him from his state with a wennion,[345] then drawing out his knife most iracundi-ously[346] at one whisk lopped off his head, and stripped him out of his golden demy or mandillion,[347] and flayed him, and thrust him down his pudding-house[348] at a gob. Yet

338. Bowls, drinking-cups.
339. Tyrant of Syracuse, 361–289. B.C.
340. Tyrant of Syracuse, fourth century B.C., notorious for plunder-ing shrines.
341. Joseph Justice Scaliger (1540–1609), or Julius Caesar Scaliger (1484–1558), both brilliant scholars.
342. Marrowbones, knees.
343. Hay-rakes.   344. Solemnly.
345. With a vengeance.   346. Angrily.
347. *Demy or mandillion*: Sleeveless coat.   348. Stomach.

long it prospered not with him (so revengeful a just Jupiter is the red herring), for as he tare him from his throne, and uncased him of his habiliments, so, in small devolution of years, from his throne was he chased, and clean stripped out of his royalty, and glad to go play the schoolmaster at Corinth, and take a rod in his hand for his sceptre, and horn-book pigmies for his subjects, *id est* (as I intimated some dozen lines before) of a tyrant to become a frowning pedant or schoolmaster.

Many of you have read these stories, and could never pick out any such English. No more would you of the Ismael Persians' Haly, or Mortus Ali,[349] they worship, whose true etimology is, *mortuum halec*, a dead red herring and no other, though by corruption of speech they false dialect and miss-sound it. Let any Persian oppugn [350] this, and, in spite of his hairy tuft or love-lock he leaves on the top of his crown, to be pulled up or pulleyed up to heaven by, I'll set my foot to his and fight it out with him, that their fopperly [351] god is not so good as a red herring. To recount *ab ovo*,[352] or from the church-book [353] of his birth how the herring first came to be a fish, and then how he came to be King of Fishes and gradationately how from white to red he changed, would require as massy a tome as Holinshed.[354] But in half a pennyworth of paper I will epitomize them. Let me see, hath anybody in Yarmouth heard of Leander and Hero, of whom divine Musaeus sung, and a diviner muse than him, Kit Marlowe? [355]

Two faithful lovers they were, as every apprentice in Paul's churchyard [356] will tell you for your love, and sell you for your money. The one dwelt at Abidos in Asia, which was

349. Whom, according to Hackluyt, the Persians regarded as Mahomet's true successor.

350. Oppose, controvert. 351. Foolish.

352. 'From the egg'. 353. Parish register.

354. Raphael Holinshead, author of *Chronicles of England, Scotland and Ireland* (1577, enlarged 1586).

355. Marlowe's *Hero and Leander*, the chief source of which was the poem by Musaeus, a fifth-century Alexandrian.

356. Where booksellers had their stalls.

Leander; the other, which was Hero, his mistress or Delia, at Sestos in Europe, and she was a pretty pinkany [357] and Venus' priest. And but an arm of the sea divided them; it divided them and it divided them not, for over that arm of the sea could be made a long arm. In their parents the most division rested, and their towns, like Yarmouth and Leystoffe, were still at wrig-wrag, and sucked from their mothers' teats serpentine hatred one against each other. Which drove Leander when he durst not deal above-board, or be seen aboard any ship, to sail to his lady dear, to play the didopper [358] and ducking water-spaniel [359] to swim to her, nor that in the day but by owl-light.

What will not blind night do for blind Cupid? And what will not blind Cupid do in the night, which is his blindman's holiday? [360] By the sea on the other side stood Hero's tower, such another tower as one of our Irish castles, that is not so wide as a belfry and a cobbler cannot jert [361] out his elbows in: a cage or pigeonhouse, romthsome [362] enough to comprehend her and the toothless trot [363] her nurse who was her only chatmate and chambermaid, consultively [364] by her parents being so encloistered from resort that she might live chaste vestal priest to Venus, the Queen of Unchastity. She would none of that, she thanked them, for she was better provided, and that which they thought served their turn best of sequestering her from company, served her turn best to embrace the company she desired. Fate is a spaniel that you cannot beat from you; the more you think to cross it, the more you bless it and further it.

Neither her father nor mother vowed chastity when she was begot. Therefore she thought they begat her not to live chaste, and either she must prove herself a bastard, or show

---

357. Pigsney, term of endearment.

358. Dabchick, a bird supposed to hide under water.

359. *Ducking water spaniel*: 'Used in falconry to put up water birds' (M.).

360. Dusk. 361. Jerk.

362. Spacious, roomy. 363. Hag, beldame.

364. Deliberately.

herself like them. Of Leander you may write upon, and it is written upon, she liked well; and for all he was a naked man and clean despoiled to the skin when he crawled through the brackish suds to scale her tower, all the strength of it could not hold him out. Oh, ware a naked man. Cithereare's nuns [365] have no power to resist him; and some such quality is ascribed to the lion. Were he never so naked when he came to her, because he should not scare her she found a means to cover him in her bed; and for he might not take cold after his swimming, she lay close by him to keep him warm. This scuffling or bo-peep in the dark they had awhile without weam or brack,[366] and the old nurse (as there be three things seldom in their right kind till they be old: a bawd, a witch and a midwife) executed the huckstering [367] office of her years very charily and circumspectly, till their sliding stars revolted from them. And then, for seven days together, the wind and the Hellespont contended which should howl louder. The waves dashed up to the clouds, and the clouds on the other side spit and drivelled upon them as fast.

Hero wept as trickling from the heavens, to think that heaven should so divorce them. Leander stormed worse than the storms, that by them he should be so restrained from his Cynthia. At Sestos was his soul, and he could not abide to tarry in Abidos. Rain, snow, hail or blow it how it could, into the pitchy Hellespont he leapt when the moon and all her torch-bearers were afraid to peep out their heads. But he was peppered for it; he had as good have took meat, drink and leisure, for the churlish frampold [368] waters gave him his bellyful of fish-broth, ere out of their laundry or wash-house they would grant him his coquet [369] or *transire*;[370] and

365. Harlots (Cytherea = Venus, Venus' nun = prostitute).
366. Without let or hindrance.
367. Dealing in petty commerce.
368. Bad-tempered.
369. Warrant certifying that goods have passed through the customs.
370. (Permission) to cross.

not only that, but they sealed him his *quietus est* [371] for curveting [372] any more to the maiden tower, and tossed his dead carcass, well bathed or parboiled, to the sandy threshold of his leman or orange,[373] for a disjune or morning breakfast. All that livelong night could she not sleep, she was so troubled with the rheum, which was a sign she should hear of some drowning. Yet towards cock-crowing she caught a little slumber, and then she dreamed that Leander and she were playing at checkstone [374] with pearls in the bottom of the sea.

You may see dreams are not so vain as they are preached of, though not in vain preachers inveigh against them and bend themselves out of the peoples' minds to exhale their foolish superstition. The rheum is student's disease, and who study most dream most. The labouring men's hands glow and blister after their day's work; the glowing and blistering of our brains after our day-labouring cogitations are dreams, and those dreams are reeking vapours of no impression if our mateless couches be not half empty. Hero hoped, and therefore she dreamed (as all hope is but a dream). Her hope was where her heart was, and her heart winding and turning with the wind, that might wind her heart-of-gold to her or else turn him from her. Hope and fear both combatted in her, and both these are wakeful, which made her at break of day (what an old crone is the day that is so long a-breaking) to unloop her luket or casement to look whence the blasts came, or what gait or pace the sea kept; when forthwith her eyes bred her eye-sore, the first white whereon their transpiercing arrows stuck being the breathless corpse of Leander. With the sudden contemplation of this piteous spectacle of her love, sodden to haddock's meat, her sorrow could not but be indefinite, if her delight in him were but indifferent; and there is no woman but delights in sorrow, or she would not use it so lightly for everything.

371. Release from life (literally 'he is quit').
372. Leaping (as on horseback).
373. Pun on leman, lover.
374. Children's game played with pebbles.

Down she ran in her loose nightgown, and her hair about her ears (even as Semiramis [375] ran out with her lie-pot [376] in her hand, and her black dangling tresses about her shoulders with her ivory comb ensnarled in them, when she heard that Babylon was taken), and thought to have kissed his dead corpse alive again, but as on his blue-jellied-sturgeon lips she was about to clap one of those warm plaisters,[377] boisterous woolpacks of ridged tides came rolling in and raught him from her (with a mind belike to carry him back to Abidos). At that she became a frantic Bacchanal outright, and made no more bones, but sprang after him, and so resigned up her priesthood, and left work for Musaeus and Kit Marlowe.[378] The gods, and gods and goddesses all on a row, bread and crow,[379] from Ops to Pomona, the first apple-wife, were so dumped [380] with this miserable wrack that they began to abhor all moisture for the sea's sake. And Jupiter could not endure Ganymede, his cup-bearer, to come in his presence, both for the dislike he bore to Neptune's baleful liquor, as also that he was so like to Leander. The sun was so in his mumps upon it, that it was almost noon before he could go to cart that day, and then with so ill a will he went, that he had thought to have toppled his burning car or hurry-curry [381] into the sea (as Phaeton did) to scorch it and dry it up; and at night, when he was begrimed with dust and sweat of his journey, he would not descend as he was wont to wash him in the ocean, but under a tree laid him down to rest in his clothes all night, and so did the scowling moon under another fast by him, which of that are behighted [382] the trees of the sun and moon, and are the same that Sir John Mandeville tells us [383] he spoke

375. Queen of Nineveh after Ninus' death.

376. Containing hair-lotion.

377. Plasters (as for healing a wound).

378. Though in fact this later part of *Hero and Leander* was written by Chapman.

379. *bread and crow*: Meaning unknown.

380. Depressed. 381. Fast-moving chariot. 382. Called.

383. In *The Voyage of Sir John Mandeville* (c. 1360), a compilation of travel stories sometimes attributed to Jean d'Outremeuse.

with, and that spoke to Alexander. Venus, for Hero was her priest, and Juno Lucina, the midwife's goddess, for she was now quickened and cast away by the cruelty of Aeolus, took bread and salt and ate it that they would be smartly revenged on that truculent jailer, and they forgot it not, for Venus made his son and his daughter to commit incest together. Lucina, that there might be some lasting characters of his shame, helped to bring her to bed of a goodly boy, and Aeolus bolting out all this heaped murder upon murder.

The dint of destiny could not be repealed in the reviving of Hero and Leander, but their heavenly-hoods in their synod thus decreed, that, for they were either of them seaborderers and drowned in the sea, still to the sea they must belong, and be divided in habitation after death as they were in their lifetime. Leander, for that in a cold dark testy night he had his passport to Charon, they terminated to the unquiet cold coast of Iceland, where half the year is nothing but murk-light, and to that fish translated him which of us is termed ling. Hero, for that she was pagled[384] and timpanized,[385] and sustained two losses under one, they footballed their heads together, and protested to make the stem of her loins of all fishes the flaunting Fabian or Palmerin[386] of England, which is Cadwallader Herring; and, as their meetings were but seldom, and not so oft as welcome, so but seldom should they meet in the heel of the week at the best men's tables, upon Fridays and Saturdays, the holy time of Lent exempted, and then they might be at meat and meal for seven weeks together.

The nurse or Mother Mampudding[387] that was a-cowering on the back side whiles these things were a-tragedizing, led by the scritch or outcry to the prospect of this sorrowful

384. Pregnant.
385. Swollen.
386. A reference to a Spanish romance by Luis Hurtado.
387. M. quotes Stow on a sailors' tavern: 'Amongst others, she, Mother Mumpudding (as they termed her), for many years kept this house.'

heigh-ho, as soon as, through the ravelled buttonholes of her blear eyes, she had sucked in and received such a revelation of Doomsday, and that she saw her mistress mounted a-cockhorse and hoisted away to hell or to heaven on the backs of those rough-headed ruffians, down she sunk to the earth, as dead as a door-nail, and never mumped crust after. Whereof their supernalities,[388] having a drop or two of pity left of the huge hogshead of tears they spent for Hero and Leander, seemed to be something sorry, though they could not weep for it, and because they would be sure to have a medicine that should make them weep at all times, to that kind of grain they turned her which we call mustard-seed, as well for she was a shrewish snappish bawd, that would bite off a man's nose with an answer and had rheumatic sore eyes that ran always, as that she might accompany Hero and Leander after death, as in her lifetime. And hence it is that mustard bites a man so by the nose and makes him weep and water his plants when he tasteth it; and that Hero and Leander, the red herring and ling, never come to the board without mustard, their waiting-maid; and, if you mark it, mustard looks of the tanned-wainscot hue of such a withered wrinklefaced beldam as she was that was altered thereinto. Loving Hero, however altered, had a smack of love still, and therefore to the coast of Loving-land (to Yarmouth near adjoining and within her liberties of Kirtley Road) she accustomed to come in pilgrimage every year, but contentions arising there, and she remembering the event of the contentions betwixt Sestos and Abidos, that wrought both Leander's death and hers, shunneth it of late, and retireth more northwards. So she shunneth unquiet Humber, because Elstred [389] was drowned there, and the Scots Seas, as before, and every other sea where any blood hath been spilt, for her own sea's sake, that spilt her sweet sweetheart's blood and hers.

Whippet, turn to a new lesson, and strike we up 'John

388. The supernal gods.
389. The daughter of Humber, drowned in the Severn. Humber himself was drowned in the river named after him.

for the King', or tell how the herring scrambled up to be king of all fishes. So it fell upon a time and tide, though not upon a holiday, a falconer bringing over certain hawks out of Ireland, and airing them above hatches on ship-board, and giving them stones to cast and scour,[390] one of them broke loose from his fist ere he was aware; which being in her kingdom when she was got upon her wings, and finding herself empty gorged after her casting, up to heaven she towered to seek prey, but there being no game to please her, down she fluttered to the sea again, and a speckled fish playing above the water, at it she strook, mistaking it for a partridge. A shark or tuberon, that lay gaping for the flying fish hard by, what did me he, but, seeing the mark fall so just in his mouth, chopped aloft and snapped her up, bells and all at a mouthful. The news of this murderous act, carried by the king's fisher to the ears of the land fowls, there was nothing but 'arm, arm, arm, to sea, to sea', swallow and titmouse, to take chastisement of that trespass of blood and death committed against a peer of their blood royal. Preparation was made, the muster taken, the leaders allotted, and had their bills to take up pay. An old goshawk for general was appointed; for marshal of the field, a sparrowhawk, whom for no further desert they put in office, but because it was one of their lineage had sustained that wrong, and they thought they would be more implacable in condoling and commiserating. The peacocks with their spotted coats and affrighting voices for heralds they pricked [391] and enlisted, and the cockadoodling cocks for their trumpeters (look upon any cock and look upon any trumpeter, and see if he look not as red as a cock after his trumpeting, and a cock as red as he after his crowing). The kestrils or windfuckers that, filling themselves with wind, fly against the wind evermore, for their full-sailed standardbearers; the cranes for pikemen, and the woodcocks for demilances,[392] and so of the rest every one according to that place by nature he was most

390. *to cast and scour*: To make them vomit.
391. Chose.
392. Those armed with short lances.

apt for. Away to the land's end they trig,[393] all the sky-bred chirpers of them. When they came there, *aequora nos terrent et ponti tristis imago*,[394] they had wings of goodwill to fly with, but no webs on their feet to swim with; for, except the waterfowls had mercy upon them and stood their faithful confederates and back-friends,[395] on their backs to transport them, they might return home like good fools and gather straws to build their nests, or fall to their old trade of picking worms. In sum, to the water fouls unanimately they recourse, and besought duck and drake, swan and goose, halcyons and sea-pies, cormorants and sea-gulls, of their oary assistance and aidful furtherance in this action.

They were not obdurate to be entreated, though they had little cause to revenge the hawks' quarrel from them, having received so many high displeasures and slaughters and rapines of their race; yet in a general prosecution private feuds they trod underfoot, and submitted their endeavours to be at their limitation in everything.

The puffin, that is half-fish half-flesh (a John Indifferent,[396] and an Ambodexter [397] betwixt either), bewrayed this conspiracy to Protaeus' herds or the fraternity of fishes; which the greater giants of Russia and Iceland, as the whale, the sea-horse, the norse, the wasserman,[398] the dolphin, the grampoys, fleered and jeered at as a ridiculous danger, but the lesser pigmies and spawn of them thought it meet to provide for themselves betime, and elect a king amongst them that might derain [399] them to battle, and under whose colours they might march against these birds of a feather, that had so colleagued themselves to destroy them.

Who this king should be, beshackled their wits and laid them a-dry ground everyone. No ravening fish they would

---

393. Trudge.
394. 'The seas terrify us and the sad aspect of the deep' (Ovid).
395. Here meaning allies, backers.
396. Jack o' both sides (M.).
397. Vice character in the play *Cambyses*.
398. Merman.
399. Draw up.

put in arms, for fear after he had averted their foes and
fleshed himself in blood, for interchange of diet, he would
raven up them.

Some politic delegatory Scipio, or witty-pated Petito,[400]
like the heir of Laertes *per aspherisin*,[401] Ulysses (well-
known unto them by his prolixious seawandering and dancing on their topless tottering hills), they would single forth, if
it might be, whom they might depose when they list, if he
should begin to tyrannize, and such a one as of himself were
able to make a sound party if all failed, and bid base to [402]
the enemy with his own kindred and followers.

None won the day in this but the herring, whom all their
clamorous suffrages saluted, with *Vive le Roy*, 'God save the
King, God save the King', save only the plaice and the butt,
that made wry mouths at him, and for their mocking have
wry mouths ever since, and the herring ever since wears a
coronet on his head, in token that he is as he is. Which had
the worst end of the staff in that sea journey or canvazado,[403]
or whether some fowler with his nets (as this host of feather-
mongers were getting up to ride double) involved or entangled them, or the water fowls played them false (as there
is no more love betwixt them than betwixt sailors and land
soldiers), and threw them off their backs, and let them drown
when they were launched into the deep, I leave to some Al-
fonsus,[404] Poggius [405] or Aesope to unwrap, for my pen is
tired in it. But this is notorious: the herring, from that time
to this, hath gone with an army, and never stirs abroad
without it. And when he stirs abroad with it, he sends out his
scouts or sentinels before him, that oftentimes are intercepted, and by their parti-coloured liveries descried, whom
the mariners after they have took, use in this sort: eight

400. Meaning unknown.

401. M. suggests this means 'in the abstract', Laertes having little
property to bequeath Ulysses.

402. Bring low.

403. *journey or canvazado*: Day's fighting or sudden attack.

404. Petrus Alfunsi (1062–1110) whose tales, *Disciplina Clericalis*,
were sometimes printed with Aesop's Fables.

405. Poggio, another writer of fables.

or nine times they swinge them about the mainmast, and bid them bring them so many last [406] of herrings as they have swinged them times, and that shall be their ransome, and so throw them into the sea again. King, by your leave, for in your kingship I must leave you, and repeat how from white to red you chameleonized.

It is to be read, or to be heard of, how in the punyship or nonage [407] of Cerdick sands, when the best houses and walls there were of mud or canvas, or poldavies entiltments,[408] a fisherman of Yarmouth, having drawn so many herrings he wist not what to do withal, hung the residue that he could not sell nor spend in the sooty roof of his shed a-drying; or say thus, his shed was a cabinet in *decimo sexto*,[409] builded on four crutches, and he had no room in it but in that garret or *excelsis* [410] to lodge them, where if they were dry, let them be dry, for in the sea they had drunk too much, and now he would force them do penance for it.

The weather was cold, and good fires he kept (as fishermen, what hardness soever they endure at sea, they will make all smoke but they will make amends for it when they come to land), and what with his firing and smoking, or smoky firing, in that his narrow lobby, his herrings, which were as white as whale's bone when he hung them up, now looked as red as a lobster. It was four or five days before either he or his wife espied it, and when they espied it, they fell down on their knees and blessed themselves, and cried 'A miracle, a miracle!' and with the proclaiming it among their neighbours they could not be content, but to the Court the fishermen would and present it to the King, then lying at Burgh Castle two miles off.

Of this Burgh Castle, because it is so ancient, and there hath been a city there, I will enter into some more special mention. The flood Waveney, running through many

---

406. Over 10,000.   407. Infancy.

408. *poldavies entiltments*: Awnings, coverings of coarse linen.

409. Very small (literally the size of a page in a book, one-sixteenth the normal size).

410. High place.

owns of high Suffolk up to Bungey, and from thence encroaching nearer and nearer to the sea, with his twining and winding it cuts out an island of some amplitude, named Lovingland. The head town in that island is Leystofe,[411] in which be it known to all men I was born, though my father sprang from the Nashes of Herefordshire.

The next town from Leystofe towards Yarmouth is Corton, and next Gorlston. More inwardly on the left hand, where Waveney and the river Jerus mix their waters, Cnoberi Urbs, the City of Cnober, at this day termed Burgh or Burgh Castle, had his being.

The city and castle, saith Bede and Master Camden, or rather Master Camden out of Bede, by the woods about it, and the driving of the sea up to it, was most pleasant. In it one Fursaeus, a Scot, builded a monastery, at whose persuasion Sigebert, King of the East Angles, gave over his kingdom and led a monastical life there; but forth of that monastery he was haled against his will, to encourage his subjects in their battle against the Mercians, where he perished with them.

Nothing of that castle save tattered [412] ragged walls now remains, framed four-square and overgrown with briars and bushes, in the stubbing up of which, erstwhiles they dig up Roman coins, and buoys and anchors. Well, thither our fisherman set the best leg before, and unfardled [413] to the King his whole satchel of wonders. The King was as superstitious in worshipping those miraculous herrings as the fisherman, licensed him to carry them up and down the realm for strange monsters, giving to Cerdick sands (the birth of such monstrosities) many privileges, and, in that the quantity of them that were caught so increased, he assigned a broken sluice in the Island of Lovingland, called Herring Fleet, where they should disburden and discharge their boats of them, and render him custom. Our herring

411. Lowestoft.
412. 'Tartered' in 1599 edition, ('tattered' in Harleian Miscellany, 1745).
413. Unloaded.

smoker, having won his monster's stall throughout England, spirted overseas to Rome with a pedlar's pack of them, in the papal chair of Vigilius, he that first instituted saints' eves or vigils to be fasted.[414] By that time he came thither he had but three of his herrings left, for by the way he fell into the thievish hands of malcontents and of launce-knights,[415] of whom he was not only robbed of all his money, but was fain to redeem his life besides with the better part of his ambry[416] of burnished fishes.

These herrings three he rubbed and curried over[417] till his arms ached again, to make them glow like a Turkie[418] brooch or a London vintner's sign, thick-jagged, and round-fringed with theaming[419] arsedine,[420] and folding them in a diaper napkin as lily-white as a ladies' marrying-smock, to the market-stead of Rome he was so bold as to prefer them; and there, on a high stool, unbraced and unlaced them to any chapman's eye that would buy them. The Pope's caterer, casting a lickerous[421] glance that way, asked what it was he had to sell. 'The King of Fishes', he answered. 'The King of Fishes?' replied he. 'What is the price of him?' 'A hundred ducats', he told him. 'A hundred ducats?' quoth the Pope's caterer. 'That is a kingly price indeed. It is for no private man to deal with him.' 'Then he is for me', said the fisherman, and so unsheathed his cuttle-bong,[422] and from the nape of the neck to the tail dismembered him and paunched him up at a mouthful. Home went his Beatitude's caterer with a flea in his ear, and discoursed to His Holiness what had happened. 'Is it the King of Fishes?' The Pope frowningly shook him up like a cat in a blanket. 'And is there any man to have him but I that am King of Kings and

414. *papal chair ... fasted*: Vigilius was Pope, 537–555. M. points out that vigils were instituted earlier than this, and calls Nashe's observation 'a piece of popular etymology'.

415. Lance-knights, mercenary foot-soldiers.

416. Store.   417. Rubbed, treated.

418. Turquoise.   419. Meaning unknown.

420. Copper alloy used as leaf-gold.

421. Lecherous.

422. Knife used for cutting purses.

Lord of Lords? Go, give him his price, I command thee, and let me taste of him incontinently.'[423] Back returned the caterer like a dog that had lost his tail, and poured down the herring merchant his hundred ducats for one of those two of the King of Fishes unsold; which then he would not take, but stood upon two hundred. Thereupon they broke off, the one urging that he had offered it him so before, and the other that he might have took him at his proffer, which since he refused and now halpered[424] with him, as he eat up the first, so would he eat up the second, and let Pope or Patriarch of Constantinople fetch it out of his belly if they could. He was as good as his word, and had no sooner spoke the word, but he did as he spoke. With a heavy heart to the palace the yeoman of the mouth departed, and rehearsed this second ill success, wherewith Peter's successor was so in his mulligrums[425] that he had thought to have buffeted him and cursed him with bell, book and candle; but he ruled his reason, and bade him, though it cost a million, to let him have that third that rested behind, and hie him expeditely thither, lest some other snatched it up, and as fast from thence again, for he swore by his triple crown, no crum of refection would he gnaw upon, till he had sweetened his lips with it.

So said, so done. Thither he flew as swift as Mercury, and threw him his two hundred ducats as before demanded. It would not fadge,[426] for then the market was raised to three hundred, and the caterer grumbling thereat, the fisher swain was forward to fettle him to his tools, and tire upon it, as on the other two, had not he held his hands and desired him to keep the peace, for no money should part them. With that speech he was qualified, and pursed the three hundred ducats, and delivered him the King of Fishes, teaching him how to geremumble[427] it, sauce it, and dress it, and so sent him away a glad man. All the Pope's cooks in their white

423. Immediately.
424. Hesitated to come to an agreeement, 'dithered'.
425. Mulligrubs, a fit of depression.
426. Suffice. 427. (?) Gut, disembowel.

sleeves and linen aprons met him middle way, to entertain and receive the King of Fishes, and together by the ears they went, who should first handle him or touch him. But the clerk of the kitchen appeased that strife, and would admit none but himself to have the scorching and carbonadoing of it, and he kissed his hand thrice, and made as many humblessos ere he would finger it; and such obeisances performed, he dressed it as he was enjoined, kneeling on his knees and mumbling twenty Ave Mary's to himself in the sacrificing of it on the coals, that his diligent service in the broiling and combustion of it, both to his Kingship and to his Fatherhood, might not seem unmeritorious. The fire had not pierced it, but it being a sweaty loggerhead greasy sowter,[428] endungeoned in his pocket a twelvemonth, stunk so over the Pope's palace, that not a scullion but cried 'Foh!', and those which at the first flocked the fastest about it now fled the most from it, and sought more to rid their hands of it than before they sought to bless their hands with it. With much stopping of their noses, between two dishes they stewed it and served it up. It was not come within three chambers of the Pope but he smelt it, and upon smelling of it enquiring what it should be that sent forth such a puissant perfume, the standers-by declared that it was the King of Fishes. 'I conceited no less,' said the Pope, 'for less than a king he could not be that had so strong a scent. And if his breath be so strong, what is he himself? Like a great king, like a strong king, I will use him. Let him be carried back, I say, and my Cardinals shall fetch him in with dirge and processions under my canopy.'

Though they were double and double weary of him, yet his edict being a law, to the kitchen they returned him, whither by and by the whole College of scarlet Cardinals, with their crosiers, their censers, their hostes, their *Agnus Dei*'s and crucifixes, flocked together in heaps as it had been to the conclave or a general council, and the senior Cardinal that stood next in election to be Pope, heaved him up from

428. Literally a stupid greasy shoemaker.

the dresser with a dirge of *De profundis natus est fex;*[429] *rex* he should have said, and so have made true Latin, but the spirable[430] odour and pestilent steam ascending from it put him out of his bias of congruity, and, as true as the truest Latin of Priscian, would have queazened[431] him like the damp that 'took both Bell and Baram[432] away, and many a worthy man that day', if he had not been protected under the Pope's canopy, and the other Cardinals, with their holy-water sprinkles, quenched his foggy fume and evaporating. About and about the inward and base court they circumducted him, with Kyrie Eleison and Halleluiah, and the chanters in their golden copes and white surplices chanted it out above *gloria patri* in praising of him. The organs played, the ordnance at the Castle of Saint Angelo's went off, and all wind instruments blew as loud as the wind in winter in his passado[433] to the Pope's ordinary or dining chamber, where having set him down, upon their faces they fell flat, and licked every one his ell of dust, in ducking on all four unto him.

The busy epitasis[434] of the comedy was when the dishes were uncovered and the swarthrutter sour[435] took air. For then he made such an air, as Alcides himself that cleansed the stables of Augaeus nor any hostler was able to endure.

This at once, the Pope it popped under-board, and out of his palace worse it scared him than Neptune's Phocases,[436] that scared the horses of Hippolytus, or the harpies, Jupiter's dogs, sent to vex Phineus.[437] The Cardinals were at their *ora pro nobis*, and held this suffocation a meet sufferance for

429. Faeces.   430. Inhaled.

431. Choked.

432. M. suggests a reference to some lost ballad.

433. A thrust in fencing.

434. 'That part of the play where the plot thickens' (NED).

435. Perhaps a reference to a ballad (M.). Swart-rutters were bands of irregular troopers in the Low Countries.

436. Phocae are Neptune's team of sea-calves. M. points out that it was a bull that frightened Hippolytus' horses.

437. It was Helios, the sun-god, who sent the furies, as punishment for choosing blindness rather than death.

so contemning the King of Fishes and his subjects, and fleshly surfeiting in their carnivals. 'Negromantick sorcery, negromantick sorcery, some evil spirit of an heretic it is which thus molesteth his Apostolicship!' The friars and monks caterwauled, from the abbots and priors to the novices, 'wherefore *tanquam in circo*,[438] we will trounce him in a circle, and make him tell what lanternman or groom of Hecate's close-stool [439] he is that thus nefariously and proditoriously [440] prophanes and penetrates our holy father's nostrils'. What needs there any more embages? [441] The ring-roll [442] or ringed circle was compassed and chalked out, and the King of Fishes, by the name of the King of Fishes, conjured to appear in the centre of it. But *surdo cantant absurdi, sive surdum incantant fratres sordidi*: [443] he was a king absolute, would not be at every man's call, and if Friar Pendela [444] and his fellows had anything to say to him, in his admiral court of the sea let them seek him, and neither in Hull, Hell nor Halifax.

They, seeing that by their charms and spells they could spell nothing of him, fell to a more charitable purpose, that it might be the distressed soul of some king that was drowned, who, being long in Purgatory, and not relieved by the prayers of the Church, had leave in that disguised form to have egress and regress to Rome, to crave their benevolences of dirges, trentals [445] and so forth, to help him onward on his journey to *Limbo patrum* [446] or Elisium, and because they would not easily believe what tortures in Purgatory he had sustained unless they were eye-witnesses of them, he thought to represent to all their senses the image and idea of his combustion and broiling there, and the horrible stench of

438. 'As if in the circus or arena'.   439. Privy.
440. Treacherously.   441. Equivocations, circumlocutions.
442. Small ring.
443. 'Fools sing to the deaf; evil brothers bewitch a deaf man.'
444. Perhaps a reference to a popular song with the line 'Friar how fares thy bandelow, bandelow'; perhaps identified with 'Friar Sandelo', *Faustus*, III, 2.
445. Correctly a sequence of thirty Requiem masses.
446. 'The limbo, where our fathers have gone before'.

his sins accompanying, both under his frying and broiling on the coals in the Pope's kitchen, and the intolerable smell or stink he sent forth under either. *Una voce* [447] in this spleen to Pope Vigilius they ran, and craved that this King of Fishes might first have Christian burial; next, that he might have masses sung for him; and last, that for a saint he would canonize him. All these he granted, to be rid of his filthy redolence, and his chief casket wherein he put all his jewels he made the coffin of his enclosure, and for his ensainting, look the almanac in the beginning of April, and see if you can find out such a saint as Saint Gildarde, which in honour of this gilded fish the Pope so ensainted. Nor there he rested and stopped, but in the mitigation of the very embers whereupon he was singed (that after he was taken off them, fumed most fulsomely of his fatty droppings) he ordained ember weeks in their memory to be fasted everlastingly.

I had well nigh forgot a special point of my Romish history, and that is how Madame Celina Cornficia, one of the curiosest courtesans of Rome, when the fame of the king of fishes was canon-roared in her ears, she sent all her jewels to the jewish lombard to pawn, to buy and encaptive him to her trencher, but her purveyor came a day after the fair, and as he came so he fared, for not a scrap of him but the cobs [448] of the two herrings the fisherman had eaten remained of him, and those cobs, rather than he would go home with a sleeveless [449] answer, he bought at the rate of fourscore ducats – they were rich cobs [450] you must rate them, and of them all cobbing country chuffs which make their bellies and their bags their gods are called rich cobs. Every man will not clap hands to this tale; the Norwichers imprimis, who say the first gilding of herrings was deducted from them, and after this guise they tune the accent of their speech, how that when Castor was Norwich (a town two mile beyond this Norwich, that is termed to this day Norwich Castor, and having monuments of a castle in it environing fifty acres of ground, and ringbolts in the walls

447. 'Unanimously'. 448. Heads.
449. Useless. 450. Misers.

whereto ships were fastened) our Norwich now upon her legs was a poor fisher town, and the sea sprawled and springed up to her common stairs in Confur Street.

All this may pass in the Queen's peace, and no man say bo to it. But bawwaw, quoth Bagshaw,[451] to that which drawlatcheth[452] behind, of the first taking of herrings there, and currying and gilding them amongst them, whereof, if they could whisper to us any simple likelihood, or rawboned carcass of reason, more than their imaginary dream of Guilding Cross in their parish of St Saviour's (now stumped up by the roots) so named, as they would have it, of the smoky gilding of herrings there first invented, I could well have allowed of, but they must bring better cards ere they win it from Yarmouth.

As good a toy to mock an ape was it of him that showed a country fellow the Red Sea, where all the red herrings were made (as some places in the sea, where the sun is most transpiercing and beats with his rays ferventest, will look as red as blood), and the jest of a scholar in Cambridge, that standing angling on the town bridge there, as the country people on the market day passed by, secretly baited his hook with a red herring with a bell about the neck, and so conveying it into the water that no man perceived it, all on the sudden, when he had a competent throng gathered about him, up he twitched it again and laid it openly before them; whereat the gaping rural fools, driven into no less admiration than the common people about London some few years since were at the bubbling of Moorditch,[453] sware by their christendoms that, as many days and years as they had lived, they never saw such a miracle of a red herring taken in the fresh-water before. That greedy seagull Ignorance is apt to devour anything. For a new Messias they are ready to expect of the bedlam hatmäker's wife by London Bridge, he

451. Bagshaw is Bagshot in Surrey, much pestered by highwaymen, 'baw waw' (or 'bow wow') being commonly associated with references to it in Elizabethan plays (F.P.W.).

452. Lags, dawdles (NED).

453. *the bubbling of Moorditch*: Meaning unknown.

that proclaims himself Elias,[454] and saith he is inspired with mutton and porridge. And with them it is current that Don Sebastian, King of Portugal (slain twenty years since with Stukeley at the Battle of Alcazar), is raised from the dead like Lazarus, and alive to be seen at Venice.[455] Let them look to themselves as they will, for I am theirs to gull them better than ever I have done. And this I am sure: I have distributed gudgeon dole [456] amongst them, as God's plenty as any stripling of my slender portion of wit, far or near. They needs will have it so, much good do it them, I cannot do withal. For if but carelessly betwixt sleeping and waking I write I know not what against plebeian publicans and sinners (no better than the sworn brothers of candlestick turners and tinkers) and leave some terms in suspense that my post-haste want of argent will not give me elbow-room enough to explain or examine as I would, out steps me an infant squib of the Inns of Court, that hath not half greased his dining cap or scarce warmed his lawyer's cushion, and he, to approve himself an extravagant statesman, catcheth hold of a rush, and absolutely concludeth it is meant of the Emperor of Russia and that it will utterly mar the traffic into that country if all the pamphlets be not called in and suppressed, wherein that libelling word is mentioned. Another, if but a head or a tail of any beast he boasts of in his crest or his scutcheon to be reckoned up by chance in a volume where a man hath just occasion to reckon up all beasts in armory,[457] he straight engageth himself by the honour of his house and his never reculed [458] sword, to thresh down the hairy roof of that brain that so seditiously mutinied against him, with the mortiferous bastinado, or cast such an uncurable Italian trench in his face, as not the basest creeper upon pattens by the highway side but shall

454. Perhaps a reference to a writer called Durden who called himself Elias (F.P.W.).

455. A reference to the several pretenders who claimed to be Don Sebastian after his death in 1578.

456. Payment for the gullible.

457. Heraldry.   458. Retreated, beaten.

abhor him worse than the carrion of a dead corse, or a man hanged up in gibbets.

I will deal more boldly, and yet it shall be securely and in the way of honesty, to a number of God's fools that for their wealth might be deep wise men and so forth (as nowadays in the opinion of the best lawyers of England there is no wisdom without wealth, allege what you can to the contrary of all the beggarly sages of Greece), these, I say, out of some discourses of mine, which were a mingle-mangle cum purre [459] and I know not what to make of myself, have fished out such a deep politic state meaning as if I had all the secrets of court or commonwealth at my fingers' ends. Talk I of a bear, 'Oh it is such a man that emblazons him in his arms'; or of a wolf, a fox, a chamelion, any lording whom they do not affect [460] it is meant by. The great potentate, stirred up with those perverse applications, not looking into the text itself, but the ridiculous comment, or if he looks into it follows no other more charitable comment than that, straight thunders out his displeasure and showers down the whole tempest of his indignation upon me, and to amend the matter, and fully absolve himself of this rash error of misconstruing, he commits it over to be prosecuted by a worse misconstruer than himself, *videlicet* his learned counsel (God forgive me if I slander them with that title of learned, for generally they are not), and they, being compounded of nothing but vociferation and clamour, rage and fly out they care not how against a man's life, his person, his parentage, two hours before they come to the point, little remembering their own privy scrapes with their laundresses, or their night walks to Pancredge,[461] together with the hobnailed houses of their carterly ancestry from whence they are sprung, that have cold plough-jade's buttocks time out of mind with the breath of their whistling, and with retailing their dung to manure lands and selling straw and chaff

459. *mingle-mangle cum purre*: Said to be a call to pigs to come to the trough.
460. Like, approve of.
461. Pancras, a district of unsavoury reputation.

scratched up the pence to make them gentlemen. But, Lord, how miserably do these ethnics,[462] when they once march to the purpose, set words on the tenters,[463] never reading to a period (which you shall scarce find in thirty sheets of a lawyer's declaration) whereby they might comprehend the entire sense of the writer together, but disjoint and tear every syllable betwixt their teeth severally. And if by no means they can make it odious, they will be sure to bring it in disgrace by ill-favoured mouthing and missounding it. These be those that use men's writings like brute beasts, to make them draw which way they list, as a principal agent in church controversies of this our time complaineth. I have read a tale of a poor man and an advocate, which poor man complained to the King of wrong that the advocate had done him in taking away his cow. The King made him no answer but this, that he would send for the advocate and hear what he could say. 'Nay,' quoth the poor man, 'if you be at that pass that you will pause to hear what he will say, I have utterly lost my cow, for he hath words enough to make fools of ten thousand.' So he that shall have his lines bandied by our usual plodders in Fitzherbert,[464] let him not care whether they be right or wrong, for they will writhe and turn them as they list, and make the author believe he meant that which he never did mean; and, for a knitting-up conclusion his credit is unreprievably lost, that on bare suspicion in such cases shall but have his name controverted amongst them. And if I should fall into their hands, I would be pressed to death for obstinate silence, and never seek to clear myself, for it is in vain, since both they will confound a man's memory with their tedious babbling, and in the first three words of his Apology, with impudent exclamations interrupt him, whenas their mercenary tongues (lie they never so loudly) without check or control must have their free passage for five hours together.

462. Pagans, heathens.
463. Strained, overstretched.
464. Sir Anthony Fitzherbert (1470–1538); a judge with many legal works attributed to him.

I speak of the worser sort, not of the best, whom I hold in high admiration, as well for their singular gifts of art and nature as their untainted consciences with corruption. And from some of them I avow I have heard as excellent things flow as ever I observed in Tully or Demosthenes. Those that were present at the arraignment of Lopus [465] (to insist in no other particular) hereof I am sure will bear me record. Latinless dolts, saturnine heavy-headed blunderers, my invective hath relation to, such as count all arts puppet-plays and pretty rattles to please children in comparison of their confused barbarous law, which if it were set down in any Christian language but the Gretan tongue, it would never grieve a man to study it.

Neither Ovid nor Ariosto could by any persuasions of their parents be induced to study civil law, for the harshness of it. How much more, had they been alive at this day and born in our nation, would they have consented to study this uncivil Norman hotchpotch, this sow of lead, that hath never a ring at the end to lift it up by, is without head or foot, the deformest monster that may be? I stand lawing [466] here, what with these lawyers and self-conceited misinterpreters, so long that my red herring, which was hot broiling on the coals, is waxed stark cold for want of blowing. Have with them for a riddle or two, only to set their wits a-nibbling and their jobbernowls [467] a-working, and so goodnight to their signories, but with this indictment and caution: that, though there be neither rhyme nor reason in it (as by my good will there shall not), they, according to their accustomed gentle favours, whether I will or no, shall supply it with either, and run over all the peers of the land in peevish moralizing and anatomizing of it.

There was a herring, or there was not, for it was but a cropshin [468] one of the refuse sort of herrings, and this her-

---

465. Dr Lopez, accused of a plot against the Queen's life and tried in 1594.
466. Playing the lawyer, arguing.
467. Blockheads.
468. Part of a herring.

ring or this cropshin was censed and thurified[469] in the
smoke and had got him a suit of durance that would last
longer than one of Erra Pater's almanacs [470] or a constable's brown bill, only his head was in his tail and that
made his breath so strong that no man could abide him.
Well, he was a Triton of his time, and a sweet singing
calendar to the state, yet not beloved of the showery
Pleiades or the Colossus of the sun, however he thought
himself another *tumidus Antimachus*,[471] as complete an
Adelantado [472] as he that is known by wearing a cloak of
tuftaffatie [473] eighteen year. And to Lady Turbot there is
no demur but he would needs go a-wooing, and offered her
for a dower whole hecatombs [474] and a two-hand-sword. She
stared upon him with Megaera's [475] eyes, like Iris the messenger of Juno, and bad him go eat a fool's head and garlic, for she would none of him. Thereupon particularly
strictly and usually he replied that though thunder ne'er
lights on Phoebus' tree,[476] and Amphion, that worthy
musician, was husband to Niobe, and there was no such
acceptable incense to the heavens as the blood of a traitor,
revenged he would be by one Chimera of imagination or
other, and hamper and embrace [477] her in those mortal
straits for her disdain, that, in spite of divine symmetry
and miniature, into her busky grove she should let him enter,
and bid adieu, sweet lord, or the cramp of death should
wrest her heart-strings.

This speech was no spirable odour to the Achelous of her

469. Perfumed with incense.
470. Published *c.* 1535, (Erra Pater unidentified, probably fictitious).
471. 'Swollen' Antimachus; a verbose hellenistic love-elegist.
472. Spanish governor.
473. A velvety kind of taffeta, arranged in tufts.
474. Massed sacrificial offerings.
475. One of the Erinyes, goddesses of vengeance sometimes
represented as like the Gorgons, whose looks turned the beholder to
stone.
476. The laurel.
477. Ensnare.

audience.[478] Wherefore she charged him by the extreme lineaments of the Erimanthian bear,[479] and by the privy fistula of the Pierides,[480] to commit no more such excruciating syllables to the yielding air, for she would sooner make her a Frenchhood of a cowshard [481] and a gown of spiders' webs, with the sleeves drawn out with cabbages, than be so contaminated any more with his abortive loathly motives. With this, in an Olympic rage, he calls for a clean shirt, and puts on five pair of buskins, and seeketh out eloquent Xenophon,[482] out of whose mouth the Muses spake, to declame in open court against her.

The action is entered the complaint of her withered brows presented, of a violent rape of his heart she is indicted and convinced. The circumstance that follows you may imagine or suppose; or, without supposing or imagining, I will tell you. The nut was cracked, the strife discussed, and the centre of her heart laid open, and to this wild of sorrows of excruciament she was confined either to be held a flat thornback or sharp pricking dog-fish to the weal public, or seal herself close to his seal-skinned rivelled [483] lips, and suffer herself as a spirit to be conjured into the hellish circle of his embraces.

It would not be, good cropshin; Madame Turbot could not away with such a dry, withered carcass to lie by her. *Currat rex, vivat lex*: [484] come what would, she would none of him. Wherefore, as a poisoner of mankind with her beauty she was adjudged to be boiled to death in hot scalding water, and to have her posterity throughly sauced and soused and pickled in barrels of brinish tears, so ruthful and dolorous that the inhabitants of Bosphorus should be laxative in deploring it. Oh, for a legion of mice-eyed decipherers and

478. *This speech ... audience*: This passage 'seems to have no meaning whatever' (M.).
479. Callisto, turned into a bear and placed in the sky as Arctos.
480. *privy ... Pierides*: Private pipe of the Muses.
481. Cow-turd.
482. Ephesian poet of second century A.D.   483. Wrinkled.
484. 'Let the king run, long live the law'; usually the other way round (*vivat rex*, etc.)

calculators upon characters, now to augurate what I mean by this. The devil, if it stood upon his salvation, cannot do it, much less petty devils and cruel Rhadamants [485] upon earth (elsewhere in France and Italy *subintelligitur,* [486] and not in our aspicious [487] island climate), men that have no means to purchase credit with their prince, but by putting him still in fear, and beating into his opinion that they are the only preservers of his life, in sitting up night and day insifting out treasons, when they are the most traitors themselves, to his life, health and quiet, in continual commacerating [488] him with dread and terror, when but to get a pension or bring him in their debt, next to God, for upholding his vital breath, it is neither so, nor so, but some fool, some drunken man, some mad man in an intoxicate humour hath uttered he knew not what, and they, being starved for intelligence or want of employment, take hold of it with tooth and nail, and in spite of all the waiters, will violently break into the King's chamber, and awake him at midnight to reveal it.

Say that a more piercing Linceus' [489] sight should dive into the entrails of this insinuating parasite's knavery. To the strappado and the stretching torture he will refer it for trial, and there either tear him limb from limb, but he will extract some capital confession from him that shall concern the Prince's life and his crown and dignity, and bring himself in such necessary request about his Prince as he may hold for his right hand and the only staff of his royalty, and think he were undone if he were without him, when the poor fellow so tyrannously handled would rather in that extremity of convulsion confess he crucified Jesus Christ than abide it any longer. I am not against it, for God forbid I should, that it behooves all loyal true subjects to be vigilant and jealous for their prince's safety, and, certain, too jealous

485. Rhadamanthus, one of the three judges of the dead.
486. 'It is understood'.
487. Presumably 'auspicious'.
488. Tormenting.
489. Look-out man on the Argo, proverbially sharp-eyed.

and vigilant of it they cannot be if they be good princes that reign over them, nor use too many means of disquisition by tortures or otherwise to discover treasons pretended against them; but upon the least wagging of a straw to put them in fear where no fear is, and make a hurly-burly in the realm upon 'had I wist', not so much for any zeal or love to their princes, or tender care of their preservation, as to pick thanks and curry a little favour that thereby they may lay the foundation to build a suit on or cross some great enemy they have, I will maintain it is most lewd and detestable. I accuse none, but such there have been belonging to princes in former ages, if there be not at this hour.

Stay, let me look about. Where am I? In my text, or out of it? Not out, for a groat; [490] out, for an angel. [491] Nay, I'll lay no wagers, for now I perponder more sadly [492] upon it, I think I am out indeed. Bear with it, it was a pretty parenthesis of princes and their parasites, which shall do you no harm, for I will cloy you with herring before we part.

Will you have the other riddle of the cropshin to make up the pair that I promised you? You shall, you shall (not have it, I mean) but bear with me, for I cannot spare it, and I persuade myself you will be well contented to spare it except it were better than the former. And yet I pray you what fault can you find with the former? Hath it any more sense in it than it should have? Is it not right of the merry cobbler's cut in that witty play of *The Case is Altered*? [493]

I will speak a proud word, though it may be counted arrogancy in me to praise mine own stuff. If it be not more absurd than *Philips, his Venus*, [494] *The White Tragedy* or *The Green Knight*, or I can tell what English to make of it in part or in whole, I wish, in the foulest weather that is,

---

490. The groat was a fourpenny-piece.
491. The angel was worth fifty pence in Edward VI's time.
492. Seriously.
493. Play by Ben Jonson *c.* 1598.
494. *Philippes Venus*, published 1591; author given as Jo. M.

to go in cut Spanish leather shoes or silk stockings or to stand barehead to a nobleman and not get of him the price of a periwig to cover my bare crown, no, not so much as a pipe of tobacco to raise my spirits and warm my brain.

My readers peradventure may see more into it than I can. For in comparison of them, in whatsoever I set forth, I am *Bernardus non vidit omnia*,[495] as blind as blind Bayard,[496] and have the eyes of a beetle. Nothing from them is obscure, they being quicker sighted than the sun to spy in his beams the motes that are not, and able to transform the lightest murmuring gnat to an elephant. Carp or descant they as their spleen moves them, my spleen moves me not to file my hands with them, but to fall a crash [497] more to the red herring.

How many be there in the world that childishly deprave [498] alchemy, and cannot spell the first letter of it! In the black book of which ignorant band of scorners it may be I am scorned up with the highest. If I be, I must entreat them to wipe me out, for the red herring hath lately been my ghostly father to convert me to their faith; the *probatum est* [499] of whose transfiguration *ex Luna in Solem*,[500] from his dusky tin hue into a perfect golden blandishment, only by the foggy smoke of the grossest kind of fire that is, illumines my speculative soul, what much more, not sophisticate or superficial effects, but absolute essential alterations of metals, there may be made by an artificial repurified flame and diverse other helps of nature added besides.

Cornelius Agrippa maketh mention of some philosophers that held the skin of the sheep that bare the golden fleece to be nothing but a book of alchemy written upon it. So if

495. 'Can it have originated in a jesting allusion to the story of St Bernard riding all day by the Lake of Lausanne, so absorbed in meditation that he did not see it?' (M.).

466. Magic horse given by Charlemagne to Renaud.

497. A dance or tune.   498. Decry, disparage.

499. 'It is proved'.

500. 'From the moon to the sun'.

we should examine matters to the proof, we should find the red herring's skin to be little less. The accidens of alchemy I will swear it is, be it but for that experiment of his smoking alone, and, which is a secret that all tapsters will curse me for blabbing, in his skin there is plain witchcraft. For do but rub a can or quart pot round about the mouth with it, let the cunningest lickspigot swelt his heart out, the beer shall never foam or froth in the cup, whereby to deceive men of their measure, but be as settled as if it stood all night.

Next, to draw on hounds to a scent, to a red herring skin there is nothing comparable. The round or cob[501] of it dried and beaten to powder is *ipse ille*[502] against the stone; and of the whole body of itself, the finest ladies beyond seas frame their kickshaws.[503]

The rebel Jack Cade was the first that devised to put red herrings in cades,[504] and from him they have their name. Now as we call it the swinging of herrings when we cade them, so in a halter was he swung and trussed up as hard and round as any cade of herring he trussed up in his time, and perhaps of his being so swung and trussed up, having first found out the trick to cade herring, they would so much honour him in his death as not only to call it swinging, but cading of herring also. If the text will bear this, we will force it to bear more, but it shall be but the weight of a straw, or the weight of Jack Straw[505] more; who, with the same *Graeca fide*[506] I marted unto you the former, was the first that put the red herring in straw over head and ears like beggars, and the fishermen upon that jack-strawed him ever after. And some, for he was so beggarly a knave that challenged to be a gentleman, and had no wit nor wealth but what he got by the warm wrapping up of herring,

501. (?) Head.   502. 'He himself'.
503. Fancy dishes in cookery.
504. Kegs holding 720 herrings.
505. Rebel leader in 1381.
506. M. suggests meaning 'cash down', the Greeks being hard-headed businessmen.

raised this proverb of him: 'Gentleman Jack Herring,[507] that puts his breeches on his head for want of wearing'. Other disgraceful proverbs of the herring there be, as 'Ne'er a barrel better herring, neither flesh nor fish, nor good red herring', which those that have bitten with ill bargains of either sort have dribbled forth[508] in revenge, and yet not have them from Yarmouth; many coast towns besides it enterprising to curry, salt and pickle up herrings, but mar them because they want the right feat how to salt and season them. So I could pluck a crow[509] with poet Martial for calling it *putre halec*, 'the scald[510] rotten herring', but he meant that of the fat reasty[511] Scottish herrings, which will endure no salt, and in one month (bestow what cost on them you will) wax rammish[512] if they be kept, whereas our embarrelled white herrings, flourishing with the stately brand of Yarmouth upon them, *scilicet*[513] the three half-lions and the three half-fishes with the crown over the head, last in long voyages, better than the red herring, and not only are famous at Roan, Paris, Diepe, Cane (whereof the first, which is Roan, serveth all the high countries of France with it, and Diepe, which is the last save one, victuals all Picardy with it), but here at home is made account of like a marquis and received at Court right solemnly. I care not much if I rehearse to you the manner, and that is thus.

Every year about Lent tide, the sheriffs of Norwich bake certain herring pies (four-and-twenty, as I take it) and send them as a homage to the Lord of Caster hard by there, for lands that they hold of him; who presently upon the like tenure, in bouncing hampers, covered over with his cloth of arms, sees them conveyed to the Court in the best equipage. At Court when they arrived, his man rudely enters not

507. 'It seems to allude to the dressing of herrings with the tail in the mouth – as fried whiting are served at present' (M.).

508. 'Let forth or utter as in driblets' (NED).

509. Have an argument (pick a bone).

510. Putrid, contemptible.

511. Rancid.

512. Rank, of a bad smell.

513. Namely, to wit

at first but knocketh very civilly, and then officers come and fetch him with torchlight, where having disfraughted and unloaded his luggage, to supper he sets him down like a lord, with his wax lights before him, and hath his mess of meat allowed him with the largest, and his horses (*quatenus* horses [514]) are provendered as epicurely. After this, some four mark fee towards his charges is tendered him, and he jogs home again merrily.

A white pickled herring? Why, it is meat for a prince. Haunce Vandervecke [515] of Rotterdam, as a Dutch post informed me, in bare pickled herring laid out twenty thousand pound the last fishing. He had lost his drinking belike, and thought to store himself of medicines enough to recover it.

Noble Caesarian Charlemagne herring, Pliny and Gesner [516] were to blame they slubbered thee over so negligently. I do not see why any man should envy thee, since thou art none of these lurcones or epulones,[517] gluttons or fleshpots of Egypt (as one that writes of the Christians' captivity under the Turk enstyleth us English men), nor livest thou by the unliving or eviscerating of others, as most fishes do, or by any extraordinary filth whatsoever, but, as the chameleon liveth by the air and the salamander by the fire, so only by the water art thou nourished and nought else, and must swim as well dead as live.

Be of good cheer, my weary readers, for I have espied land, as Diogenes [518] said to his weary scholars when he had read to a waste leaf. Fishermen, I hope, will not find fault with me for fishing before the net, or making all fish that comes to the net in this history, since, as the Athenians bragged they were the first that invented wrastling, and one Ericthonius amongst them that he was the first that

514. As horses go, seeing they are horses.
515. Hans van den Veken, a Dutch merchant with a share in the ship seized by the 'pirate', Gilbert Lee, in 1588 (F.P.W.).
516. i.e., the great antiquarians had neglected the red herring.
517. *lurcones or epulones*: Meaning unknown.
518. 'An incipient Wellerism' (H.).

joined horses in collar couples for drawing, so I am the first that ever set quill to paper in praise of any fish or fishermen.

Not one of the poets aforetime could give you or the sea a good word. Ovid saith *Nimium ne credite ponto*: the sea is a slippery companion, take heed how you trust him, and further *Periurii poenas repetit ille locus*: it is a place like hell, good for nothing but to punish perjurers. With innumerable invectives more against it throughout in every book.

Plautus in his *Rudens* bringeth in fishermen cowthring [519] and quaking, dung-wet after a storm, and complaining their miserable case in this form: *Captamus cibum e mari; si eventus non venit, neque quicquam captum est piscium, salsi lautique domum redimus clanculum, dormimus incoenati* ('All the meat that we eat we catch out of the sea, and if there we miss, well washed and salted, we sneak home to bed supperless'). And upon the tail of it he brings in a parasite that flouteth and bourdeth [520] them thus: *Heus vos familica gens hominum ut vivitis? ut peritis?*: hough, you hunger-starved gubbins or offals of men, how thrive you, how perish you? And they, cringing in their necks, like rats smothered in the hold, poorly replicated *Vivimus fame, speque, sitique,* with hunger and hope and thirst we content ourselves. If you would not misconceit that I studiously intended your defamation, you should have thick hailshot of these.

Not the lousy riddle [521] wherewith fishermen constrained, some say, Homer, some say another philosopher, to drown himself because he could not expound it, but should be dressed and set before you *supernagulum*,[522] with eight-score more galliard cross-points [523] and kickshiwinshes [524] of giddy earwig brains, were it not I thought you too fretful and choleric with feeding altogether on salt meats to have

519. Shaking, trembling.
520. Mocks and makes fun of.
521. An allusion to the story in one of the spurious 'lives' of Homer that he died when unable to solve a riddle concerning life.
522. See Nashe's note in *Pierce Penniless*, p. 105.
523. Steps in dancing.   524. 'Fantastic devices' (M.).

the secrets of your trade in public displayed. Will this appease you, that you are the predecessors of the Apostles, who were poorer fishermen than you, that for your seeing wonders in the deep, you may be the sons and heirs of the prophet Jonas, that you are all cavaliers and gentlemen since the King of Fishes vouchsafed you for his subjects, that for your selling smoke [525] you may be courtiers, for your keeping of fasting-days Friar Observants, and lastly, that, look in what town there is the sign of The Three Mariners, the huffcapest [526] drink in that house you shall be sure of always?

No more can I do for you than I have done, were you my god-children every one. God make you his children and keep you from the Dunkirks,[527] and then I doubt not but when you are driven into harbour by fould weather, the cans shall walk to the health of *Nashe's Lenten Stuff* and the praise of the red herring, and even those that attend upon the pitch-kettle [528] will be drunk to my good fortunes and recommendations. One boon you must not refuse me in, if you be *boni socii* [529] and sweet Olivers,[530] that you let not your rusty swords sleep in their scabbards, but lash them out in my quarrel as hotly as if you were to cut cables or hew the main mast overboard, when you hear me mangled and torn in men's mouths about this playing with a shuttlecock or tossing empty bladders in the air.

Alas, poor hungerstarved muse, we shall have some spawn of a goose-quill or over-worn pander quirking and girding,[531] was it so hard-driven that it had nothing to feed upon but a red herring? Another drudge of the pudding-house [532] (all

525. A reference to the story of one who, promising to use his influence with his master, took bribes; he was publicly asphyxiated as 'they which sell smoke should so perish with smoke' (Greene's *Farewell to Folly*) (M.).

526. Headiest, strongest.

527. Dunkirk pirates.

528. Vessel for boiling pitch, especially on board ship.

529. 'Good companions'.

530. Good fellows.

531. Quipping and scoffing.   532. Stomach.

whose lawful means to live by throughout the whole year will scarce purchase him a red herring) says I might as well have writ of a dog's turd (in his teeth surreverence [533]). But let none of these scum of the suburbs be too vinegar-tart with me; for if they be, I'll take mine oath upon a red herring and eat it to prove that their fathers, their grandfathers, and their great-grandfathers, or any other of their kin were scullion's dishwash and dirty draff and swill, set against a red herring. The puissant red herring, the golden Hesperides red herring, the Meonian [534] red herring, the red herring of Red Herrings' Hall, every pregnant peculiar of whose resplendent laud and honour to delineate and adumbrate to the ample life were a work that would drink dry fourscore and eighteen Castalian fountains of eloquence, consume another Athens of fecundity, and abate the haughtiest poetical fury twixt this and the burning zone and the tropic of Cancer. My conceit is cast into a sweating sickness, with ascending these few steps of his renown. Into what a hot broiling Saint Lawrence fever [535] would it relapse then, should I spend the whole bag of my wind in climbing up to the lofty mountain-crest of his trophies? But no more wind will I spend on it but this: Saint Denis

<blockquote>
for France, Saint James for Spain, Saint
Patrick for Ireland, Saint George for
England, and the red herring
for Yarmouth.
</blockquote>

533. Great reverence.
534. Homeric.
535. Alluding to martyrdom by broiling.

6

The Choice of Valentines

To the Right Honourable the Lord S.[1]

Pardon, sweet flower of matchless poetry,
    And fairest bud the red rose ever bare,
    Although my muse divorc'd from deeper care
    Presents thee with a wanton elegy.[2]
Ne blame my verse of loose unchastity
    For painting forth the things that hidden are,
    Since all men act what I in speech declare,
    Only induced by variety.[3]
Complaints and praises everyone can write,
    And passion-out their pangs in stately rhymes,
    But of love's pleasures none did ever write
    That hath succeeded in these latter times.
Accept of it, dear Lord, in gentle gree,[4]
    And better lines ere long shall honour thee.

THE CHOOSING OF VALENTINES

It was the merry month of February,
    When young men in their jolly roguery
Rose early in the morn 'fore break of day
    To seek them valentines so trim and gay,
With whom they may consort in summer-sheen
    And dance the heidegeies [5] on our town-green,
As Ale's [6] at Easter or at Pentecost

1. Probably Ferdinando Stanley, Lord Strange, Earl of Derby.
2. Used very loosely, here meaning love-poem.
3. The motivation of the poem is an artistic desire to broaden the scope of poetry.
4. Good will.
5. An incomplete manuscript text reads 'the high degrees'.
6. M. emends to 'At Ale's', an ale-drinking festival.

Perambulate the fields that flourish most,
And go to some village abordering near
   To taste the cream and cakes and such good cheer,
Or see a play of strange morality
   Showen by bachelry of Manningtree;[7]
Whereto the country franklins [8] flock-meal [9] swarm,
   And John and Joan come marching arm in arm
Even on the hallows [10] of that blessed saint
   That doth true lovers with those joys acquaint,
I went, poor pilgrim, to my lady's shrine
   To see if she would be my valentine.
But woe, alas, she was not be found,
   For she was shifted to an Upper Ground.[11]
Good Justice Dudgeon-haft and Crabtree-Face [12]
   With bills and staves had scar'd her from the place;
And now she was compell'd for sanctuary
   To fly unto an house of venery.
Thither went I, and boldly made enquire
   If they had hackneys [13] to let out to hire,
And what they crav'd by order of their trade
   To let one ride a journey on a jade.
Therewith out stepped a foggy [14] three-chin'd dame,
   That us'd to take young wenches for to tame,
And ask'd me if I meant as I profess'd,
   Or only ask'd a question but in jest,
'In jest?' quoth I. 'That term it as you will:
   I come for game, therefore give me my Jill.'
'Why, sir,' quoth she, 'if that be your demand,
   Come, lay me a God's-penny [15] in my hand;
For in our oratory sikerly [16]
   None enters here to do his nicery

7. Young men acting in the Morality plays often referred to as
still being performed at Manningtree, Essex.
8. Freeholders.   9. In great numbers.
10. Saints' days.
11. A street of low repute in Southwark.
12. Fictitious names for severe, puritanical officers.
13. Prostitutes.   14. Fat, gross.
15. Deposit.   16. Certainly.

But he must pay his offertory first,
    And then perhaps we'll ease him of his thirst.'
I, hearing her so earnest for the box,
    Gave her her due, and she the door unlocks.
In am I enter'd: Venus be my speed.
    But where's this female that must do this deed?
By blind meanders, and by crankled [17] ways
    She leads me onward (as my author says),
Until we came within a shady loft
    Where Venus' bouncing vestals skirmish oft.
And there she set me in a leather chair,
    And brought me forth of pretty trulls a pair,
To choose of them which might content mine eye;
    But her I sought I could nowhere espy.
I spake them fair, and wish'd them well to fare,
    Yet so it is, I must have fresher ware.
Wherefore, dame bawd, as dainty as you be,
    Fetch gentle Mistress Francis forth to me.
'By Halydame,' quoth she, 'and God's own mother,
    I well perceive you are a wily brother.
For if there be a morsel of more price,
    You'll smell it out though I be ne'er so nice.
As you desire, so shall you swive [18] with her,
    But think your purse-strings shall abuy it dear;
For he that will eat quails must lavish crowns,
    And Mistress Francis in her velvet gowns,
And ruffs and periwigs as fresh as May
    Cannot be kept with half-a-crown a day.'
'Of price, good hostess, we will not debate,
    Though you assize [19] me at the highest rate.
Only conduct me to this bonny belle,
    And ten good gobs [20] I will unto thee tell [21]
Of gold or silver, which shall like thee best,
    So much do I her company request.'
Away she went: so sweet a thing is gold

17. Twisted.
18. Have intercourse.
19. Assess.
20. Lumps.
21. Count out.

That (mauger) [22] will invade the strongest hold.
Hey-ho, she comes, that hath my heart in keep:
  Sing lullaby, my cares, and fall asleep.
Sweeping she comes, as she would brush the ground:
  Her rattling silks my senses do confound.
Oh, I am ravish'd! Void the chamber straight,
  For I must needs upon her with my weight.
'My Tomalin', quoth she, and then she smil'd.
  'Ay, ay', quoth I. So more men are beguil'd
With smiles, with flattering words and feined cheer,
  When in their deeds their falsehood doth appear.
'As how, my lambkin?' blushing she replied.
  'Because I in this dancing school abide?
If that be it that breeds this discontent,
  We will remove the camp incontinent. [23]
For shelter only, sweetheart, came I hither,
  And to avoid the troublous stormy weather.
But now the coast is clear we will be gone,
  Since but thy self true lover have I none.'
With that, she sprung full lightly to my lips,
  And fast about the neck me colls and clips. [24]
She wanton faints and falls upon her bed,
  And often tosseth to and fro her head.
She shuts her eyes and waggles with her tongue:
  Oh, who is able to abstain so long?
I come, I come; sweet lining [25] be thy leave.
  Softly my fingers up these curtains heave
And make me happy stealing by degrees.
  First bare her legs, then creep up to her knees.
From thence ascend unto her manly thigh
  (A pox on lingering when I am so nigh).
Smock, climb a-pace, that I may see my joys.
  Oh, heaven and paradise are all but toys
Compared with this sight I now behold,

22. In spite of everything.   23. Immediately.
24. Hugs and embraces.
25. *sweet . . . leave*: A textual variant is 'limmem', possibly meaning
'leman', or lover. 'Be' should then read 'by'.

Which well might keep a man from being old.
A pretty rising womb without a weam,[26]
  That shone as bright as any silver stream,
And bare out like the bending of an hill,
  At whose decline a fountain dwelleth still,
That hath his mouth beset with ugly briars
  Resembling much a dusky net of wires.
A lofty buttock barr'd with azure veins,
  Whose comely swelling, when my hand distrains,
Or wanton checketh with a harmess stype,[27]
  It makes the fruits of love eftsoon be ripe,
And pleasure pluck'd too timely from the stem,
  To die ere it hath seen Jerusalem.
Oh gods, that ever any thing so sweet
  So suddenly should fade away and fleet.
Her arms are spread, and I am all unarm'd.
  Like one with Ovid's cursed hemlock [28] charm'd,
So are my limbs unwieldy for the fight,
  That spend their strength in thought of their delight.
What shall I do to show myself a man?
  It will not be for aught that beauty can.
I kiss, I clap,[29] I feel, I view at will,
  Yet dead he lies not thinking good or ill.
'Unhappy me,' quoth she, 'and will't not stand?
  Come, let me rub and chafe it with my hand.
Perhaps the silly worm is laboured sore,
  And wearied that it can do no more.
If it be so (as I am great a-dread)
  I wish ten thousand times that I were dead.
How ere it is, no means shall want in me,
  That may avail to his recovery.'
Which said, she took and rolled it on her thigh,

26. Blemish.
27. Unknown.
28. cf. 'Yet like as if cold hemlock I had drunk, it mock'd me, hung down the head, and sunk', Marlowe's translation of Ovid's *Elegies*, 3, 6, 13–14.
29. Clasp.

462

And when she looked on't, she would weep and sigh,
And dandled it and danc'd it up and down,
   Not ceasing, till she raise it from his swoon.
And then he flew on her as he were wood,[30]
   And on her breach did thack [31] and foin [32] a-good.
He rubb'd and prick'd and pierc'd her to the bones,
   Digging as far as eath [33] he might for stones.
Now high, now low, now striking short and thick,
   Now diving deep he touch'd her to the quick.
Now with a gird [34] he would his course rebate.
   Straight would he take him to a stately gait.
Play while him list, and thrust he ne'er so hard,
   Poor patient Grisel [35] lieth at his ward,
And gives and takes as blithe and free as May,
   And e'er more meets him in the middle way.
On him her eyes continually were fix'd,
   With her eye-beams his melting looks were mix'd,
Which like the sun, that twixt two glasses plays
   From one to th'other casts rebounding rays.
He like a star, that to reguild his beams
   Sucks in the influence of Phoebus' streams,
Imbathes the lines of his descending light
   In the bright fountains of her clearest sight.
She fair as fairest planet in the sky
   Her purity to no man doth deny.
The very chamber, that enclouds her shine,
   Looks like the palace of that God divine,
Who leads the day about the zodiak,
   And every even descends to th'ocean lake.
So fierce and fervent is her radiance,
   Such fiery stakes she darts at every glance,
She might enflame the icy limbs of age,

30. Mad.   31. Strike.
32. Thrust.
33. Easily.
34. Suddenly.
35. In Chaucer's *Clerk's Tale*; since then an emblem of long-suffering womankind.

And make pale death his surquedry [36] assuage
To stand and gaze upon her orient lamps
   Where Cupid all his chiefest joys encamps,
And sits and plays with every atomy
   That in her sunbeams swarm abundantly.
Thus gazing, and thus striving we persever,
   But what so firm that may continue ever?
'Oh, not so fast!' my ravish'd mistress cries,
   'Lest my content, that on thy life relies,
Be brought too soon from his delightful seat,
   And me unwares of hoped bliss defeat.
Together let our equal motions stir;
   Together let us live and die, my dear.
Together let us march unto content,
   And be consumed with one blandishment.'
As she prescrib'd, so kept we crotchet-time,
   And every stroke in order like a chime.
Whilst she, that had preserv'd me by her pity,
   Unto our music fram'd a groaning ditty.
Alas, alas, that love should be a sin,
   Even now my bliss and sorrow doth begin.
Hold wide thy lap, my love Danaë, [37]
   And entertain the golden shower so free,
That trilling falls into thy treasury,
   As April-drops not half so pleasant be,
Nor Nilus' overflow to Egypt plains,
   As this sweet-stream, that all her joints imbanes. [38]
With 'Oh' and 'Oh', she itching moves her hips,
   And to and fro full lightly starts and skips.
She jerks her legs, and sprawleth with her heels,
   No tongue may tell the solace that she feels.
'I faint, I yield: Oh, death rock me asleep.' [39]
   'Sleep, sleep, desire, entombed in the deep.'

36. Pride.
37. To whom Jove came in a shower of gold.
38. Unknown.
39. *Oh, death ... asleep*: First line of song attributed to Anne
Boleyn.

'Not so, my dear', my dearest saint replied,
   'For from us yet thy spirit may not glide
Until the sinowy channels of our blood
   Withold their source from this imprison'd flood;
And then will we (that "then" will come too soon)
   Dissolved lie as though our days were done.
The whilst I speak, my soul is fleeting hence,
   And life forsakes his fleshly residence.
Stay, stay, sweet joy, and leave me not forlorn.
   Why shouldst thou fade that art but newly born?
Stay but an hour; an hour is not so much.
   But half an hour, if that thy haste be such.
Nay, but a quarter: I will ask no more,
   That thy departure (which torments me sore)
May be alightened with a little pause,
   And take away this passion's sudden cause.
He hears me not, hard-hearted as he is:
   He is the son of Time and hates my bliss.
Time ne'er looks back, the river ne'er return;
   A second spring must help me or I burn.
No, no, the well is dry that should refresh me.
   The glass is run of all my destiny.
Nature of winter learneth niggardize,
   Who, as he overbears [40] the stream with ice,
That man nor beast may of their pleasance taste,
   So shuts she up her conduit all in haste,
And will not let her nectar overflow,
   Lest mortal men immortal joys should know.
Adieu, unconstant love, to thy disport.
   Adieu, false mirth, and melody too short.
Adieu, faint-hearted instrument of lust,
   That falsely hast betray'd our equal trust.
Henceforth no more will I implore thine aid,
   Or thee, or men, of cowardize upbraid.
My little dildo shall supply their kind,
   A knave that moves as light as leaves by wind,
That bendeth not, nor foldest any deal,

40. (?) Over-bars.

465

But stands as stiff as he were made of steel,
And plays at peacock twixt my legs right blithe,
　　And doth my tickling swage with many a sigh.
For, by Saint Runyon, he'll refresh me well,
　　And never make my tender belly swell.'
Poor Priapus, whose triumph now must fall,
　　Except thou thrust this weakling to the wall,
Behold how he usurps in bed and bower,
　　And undermines thy kingdom every hour.
How sly he creeps betwixt the bark and tree,
　　And sucks the sap, whilst sleep detaineth thee.
He is my mistress' page at every stound,[41]
　　And soon will tent a deep intrenched wound.
He waits on courtly nymphs that be so coy,
　　And bids them scorn the blind-alluring boy.
He gives young girls their gamesome sustenance,
　　And every gaping mouth his full sufficience.
He fortifies disdain with foreign arts,
　　And wanton-chaste deludes all loving hearts.
If any wight a cruel mistress serves,
　　Or in despair, unhappy pines and sterves,[42]
Curse eunuch dildo, senseless, counterfeit,
　　Who sooth may fill, but never can beget.
But if revenge enraged with despair
　　That such a dwarf his wellfare should impair,
Would fain this woman's secretary know,
　　Let him attend the marks that I shall show.
He is a youth almost two handfuls high,
　　Straight, round, and plumb,[43] yet having but one eye,
Wherein the rheum so fervently doth rain,
　　That Stygian gulf may scarce his tears contain;
Attired in white velvet or in silk,
　　And nourish'd with hot water or with milk;
Arm'd otherwhile in thick congealed glass,
　　When he more glib to hell below would pass,
Upon a chariot of five wheels he rides,

41. Moment.　　　　42. Dies.
43. Upright.

466

The which an arm-strong driver steadfast guides,
And often alters pace as ways grow deep
  (For who in paths unknown one gate can keep?).
Sometimes he smoothly slideth down the hill,
  Another while the stones his feet do kill.
In clammy ways he treadeth by and by,
  And plasheth and sprayeth all that be him nigh.
So fares this jolly rider in his race,
  Plunging and sourcing [44] forward in like case,
Bedash'd, bespirted, and beplodded foul,
  God give thee shame, thou blind misshapen owl.
Fie, fie, for grief: a lady's chamberlain,
  And canst not thou thy tattling tongue refrain?
I read thee, beardless blab, beware of stripes,
  And be advised what thou vainly pipes.
Thou wilt be whipp'd with nettles for this gear,
  If Cicely show but of thy knavery here.
Saint Denis shield me from such female sprites!
  Regard not, dames, what Cupid's poet writes.
I penn'd this story only for myself,
  Who giving suck unto a childish elf,
And quite discourag'd in my nursery,
  Since all my store seems to her penury.
I am not as was Hercules the stout,
  That to the seventh journey could hold out.
I want those herbs and roots of Indian soil,
  That strengthen weary members in their toil.
Drugs and electuaries of new device
  Do shun my purse, that trembles at the price.
Sufficeth, all I have I yield her whole,
  Which for a poor man is a princely dole.
I pay our hostess scot and lot at most,
  And look as lean and lank as any ghost.
What can be added more to my renown?
  She lieth breathless; I am taken down.
The waves do swell, the tides climb o'er the banks,
  Judge, gentlemen, if I deserve not thanks.

44. Surging.

And so good night unto you every one,
   For lo, our thread is spun, our play is done.
Claudito iam rivos Priape, sat prata biberunt.

THO. NASH.

Thus hath my pen presum'd to please my friend;
   Oh mightst thou likewise please Apollo's eye.
   No: Honour brooks no such impiety.
   Yet Ovid's wanton Muse did not offend.
He is the fountain whence my streams do flow.
   Forgive me if I speak as I was taught,
   Alike to women, utter all I know,
   As longing to unlade so bad a fraught.
My mind once purg'd of such lascivious wit,
   With purified words and hallow'd verse
   Thy praises in large volumes shall rehearse,
   That better may thy graver view befit.
Meanwhile yet rests, you smile at what I write,
   Or for attempting, banish me your sight.

THOMAS NASH.

PART III

I

from *The Anatomy of Absurdity*

PRODIGAL SONS

GOOD counsel is never remembered nor respected till men have given their farewell to felicity and have been overwhelmed in the extremity of adversity. Young men think it a disgrace to youth to embrace the studies of age, counting their fathers fools whiles they strive to make them wise, casting that away at a cast at dice which cost their dads a year's toil, spending that in their velvets which was raked up in a russet coat; so that their revenues racked, and their rents raised to the uttermost, is scarce enough to maintain one's ruffling pride which was wont to be many poor men's relief. These young gallants having lewdly spent their patrimony, fall to begging of poor men's houses[1] over their heads as the last refuge of their riot,[2] removing the ancient bounds of lands to support their decayed port, rather coveting to enclose that which was wont to be common than they would want[3] to maintain their private prodigality.

The Anatomy of Absurdity (M., I, 33).

POOR SCHOLARS

Learning nowadays gets no living if it come empty-handed. Promotion, which was wont to be the free-propounded palm of pains,[4] is by many men's lamentable practice become a purchase. Whenas wits of more towardness[5] shall have spent some time in the university and have as it were tasted the elements of art and laid the foundation of knowledge, if

---

1. A reference to corrupt ways of obtaining property.
2. As the last resort after their period of depravity and dissipation.
3. Fail, be in want.
4. *free . . . pains*: Liberally offered reward of hard work.
5. Precocity, forwardness.

by the death of some friend they should be withdrawn from their studies, as yet altogether raw and so consequently unfit for any calling in the Commonwealth, where should they find a friend to be unto them instead of a father, or one to perfect that which their deceased parents began? Nay, they may well betake themselves to some trade of husbandry for any maintenance they get in the way of alms at the university, or else take upon them to teach, being more fit to be taught, and perch into the pulpit, their knowledge being yet unperfect, very zealously preaching, being as yet scarce grounded in religious principles. How can those men call home the lost sheep that are gone astray, coming into the ministry before their wits be staid? This green fruit, being gathered before it be ripe, is rotten before it be mellow, and infected with schisms before they have learnt to bridle their affections, affecting innovations as newfangled, and enterprising alterations whereby the Church is mangled.

The Anatomy of Absurdity. (M., I, 37).

ADVICE TO SCHOLARS

There be three things which are wont to slack young students' endeavour: negligence, want of wisdom, and fortune. Negligence, whenas we either altogether pretermit [6] or more lightly pass over the thing we ought seriously to ponder. Want of wisdom when we observe no method in reading. Fortune is in the event of chance, either naturally happening, or whenas by poverty or some infirmity or natural dullness we are withdrawn from our studies and alienated from our intended enterprise by the imagination of the rareness of learned men. But as touching these three: for the first, that is to say negligent sloth, he is to be warned; for the second, he is to be instructed; for the third, he is to be helped. Let his reading be temperate, whereunto wisdom, not weariness, must prescribe an end. For, as immoderate fast, excessive abstinence and inordinate watchings are argued of intemperance, perishing with their immoderate

6. Ignore.

use, so that these things never after can be performed as they ought in any measure; so the intemperate study of reading incurreth reprehension, and that which is laudable in his kind is blameworthy by the abuse. Reading, two ways is loathsome to the mind and troublesome to the spirit, both by the quality, namely if it be more obscure, and also by the quantity if it be more tedious, in either of which we ought to use great moderation lest that which is ordained to the refreshing of our wits be abused to the dulling of our senses. We read many things, lest by letting them pass we should seem to despise them. Some things we read lest we should seem to be ignorant in them. Other things we read not that we may embrace them, but eschew them. Our learning ought to be our lives' amendment, and the fruits of our private study ought to appear in our public behaviour.

The Anatomy of Absurdity (M., I, 42–3).

2

from *Preface to Greene's* Menaphon

ENGLISH SENECA, WHOLE HAMLETS AND ST JOHN'S IN CAMBRIDGE

IT is a common practice nowadays amongst a sort[1] of shifting companions, that run through every art and thrive by none, to leave the trade of Noverint,[2] whereto they were born, and busy themselves with the endeavours of art, that could scarcely latinize their neck-verse[3] if they should have need. Yet English Seneca[4] read by candlelight yields many good sentences, as 'Blood is a beggar,' and so forth; and if you entreat him fair in a frosty morning, he will afford you whole Hamlets,[5] I should say handfuls, of tragical speeches. But oh grief! *Tempus edax rerum*: [6] what's that will last always? The sea exhaled by drops will in continuance be dry, and Seneca, let blood line by line and page by page, at length must needs die to our stage; which makes his famished followers to imitate the kid in Aesop,[7] who, enamoured with the fox's newfangles, forsook all hopes of life to leap into a new occupation. And these men, renouncing all possibilities of credit or estimation, to intermeddle with Italian translations, wherein how poorly they have plodded (as those that are neither provenzal men nor are

1. Gang.   2. Scrivener.
3. Verses recited before execution on the gallows.
4. Probably *Seneca his Ten Tragedies translated into English*, 1581.
5. A much-debated reference, in that Thomas Kyd has probably been obliquely referred to as one of the 'shifting companions' who rely on 'English Seneca', and may therefore be regarded as the author of the old version of *Hamlet*. Hibbard's view is that the 'puzzles in it [the Preface] may well be deliberate' and that the case is non-proven.
6. 'Time, the consumer of all things' (Seneca).
7. Not in Aesop, but in the May Eclogue of Spenser's *Shepherd's Calendar*; ('kid' probably a play on Kyd).

474

able to distinguish of articles [8]), let all indifferent gentlemen that have travelled in that tongue discern by their two-penny pamphlets. And no marvel though their home-born mediocrity be such in this matter; for what can be hoped of those that thrust Elizium into hell, and have not learned, so long as they have lived in the spheres, the just measure of the horizon without an hexameter? Sufficeth them to bodge up a blank verse with ifs and ands, and otherwhile for recreation after their candle-stuff, having starched their beards most curiously, to make a peripatetical [9] path into the inner parts of the City, and spend two or three hours in turning over French Dowdy,[10] where they can attract more infection in one minute than they can do eloquence all days of their life by conversing with any authors of like argument.

But lest in this declamatory vein I should condemn all and commend none, I will propound to your learned imitation those men of import that have laboured with credit in this laudable kind of translation. In the forefront of whom I cannot but place that aged father Erasmus, that investest most of our Greek writers in the robes of the ancient Romans; in whose traces Philip Melancthon, Sadolet, Plantine, and many other reverent Germans insisting, have re-edified the ruins of our decayed libraries, and marvellously enriched the Latin tongue with the expense of their toil. Not long after, their emulation being transported into England, every private scholar, William Turner,[11] and who not, began to vaunt their smattering of Latin in English impressions.

But amongst others in that age, Sir Thomas Elyot's [12]

8. *provenzal* ... *articles*: Meaning unknown, though it would make sense if 'neither ... nor' became 'either ... or'.

9. Apparently implying a stiff and stately walk (M.).

10. *inner parts* ... *French Dowdy*: Perhaps a reference to book-sellers in St Paul's churchyard and lewd French literature to be bought there, ('dowdy' sometimes meant slut or prostitute).

11. d. 1568, Cambridge scholar, zealous Protestant.

12. 1490?–1546, author of *The Book named the Governor*, a treatise on education, 1531, and *The Castle of Health*, 1539.

elegance did sever itself from all equals, although Sir Thomas More with his comical wit at that instant was not altogether idle. Yet was not Knowledge fully confirmed in her monarchy amongst us, till that most famous and fortunate nurse of all learning, Saint John's in Cambridge, that at that time was as an university within itself, shining so far above all other houses, halls and hospitals whatsoever, that no college in the town was able to compare with the tithe of her students; having (as I have heard grave men of credit report) more candles lit in it every winter morning before four of the clock than the four-of-the-clock bell gave strokes; till she, I say, as a pitying mother put to her helping hand and sent, from her fruitful womb, sufficient scholars, both to support her own weal, as also to supply all other inferior foundations' defects, and namely that royal erection of Trinity College, which the University Orator,[13] in an Epistle to the Duke of Somerset, aptly termed *Colonia deducta*[14] from the suburbs of Saint John's. In which extraordinary conception, *uno partu in rempublicam prodiere*[15] the Exchequer of Eloquence, Sir John Cheke,[16] a man of men, supernaturally traded in all tongues, Sir John Mason, Doctor Watson, Redman, Ascham, Grindall, Lever, Pilkington: all which have, either by their private readings or public works, repurged the errors of art, expelled from their purity, and set before our eyes a more perfect method of study.

To the Gentlemen Students of both Universities
(*Preface to Greene's* Menaphon) (M., III, 315–17).

13. Ascham, Public Orator of the University, 1546–54.
14. Colony founded.
15. 'From a single consignment, there appeared on the public stage ...'
16. Professor of Greek at Cambridge, 1540–51; Public Orator, 1544–6.

3

from *Strange News*

ROBERT GREENE[1]

IN short terms thus I demur upon thy long Kentish-tailed[2] declaration against Greene.

He inherited more virtues than vices: a jolly long red peak, like the spire of a steeple, he cherished continually without cutting, whereat a man might hang a jewel, it was so sharp and pendent.

Why should art answer for the infirmities of manners? He had his faults, and thou thy follies.

Debt and deadly sin, who is not subject to? With any notorious crime I never knew him tainted (and yet tainting is no infamous surgery for him that hath been in so many hot skirmishes).

A good fellow he was, and would have drunk with thee for more angels[3] than the lord[4] thou libeledst on gave thee in Christ's College; and in one year he pissed as much against the walls as thou and thy two brothers spent in three.

In a night and a day would he have yarked up a pamphlet as well as in seven year, and glad was that printer that might be so blest to pay him dear for the very dregs of his wit.

He made no account of winning credit by his works, as thou dost; thou dost no good works, but thinks to be famoused by a strong faith of thy own worthiness. His only

1. 1560?–92, romancer (author of *Perimedes the Blacksmith* and *Menaphon*) and playwright (*Friar Bacon and Friar Bungay*, *Alphonsus* and *A Looking-Glass for London and England*). See also Introduction, p. 26.
2. A reference to the legend that Kentishmen had tails, given as punishment for cutting off the tail of Thomas à Becket's horse.
3. Coins, at times worth as much as fifty pence.
4. Earl of Oxford ('thou' = Harvey).

care was to have a spell in his purse to conjure up a good cup of wine with at all times.

For the lousy circumstance of his poverty before his death, and sending that miserable writ to his wife, it cannot be but thou liest, learned Gabriel.

I and one of my fellows, William Monox (hast thou never heard of him and his great dagger?), were in company with him a month before he died, at that fatal banquet of rhenish wine and pickled herring (if thou wilt needs have it so), and then the inventory of his apparel came to more than three shillings (though thou sayest the contrary). I know a broker in a spruce leather jerkin with a great number of gold rings on his fingers and a bunch of keys at his girdle shall give you thirty shillings for the doublet alone, if you can help him to it. Hark in your ear, he had a very fair cloak with sleeves, of a grave goose-turd green; it would serve you as fine as may be. No more words, if you be wise, play the good husband and listen after it: you may buy it ten shillings better cheap than it cost him. By St Silver, it is good to be circumspect in casting for the world;[5] there's a great many ropes go to ten shillings. If you want a greasy pair of silk stockings also, to show yourself in at the Court, they are there to be had too amongst his moveables. *Frustra fit per plura quod fieri potest per pauciora*: it is policy to take a rich pennyworth whiles it is offered.
Strange News or The Four Letters Confuted (M., I, 287–8).

5. *casting ... world*: Attempting to get on in the world.

4

from *Christ's Tears over Jerusalem*

ATHEISTS

M O S T of them, because they cannot grossly palpabrize[1]
or feel God with their bodily fingers, confidently and grossly
discard Him. 'Those that come to God must believe that
God is, and that He is a rewarder of them that seek Him'
(Hebrews 11). They, coming against God, believe that He is
not, and that those prosper best, and are best rewarded,
that set Him at naught. 'The heavens declare the glory of
God, and the firmament showeth His handiwork; one
generation telleth another of the wonders He hath done'
(Psalm 18). Yet will not these faithless contradictors suffer
any glory to be ascribed to Him. Stoutly they refragate[2]
and withstand, that the firmament is not His handiwork,
nor will they credit one generation telling another of His
wonders. They follow the Pironicks,[3] whose position and
opinion it is that there is no hell or misery but opinion.
Impudently they persist in it, that the late discovered
Indians are able to show antiquities thousands[4] before
Adam.

With Cornelius Tacitus, they make Moses a wise provident
man, well seen in the Egyptian learning, but deny he had
any divine assistance in the greatest of his miracles. The
water, they say, which he struck out of a rock in the wilder-
ness, was not by any supernatural work of GOD, but by
watching to what part the wild-asses repaired for drink.

With Albumazar, they hold that his leading the children
of Israel over the Red Sea was no more but observing the
influence of stars and waning season of the moon that

1. Touch, make palpable.   2. Controvert, gainsay.
3. M. suggests followers of Pyrrho of Elis, said to have affirmed
nothing in his philosophy.
4. i.e. of years.

withdraweth the tides. They seek not to know God in His works, or in His son Christ Jesus, but by His substance, His form, or the place wherein He doth exist. Because some late writers[5] of our side have sought to discredit the story of Judith, of Susannah and Daniel, and of Bell and the Dragon, they think they may thrust all the rest of the Bible in like manner into the Jewish Thalmud, and tax it for a fabulous legend.

Christ's Tears over Jerusalem (M., II, 115–16).

FROST-BITTEN INTELLECT

I am at my wits' end, when I view how coldly, in comparison of other countrymen, our Englishmen write. How in their books of confutation they show no wit or courage as well as learning. In all other things Englishmen are the stoutest of all others, but being scholars and living in their own native soil, their brains are so pestered with full platters that they have no room to bestir them. Fie, fie, shall we, because we have lead and tin mines in England, have lead and tin muses? For shame, bury not your spirits in beefpots. Let not the Italians call you dull-headed *tramontani*.[6] So many dunces in Cambridge and Oxford are entertained as chief members into societies, under pretence, though they have no great learning, yet there is in them zeal and religion, that scarce the least hope is left us we should have any hereafter but blocks and images to confute blocks and images. That of Terence is oraculized: *Patres aequum censere nos adolescentulos ilico a pueris fieri senes*[7] ('Our fathers are now grown to such austerity as they would have us straight of children to become old men'). They will allow no time for a grey beard to grow in. If at the first peeping out of the shell a young student sets not a grave face on it, or seems not mortifiedly religious (have he never so good a wit, be he never so fine a scholar), he is cast off

5. Probably Puritan attacks on the Apocrypha (M.).
6. Foreigners, from beyond the Alps.
7. Terence, *Heautontimorumenos*, I, 4, 1–3.

and discouraged. They set not before their eyes how all were not called at the first hour of the day, for then had none of us ever been called. That not the first son that promised his father to go into the vineyard went, but he that refused and said he would not, went. That those blossoms which peep forth in the beginning of the spring are frost-bitten and die ere they can come to be fruit. That religion which is soon ripe is soon rotten.

Christ's Tears over Jerusalem (M., II, 122–3).

GORGEOUS LADIES OF THE COURT

Just to dinner they will arise, and after dinner go to bed again, and lie until supper. Yea, sometimes, by no sickness occasioned, they will lie in bed three days together, provided every morning before four o'clock they have their broths and their cullises [8] with pearl and gold sodden in them. If haply they break their hours and rise more early to go a-banqueting, they stand practising half a day with their looking-glasses, how to pierce and to glance and to look alluringly amiable. Their feet are not so well framed to the measures as are their eyes to move and bewitch. Even as angels are painted in church-windows with glorious golden fronts beset with sunbeams, so beset they their foreheads on either side with glorious borrowed gleamy bushes; which, rightly interpreted, should signify beauty to sell, since a bush [9] is not else hanged forth but to invite men to buy. And in Italy, where they set any beast to sale, they crown his head with garlands, and bedeck it with gaudy blossoms, as full as ever it may stick.

Their heads, with their top and top-gallant lawn baby-caps and snow-resembled silver curlings, they make a plain puppet stage of. Their breasts they embusk up on high, and their round roseate buds immodestly lay forth, to show at their hands there is fruit to be hoped. In their curious antic-woven garments, they imitate and mock the worms

8. Strong broths (e.g. beef-tea).
9. The ivy-bush was the vintners' sign.

and adders that must eat them. They show the swellings of their mind in the swellings and plumpings out of their apparel. Gorgeous ladies of the Court, never was I admitted so near any of you as to see how you torture poor old Time with sponging, pinning and pouncing;[10] but they say, his sickle you have burst in twain to make your periwigs more elevated arches of.

I dare not meddle with ye, since the philosopher [11] that too intentively gazed on the stars stumbled and fell into a ditch; and many gazing too immoderately on our earthly stars fall in the end into the ditch of all uncleanness. Only this humble caveat let me give you by the way, that you look the devil come not to you in the likeness of a tailor or painter; that however you disguise your bodies, you lay not on your colours so thick that they sink into your souls. That your skins being too white without, your souls be not all black within.

It is not your pinches,[12] your purls,[13] your flowery jaggings,[14] superfluous interlacings, and puffings up, that can any way offend God, but the puffings up of your souls which therein you express. For as the biting of a bullet is not that which poisons the bullet, but the lying of the gunpowder in the dint of the biting, so it is not the wearing of costly burnished apparel that shall be objected unto you for sin, but the pride of your hearts, which, like the moth, lies closely shrouded amongst the thrids of that apparel. Nothing else is garish apparel but Pride's ulcer broken forth. How will you attire yourselves, what gown, what head-tire will you put on, when you shall live in hell amongst hags and devils?

As many jags, blisters and scars shall toads, cankers and serpents make on your pure skins in the grave, as now you have cuts, jags or raisings upon your garments. In the marrow of your bones snakes shall breed. Your mornlike crystal

10. Ornamenting by cutting eyelet-holes, scalloping edges, etc.
11. Thales of Miletus.
12. Pleats, gatherings in skirt, etc.
13. Frills.   14. Fringes.

countenances shall be netted over and, masker-like, cawl-
vizarded with crawling venomous worms. Your orient teeth
toads shall steal into their heads for pearl; of the jelly of
your decayed eyes shall they engender them young. In their
hollow caves (their transplendent juice so pollutionately employed) shelly snails shall keep house.

Christ's Tears over Jerusalem (M., II, 137–9).

STEWS AND STRUMPETS

London, what are thy suburbs but licensed stews? Can it be
so many brothel-houses of salary sensuality and six-penny
whoredom (the next door to the magistrates) should be set
up and maintained, if bribes did not bestir them? I accuse
none, but certainly justice somewhere is corrupted. Whole
hospitals of ten-times-a-day dishonested strumpets have we
cloistered together. Night and day the entrance unto them
is as free as to a tavern. Not one of them but hath a hundred retainers. Prentices and poor servants they encourage
to rob their masters. Gentlemen's purses and pockets they
will dive into and pick, even whiles they are dallying with
them.

No Smithfield [15] ruffianly swashbuckler will come off with
such harsh hell-raking oaths as they. Every one of them is
a gentlewoman, and either the wife of two husbands, or a
bed-wedded bride before she was ten years old. The speech-
shunning sores and sight-irking botches of their unsatiate
intemperance they will unblushingly lay forth and jestingly
brag of, wherever they haunt. To church they never repair.
Not in all their whole life would they hear of GOD, if it
were not for their huge swearing and foreswearing by Him.

Great cunning do they ascribe to their art, as the discern-
ing, by the very countenance, a man that hath crowns in
his purse; the fine closing in with [16] the next Justice, or
Alderman's deputy of the ward; the winning love of neigh-

15. Duelling ground, and resort of rough types and criminals.
16. *closing in with* : Getting on good terms with.

bours round about to repel violence if haply their houses should be environed, or any in them prove unruly, being pilled and pould [17] too unconscionably. They forecast for backdoors, to come in and out by, undiscovered. Sliding windows also and trapdoors in floors to hide whores behind and under, with false counterfeit panes in walls, to be opened and shut like a wicket. Some one gentleman generally acquainted they give his admission unto sans fee, and free privilege thenceforward in their nunnery to procure them frequentence. Awake your wits, grave authorized lawdistributors, and show yourselves as insinuative-subtle in smoking this city-sodoming trade out of his starting-holes as the professors of it are in underpropping it. Either you do not or will not descend into their deep-juggling legerdemain. Any excuse or unlikely pretext goes for payment. Set up a shop of incontinency whoso will, let him have but one letter of an honest name to grace it. In such a place dwells a wise woman that tells fortunes, and she, under that shadow, hath her house never empty of forlorn unfortunate dames, married to old husbands.

Christ's Tears over Jerusalem (M., II, 148, 152).

PRAYER FOR LONDON

Comfort us, Lord; we mourn, our bread is mingled with ashes and our drink with tears. With so many funerals are we oppressed that we have no leisure to weep for our sins, for howling for our sons and daughters. Oh, hear the voice of our howling, withdraw Thy hand from us, and we will draw near unto Thee.

Come, Lord Jesu, come, for as thou art Jesus, thou art pitiful. Challenge some part of our sin-procured scourge to thy cross. Let it not be said that thou but half-satisfiedst for sin. We believe thee to be an absolute satisfier for sin. As we believe, so for thy merit's sake we beseech thee let it happen unto us.

Thus ought every Christian in London, from the highest to

17. Peeled and polled, skinned and shaven.

the lowest, to pray. From God's justice we must appeal to His mercy. As the French King, Francis the First, a woman kneeling to him for justice, said unto her: 'Stand up, woman, for justice I owe thee; if thou begst anything, beg for mercy.' So if we beg of God for anything, let us beg for mercy, for justice He owes us. Mercy, mercy, Oh grant us, heavenly Father, for Thy mercy.

Christ's Tears over Jerusalem (M., II, 174–5).

5

from *Have with You to Saffron Walden*

HIS education will I handle next, wherein he ran through
Didymus or Diomedes'[1] six thousand books of the art of
grammar, besides learned to write a fair capital roman
hand that might well serve for a boon-grace[2] to such men
as ride with their face towards the horse-tail, or set on the
pillory for cozenage[3] or perjury. Many a copy-holder[4] or
magistral scribe, that holds all his living by setting schoolboys copies, comes short of the like gift. An old doctor of
Oxford showed me Latin verses of his, in that flourishing
flantitanting[5] gouty Omega fist,[6] which he presented unto
him (as a bribe) to get leave to play, when he was in the
height or prime of his *Puer es, cupis atque doceri.*[7] A good
quality or qualification, I promise you truly, to keep him out
of the danger of the statute gainst wilful vagabonds, rogues
and beggars.

But in his grammar years (take me thus far with you) he
was a very graceless litigious youth, and one that would pick
quarrels with old Gulielmus Lily's *Syntaxis* and *Prosodia*[8]
every hour of the day. A desperate stabber with pen-knives,

1. Didymus was a famous Greek scholar, b. 63 B.C. Diomedes a
Roman grammarian of the fourth century A.D. Cornelius Agrippa and
Bodin are Nashe's probable authorities on their output.
2. Bongrace, shield fixed to hat normally as sunshade; here perhaps
as placard advertising name and offence.
3. Cheating.
4. Literally one who holds his estate in copyhold, here a punning
reference presumably to scribes getting schoolboys to do their work.
5. Flaunting (only use: NED).
6. Writing 'with great rounded curves' like the Greek letter (M.).
7. 'You are a boy, and want to be taught' (from Lily's *Short Introduction of Grammar*, 1577).
8. Syntax and prosody taught in the school books.

and whom he could not overcome in disputation he would
be sure to break his head with his pen and ink-horn. His
father prophesied by that his venturous manhood and
valour, he would prove another Saint Thomas à Beckett to
the Church. But his mother doubted him much, by reason
of certain strange dreams she had when she was first quick
with child of him, which well she hoped were but idle swimming fancies of no consequence, till, being advised by a
cunning man (her friend, that was very far in her books),
one time she slept in a sheep's skin all night, to the intent
to dream true; another time under a laurel tree; a third time
on the bare ground stark naked, and last on a dead man's
tomb or grave-stone in the church in a hot summer's afternoon, when, no barrel better herring,[9] she sped even as she
did before.

For first she dreamed her womb was turned to such another hollow vessel full of disquiet fiends as Solomon's
brazen bowl,[10] wherein were shut so many thousands of
devils; which, deep hidden under ground, long after the
Babylonians, digging for metals, chanced to light upon, and,
mistaking it for treasure, break it ope very greedily, when,
as out of Pandora's box of maladies, which Epimetheus
opened, all manner of evils flew into the world, so all manner of devils then broke loose amongst human kind. Therein her drowsy divination not much deceived her; for never
were Empedocles' devils [11] so tossed from the air into the
sea, and from the sea to the earth, and from the earth to the
air again exhaled by the sun, or driven up by winds and
tempests, as his discontented poverty (more disquiet than
the Irish seas) hath driven him from one profession to
another. Divinity, the heaven of all arts, for a while drew
his thoughts unto it, but shortly after, the world, the flesh
and the devil withdrew him from that, and needs he would
be of a more gentleman-like lusty cut; whereupon he fell to
a moral epistling and poetry. He fell, I may well say, and

9. *no barrel better herring*: It made no difference, (proverbial).
10. A story in Scot's *Discovery of Witchcraft*, 1584.
11. Meaning unknown.

made the price of wit and poetry fall with him, when he first began to be a fripler [12] or broker in that trade. Yea, from the air he fell to the sea (that my comparison may hold in every point), which is, he would needs cross the seas [13] to fetch home two pennyworth of Tuscanism. [14] From the sea to the earth again he was tossed, *videlicet* [15] shortly after he became a roguish commenter upon earthquakes, [16] as by the famous epistles (by his own mouth only made famous) may more largely appear. *Ultima linea rerum*, [17] his final entrancing from the earth to the skies, was his key-cold defence of the clergy in the tractate of Pap-hatchet, [18] intermingled, like a small fleet of galleys, in the huge Armada against me.

The second dream his mother had was that she was delivered of a caliver [19] or hand-gun, which in the discharging burst. I pray God, with all my heart, that this caliver or cavalier of poetry, this hand-gun or elder-gun, [20] that shoots nothing but pellets of chewed paper, in the discharging burst not.

A third time in her sleep she apprehended and imagined that out of her belly there grew a rare garden bed, overrun with garish weeds innumerable, which had only one slip in it of herb-of-grace, not budding at the top neither, but, like the flower narcissus, having flowers only at the root; whereby she augured and conjectured, however he made some show of grace in his youth, when he came to the top or heighth of his best proof he would be found a barren stalk

12. Pawnbroker.

13. Harvey was once expecting to go abroad, but there is no evidence that he did so.

14. A reference to Harvey's poem *Speculum Tuscanismi*, generally seen as an attack on the Earl of Oxford.

15. 'That is'.

16. Harvey describes the earthquake of 6 April in *Three Proper Letters*, 1580.

17. 'The final goal of things' (Horace).

18. Harvey's attack in *Pierce's Supererogation* on Lyly, supposed author of the anti-Puritan pamphlet *Pap with a Hatchet*.

19. Musket.

20. Pop-gun made with a hollow shoot of elder-wood (NED).

without fruit. At the same time (over and above) she thought that, instead of a boy (which she desired), she was delivered and brought to bed of one of these kestrel birds called a windfucker. Whether it be verifiable or only probably surmised, I am uncertain; but constantly up and down it is bruited [21] how he pissed ink as soon as ever he was born, and that the first clout he fouled was a sheet of paper, whence some mad wits given to descant, even as Herodotus held that the Ethiopians' seed of generation was as black as ink, so haply they unhappily would conclude, an incubus in the likeness of an ink-bottle had carnal copulation with his mother when he was begotten . . .

I have a tale at my tongue's end, if I can happen upon it, of his hobby-horse revelling and domineering at Audley End, when the Queen was there; to which place Gabriel, to do his country more worship and glory, came ruffling it out, huffty-tuffty,[22] in his suit of velvet . . .

There did this our Talatamtana or Doctor Hum [23] thrust himself into the thickest ranks of the noblemen and gallants, and whatsoever they were arguing of, he would not miss to catch hold of, or strike in at the one end, and take the theme out of their mouths, or it should go hard. In self-same order was he at his pretty toys [24] and amorous glances and purposes with the damsels, and putting bawdy riddles unto them. In fine, some disputations there were, and he made an oration before the Maids of Honour, and not before Her Majesty as heretofore [25] I misinformedly set down. . . . The process of that oration was of the same woof and thread with the beginning, demurely and maidenly scoffing, and blushingly wantoning and making love to those soft-skinned souls and sweet nymphs of Helicon, betwixt a kind of careless rude ruffianism and curious finical [26] compliment, both which he more expres-

21. Told ('noised abroad').   22. Swaggering.
23. *Talatamtana . . . Hum*: Meaning unknown.
24. Tricks.
25. i.e. in *Strange News* (M., I, 276).
26. Finicking, over-refined.

sed by his countenance than any good jests that he uttered. This finished (though not for the finishing or pronouncing of this) by some better friends than he was worthy of, and that afterward found him unworthy of the graces they had bestowed upon him, he was brought to kiss the Queen's hand, and it pleased Her Highness to say (as in my former books I have cited) that he looked something like an Italian.

No other incitement he needed to rouse his plumes, prick up his ears, and run away with the bridle betwixt his teeth, and take it upon him (of his own original engrafted disposition thereto he wanting no aptness); but now he was an insulting monarch above Monarcho,[27] the Italian that ware crowns on his shoes, and quite renounced his natural English accents and gestures and wrested himself wholly to the Italian punctilios,[28] speaking our homely island tongue strangely, as if he were but a raw practitioner in it, and but ten days before had entertained a school-master to teach him to pronounce it . . .

His father he undid to furnish him to the Court once more, where presenting himself in all the colours of the rainbow, and a pair of moustaches like a black horse-tail tied up in a knot, with two tufts sticking out on each side, he was asked by no mean personage *Unde haec insania?* ('Whence proceedeth this folly or madness?'), and he replied with that weather-beaten piece of a verse out of the Grammar, *Semel insanivimus omnes* ('Once in our days there is none of us but have played the idiots'). And so he was counted, and bad stand-by for a nodgscombe.[29] He[30] that most patronized him, prying more searchingly into him, and finding that he was more meet to make sport with than any way deeply to be employed, with fair words shook him off, and told him he was fitter for the university than

---

27. The supposed name of an eccentric hanger-on at the Court.
28. Niceties of etiquette.
29. Ninny (NED has earlier word 'nodgecock' with same meaning).
30. Probably the Earl of Leicester.

for the Court or his turn, and so bad God prosper his studies, and sent for another secretary to Oxford...

A gentleman, a friend of mine that was no stranger to such bandyings as had passed betwixt us, was desirous to see how he looked since my strappadoing and torturing him; in which spleen [31] he went and enquired for him. Answer was made he was but new-risen, and if it would please him to stay he would come down to him anon. Two hours good by the clock he attended his pleasure, whiles he (as some of his fellow inmates have since related unto me) stood acting by the glass all his gestures he was to use all the day after, and currying [32] and smudging [33] and pranking [34] himself unmeasurably. *Post varios casus*,[35] his case of tooth-pikes, his comb-case, his case of head-brushes and beard-brushes run over, and *tot discrimina rerum*,[36] rubbing-cloths of all kinds; down he came, and after *bazelos manus*,[37] with amplifications and compliments he belaboured him till his ears tingled and his feet ached again. Never was man so surfeited and over-gorged with English as he cloyed him with his generous spirits, renumeration of gratuities, stopping the posterns of ingratitude, bearing the lancer too severe into his imperfections, and traversing the ample forest of interlocutions. The gentleman swore to me that upon his first apparition, till he disclosed himself, he took him for an usher of a dancing-school; neither doth he greatly differ from it, for no usher of a dancing-school was ever such a *Bassia Dona* or *Bassia de umbra des los pedes*,[38] a kisser of the shadow of your feet's shadow, as he is. I have perused verses of his, written under his own hand to Sir Philip Sidney, wherein he courted him as he were an-

31. Mood, humour.
32. Furbishing, polishing up.
33. Adorning.   34. Dressing up.
35. 'After various hindrances'.
36. 'And so many troubles'.
37. Ceremonial kissing of hands.
38. Giver of kisses; a reference to courtly terms in which civilities were exchanged.

other Cyparissus[39] or Ganymede. The last Gordian true-love's knot or knitting-up of them is this:

Sum iecur ex quo te primum Sydnee vidi,
Os oculosque regit, cogit amare iecur.[40]

'All liver am I, Sidney, since I saw thee;
My mouth, eyes, rules it, and to love doth draw me.'

Not half a year since, coming out of Lincolnshire, it was my hap to take Cambridge in my way, where I had not been in six year before, when, by wonderful destiny, who, in the same inn and very next chamber to me, parted but by a wainscot door that was nailed up, either unwitting of other, should be lodged but his Gabrielship, that, in a manner, had lived as long a pilgrim from thence as I? Every circumstance I cannot stand to reckon up, as how we came to take knowledge of one another's being there, or what a stomach I had to have scratched with him,[41] but that the nature of the place hindered me, where it is as ill as petty treason to look but awry on the sacred person of a doctor, and I had plotted my revenge otherwise; as also of a meeting or conference on his part desired, wherein all quarrels might be discussed and drawn to an atonement, but *non vult fac*,[42] I had no fancy to it, for once before I had been so cozened by his colloguing,[43] though personally we never met face to face, yet by trouchmen[44] and vaunt-couriers[45] betwixt us. Nor could it settle in my conscience to lose so much pains I had took in new-arraying and furbishing him, or that a public wrong in print was to be so slightly slubbered over in private, with 'Come, come, give me your hand, let us be friends, and thereupon I drink to you.' And a further doubt there was if I had tasted of his beef and porridge at Trinity

39. A beautiful boy in Ovid's *Metamorphoses* (X, 106).
40. From Harvey's *Gratulationes Valdinenses*.
41. *what a stomach . . . him*: 'How I wanted to have a go at him'.
42. M. suggests should read *'non velit fac'* or *'non velle fac'* ('assume that he won't').
43. Blandishment.   44. Go-betweens.
45. Messengers.

Hall, as he desired (*notandum est*,[46] for the whole fortnight together that he was in Cambridge, his commons ran in the College detriments, as the greatest courtesy he could do the house whereof he was, was to eat up their meat and never pay anything): if I had, I say, rushed in myself and two or three hungry fellows more, and cried 'Do you want any guests? What, nothing but bare commons?', it had been a question (considering the good-will that is betwixt us) whether he would have lent me a precious dram more than ordinary to help digestion. He may be such another crafty mortaring[47] drugger, or Italian porridge seasoner[48] for anything I ever saw in his complexion.

The word complexion is dropped forth in good time, for to describe to you his complexion and composition entered I into this tale by the way, or tale I found in my way riding up to London. It is of an adust[49] swarth[50] choleric dye, like resty[51] bacon, or a dried skate-fish; so lean and so meagre that you would think (like the Turks[52]) he observed four Lents in a year, or take him for the gentleman's man in *The Courtier*,[53] who was so thin-cheeked and gaunt and starved, that, as he was blowing the fire with his mouth, the smoke took him up, like a light straw, and carried him to the top or funnel of the chimney, where he had flown out God knows whither, if there had not been cross-bars overwhart that stayed him. His skin riddled and crumpled like a piece of burnt parchment; and more channels and creases he hath in his face than there be fairy circles on Salisbury Plain, and wrinkles and frets of old age than characters on Christ's Sepulchre in Mount Calvary, on which everyone that comes scrapes his name and sets his mark to show that he hath been there; so that whosoever shall behold him,

---

46. 'Let it be noted'.
47. Using the mortar and pestle.
48. *Italian . . . seasoner*: Poisoner.
49. Burnt.
50. Dark, swarthy.　　　　　51. Rancid.
52. Hakluyt reports this of the Russians.
53. Castiglione's *Il Cortegiano*, translated by Hoby, 1561.

Esse putet Boreae triste furentis opus [54]

will swear on a book I have brought him low and shrewdly broken him. Which more to confirm, look on his head, and you shall find a grey hair for every line I have writ against him; and you shall have all his beard white too, by that time he hath read over this book.

For his stature, he is such another pretty Jack-a-Lent [55] as boys throw at in the street, and looks, in his black suit of velvet, like one of these jet drops which divers wear at their ears instead of a jewel. A smudge [56] piece of a handsome fellow it hath been in his days, but now he is old and past his best, and fit for nothing but to be a nobleman's porter or a Knight of Windsor, [57] cares have so crazed him, and disgraces to the very bones consumed him; amongst which his missing of the University Oratorship, wherein Doctor Perne [58] besteaded [59] him, wrought not the lightliest with him. And if none of them were, his course of life is such as would make any man look ill on it, for he will endure more hardness than a camel, who in the burning sands will live four days without water and feeds on nothing but thistles and wormwood and suchlike; no more doth he feed on anything, when he is at Saffron Walden, but sheep's trotters, porknells, [60] and buttered roots; and otherwhile in an hexameter meditation, [61] or when he is inventing a new part of Tully, [62] or hatching such another paradox as that

54. 'Must see it as the sad work of the North wind' (Ovid).
55. 'Figure of a man set up to be pelted' (NED).
56. Neat, spruce.
57. Old pensioners lodged at Windsor.
58. Harvey was defeated by Anthony Wingfield, supported by Dr Andrew Perne, in his candidature for the appointment in 1579.
59. Advanced another instead of him.
60. (?) Offal.
61. Allusion to Harvey's enthusiasm for the hexameter line in English verse.
62. A book was published in 1583, advertised as a newly discovered work by Cicero; but there is no evidence for Harvey's authorship of it.

of Nicholaus Copernicus[63] was, who held that the sun remains immoveable in the centre of the world and that the earth is moved about the sun, he would be so rapt that he would remain three days and neither eat nor drink, and within doors he will keep seven year together, and come not abroad so much as to church ...

Pierce's Supererogation[64] printed, the change whereof the Doctor had promised to defray and be countable to Wolfe[65] for, amounting (with his diet) to thirty-six pounds, from Saffron Walden no argent would be heard of, wherefore down he must go amongst his tenants, as he pretended (which are no other than a company of beggars, that lie in an out-barn of his mother's sometimes) and fetch up the grand sums, or *legem pone*.[66]

To accomplish this, Wolfe procured him horses and money for his expenses, lent him one of his prentices (for a serving creature) to grace him, clapping an old blue coat on his back, which was one of my Lord of Hertford's liveries (he pulling the badge off), and so away they went. Saint Christopher be their speed, and send them well back again. But so prays not our Dominico Civilian, for he had no such determination; but as soon as ever he had left London behind him, he insinuated with this Juventus[67] to run away from his master and take him for his good lord and supporter. The page was easily mellowed with his attractive eloquence, as what heart of adamant or enclosed in a crocodile's skin (which no iron will pierce) that hath the power to withstand the Mercurian heavenly charm of his rhetoric? With him he stays half a year, rubbing his toes, and following him with his sprinkling-glass and his box of kissing-comfits from place to place; whiles his master, fretting and chafing to be thus colted[68] of both of them, is ready

63. In *De Revolutionibus Orbium Coelestium*, 1543.
64. Published 1593.
65. John Wolfe, the printer.
66. Proverbially meaning 'cash payment' (from the Psalm set for the twenty-fifth morning, 25 March being Quarter Day).
67. Youth.   68. Cheated.

to send out process for the Doctor and get his novice cried in every market town in Essex. But they prevented him, for the imp or stripling, being almost starved in this time of his being with him, gave him warning he would no longer serve him, but would home to his master whatever shift [69] he made.

Gabriel thought it not amiss to take him at his word, because his clothes were all greasy and worn out, and he is never wont to keep any man longer than the suit lasteth he brings with him, and then turn him to grass and get one in new trappings; and ever pick quarrels with him before the year's end, because he would be sure to pay him no wages. Yet in his provident forecast he concluded it better policy for him to send him back to his master than he should go of his own accord; and whereas he was to make a journey to London within a week or such a matter, to have his blue coat (being destitute of ever another trencher-carrier) credit him up, though it were threadbare. So considered, and so done; at an inn at Islington he alights and there keeps him aloof, London being too hot for him. His retinue or attendant, with a whole cloak-bag full of commendations to his master, he dismisseth, and instead of the thirty-six pounds he ought [70] him, willed him to certify him that very shortly he would send him a couple of hens to shrove with.[71]

Wolfe, receiving this message, and holding himself palpably flouted therein, went and fee'd bailies, and gets one Scarlet,[72] a friend of his, to go and draw him forth and hold him with a tale whiles they might steal on him and arrest him. The watch-word given them when they should seize upon him was 'Wolfe, I must needs say, hath used you very grossly.' And to the intent he might suspect nothing by Scarlet's coming, there was a kind letter framed in Wolfe's name, with 'To the right worshipful of the laws' in a great text hand for superscription on the outside; and underneath

69. Trick for putting him off.
70. Owed.
71. Have for his Shrovetide feast.
72. Possibly T. Scarlet, printer of *The Unfortunate Traveller*.

at the bottom 'Your Worship's ever to command, and pressed to do you service, John Wolfe.' The contents of it were about the talking with his lawyer, and the eager proceeding of his sister-in-law [73] against him.

This letter delivered and read, and Scarlet and he (after the tasting of a cup of dead beer that had stood palling [74] by him in a pot three days) descending into some conference, he began to find himself ill-apaid [75] with Wolfe's encroaching upon him and asking him money for the printing of his book, and his diet whiles he was close prisoner, attending and toiling about it, and objecting how other men of less desert were liberally recompensed for their pains, whereas he, whose worth overbalanced the proudest, must be constrained to hire men to make themselves rich. 'I appeal to you,' quoth he, 'whether ever any man's works sold like mine.' 'Ay, even from a child, good Master Doctor,' replied Scarlet, and made a mouth at him over his shoulder, so soothing him on forward till the bailie's cue came of Wolfe's abusing him very grossly; which they not failing to take at the first rebound, stepped into the room boldly (as they were two well-bumbasted [76] swaggering fat-bellies, having faces as broad as the back of a chimney and as big as a town bag-pudding [77]) and clapping the Doctor with a lusty blow on the shoulder, that made his legs bow under him and his guts cry quag again, 'By your leave,' they said unto him (in a thundering yeoman's usher's diapason), 'in God's name and the Queen's we do arrest you.'

Without more pause, away they hurried him, and made him believe they would carry him into the City where his creditor was, when coming under Newgate, they told him they had occasion to go speak with one there, and so thrust him in before them for good manners' sake, because he was a Doctor and their better, bidding the Keeper, as soon as ever he was in, to take charge of him.

73. Martha Harvey, widow of Gabriel's brother, John, after whose death (1592) she went to law in a dispute over the property.
74. Going stale.   75. Dissatisfied, angry.
76. Well-stuffed.   77. A kind of haggis.

Some lofty tragical poet help me, that is daily conversant in the fierce encounters of raw-head and bloody-bones,[78] and whose pen, like the ploughs in Spain that often stumble on gold veins, still splits and stumps itself against old iron and raking o'er battered armour and broken truncheons, to recount and express the more than Herculean fury he was in when he saw he was so notably betrayed and bought and sold. He fumed, he stamped, he buffeted himself about the face, beat his head against the walls, and was ready to bite the flesh off his arms if they had not hindered him. Out of doors he would have gone (as I cannot blame him) or he swore he would tear down the walls and set the house on fire if they resisted him. 'Whither,' quoth he, 'you villains, have you brought me?' 'To Newgate, good Master Doctor,' with a low leg they made answer. 'I know not where I am.' 'In Newgate,' again replied they, 'good Master Doctor.' 'Into some blind corner you have drawn me to be murdered.' 'To no place,' replied they the third time, 'but to Newgate, good Master Doctor.' 'Murder, murder!' he cried out; 'somebody break in or they will murder me!' 'No murder, but an action of debt,' said they, 'good Master Doctor.' 'Oh you profane plebeians!' exclaimed he: 'I will massacre, I will crucify you for presuming to lay hands thus on my reverent person.'

All this would not serve him, no more than Hacket's counterfeit madness [79] would keep him from the gallows, but he was had and showed his lodgings where he should lie by it, and willed to deliver up his weapon. That wrung him on the withers worse than all the rest. 'What? My arms, my defence, my weapon, my dagger?' quoth he. 'My life then, I see, is conspired against, when you seek to bereave me of the instruments that should secure it.' They rattled him up soundly, and told him if he would be conformable to the order of the prison, so it was; otherwise he should be forced.

Force him no forces, no such mechanical [80] drudges

---

78. *raw-head and bloody-bones*: Proverbial names to frighten children.

79. William Hacket, a visionary, proclaimed as Christ by supporters, and executed.   80. Labouring.

should have the honour of his artillery. Marry, if some worthy magistrate came (as their master or mistress, it might be), upon good conditions for his life's safety and reservation, he would surrender. The mistress of the house (her husband being absent), understanding of his folly, came up to him and went about to persuade him. At her sight somewhat calmed he was, as it is a true amorous knight and hath no power to deny anything to ladies and gentlewomen, and he told her if she would command her servants forth (whom he scorned should have their eyes so much illuminated as to behold any martial engine of his), he would in all humility despoil himself of it. She so far yielded to him; when, as soon as they were out, he runs and swaps the door to, and draws his dagger upon her with 'Oh I will kill thee! What could I do to thee now!' And so extremely terrified her, that she scritched out to her servants, who burst in in heaps, thinking he would have ravished her.

Never was our Taptharatharath [81] (though he hath run through many briars [82]) in the like ruthful pickle he was then, for to the bolts [83] he must, amongst thieves and rogues, and taste of the widow's alms [84] for drawing his dagger in a prison; from which there was no deliverance, if basely he had not fallen upon his knees and asked her forgiveness.

Dinner being ready, he was called down, and there being a better man than he present, who was placed at the upper end of the board, for very spite that he might not sit highest, he straight flung to his chamber again, and vowed by heaven and earth and all the flesh on his back, he would famish himself before he eat a bit of meat as long as he was in Newgate. How inviolably he kept it, I will not conceal from you. About a two hours after, when he felt his craw [85] empty, and his stomach began to wamble, he writ a supplication to his hostess that he might speak with her. To whom (at her approaching) he recited what a rash vow he

81. Meaning unknown.
82. Lived through many difficulties.
83. Fetters.   84. Leg-irons.
85. Literally a bird's crop.

had made, and what a commotion there was in his entrails or pudding-house, for want of food; wherefore if she would steal to him a bit secretly and let there be no words of it, he would, ay marry would he (when he was released) perform mountains. She (in pity of him) seeing him a brain-sick bedlam and an innocent, that had no sense to govern himself, being loth he should be damned and go to hell for a meal's meat, having vowed and through famine ready to break it, got her husband to go forth with him out of doors, to some cook's shop at Pie Corner [86] thereabouts, or (as others will have it) to the tap-house under the prison, where having eaten sufficient his hungry body to sustain, the devil a scute [87] had he to pay the reckoning, but the Keeper's credit must go for it.

How he got out of this Castle Dolorous, if any be with child to know, let them enquire of the Minister then serving at Saint Alban's in Wood Street, who in Christian charity, only for the name's sake [88] (not being acquainted with him before), entered bond for him to answer it at law and, satisfied the house for his lodging and mangery.[89] But being restored to the open air, the case with him was little altered, for no roof had he to hide his noddle in, or whither he might go to set up his rest, but in the streets under a bulk he should have been constrained to have kennelled and chalked out his cabin, if the said Minister had not the second time stood his friend, and preferred him to a chamber at one Rolfe's, a sergeant's in Wood Street whom, as I take it, he also proved to be equally bound with him for his new cousin's appearance to the law, which he never did, but left both of them in the lurch for him, and running in debt with Rolfe beside for house-room and diet, one day when he was from home, he closely conveyed away his trunk forth out of doors, and showed him a fair pair of heels.

At Saffron Walden, for the most part, from that his

86. Between Newgate and Smithfield, famous for cooks' shops.
87. Colloquial for a coin of small value.
88. His name was Robert Harvey.
89. Food.

flight to this present hath he mewed and cooped up himself
invisible, being counted for dead, and no tidings of him, till
I came in the wind of him at Cambridge. And so I wind
up his thread of life, which, I fear, I have drawn out too
large, although in three-quarters of it (of purpose to curtail
it) I have left descant and tasked me to plainsong; whereof
that it is any other than plain truth let no man distrust, it
being by good men and true (word for word as I let fly
amongst you) to me in the fear of God uttered, all yet alive
to confirm it. Wherefore settle your faith immovably, and
now you have heard his life, judge of his doctrine accordingly.

Have with you to Saffron Walden
(M., III, 60–62; 73; 75; 76; 79; 91–94; 96–102).

MORE ABOUT PENGUINS, PELICANS
AND PUFFINS

PENGUIN CLASSICS

A selection

LEO TOLSTOY

THE KREUTZER SONATA
AND OTHER STORIES

Translated by David McDuff

PROPERTIUS

THE POEMS

Translated by W. G. Shepherd and Introduced by Betty Radice

HENRY MAYHEW

LONDON LABOUR AND THE LONDON POOR

Selected and Introduced by Victor Neuburg

SOREN KIERKEGAARD

FEAR AND TREMBLING

Translated by Alistair Hannay

HENRY JAMES

AN INTERNATIONAL EPISODE
AND OTHER STORIES

Edited by S. Gorley Putt

SELECTIONS FROM THE CARMINA BURANA

Translated by David Parlett

FYODOR DOSTOYEVSKY

THE HOUSE OF THE DEAD

Translated by David McDuff

SEVEN VIKING ROMANCES

Translated by Hermann Pálsson and Paul Edwards

PENGUIN CLASSICS

A selection

PENGUIN CLASSICS

A selection

CLASSICS IN TRANSLATION IN PENGUINS

☐ *Remembrance of Things Past* **Marcel Proust**

☐ Volume One: *Swann's Way, Within a Budding Grove* £7.50
☐ Volume Two: *The Guermantes Way, Cities of the Plain* £7.50
☐ Volume Three: *The Captive, The Fugitive, Time Regained* £7.50

Terence Kilmartin's acclaimed revised version of C. K. Scott Moncrieff's original translation, published in paperback for the first time.

☐ *The Canterbury Tales* **Geoffrey Chaucer** £2.50

'Every age is a Canterbury Pilgrimage . . . nor can a child be born who is not one of these characters of Chaucer' – William Blake

☐ *Gargantua & Pantagruel* **Rabelais** £3.95

The fantastic adventures of two giants through which Rabelais (1495–1553) caricatured his life and times in a masterpiece of exuberance and glorious exaggeration.

☐ *The Brothers Karamazov* **Fyodor Dostoevsky** £3.95

A detective story on many levels, profoundly involving the question of the existence of God, Dostoevsky's great drama of parricide and fraternal jealousy triumphantly fulfilled his aim: 'to find the man in man . . . [to] depict all the depths of the human soul.'

☐ *Fables of Aesop* £1.95

This translation recovers all the old magic of fables in which, too often, the fox steps forward as the cynical hero and a lamb is an ass to lie down with a lion.

☐ *The Three Theban Plays* **Sophocles** £2.95

A new translation, by Robert Fagles, of *Antigone, Oedipus the King* and *Oedipus at Colonus*, plays all based on the legend of the royal house of Thebes.

CLASSICS IN TRANSLATION
IN PENGUINS

☐ *The Treasure of the City of Ladies*
Christine de Pisan £2.95

This practical survival handbook for women (whether royal courtiers or prostitutes) paints a vivid picture of their lives and preoccupations in France, *c.* 1405. First English translation.

☐ *Berlin Alexanderplatz* **Alfred Döblin** £4.95

The picaresque tale of an ex-murderer's progress through underworld Berlin. 'One of the great experimental fictions . . . the German equivalent of *Ulysses* and Dos Passos' *U.S.A.*' – *Time Out*

☐ *Metamorphoses* **Ovid** £2.50

The whole of Western literature has found inspiration in Ovid's poem, a golden treasury of myths and legends that are linked by the theme of transformation.

☐ *Darkness at Noon* **Arthur Koestler** £1.95

'Koestler approaches the problem of ends and means, of love and truth and social organization, through the thoughts of an Old Bolshevik, Rubashov, as he awaits death in a G.P.U. prison' – *New Statesman*

☐ *War and Peace* **Leo Tolstoy** £4.95

'A complete picture of human life;' wrote one critic, 'a complete picture of the Russia of that day; a complete picture of everything in which people place their happiness and greatness, their grief and humiliation.'

☐ *The Divine Comedy: 1 Hell* **Dante** £2.25

A new translation by Mark Musa, in which the poet is conducted by the spirit of Virgil down through the twenty-four closely described circles of hell.

CLASSICS IN TRANSLATION
IN PENGUINS

☐ *The Magic Mountain* **Thomas Mann** £3.95

Set in a sanatorium high in the Swiss Alps, this is modern German literature's most spectacular exploration of love and death, and the relationships between them.

☐ *The Good Soldier Švejk* **Jaroslav Hašek** £4.95

The first complete English translation, with illustrations by Josef Lada. 'Hašek was a humorist of the highest calibre . . . A later age will perhaps put him on a level with Cervantes and Rabelais' – Max Brod

These books should be available at all good bookshops or news-agents, but if you live in the UK or the Republic of Ireland and have difficulty in getting to a bookshop, they can be ordered by post. Please indicate the titles required and fill in the form below.

NAME _____ BLOCK CAPITALS

ADDRESS _____

_____

_____

Enclose a cheque or postal order payable to The Penguin Bookshop to cover the total price of books ordered, plus 50p for postage. Readers in the Republic of Ireland should send £I R equivalent to the sterling prices, plus 67p for postage. Send to: The Penguin Book-shop, 54/56 Bridlesmith Gate, Nottingham, NG1 2GP.

You can also order by phoning (0602) 599295, and quoting your Barclaycard or Access number.

Every effort is made to ensure the accuracy of the price and availability of books at the time of going to press, but it is sometimes necessary to increase prices and in these circumstances retail prices may be shown on the covers of books which may differ from the prices shown in this list or elsewhere. This list is not an offer to supply any book.

This order service is only available to residents in the UK and the Republic of Ireland.

● ● ●